PRAISE FOR
BLOOD OF THE LAMB

"Wow . . . totally unlike any novel ever written about vampires, or secret societies, or Roman art mysteries, or Vatican conspiracies. But Sam Cabot has combined all of these in this refreshing potpourri that provides us surprising and wonderful insights into each—and at the same time, endless fun!"

—*New York Times* bestselling author
Katherine Neville

"You never quite catch your breath as the secrets unfold one at a time, all the while building to a first-class conclusion. History, secrets, conspiracies, adventure. What more could you want from a thriller?"

—*New York Times* bestselling author Steve Berry

"Just when you thought vampires were so last year, Sam Cabot's *Blood of the Lamb* offers up a fresh, compelling history of the vampire. Like all great works in the genre, this one makes us think deeply about what it really means to be human. Hope there will be more in this vein!"

—Leslie S. Klinger, editor of *The New Annotated Dracula*

"Firmly located in Dan Brown territory, this religious-themed thriller combines historical mystery with modern-day intrigue. . . . One thing is crystal clear: [Cabot has] produced a first-rate thriller."   —*Booklist*

continued . . .

BLOOD

of the

LAMB

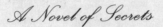

A Novel of Secrets

SAM CABOT

A SIGNET BOOK

SIGNET
Published by the Penguin Group
Penguin Group (USA) LLC, 375 Hudson Street,
New York, New York 10014

USA | Canada | UK | Ireland | Australia | New Zealand | India | South Africa | China
penguin.com
A Penguin Random House Company

Published by Signet, an imprint of New American Library, a division of Penguin Group
(USA) LLC. Previously published in a Blue Rider edition.

First Signet Printing, July 2014

 REGISTERED TRADEMARK—MARCA REGISTRADA

ISBN 978-0-451-46689-1

Printed in the United States of America
1   3   5   7   9   10   8   6   4   2

Rome

VATICAN CITY

Thomas's Room
Exit
Library
Cardinal's Office
Saint Peter's Square
Saint Peter's Basilica
Gendarmerie Office

Palace of Justice
Tiber
Santa Maria Maddalena
Pantheon
Trevi Fountain
Piazza del Colosseo
Colosseum

JANICULUM HILL
TRASTEVERE

Tiber

Palazzo Farnese

Santa Maria dell'Orazione e Morte

Ponte Sisto Bridge

ORTO BOTANICO

Piazza Trilussa

Apothecary

Santa Maria della Scala

Spencer's House

Livia's House

Il Pasquino

Tempietto

Santa Maria in Trastevere

Ellen's Apartment

Piazza di San Cosimato

Ministero della Pubblica Istruzione

Trastevere

TIBER ISLAND

Basilica of Santa Cecilia

Santa Maria dell'Orto

Tiber

• San Francesco a Ripa

PROLOGUE

◆〇◆

April 21, 1992

He wasn't prepared.

He never could have been. As the Fire rose in him he understood that.

They'd discussed it, so deeply and so long. The right thing, or wrong? She'd cautioned, counseled patience. But he knew what he wanted, knew with a certainty rock-solid and also rolling, cresting, an endless ocean wave. She wanted the same—he knew that. Her restraint was an attempt to protect him from irreparable error—if error it were. It wasn't, he was sure: the reverse, it was the choice that could join them together, give each to the other in ways beyond, even, the love and the bond they already shared.

They decided; and once *whether* was behind them, *when* and *where* became simple. Now: this soft spring dusk, the sky fading from violet to onyx as it had the night she'd first revealed to him that this was possible. Here: in the parlor of her ancient home, a tower that had stood centuries upon this spot and watched Rome grow around it, watched the world change.

In the dark and silent room she lit no lamps, put on no music. The streetlight's distant gleam, footsteps in the piazza below: "It's enough," she whispered. They'd had wine, velvety Barbaresco, but now the wineglasses stood forgotten. On a cloth of cobalt silk spread across an intricate carpet, she leaned over him, the pale streaks in her long black hair glittering in the dim light. Silver to his gold, as her green eyes were ocean to his sky. She paused for a moment, but she didn't ask if he was sure; the time for that had passed. She brushed his lips once with hers. He was seized, suddenly, with a yearning to wrap his arms tight around her, to press her body against his, but he didn't move. He couldn't move.

She took his hand. She kissed his palm and a moan escaped him. She moved her lips slowly to his wrist. Another kiss, another moan. Then a fierce sharp pain, a searing that flashed to shoulder and fingertips. It faded as fast as it had come, to nothing, to numbness. Time passed; he didn't know how much.

And now this. Everywhere, every cell—he swore he could feel them each, individually—in every one, a warmth, a generous, suffusing heat began, intensified, rose. The sense of it made him joyous, wild. As it heightened he was sure he was ablaze, would be consumed by fire from within, and he couldn't stop himself: he laughed.

Slowly, the burning faded, too. He turned amazed eyes to her. She was smiling. Her breath, her blood, her gardenia scent: he knew them all; his blood knew them all as it knew, as he knew, the cat out on the cobblestones licking its paw, the soft murmur of lovers crossing the piazza, hand in hand. Intoxicating perfume drifted in the open window: the blossoms on the magnolias, too faint for him before. Somewhere, not close, someone played a piano. He heard the instrument. And he heard the distance.

He had Changed.

I

———◦———

May 27, 1849

Dear Margaret,

I write to you tonight on a matter of utmost consequence. Please, my friend, give your gravest consideration to what I am about to ask of you. I am guilty, I know, of a fondness for the grand gesture, and I imagine you are rolling your eyes at yet more melodrama from your little poet; but I am in earnest when I say that what is contained herein, as fantastic as you may find it, is simply—and momentously—the truth.

With this letter I send you a small sealed box. It holds a copy I made of a document obtained from the Library of the Vatican itself. Obtained! Margaret, I stole it! As you no doubt know by now, Pius the Ninth has fled, taking refuge from our righteous cause in the Kingdom of the Two Sicilies. Here in Rome his craven disappearance had been rumored for months— thus the Pope defends his faith? Hah!—but we were not assured of it until this Easter last. As the news spread our soldiers were hard put to choose between festivity and fury. The coward Pope has summoned the French—the French!—and crawled away.

In the end, being unable to dissuade my men from their consuming rage, I chose to channel it. I led them to the very gates of the Vatican, barely more than a howling mob. (Barely, but yet more: soldiers still, and under my command. Since receiving my commission from General Garibaldi, your fat and laughing poet has become a very good officer; indeed I have!) They would have eagerly stormed the walls at any spot, but I conducted them to the gate nearest the Library, though the purposeful nature of my orders was, perhaps, not apparent.

Wait, I hear your voice, and you are shocked: **Wild soldiers, marauding through that storehouse of wisdom? Papal possessions or not, the glories contained therein are world treasures! You, Mario, deliberately led soldiers thence?** *Margaret, your reverence for learning causes horror to ring loud, drowning out the* **bravo!** *you are no doubt otherwise heaping upon me for my martial prowess.*

Withhold your judgment, I beg of you. I was in search of the very document, a copy of which I send you now, and under cover of my soldiers' rampages, I found it. Immediately, I ordered them out, and they obeyed. Yes, there was damage, and there was pilfering; these were unavoidable, my intent being to create a chaos in which my retrieval of these papers would go unnoticed.

This document, dear friend, will shatter the Church.

I retain the original, and believe me when I tell you I have taken steps tō conceal it well, in a place that will resist flames, floods, and the predations of the French. I fully intend and expect to employ it my-

self, at a moment of my choosing, to maximum effect.

But Louis Napoleon's army, led by that jellyfish Charles Oudinot, remains camped outside the city. We were told they were impartial, come to mediate between Pius the Ninth and his subjects—his subjects! my God!—but Oudinot has thrown his lot in with the Papacy. I cannot say this surprised me; his master is that Napoleon elected President by free vote of his people, who is rumored on the verge of declaring himself their Emperor. Emperor, Margaret! Does he intend to be Caligula, or perhaps to rule Cathay?

This is why I write to you now. It is likely but a matter of time before Oudinot takes action on behalf of Pius the Ninth and lays siege. If he does he will succeed. It is that simple. Our army will be defeated. But we will not. This document, Margaret, will be the salvation of the Republican cause. Of more than that! It will throw the Papal boot from the neck of the Italian people, of my people, and be the agent of its fall from the necks of those who love freedom in every corner of the world.

But know this: once the inner cabal of the Church understands that it is gone they will stop at nothing to get it back. Thus your friend, full of buoyant confidence though I am, might at some point be no more. Improbable, Margaret, so do not fear—I am a hard man to kill. More credible is the prospect that, despite all my planning, the document itself will be destroyed; or that I will be prevented from recovering it to make the use of it that I so ardently wish and so wholly intend.

Why not, then, just say where the document is, instead of this overwrought business of copies, locked boxes, and other absurdly theatrical goings-on? you ask, and though I shall not tell you where it is, I will say how very much I am enjoying this imaginary conversation, hearing your voice once again! I shall not tell you, because, although I am consigning this package to a trusted (and well paid!) courier, the possibility exists that it will be intercepted and this letter read by eyes for whom it is not intended. (And if you who are reading this are not Margaret Fuller, I say: shame on you, sir!) No, the hiding place of the original document is my secret alone. But, dear Margaret, as you have been in our mutual explorations of scholarship, of literature, and of statecraft, I am asking you in this, also, to be my invaluable collaborator. I send you this copy of the document sealed and ask you to retain it thus. Margaret, do not read it. I promise you what is found therein will tell a tale you would scarcely credit. You will think your good friend mad, but I assure you, I am not. I beg you, follow these instructions faithfully. Keep this box unopened and always near you; and tell none you have received it.

In the months to come, once the impending battles have been fought and decided, I will send word. But if you have not heard from me in a year's time, take this box to safety. If he still lives, deliver it into the hands of General Garibaldi. He will read the document and, though at first he will recoil, if he is the man I know him to be, he will acknowledge the truth and understand the use of it. If he lives not, Margaret, you must publish the document yourself. Re-

member, as you know me, and on our friendship, I
pledge to you that this document is no fiction and the
bargain it makes is irrefutable and real. The other
signatory—my people—retain possession of their
original manuscript, signed and sealed as is the Vat-
ican's that I have hidden. Once your copy has seen
the light of day, though the world may at first refuse
to believe, my people will have no choice but to bring
their copy forward. Then will the Papacy and the
Church come crashing down, and a new era begin!

Ah, Margaret, how often and how fondly do I
think of you, imagining you intensely at your work,
quietly at your reading, joyously with your family!
How I miss you! The brilliance of your arguments,
the passion of your debate. Here in the Army of the
Republic, I find much excitement, but little, alas, in
the way of conversation.

Spencer, of course, predicted this, arguing against
my decision to offer my services to General Gari-
baldi. He takes, as might be expected, a longer view
of the unfolding of history than I myself. I would
send you his greetings, but I cannot, because he has,
at my insistence, left Rome. My thought was not so
much of danger to him, but to the objects in his col-
lection. Planned or unplanned, destruction in war
is inevitable; what good, I argued, is a historian
without relics of the past, the very objects that prove
history? So (upon a laden oxcart, with another fol-
lowing, how you would have laughed!) Spencer has
gone to the Piedmont. The result of my silver tongue
is that I sit in a leaking tent eating badly boiled po-
lenta, while he sips cognac in a warm villa in the
North.

Oh, but how I digress! Your poet is a willing, even an eager, soldier, but a lonely one, and apparently no less garrulous than in civilian life.

Your dashing Giovanni cuts a grand figure in Riete, I am sure; you must send him my compliments. And little Nino is no doubt flourishing. I look forward eagerly to the day when, in a free and united Italy, we are all together once more!

Until that day, Margaret, please: upon our friendship, promise me, though I am not there to hear it, that you will faithfully accomplish what I have asked of you.

Until we meet again, dear friend, I remain

Devotedly yours,
Mario Damiani

2

⬥◇⬥

July 5, 1850

They didn't roar. Flames. They didn't roar; and pumping his thick legs as hard as he could, slipping and stumbling on the rough stones of Via della Madonna dell'Orto, plowing through the bedlam of shouts, carts, and the ripe smell of fear, Mario Damiani laughed. The celebrated poet, renowned for his love of the concrete and real, of physical facts and sensory truths, was surprised to find a cliché untrue? Damiani's experience of fire was, naturally, limited, but not entirely lacking. Caged fires had warmed his homes and cooked his meals, had lit gas lamps and other men's cigars. Not one of them had roared. The flames he and all around him now raced to escape were of a wildly grander scale, but still distant—though a single errant cannonball from the French position on the Gianicolo and more were sure to bloom. These flames snickered, sizzled, whispered, telling of the mindless destruction of places he had loved. They broke his heart, but they didn't roar, and he laughed to acknowledge the fool he was.

Not entirely a fool, though. A sharp turn, another minute's elbowing through frantic, fleeing crowds, and before him, suddenly, the gates leading to the dark, aloof façade of the Basilica of Santa Cecilia. Cecilia, patron saint of poets. **How apt,** Damiani thought, **and how marvelously arbitrary.** His choice of this place, like the others he'd hastily visited tonight, was dictated by happenstance: all were churches on the path from his home to the river, and his little notebook of praise poems already held a page celebrating each. Damiani creaked open the courtyard gate, closed it behind him, and stood panting. Perspiration dripped from his brow. He wiped it with his sleeve, grinning to think how horrified Spencer would be by the gesture. Damiani, a year a rough soldier, would have to relearn gentlemanly ways when he reached the North. As his breathing slowed he crept across the courtyard, keeping to the shadows.

This was the last place he'd visit tonight. Six times already, Damiani had torn poems from the notebook and concealed them. Across the bottom of five he'd block-printed five letters with an artist's lead—inelegant but serviceable, and it was wartime, after all—and he'd hidden each where it would be safe for as long as it would need to be. Here in Santa Cecilia, he'd do something different. The page from his notebook that he'd hide here held no poem. It bore only the last five block letters, the final pieces of the puzzle.

He pulled open the basilica's heavy door and slipped inside. Shouts and panicked footfalls fell away, replaced by the patient hush of old, worn stone. Traces of incense lingered in the cool air, hardly discernible to most, perhaps, but murmuring to Damiani of desert caravans and exotic Eastern cities. Lately, Spencer had been wanting to travel, to see distant lands and wonders. Damiani had always maintained that Rome was enough to satisfy the soul of any man; but now, for the first time, he felt something of Spencer's yearning. Yes, he decided: once reunited, he and Spencer would travel, to see miracles and marvels. Perhaps Spencer, though he'd always scoffed at the idea of going west to the young land, might be persuaded to journey to America, to see cities of vigor, of ferment.

Damiani shook his head and grinned. **Fine, Mario. An Atlantic crossing. Perhaps you'd care to find your way out of Rome first?**

Three votive candles, evidence of someone's concern for the next world even as Louis Napoleon's soldiers tramped the streets of this one, provided the basilica's only light. No matter; Damiani saw well in the dark, and had spent countless hours in this place. He trotted up the center aisle, knelt, and crossed himself. It was an old habit, one he'd found he could not break. Spencer had accused him of not trying so very hard to break it, of actually enjoying the atavistic nature of the gesture. Well, perhaps.

Rising, he vaulted the altar rail.

There he knelt again. Before him lay Stefano Maderno's breathtaking, delicate statue of Santa Cecilia, head so oddly turned away from those who looked on her. The executioner's sword had fallen on Cecilia three times, but her neck had not been severed, and for three days she hadn't died. A beautiful, terrible thing for a sculptor to depict; made more terrible, and more wondrous, by the model Maderno had used: the remains of the saint herself, uncorrupted when disinterred twelve hundred years after death.

Terrible, wondrous, and to the Noantri, Damiani's people, a particular and secret astonishment.

For Damiani, it was a bittersweet thing that his chase

should end here, at the small, tender work he loved most of all Rome's glories. From his notebook he tore the leaf, blank but for the five lead letters. He folded the paper and, after a brief pause, slid it deep into a gap at the statue's base. He reached out when he was done to trace his finger on the thin line across the saint's marble throat, where her life should have left her but had not. Then he rose, crossed himself again (hearing, in his mind, Spencer's sigh), and, after a glance about him (even in the dark, he knew the angels, he knew the saints), made his way back up the center aisle.

Opening the groaning church door, Damiani flinched at the way the din of the invaded streets splintered the stillness. Across the courtyard he took a deep breath and pushed through the gate. Here, as before, swarming people, burdened wagons, horses and donkeys being ridden or desperately pulled along. Damiani laughed again, as Spencer's sardonic voice rang inside his head. **Really, Mario. Such vast drama—is it necessary? Concealed clues, a hunt for treasure—it seems like a great deal of bother.**

Oh, Spencer, Damiani thought, hurrying on the ancient stones (did he hear the snort of warhorses, the instep tramp of troops?). **Oh, yes, a great deal of bother. But when you find the treasure, when you hold in your hands the document itself, you'll understand why.** Rash and reckless Damiani, who never planned anything beyond the next line of verse, had hidden the document a year ago. Had first made a copy and sent it out of Rome. Now, this evening, he'd left a note in Spencer's study at the deserted villa: *Look to your poem.* It was an instruction that would be cryptic to all but Spencer, and with it he was proposing to lead his historian lover in a merry dance. All this should in itself convince anyone of the gravity of his intention.

Except, of course, Spencer would laugh at him in any case, as they sat sipping cognac in the Piedmont. None of the steps Damiani had taken to secure the document would be of the least importance except in the case of his own death. He raced now to render them all useless, for he did not intend to die.

On Via di Santa Cecilia he charged left, toward Via dei Genovesi, the river, his hidden boat, and, if his purse of gold had been of any use, his hidden boatman. He'd reach the mooring well before the arranged time. If the boatman had been seized with fear and had fled? Mario would handle the boat himself. If the boat was gone? He'd jump into the Tiber and swim until he reached a French-free shore. He'd fight his way to the Piedmont, sweep triumphantly into the villa, drink the excellent wine Spencer could be trusted to lay in wherever he found himself, and make poems until his moment came. Then he'd return and retrieve his hidden treasure, and the world would change.

He plowed headlong through the tumult, his ears so full of shouts and his own labored breathing that he didn't hear the clip-clop of horses' hooves until the horses themselves pranced into Via di Santa Cecilia, practically on top of him.

Damiani pressed into the shadow of an overhanging window. The street's panic swelled, though most of these people had nothing to fear from the French. Nothing immediate, in any case. Damiani himself was a different matter. He still wore the trousers and rough cotton shirt of Garibaldi's troops, though he'd prudently thrown aside the officer's coat he'd so proudly donned the year before. The general himself, seeing Rome was lost, had wisely negotiated a truce and taken his army north. Oudinot's plans to deliver Garibaldi with Louis Napoleon's compliments into the hands of the Pope being thus foiled, his troops were now hunting soldiers who had remained in Rome—men like Mario Damiani.

Were hunting, and had found. Shouting, the lead cavalryman reined his horse so hard it reared, and charged forward with his saber raised.

An instant to decide: left? right? Damiani had once assured a friend he was a hard man to kill, and so he was; but to capture would be easier, and especially compassed round, as now, with tons of stone and horseflesh. To his right, down Via dei Genovesi, lay the river, so close he could smell its damp stone channels: but that street was wide enough for horses. Even if he were to successfully bolt, a straining fat poet is no match for a galloping horse. In the dark wall on his left, a slice of deeper darkness: an alley's opening. It would be more useful if this alley connected to another street, which Damiani, who had walked every public inch of Trastevere (and many of the private inches, too) knew it did not. Still, the horses couldn't follow. If the cavalrymen dismounted and chased him on foot, perhaps the shadows of the tiny inner piazza would shelter him until they gave up, decided he'd ducked into a doorway, and went away. Fighting foot soldiers, if it came to that, would still be preferable to fighting horses. He exploded out from the wall.

The soldiers, without pause, swung off their horses and swarmed after. Damiani crouched behind the piazza's absurdly tinkling fountain. The French captain gave an order: one man with him, circling left, two more going right. The rest remounted at the alley's mouth. One of each stalking pair tested doors while the other watched the shadows. These men might be French fops, but they were no fools and they were closing like pincers. Still, they were only four. Damiani was Blessed with tremendous strength, in the way of his people, and it was not unreasonable that he could defeat four Frenchmen. But then what? Into the street again, to where the rest of the troop waited? Diving under the horses' bellies to escape?

That, he thought as the first to see him shouted, was a question for later.

They rushed him; he leapt back from the fountain to a recessed doorway. Let them come at him from the front. Let them come.

They came. The captain first, a privilege of rank. Ducking the saber-swinging arm, Damiani rammed his shoulder into the man, throwing him into the soldier behind. For a moment all movement stopped. Any plan they'd had to attack him singly, as gentlemen would, was abandoned now that they saw his strength; and he'd just made a fool of their captain. All four charged in a gale of shouts and swords. He felt the sting of a blade on his wrist, then a fiery slice down the length of his thigh. Meaningless in the end but distracting in the moment, as pain always was. Two soldiers tackled him, knocking out his breath, throwing him down. He shoved a hand up under one man's sweaty chin, pushed and pushed, straining until suddenly the man tumbled off; but the other was still pummeling him and two more dove down hard. Damiani's head rang. He drew a great breath and with a roar and a thrashing of arms, he erupted. Jumping to his feet, he hurled one man against the wall,

punched another squarely on his thin French mustache.
But still they came, fists and sabers sweeping the night
air.

Mario, Damiani thought, **this may not turn out as
well for you as you hoped.** He ducked a blade that
chipped the doorpost where his head had just been, then
twisted his arm to throw off a hand clamping his wrist.
That hand, though, did not yield. Its strength was as
great as his, and it yanked him left, then backward. Damiani braced to slam the wall. Instead he fell flat on his
back in darkness. An urgent voice whispered, "Come!"
and a door was slammed and barred against angry
French pounding. Damiani jumped up and ran, following a shadow down a dark passage, followed himself by a
tall shadow behind.

The thumps and angry cries faded as Damiani and his
rescuers—his own people, he now knew—emerged into
another alley. A horn sounded, the French patrol raising
the alarm. "They will be everywhere now," the man behind Damiani said, a calm dark voice Damiani simultaneously recognized and was astounded to hear. "We
cannot risk the streets. Filippo, that door. Ahead, on
your left." The lock would not give, but Filippo—
Filippo Croce, it must be; he was the other man's personal secretary—threw his shoulder against it twice. The
wood shrieked as it tore. A nail plinked on the cobblestones. The door, complaining, opened, and the three
stepped through.

The light in the room was low but the aroma was
unmistakable. Before Filippo lit a torch, Damiani, hands
on knees as he drew breath, knew they had entered a
stable. Dancing shadows showed him to be correct. The
smells of dung and hay thickened the air, but the place

was silent: the horses were all in the North, under the backsides of Garibaldi's troops.

"Thank you," Damiani panted, still bent over. He rubbed the wound on his leg, painful but not as deep as he'd thought. "How did you find me? Or am I just lucky beyond belief?"

The tall man shook his head. In his deep, slow voice, he said, "We have been searching for you, Mario. Do I have to tell you why?"

A jolt caused Damiani's heart to skip. Heat suffusing his skin, he straightened slowly. After a moment he replied, "No, Lord."

"Then tell me where the document is hidden."

Another moment; another breath. In a voice at once trembling and sure, Damiani said again, "No, Lord."

"Mario." A shake of the dark head. "I understand your cause. I know you believe I do not, but I do. It is not time. The time will come, but it is not come yet."

"Lord." Damiani steadied his voice. "My Lord, the time will not 'come.' In all these years it has not yet come. We must make it come."

"We cannot. To everything there is a season."

Damiani blinked. "You'd quote Scripture to me? On this question?"

"And why not? Your argument, as I understand it, is with the papacy, not the Church."

"If only the papacy allowed for the distinction!"

All three froze as rushing footsteps and jangling swordbelts in the next street told them the French were near.

The tall man said, "We cannot debate now. You must give me the Church's copy of the Concordat that you have stolen. You will come to understand when you have lived as long as I have."

"It is precisely those years that blind you to the chance these times create! The world has changed. It will continue to change. Reason and scientific thought gain the upper hand. We no longer need the Church!"

"You are wrong, Mario." A slight nod signaled Filippo; Damiani saw it, but not in time. Together the two threw themselves on him, and though he was strong, they were stronger. He kicked and heaved, but heard a clanking, felt a constriction, found his arms and chest bound in iron. Filippo wound the chain tight and fastened it about a post. Trussed, Damiani lay on his back in the straw, staring up at the others.

"Filippo," said the tall man. "Leave us."

"My Lord—"

"Leave us!"

After a moment Filippo bowed and obeyed.

Damiani tugged at his chains, feeling them bruise his arms. Perhaps he could break them or tear down the post, but it would take time.

"Mario." The words came gently. "Tell me."

Damiani did not speak.

"This is useless, Mario. Garibaldi's army is defeated and the Pope still rules. The Noantri must keep peace with the papacy and the Church."

"Peace!" Damiani repeated bitterly. "This is not peace! This is serfdom! We wait, and wait, concealing ourselves, feigning and dissembling. You know what our lives are! But we need not! When the agreement comes to light, when the Church falls—"

"*It is not time!* If the Church falls, we also fall. The life you've had—the villa, your poetry, your fame—you are a wonderful poet, Mario. A great talent."

Damiani stared stonily, not acknowledging the compliment, and the other man sighed and went on. "This agreement you so despise is what allows it all. You did not know the times before." He paused. "You have been impatient, a hothead from the day you joined us. I should not have permitted it."

"No, I didn't know those times," Damiani retorted. "But these are different times. You are living in the past. I am looking to the future."

"The future." The tall man's voice held a new, sad note. "Do you not understand? Unless you give me the stolen document, I cannot let you live."

Damiani's blood ran cold.

"This is not something I want to do," the other went on. "It will haunt me forever, I fear. But my responsibility is to our people. If you live, though it take years, you will retrieve the document and you will publish it. Am I wrong?"

Slowly, Damiani shook his head.

"Then, unless you return it to me, you cannot live."

"My Lord." Damiani's voice was ragged. He tried to strengthen it. "Do not do this, I beg of you." Meeting the steady, silent gaze, he said, "It will be futile in any case. I made a copy. I gave it to a friend."

The dark eyes held him. "No, you did not."

"I did. With instructions to publish it, in the event of my death."

"To whom?" A contemplative frown. "Not to Spencer George, I think. He's been ensconced in the North for some time. And would not, I think, approve of your actions, if he knew."

"No, he wouldn't. He is a historian. His view is long." Damiani said this calmly. He hoped he was wrong; but, for Spencer's sake, he hoped he was convincing.

"If it's true you've made a copy, you have put a friend in danger. It is not only we who will be searching. Did you think the Vatican would not discover your theft, not chase after what they've lost?"

"In truth, my Lord, I thought only they would. I did not think I had anything to fear from our own people."

A thought seemed to come to the tall man. In a voice equal parts wonder and disappointment, he asked, "Is this why you joined Garibaldi's army? With this sole intention: to put yourself into a position to raid the Vatican Archives?"

Bound and prone, Damiani had to laugh. "Sir. You think too highly of my cunning. I never understood what I might bring about until I found myself with my troops at the gates of the Vatican. No, my Lord, I joined the Army of the Republic to unite Italy and throw off the papal yoke, not just from the necks of our people, but of all people."

"Ah, Mario, you laugh. It was that laugh, that excitement, your boundless joy in life, that convinced me you could be one of us. Please, remain one of us. Tell me where the document has gone. Allow me to free you and all will be as before."

Damiani breathed deeply. He smelled the straw he lay in, saw shadows flicker on the walls. He drew another breath and said, "No."

"We will find it, Mario. We will find your friend. This is a grand gesture, but it will be in vain." After a long, silent time, the tall man nodded. "I see. I'm sorry, then. Very sorry."

He turned and strode to the rear of the stable. A great wave of fear broke over Damiani, banished, to his surprise, almost immediately by this thought: **All men die. In the**

end, you are a man, Mario, as you were at the beginning. It calmed him, that realization; and another thought
almost made him smile. Margaret would succeed. The
death of Mario Damiani would mean something, mean
more, even, than his life. Margaret Fuller, well-known and
wealthy, famously resolute in her endeavors, beyond the
reach of both the Pope and the Noantri, would bring
about the liberation of his people and the destruction of
the Church. **It's in your hands now, my friend. I know
you will not fail.** Damiani was thinking this when the
other man returned, carrying a blacksmith's hammer.

"Mario?"

He waited, but Damiani did not speak.

Finally: "I understand. At least, I will not make you
suffer." He swung the hammer high above his head and
down again with rushing force. Pain seared Damiani's
skull and blackness flooded in. Through it, he saw the
other man take the torch from the wall and set it to the
straw. As the world faded, Damiani had to laugh one last
time. Flames, when they were racing to devour you, did,
indeed, roar.

3

September 14, 2012

This document, dear friend, will shatter the Church.

Father Thomas Kelly read the words again, absently tapping a pencil on the table, an old seminary habit. A glare from his left and a "shush!" from his right; he grabbed the pencil up guiltily, offered an abashed smile. Serious researchers, brooking no distractions, were clearly to be found in London's Transcendentalist Archives. Thomas sympathized. He was one himself. How else to explain his joy in rooting through these (rather ill kept, if truth be told) shelves and boxes, searching for a path probably not there to find?

And while he was on sabbatical, too.

Unlike many of his fellow Jesuit scholars, Thomas Kelly enjoyed teaching undergraduates, feeding happily off their enthusiasm and energy; but they required direction to the same strong degree that they resented receiving it. His own student days were barely a decade behind him, and his occasionally headstrong approach to his studies was still a clear enough memory that he couldn't fault them. Teaching did sometimes feel like sailing into a headwind, though. Exhilarating, but exhausting. Time without classes was restorative, no question.

More so if you actually used it productively, of course. Or, on the other hand, found a way to relax. Maybe he should go down to the Thames and sail a real boat, not a metaphorical one. Instead of spending his days sifting through the disordered collection of papers left behind in 1850 when the American journalist Margaret Fuller sailed for New York. Although, he reminded himself, that journey ended in a shipwreck that took the lives of all the passengers, Fuller included, and most of the crew. So much for real boats.

Thomas glanced at his watch. What he *should* do was stop daydreaming and get back to campus. He had a meeting soon at his office at Heythrop College with a student whose thesis he'd agreed to advise even while theoretically student-free. Why not? His own academic career had received generous help from some of the Church's top scholars. Now that he was regarded as in those ranks—a standing Thomas viewed with skepticism, but there it was—it was his duty to offer help in the same spirit.

It was not an entirely altruistic gesture, though. What was? On days like this it was good to feel you'd gotten something done. Thomas's morning had been a waste. The letter with the dire phrase ("shatter the Church," indeed!) had been written by Mario Damiani, a fiery anti-Papist poet of the Risorgimento—the nineteenth-century uprising of the Italian people against the power of the Church. Thomas considered the idea that any document could be that dangerous flatly absurd. For one thing, Damiani's politics plus his tendency toward hyperbole suggested he might be putting forth more hope than fact. For another—and Thomas said this as a churchman who'd himself been through a momentous crisis of faith, who loved his Church yet saw it with clear eyes—if the scandals, disasters, and wrong turns of the past decades, or millennia, hadn't shattered the Church, he suspected there wasn't much that could.

He was curious about what Damiani thought had that power, though; but his real interest in Damiani grew from another part of this letter. Thomas's focus as a scholar encompassed the Risorgimento and the other Italian political movements of the time. He'd written a number of groundbreaking papers, and two books, in that area, and when he'd found Damiani's letter to Fuller the implications made his scholar's heart pound. The Vatican Archives had been looted in 1849. The letter made it clear Damiani had been involved; in fact it claimed he'd led the troops himself, though Thomas suspected the poet of being a bit of a blowhard. Church scholars had long given up hope of recovering treasures stolen in that raid, partly because Vatican record-keeping had been so imprecise it was hard to know exactly what was gone. But no one, to Thomas's knowledge, had taken the route he was following: through Garibaldi's partisans.

He'd struck a vein with this letter: Damiani had sent a copy of something to Margaret Fuller and hidden the original. Whatever it was, the copy no doubt went down with Fuller, and the location of the original must have died with Damiani. But maybe he'd done it more than once, or maybe others had done the same—hidden things or sent them away. A study of Damiani's papers and those of his circle might, just possibly, lead somewhere new.

It was the lot of historians to interpret events, to stand to the side and study, not participate. Thomas had chosen that role and for the most part was content. But as he gathered his coat, laptop, notepad, briefcase, and errant pencil, he thought—not for the first time—how satisfying it would be to be instrumental, just once. To be a part of history instead of a follower of it. One small discovery, one document found because Thomas Kelly had thought to look where others hadn't—well, well, if that wasn't the sin of pride rearing its ugly head. Thomas grinned and, probably to the gratification of the other researchers, left the Transcendentalist Archive.

Heythrop College stood at the other side of Holland Park. Since coming to London from Boston seven years earlier, Thomas had become rather the sedentary scholar. A fast walk, he decided, would do him good, and he trotted down the steps and into the park. The brilliant gold of linden leaves overhead and their crunch underfoot called forth from him a silent prayer of thanks. Thomas loved the change of seasons, both the fact of it and the idea. Yellow leaves, bare branches, pale buds, bursting blooms, then yellow leaves again: it all happened whether you wanted it to or not. If at the height of summer you couldn't quite believe in winter, if in the depths of winter you thought summer would never be back—it didn't matter. Flowers, autumn colors, snowfall, they were all on the way; faith not required. For Thomas, that very fact was enough to bolster faith.

He'd traversed the park, reached the campus, and was climbing the stone steps to the doors of Charles Hall when his cell phone rang. Juggling briefcase and office keys, he stuck the phone to his ear. "Thomas Kelly."

"*Buongiorno*, Thomas. It's Lorenzo."

"Father!" Thomas stopped, smiling in delight and surprise. He hadn't spoken to Lorenzo Cardinal Cossa in three or four months. His own fault, he knew. His former thesis adviser—and spiritual adviser and friend, more to the point—had much to occupy him since his move to the Vatican four years ago. It was Thomas who should have made the effort to keep in better touch. "An unexpected pleasure! How are you?"

"Very, very well, Thomas. And you?"

"I'm fine, thanks."

"You sound out of breath."

"Rushing as usual, is all."

"With your coat unbuttoned and your arms laden."

"I'm afraid so."

"You're busy."

"Always. But don't—"

"You're about to be busier. Thomas, I need you."

"Of course." Thomas shifted his load and started up the stairs again. "Tell me what I can do."

"Here."

"I'm sorry?"

"Here, Thomas. I need you in Rome. And now. As soon as you can get here. Much is happening. The day has finally come."

"I—I'm sorry. I'm lost. What day? What's happened? Is everything all right?"

"Much better than all right. I've wanted to call you for the last few months, since Father Bruguès took ill, but of course that wasn't possible. But now it's official. Two weeks ago he took a well-earned retirement. Thomas, I've been honored with both of his positions. I've been made Archivist and Librarian of the Vatican."

"Oh!" Thomas stopped again, causing a rushing student to plow into him. The student, seeing he was on the phone, mouthed, *Sorry, Father*. Thomas smiled and waved him off. "Oh, that's wonderful! Congratulations! Both positions—what an honor."

"And a responsibility. Thank you, Thomas. Now come help me."

"I— My classes, my students . . ."

"You're on sabbatical, aren't you?"

"I'm advising three theses."

"Our Lord has given us glorious new technologies to allow you to do that from here."

"I—"

"Thomas. You and I spoke about this back in Boston, when it was barely a dream. This priceless, irreplaceable, and deeply chaotic collection needs a comprehensive stewardship, an approach of methodical care it hasn't seen yet. The opportunity to participate in that work was why I came to Rome. The chance to take the lead in it has been what I've wanted most, for a very long time, and I don't deny it. Assisting Monsignor Bruguès was the beginning. Now the entire Library has been given into my care. It's always been my intention that you should have a role."

"Yes, of course." Thomas entered the building and turned down the hallway. Outside his office the waiting student jumped to his feet. Thomas held up a delaying finger, unlocked the door, and shut it behind him. "And I hope—"

"A specific role," Lorenzo went on. "The overall work is important, but there's a particular task I need you for. Your skills and your knowledge. It's something we haven't discussed yet. I was waiting for the right time, and now the time has come."

"I'm supposed to start teaching again in the spring semester," Thomas said weakly.

Lorenzo Cossa sighed. "Your obsessiveness as a scholar is the positive side, I suppose, of your . . . lack of flexibility. Thomas, I'm a Cardinal. I'm the Vatican Librarian and Archivist. I can get you reassigned and Heythrop College will be proud, not dismayed. I promise you. Please, come help me here."

Thomas shrugged out of his coat, looking around. His plants, his pictures, his books and papers. Seven years of settling in. He tossed the coat on the chair. "Yes," he told the Cardinal. "Of course."

The call to the priesthood had been the most compelling force in Thomas Kelly's life. A rangy Irish redhead, he'd found baseball, girls, and garage bands also part of his South Boston youth, and he had a nodding acquaintance with illicitly acquired six-packs and smokable non-tobacco products. But behind it all, beyond the breathless rush of childhood and above the clang and crash of adolescence, hovered something still and silent. Something as calm and deep, endless and inviting, as the sea. Later he would come to understand this as faith; early on, he only knew the peace, the sense of being home, that he felt at Mass. It took him years to recognize most people didn't feel what he did, even longer to see the path open to him. When he understood, he took to his vocation with joy and gratitude.

He'd been an exemplary seminarian, drawn to the cerebral, scholarly life. After ordination he'd headed along an academic route, happily exploring obscure byways of Church history. His powerful intuitive gift for research had drawn the attention of other scholars, of journals and publishers. Doctoral, postdoctoral, and teaching positions had sought him out, for which he was thankful. Whatever intellectual talents he possessed were matched— no, actually, overshadowed—by a pronounced clumsiness as a pastoral counselor. His efforts to comfort the occasional undergraduate or old friend who came to him at times of crisis only left Thomas feeling intrusive, cliché-ridden. He greatly admired priests who ministered directly to people's spiritual needs, but he accepted that his own contribution to his Church would be less immediate, more ethereal. That his work was unlikely to rock anybody's world, however, did not lessen his joy or confidence in his vocation and the direction he'd chosen within it.

It had therefore been a shock to him when, the fourth winter after ordination, he'd found himself plunged into a terrifying abyss by a single word.

In the midst of consoling the young widow of a high school classmate who'd died unexpectedly (one of those times when Thomas felt it his duty to attempt the solace a priest should be able to offer), a previously unheard voice came whispering inside his own mind. "The Lord has a plan for each of us," he'd said to the distraught woman. "It's not ours to know, but you must never doubt it exists. To everything, there is a season, and a time—" He'd stopped, dumbfounded, hearing a silent question: **Really?**

The widow, mistaking his stillness for pastoral manner, smiled sadly and completed the phrase. "—to every purpose under heaven. Yes, Father, of course." She had, he recalled, taken strength from whatever he'd gone on to say and left with renewed hope. He, on the other hand, sat motionless in his study for the rest of the day. The afternoon faded and the streetlights spread an anemic glow across the slushy sidewalks. The voice that had asked the question didn't stop, asking others, all different but with only one meaning. **Are you sure? How can you be? Isn't it convenient that God has for each of us what we most desperately want—a purpose, a reason to exist—but keeps it secret? Thomas,** the voice whispered, **you're a smart man. Isn't it just as likely we invented all this, a huge absurd theological security blanket, because we're scared? That nothing has purpose, nothing has meaning, and God is just a lullaby we sing to ourselves? Thomas—really?**

"Thomas, the only men of God who've never felt what you're feeling now are sheep. Hah! Lambs of God. Followers. Not thinkers." In his austere, book-crammed study Lorenzo Cossa flicked the Red Sox lighter Thomas had brought as a gift and grunted in satisfaction at the steadiness of the flame. He pulled in air until his cigar glowed, and settled his long, gaunt frame in an armchair. "It's a crisis of faith. Everyone goes through it."

"Yes, Father."

"Doesn't help at all, does it? Knowing that?"

Thomas shook his head. Three weeks after his counseling session with the widow, he was still spiritually dazed and unable to find footing. He'd requested a leave and flown off to Chicago, hoping his mentor could help him make sense of this onslaught of uncertainty.

When Thomas was in graduate school at Boston College, Monsignor Lorenzo Cossa's history seminars were legendary for their rigorous intellectual demands and equally for the priest's galvanizing oratory. Monsignor Cossa maintained the Church had long ago strayed from the spiritual high road and, far from being a path to salvation in the debased world, was itself in danger of being devoured by it. This wasn't a belief Thomas shared—where was the Church, and where was it needed, if not in the world?—but such was the flair of Lorenzo Cossa's rhetoric that Thomas would have studied algebra with him for the pleasure of hearing him talk. That his courses fit Thomas's interests was a bonus. That Lorenzo Cossa seized on Thomas Kelly as the most promising student he'd had in years was a mixed blessing. He leaned harder on Thomas than on other students; but even alone in the library at three a.m. Thomas understood he was being forced to do his cerebral best, and, though exhausted, was grateful. The year after Thomas got his doctorate, Monsignor Cossa had been elevated and given charge of Church educational programs in the Midwest. They'd remained in touch, but such was the power of this earthquake that Thomas knew the telephone and computer screen would be powerless against it.

"No," Thomas said, in Lorenzo—now Bishop—Cossa's study. "It doesn't help."

The Bishop wasn't fazed. "Of course not. It's like going to the dentist. Knowing everyone who ever sat in that chair suffered the same agonies doesn't reduce your pain. But remember this: they all survived."

"I'm not sure about that. Some men leave the priesthood. Some leave the Church."

Around the cigar, Lorenzo grinned. "I was talking about the dentist. Thomas, in all seriousness. Yours is one of the strongest vocations I've ever come across. But what made you think you'd never have doubts? Jesus himself had doubts. Doubt is the coin which buys our faith. That this never happened to you before might be lucky or unlucky. You're farther down the road than most when the first crisis comes. But eventually everyone arrives at this chasm and has to find a way to jump it."

"First crisis? I can expect this to happen again?"

"Forget I said that."

"No, it's actually hopeful. It almost gives a context."

Lorenzo regarded Thomas in silence. Knocking ash from his cigar, he said, "I saw this coming."

"You did? Why didn't—why didn't I?"

"Why didn't I warn you, you mean. Could I have said anything you'd have believed? What's happened to you is one of the hazards of scholarship. Knowledge is power, isn't that what we say? But power corrupts. An institution based on knowledge and learning can't help but be a corrupt institution."

"You're calling the Church corrupt?"

"There's the flaw!" With a joy Thomas remembered from the classroom, Lorenzo pounced. "The Church isn't based on knowledge! It's built on faith! What drew you to the priesthood, Thomas? The spiritual magnet of faith. Indefinable. Mystical, even. If you'd chosen the contemplative life and locked yourself in a monastery you'd have been fine. But you made the mistake of engaging your faith with the world. In your case, through the study of history."

"With you as my guide."

"Yes, all right, I made the same mistake. And had a similar crisis, if that's what you're fishing for. Until I realized that all the knowledge in the world can't stand against faith. No matter what you learn, Thomas, your faith is still there behind it all. The magnet's still pulling." The Bishop's cigar had gone out; he lit it, puffed on it, and resumed.

"It's the learning that's troubling you, isn't it? The evidence is too heavy to ignore: that no one associated with this enterprise, by which I mean the Church, is divine, with the exception of our Lord. It's a shining exception. But the discovery makes you wonder. Thomas, I want you to remember this: Knowledge is about facts. Faith is concerned with truth. They're not necessarily the same. That's what you've flown halfway across the country to discuss, isn't it? Come, it's time for dinner. I don't think there was ever a discussion of faith not improved by a bottle of wine."

That evening didn't set Thomas back on firm ground, but it gave him a life preserver to cling to in the frightening waters of misgiving. They talked for three days; it was, finally, a practical suggestion by the Bishop that realigned the world, showed Thomas a direction to follow while he waited to see if his faith would return.

"One of your strengths as a historian," Lorenzo said as morning sun poured through the window, "has always been your broad range of interests. Periods, places. Now I'm going to suggest another approach. Something different has happened to you, Thomas, and perhaps it calls for a response in kind." The Bishop stretched out and crossed his legs. "The intellectual life of the nineteenth century, in America and Europe, revolved around faith. What it was, who had it, where and when it was needed. It was a powerful set of questions, sometimes created by, and sometimes creating, political and military movements. Questions of faith moving secular societies. I'm suggesting you focus your attention in that arena."

Thomas considered. "Randomly? Or do you have something specific in mind?"

"Of course I do. You sure I can't give you one of these?" He gestured to the humidor. As always, Thomas shook his head. He couldn't think of half a dozen times outside of meals and the celebration of Mass that he'd seen Lorenzo without a cigar. Early on he used to take one to be polite, but he'd never enjoyed them, and their friendship hadn't required that sort of courtesy for years.

"I want you to head straight for the lion's den," Lorenzo said, drawing on his cigar to get it going. "In the nineteenth century, before there was an Italy, rebellions up and down the peninsula raised questions about the secular power of the papacy. The Church in the world, Thomas."

"Your favorite subject."

Lorenzo rolled his eyes in mock despair. "*In* the world, *of* the world—completely different states! Have you learned nothing, Father Kelly?"

If he'd learned nothing else, Thomas had learned that particular distinction well and truly in his years with Lorenzo Cossa. He couldn't help grinning.

Lorenzo grunted. "You're having me on, aren't you? I suppose that's a good sign, that your sense of humor, such as it is, is returning. May I get back to the nineteenth century?"

"Please."

"The questions about the Church's secular power became questions about spiritual power. Do you see what I'm saying? These men followed their doubts to their logical end. Don't run from that: study it. If your faith is strong—as I know it is—you'll survive this encounter and be the better for it."

"And if not?"

Lorenzo held Thomas's eyes. "I'm offering no promises. But at the least, you'll have added to the store of human knowledge. Is that, in itself, such a poor goal?"

It had not been, and Thomas had worked toward it, at first mechanically, then with growing animation. Lorenzo's prescription had proven to be precisely the cure for Thomas's spiritual ailment. Close study of the words and actions of men whose sworn enemy was the Church gave Thomas the tools, the time, and in some way the courage, to sort out the roots of his own faith and the roots of his doubts. The doubts, he'd begun to understand, flowed from received wisdom, unexamined assumptions. **Thomas—really?** The faith sprang from someplace simpler, deeper: the peace he'd always felt in the presence of God. The questions the new voice was asking were only that: questions. Not sly statements of fact, just uncertainties. Legitimate; but standing against them was that undeniable, palpable sense of being home.

Thomas was rock-certain that without Lorenzo's help then, and in the late-night calls in the weeks and months that followed, he'd have made the huge and heavy mistake of valuing the new voice over the old peace. He'd have left his vocation; he'd have left the Church. Now, eight years later, with Thomas secure in his decision and the direction of his life, Lorenzo was asking Thomas for help.

How could he say no?

4

◇

Lorenzo Cardinal Cossa replaced the ornate receiver and stared sourly at the telephone on his desk. How much had been spent to rewire these ridiculous porcelain antiques to modern standards? He relit his cigar, sighing. That they'd go to that trouble proved, yet again, the soundness of his argument: the Church, Lorenzo Cossa's home, his chosen and very nearly his sole family, had lost its bearings. Was wandering in the wilderness. The useful elements of the modern world—functioning electronics, for example, and comfortable clothing—it eschewed in favor of gilt and ermine. But suggest a Latin Mass, or offer the once-obvious idea that the contemplation of a saint's relics could be of spiritual use, and you were derided as pathetically old-fashioned.

All right, then, he was. And from now on, he'd use his cell phone.

As he puffed the cigar, the Cardinal's mood improved. Thomas was coming, would be here in two days. Unlike Lorenzo, Thomas didn't grow short-tempered at the Church's frivolities; he either shrugged them off, or actually didn't notice them, so focused was he on the high-altitude joys of recondite research. Not only a born churchman, a born Jesuit. Born and, once Lorenzo had found him, led, directed, and guided. Thomas Kelly had been that once-in-a-lifetime gifted student, and Lorenzo Cossa had uttered daily prayers of thanks for him. The Good Lord knew what he was doing when he sent Thomas to Lorenzo. In fact Lorenzo saw it as a sign: his time was coming.

And now, had come.

Many of those around Lorenzo assumed that, having achieved his current exalted positions (both at once!), he'd fulfilled his ambitions and would now happily putter among the manuscripts and books for the rest of his days. A valued and important cardinal, a senior official, and a trusted adviser, yes, of course—but sidelined, as the Librarians always were.

Not true. Oh, no, not true. Lorenzo's work had just begun.

5

The wind made a grab for Livia Pietro's hat as she raced out the door. The magnolia's thick green leaves gleamed in the sunlight but she dashed by without a glance, charging across the uneven stones of Piazza Trilussa, heading for the bridge. A strong breeze carried the loamy scent of the Tiber; the more she sped up the harder it pushed against her. As an external manifestation of her internal state, that was perfect; she'd have laughed if she hadn't felt queasy. She didn't remove the wide straw hat, only clamped her hand on it as she ran. She felt foolish, hand square on head like that, though her neighbors' indulgent smiles would have told her—if she hadn't already known—that eccentricity from her was nothing new. The hats, the sunglasses, her ancient tower house, the gray streaks she refused to banish from her long, dark hair, and, worst, her unmarried state at the age of gray streaks, all conspired, though her academic status provided a partial explanation. (*"Professor-essa,"* they'd confide to one another knowingly.) Gossip, Livia was resigned, was inevitable. Through friendliness and liberal spending in the local shops she managed at least to keep the gossip benign.

A horn bleated. She let a *motorino* pass, then darted across the road in a nimble dance with oncoming traffic.

She hurried over the bridge as fast as she dared, though not as fast as she could. Among Livia's Blessings were agility and speed. A horsewoman in her youth, she retained a high level of athletic skill. But a middle-aged *professoressa* speeding like Mercury along the Ponte Sisto would invite exactly the kind of attention Livia was at pains to avoid.

Odd, she thought as she ran, to be rushing someplace she so very much didn't want to go; but a Summons was neither a happy event nor an occasion for choice. Although the Conclave met regularly to debate issues of importance to the Community, it was possible to live a long and happy life without ever being Summoned before it. In fact that was the experience of most Noantri; but this was Livia's second time.

Worse, she feared this Summons was not unrelated to the first.

Across the river she cut left, onto Via Giulia, where the cobbles led past the Palazzo Farnese's ivy-draped wall. The Fontana del Mascherone—the Big Mask Fountain— looked particularly apprehensive and unhappy today. Before her Michelangelo's bridge curved over the road. Livia loved that bridge, its perfect arch and trailing leaves, but right now her heart lurched at the sight. Immediately past it stood, to the right, an apartment building where people lived comfortable, normal lives; and to the left, her destination: Santa Maria dell'Orazione e Morte.

The art historian in her wanted to stop and stand, to drink in the church's bone-bedecked façade, her eyes tracing the path the sculptor took as, inch by inch, he'd coaxed cherubs and skulls from the stone. At times, before a statue or a painting, Livia felt tiny contractions in her arms and hands. Her body, more insightful by far than her mind or even her heart, was re-creating the artist's movements, teaching her how the piece had come to life. Those moments of perception, which after so many years still thrilled her, had been part of the Change for Livia; the works where she felt them were the ones she knew and loved best.

This church's façade was one of those, but she didn't linger. She slipped a five-euro note from her pocket and slid it into the collection slot. In that same movement she found and threw the hidden switch to unlatch the church door. Each Noantri Summoned before the Conclave was told about the switch and how to operate it. Livia had been told the first time; now, she regretted to say, she knew.

Inside the church she took off her dark glasses and moved through the sanctuary to a point behind the altar. The crypt door stood ajar. She removed her hat, smoothed her hair, listened for a moment to the thumping of her heart, and headed down the uneven stone steps into the dank air of the crypt.

At least she was on time.

The stairway curved down to a brick-arched, stone-floored room whose niches held meticulously stacked bones and pyramids of skulls. Rosettes made from hands and arcs made from ribs adorned the walls. Four centuries of the poor and the unclaimed had found sanctified ground here, their bones painstakingly cleaned and positioned for the devout to reflect upon as they prayed. Not for the first time, Livia considered the oddness of her people's penchant for the trappings of death. It was akin, she had decided, to the woven streams that flowed through the carpets of the Bedouins.

This church, though, odd as it was, was an excellent choice for meetings of the Conclave. Like so many of Rome's small churches, Santa Maria dell'Orazione was now rarely used, and the crypt visited even less often. A discreet and sizable annual contribution from the Noantri to the church's burial society procured private access to the crypt at any time; thus the latch in the collection box. For uninterrupted meditation, officially, and no priest or bone cleaner had yet sought to investigate more deeply. The Conclave would be undisturbed, and the weight of centuries in the scents of earth and rock would, as always, serve to remind those who met here of the consequence of their deliberations.

The crypt housed an eternal flame, also appropriate. Its flicker was often the only illumination, but now, as was usual when the Conclave met, great iron candelabra on either side of the room cast pools of wavering light. Puffs of air from cracks in the ancient walls danced shadows against the blacker darkness. As she stepped through the doorway, Livia heard no sound but her own footsteps and their timid echoes, fading as she walked forward and stood before the Conclave.

All were assembled, silent, waiting: the twelve Counsellors sitting in rows right and left, and between them the Pontifex, whose dark gaze made Livia uneasy even when she encountered him in the most casual of circumstances. Here, in the hush of stones and skeletons, it was all she could do not to squirm. She stood silent; it was protocol that the Pontifex should speak first, though in truth Livia could not, at that moment, have spoken at all. A shuddering conflict had enveloped her, familiar from her first Summoning. Like all Noantri, Livia felt an immediate comfort, a sense of grateful belonging, in

a group of her own people. It was physical and instanta-
neous, a calling of blood to blood. The relief of it had
flooded around her when she walked into the crypt. But
here, it was illusion. These black-robed Counsellors were
not her friends. Standing before them the first time,
she'd sensed individual flashes of sympathy behind the
unanimous disapproval. This time, though she didn't
yet know why she was here, nothing but anger filled the
dank air.

"Livia Pietro," the Pontifex said, his deep, slow voice
echoing in the stone chamber. "I'm dismayed to see you
before us once again."

Not as much as I am, Livia thought, but she only
nodded in acknowledgment.

"Years ago, when you were called here," the Pontifex
went on, "you spoke eloquently. You admitted your
error in judgment, but you pleaded movingly the case of
Jonah Richter. Your plea was heard. He was initiated
and allowed to remain. Many of us, through the years,
have made similar mistakes in the name of love." Though
the Pontifex's eyes did not stray from Livia, the black-
robed man at the end of the row to his left—the position
of the Conclave's newest member—lowered his gaze.
Livia struggled not to do the same. "In the event," the
deep voice continued, "your breaking of the Law seems
to have been in vain. Jonah Richter left you not long
after he became one of us. You look surprised that I
know this."

"We were—we were in Berlin at the time, my Lord."

"Because we allowed him to remain, did you think
we would not be watching him? The New always bear
watching, Livia."

Now Livia did look away, her face hot. Her separation

from Jonah was no secret, but she hadn't understood it to have happened in a public spotlight, either.

"Livia," the Pontifex said in tones that were, to her surprise, gentle, "we haven't called you before us to settle that account. This Conclave deliberated and, once you'd made Jonah Richter Noantri, permitted him to continue. That was our decision. Nor could any reproach from us be as painful as his forsaking you has already been, I'm sure. That's the way it is with affairs of the heart." Livia looked back up, meeting his dark eyes as he said, "No, we're here because of a different betrayal. Larger and much more dangerous."

He turned to the woman on his immediate right. Senior in the Conclave and one of the Eldest—like the Pontifex, a bridge to the times Before—she was known to Livia as Rosa Cartelli, although of course that would not have been her name at birth.

"We have received a letter." Cartelli's words were clipped and businesslike. "From Jonah Richter. In German," she added. Livia heard clearly the contempt in Cartelli's voice. To the Counsellors, from various lands and all highly learned, Jonah's native tongue wouldn't have presented a problem; but by tradition, communication with the Conclave was initiated in Latin. From courtesy, the Counsellors usually replied in the language of the petitioner; with Livia called before them, all were speaking Italian. But the choice was always theirs. That Jonah had defied tradition this way did not bode well.

"The letter is a threat," Cartelli said flatly. "He is telling us to choose: either we can make public the contents of the Concordat, or he will."

"But . . ." Livia was at a loss.

"Do you doubt he would carry this through?" the Pontifex asked.

After a moment Livia shook her head. "No, Lord. Jonah is . . . impatient. He feels the Concordat constricts us all. There are many who think the same way," she added. "Who feel it is past time we stepped into the light. And that the world is ready to accept us."

Why had she said that? To defend Jonah? After all this time and in these circumstances? Absurd.

"Yes," the Pontifex said patiently. "I know that. They are wrong."

Livia glanced at the faces of the Counsellors. Most appeared in calm agreement with the Pontifex—as, on this point, despite having just articulated the opposing view, Livia was herself. Three Counsellors, however, glared with an accusatory fierceness that could only mask doubt. Well, why would that not be? Unveiling was a topic of endless interest to, and discussion within, the Community; why wouldn't it be debated in the Conclave as well? Still, whatever their individual beliefs, none of the Counsellors spoke, save one: a woman two seats from Cartelli, whose features were Asian and whose name Livia didn't know. "They are wrong," she echoed the Pontifex in a soft, clear voice, "and there are others in our Community more radical than Jonah Richter who would seize on the chaos this revelation would cause to advance plans yet more perilous."

Livia waited for more explanation; none was forthcoming, but she didn't doubt that what the Counsellor had said was true. She looked again to the Pontifex. "But, Lord, this threat. Why would any of the Unchanged believe him? He can try to reveal whatever he wants—he'll sound like a ranting fool. Surely this isn't any real danger."

"It could be." The man at the end, the one who'd looked away when the Pontifex talked of mistakes made for love, spoke now. "If he can prove it."

"But how could he?"

"The Vatican's copy of the Concordat disappeared in 1849," the Counsellor said.

Taken aback, Livia asked, "It did?"

"Yes. And Jonah Richter claims to have it."

"Is that possible?"

The Counsellor looked to the Pontifex. "The man who stole and hid it," the Pontifex said, "a poet by the name of Mario Damiani, was one of us—a Noantri who believed as Jonah does. Damiani died without revealing its location." The Pontifex spoke steadily, but a shadow passed over his face that Livia thought was not from the flickering candles. "We made a search. I can assure you the Church did also, starting even before the Pope returned from Naples to reestablish his rule in Rome. The Vatican eventually concluded their copy had been misplaced, or possibly destroyed, in the looting and the subsequent attempt to restore order. For the past century and a half they've believed it most likely lost somewhere in the vast disorganization of their collection."

Livia nodded slowly. "It would be plausible. Artworks and documents surface in the Vatican all the time. Sometimes centuries after they disappear."

"The cumbersome bureaucracy at the Vatican—in the Church in general, in fact—has always worked in our favor. The very fact that the Concordat never came to light convinced the Church it hadn't fallen into the wrong hands. For our part, the Conclave was satisfied it had either been destroyed or was hidden so well it would never be found. But Jonah Richter claims he's discovered its hiding place and will reveal its location unless we reveal its contents. That, of course, would be tantamount to Unveiling."

Livia tried to think clearly. "Is it possible Damiani never took it at all? That Jonah knows that story and is bluffing?"

"Jonah Richter might be bluffing, but Mario Damiani did steal the Concordat. He made a copy."

The Pontifex turned to a round man, an American, Livia recalled, named Horace Sumner. "He sent it to a friend, a journalist named Margaret Fuller," Sumner said. "Sealed in a silver box. He instructed Fuller not to read it, and we don't believe she did. In any case she didn't speak about it and she died within a year, in a shipwreck. Her papers and possessions were all lost— except for the silver box, which we were able to retrieve. We've read the copy. It's the Concordat, word for word."

Livia understood. Though the general terms of the Concordat were known to all in the Community, none but the Conclave had seen it. Mario Damiani couldn't have quoted it unless he had it before him.

"Jonah Richter has given us a deadline. Impudent man!" Cartelli's anger was barely contained. "Three days hence, on the feast day of San Gennaro. How symbolic." Her curled lip told Livia that if they'd been alone, woman to woman, Cartelli's next words would have been, *Really, what did you ever see in him?*

"Richter has since gone into hiding," the Pontifex said. "Because of the way he phrased his threat, we don't believe he has the document with him. We think he's discovered its location but left it where it was."

"Why would he do that?"

"Perhaps it's in a place too public, or too private, for easy access. Now, we could find him and eliminate the immediate danger." The casualness with which the words were uttered, in this crypt of the dead, chilled Livia's blood. "But that won't lead us to the Concordat. Unless we find *it,* we're at risk of this happening again. Livia, *you* must find them both. Jonah Richter and the Concordat. He is your responsibility. You know him well, know how he thinks. Do whatever he did, follow whatever trails he followed. Find them before the deadline."

"And then?" She asked this with a tremor in her voice, because she knew the answer.

"You will bring us the Concordat. And you will kill Jonah Richter."

6

Forty-eight hours ago Thomas Kelly had been in cool, fall-fresh London, facing a comfortably predictable day of students, books, and his plant-filled office. Now he sat in a silk armchair watching dust motes dance on a shaft of sunlight at the Vatican. He was still trying to comprehend this shift in the pattern of his life when his thoughts were interrupted by a cheerful young priest, an African with a lilting voice, who led him across the anteroom and ushered him through a grand pair of doors. Lorenzo Cossa looked up from behind a gilt-trimmed desk.

"Your Eminence!" Thomas couldn't help grinning. "You look well." The Cardinal was thin as ever, but a glow of purpose suffused his sharp features. Thomas knew that look: Lorenzo Cossa was at the start of a major new work. Neither the Cardinal nor anyone else involved would be sleeping much for a while.

"You're clearly flourishing yourself, Thomas." Lorenzo stood and came out from behind the desk, looking his protégé over as the African priest left, discreetly shutting the door. "Come, sit. There? Here? Shall we try them all?" With theatrical despair he waved a hand, taking in the throng of furniture, the inlays and rare woods; and the silk-covered wall panels, the marble statuary, the paintings. "What do you think? Too early to redecorate?"

"You haven't changed." The suite, like every inch of the Vatican, was luxurious and ornate, these rooms even more than some because they were the office of a cardinal. Most Princes of the Church took seriously their status as Princes. But Lorenzo had always found luxury distasteful. "All that gilt," he'd say, shaking his head. "Distracting. We have work to do." If Lorenzo had his way, Thomas knew, this room would be emptied and painted white. Filing cabinets would replace cherubs; bookcases would line the walls where Renaissance Madonnas now hung. Everything would go but the desk—and the humidor.

"And you, Thomas? Have you changed your ways? One of the advantages of Rome over home—I can smoke wherever I want. Father Ateba's arranging for coffee. Can I offer you a cigar?"

"No, thanks." Thomas sat in a velvet armchair, smoothing his cassock under him. He rarely wore it, preferring to teach in jacket and collar; but presenting himself at the Vatican for the first time seemed to call for more formal attire.

"You can wear whatever you want, by the way," Lorenzo grunted, appearing, as so often, to read Thomas's mind. He himself was in a black jacket and shirt. A heavy gold chain draped into his jacket pocket, where his cardinal's cross was tucked to keep it out of the way of his work. That and the gold ring on the hand that had swept the air were the only changes Thomas could see in the cantankerous scholar he'd met years ago. "I want you focused on your work, not the trim on your ferraiolo. They take the trappings seriously here but don't let that fool you. A lot of what goes on is less pious than you'd think. Than you'd hope. More of a business, sometimes, than God's holy work." Briefly, Lorenzo glared; then he relaxed. He thumbed an onyx lighter, puffed his cigar. "That's why you're here." He settled against the gilt and velvet of an armchair and looked at Thomas steadily. "The Church was founded by our Lord, but it's run by men. Good men, most of them, and some not, and all of them—all of us—make mistakes. Sometimes those mistakes, large or small, come back to haunt us. You've seen that happen."

Thomas nodded, unsure where Lorenzo was headed.

"A serious mistake was made six hundred years ago. I'd like to undo it, but I can't. The best I can do is make sure it never comes to light." Lorenzo tapped ash from his cigar. "In 1431, shortly after he became Pope, Martin the Fifth signed an agreement known as the Concordat. The Church has been living with its provisions ever since. It was wrong to sign it, wrong to abide by it, but at this point the Church would be seriously damaged if its existence became known. Much more than the damage that's already been done by continuing to follow it."

Thomas frowned in thought. "The Concordat? I haven't heard of it."

"No, you wouldn't have. It's hidden even from you deeply learned scholars. It's a secret even most cardinals aren't privy to."

"I see. But now that you're Archivist and Librarian—"

"That's what they think. But I was familiar with it already. I've known for some time."

"This Concordat—it's an agreement with whom?"

"I can't tell you that. When you read it you'll know,

but until then— Thomas, I'm afraid of what it will do to you, to your faith, to hear me tell it without proof."

Thomas stared, and then laughed. "My faith? I've been through that fire and out the other side. Thanks to you. Whatever this is about, it can't be worse than that was."

"You're wrong." Flatly, Lorenzo returned Thomas's gaze. A silence stretched, and Thomas became aware of an unseen clock ticking in some distant corner.

Lorenzo shifted, puffed on the cigar again. "The Concordat is missing."

"Missing?"

"The Vatican copy. The other party has evidently been able to keep track of theirs through the centuries—at least, I haven't heard otherwise. Ours, however, seems to have vanished sometime after 1802. That's the last time a comprehensive inventory was attempted. Though even then, I can't be sure the records are accurate." Lorenzo shook his head. "I told you: this collection is chaotic. Disastrously so."

"But the renovation—the entire Library was closed for three years."

"Renovated chaos is still chaos. That was all about electronic security chips, computer workstations, and bombproof bunkers. What's here, and where it is—still anybody's guess."

The door opened and the young priest returned, bearing a silver coffee service and china cups. "Thank you, Father," Lorenzo said. "You didn't have to bring it in yourself. They tell me that's what the valet is for."

The priest smiled. "I had a sense you wanted a certain level of discretion, Eminence. And coffee is not so heavy."

"A fine young man, that," Lorenzo told Thomas once Father Ateba was gone. "He has a future here in Rome. Or he could go back to Cameroon, and he'll become a bishop, without question. The future of the Church lies in Africa. In Latin America. In Asia! Do you know why?"

Thomas took the coffee Lorenzo handed him and added cream and sugar, marveling at the delicate porcelain. "You're about to tell me, aren't you?"

"To enlighten you, yes!" Lorenzo's tone was self-mocking but he continued seriously. "Because they believe. It's about faith with them—with us it's logic, it's reason, it's rationalism. Other words for compromise. So-called fairness—accommodation!—they'll be the death of this Church. Oh, wipe off that smile."

"It's a pleasure to hear you fume again, is all. Your Eminence."

"Yes, fine. You think I'm Cardinal Chicken Little. Still, indulge me. This is serious business. I may be wrong, and you're certainly entitled to keep that thought in your head as you do your work, as long as you do it. I need you to find the Church's copy of the Concordat. That's why I called you here. I had a search made when I took this office. No trace of it's turned up. But we need to find it. Before someone stumbles over it by accident and everything comes out."

Thomas sat back against the chair and let his gaze wander the high-ceilinged room. The weight of history was palpable in the paintings and the statues, in the thick, figured carpets. The worries and triumphs, the work and the scheming—the prayers and uncertainties—of centuries of churchmen could be breathed in with the air. Two days ago, he'd sat in a dusty archive in London, reading a letter from an implacable enemy of this place, and now, he was breathing this air. He set down his coffee cup.

"It's not here."

Whatever Lorenzo had been expecting Thomas to say, it clearly wasn't that. "Excuse me? You've suddenly developed unshakable faith, and it's not in vital theological doctrine but in the efficiency of the Archivist's staff? Just because we can't find it, you conclude it's not here?"

"That's not what I mean. I've never heard of this Concordat until today, but . . . Does the name Mario Damiani mean anything to you?"

"No. Should it?"

"Possibly." Thomas resettled himself, hearing his cassock rustle. "Damiani was a poet of the Risorgimento. A captain in Garibaldi's army. It's likely he was involved in the looting of the Archives in 1849."

Lorenzo's gaze was steady. "You think that was when the Concordat disappeared?"

"I think he stole it. Deliberately."

"Do you now? Based on what?"

"There's a letter he wrote to Margaret Fuller. The American journalist?" No light went on in the Cardinal's eyes, but it didn't matter. "It's what I've been doing in London. Going through Fuller's papers. She was enormously important in Italy. Her reporting shaped the American view of the uprising and helped make Garibaldi a hero. She was married to a partisan, knew them all, and didn't pretend to be objective. Damiani and she were particularly close. In his letter he tells her he stole something from the Vatican. He's coy about what it is, but calls it, quote, 'a document that will shatter the Church.'"

Briefly, Lorenzo was silent. Then: "No, I don't think so. If he had it and knew what it was, why didn't he use it?"

"I'm not sure he got the chance. He claims to have hidden it somewhere safe. He made a copy and sent that to Fuller with instructions not to read it, but to take it to Garibaldi if anything happened to him. Something did, though it's not clear what. That letter, from 1849 just before the French entered Rome, is the last time he's heard from."

Lorenzo sat very still. "There's a copy?"

Thomas shook his head. "Fuller headed for New York a year later, on a sailing ship. No one's ever been sure why."

"Why she went? Or why a sailing ship?"

"Either. But both make sense in light of Damiani's letter. He tells Fuller to take care, because the Vatican will be after the document, and to give it to Garibaldi if she hasn't heard from Damiani in a year. By then Garibaldi was already in New York. Steamships had just begun to cross the Atlantic, faster than sailing ships but also bigger. More danger of being followed. On Fuller's ship, besides her family, there was only one other passenger, an American named Horace Sumner, who boarded at the last minute. The ship turned out to be a legendary mistake, though: they sank in a storm within sight of the New York coast. Most of the bodies were never found, and all Fuller's papers were lost. Besides her published books and articles, she only left behind a few scattered items."

"Which you, my eminent scholar, have discovered?"

With a grin, Thomas said, "This is my period, you know."

"Well, don't you look pleased with yourself? I seem to recall it wasn't your period until some wise man recommended it to you. Nevertheless, a little back-patting might be in order, if you're correct." The Cardinal smoked in silence for a time. Finally he said, "If that document was the Concordat, it would answer two questions: why we haven't located it here, and why it hasn't come to light."

"Exactly."

"Well." Lorenzo laid his cigar in a crystal ashtray. "Do you think you can find it?"

"I have no idea. But why not leave it hidden?"

"You mean, since it hasn't been found in all these years, assume it won't be? For two reasons. First, we're not sure Damiani—is that his name?—was talking about the Concordat. I'd hate to think he'd unearthed yet another document equally dangerous, and I'd like to know. For another, assuming it *is* the Concordat, it's too big a risk. Maybe it's been destroyed by now, but if it hasn't, it could still be found. Someone will be digging a foundation or knocking down a wall, leafing through an old book or reframing a picture . . . No, what I need is either the thing itself or some believable proof it's gone for good. Can you bring me that?"

"I really don't know. Do you want me looking for the Concordat, whatever it is, or the document Damiani stole and hid, whatever *it* is?"

"Both. Pursue whatever trails make sense. But I have a feeling you might be right. Follow your poet. Find what he stole. If it's the Concordat, you will have done your Church a great service."

In the opulent room with the unseen clock faintly ticking, Thomas nodded. "I'll start this afternoon."

7

Standing in the dank silence of the bone-decked crypt, Livia Pietro struggled to find her voice. She'd been given the instructions of the Conclave, delivered by the Pontifex himself; no argument was possible, but still, she spoke. "My Lord. I can't."

"On the contrary," the Pontifex replied calmly. "You will kill Jonah Richter, or we will. He is your Disciple. He is your responsibility."

Livia felt faint. Of course he was right. She knew the Law. Her first transgression—bringing Jonah into the Community without prior permission—had been a major one, and it was by grace of the Conclave that she hadn't been exiled for it. They wouldn't be so lenient again.

"The search for the Concordat, right now, takes precedence over the search for Jonah Richter," said the American, Horace Sumner. At that, Livia felt a spark of hope. Perhaps if she found the document and returned it, Jonah would be spared. He was impatient, yes, but he was still New, and he was young. He could be made to understand—to see that many others had thought through the position he'd taken and that the results of Unveiling would not be what he hoped.

Sumner went on. "As far as that, we've fallen into a bit of luck. A priest has recently arrived in Rome, sent for by the new Librarian of the Vatican. Father Thomas Kelly, from Boston by way of London. Father Kelly's field is the history of the Church. His specialization is Italy in the nineteenth century."

"The Cardinal is searching for the Vatican's copy of the Concordat," Cartelli said. "He had people comb through the collection when he arrived, and of course they didn't find it. He knows when it was last seen, thus more or less when it disappeared. Our sources say he's brought Father Kelly here because of that expertise, but we think the priest doesn't know the nature of the document."

Livia looked from Cartelli to Sumner. "An odd coincidence. The timing, I mean."

"No." Sumner shook his head. "It's more likely that Jonah Richter, seeing the Cardinal make such a serious effort to locate the Concordat, feels his hand's been forced and so is forcing ours."

The scholar in Livia, trying to stay calm, focused on an unanswered question. "Why, in fact, is the Cardinal making this effort? From what you say, the Archivists before him have been content to let this secret lie."

The Pontifex spoke. "Just as we have always been divided between those who are grateful for the Concordat and willing to abide by its provisions and those who believe it constricts us and that the time is past for Unveiling, the Church has had for centuries its own internal debate. Among those in the Church who know about the Concordat, all—*all*, Livia—find it repugnant. But an extremist faction feels that in agreeing to it, Martin the Fifth poisoned the Church's very soul. They believe any relationship with us beyond the murderous enmity of old is a tragic and irresponsible mistake and argue

Martin's act delegitimizes him and all Popes since. That it is proof he was never fit to lead the Church. They maintain it was we who engineered Martin's rise, in exchange for this contract. A charge," he added with a small smile, "not entirely without merit. We didn't engineer it, but once assured of the transformation in our lives Martin was prepared to bring about, we . . . took part in events already under way."

"A fine distinction," Cartelli sniffed, "which is lost on the extremists. A sour and unsubtle crowd. Their dearest wish is to go back to the apostolic line of the man who would have been John the Twenty-third, now called Antipope. It was he who was defeated by Martin."

Livia considered this. "They want to install whoever's in that line today, as Pope? The Church would never allow it."

"Whether they would or wouldn't does not signify!" Cartelli snapped. "For myself, I believe they might indeed. But can you not see the danger of the argument erupting, irrespective of who wins it? If the Church were to split publicly on this issue, our existence would be revealed. In order to gain sympathy for their cause, the militant faction would paint us in the darkest of colors. Vicious and bloody rhetoric would be used to terrify the faithful, as in years past. The power struggle within the Church would be couched in terms of us: *Are you a true and pious child of the Holy Mother Church? Or a friend of the Godless Noantri?* Those currently in power would try to make people understand the Concordat as a lesser-of-two-evils way to keep the wicked Noantri under control. The others would claim no compromise is possible with such demons. And no one, Livia Pietro, would claim us as their friends."

Ice sat in Livia's stomach; she wanted to argue, but long experience of the world silenced her. Cartelli, in fact, was probably correct.

"The new Librarian," the Pontifex said, and Livia was grateful for his calm, measured tones, "Lorenzo Cardinal Cossa, is of the extremist camp. He would happily use the Concordat as a scourge against us. But he is bound by obedience to his Church. We believe his search for the lost copy, therefore, is his attempt to do the next best thing: to ensure this compromise never comes to light."

"I see," Livia said slowly. "But if it does—"

"If Jonah Richter were to reveal the contents of the Concordat and prove its existence, the Cardinal, we think, would be bitterly grateful. The ensuing hysteria within the Church—and around the world—would set him free to argue to the current Pope and the Church powers that nothing could restore the Church's legitimacy but an abrogation of the Concordat and the destruction of the Noantri."

The Pontifex paused, then spoke like iron. "That will not happen." His echoing voice seemed to agitate the shadows, to make the bones dance on the candlelit walls. Livia did not doubt him. One of the Eldest, the Pontifex was a man of great learning, wise judgment, and respected counsel. And something more, also: a depth and delicacy of understanding of the Community, their lives and their situation, that set him apart and above. There were those, like Jonah, who believed that they needed no Conclave and no leader and, after Unveiling, would have none. But while they had a leader, no Noantri had ever argued that another was more suited than this man.

In a quiet voice, the Pontifex spoke again. "That Cardinal Cossa has not already begun this argument within the Church indicates, we believe, that he does not know about Jonah Richter's threat. Nor will he. As I said, if you make no progress in your search for the Concordat, the Conclave will attend to Jonah Richter. But there will be other Jonahs, other cardinals. Until the world becomes more enlightened, this danger will be with us. The document must be recovered."

In the silence, all eyes rested upon Livia. It seemed to her she was seeing the Pontifex, the entire Conclave, from a great distance; but with exquisite clarity just the same.

"The priest," she heard herself say. "Father Kelly."

"You will need him," the Pontifex replied. "We're fairly certain Mario Damiani left instructions of some sort to the place where he hid the Concordat, where Jonah Richter stumbled upon it."

"'Stumbled upon'!" Cartelli scoffed. "More likely, has been obsessively searching for it under our very noses."

"Perhaps," the Pontifex said evenly. "In any case, Mario Damiani was a man with enormous contempt for the Church. A very intelligent man, also. He would have understood the Concordat might have to pass decades, perhaps centuries, in its hiding place. Concealing it on Church property would be a sensible decision: Church-owned buildings are the last to be demolished, are rarely even renovated beyond minimal structural repair. Such a course would have appealed to Damiani's sense of irony, also. He'd have chosen carefully, appropriately. If Jonah Richter has already located the document's hiding place, an expert in Church history might be able to right the balance."

"Also," said Cartelli drily, "we do not like the idea of a priest running around loose, digging into our past. We'd like an eye kept on him."

"So you want me to enlist Father Kelly in my search?"

"Or offer to aid his," said the Pontifex. "An art historian who's lived a long time in Rome—you could be valuable to him. Our information is that Father Kelly is an obsessive researcher. He's been charged with an important task. He might welcome the help. But bear in mind, the priest has no deadline and feels no sense of urgency. We do."

"If he refuses?"

"Persuade him."

"If that involves telling him—the truth? About the Noantri?"

The Counsellors glanced at one another. The Pontifex didn't take his eyes off Livia. "Then you will tell him. We have debated this. Father Kelly is a scholar of great achievement and deep intellectual curiosity. It strains credulity to think that Cardinal Cossa expected once he found the Concordat, he would not read it."

"Does he believe as Cardinal Cossa does, about us?"

"They all do," Cartelli said with disgust.

The Pontifex, for the first time, turned on Cartelli a look of mild impatience; but he didn't correct her.

"If Father Kelly doesn't yet know the contents of the Concordat, he most likely doesn't know the truth of our existence, either," he said. "But Cardinal Cossa has been grooming this young man for some time. He probably intended to make him privy to that secret as he advanced in the Church. Father Kelly will almost certainly know one day."

"And so you are giving me permission to tell him now?"

"My," Cartelli said, "why suddenly so obedient? I don't recall you asking for permission the last time."

Livia's cheeks burned. The last time: when she had told Jonah. Revealed what she was, who the Noantri were. She had wanted to share with him the deepest part of herself, and to make him comprehend her certainty and her fears: what could be theirs in a life together, and what could not. The risk had been that he'd react as so many always had, with fear, with revulsion. She'd wanted him to know she understood that and was willing to take that chance, for him. From the start of time lovers had promised to climb the highest mountain, swim the deepest ocean, to prove their love, but Livia had offered Jonah a greater gift: their love itself, to claim or destroy.

And he'd been neither afraid nor repulsed. Nor merely accepting. Amused, at first, believing she was joking with him. Then, once persuaded, he was thrilled, and soon was asking, pleading, to join her. To be Noantri, too. She had thought, at the time, that it was from love. That he wanted to be everything she was.

"Livia." The dark voice came to her as though from far away. "Livia. You must begin." She looked up to see the Pontifex leaning forward in the flickering light. "Time is short." He smiled a tiny smile, acknowledging the irony in that statement.

"My Lord," she said. "I may not succeed."

He shook his head. "You will. You will search until you find the Concordat. If the deadline is near and you haven't found it yet, you will continue the search and we will see to Jonah Richter." He sat back again. "Jonah cannot escape this sentence, Livia. It will be far better for him if you are the one to carry it out."

The Counsellors, the Pontifex, all sat motionless, eyes on Livia in the candlelit gloom. She had been given her instructions and dismissed; she understood that.

Still, in a shocking breach of protocol, as though she were not part of the proceedings, but only watching, she heard her own voice whisper, "Is there no other way?"

The Pontifex may have been about to speak, but Cartelli slapped the arm of her chair. The sound rattled like a gunshot. "*What* other way? Are you a fool, too? Or"—her eyes narrowed in her wrinkled face—"are you in sympathy with Jonah Richter? Do you, also, believe the time for Unveiling has come?"

Livia shook her head. "No, no. I wish I could say I think so. But I don't believe it has."

"Then go. Do as you've been told. Or six centuries of peace will be destroyed. The fires will come again. In fear and raging fury we will be hunted, driven out, and we will die. You did not know those times. I did. We did." She nodded to the Pontifex, to a few of the others. "All this will be repeated, magnified a thousand times, if the world learns once again whom to label 'vampire.'"

8

The blue eyes that had watched Livia Pietro enter the church now saw her emerge, pale and shaken. She shut the door gently, as though it were fragile, and stood unmoving on the cobblestones until a gust tangled her long black hair. That seemed to wake her: she smoothed her hand over her head and put on her hat. The watcher's heart leapt. He remembered the feel of her hair, thick and untamed, under his own hand. Her skin, also, supple velvet despite her age. He smiled, understanding now what he hadn't the first time he touched her: the full and double meaning there. And the scent of her. He stood behind a closed window in a flat across Via Giulia, so what stirred him now must be not real, but remembrance. Still, he caught his breath. Few of the Noantri wore perfume. To senses awakened by the Change, the world offered sights, sounds, and aromas in infinite and startling intricacy. Not the least of these was the scent of one another; few cared to mask or even augment this signature. With this, as with so many of the Community's customs, his Livia was out of step. She delighted in a range of essences, rare and delicate, each applied with a fine hand—and each acting on him differently but irresistibly. He had tried, so many times and in so many ways, to persuade her of what was clear to him: that her unconcern with Noantri convention proved that what she claimed to want—a comfortable, invisible, assimilated life—was not her real desire.

His Livia. He shook his head. He still thought of her that way. They hadn't spoken in more than two years, and if he was correct, she'd just been instructed to kill him.

Jonah Richter had known his letter to the Conclave would call them into full battle mode—meaning, first, mind-numbing assemblies and debates. Ultimately, though, they'd have to act. He suspected he knew what form their response would take, and apparently he'd been right. Livia had been Summoned, had gone in looking apprehensive, and come out looking like hell. Maybe he was flattering himself; but if the Conclave had been as alarmed by his threat as he expected, his destruction was an obvious solution. Livia—the Noantri who had Made him and thus the only Noantri inherently dangerous to him— was its obvious agent.

Many of his friends, Noantri who believed as he did about Unveiling, claimed the Noantri were superior to the Unchanged. Some had taken, in fact, to ostentatiously dropping "Unchanged" in favor of "Mortal," a label so fraught that its use had been abandoned by the Community long ago. The extremist opinion held that, far from being forced into hidden, constricted lives, the Noantri ought to rule. That their fine sensibilities, acquired wisdom, and distant view of unrolling time made them better suited to governing than were the limited Unchanged.

Jonah did not share this viewpoint, and he sniffed the stench of egotism in those who did. He suspected that each saw himself—or herself—as the Emperor of All when the transition came. And he remained skeptical at the idea that it was possible to benignly rule those who were, not to put too fine a point on it, your food source.

The vision shared by Jonah and his group was a different one. After Unveiling, the Unchanged would understand two things: that the Noantri were not a threat; and that to be Noantri was to live so completely, to have senses so finely tuned and a mind so fully awake, that everyone would want to Change.

And where would nourishment come from, when all blood was Noantri blood? The would-be Emperors sneered this question in the Noantri coffeehouses and bars, the baths and gathering places. The answer—offered patiently by partisans like Jonah, edgily by those less tolerant—was: science. Human blood, after all, was only a chemical compound. It could be cloned, synthesized, grown. Why not? Promising work was already coming out of Japan. More would follow. Until then, the Unchanged already donated blood by the barrelful, some of which found its covert way to the Noantri as it had for centuries. More to the point, many sold their blood to pay their rent or buy their beer. Why wouldn't they keep that practice up, especially at the prices the Noantri could offer?

The arguments went on and on. Talk of Unveiling was everywhere; according to those Elder than Jonah, it always had been, since the day the Concordat was signed. The Conclave had no objection to the discussion, in fact was willing at any time to hear a new line of reasoning pro or con. The position of the Conclave, however, had never yet been affected by argument. Unveiling would happen in time; this was not the time.

But it was. Jonah was tired of hearing the arguments.

He was tired of pretending, of evading questions with a smile. He had become afraid, suddenly, of losing the friends of his youth, as he saw them change, saw their faces line and their eyes soften. Livia had tried to comfort him, telling him these losses were part of the dark side of Noantri life, unavoidable and balanced by so much else. She repeated to him an aphorism, a saying of the Noantri: The Unchanged change; only the Changed remain unchanging. But her voice held sorrow as she thought of people she'd loved, long gone; and far from being persuaded to accept his friends' bad fortune, Jonah had begun to see an entirely different course of action.

Livia, he thought now, as he watched her turn and start slowly down the street. **You'll come to understand. This is, without question, the right thing. Even the members of the Conclave will be glad this happened, once it's over. Then maybe—maybe—you and I can be together again. In any case, don't worry; you won't be killing me.**

9

In the vast, marble-floored hush of the Vatican Library's *Manoscritti* Reading Room, Father Thomas Kelly jotted on a notepad, then pocketed his pencil to keep his bad habit at bay. No pencil-tapping here. Along with no photography, no food or drink, no ink pens, and no humming to yourself. And no touching the books without white cotton gloves. Ah, intellectual freedom.

Not that he minded the restrictions, really. He was amazed just to be here. He wanted nothing more than to wander through the bright rooms, along shadowed corridors, past towering windows, and across the thresholds of low, hidden doors. He yearned to unlatch cabinets, slide drawers, climb ladders. But you couldn't. You sat and looked through the electronic catalog, a legacy of a previous Librarian's reorganization of the treasures in his charge. You requested the items you wanted to study, and they were delivered to you.

Thomas's clerical collar brought him considerable deference from the staff, but he had no freer access than any other scholar. Lorenzo, of course, could have arranged for Thomas to enter any room he wanted, handle any document he cared to, without interference. That arrangement would have been highly unusual, though, and would not pass unnoticed. Because of the sensitive nature of Thomas's research, Lorenzo had asked him to work within the system. "Unless it becomes absolutely necessary," he'd added. "If it is, let me know and I'll say the word."

Thomas had been tempted, just so he could wander those corridors; but that would be overweening and wrong. For the task Lorenzo had charged him with, the system was working fine. Right now, better than fine.

A day of intense research here, added to the work he'd been doing in London for the past few years, had Thomas convinced he was one of the world's leading experts on the looting of the Vatican Library in 1849. That, in itself, was no great accomplishment; but he was also more sure than ever that it was then that *Sottotenente* Mario Damiani—who, braggart though he may have been, did actually seem to have led the raid—had stolen the Concordat. What the Concordat was and why this mattered so much, Thomas still had no idea. All in good time, though: Lorenzo had brought him here to discover its hiding place, not its meaning.

Methodical scholar that Thomas was, he'd spent his first afternoon following the few faint trails the first search team had found, just to make sure they'd missed nothing. When those trails faded out, he'd gone back to his original thought and begun tracking down Mario Damiani.

All day yesterday he'd uncovered nothing but the facts of Damiani's life and work and his service in Garibàldi's Republican Army. Some of what he found was straight information, and some of it had to be read between the lines; some he'd already known and some he hadn't; much was of interest to the scholar in him but little to the newly minted detective. But with the fresh new morning came a new thought and a hopeful find.

Damiani had written in Romanesco, the traditional dialect of Rome, a choice of some Republican patriots of his era that Thomas, if he were being honest, would have to call a self-limiting affectation. In Thomas's opinion, Romanesco wasn't different enough from Italian to make using it the statement of fierce independence the partisans intended; it was, though, just different enough to be irritating to the Italian speaker trying to read it. For scholarly purposes Thomas had long since become fluent in Romanesco, as well as a number of other Italian dialects, dead and living. Hoping to get an idea of who Mario Damiani had really been, of how he'd thought and therefore where he might have taken something as precious as the Concordat, Thomas had requested the Library's volumes of Damiani's works. When they arrived they told him little, but by then he was off on a different trail.

Waiting for the volumes to be excavated from whatever deep vault they were buried in, he'd stayed at the catalog computer and clicked idly through the list of other Romanesco poets, thinking perhaps the works of Damiani's fellow fiery patriots might help his project of getting inside the man's mind. The catalog included thumbnail images, usually the front covers of the works in question. Some seemed promising, and Thomas slipped his pencil from his pocket once or twice to make notes, books to request later if he needed them. At the end of the list he found a grouping of uncategorizable odds and ends: letters, records, fragments. An item listed as "Poems, handwritten, anonymous, damaged" caught his eye. He clicked on the thumbnail image to enlarge it. The item was a pasteboard-covered notebook, bent and beat. How extensive the damage to the pages might be, Thomas couldn't tell, but the front cover was in good enough shape that he could read the handwritten inscription on it: *Poesie d'Amore, per Trastevere, Gennaio 1847.* **Love Poems, for Trastevere, January 1847.** He hadn't been able to make out the words when the image was small, but the handwriting had seemed familiar. Now he could see he was right: it was Damiani's.

Thomas put in an immediate request for the notebook, and it was delivered soon after Damiani's other works on a silent-wheeled cart by a thin, solemn clerk who whispered, *"Prego, Padre,"* and slipped away. Thomas's white-gloved fingers put down the volume he'd been holding and took up the notebook. He leafed through it with a delicacy that belied the pounding of his heart. Could it be this easy? The stolen document, slipped into a notebook, then lost all these years because of a lack of attribution? Thomas imagined the Concordat rustling out of the pages, saw himself racing through the echoing hallways, bearing it triumphantly to Lorenzo; and he laughed out loud—provoking frowns from other researchers, which seemed to be his lot—when he turned the final pages. Of course it wasn't there. Nothing fell out, though the book was in sorry shape: back cover gone, some pages torn and some missing, looking as though it had been stepped on more than once. **Oh, Thomas. Still a hopeless romantic.**

He glanced at some of the poems. Just as the cover promised, they were love poems, or at least, poems of praise, to the buildings and streets, the statues and fountains of Trastevere. None of the poems was titled; it was left to the reader to work out the subject of each. A few seemed obvious to Thomas:

Du' angioloni de quell'angiolo stanno de guardia
ar martiro, buttato ggiù in ner pozzo

two angels of that angel keep their watch
over the martyr, thrown into the well

That had to be San Callisto, where two of Bernini's
angels gazed perpetually across the church to the pit
where the martyred Pope had died. Or

Cosmologgje de colore, rosso-sangue, bianche,
e le curve llustre de li pini in ombre de verde

cosmologies of color, blood-red, white,
and shining curves of pines in shades of green

What came to mind was the floor—Cosmatesque,
the style was called—at San Crisogono. Many churches
had similar floors, but these colors were associated, in
Thomas's mind at least, with that one. And *Cosmolog-*
gje/Cosmatesco, was it wordplay? Maybe. But maybe
not . . .

Well, it had been his plan to spend the morning
studying Damiani's work. He might as well start here.
He settled over the notebook, forearms on the table. He
read a poem, turned a page, read another. So absorbed
was he in the words he was reading that he actually
jumped when a soft voice spoke beside him.

"Mario Damiani! I thought no one read him anymore but me!"

Thomas blinked, taking in the sight: a woman in a
flowing flowered skirt, a blouse, and a complicated jacket
(how did women know how to wear things like that?)

was removing large sunglasses and smiling in surprise. She took off a straw hat and smoothed her dark hair. She'd spoken in English, and, extending her hand, in English went on. "Livia Pietro. I'm an art historian."

Thomas took her hand automatically. Her grip was strong and cool, and her eyes were an extraordinary green: silver-flecked, deep and dark. Moonlight on the ocean. Thomas realized he was staring. "Thomas Kelly," he said. He started to stand, but she slid out the chair next to him and sat. He dropped back into his own chair and added, "A historian, too, but of the Church. From Boston."

"I know." Livia Pietro dropped her voice to a whisper as two scholars by the window frowned over at them. She laid her hat on the table and gave Thomas a mischievous smile.

"That I'm an American?" Thomas matched her whisper. "Is it that obvious?"

"Well, you Americans do sit, walk, and hold yourselves in your own way. You're not hard to spot. But no: I meant, that you're a historian. The collar might suggest theologian, but you're reading Damiani, a fellow not known for his religious subtlety."

"Brava." Thomas smiled. "Some fine deduction."

"Why, thank you, Father. I've studied Damiani myself, here and there. He was an excellent poet. Complicated, elliptical, but well worth the effort. May I?"

Livia Pietro unzipped her shoulder bag and removed white cotton gloves, pulled them on, and lifted a volume off the pile. **Prepared and making herself at home,** Thomas thought. Academic protocol demanded that he object, stake his claim now, or risk losing his proprietary rights to Damiani's volumes. But Pietro's good humor was appealing, and it occurred to Thomas that if she knew Damiani's work well, perhaps she could help him get inside the poet's head.

She looked up and asked, "Do you read Romanesco? Few non-Italians do. Few Italians these days, actually."

"My main subject is the Church in the nineteenth century, on the Italian peninsula and elsewhere around Europe, as affected by the political movements of the time. Many primary sources have never been translated. I found it easier—" At Livia Pietro's smile, Thomas stopped short, hearing with something like horror his own pedantic tones. "I'm sorry. I think I spend too much time with undergraduates. Yes, I read Romanesco."

"So do I. What's this?" With a quick, conspiratorial movement, Livia Pietro slid the battered notebook along the tabletop. One finger keeping Thomas's place, she leafed through the pages. Her green eyes seemed to sparkle. "Is this Damiani's? I don't know these."

Thomas, who until that moment had not known eyes sparkled except in novels, said, "Yes, I think so. It was cataloged with the miscellanea. I doubt if anyone's looked at it since it was accessioned. If they had, the handwriting would've—"

"Yes," she said. "I agree. How exciting! You've made a discovery. Added to the store of human knowledge." Her brows knit. "But look—missing pages. I wonder why."

"I assume, poems that didn't go well."

"Perhaps," she said doubtfully. "But look at some of these. Cross-outs, rewrites, arrows, more cross-outs, lines up the margins. He didn't seem to mind poems that needed work."

"Maybe he thought these couldn't be saved."

"Ummm." Livia Pietro came dangerously close to humming to herself, Thomas thought, as she turned the pages of the small notebook. "Interesting." She nodded, said, "Ummm," again, and settled over the volume. After a moment, Thomas pulled his own chair closer and read along with her.

IO

---◇---

Under the glorious blue Rome sky the buildings of La Sapienza positively glowed with learning. Anna Jagiellon flopped down against the trunk of a golden-leafed *platano*. The morning was fresh and clear and she had an hour before her next class: twentieth-century Russian poetry, a miraculous trifecta of a fascinating subject, presented in a creatively organized curriculum, taught by, for once, a professor who, though Mortal, wasn't an idiot. Not only not an idiot, the man was hot: a grinning swarthy Serb. She'd caught the way he looked at her as she studiously took her notes, seen the corners of his mouth tug up when she swept her long blond hair back from her forehead. She'd have taken a run at him already, but her current life was a comfortable one that she wasn't prepared to complicate for a few rolls in the hay. Especially now, with her goal suddenly, after so long, within sight. If she was able to accomplish her objective, she and the Serb could take it up then. At that point they'd be fair game for each other.

Not that there was anything fair going on when a Noantri made a play for one of the Unchanged. The Noantri body was so intensely and elusively irresistible to Mortal senses that Noantri custom declared seducing the Unchanged unacceptable. Amazing, Anna thought, how her people had the same wide streak of pious hypocrisy as Mortals, who outlawed double-dealing, drunkenness, and debauchery and then feverishly committed every sin they had time for. In her Community, it was the same. If every Noantri who took a Mortal lover were punished, the Conclave would have time for little else. And, Anna suspected, would be missing a few of its own members.

Now that she was settled in the shade she pulled off her hat, a red straw Jason Wu, fizzy with random bits of crimson netting that would have done her no good if she'd actually needed to veil her features, if she'd had to go about with that air of elegant mystery women had affected a hundred years ago. Aha, progress! A century and now she could uncover her face.

Honestly, how could these Mortals stand it?

Of all the identities, professions, and trades Anna Jagiellon had had through a long, long life, being a university student was the one she returned to most often. True, her considerable intellect was rarely challenged except by Noantri professors, who, recognizing their own, quietly tailored assignments to take into account, and take advantage of, not only her intelligence but also the years of learning already behind her. Still, even without that, she'd found enough new knowledge at universities to keep her interested, and her own impatience and restlessness found an echo in the yeasty fervor of young Mortals. Mortals, damn it. She used the politically correct "Unchanged," or "Gli Altri"—"the others," as opposed to her own peoples' "Noantri," which meant "we others"—when she had to, but she hated those terms. It wasn't, as she pointed out to nods and mumbled agreement in the Circolo degli Artisti café, in that back room where you'd always find a compatible few, that they were *other* or *not changed* that made the vast majority of humans different from, and yes, lesser than, Noantri. It was that they were *mortal*. It was that they would die.

That kind of talk, naturally, was dangerous. It had gotten her exiled nearly a century and a half ago, sent to Buenos Aires. Far from Europe, but not any kind of hardship, not for her. The beautiful, wealthy, and wild port city had adored the beautiful, wealthy, and wild young Hungarian. She'd loved it back, its burning sun and broad, sparkling river, its *confiterías* where she sipped *café con leche* all day, and its sultry clubs where she danced all night. She'd considered turning her back on the Old World and making the New her home. But though the Noantri Community in Argentina was large, Rome was the center of the oppressor's power and also of her people's. Her people, her hidden, optimistic, absurdly contented people, who had every right to the entire pie and were grateful for the crumbs. The Conclave had eventually lifted her sentence, not called her back but allowed her to return if she chose. She did.

She was braiding her long pale hair over her shoulder, looking forward to an hour of reading Akhmatova, when her cell phone rang. "I Will Follow You into the Dark," which meant that fool, Jorge. Maybe she shouldn't have given him his own ring tone. Then whenever he called she'd have a few more exasperation-free seconds between the time the phone rang and the time she knew who it was.

"*Pronto*, Jorge." He'd speak in Spanish, she knew; his Italian, though earnest, was clumsy, and his laughable attempts to master even a few words of her native Hungarian were pathetic. If she'd wanted to make him comfortable she'd have picked up with, "*Bueno.*" But Jorge was more useful if he wasn't comfortable. He tried harder to please.

"Anna." She could tell from that one word that he was excited. "I'm in the Vatican Library," he said. Yes, in Spanish and just a notch above a whisper.

She blew out a sigh, answered in Spanish to move this conversation along. "That's where you're supposed to be, Jorge. Did you call to tell me that?"

"No! No, of course not. I've been watching that priest the way you said to—"

"Good boy," Anna said, knowing he'd beam and completely miss her acid sarcasm.

"Thank you." God, it sounded like he was blushing! "For the last two days he's been asking for books by nineteenth-century Republican poets."

"And . . . ?" He might miss sarcasm but he'd hear impatience, at this high level anyway.

"And someone came to join him today," Jorge hurried on. "One of us."

Anna sat straighter. All right, the boy might be on to something. "Who? What do you mean, 'to join him'?"

"She introduced herself but I didn't hear. A woman, with long black hair. Some gray streaks," he added, with clear pride in his powers of observation.

"When you get a chance"—she suggested the obvious—"you might check the registry. Wouldn't she have had to sign in?"

"Yes, she would've." Again, sarcasm flew over his head. She wondered if that was a hearing defect, or a mental one. "I'll go look. But here's why I called."

"Oh, you mean there's a point?"

"Anna!" Finally, he was wounded. "The priest asked

for a book, and when she saw it she got excited. They're leaning over it and reading it together."

He stopped again. Sometimes Anna doubted herself: Were the Noantri really the right choice to rule the world, if the Community included morons like Jorge? And like herself, whose fault Jorge was in the first place?

"Jorge," she said carefully, "what is the book?"

"Poetry," he answered promptly. "Nineteenth century, but unattributed until now. The priest thinks it's Mario Damiani's. Anna, wasn't he one of—"

"Yes. Does she agree? The black-haired woman?"

"Yes, and she—"

"Get it."

"What?"

"The book, Jorge! I want that book! Do you understand me?"

"I—yes, but—"

"Call me when you have it." Anna added, *"Ciao,"* then thumbed the phone off with perhaps more force than necessary. She settled back against the tree trunk and took out a cigarette. Few of the Noantri smoked. A real pity, she'd always thought; it was a great pleasure, and the health dangers of this habit meant nothing to them. Of course, the problem was the fire. You needed a flame to get your cigarette going and it burned at its tip the whole time. Well, what of it? These miniature embers, so easily smashed out on the bottom of your shoe? Her people had been afraid of fire, and so much else, for far too long.

She drew in smoke and streamed it out contentedly. The Conclave had sources in the Vatican; well, good for them. So did Anna and her friends. She'd been told about Father Thomas Kelly, called to the Vatican to root through the Archives in clear—and clearly desperate—search of something. Now he'd been joined by a Noantri with Vatican Library credentials, thus obviously a scholar. And there they were, getting excited together over a book of Noantri poetry.

Of course, it could mean nothing. Just some academics getting their bookish thrills.

Though if it meant nothing, why was Anna's skin tingling like this?

II

———◦———

"Interesting," Livia Pietro said again, still studying the pages of the poetry notebook.

Thomas, who'd been contentedly reading the poems alongside her, looked up. "What's interesting?"

Now she turned to him, considering. "Do you know Trastevere well?"

"I'm afraid I don't. It's across the Tiber from Rome proper and therefore through the centuries a neighborhood of noncitizens when only citizens were allowed to live within the city walls. It housed the Jewish ghetto until the ghetto was dissolved and has always been a magnet for people of many nationalities because of its proximity to the docks. It has a Bohemian reputation but has gentrified lately, with writers, galleries, cafés— you're smiling again. I've gone beyond pedantic into pompous, haven't I?"

"Just a little, around the edges. But you're spot-on. Damiani lived there, and as it happens, so do I. It's an extraordinary place. Though I suppose," she added, "most people feel that way about their hometowns. You probably find Boston extraordinary."

"Yes, I do." Thomas thought it sweetly polite of her to be at pains not to rank her hometown above his own. Though he had yet to meet a Roman who didn't consider everywhere else inferior to Rome. "It does seem a fascinating place. Trastevere," he said. "Damiani obviously thought so, writing love poems to it. Is that what you meant by 'interesting'—that he wrote love poems to buildings?"

"No." She shook her head thoughtfully. "We actually have a tradition of that here. But look. You wouldn't know this, but . . . These pages, there are forty or so poems here. Some are clearly in praise of what could be called major sites—important churches, statues, piazzas."

"You can tell which they are?"

"A few. They're unmistakable. Here—the martyr in the well has to be San Callisto."

"Yes, I thought so, too."

She glanced sideways with a smile. "Did you?" Then back to the book. "And here's Fontana dell'Acqua Paola, and I think I see Porta Settimiana. But there are so many poems. Some seem to be about places that are relatively insignificant. And I think some major places are missing."

"Well," Thomas said, "a lover writing love poems—he might find praiseworthy what others consider insignificant."

"Undeniably true." She inclined her head. "Still, there are one or two churches, for example, that no lover of Trastevere would ignore. What I'm wondering is whether the missing pages were about those places."

"They might have been. There's no way to know, though."

"I'm not so sure. I—" Livia Pietro snapped her head around. The solemn clerk who'd brought Thomas's materials wheeled his cart past their table. Livia Pietro's

green eyes seemed for a moment to flash, another thing
Thomas had thought eyes didn't actually do. The clerk,
paying no attention to them, crossed the room to collect
books left by a researcher finished for the day. Livia Pietro watched him wordlessly, then turned back to Thomas.
"If you look at how the—"

Stopping, she leapt to her feet. Before Thomas had
quite registered that she was standing in front of him, he
felt himself gripped from behind and flung onto the cold
stone floor. The echoes of clattering chairs pinged around
the room, mixing with shouts from affronted scholars
and from Livia Pietro, who, in a flurry of complicated
jacket and skirt, seemed to be struggling with the silent
clerk over Damiani's notebook. Thomas was briefly immobile in confusion—What was going on? Why had the
clerk thrown him out of his chair? How had he come back
across the room so fast?—but when a falling book thunked
onto his forehead he unfroze and grabbed for the clerk's
ankle. All he got was trouser leg, so he yanked on that.
Thrown off balance, the clerk tottered and fell but rolled
to his feet again. He ignored Thomas, who was clumsily
trying to free himself from books and furniture. The clerk
and Livia Pietro faced each other. For a half second both
stood as still as the marble statues that stared disapprovingly from niches along the walls.

Then movement: the clerk's eyes, fixing on the notebook in Livia Pietro's hand. He lunged. Thomas, halfway to his feet, body-blocked him with a South Boston
street corner move. As the clerk crashed to the floor and
a chair toppled onto him, something brushed by Thomas:
the complicated jacket of Livia Pietro, who, shoulder
bag and hat in one hand and notebook in the other, was
racing across the marble floor.

Appalled, Thomas yelled, "Wait!" He was aghast at the sudden thought he'd gotten it wrong: Livia Pietro was stealing the notebook and the clerk had been trying to stop her. Thomas glanced down, saw the man trying to untangle himself from a heavy chair. No time to help: Pietro had turned a corner. In a hail of *"Silenzio!"* from the other researchers, Thomas sprinted after her.

12

◆—◇—◆

Livia cracked the hidden door just enough to see Thomas Kelly race around the corner and skid to a bewildered stop a few yards past her in the bright, empty hall. A crash from the reading room announced the clerk was free of the chair; pounding footsteps said he was coming after them. If the Gendarmes weren't also, they would be any moment. Livia cursed herself for a fool. Why hadn't she been on her guard from the moment she became aware of the clerk? Of course a number of Noantri were in service at the Vatican—it only seemed prudent—but this was someone she didn't know. That should have rung an alarm, but it hadn't.

Or perhaps it had, but she'd been so intent on her mission and on Thomas Kelly's discovery that she'd ignored it. The priest's find, this notebook, could be crucial. She thought she'd seen a pattern to the places not written about, something Thomas Kelly wouldn't have noticed because he didn't know Trastevere. She might be wrong, or the pattern might be there but mean nothing. Until she was sure, however, she wasn't giving the notebook up. Not to the priest, and especially not to a sticky-fingered fellow Noantri.

Briefly she considered leaving the priest behind. He'd only slow her, and what did he really have to offer? Well, she reflected, he did read Romanesco, possibly better than she. If she was right about the pattern of what was missing in the notebook, and if the poems that remained turned out to be important, another viewpoint on Damiani's elliptical verse might come in handy. So, given the nature of the buildings, might an expert in Church history. Most importantly, the Conclave had told her to make use of, and keep an eye on, this priest. Obeying the Conclave in letter as well as spirit struck her as wise, right now.

Livia pushed the door open and showed herself.

"Father Kelly. Quickly! In here." The priest spun in surprise. She held out the notebook. Kelly dashed toward her; she seized his arm and yanked him through the door, then slammed it shut.

"I— What—"

"Shh," she commanded. "Come." She grasped the priest's arm and started towing him down the corridor. She knew he couldn't see a thing. Her own eyes, much sharper than his, could barely tell floor from walls in the faint light seeping through the high openings. In the rooms on either side, those slits would be invisible, shadows in moldings near the ceiling. The door she'd just slammed, too, was imperceptible once shut. The Vatican was riddled with hidden passages and the Library was no exception. Most were built to allow servants to travel invisibly. Some had been created to facilitate other exchanges or escapes. Over many years, in the course of many legitimate research projects in various libraries, museums, and study centers around the world—her scholar's credentials were impeccable—Livia had occasionally passed time wandering where she wasn't supposed to be. Those explorations had yielded a number of doors and passages and occasionally led her to some interesting scholarship. Some secret doors, like the one to this passage, were never meant to be locked and gave easily once you'd found the hidden latch. Others required more finesse. To aid in her private research projects, Livia had acquired locksmith's tools and the skills to use them, but she was glad not to be slowed down by the need for them now.

Of course, the clerk wouldn't be slowed down, either. Even if he didn't know about this passageway, he'd find it. His heightened Noantri senses would lead him to her, by scent if all else failed. But she and the priest had a good head start. Livia's hope was that by the time the clerk discovered the hidden latch, they'd be out the passage's other end.

If, that was, Father Kelly could be persuaded to keep going. Shocked into silence by her sudden appearance and by her manhandling, apparently he'd now recovered. He tugged and twisted, trying to free himself or at least stop their progress. In the face of her strength he couldn't do either, which added to his confusion and panic. He dug in his heels and shouted, "No! Wait! What's going on?"

She stopped and turned, catching him gently so his momentum wouldn't plow him into her. "I'll explain," she said. "But not here. Stay quiet. We need to get out." She added, "I have Damiani's notebook."

"I know you do! You stole it! We've got to go back."

"There's no time. Come." She started forward again, hauling him with her.

"Don't pull! Let me go!"

Father Kelly sounded so surprised, so offended at her unexpected might, that Livia almost laughed. Normally, like most Noantri, Livia hid her Blessings—her strength, her agility—from the Unchanged, to avoid provoking exactly this unease. She released his arm. "You don't have to come. You can stay here. Work your way back along that corridor. Or shout and they'll find you. But I'm taking the notebook and if you don't come, you won't know why."

"You can't! It's—" He stopped. When he spoke again his voice was calm. "You came here for that notebook. You're not studying Damiani any more than I am. Who are you?"

"I'm an art historian, as I told you, and on the contrary, I'm studying Damiani exactly as much as you are. I didn't know about the notebook, though I'm very glad you found it. But I didn't come for it. I came for you."

A pause. "What?"

"I need your help. And I can help you. We're both after the same thing."

He said nothing. His eyes were wide in the dark and she held them with her own though he probably couldn't see it. "I'm searching for the same thing you are," she said. "We have to find it, and more urgently than I think you know."

"*We?* Are you—"

"Wait!" She touched a finger to his lips. He startled. She listened, spoke again. "He's found the door. He could find the catch at any moment. Come, or stay." The priest didn't move. "Father Kelly. To find the Concordat, you must come with me." She heard his sharp intake of breath.

"What do you know about the Concordat?"

"More than you. You've been told to find it and

you've been told it's dangerous, but you don't know its contents, do you? I do."

"All I know is that it's a secret the Church guards closely."

"You doubt me. You have that right. But I'm telling the truth."

"Why are you looking for it?"

"Not now. Come." Instead of seizing his arm again, she gently took his hand. He startled once more, but while he didn't fold his fingers onto hers, he didn't pull away, either. She waited, then gave a soft tug. After a moment he took a step toward her.

They made their way down the servants' passage, Livia listening for the clerk's progress. A tiny click—he'd found the latch. She sped up, as sure-footed as the priest was stumbling. Twice she had to keep him from falling, losing precious seconds each time. Without him she'd have eluded the clerk for sure, but now it was touch and go. The rhythm and minutely rising volume of the clerk's steps behind them told her he'd shortened the distance, was quite close by the time she and Father Kelly emerged through another hidden door into a tiny anteroom. Kelly blinked in the sudden wash of light. Livia slipped on her sunglasses and fixed her hat. "Be casual," she instructed, and stepped through a low archway into the Vatican Museum's Galleria Clementina.

Thomas Kelly alternately beside and behind her, Livia wove through crowds of shuffling tourists, keeping up a hurried but informed commentary on the paintings, statuary, and artifacts they passed. She was a private tour guide steering a visiting priest through the treasures of the Galleria Clementina and then into the Museum of Pagan Antiquities, behind in their schedule but still fo-

cusing on the art as they rushed. No one seemed to notice them, not even the security guards strolling casually,
protecting the art while not alarming the tourists. One
of those officers was Noantri, a man Livia recognized.
They exchanged the tiniest of nods. Could she count on
him to stop the clerk if it came to that? She wasn't sure;
best not to chance it.

The clerk, of course, had found his way through the
passage and was on their trail. He was two rooms behind them; Livia easily picked his footsteps out. Unlikely
that he'd risk a confrontation in this crowd. He'd follow
them, waiting for his chance. She heard him speed up as
she and Thomas Kelly maneuvered through the crush of
people and started circling down the bronze spiral staircase. As they reached the bottom, he took the first steps
down. The same thick crowd that slowed them would
hinder him, but still he'd be no more than a few seconds
behind when they burst out into the bright, crowded
piazza.

Burst they did, and as Livia feared, alarms began to
shrill and clang when the notebook in her bag crossed
the Vatican's threshold. Cardinal Fariña's parting gift,
the new security system; she'd known it was a risk.
Quick-walking beside her, Thomas Kelly blanched.

"Fifty people came out when we did." She spoke low,
keeping a merry smile, not looking at him or changing
pace. "Forty-five of them look more suspicious than a
middle-aged lady tour guide and a priest. Just stay with
me." Ignoring the alarms and the security guards now
running through the crowd, she clasped Father Kelly's
arm again and took off striding past the gelato and torta
carts.

Camera-draped tourists flowed through the piazza,

swarming after colorful umbrellas and pennants on poles. They circled water- and trinket-sellers like feeding fish. At the curb, buses disgorged them and, more importantly, waited in patient lines to scoop them up again.

"What are you—"

"Shhh." Livia scanned the crowd. The visored Taiwanese would do them no good, and the Americans were just arriving, but beyond, a group of mixed Europeans— Italians, Poles, and a gaggle speaking Greek—were loading onto a bright blue bus. "Come." When they were close to the bus, she slowed, waiting until the guide turned away to answer the inevitable question from the inevitable guidebook-thumbing tourist. "Now!" she said, and hopped onto the stairs and into the bus. The engine was already running. She moved through to the back, smiling at her fellow passengers as though they'd been together for days on this whirlwind tour of Italy. She'd found a seat and was looking through the window when Thomas Kelly dropped beside her.

"Are you crazy?" he demanded in a whisper.

She turned to him with a smile. He was red-faced and sweating. "You're a tourist," she said quietly. "Act like one."

He dropped his voice. "Give me the notebook."

"I will. I will, and you can replace it in the Library. But we need it first."

"Need it for what? You can*not* just *do* that." He was spluttering sotto voce. "Who *are* you?"

"A historian, as you are. We can't talk now. Wait until we get where we're going."

"No. Give me the notebook or I'll call the police."

"No, you won't."

"I will!"

The harried guide climbed the stairs. The driver left the door open for the last of the straggling tourists.

"You could have called for help at any time in the museum," Livia said, "but here you are. You're curious." On his face, guilt fleetingly eclipsed confusion and anger. "Father Kelly, trust me, please. We're after the same thing: the lost copy of the Concordat. Damiani's notebook may be vital, and as soon as we get somewhere safe I'll tell you why."

"Safe? We were perfectly safe until you stole it!"

"No. The clerk was trying to steal it. I stopped him."

"The clerk? Who is he?"

"I don't know."

Kelly frowned. "It's ridiculous anyway. Why would he bring it to me and then try to steal it? He could've stolen it anytime, if that's what he wanted."

"I think it was my interest in it that called his attention. My interest coupled with yours, I mean. I think he was in the Library to watch you."

"Me? To watch me? And you say you came for me? I see. Thomas Kelly from Boston is the clueless center of a vast Vatican conspiracy. That's what you mean?"

"When you put it that way—"

"Well, maybe it's okay." The priest threw up his hands. "Maybe that clerk is after the same thing we are, too. Just another member of our happy clan."

The desperate edge of Father Kelly's sarcasm was impossible to miss, but she answered him seriously. "No. If the people who sent me already had an agent in the Vatican Library, they'd have told me. I'm afraid he might be working for the other side."

"*What* other side?"

She touched his arm and nodded to the aisle, where

the guide was working his way along, greeting the group, answering questions. "Don't say anything. You don't speak Italian."

"Of course I—"

She stopped him with a look.

When the guide reached them he gave them a quizzical raise of the eyebrows. Before he could speak, Livia grinned and said in Italian, "Hi! Are you the new guide? Where's Aldo?"

"Aldo? Who is he?"

"Our guide from this morning. And yesterday, too. He's so funny! He made us laugh so hard when we were at the Trevi Fountain, didn't he, Thomas? Even though Thomas doesn't really speak Italian, but he understood Aldo! Everyone did, even those sour Scots! Does Aldo have the afternoon off or something?"

"*Signora*," the guide said carefully, "I have been with this group since Saturday. There is no one named Aldo."

"Oh, but—" Livia suddenly stopped. She looked blankly at the guide and glanced around. "Oh!" She clapped her hands together, then buried her face in them. "Thomas!" she said in English, muffled and laughing. "We're on the wrong bus!"

"*Signora*—"

She dropped her hands, switched to Italian again. "Our bus was blue, too! And we were so late that I was afraid everyone would be mad—oh, this is mortifying!" She craned her neck to look out the window, then giggled like a schoolgirl caught in a prank. "It's gone! We're so late they already left!" She rooted around in her bag and dug out her cell phone. "Don't worry." She peered at the guide's name tag. "Sergio? Don't worry, Sergio. I'll text Aldo. It's lucky he gave us his phone number! I thought, why would we ever need that, but you see? He was right! Where are you going next?" Her thumbs hovered above her phone's buttons. "This group—where are you going?"

Sergio blinked. "To the Colosseum, *Signora*."

"So were we! Oh, good! Oh, marvelous! I'll text Aldo and tell him not to worry about us and we'll just get off and meet the group there and thank you so much, Sergio! I'm sorry to cause you trouble! Oh, how ridiculous!" She laughed again and bent over her phone, thumbing rapidly. "Thomas, what a pair of idiots we are! Why didn't you say something? You know I have no sense of direction! This is so funny!" She was still giggling and thumbing when Sergio nodded, said something about having been put to no trouble at all, and walked quickly back up the aisle.

13

The doors finally closed and the tour bus inched along the curb in front of the Vatican, the driver eagle-eyed for a gap in the traffic.

"Look." Pietro nodded back toward the piazza. Thomas leaned across her. The clerk, in the center of the tourist scrum, snapped his head left, right, left again, clearly at a loss and clearly livid. In the patternless milling another disruption caught Thomas's eye: two men in blue uniforms and a third in a dark suit charging the wrong way through the entry and shouldering through the crowd. Gendarmerie: the Vatican Police. Thomas saw the clerk catch sight of them, too, and fade back into the shadows. **Why?** Thomas wondered. The Gendarmes would have been alerted by the alarm, but they wouldn't know what they were chasing. The clerk not only knew what, but whom. Why not race over to the police and tell them? Help them?

Unless what Pietro had said was true: the clerk had been trying to steal the book for himself.

Thomas flopped back against his seat as the bus found an opening and dove into the stream of cars. What was he doing? **This is pride, Thomas. The sin of pride. You should have stood your ground in the passageway and shouted for help. You should have** summoned a guard on the piazza as soon as the alarm bells rang. You should have wrestled Damiani's notebook right out of this mad historian's hands. Though he wasn't quite sure how he'd have done that, given her baffling physical strength. Admittedly he had little experience of the female body, but he'd seen her outwrestle the clerk and he'd felt her iron grip—he touched his arm; it was tender and, under his sleeve, no doubt turning colors—and he didn't think he was wrong in suspecting Livia Pietro was, comparatively, a powerhouse. Still, that he'd likely lose a cage match against her didn't mean he shouldn't have tried. But she was right. He was, as ever, curious. Pride: his right to have his questions answered trumping ethical impera-tives, like Thou Shalt Not Steal.

He turned his head to look at Livia Pietro. She was still watching out the window.

"Well," Thomas said softly. "Gendarmes. You'd think someone had committed a crime. Theft, perhaps. I won-der if they're worried, the criminals."

At that she sat back also, and shrugged. "There's nothing I can do."

"I can."

She raised an eyebrow to him. She hadn't removed her sunglasses, dark against her pale skin. Thomas found him-self, irrelevantly and annoyingly, wanting to see those ocean-in-moonlight eyes again. Those eyes that had found their way so easily through the black passages in the Vati-can, where he'd been blind as a bat. He pushed away the thought of Pietro's eyes as she asked, "You can what?"

"Back them off," he answered. "But you'll have to give me the notebook." If she did, he'd call Lorenzo. The Cardinal would tell the Gendarmerie it was just a misunderstanding. The police wouldn't argue with the Librarian. They'd smell a fix but they'd drop it. Then Livia Pietro would owe Thomas, and he'd insist she tell him what the Concordat was and how she knew about it. And why she wanted it. And who—

"No." Livia Pietro looked straight at him, planting her handbag more solidly on her lap as though issuing a dare.

Thomas, after a moment, settled again in his seat and stared at nothing. He should probably call Lorenzo anyway. He was cheered by the thought that Lorenzo would by now have gotten a report and that the events in the reading room would make Thomas look like a hero: madwoman steals book, clerk fails to stop her, Thomas runs after her. The body-block he'd thrown on the clerk might put things in a different light but even if Lorenzo heard about that—even from the clerk himself—the Cardinal would believe the Thomas-the-Hero version until he was forced to think otherwise. Which would be never, if Thomas called right now.

But he didn't. He meditated on the relationship between curiosity and pride, a relationship he hadn't noted before, as the tour bus honked its way down the Lungotevere, headed for the bridge.

The bus was pulling up at Piazza del Colosseo when Pietro, once again peering out the window, stiffened. "Gendarmes," she said quietly. Thomas looked past her, saw the same two uniformed men he'd seen at the Vatican now emerge from a tiny black-and-white Alfa Romeo. The man in the dark suit was already in the piazza, scanning the crowd from beside an unmarked Peugeot. The comfortable vehicle, a privilege of rank. "I didn't think they saw us get on this bus," she said.

Light dawned for Thomas. "I'm sure they didn't," he replied, with a smug smile he couldn't help.

"Then how?"

"That book." He thumbed at her bag. "Cardinal Fariña, before he retired. He spent years renovating the Library and Archives. Most of it was about security. The chip that set off the alarms, I'll bet it's also got a GPS. They tracked us. *Professoressa* Pietro? You're busted."

To his surprise she grinned as their bus squealed to a stop. "Think so? Watch." She pulled the notebook from her bag and turned it over, to the marbleized paper that had once been the last leaf inside the missing back cover. The security chip, wafer-thin and about an inch square, was attached to the blank page before that. Which, after Pietro gave it a quick rip, was no longer attached to the book.

"*What*? No! You can't!" Thomas, appalled, grabbed for the notebook but as always, she was faster. She stuck the book deep in her shoulder bag and the chip in the pocket of her flowing skirt. A part of Thomas, nonplussed, thought, **A lot of good that'll do: it's still on you. Why not toss it?** The rest of him was appalled to see himself abetting this thievery, even if only in his head. Pietro jumped to her feet as the rear door opened. Thomas couldn't believe he'd just sat and watched her vandalize a book from the Vatican Library. He was nearly ready to stay behind. Let her hop off the bus and get scooped up by the Gendarmes. On the other hand, that might not happen. If it didn't this would be a ridiculous time to stand on principle and lose the notebook. **In for a penny, in for the crown jewels.** He stood.

The doors opened and Pietro jumped out onto a bright sidewalk boiling with tourists. The crumbling hulk of the Colosseum towered a half-block in front of them, but Pietro dashed the other way, across the street. She wove between taxis, sedans, and Smart cars. Thomas, close in her slipstream and fully expecting to get flattened, muttered an automatic Hail Mary. Though he wondered whether prayer was effective when you were stealing from the Vatican. At least he was wearing his clerical collar. Maybe people would try harder not to hit a priest. In the end both he and Pietro made it across unsquashed, and Thomas caught up with her at the entrance to the Colosseo Metro station—caught up only because she'd screeched to a halt.

Standing between them and the turnstiles was the clerk.

Clerk before, Gendarmes behind, end of the road, *Professoressa;* but before Thomas quite finished that thought Pietro said, "Do you have a ticket?"

It took him a moment to understand she was speaking to him, not the clerk, and what the question meant. "A monthly," he stammered.

"Use it now. Wait for me."

He could see the Gendarmes, one of the uniformed men with a handheld device, the other frantically and uselessly trying to stop the traffic. They dodged and wove as Thomas and Livia had done, working their way across the frenzied lanes. A screech of brakes, a scream of metal on metal, a tinkle of breaking glass, and then a symphony of curses and car horns. Thomas stared into the street and saw the Gendarmes still coming, crumpled fenders, stopped cars, and furious motorists in their wake. One way or another, Thomas decided, the far side of the turnstile might be the place to be during whatever mayhem was about to erupt. He swiped his card; the clerk paid no attention to him, but stepped up to Pietro, to block her way.

Thomas expected her to sidestep. She didn't. Instead, she charged right at him. The clerk was as surprised as Thomas, probably even more when Pietro tackled him. They tussled, twisted, and rolled, scattering shrieking tourists and Romans. The Gendarmes reached the curb outside and pushed past the souvenir carts. In a swirl of flowered skirt and complicated jacket Livia Pietro leapt to her feet. She snatched her hat and sunglasses up from the tile floor and shouted, "Go!"

Thomas was rooted in place until he saw Pietro neatly vault the turnstile and race down the escalator steps. **Turnstile jumping, well, why not?** Thomas took off after her, though he wondered exactly why: the Gendarmes would do the same, would be along any moment, would either grab her in the station or have Carabinieri waiting at the next stop if she managed to get on a train. Whatever happened now, Thomas would be well out of it. He decided to watch the denouement from a distance, then go report to Lorenzo.

The first thing he saw when he reached the platform was the countdown clock, claiming a train would be along in under three minutes. The second was Pietro, sunglasses and hat replaced, calmly waiting for it. He turned back to the escalator to follow the progress of the Gendarmes. Only they weren't there. All he saw was the escalator's steady stream of well-dressed locals and backpacked tourists, undisturbed by a ripple of charging policemen.

Pietro, as though she felt Thomas watching her, turned to him and smiled. After an uncertain moment he walked down the platform to her. "The Gendarmes are coming, you know."

She didn't answer, just kept smiling. The Gendarmes didn't come. The train did. Pietro got on. Thomas, wondering what had become of the Thomas Kelly he'd been for thirty-four years, followed her through the closing doors.

14

No law enforcement officers—not Gendarmes, not Carabinieri—burst onto the Metro train at the next stop. None were waiting on the platform ready to pounce when they left the subway car at Piramide, nor were any lurking by the station when they emerged to switch to the bus.

Livia would have been surprised if they had been.

On the Metro ride, when the rumbling of wheels could have covered the sounds of their conversation, there was no conversation: the priest had been stonily silent. During the short bus ride to Trastevere he'd hissed a question or two but the bus was packed and Livia refused to speak. When they alit in front of the giant palazzo of the Ministero della Pubblica Istruzione, she and Kelly were finally alone. Livia, as always on these streets, felt a calm, a comfort. She'd been born in Trastevere, and though she'd lived for years at a time in other places—a necessity of Noantri life—her home was here.

As soon as she started forward she could feel Thomas Kelly about to start grilling her. The streets were still too crowded, though, so she walked just a little too fast for him, staying ahead until they reached the cobblestones of Piazza di San Cosimato. Two Carabinieri moving purposefully through the piazza made the priest draw a sharp breath. Livia smiled at them and they smiled back, one touching his cap in greeting. *"Buona-sera, Professoressa."* They strode on past.

"They're going for coffee," Livia told Thomas Kelly. "That's why they look so determined. Nothing to do with us." She continued to quick-walk through the cobbled streets, the priest truculent but sticking with her. Once past the fountain outside Santa Maria in Trastevere, the crowds thinned and Livia slowed her pace.

"Why have we come here? What's going on?" When she didn't answer, Thomas Kelly grumped, "They'll find us, you know," amending it after a moment to, "They'll find you. Or maybe that clerk will, first. He seems to be persistent."

"The Gendarmes never saw us," she reminded him. They turned the corner by the ancient hospital. "And they have their chip."

He stopped. "They do?"

She grinned. "If you'd asked while we were on the train, instead of shooting daggers out of your eyes, I'd have told you." She tucked her arm in his to get him moving again. "I shoved it into the clerk's pocket when we had that little scuffle. So I don't think he'll be an immediate problem, either."

"I— Is that why you tackled him?"

"Well, it wasn't because I enjoy your American football." Her shoulder still hurt where she'd banged up against a turnstile. So did her shin where the clerk had kicked her. Neither injury was as painful now as when they'd happened, but what drew people to contact sports—especially the Unchanged, who healed much more slowly than Noantri—she would never know.

They'd just come into the small piazza in front of Santa Maria della Scala when the priest broke another dark silence to ask, "Where are we going?" His tone implied he was nearing the end of his patience. She couldn't blame him; luckily, they'd arrived.

"To see a friend." Across the square from the church stood an old house, less impressive from without, she knew, than from within. Livia stepped to the door and clanked the ring in the brass lion's mouth.

A few moments' wait, and the door was opened to them by Spencer George himself. He wore a chocolate cashmere sweater and tan trousers, his feet encased in butter-colored leather slippers. Livia always enjoyed the sight of Spencer, who seemed to delight in his own excellent taste. Though in little else: his thinning brown hair topped a long face perpetually on the verge of a glower. They were old friends, but she hadn't expected a warm welcome today, and she wasn't mistaken.

"Livia. What a pleasure." Spencer spoke in dry, guarded tones, and in English, his native tongue.

From courtesy—he was Elder—she replied in English, too. "You know, then?"

"Oh, I think everyone knows."

She wasn't surprised. Meetings of the full Conclave were infrequent enough to be noteworthy in themselves. No one appeared before the Conclave except by Summons. If Livia Pietro had been spotted going into Santa Maria dell'Orazione e Morte—for a second time—the Noantri grapevine would have sizzled with the news.

"I must admit I was halfway expecting you," Spencer said.

"And hoping I wouldn't come."

"On the contrary. I don't know what your instructions are but I'll be glad to help if I'm able. Though I rather think I won't be."

"Why not?"

"Because whatever it's about, if the Conclave had any hope of me, they'd have called me in, too. Who's your friend?"

The tone in which Spencer said "friend" implied it wasn't the first word that had come to mind. Livia smiled and said, "Father Thomas Kelly."

Spencer waited, but she didn't go on. Thomas Kelly turned to her, about to speak, but she shook her head. After a long stare of clear distaste at the priest, Spencer shrugged and stepped aside. "All right, then. Come in."

He led them through the entrance hall and upstairs to his study. At various periods, both since Livia had known him and before, Spencer had kept a full staff. At others he'd had a butler or valet; moving with the times, he now had a cleaning woman who came twice a week, and a cook. Some of the Noantri were indifferent to food and drink. Others, though they appreciated the pleasures of the palate, didn't go to the trouble of keeping stocked pantries or fully equipped kitchens. Livia herself was in that camp. She enjoyed a leisurely meal in the presence of friends, both Noantri and Unchanged; but at home, except for the *gelato al pompelmo rosso* that she bought by the liter, her larder was generally bare. Spencer, though, had been a gourmand before he became Noantri. The rest of the staff came and went with current fashion, the better for Spencer to blend in. A cook was nonnegotiable.

He rang for the current one as Livia and Thomas Kelly seated themselves in heavy leather chairs. "You'll have

coffee?" Spencer said to Father Kelly. Livia smiled to herself. Spencer had little use for priests, but less for discour-
tesy. The priest was in his house; civility would prevail.

Despite Father Kelly's confusion and his angry impatience, Livia caught him peering around the room at the
maps and prints on Spencer's walls, the odd arcana on
the shelves and polished tables. **We historians,** she
thought, **we're all alike.** Spencer's house had always
been too overstuffed for her liking, but it suited its
owner well enough. Livia took pleasure in surrounding
herself with objects of beauty. Spencer, however, collected first for interest and meaning; beauty, if any, was a
secondary concern. He was also a historian, but his
study was their people.

The cook appeared; coffee was requested. When she'd
gone, Spencer settled himself, tugging at his trouser
legs. "So you've come for my help. What can I do?" He
looked at Livia and then, pointedly, at Thomas Kelly.

"It's more complicated than that," Livia said. "I
wouldn't feel right if I didn't tell you this from the start:
the Gendarmerie are after us."

"The Gendarmerie?" Spencer's eyebrows rose. "Not
the Carabinieri? My, what have you done?"

"We stole a book from the Vatican Library. I stole it,"
she amended, in response to a strangled sound from
Thomas Kelly.

"Well, good for you. Presumably because it will help
you do whatever you've been instructed to do? Can I
expect those strapping young gentlemen to arrive at any
moment, then? I can ring for more coffee."

"No, we've taken care of them for a while, I think."

"How grand. But really, Livia, before we continue,
you'll have to explain the priest to me."

"I speak English, you know," snapped Thomas Kelly.

"No, I didn't know," Spencer drawled. "Then perhaps you'll be good enough to explain yourself?"

"If I had any idea at all, I'd be glad to. As it is, I'm at a loss. I don't know why I'm here, and I should probably leave." He turned to Livia. "With the notebook."

"Notebook?" Spencer inquired mildly.

"The one I stole." Livia felt a surge of sympathy for the priest. "I asked Father Kelly to come with me. He doesn't know why yet."

Thomas Kelly started to splutter at "asked" but before he could speak the cook reentered with a tray.

"Excellent," said Spencer, and it was unclear whether he was referring to the situation or the refreshments. He thanked the cook, dismissed her, and poured out from a silver service into fine china cups. With silver tongs he placed two small biscotti on each saucer. Father Kelly accepted the offered cup a little desperately, Livia thought. Spencer said, "You can explain to us both, then, Livia, why you've brought me a priest."

Livia took a sip of Spencer's always superb coffee, then put the cup on the inlaid side table. "I was called before the Conclave yesterday."

"I think I mentioned: everyone knows that."

"Does everyone know why?"

"Of course not."

"The Vatican's copy of the Concordat, it seems, disappeared a century or so ago," Livia said. "Now it appears to have been found. Not by the Vatican."

Before Spencer could speak Thomas Kelly blurted, "It's been found? Found where?"

With a wave of his cup toward Father Kelly, Spencer asked, "How much does he know?"

"His name is Thomas Kelly!" The priest sat forward, red-faced. "He's from Boston, he was brought here two days ago by Lorenzo Cardinal Cossa to find this mysterious Concordat, and he's about to call the Cardinal and tell him you people know where it is and he can come get it himself."

Spencer gazed at him, unruffled. "If you think invoking a cardinal in this house is going to occasion fear and trembling, you're misinformed, Father. What I'm asking is, are you aware of the contents of 'this mysterious Concordat'?"

Thomas Kelly met Spencer's stare. The bellicose set of his shoulders made it clear to Livia how very much he wanted to tell Spencer he knew everything he needed to know about anything and Spencer could go climb a tree, or whatever insult they'd use in Boston. Instead, after a frustrated breath, he said, "I'm told it's an agreement between the Church and another group. I don't know who the others are or what it binds each to do but Cardinal Cossa has impressed upon me that it's secret and highly dangerous. That public knowledge of so much as its existence, never mind its details, could seriously damage the Church. Which, with all due respect to the Cardinal, strikes me as alarmist poppycock."

Spencer's only response was a small, amused smile.

Livia said, "No, Father. It's true."

Thomas Kelly gave her a hard look, and then shrugged. "If you say so. I have no way to judge and I'm close to not caring. My job was to find it, and I seem to have done that." He stood. "Give me the notebook."

"Sit down," said Spencer. In all these years Livia had never heard Spencer raise his voice; but she also didn't know anyone who didn't obey without a second's pause the granite tone he'd used just now.

Father Kelly, to her surprise, remained on his feet, gave Spencer a calm, wordless stare, then turned back to her. "Give me the notebook."

"Father," she said, "please, hear me out. The Concordat's been found but I—we—don't have it. None of us know where it is, except the man who discovered it."

"Ah," said Spencer, overriding whatever the priest might have been about to say. "And who is that? I assume there's some reason the Conclave didn't just ask the finder to gift wrap it and send it over. And some reason, Livia, why you were chosen."

Spencer's gaze was at once stern and sympathetic. Livia's cheeks burned. She nodded to confirm his guess. "It's Jonah." From the corner of her eye she saw Thomas Kelly give her an odd look. He didn't sit down, but he stayed silent.

"Oh," said Spencer. "Oh, my. I'm beginning to understand. Your young man isn't at all interested in placing it in the hands of the Conclave, is he? Nor of the Vatican. Let me guess. He's threatening to make it public."

"Yes."

"But he hasn't yet. So he's making demands, in return for silence. What could he possibly be asking for?"

"What could he possibly want? It's not about that. He's just giving the Conclave a chance to do it formally. He says either they publish the contents or he will."

"Really? Is he that militant? I had no idea."

"It was one of the . . . reasons for our split. I tried to tell him the New often feel that way, but that over time he'd come to understand."

"Apparently he hasn't. And what does the Conclave expect of you? Surely they're capable of searching out and dealing with a renegade on their own?"

Livia's heart skipped at "dealing with." "Of course. But they don't just want Jonah. They want the Concordat. So this can't happen again. They think I can find both him and it because I know him so well."

"And because he's your responsibility," Spencer said, sounding severe. Spencer had his own opinions on some of the Laws, but the accountability of a Lord for a Disciple was one he believed in strongly. It was, she suspected, one reason he had never become anyone's Lord.

"Yes," she acknowledged. Her face flushed but she met Spencer's gaze. "That's right."

"Are they correct? Can you call him up and have a nice chat, during which he'll gladly disclose the location of his hidey-hole? Or skip over that step and go fetch the Concordat directly because you already know where that place might be?"

She shook her head. "For one thing, they think he's not the one who hid it. He only says he knows where it is—it's likely what's happened is, he's somehow found its hiding place. For another . . . It's been a long time, Spencer. I don't think I know him anymore."

Spencer nodded. "Well, I must admit to feeling a certain amount of sympathy."

Livia was about to thank him when she realized he didn't mean for her. "Spencer, you can't agree? That the Concordat should be made public?"

"No," Spencer sighed. "No, of course not. Though in a perfect world making it public would yield benefits all around. But in a perfect world we wouldn't have needed it in the first place."

"One of the benefits of making it public," Thomas Kelly snapped, "is that some of the rest of us might have an idea what you're talking about."

Spencer turned to stare at the priest. "Livia," he said, "why is he here?"

"The Conclave instructed me to . . . involve Father Kelly in the search. Because his search is the same."

"Wait—they did?" Kelly said. "But we just met. Because you saw I had all those poetry books . . ."

She watched understanding dawn in his eyes. "I'm sorry."

"Let me understand something," Spencer said. "You"—to Thomas Kelly—"were brought here just recently, by the new Librarian, to find the Vatican's Concordat? Does the Cardinal know what the Conclave knows—that Jonah Richter has found it?"

"I'm sure he doesn't," the priest replied tightly, "because he wouldn't have had me looking through the Archives then, would he?"

"Your tone aside, I think you're correct. In which case, I have two questions. One, it's an odd coincidence, don't you think, that your search should come just when the Concordat has reappeared? But two, and more to the point, what possible help can you be to Livia? Livia, why not let me show him out? Without, of course, this stolen notebook. If you feel you need that to complete your task."

"For one thing," Livia replied, "he found the notebook."

"And for another, he's not leaving without it," Thomas Kelly said. "I'll call the Gendarmes if I have to."

Spencer rolled his eyes.

Livia said, gently, "Spencer? There's something else. The notebook is Mario Damiani's."

Color drained from Spencer's face.

"I'm sorry," Livia said. "I was told at the Conclave that it was he who stole the Concordat. When the Vatican Library was looted."

After a long moment, her old friend slowly shook his head. "Well, well. Mario. There were always rumors that he'd done something big and bad, and had had to go to ground. I put them down to the fact that he was gone and therefore ripe to become the stuff of legend. I knew he wasn't in hiding. He wouldn't have vanished for all time without a word to me. Mario. I waited, you know. In the North. I really thought he'd come." Spencer trailed off. Livia shot the priest a look to keep him quiet. At last Spencer roused himself. "The Conclave," he said. "Have they known for long?"

"That Damiani stole it? Apparently since it happened. Back then, when it never turned up and a search didn't find it, the Conclave was satisfied it had been destroyed. Or at least hidden too well to be found."

"Did they tell you how he . . . What happened to him?"

"No."

Spencer nodded and finished his coffee, gazing at nothing. A tiny smile tugged the corners of his mouth. "That explains, then, why you were called in, but I was not."

Thomas Kelly now spoke, his scholar's curiosity clearly overpowering, for the moment, his anger and confusion. "I was right, then. It was the Concordat that Damiani's letter referred to."

Livia looked up at him. "What letter?"

Abruptly, Thomas Kelly sat again. "You have your secrets. I have mine. What are we talking about?"

As if from far away, Spencer asked, "Livia? May I see the notebook?"

Livia slipped it from her bag. She was prepared to fend off the priest, but although he didn't take his eyes from it once she produced it, he didn't grab for it, either. Handing it to Spencer, she said, "I think it might tell us where the Concordat is."

"How?" Spencer asked absently. He began slowly to turn the ragged pages.

"It's a book of praise poems. To churches, piazzas, fountains—various places in Trastevere."

"He was working on that, yes. This is it?" Spencer smiled. "Ah, yes. They're all *cinquini*—he invented the form, you know. A-B-A-B-A. He had to be different."

"Seven pages are missing. One of them might be a poem to the hiding place." She watched Spencer as he read a page of faded handwriting. "Are you all right?"

"Something about this book . . . I don't know what, but it's oddly familiar."

"You must have seen any number of Damiani's note-books."

"No, it's more than that." Spencer fingered the paper. "But to what you were saying: if one of the missing poems identifies the Concordat's location, what about the others? Why are seven missing?"

"They're red herrings?"

"To mislead whom?" Spencer looked up skeptically. "And what's your plan, then? To discover what land-marks are missing and go to each?"

"I can't come up with anything better," Livia admit-ted.

"I'm not sure how you would even make that deter-mination," Spencer said. "And the priest?"

"Is a Church historian. If any—or all—of these missing places are churches, he might—"

"All right!" Thomas Kelly exploded. "The priest is tired of being talked about in the third person and tired of feeling like he's—like I'm in a play without a script! Who's the Conclave? What's the Concordat? What's Mario Damiani to you? Who are you people?"

Livia and Spencer looked at each other.

"All right," Kelly said again. "Tell me or I'm leaving. I'll call the Gendarmerie and the Cardinal the minute I'm out the door. The Gendarmes will come for the book and the Cardinal will tell me what's going on."

He stood once more. Livia did, also, though she wasn't sure what she was about to do. Stop him, certainly. The Conclave wanted him involved; the Conclave would have him. But how? She could keep him here, but she couldn't force him to help her. He already knew this search was of great importance to his Church, yet he was ready to leave, so that argument wouldn't persuade him. And though the damage to his Church was certain and irreparable if the Concordat was revealed, she didn't have its interests at heart and he wouldn't believe her if she said she did.

It was her Community who concerned her.

It was Jonah.

She still had hopes of saving Jonah from his sentence; but if she didn't find the document, his death was certain.

And if he found a way to carry out his threat before the Conclave destroyed him, then the inevitable, unthinkable consequence would be the devastation of her people. The obliteration of six centuries of release from the terror and peril that had filled all the countless years before.

The priest still stood at the doorway, frustrated, furious, and ready to bolt. **He'll never understand what's at stake,** she finally admitted to herself, **without the truth.** She looked to Spencer for help, but he sat with the notebook, lost in its pages, as though she and Thomas Kelly weren't there.

"Father," Livia said, laying a hand on the priest's arm. "Please. Sit down."

15

Thomas Kelly charged down the stairs to the front door. He threw it open with such ferocity that the ring clanged against the lion's mouth. Turning blindly right, he swept around the corner and ran on, stopping only when, another block later, he found himself half-hidden by the tables and umbrellas of an outdoor café. His heart still pounded wildly. He drew a deep breath and peered back past the patrons sipping their espressos, reading their papers, and talking on their cell phones.

No one. He wasn't being followed.

In fact, he hadn't been followed down the stairs, he realized, playing the scene back for himself. His crashing steps were the only footfalls. Livia Pietro, after her insane words and the historian's calm, shocking display, hadn't even stood when he ran off. Nor had her mad friend. They weren't coming after him. He was safe.

Safe from what? What had just happened? What did any of this mean? Who were these people and why had they gone to all this trouble to terrify him? Which was obviously what it was about. These lunatics were playing with his mind. To distract him, that must be it. Yes, of course. To make him useless. To prevent him from finding the Concordat before they did. Why? Why did they want it? What was this document, that people would go to such elaborate lengths? Because it indisputably wasn't the document they'd described to him.

His heart had just about come back to normal now. He took out his cell phone. Before he could make his call he saw on its screen that he had seven messages from the Cardinal. He thumbed the button and stood staring back through the umbrellas toward the House of Crazy People.

Lorenzo picked up at once. "Thomas! Where are you? What's going on? Why didn't you answer my calls?"

"I didn't get them. I had my phone off. In the Library, so I wouldn't disturb people, and then I—"

"Well, apparently you disturbed a lot of people. What on earth happened? The reports say a fight, a stolen book? Which hasn't been recovered, though the thief's in custody. Where are you? What happened? What book, and do you have it?"

"In Trastevere. No. It's a little hard to explain. He's not the thief. The clerk. She said he was trying to steal it but he was trying to stop her. She stole it. A notebook of Mario Damiani's. She still has it but I know where it is. I—" **You what, Thomas? Ran away? Because two mad people told you a crazy story?** Out here in the sunny morning on this quiet cobbled street, he found himself unable to admit anything so ridiculous. "A historian who lives in Trastevere. Across from Santa Maria della Scala. We took it to him. They're up there now, the two of them. You can send the Gendarmes. The reason they think they have the thief—the Gendarmes think that, I mean—is because she stuffed the chip in his pocket. The clerk's pocket. But make sure they're armed, because they're crazy. Not the Gendarmes are crazy. These people. They're crazy."

"Thomas?"

"I should've taken the book from her, but she was saying such insane things. Who they were, what the Concordat is. Insane. And then—what he did—still, I shouldn't have left it. Maybe I should go back. Yes. I'll go back. I—"

"Thomas."

"There's no—"

"Thomas."

"I had—"

"Father Kelly!"

The last time Thomas had heard his name in those tones was during his second week in graduate school. A fellow student in his Augustinian Thought seminar had remarked that feeding the poor and fasting were two sides of the same coin, which set Thomas to wondering what the obligations of the poor really were on fast days. Apparently he'd been so deep in thought that he'd missed the next discussion question, and Lorenzo Cossa, not yet a cardinal but already a legend, had not been pleased.

"Father Kelly! Get hold of yourself!"

Thomas swallowed. "I'm sorry, Father. I've been babbling, haven't I? I'm sorry."

"Thomas. The people who have the book—have they left the house?"

"No, I don't think so. I'll go back and get it."

"You won't. I'm sending the police."

"For the book?"

"Stay until they get there to make sure those people don't leave. If they do, don't confront them. Just keep tabs on them and call me. If they don't, then soon as the Carabinieri show up, come here."

"The Carabinieri? Not the Gendarmerie?"

"Do you know where the nearest taxi stand is?"

"I—"

"If you're near Santa Maria della Scala, there's one in Piazza Trilussa. When the police arrive, get in a cab and come here. I'll be waiting."

The Cardinal clicked off.

16

◇

Lorenzo Cardinal Cossa sat motionless behind his ornate desk. He'd already instructed Father Ateba to bring Father Kelly in the moment he arrived, and he'd called the Gendarmes and told them to release the hapless clerk. Before any of that he'd called his nephew, Raffaele Orsini. He'd found the young Carabiniere on duty but available to do a favor for his uncle. That meant Raffaele's partner was probably not around, the anticlerical detective whose name Lorenzo could never remember—Giulio Aventino, that was it. Julius Caesar of the Aventine Hill, Raffaele called him. How much clearer could it be that the man was from an old Rome family, one that predated possibly the founding, and at least the growth to power, of the Church? And, according to Raffaele, he had a chip on his shoulder about it. Detective Julius Caesar; but Lorenzo, even as his lip curled with disgust, realized he was directing his bile at the absent detective in order to avoid focusing on his real and looming problem.

Even allowing for Rome traffic, Thomas would be here in fifteen minutes.

What then?

Lorenzo sighed. Was there really any question? Thomas had indeed been babbling, and Thomas Kelly didn't babble.

Something had badly shaken him up, frightened him—
something he didn't understand. The woman from the
Library who'd stolen the book, and the historian who
lived in Trastevere: they'd terrified Father Kelly. He'd
said they were crazy, but Lorenzo had heard the tiny
note of doubt in Thomas's voice.

There was only one possibility.

They'd told him the truth.

17

Gendarme *Vice Assistente* Luigi Esposito slammed his fist on his desk and clenched his jaw shut. Back home in Naples he'd be cursing a blue streak but in the years since he'd come up to Rome to join the Gendarmerie he'd learned to keep his language clean. Well, no. He'd learned to keep his mouth completely closed on infuriating occasions like this, so he wouldn't risk filling the security offices of the Holy See with the words the situation called for.

It was bad enough he'd had to go racing through the traffic-choked streets of Rome in the company of two provincial dolts whose entire ambition extended to putting in their years finding tourists' lost purses and then retiring on their piddling Gendarme pensions. Though at least the chase, as opposed to most of the work Luigi did here, had gotten his blood moving. They'd caught their quarry, too, a pale, sniveling clerk who'd stolen a book from the Vatican Library.

The uniformed idiots Luigi was saddled with laughed uproariously at how stupid he must be, this Argentinian punk, to work at the Library and not even think about the GPS-alarm chip in the book. And when it set off the alarm, to rip it out, stash the book somewhere—and forget he had the chip still on him! Oh, what a *scemo*!

Gritting his teeth, Luigi had thought, **No. You're the** *scemi*. **No one's that dumb, with the possible exceptions of yourselves.** Keeping the chip was clearly a well-thought-out red herring. The clerk had passed the stolen book to a confederate—probably the black-haired woman he'd pretended to be scuffling with—and kept the chip so they'd focus on him while she got away. This suggested to Luigi an organized burglary ring. Perhaps specializing in antique manuscripts, or perhaps just in stealing from the Vatican. Why not? There was wealth here beyond comprehension. Furthermore, as far as Luigi could tell, the possessions of the Vatican were like an iceberg. The ten percent that was visible was impressive enough, but the rest, besides being nine times greater, was hidden in murky waters. If you could get a precious item beyond the walls, there was a good chance no one would miss it. Which didn't mean it was easy to steal from the Vatican, but it was possible, and probably, if you were a certain kind of crook, irresistibly tempting.

Luigi was a cop, not a crook. Scratching out his childhood on the cobblestones of Naples, he'd dipped a toe in criminal waters. Which of his friends hadn't? He'd boosted the odd TV, raced off with the occasional dangling purse, run errands for a few local *malavitosi*. But it wasn't for him. He watched his pal Nino get sent away to reform school, which everyone knew was six kinds of hell; and then his cousin Angelo, at fifteen, was one night advised to leave Naples immediately and plan not to come back. Angelo kissed his tearful mother and didn't even pack a suitcase. Luigi could see early on that there was toughness and its attendant respect, but no real future, in crime.

There was a future, however, and other advantages,

too, on the police. You could be tough and respected, and it was also useful to be smart. Luigi joined the local force, but ran up against a difficulty. His past as a booster and errand-runner wasn't enough to blackball him. This was Naples, after all; if the police only accepted lily-white recruits, there wouldn't be a dozen cops in the city. But Luigi had been smarter and more enterprising than most *ragazzi*, reliable, able to think on his feet. Every *malavitoso* in Naples coveted his services. If he'd elected to join one crime family over another, the loser would have felt regret and congratulated the chosen. When he turned his back on them all and declared his loyalty to the other side, it stung. The investigation of crime depends on the cultivation of sources and mutual back-scratching; but no matter what Luigi Esposito offered, the word was out. No crook in Naples would talk to him. All doors were shut.

Luigi knew a cobblestone ceiling when he saw one. He began to despair at the vision of a future spent patrolling garbage-strewn alleyways and directing traffic on fume-filled streets.

One day, as he was responding to a purse-snatching on Via Santa Chiara, in the heart of his old neighborhood, inspiration struck. The American tourist's pocketbook was long gone—when would they learn not to dangle their bags so condescendingly from their fingertips?— but after he made short work of the report he took his hat off and entered the quiet church. Old Father Carmelo was delighted to see Luigi Esposito and to find he'd done so well. By which, given the nature of the parish, the priest meant that Luigi had graduated from high school and wasn't in jail. Luigi confided his problem to Father Carmelo, who had a word with a seminary mate whose cousin was a bishop, and so on, and Luigi had gone up to Rome.

It was quite an honor, so he was told, to serve on the Gendarmerie. That might be true, but Luigi soon discovered it to be an honor reserved for men like himself: people who knew people. Talent for the job, which Luigi happened to have, was secondary. In one way that was good. Surrounded by dull lumps of coal, a diamond shines all the brighter. Luigi, unsure he was a diamond but demonstrably not as dull as most of his colleagues, rose to the rank of *vice assistente* in an impressively short time. *Vice assistente* was a detective's title; the problem was that the Gendarmerie had nothing much to detect. The pickpockets of Saint Peter's Square needed chasing, and the occasional nut who insisted on speaking to the *Papa*—or insisted he *was* the *Papa*—needed to be quietly shooed from the premises. But anything juicy, any criminal activity an investigator could sink his teeth into, ran headfirst into the fact that as far as the Holy See was concerned, silence was golden. *Make It Go Away* was the Gendarme's first directive. Find out who did whatever it was, and then explain in a soft and calm way that a dossier had been compiled and they'd best get themselves gone and keep quiet, did they understand? They always did, and the investigations of the few real crimes Luigi had come up against had ended as compiled dossiers in his desk. It was enough to turn a cop into a cynic.

Or to make him long for another move. Luigi began to dream of the Carabinieri. For a kid from Naples by way of the Gendarmerie, this was close to an impossible dream, based equally on the Carabinieri's heavy pro-Rome bias and the fact that Luigi had little to show for his six years on the Gendarmes.

Until today. This could have been it; this could have been big. Luigi could see that this Argentinian, this Jorge Ocampo, was no *scemo* and he hadn't acted alone. When they caught him he didn't have the stolen book. But Luigi had him. Luigi began his interrogation and it was only a matter of time before he'd have broken the punk down. That would have led to his confederates. As the detective on the case—as, in fact, the man who'd personally tackled the clerk after his bogus fight with the woman (though the skinny kid was unaccountably strong and it had taken all three Gendarmes to subdue him), Luigi would be in a fine position to make Carabinieri hay while this sun shone.

He was, he thought, not far—a few minutes, half an hour—from pulverizing the kid's innocent-victim act and getting him to spill it, when his *soprintendente* interrupted him. A call had come from the Cardinal Librarian: it was all a mistake. Nothing had been taken. Nothing was wrong. A faulty alarm system, a chip fallen from a book. A big uproar over zilch. Let the kid go.

Expressing his disappointment and his outrage to the *soprintendente* had gotten Luigi nowhere, not even winning him a sympathetic shrug. "We work for them, Esposito," had been his boss's cold reply. "Most of us are grateful for the opportunity to serve."

Thus it was that the Argentinian, pale and confused but not checking this gift horse's mouth, scuttled away, and Luigi Esposito smashed his fist on his desk and bottled up the curses that threatened to singe the office's air. A cardinal! Luigi's blue Carabinieri uniform torn from his grasp by a cardinal who was no doubt embarrassed by the traffic-disaster chase and the Metro-stop dustup. Not to mention the obvious involvement of Library staff. Like all of them, the Cardinal Librarian only *Wanted It to Go Away* and probably considered a missing book a small price to pay for maintaining dignity and decorum at the Holy See.

Luigi stepped outside. He'd been trying to cut down but this situation called for a smoke. He lit up, pulled deeply, and looked around at the groomed, disciplined, cross-eyed boring perfection of this place.

Maybe it was the change in perspective, or maybe the nicotine jolting his brain, but as he was grinding out the cigarette Luigi had a thought. The Librarian, Cardinal Cossa, wanted the problem to go away *from the Vatican*. If Luigi was right, though, this wasn't a Vatican crime, as such. It was a burglary ring, a criminal racket, an organized conspiracy, targeting the Vatican but possibly other places, too. Secular places. With at least one member inside the Vatican Library and others outside it. If Luigi could crack this racket, could at a minimum point the secular authorities in the right direction, that could be the feather his cap needed to get him in the Carabinieri's door.

18

Jorge Ocampo stood still, an island buffeted by the waves of tourists in Saint Peter's Square. The Gendarmes had escorted him out after that belligerent Neapolitan detective had suddenly decided to let him go. Jorge had been pleased that his protestations of innocence had finally gotten through to the man.

His satisfaction was short-lived, though.

Anna was angry. Very angry.

He flinched at the voice issuing from the phone at his ear. "Forget it, Jorge. Go home. Go take a nice coffee. Go back to Argentina! I don't care. You're an idiot! Worse than useless. I'll do it myself. No—I'll find someone else. Franklin, from California—yes, I'll call him."

Jorge's blood froze. Franklin had recently joined the group that met in the back room of Circolo degli Artisti, where Anna led them in planning the world they would create once the Noantri took their rightful places. Franklin was young, Newer than Jorge, and impassioned. He believed in Anna and their mission, and the last thing Jorge wanted was to give up his place at Anna's side to the fresh-faced American.

"No, no, Anna!" Jorge heard himself croaking. He swallowed and went on, "I'm sorry. Let me try again.

I'll find the book. I'll find out who that woman is and I'll get it from her. I'll get it for you, Anna. I will."

"You can't, Jorge. You're not the man for the job."

"I am!"

A short pause. "I don't know."

"Anna—"

"All right. One more chance. Do not screw this up, Jorge."

"I won't! I'll find out—"

"I already know who she is."

"What?"

With an exasperated sigh: "I asked around. Livia Pietro. An art historian. Three different people recognized her from your description. Not even Noantri—they were Mortals, art students. She's well-known. She lives in Trastevere, in that really old house in Piazza dei Renzi that used to be the watchtower. Do you think that gives you enough to go on, Jorge? Do you think you can do it right this time?"

"Yes! Yes, Anna. Thank you. I'll go there now. I'll get the book."

"You'd better." She clicked off.

Jorge slipped his phone back into his pocket and wiped the sweat from his upper lip. He stood for a moment more, watching the crowds surge this way and that in their eagerness to take in everything they could in their time here. Benighted fools, Anna called them. Far too shortsighted to understand their own best interests from one day to the next. No wonder they'd made such a mess of the world! They fundamentally didn't care about anything that didn't affect them immediately, because in their hearts they knew they'd be gone by the time things got bad.

Was what she said true? Anna was deeply passionate and completely serious about everything she believed, but still, Jorge wasn't sure. He didn't remember feeling that way when he was Mortal. His Change was much more recent than Anna's. She'd been Noantri for four hundred years, so maybe she'd forgotten. Back home in Argentina, where they'd met, Jorge had joined the Communist Party because he and his comrades shared the revolutionary dream of a better future. They knew freedom fighters like themselves were unlikely to live to see it, but they were willing to fight and die for the dream.

Though he couldn't deny that a longer view had its advantages, too. And Anna had done a great deal of thinking about these things. She had been a member of the Party, also, and had urged resistance to the military dictatorship with fiery speeches and acts of breathtaking bravery. Even now, when he understood that, being Noantri, she hadn't been risking, perhaps, quite what he and his friends had, his heart still swelled with pride at her fierce valor.

Bueno. Enough dreaming. The parking lot, that's where he needed to go now, to fetch his *motorino.* As he turned to head in that direction he pulled out the phone again to switch the ringer on. It was required to be off in the Library, and with all that had happened he hadn't thought about it since. He and Anna had just hung up, but she might call back. With new instructions, or to say she'd thought it over and she understood that it wasn't his fault. She had her own ring tone, Anna did: Fuerte Apache's "Vida Clandestina." Hearing it always caused a clash of emotions in Jorge: joy that Anna was calling him and a stab of longing for home. He missed home.

Sometimes, before he caught himself, he almost, almost, wished he'd never met Anna, never become Noantri. That the vicious military dictatorship of his beloved Argentina had made him a *desaparecido* like so many of his friends. That he'd died a martyr hero of La Guerra Sucia. It was the fate he was surely headed for until Anna intervened.

But those moments passed. How could he not want what he now had, what everyone would want if they knew it was possible? He had eternal life! He had the power to heal his body, develop his talents, advance his mind! Anna had told him how it would be, in those moments after the Fire, after the Change, when he lay paralyzed and bewildered. He'd been dying, she said; she'd had no choice. He would be grateful, she promised; he'd welcome what she'd done, when he understood. When he learned what she was, and what he now was. The news that he'd been dying had surprised him—the wound was excruciating, but even as he lay writhing he'd known the pain was from a bullet-shattered collarbone— but Anna had risked a great deal, she explained later, to save him. She'd chased off his assailants, but the real risk was what came next. To make someone Noantri without the Conclave's prior assent was forbidden; for Anna, already in exile for previous infractions of the Law, the penalty for such an action could be— Jorge shuddered. He wouldn't think of it. What she had done for him, without his asking or even knowing to ask, proved her love. He owed her this wondrous new life, and he would do whatever Anna needed, whatever Anna desired, for as long as she wanted him to.

For eternity.

And Anna, Anna had a goal! The world would not

remain as it was, continuing, day to day, day to day . . .
Anna's ambition held that everyone, Mortal and Noantri, deserved to lead rich and magnificent lives. Lives like
hers. It wouldn't be long now until her plans—their
plans—succeeded. When they were triumphant and Noantri jurisdiction was established, he could go home
then. Once the Church was destroyed, there'd be no
reason for Rome to remain the center of Noantri power.
He and Anna would go back to Argentina. She would
rule from Buenos Aires, and they would be happy.

The ringer was on now, but although Jorge stared at
the phone as he walked, it sat inert in his hand. Resigned, he put it away when he reached the parking area
and took out his keys. He mounted the *motorino*, revved
the engine, and headed for Trastevere, as Anna had told
him to do.

19

For the second time that day Thomas Kelly charged blindly out a door. His racing footsteps slapped and echoed through the ornate marble corridors as he ran from the Librarian's suite the way he had from the House of Crazy People. But this time it was much, much worse. Because according to Lorenzo, according to Cardinal Cossa, according to Thomas's friend and rock and spiritual anchor, those people weren't crazy.

It was a nightmare. Wait, yes, that was it! Literally. It was a nightmare, this whole day. He was actually asleep in his bed in the *residenza*, exhausted, disoriented, probably even under the influence of Lorenzo's good red wine from dinner. A nightmare. Thomas slowed his footsteps and waited: in his experience, once you knew you were having a nightmare, you woke up.

He didn't wake up. The crowds still milled in Saint Peter's Square, cameras clicked, groups of tourists swirled this way and that. The vast curve of the Colonnade swept away to encircle the great piazza on two sides, but Thomas saw no grandeur now: only vertigo.

It wasn't a nightmare, then. It was a horror worse than that.

Picking up his pace again, he made his way to Via del Pellegrino. When Lorenzo had informed him he'd be staying in the Jesuit *residenza* inside the Holy See while on this mission, he'd been awed and thrilled. Now all he wanted was to leave as soon as he could, to run as fast as he could, to flee from here to somewhere far, far away.

He heard, *"Buongiorno, Padre,"* as he brushed past another priest, a man heading out into the sunshine, a man who still lived in a normal world. He couldn't answer. At the door to his room he jabbed the key at the lock, could not find the keyhole. **Get a hold of yourself, Thomas!** Who had said that? Lorenzo! Lorenzo dared! Lorenzo Cardinal Cossa, who'd proved, in this last hour, that he'd been lying to Thomas since the day they'd met.

An hour before, in a different lifetime, Thomas had waited in Trastevere as Lorenzo had requested until he'd seen a dark blue Carabinieri Lancia roll to a stop near the café that shielded him. The car parked where it couldn't be seen from the small piazza at Santa Maria della Scala, and when the business-suited young man who got out rounded the corner, he glanced toward the historian's house. All right, the police were here. Thomas jogged to Piazza Trilussa and got in the first cab at the stand. The cab bounced over the cobbles, swung onto Ponte Garibaldi to cross the Tiber, and headed up the broad, busy street on the other side. Thomas tried to think of nothing at all as the *platano* trees slipped rhythmically past the windows. By the time he arrived at the Vatican he'd calmed down. He paid the driver and reported to the Librarian's suite.

He hadn't been kept waiting this time. He was shown in immediately by the young African priest. As Thomas thought back now, did he see a glint in the young man's eye? Did he know, too? Lorenzo had said not, had said no one knew except a very few in the Church's highest ranks. But how could Thomas trust anything Lorenzo said ever again?

When Thomas arrived Lorenzo had dismissed the young priest, pointed Thomas to a chair, and poured cognac into crystal snifters. Thomas, even at this ridiculously early hour, had been grateful for that, but the strong drink made what followed even more surreal.

"Thomas," Lorenzo had said in quiet, measured tones, "tell me what happened. Start in the Library."

So Thomas had recounted the meeting with Livia Pietro, the fight, the flight. Lorenzo said nothing, just sat puffing on a cigar, his eyes searching Thomas's face. Thomas, sure by then the whole thing was an inexplicably elaborate attempt to terrorize him, felt calm, almost amused; but suddenly, when he reached the discussion in Spencer George's study, he had trouble going on. Lorenzo advised him to finish his cognac, and gave him more.

"What happened there, Thomas?" Lorenzo asked. "What did they tell you?"

Feeling the comforting burn of excellent liquor, Thomas continued. "At first, nothing. Just that someone they both seemed to know, someone named Jonah, knew where the Concordat was. And that she—Livia Pietro— was ordered to find it by some group they call the Conclave. Whoever they are, they told her to get me to help her. They know why I'm here."

He looked to Lorenzo but Lorenzo just nodded.

Thomas said, "She's afraid of them, or of something, but I don't know what. He—" Spencer George's face flashed in front of Thomas and his stomach clenched. "Nasty, sneering man. He—he—"

"He what, Thomas?"

Thomas took another sip. The cognac was warming him. He felt it in his fingertips and along the back of his neck. He was loose, he was safe. "I wouldn't help them. They wouldn't tell me how they knew about the Concordat or what it was or why they wanted it, and finally I told them I'd leave unless they did. I started to go and she said no, sit down, and she told me what they are— what they say they are. Do they believe it themselves?" he suddenly wondered. "Can they be that crazy? How could anyone—"

"Thomas. What did they say?"

Thomas snapped his eyes back to Lorenzo. "Yes. I'm sorry. She said . . ." He drew his brows together and concentrated, peering down at the light reflected in the amber liquid he was holding. As he spoke, the glow shimmered and danced. "She kept using the word 'Noantri.' It's a Romanesco word, a contraction of *noi altri*. It means 'we others,' and residents of Trastevere use it about themselves but she said even though that's what most people mean by it, it didn't just mean that—it meant her people."

"Her people? Thomas, who are her people?"

Thomas lifted his eyes again to meet Lorenzo's. Why was the Cardinal looking so solemn? Thomas burst into a grin. He realized he was tipsy and that this was the most absurd thing he'd ever say to Lorenzo. Dramatically, he lifted his hand toward the ceiling. "*Vampires!*" He started to laugh. Guffaws rocked him and he shook helplessly. The cognac sloshed in his snifter as he cracked up.

Lorenzo reached forward and took the glass from Thomas's hand. He set it down and softly asked, "What else?"

Instantly, the comic mood vanished; instantly, Thomas was sober. "The historian," he heard his own voice in monotone. "I refused to believe them, anything so ludicrous. He said all right then, I should leave, but she said it was important that I stay, important that I help them. So the historian—Spencer George, yes, that's his name—he shrugged and picked up a knife from his desk. He took the flowers from a glass vase—I think they were irises, but I'm not good with flowers—"

"Thomas?"

"He laid them very carefully on the tray. As though he cared about them. He brought the vase and put it on the table right in front of me and then he took the knife and he slit his wrist."

Thomas stopped. Lorenzo repeated, "He slit his wrist."

As though from far away, Thomas noted that Lorenzo phrased that as a statement, not a question. "Over the vase. Blood spurted into the water. Bright red . . . But right away, right *away*, it started to heal. It was a deep wound. He showed it to me, turned his wrist up right in front of me, and I watched it heal. I could see it. The bleeding stopped; the skin moved, crawled together almost. The blood in the water hadn't even mixed, it was still making little trailing threads, and he wasn't bleeding anymore." Thomas looked up at Lorenzo. "How did he do that? What kind of trick . . . ?"

Lorenzo was shaking his head.

"She didn't move," Thomas said. "She just sat there drinking her coffee. As though there weren't . . . weren't blood in the vase. Then he did it again. He did it to his other wrist. The same thing, more blood in the water, and when that one had started to heal he showed me the other one again. It was barely a pink scratch. 'Well,' he said, 'is that dramatic enough? Father?' I didn't answer so he said, 'Livia, I don't think he's convinced.' Then he smiled and handed me the knife. It was bloody. He opened his shirt and tapped himself on the chest. On the heart."

"What did you do?"

"I dropped the knife and ran."

That was it. That was the moment Thomas expected Lorenzo to grin, also, to laugh as hard as Thomas just had, and to explain to him what the Concordat really was, who the other signatory really was, and what the gang of book thieves/terrorists/merry prankster lunatics he'd encountered was really up to.

Lorenzo had not.

Quite, quite the opposite. He'd apologized for withholding this information from Thomas for so long, and said that Thomas's reaction now was proof that he'd been correct in doing so. That of all the Church's secrets, all its hidden truths, the truth of the Concordat was the most difficult for any devout man to learn. That the Noantri, begotten of Satan and birthed in hell, walked the earth. That they had as their purpose the degradation of men's bodies and the destruction of men's souls. That the Noantri promise of eternal life, meaning as it did a never-ending earthly existence and not a rebirth in the presence of the Lord, was a foul and futile pledge.

And that the Church had made a contract with them. And had held to it, to the mutual benefit of both groups, for six hundred years.

20

◄○►

Thomas Kelly yanked open drawers and grabbed fistfuls of freshly pressed shirts. He pulled jackets and their hangers from the closet, swept the desk clean of pens and notepads, and stuffed everything recklessly into his suitcase. He was normally neat and methodical about his packing, as he was about everything, but nothing right now was normal and the only thing that mattered was to get away from here. To where? He didn't care. The next plane out of Rome, wherever it was going. Beijing, New York, Kuwait City. Somewhere he knew no one, no one knew him, and he could try to understand what had happened to him this day.

The drawers and closets were emptied and the suit-case mashed shut when Thomas, loading his pockets with his passport and wallet, heard his cell phone ring. No! Whoever it was, let them— But conscientious habit had by then forced the phone from the top of the bureau into his hand. An unknown number, a Rome code. Again unconscious routine took over; he'd been at the service of others, trying to be of use, for so long. Before he quite knew what he was doing he'd answered it.

"Thomas Kelly."

"*Buongiorno*, Father." An unrecognized voice, speaking, after that first word, in an English lightly accented.

"You don't know me but we have reason to work together. You must bring me the Concordat."

Thomas stopped in the middle of his room, suitcase waiting on the bed. "Who are you? What do you mean?"

"Who I am is not important. You will be more interested, perhaps, in whom I know."

"What are you—"

"Thomas." A new and this time familiar voice. "It's Lorenzo. Whatever this man tells you to do, don't do it!"

"What— What are—"

Through the phone, Thomas heard muffled, unintelligible sounds. Then the other voice was back. "He is a brave man, your friend. Surprising, for a man of the Church. You're usually such cowards. Father Kelly, I don't have much time and neither do you. You'll bring me the Concordat or your friend will die."

Thomas sank into the armchair. He bent forward over the phone. Weakly, he said, "What?"

"My people need that document. It's time the hypocrisy and evil of your Church was revealed for the world to see. Your friend the Cardinal wanted you to find it so he could hide it again and save your Church. Now you'll have to find it to save *him*. He's here with us, and not, believe me, by his own choice. If you don't bring us the Concordat, he will die." A brief pause. "No, better. Yes, much better. He won't die. He'll never die. I'll make him one of us." Thomas heard a horrified intake of breath that could only have come from Lorenzo. "Yes, a marvelous idea," the voice continued. "I'll give your friend eternal life. Isn't that what you men of the Church are always going on about? Eternal life. Won't he love that?"

A foul and futile promise. Lorenzo's words rang in Thomas's head. **The destruction of men's souls.**

"No," Thomas said. "This isn't happening. This isn't real."

"I'm sorry. I'm afraid it is. You'll go back to those of our people you've already met, the two who are searching, and you'll help them. You'll find the Concordat and bring it to me or I'll have the pleasure of welcoming your friend into our Community. We're not unrepresented in your Church, but he'll be our first cardinal. Quite an honor, wouldn't you say?"

"No!" Thomas heard Lorenzo yelling from a distance. "Thomas! Don't help him! They—" His words were cut off.

"Oh, yes, he's very brave." The voice was mocking now. "Willing to die for his Church and his God, I have no doubt. But sadly, I don't think he's going to get that chance. Go join the search for the Concordat, Father Kelly, and wait for my next call."

The connection was cut.

21

Livia Pietro leaned over a map of Trastevere as the area had been in 1840. It had been Spencer's idea to photocopy the map, one of the antique treasures of his collection, and use it to plot the locations of Damiani's subjects. Truth be told, not very much had altered in the district since this map was made, but Spencer thought it would be useful to get as close to Mario Damiani's standpoint as they could.

Livia could see how hard this was for Spencer. She hadn't known Damiani—her own Change had come about during the First World War—and Spencer had never been one to reveal his feelings. But he and Damiani had been together for many decades; as Livia understood it, nearly a century. Noantri unions were the same as those the Unchanged made and also different. Couples came together for the same reasons: an ultimately indefinable compatibility of qualities physical, intellectual, emotional, and spiritual. Among the Unchanged, pairings that started well sometimes came apart nevertheless, as life's events strained them, as the partners grew and became different people from the ones they'd been.

For the Noantri, the challenge was the same, and it was magnified by stretching over greater expanses of time. Through decades and centuries, personalities and behaviors altering as new knowledge, new views, and new experiences were added, a couple could easily find themselves, at last, totally unknown to each other.

But sometimes, the reverse. Sometimes the wealth of years only gave power to a couple's love. Possibly it was the fact that the two had always been opposites that was the strength of Spencer's relationship with Mario Damiani. Livia, despite what she'd led Father Kelly to believe, had known little about Damiani until yesterday, when she'd received the instructions of the Conclave. She'd researched him extensively before heading, just that morning, to the Vatican Library. From what she'd learned, Damiani had been everything Spencer wasn't: enthusiastic, open, optimistic, and spontaneous. Among the Noantri of Rome, she'd discovered, their mutual devotion had been legendary.

"I get the feeling Mario Damiani knew every inch of Trastevere," Livia ventured, glancing at Spencer as she spoke. Working with Damiani's notebook and the map, the two of them were trying to decipher Damiani's passionate, elliptical references and locate the poems' subjects. They'd been at it for nearly two hours, ever since Thomas Kelly had bolted. Spencer, for his part, was delighted to be rid of the priest. Livia, though dismayed, could see that for her to go after Father Kelly would only terrify him more. She had thought, from their short acquaintance, that he might actually be strong enough to accept the difficult truth he was being told. She'd been wrong. She felt bad for him, and worried about the Conclave's reaction when they found out. But perhaps it wouldn't matter, after all, whether he was involved. His knowledge might have been useful, but Damiani's notebook was likely to be the real treasure here. So while

Spencer had calmly rinsed out the vase he'd used as a prop in his theatrical display—*Signora* Russo, his cook, was Unchanged, so it wouldn't do for her to come upon it—Livia unrolled the map and began.

"When we met, Mario had been Noantri twenty years, I nearly two hundred." Spencer answered Livia without looking up. "In all the time we were together we never traveled far. Mario didn't care to. Rome, and particularly Trastevere, had his heart. I'd always traveled, even before my Change. I wanted to go back to Asia, but Mario could never be persuaded. He did say he might want to see the New World one day, maybe New York, but such . . . coarseness . . . held no interest for me. So we remained in Rome." Spencer trailed off into a pensive silence. Livia let him be.

"There," Spencer said after a moment, in stronger tones. He laid down his pencil. "I think that's the last of them." He frowned down at the map and then at the notebook. "I have to tell you, though, that whatever was bothering me earlier has not gone away. Something about these poems is so familiar. . . ."

"It's not just that you knew he was working on them?" Livia studied the map, now that they'd completed it, looking for a pattern in the places Damiani had chosen to celebrate.

"I knew it, but I hadn't seen them. He never showed me his work until it was finished. Something here . . . Something about the notebook itself, I think. I—"

The clanking of the brass ring on the front door interrupted him. Livia and Spencer exchanged glances; then Spencer crossed the room to peer through the window overlooking the piazza. "Oh," he said. "My, my. Livia, come see this, and tell me what you want me to do."

22

———◦———

Carabiniere *Sergente* Raffaele Orsini scratched his chin (where his stubble was kept at fashionable two-day length by Elena's birthday gift of a beard trimmer) and resettled in his café chair. Even the best of chairs could get a little uncomfortable after an hour and a half.

Giulio Aventino, his partner and senior, was probably back at the station by now, and livid that the *maresciallo* had given Raffaele permission to do this surveillance. If Giulio had been there when the request had come in he'd have fought it, though the *maresciallo* would've overruled him and Raffaele would be here anyway. That was politics, not piety, Raffaele knew: an uncomplicated favor like this for the Vatican was the sort the Carabinieri were only too happy to grant, so that when someday the police needed to, for example, follow a suspect into San Pietro, the Curia would respond in kind. Everyone scratched one another's backs, that was the Italian way, and Giulio Aventino was no different except when it came to the Church.

The senior detective wasn't just some kind of blasé unbeliever to whom the Church meant nothing. In Raffaele's view Giulio's soul seemed infused with the bitter cynicism of a heartbroken lover. Giulio Aventino had been devout once, Raffaele was sure of it. Now, his religion was his work. As his sergeant, Raffaele applied himself to learning from a senior officer of long experience, obvious skill, and high reputation. As a man, younger but much stronger in devotion to the Holy Mother Church, he was grateful for his own faith in the face of his partner's gloom.

Here now, what was this? Raffaele, as he'd been trained to do, stayed slouched in his chair, didn't move, as though nothing was on his mind but his mid-afternoon *macchiato*. He reached for his phone, looking for all the world like a *figlio di papà* calling his girlfriend for a romantic chat. What he was, though, was a cop calling his uncle, the Cardinal, for whom the Carabinieri were doing this favor. Raffaele didn't know why he'd been asked to watch this house, and no one had come out; but he thought Lorenzo Cardinal Cossa might be interested to know that a priest had just arrived, knocked, and was standing on the threshold talking to the black-haired woman whose photo, marking her as Raffaele's surveillance target, the Cardinal had sent.

23

——◇——

Standing on the cobblestones as the echo of his knock died away, it was all Thomas Kelly could do not to turn and run. He swallowed, bile burning his throat. The idea that he'd soon once again be in the presence of those . . . those *creatures,* made his stomach curdle and his skin crawl.

He still wasn't sure he believed any of it: what he'd seen, what Lorenzo had told him. He'd given up hope that this was a simple nightmare but he was clinging to a new idea, that it was some sort of drug-induced hallucination. There'd been an accident. One of these terrible Rome drivers—some young kid on a *motorino* had almost run him down just moments ago, it was something like that. He was in a hospital all drugged up and his own subconscious had created this insane fantasy out of the depths of who-knows-where. The theory comforted him, but the problem with it was that while he waited for consciousness to return and the world to become right again, he had to take some sort of action. Although in this delusion Lorenzo Cossa had been deceiving and betraying Thomas for fifteen years, the fate threatening the Cardinal now was so horrifying that, though if any of this were true Lorenzo certainly wouldn't deserve his help, Thomas found himself unable to just abandon him. **After all,** Thomas thought, **if you don't act heroically in your own hallucination, what can you hope from yourself in real life?** Somewhere, somehow, Thomas was sure this all had to do with faith. The need to save someone whose treachery cut so deeply must be a test of faith. Thomas didn't know why his subconscious demanded this of him, but he wasn't about to let himself down.

And in a dark, far corner of his mind was a tiny stabbing pain he was trying desperately to ignore. But like a sliver of glass in his shoe, though minute it was agonizing and unremitting: the unspeakable possibility that he was wide awake and it was all true. In which case Lorenzo deserved his help even less, and needed it much more.

The door opened. Thomas stepped back involuntarily at the sight of Livia Pietro. "Don't touch me!"

"No, Father," she said quietly. "Of course not." After a moment she moved back into the foyer, holding the door wide. "Will you come in?"

Thomas found he couldn't cross the threshold, could not enter that house. They stood in silence, regarding each other. Pietro's green eyes seemed kind, even concerned, but Thomas was not going to be taken in again. "You're a monster," he rasped.

She shook her head. "I'm a person. Like you, but different from you."

A person? This creature was claiming to exist in the image of the Lord? He felt the calm that his new theory had brought him begin to slip away. "No!" he barked. "A creature with no soul." Pietro just gazed at him sadly; for some reason that pitying look enraged him more. "You sold your soul for a promise of eternal life..

But what you've bought isn't that. It's never-ending corruption. Everlasting decay!" He could feel the heat in his skin, could hear his voice rising; he knew he sounded wild but he couldn't stop himself. "Your bargain is worthless. Worthless! Your false prophet will abandon you. The End of Days will come, even for you, and—"

Pietro held up her hand. Thomas's cheeks burned; he trembled with rage. But looking at her pale face, her long dark hair—staring into her ocean-green eyes—he felt his flood of accusatory words abate. What was the point? The choice Livia Pietro and the others like her had made couldn't be undone. The sin they'd committed couldn't be confessed, expiated, forgiven. His knotted shoulders fell. Helplessness and sorrow flooded through him where, moments before, righteous anger had blazed.

"Father," Pietro said. "You left here, and I understand. What you're saying is wrong, but many think as you do. But you've come back. Why?"

No, he couldn't do this. Without the heat of his fury he felt cold and clammy, and his breathing caught as he just stood here in front of her. He couldn't go into that house. **Blood in the vase.**

"Father Kelly? Are you all right?"

"No! How could I be all right? Your . . . your 'people' . . ."

"Father." Now she spoke decisively, commandingly. "Come inside. Or leave."

Lord, Thomas prayed. **Father, help me.** He stood on the threshold another moment, a few more seconds in the cobblestoned, scooter-buzzed, sunny morning, and then he went in.

24

Livia led Thomas Kelly in silence up to Spencer's study. In the doorway, the priest stopped and peered apprehensively into the room.

"Where is he?"

"I asked Spencer to give us some time alone."

Livia sensed his relief, but he straightened and said, "I have no reason to be alone with you."

"Would you rather Spencer were here? Come in and sit down. Please."

She sat first, to appear as unthreatening as she could manage. Thomas Kelly chose a chair in the farthest corner and barely perched on it. He continued to look around uneasily.

"Spencer removed the vase, too," she said. "Why have you come back?"

He snapped his eyes to her like a nervous cat. After a moment: "Cardinal Cossa. The Vatican Librarian."

"And Archivist. I know who he is. What about him?"

"I got a call. Some of your . . . 'people' have abducted him."

"What?" She sat forward. As she did, he drew back.

"They'll make him one of you." The priest swallowed, then set his jaw and went on. "Unless I bring them the Concordat."

"I don't understand," Livia said. "This is— Who are they?"

"I have no idea. They said to come back here and help you. They'll contact me. Once I have the Concordat I have to give it to them."

Once *you* have it? Livia thought, but only said, "When did this happen?"

"I just got the call. Not fifteen minutes ago. That's how long it took me to get here." Kelly took a handkerchief from his pocket and wiped his sweating face. "The abduction must have happened within the hour. I was with him until then. The Cardinal. He told me— He told me—"

"He told you about the Concordat. And about us. The Noantri."

Kelly nodded, looking sick.

"Father," she said gently, "what you've been told—"

"Your people promised to raise Martin the Fifth to the papacy," he blurted. "If he agreed to stop exterminating you as the Church had always done. If he allowed you to exist and proliferate and defile the world!"

"No, that—"

"And worse: Martin agreed not only to permit you to continue, but to provide you with blood from Catholic hospitals for your filthy rites. Innocent blood!"

"Father," she said firmly. "As far as they go, your facts are correct, but the motivations you ascribe are wrong. As is your characterization of my people. And you're leaving out a great deal. I suppose you haven't been told the whole truth."

"What I was told—"

"What you were told is what most of the Unchanged believe."

"'Unchanged'?"

"People like you. Please. Wait here a moment. There's something I have to do, urgently. But I want very much to discuss this with you. To tell you—"

"What? Your side? Life from the demon's point of view?"

She stood and saw him recoil. "The news you've brought is troubling. I must discuss it with . . . the people whose instructions I'm to carry out. I won't be long."

"And what am I supposed to do? Just sit here?"

"I'm asking you to wait for me. But you're not a prisoner here. You can stay or go."

She walked past him out the study door, leaving him pale and staring.

Livia found Spencer where he'd said he'd be, in the drawing room on the next floor. "Well?" Spencer looked up, slipping a bookmark into the volume in his hands. "How is he, your young priest? Has he returned to drive stakes into our hearts? Has he brought his pistol and his silver bullets?"

"He's frightened half to death. You really didn't need to break out the Grand Guignol, Spencer."

"Of course I did. He wasn't believing a word you were calmly saying. He thought you and I were both mad. Two batty people sharing a *folie à deux*."

"I could have convinced him."

"Let me remind you that although you and I have all the time in the world, your priest grows older every minute. By the time your gentle rationality persuaded him, he'd have been too doddering to be of any use. Furthermore, unless I'm wrong, ageless though we may be, we still have a deadline to meet."

Livia dropped into a chair. "You're right. And things just got worse." She told Spencer the news Father Kelly had brought.

Spencer lifted his eyebrows. "An interesting development."

"You're certainly calm about it."

"The abduction of a cardinal is not an event that disquiets me."

"Under these circumstances? This cardinal? It's intensely disquieting, I think." She took out her cell phone. "I have to tell the Conclave. They may not know." She pressed the number and lifted her phone to her ear.

After a moment: *"Salve."* Her call, as she expected, was answered by Filippo Croce, the Pontifex's personal secretary. This man, sober, trustworthy, and devoted, had been the channel for communications to the Conclave since the media for contacting that august body had been quill pen and parchment.

"Salve. Sum Livia Pietro. Quid agis?" Automatically, as her people had for centuries, Livia inquired into the state of the Community before introducing her own affairs.

"Hic nobis omnibus bene est. Quomodo auxilium vobis dare possumus?" **All is well here,** came the response. **How may we be of service?**

The brief ritual completed, Livia switched to Italian and asked to speak to the Pontifex, or, failing that, to Rosa Cartelli. She wasn't asked her mission; clearly she'd been given a priority with the Conclave that, flattering as it was, she'd have preferred not to need. She was assured the Pontifex would speak with her in short order. A brief silence, then the music of Carlo Gesualdo. As with the art hung at the Conclave offices—the paintings of artists such as Ivan Nikitin and Romualdo Locatelli—the music played, even over the phone, was the work of Noantri. Livia had always been uncomfortable with this kind of self-conscious Noantri pride; to her it bordered on separatism. As an art historian, she argued that good art was good and bad art bad, regardless of who produced it. If the paintings of Noantri artists could hang in museums and galleries around the world, as, unbeknownst to Unchanged curators and collectors, they indeed did, then Noantri could have on their walls the work of the best of their own people, and equally, the best of the Unchanged. And better music than Gesualdo's could pour from the Conclave's office phone. She rolled her eyes at Spencer. "I'm on hold."

Spencer sighed, and took the opportunity to ask, "Whom do you suppose is behind it? This abduction?"

Livia shrugged. "There are other factions, other people besides Jonah who're impatient to Unveil. Any one of them might want to force the issue the same way Jonah does."

Spencer looked skeptical. "To take this action and make this threat—to send the priest back here to us—they'd have to know what you've been told to do and why the priest is in Rome at all."

"Father Thomas Kelly," Livia told Spencer, waiting for the Pontifex to come on the line. "That's his name."

25

It was all Thomas could do to force himself to stay seated. He had to, though. If he stood, he knew he'd run again from this house, and this time he'd keep going. How long should he give her? Half of him hoped she'd never come back. The other half feared the mortal danger—no, the immortal, the eternal danger!—to Lorenzo was becoming more real with every passing second.

This was a terror he'd never encountered before. The late-night seminary arguments and wine-fueled graduate school debates about free will had never covered this territory: the possibility that a man could lose his soul not through his own choices but through the actions of another. Confession, penance, and absolution: these were central to Thomas's faith. Any man, until his dying breath, could repent and be forgiven, could enter into the presence of God though he had denied him all his life. But redemption and God's grace, lost forever because a monster chose to make you a monster, also—neither Thomas nor any of his classmates had for a moment considered this. Their sophistic deliberations of free will had swirled around well-worn issues of the Lord's omnipotence and omniscience, threadbare questions of paradox with the answers always the same: God, in his omnipotence, gives us our own power; in his omniscience he grants us knowledge, in order that we make our own choices. He does this from hope and boundless love, to give each of us the privilege of coming to him freely, of choosing to put our souls into his care.

When this nightmare ended—this drug coma, this hallucination, yes, of course it was that—Thomas hoped he'd remember the foolish naïveté and philosophical bankruptcy of his now-blasted, ever-so-clever theology.

Of course, if this was just a hallucination, and the Noantri didn't exist, then the stealing of one's soul couldn't happen, and all could go back to the way it had been before. Oh, this was marvelous! If he woke, he wouldn't need to remember what he'd just learned, because it would be useless.

And if he didn't wake, he wouldn't need to remember it, because he'd never be able to forget it.

He started when the door opened, but this time he was prepared. The silver crucifix that usually hung around his neck was gripped in his hand. He thrust it out as Livia Pietro stepped back into the room. She stopped, stared, and shook her head. "Put that away." Crossing the carpet, she sat again. "The Church has always been our enemy, Father Kelly, but we haven't been yours. To think that the sight of a cross will have any effect on me—I'm sorry, but it's narcissistic."

Thomas slowly lowered his arm as she went crisply on.

"I've relayed your news to the Conclave. It caused a good deal of unease. The situation was already serious. Now it's much worse. That Cardinal Cossa's fate should be dependent on the revelation of the Concordat—this problem is of great concern to our Noantri leaders."

Thomas had to search for his voice, but he found it. "You'll forgive me if I withhold my thanks."

She stared levelly, then continued. "The Conclave is not without resources. They're attempting to find out what they can about what's happened and to intervene if possible."

"No!" Thomas jumped up. "Any interference could jeopardize the Cardinal further!"

"According to your thinking, his position is already dire. We disagree with your characterization of us, but it's one of our First Laws that no Mortal is made Noantri against his will. It's a condition of the Concordat. That document you despise."

She glanced pointedly at his chair. Thomas, not sure he had the strength to stand in any case, sank back down.

"A brief history lesson for you, Father. First: although the Noantri did help Martin the Fifth to achieve the papacy, we weren't the central agents of his rise. He had widespread support in the Church—that is, among *your* people. We aided him because Martin was able to understand the mutual advantages the Concordat would bring to the Noantri and to the Unchanged. His rivals, the Popes of the Avignon line, were blind to these benefits. The Concordat, in essence, obligates the Catholic Church to, as you say, cease trying to annihilate us. And yes, to provide us blood from Catholic hospitals. Blood is our sustenance, Father Kelly. This is not a choice we've made—it's a simple fact. In return, we will make no one Noantri without his consent—no, more than consent: his request—and the consent of the Conclave." She glanced away as she said that and was silent for a moment. Then she brought her gaze back to him and resumed. "We also, for our part, agree to remain hidden, not revealing our true natures. Not so hidden as we once were, though: we live in Community now, with our own kind, in cities around the world. This is a great comfort to us—just to be together. Because our nourishment is assured, we have no need of stealth, of violence—or of guilt. We're no longer the feral, furtive, degraded people of the past. The Concordat has given us that."

"You still say 'people.' You are not people."

"We are. Each of us started as you are today. As a Mortal man or woman. 'Unchanged' is the word we use. The Change comes about through a microorganism introduced into the blood. It alters the structure of our DNA." She gave a slight smile. "You look surprised."

"To hear you speak of a devil's bargain in such cold and scientific terms."

"It is science—it's not supernatural. The devil, whether he exists or not, has nothing to do with this. A microbe mutated in the blood of a small number of early humans. Possibly, at first, only one. It causes a need, and a great thirst, for human blood, and grants DNA the ability to rapidly repair cells. Our cells don't deteriorate. So we don't die. That's it."

Thomas drew a breath. "I'll remind you that the very essence of evil is to be subtle. Do you really think that because your unnatural bargain was made with a microbe and not a man with horns and a tail, it's any less the work of Satan?" Who, until today, Thomas might have been willing to argue was only a metaphor, an externalized manifestation of the human capacity for cruelty. Or, alternately, a distilled and focused expression of the evil that did exist in the Universe, brought into being by, and purposefully in contradistinction to, the goodness of God. Right now, though, if Satan walked through the door wearing his horns and tail, Thomas wouldn't blink.

"Couldn't your God have created this microbe?" Pietro asked. "In fact, in your view, how else could it have gotten here?"

"The Lord also created knives and guns. He gives us the privilege of choosing whether to use them." On firmer ground now that he was engaged in theological debate, Thomas added, "People were not meant to live on this earth forever. Only through death can man achieve eternal life."

"Really, Father? Do you say that to the doctors at your hospitals? The ones who stop people from dying every day? Some of whom are Noantri, by the way."

Thomas felt the firm ground slipping. "The doctors?"

"And the lawyers, and the cabdrivers. And"—Pietro pointed to herself—"the university professors. You've lived beside us and known us all your life, Father Kelly."

"No. That can't be true."

"It is. The Noantri came into being long ago. Before your Church, before the religions and belief systems from which your Church sprang. Before written history began. We've been here since the start of humankind."

"So has evil."

"True but irrelevant."

Thomas shook his head. "Even if your explanation is correct, the microbe itself was clearly sent by Satan."

Pietro smiled. "That's not so clear to us. And to your point about eternal life, you may be right. We don't know. What we have may only be longevity. Extreme, but not eternal. Some of our scientists think we may be deteriorating, as you are, just at a rate so slow as to be undetectable."

Thomas found himself asking, in spite of his repugnance, "Can you . . . die?"

"We can. Not of natural causes, because of the rapidity of repair of our cells. And certainly not of silver bullets or stakes to the heart at a crossroads at midnight. Or an overdose of garlic."

"Or," it occurred to Thomas, "sunlight. I was with you, in the sun."

"The Change heightens all the senses and makes us extremely responsive to our environment. We hear and see exceptionally well, for example, so most of us dislike loud noises. By that same token, bright light is painful, and for those of us who're naturally pale, our skin sunburns easily. It's not dangerous but it hurts, and pain is also something we feel more acutely than you do. So we wear sunglasses. And long sleeves, and hats. It was a Noantri chemist who developed sunscreen."

"But stakes to the heart—" A scene from earlier in the day flashed before Thomas. "Surely, if I'd stabbed Spencer George in the heart . . ."

"No. It's complex and still poorly understood, but there seems to be a sort of critical mass of blood and soft tissue that, as long as it's maintained, will eventually repair or, if needed, replicate, the rest of the body. It can take a long, long time, depending on the damage, but it will happen. In this case, Spencer's heart would have stopped, and the whole thing would've been messy, but after a day or a week of deep coma he'd have been back with us."

"Rising from the coffin. That's why they say you rise from the coffin."

Pietro nodded. "That's exactly right. We don't sleep in coffins, of course not. But once buried, we can 'rise again.' It's not really that, because it's not really death. But we understand why it seems like it, to the Unchanged."

And the dead shall be raised
Incorruptible

Thomas shuddered. The gift promised to all humanity at the Last Trumpet, usurped and perverted. "But you say you can die."

"Yes. In two ways, one more widely understood than the other. First, by fire. Some chemical process involved in the Change makes our flesh more vulnerable to fire than yours. I'm not a scientist so I can't explain it but if you want—yes, all right, never mind. The result is that fire can rapidly destroy us. If our bodies are completely consumed, there's nothing left to initiate the process of regrowth."

"There's always something. A tooth, a bit of bone."

"Bone and tooth don't live in the same way. Or hair, or nails. Soft tissue is what's needed. Living tissue, containing blood, which is what can be destroyed by fire."

"And the other way?"

"Obviously, complete dismemberment would, at some point, eliminate that critical mass. How small you'd have to chop us"—to Thomas's horror, she smiled—"that's something we don't know."

"Why not?"

"Because what Noantri would volunteer for that experiment?"

"Volunteer?" A wild laugh escaped him. Fiends with

medical ethics? "Why not just, I don't know what you call it, infect a bunch of people? Then you could chop them into pieces and see if they spring back to life!"

She stared. "You can't really believe we'd do that?"

He didn't answer.

"No," she said, calmly and firmly. "We consider our Changed lives a great gift. A Blessing. What you've suggested would make any Noantri ill even to contemplate."

Thomas felt ill himself. "But you can burn. So when you reach the fires of hell . . . But how will that happen, if you don't die . . . ?"

"Well, Father, perhaps you can take comfort in the knowledge that millions of years from now, the Earth will fall into the sun. Then the Noantri will all be destroyed. We'll die, and, if there's a Last Judgment, we'll be judged."

"You can't be judged. You have no souls."

"How can you be sure?"

Thomas looked around him, for help, for guidance. He was a Jesuit; he wasn't a scientist, but he was a scholar, trained not to shy away from the conflicts between fact and faith. Nor had he, ever. Ultimately, he saw those contradictions themselves as a gift from God: they were why faith was required. If God's goodness, if even his existence, could be proved, then what was man bringing to the table? What were we offering God? Faith was what God asked of man. It was our single gift to him. The only thing man has, and the only thing God wants.

What did that mean, then? Was it possible these—these creatures, were just another form of human life? Ultimately, as Pietro said, to die, and be judged, like all others?

Thomas looked at Livia Pietro again. For a moment, he saw her eyes as kind and her face as animated by a lively intelligence. Then: **Begotten of Satan and birthed in hell!** Inside his head, as clear as if the man himself were sitting here, Thomas heard Lorenzo's roar. **The degradation of men's bodies, the destruction of men's souls. A foul and futile pledge.**

They drink human blood.

It's the essence of evil to be subtle.

Kind eyes, an intelligent face. Better men than he had been deceived by less.

Pietro had been silent, watching him. Now she spoke. "Father, I thought I might be getting through to you but I can see that I haven't. I wish you'd keep an open mind but I know this is hard for you and I can't help what you believe. I think that's enough discussion. We're wasting time. Each of us has a compelling reason to find the stolen copy of the Concordat, and a better chance of succeeding if we act together. Can you put aside your distrust and work with me?"

If only it were merely distrust, Thomas thought helplessly. Revulsion, anger, sadness, and a soul-deep despair opened a chasm within him. This was what Lorenzo had meant when he said, *I'm afraid of what it will do to you, to your faith.*

And Thomas had laughed, because he'd thought that his crisis of faith had come and gone. He saw now that he'd been a man unconcerned about spots on his skin because he'd once survived hives, only to learn, too late, that he has the plague.

"The notebook," Pietro said. "Damiani's notebook. Spencer and I have been studying it. He agrees with me that the pattern of the missing pages may be important."

Thomas stared. Was he really going to do this? As though discussing Damiani's poems, or anything, with her, was reasonable? But, without a sense that he'd decided, he heard his own voice: "How can— How can you tell? You've identified the places the missing pages refer to?"

"No. There are too many possibilities. What we did was to decipher the poems that remain. When we mapped those places out, we found a broad area from here—this house—through Trastevere to the Tiber, with no poems relating to it. It's possible Damiani was heading from here to the river, and hid the Concordat on his way. In some place, some building or statue or fountain, he'd already written about."

Thomas hesitated, then slowly said, "If I do agree to help, what use can I be?"

"You know the significance to the Church of many of these buildings much better than either Spencer or I do," Pietro came back promptly. "And if we do manage to find the right building, we'll still have to locate Damiani's hiding place within it. He was a brilliant and ironic man with a great sense of humor, I'm discovering. Especially if the building he chose was a religious property, as I suspect it was, your knowledge of Church history could be very valuable."

"I'm not sure."

"The Conclave is. And your cardinal."

Yes, the Cardinal. Lorenzo had great faith in Thomas. Not enough to tell him the truth, but enough to ask him to take on this task.

"And if we find the Concordat?" Thomas asked. "What happens then?"

"Our goals are the same: to keep it hidden."

That's your goal, Thomas thought. **And the Cardinal's. Mine, right now, is to save him. If what it takes to do that is giving the Concordat to someone who'd reveal its contents, how bad would that really be? Would it really cause the destruction of the Church?** No: the setting of the Church back on the correct path, a path Thomas could now see had been abandoned six hundred years ago. Would Thomas be able to convince Lorenzo of the rightness of this? Lorenzo had screamed, *Don't help them*; Lorenzo had been willing to sacrifice himself to protect his Church. But Lorenzo, Thomas suddenly realized, could only be anxious to maintain the status quo because all this was theoretical to him. He must never—until they'd seized him—have met one of these Noantri, never been in this insidious, seductive presence. If he had, he'd understand. He'd feel the way Thomas felt now.

Thomas swallowed and asked, "How do we begin?"

"Spencer has the notebook." Pietro's relief was palpable as she stood. "I'll get him. He—"

She stopped as the door opened. Thomas's stomach clenched at the sight of Spencer George, who stood in the doorway holding Damiani's notebook. Thomas had to stop himself from going for his crucifix again. Looking at the historian, Thomas had to admit the man looked none the worse for the great gushing of blood from his wrists a few hours earlier.

None the worse; but he did look odd.

"Livia?" Spencer George spoke in a voice distant and strange. He didn't seem to notice Thomas. "Livia, I have one of these poems."

26

◄○►

Livia's heart leapt. Spencer had one of Damiani's missing poems; Father Kelly was joining in the search. She was doing as the Conclave had instructed and now had a hope of succeeding. Maybe things would turn out all right.

Maybe Jonah wouldn't have to die.

Spencer crossed the room to a rolltop desk in the corner. Livia watched as he unlocked it and slid the cover open. Laying Damiani's notebook down, he pulled out a drawer and retrieved a small leather case, from which he took a single sheet of paper. He held the sheet, fingering its edges, his eyes moving over it as though searching for something that wasn't to be found—something he'd searched for many times before, something he had never found. Then he laid his paper gently down and opened Mario Damiani's notebook beside it.

The priest started forward but Livia put out a hand to stop him. They waited; finally, Spencer, still in a soft monotone, said, "Come and look." After a moment, "You, too, Father Kelly, you may look."

They did, and over Spencer's shoulder she could see: the paper, the handwriting, the ink were all the same. Spencer turned pages, comparing torn edges until he located the place the sheet from his desk had originally resided.

"Mario gave it to me," Spencer said. "When he was just starting this book. He was satisfied with this poem— No," Spencer interrupted himself with a sad smile. "It was Mario. He was delighted. He said whether or not the rest of the book ended up any good, this poem did just what he wanted it to and it would always be mine. I thought that's all the note meant."

Livia glanced up at him. "The note?"

From the leather case Spencer drew a second sheet. Though the paper clearly came from another source, and the ink was different, the handwriting was the same. Its single line was Italian, not Romanesco, and scribbled in haste, but no one could mistake that it had been written by Damiani. *Look to your poem*, it said.

"I thought it was a farewell." Now Spencer turned and met her eyes. "When I finally returned to Rome, this was on my desk. I thought he'd left it in case—in case something happened to him. To remind me I had the poem. Had something of him. You see?"

"Yes."

"But maybe that's not what he meant at all. Maybe he wanted me to find the Concordat. Maybe he was telling me where it is."

Heart pounding, Livia peered at the poem; over Spencer's other shoulder, Thomas Kelly did the same.

Quer sbirilluccico che jje strazzia
er gruggno, er ginocchione flesso, è 'n passettino
incontro ar Padre nostro: Lui sà ch'è la monnezza
tra dde noi che bbatte er cammino,
piede destro, poi er sinistro, che porta l'anima a la
grazzia.

The Romanesco words lay oddly on the page, their letter groupings not those found in Italian, certainly not in English. But Livia had had a lot of practice at this, as she knew Spencer also had. Nor did Thomas Kelly seem fazed. In Livia's head the poem quickly transformed.

The glow of ecstasy upon the face,
the bended knee, the humblest of steps
toward our Father: He well knows the base
and lowly are the ones who make the trek,
right foot then left, that leads the soul to grace.

"If we can understand it," she said, "if we can work it out, you're right, Spencer. Maybe that's what he meant, and this is what we need."

"Work it out?" Spencer seemed bemused.

"What it refers to!" Thomas Kelly snapped. "Where he was sending you!"

Now Spencer smiled. "I'm surprised at you, Father. A Church scholar of your supposed erudition. 'The humblest of steps.'"

Thomas Kelly flushed angrily.

"I'm sorry, Spencer," Livia said. "I don't see it either."

"On the contrary. You do." Spencer pointed out the window, at the shadowed façade of the church of Santa Maria della Scala.

27

◄◦►

Jorge Ocampo lit another cigarette and ordered another coffee. The smoke was his fifth and the coffee his third since he'd sat down in this café in Piazza della Scala. He coughed. Maybe he should cut down. Though Anna said there was no reason. His indestructible Noantri body would repair any damage he was doing. But Jorge found the coughing itself unpleasant.

Anna never coughed.

The *cameriere* brought his coffee. Jorge liked it well enough, this Italian roast, but he'd never been served a coffee here yet that had the depth and strength of an Argentinian brew. He stirred in sugar (they didn't drink it sweet enough here, either), all the while keeping an eye on the door through which the priest had disappeared. Anna would be proud of him. He'd spotted that priest, and this time, he wouldn't let him get away.

He admitted it was mostly luck, but a large part of a revolutionary fighter's skill was recognizing the luck that came his way and knowing how to use it. Speeding on his *motorino* to the home of the dark-haired Noantri woman who lived on Piazza dei Renzi, he'd almost collided with the priest who'd been with her in the Vatican Library. He spun his bike around and followed, instinct telling him this man, in such a rush, might lead him where he needed to be.

Besides, this priest had knocked him down, and he owed the man for that, he thought as he sat in the café rubbing his shoulder. Though in truth it didn't hurt anymore. An unfortunate fact about the Noantri body, Jorge had found, was that vastly heightened senses meant pain, like any other physical phenomenon, was amplified far beyond what was experienced by Mortals. But it was also true that quick healing made the pain pass rapidly. Anna had promised, since disability and death were now impossible for him, that eventually the instinctive panic and fear that serious pain occasioned would fade, also.

Jorge hoped so; meanwhile, he was happy to trade occasional bouts of panic and moments of searing pain for the irreplaceable gift his augmented senses had also brought him: the acute, almost unbearable pleasure that surged over him, enveloped him, at Anna's touch. Her velvet lips brushing his lips, his throat; her silken finger-tips stroking his face, his chest—and the beautiful blazing agony when she dug her nails into his shoulders, scraped furrows down his back: all this was his, and was worth whatever it cost.

Once or twice, Jorge had caught himself wistfully wondering what it might have been like to make love to Anna if they'd both been Mortal. If all they had were the senses they'd been born with and the desperate, thrilling urgency Jorge remembered as such a vivid part of Mortal embraces. Urgency, of course, underlay all Mortal endeavors, though in daily life it hung almost unnoticed in the background. It came from the simple knowledge that time was finite and one's supply of hours would one day be exhausted. That understanding furnished a piquancy to a Mortal's every moment that, in his unguarded thoughts, Jorge sometimes found that he missed.

But in exchange, look what he had! He had eternal life. And he had Anna.

And right now, he had a chance to make his Anna so very happy. The door he'd been assiduously watching had opened, and from it issued the priest, the black-haired *professoressa*, and a third person: a well-dressed man Jorge didn't know but one Jorge could tell by his scent was Noantri. They were walking with purpose across the little piazza, toward the church.

The *professoressa*, in her hand, gripped the stolen notebook.

Jorge stood.

28

◆◇◆

Sergente Raffaele Orsini remained seated at his table at the café in Piazza della Scala. The call he'd made half an hour ago to his uncle, Lorenzo Cardinal Cossa, about the priest's arrival at the house Raffaele had been sent to watch had gone to voice mail. He made another call now, and when the Cardinal once again didn't answer, Raffaele called the *maresciallo*.

"The subject has just come out of the house. She's with two people I don't know. One's a priest. I can't reach the Cardinal."

The cell phone in his ear was briefly silent. Raffaele could picture his boss's exasperated frown as he weighed the options. On the one hand, the *maresciallo* was losing the use of one of his men and would eventually have to account to his own superiors for Raffaele's unproductive time. Then again, this was a favor for a cardinal. Sooner or later the *maresciallo* would be able to call it in, thereby impressing his superiors with his Vatican entrée. Good personal connections with the Curia, outside the professionally cordial relationship the Carabinieri were at pains to maintain with the Church, were no small advantage for an ambitious cop on the climb. Raffaele had seen how his own stock had risen in the *maresciallo*'s calculating eyes when his uncle was elevated to cardinal and brought to Rome. He found his boss's transparency amusing, but Raffaele was an ambitious cop, too. That he was a cardinal's nephew was nothing but luck, but he wasn't ashamed to take advantage of what it could bring him. His partner and senior, Giulio Aventino, always said police work was five percent doggedness, five percent luck, and ninety percent the skill to recognize and doggedly use the luck that came your way.

Of course, Giulio Aventino must be the reason the *maresciallo* was hesitating at all over Raffaele's instructions. The work Raffaele should have been doing right now, whether in the office or in the field, would naturally have fallen to his partner. Giulio, with his mustached hangdog face, dislike of paperwork, short temper with technology, and aversion to the Church, had no doubt been grousing nonstop for the past hour and a half about his missing sergeant. This would've been true if the *maresciallo* had given Raffaele the afternoon off to see the dentist; how much truer was it now, when Giulio was left to shoulder their mutual burden because Raffaele was running some nepotistic errand for a cardinal?

Finally the *maresciallo* growled into his ear, "Stay with it. Follow her."

Curia one, Giulio nothing. Raffaele grinned to himself. But his boss's vacillation, though short, had been just long enough to bring up another problem. "They're heading for the church."

"What church, Orsini? Where are you?"

"Sorry, sir. Santa Maria della Scala. In Trastevere."

"They're going in?"

"Yes, sir."

"And one's a priest?" Another moment of thought, much more brief. "Don't go in after them. All we've been asked to do is to keep track of the woman. You sure it's her?"

"I have a photo."

"Well, whatever they're doing in there, they'll have to come out eventually. Wait for them. I don't want you barging into a church. It's always a nightmare even if a crime's been committed, and we don't know that one has. Besides," he added, "I know Santa Maria della Scala. It's small enough that they might notice you."

Showing off, Raffaele thought, but the *maresciallo* couldn't see his smile and he said nothing.

"Just wait for them," his boss said again. "If they go back to that house, keep up your surveillance. If they go somewhere else, follow them, but, Orsini, keep trying your uncle. I want you back here sometime today. Aventino is driving us all mad."

29

◇

Across the cobbled piazza, through the wrought-iron fence, and up the stairs. Not the *scala* for which the church was named; those had belonged to a nearby, long-ago-demolished house. There the miracle of an ill child's recovery had been granted to a mother praying to an icon in a stairway alcove. Thomas hadn't been to Santa Maria della Scala before, but he knew the story. He knew so many of his Church's stories.

The entry doors stood open. Thomas paused minutely and then stepped through as though he were any priest, in the company of any pair of historians, visiting any church in Rome. He felt acutely the presence of Livia Pietro beside him and that of Spencer George a few paces behind. Could they really enter a church? Step onto consecrated ground as easily as he could? A part of him expected—no, admit it, hoped—that they would be struck down at the threshold, reduced to dust and ashes for defiling the sanctified air. Though it was true his crucifix had had no effect. Nor had the midmorning light in the piazza, any more than the glare of the early sun through which he'd raced with Livia Pietro from the Vatican Library, back in the good old days a few hours ago when he thought she was merely insane.

Livia Pietro followed him and Spencer George followed her and they all crossed the wooden sill and nothing happened. Resigned, Thomas turned through the vestibule to the right-side door. He pushed it open and stopped a few steps in at the marble font to dip his fingers into the holy water and cross himself, perhaps a bit more fervently than usual. He was horrified by the idea that Pietro or Spencer George, as an element of subterfuge, might attempt to do the same. But maybe they couldn't? Maybe contact with holy water would do to them what the sight of a crucifix had not? Maybe they'd melt, and sizzle, and— **Stop it,** he ordered himself, **you sound like a Dominican.** Pietro looked at the font, at him, smiled slightly, and shook her head. Spencer George passed the font without a glance.

Thomas, behind them now, found himself blinking in the dimness. He squinted to adjust his eyes while Pietro slipped off her sunglasses and seemed quite comfortable. Spencer George had also donned shades and a hat as they left his house, even for the brief walk across the piazza. It must be habitual with them. Every time they go outdoors, the way a real person, a human person, puts on clothes. Thomas suddenly flashed on a college friend, an affable physicist who wore photosensitive glasses, their lenses darkening automatically at the first touch of bright light. . . . And a baseball cap, the physicist was rarely seen without his baseball cap . . . No. It couldn't be.

Thomas shuddered that thought off. He couldn't bear, suddenly, the close presence of the two Noantri. He strode along the center aisle toward the altar. Of course they followed. What had he expected? To avoid the sight of them, Thomas looked up, down, around. Santa Maria della Scala was itself a miracle, though a common enough miracle in Rome: its sedate, slightly crumbling façade opened from a small, dark entry into an interior well kept, grand, and imposing. A patterned stone floor—incorporating, as in so many churches, gravestones, identifying the dead who slept beneath your feet—polished wood pews, a soaring vaulted ceiling supported on marble columns; and everywhere, art. None of it, on first glance, exceptional, but its profusion making up for its lack of distinction. Paintings, frescoes, sculpture, gilded candlesticks. Crystal chandeliers over the altar and side chapels, the gift of some pious—or guilt-ridden—nineteenth-century worshipper. They struck an odd note, the chandeliers. But every church had its own oddnesses, its own eccentricities. Its own secrets.

They had come here to find one of those secrets. Father Thomas Kelly, SJ, and two vampires. Thomas felt his composure hanging by a thread.

He stopped at the altar rail, and the other two stopped beside him. "What do we do now?" Thomas spoke not out of hope of an answer, but to keep himself from losing hold.

"I think we were anticipating you'd take the lead from this point, Father Kelly," Spencer George replied. He had, Thomas noted, removed his hat. Anger flared in Thomas at the hypocrisy of the gesture.

"Just how do you expect me to do that? I didn't know Mario Damiani. I've never been in this church before. I first heard of the Concordat just a few days ago and I can't tell you how dearly I wish I never had!"

"Father." Livia Pietro spoke softly, laying a hand on his sleeve. She nodded toward two old women lighting candles in a side chapel.

Thomas pulled back from her touch and dropped his

voice to a sarcastic whisper. "Of course, we mustn't disturb the faithful. I know how that upsets you."

Spencer George rolled his eyes. Pietro said, "Actually, it does. I was raised in the same Church you were and I think faith is a precious thing, to be protected wherever it's found. But I know you don't believe that of me and I'm not asking you to. I'm suggesting that you focus on the reason we're here."

Thomas stared at her for a long moment. Then he blew out a breath and looked around helplessly.

Santa Maria della Scala had a nave and transept; it had side chapels and high windows. Great bouquets of flowers had greeted them at the church entry with still more standing in the side chapels and others flanking the altar. Because Mass had recently ended, thick incense hung heavy in the air, threading its scent through that of the flowers. What footsteps and soft words were to be heard did not disturb the peaceful hush common to so many churches. It was all comforting and familiar, and Thomas thought he felt a faint echo of his old sense of home.

But as to a hiding place for a six-hundred-year-old document that detailed a satanic bargain, he could think of none.

"This church," Spencer George said. "What's special about it?"

"You live across the piazza from it! You should know it much better than I do!"

"Really, Father? How much time do you imagine I've spent here? What is it you're thinking I would do if I came? Kneel and pray?"

"No, I can see there'd be no point. Even prayer can't save your mortgaged soul!"

"Then why would I come?"

"Spencer?" Pietro said, speaking to the historian but throwing Thomas a disapproving glance. "Did Mario come here?"

Spencer George unlocked his gaze slowly from Thomas's and looked to Pietro. He nodded. "He loved them all, these little churches. Loved them as art and as history. Once or twice I came inside this one with him. It had always been one of his particular favorites, and he became even more strongly attached to it during the Rebellion because it served as a field hospital for Garibaldi's troops. Mario was an officer in the war against papal power, you know." Spencer George looked pointedly at Thomas again. Thomas bit his lip and refused to rise to the bait. "Mario's mission," George went on, "the mission he'd given himself, was to take these little jewels back from the stranglehold of the Church and return them to aesthetics and to true spiritual meaning."

"True spiritual meaning?" Thomas hissed, finally unable to contain himself. "As though there were some question? Of the spiritual meaning of a church?"

"As it happens I agree with you. I thought his whole project was absurd. I've spent nearly three centuries in Rome avoiding every church I could."

"You'd have done better—"

"Father? Maybe we can have this conversation later?" As she spoke, Livia Pietro looked back up the center aisle. An elderly monk moved stiffly toward them, his cinctured tan habit whispering. Pietro and George smiled in greeting. Thomas struggled to do the same.

"Buongiorno, Padre," the monk greeted Thomas.

"Buongiorno, Padre," Thomas replied. He continued in Italian, "I'm Thomas Kelly. From Boston. This is Dr.

Pietro and—Dr. George. They're historians. As I am," he added.

"Giovanni Battista. Welcome to Santa Maria della Scala." The monk's thin hands were misshapen by arthritis, and his voice rattled with an old-man quaver.

"Thank you," Pietro replied politely. Spencer George murmured some noncommittal courtesy, also, though Thomas could swear his lip was curled. Pietro continued diffidently, "We've come here as part of a project. We're studying the art and history of Trastevere's churches. Each church is unique in some way and we're very interested in seeing the special pieces here."

Father Battista's thin smile told Thomas the monk was well aware of his church's relative lack of artistic riches. Nevertheless, he answered, "Then I'm sure you'll want to see the icon of Our Lady, that holy painting that cured the child. It's in the transept altar, on this side." Without waiting for an answer, he turned to lead the way. Not knowing what else to do, Thomas started after him, peering around, hoping for—what? A ray of heavenly light to strike a painting, an angelic chorus to sing as he passed a piece of sculpture? He walked behind Father Battista, surveying the sanctuary, listening distractedly to the monk's sandals slapping softly on the stone.

Sandals.

Father Battista was a Discalced Carmelite.

Discalced. Shoeless.

"Shoeless" meaning in sandals, not barefoot. They didn't go barefoot.

But they and their order's founder, Saint Teresa of Avila, were often portrayed that way. Even Bernini's celebrated sculpture of Saint Teresa depicted one bare foot peeking from under her robe.

the humblest of steps . . .
right foot then left, that leads the soul . . .

"The relic!" Thomas burst out.

The monk stopped and turned. "Father?"

"The relic," Thomas repeated, stopping also. He brought his voice under control, which could not be said of his racing heart. "Santa Teresa. It's here, isn't it? I'd like very much to see the relic."

Spencer George furrowed his brow. Livia Pietro gave Thomas a quizzical look, but Thomas kept his eyes on Father Battista.

A new interest softened the monk's lined face. "I have to admit that's a pleasant change," he said. "The veneration of relics is out of fashion lately." He gave Thomas a tentatively commiserating smile. Thomas returned it, though "lately" in this case was a relative term: the change dated from 1965, one of the results of the Second Vatican Council. That was before Thomas was born, so he'd come into a religious life that followed the Council's precepts; but the elderly Father Battista had been a young man then, Thomas realized. He wondered if the monk had already taken his vows by the time the Council met. And whether, if young Giovanni Battista had known what changes were coming, he'd have entered holy orders all the same. And if he knew what Thomas knew now? About Thomas's companions, about the Concordat's corrupt bargain? How would he feel about his Holy Mother Church then?

". . . quite a shame," Father Battista was saying. Thomas forced his attention back to the monk. "Communion with the corporeal remains of a departed saint creates an atmosphere for prayer different from any other. It brings the worshipper into an intimate relationship with sanctity. It offers an immediacy that's otherwise much more difficult to reach."

Indeed, Thomas thought. **I've heard that speech before.** Father Battista could spend a pleasant evening over cigars and brandy with Lorenzo, discussing the mistaken direction in which the Church was headed. They could talk about relics and the Latin Mass, the apostolic calling, nuns discarding their habits. Father Battista might not even care that all Lorenzo's piety was a lie.

A lie with which Thomas would never have the opportunity to confront Lorenzo—not in human form, anyway—unless he found the Concordat.

"Yes," he said to Father Battista, nodding as though in earnest agreement. "I'd like very much to see the relic."

30

———◆———

"What relic is your priest dragging us off to see?" Spencer whispered to Livia as the old monk led them down the side aisle.

"I have no idea. Or why."

She watched Father Battista and Father Kelly walk side by side a few steps ahead, a young man and an old one, sharing the same piety, the same comprehension of the world. Father Kelly's faith had been shaken by what he'd learned today, but Livia expected—she hoped—he'd recover his equilibrium. She'd meant what she told him: she did believe faith was a precious thing. Her own was more complex than his; she wasn't sure at all that that was a good thing, but it was a truth there was no point in denying.

She'd been raised to believe in the same God Thomas Kelly did, though she'd never been as ardent as he. Since her Change, she'd pondered often the question of a deity and also of an afterlife. As she'd told Father Kelly, Noantri could die, though she had not been completely forthcoming with him on that subject: of the three ways death could come to a Noantri, she'd described only two. What she'd said about fire was true, though, and she'd been just half-joking when she'd reassured him that they'd all be devoured when the sun flared out.

What then? On that large subject, she'd come to no conclusions. But she was sure of three things.

One was that she could think of no reason why a benevolent God, Thomas Kelly's God, could not be credited with creating the microbe that Blessed the Noantri with their long, rich lives. Thomas Kelly saw the microbe, and the Noantri, as evil. The Unchanged always had, and through the millennia when the Noantri's need for blood nourishment had made them an imminent threat, that view had been understandable. It wasn't true any more than evil accounted for a cat killing a mouse; but you could see the mouse's point. Which led Livia to her second article of faith: that the Concordat was an unqualified good.

The explanation Cardinal Cossa had given Thomas Kelly of how the Concordat came to be was no more the full story than Livia's account of the death of a Noantri had been. It was true as far as it went and so was the history she'd added for him in Spencer's study, but there was more she knew and hadn't told him. And there was a secret at the heart of the Concordat's story that she didn't know. That Martin the Fifth had seen the advantages of ending the Church's virulent and everlasting assault on the Noantri was true enough; but at the time of the Concordat, before Community, before the Law, the Noantri were a fragmented, furtive people. Calling a halt to the hunting, the persecution, was one thing, and would have permitted Martin to concentrate his strength on pressing matters of consolidating papal power. But to sign an agreement with her people, committing the Church to obligations in perpetuity? As a group, in 1431, the Noantri had commanded neither strength nor wealth enough to put in Martin's service in exchange. Why had he done it? And why had the Church continued to abide by it through six centuries?

Possibly the answer to that last question was simple: peace was peace. Even early on, it might have been clear to Church fathers that once the Concordat was signed, the Noantri ceased being a danger. Thus the Church could turn its attention elsewhere.

As to the larger question, though, Livia had pondered it often, but had come to accept the fact that she did not, probably would never, have an answer. That knowledge was accorded to no Unchanged save the highest ranks of the Church, and to no Noantri outside the Conclave. Ultimately, though, it didn't matter. Whatever had brought the Concordat into being was itself a Blessing.

But though most of the Unchanged didn't know the Concordat existed at all, and the Noantri knew it only insofar as they were required to follow its provisions, the third thing Livia was sure of was that the life she and her people were able to lead because of the Concordat, the life she had come into when she'd Changed, the life so rich and full they had come to think of it as Blessed, was only possible if the agreement was faithfully kept by both parties.

Jonah refused to accept this truth, but he was wrong. And only if she found the lost copy of the Concordat and delivered it to the Conclave did he have any chance of living long enough to understand that.

31

◄○►

Jorge Ocampo rose quietly from his knees. He waited a few moments and then passed between the pews to the left aisle of the church. The little group he'd slipped into the church to watch had been joined by an old monk and, after a false start in the other direction, was heading beyond the apse. He needed to keep them in view, but not to get too close. Right now the length of the church and the perfume of flowers and incense were keeping the *professoressa* from noticing him. If he were careful, if he were stealthy, that wouldn't change. He hoped the group was planning to view a piece of art or inspect something in one of the side chapels and then leave. When they turned toward the door he'd slip back outside, and as soon as they came out he'd grab the notebook and race around the corner to his *motorino*. He'd bring Anna the notebook and she'd see he was, he truly was, the man for the job.

His only worry was that they were on their way to the church offices, or even worse, to the Carmelite cloister behind Santa Maria itself. How he'd follow them then, he wasn't sure, but he'd find a way. This time, nothing was going to stop him from recovering that notebook for his Anna.

32

Thomas walked beside Father Battista, slowing his own pace to allow for the old man's painfully arthritic steps. What he wanted to do was break into a run, but that would startle the women by the candles, and a young man praying in a rear pew. Not to mention the monk. It wasn't likely that anyone, no matter how devout, had ever raced through Santa Maria della Scala to reach the church's relic.

He'd heard Spencer George's whisper to Livia Pietro. Neither of them had any idea what he was thinking and he didn't enlighten them. Let their preternatural Noantri senses find them an answer. If he was right, he'd be free of them in any case, after this.

An upholstered wooden kneeler stood at a gap in the stone railing, blocking the entrance to a side chapel where a high marble altar rose. "The Reliquary Chapel is through there." Father Battista pointed to the right, at an openwork gate in the chapel's wall. "It's visited rarely now, and we're very few here. We keep it locked."

"I appreciate your willingness to open it for me, Father," Thomas said.

"Certainly." The old monk made to roll the kneeler aside, but Thomas hurried forward to do it. At the gate to the Reliquary Chapel, under a pair of gold angels,

Father Battista hoisted a jingling key ring, selected the proper key, and turned the heavy lock.

Thomas followed the monk into a small, high-ceilinged chapel where light glowed through stained glass windows to the left and right of the altar. John of the Cross and Saint Teresa. Paintings adorned the walls, but Thomas barely gave them a glance. Ahead, behind a low stone railing, was the reason he was here. On a marble altar, a flight of solemn gold angels supported a glass-doored case, perhaps eighteen inches high. Inside it, another glass-fronted box stood on golden lion's legs. This was the reliquary itself.

Inside it rested the severed right foot of Saint Teresa.

Thomas's heart beat faster. This must be it, what Damiani meant. Foot, trek, steps—it was all here. The two Noantri exchanged glances but Thomas ignored them. He became aware that the old monk was watching his face.

"Father, would you like to be alone to pray?"

Conscious that his relief and excitement had been mistaken for devotion, and conscious also that he was about to lie to a monk in a consecrated chapel in front of a saint's relic, Thomas answered, "Yes, Father, thank you. I would."

33

Father Giovanni Battista left the Reliquary Chapel, smiling at the sound of the gate behind him clicking shut. It had been a long time—years, he thought, though his clouded memory might be muddling things again, but in any case, a long time—since he'd seen that glow in a visitor's eyes at the sight of the relic of Santa Teresa, that holy object with which he and his brothers were entrusted. He chided himself for his instinctive, mistaken dismissal of this trio. He'd assumed they were interested in Santa Maria della Scala only as art and as history. He'd supposed they'd come to see the icon, as visitors usually did. But three historians, on a project to study churches, what could he be expected to think? The young priests from America were usually the worst, too, taking pride in their own sophistication, their cynicism and worldly-wise ways. And Jesuits! Everything was reason and learning with the Jesuits. In his experience—and his experience was long; though his memory was often too foggy to detail that experience, the existence of the fog itself proved the years were there—Jesuits had no interest in mysticism, cared nothing for those rare, longed-for, and inexplicable ecstatic moments that had made Father Battista's life worth living.

Carmelite monks devoted themselves equally to meditation and service. Giovanni Battista had always considered it one of his own many failings that, though he tried his best to be diligent when performing his pastoral tasks, such as guiding visitors through Santa Maria, he much preferred the solitary, silent hours of contemplation and prayer. Vatican II, which had issued its directives nine years after Giovanni had taken his vows, had greatly disappointed him. The changes, all in the direction of secularization, had been in aid of bringing the Church nearer the flock. In Giovanni's view, this was a great mistake. The Church should be the City of Gold high on Saint Peter's rock: unattainable, but always the glowing goal to strive toward. It was the flock that needed to be helped to come nearer the Church.

But these historians, what a pleasant surprise. He'd thought only the priest would want to pause in the chapel and pray, but the woman—yes, he knew they'd been introduced, but there was no point in trying to remember her name—had given Father Battista a warm smile and a big thank-you. Such lovely, kind eyes! She'd told him he had no idea how much this meant to all of them, and even the supercilious older gent—older compared with the other two, of course just a pup to Giovanni—had nodded and smiled, also. The priest had seemed a little surprised at his companions himself, but such is the power of the Holy Spirit. Giovanni left them to it.

A warm glow filled him when he thought of the quiet delight with which his brothers would receive this story at the evening collation. Imagine: even Americans, even Jesuits, could still catch one unawares.

With a new spring in his crotchety old bones, Giovanni Battista strode forward to greet the thin young man approaching down the aisle.

34

◄○►

"Don't look so dismayed, Father," Livia said to Thomas Kelly, turning from the chapel door to face the priest.

"Well, he's disappointed," Spencer said. "He was hoping to have the relic all to himself."

"I'm the one who thought of it," Thomas Kelly snapped.

"Oh, yes, and very clever of you," Spencer acknowledged. "All those feet and steps of Mario's?"

"This is the severed limb of a saint," the priest said coldly. "Teresa of Avila. She founded the Carmelite order."

"Yes, now I remember Mario telling me about it. This chapel was locked when we came, though, so he couldn't show it to me. As it was just now. A lovely bit of subterfuge you used to get us in, by the way. Wanting to pray. My compliments."

The priest stepped forward, fists clenched. Livia couldn't blame him, and it would almost be worth letting him take a swing at Spencer just to see the look on Spencer's face. But she put up her hand. "Father Battista's not going to leave us alone in here forever. Spencer, do you think it's possible this is the place Mario wanted you to find?"

"Oh, very likely. It's right up his street. The double

meanings in the poem, plus the quirky oddness of worshipping desiccated body parts—oh, no offense, Father."

Spencer clearly meant to give offense and Thomas Kelly equally clearly took it, but to the priest's credit, he remained silent. "The chance he took," Spencer continued, "was to imagine I remembered anything at all about what this church contained. That was a mistake. If I had, though, yes, I'd have come straight to this little room."

Livia turned to the priest. "Father Kelly? Now that we're in this chapel"—to make up for Spencer's "little room"—"what are you thinking?"

Thomas Kelly didn't answer her. After a glare at Spencer, he turned and strode through the gap in the altar rail, where he stood looking up at the pair of golden boxes, one inside the other. With a sharp glance Livia pinned Spencer to his spot on the marble floor. Spencer shrugged and remained where he was as she followed the priest.

The reliquary's glass front was answered by worked gold panels on the sides and, as far as Livia could see, at the back. The box stood on its raised lion's legs, while inside, its leathery, shrunken, jewel-studded treasure wore a golden sandal and rested on a velvet cloth.

Thomas Kelly hesitated. Stretching his arm, he was just able to reach the bottom of the outer box. He hooked his fingers under the gold frame and tried to pull it open, but it didn't give. He turned to Livia, the set of his shoulder conveying, equally, failure and triumph. "It's locked."

She stepped up. "Let me try."

"I just told you. It's locked."

"And I didn't tell you, but I can open it." She slipped a probe from the zippered pocket of her shoulder bag, plus a nail file to use as a shim. Handing the bag to Spencer, she appraised the high altar and then set herself and jumped. A five-foot vertical leap from a standing start was not an everyday feat even for a Noantri, but Livia was strong and she was motivated. She landed lightly on the marble, to the priest's horrified gasp and Spencer's laughing, "Brava!" She took out her tools and had the flimsy lock open before the priest found words to express his horror.

Spencer was still laughing when she pulled the glass door wide. "Livia! I had no idea."

Livia looked down at Thomas Kelly. "Father?"

His eyes widened. "Me? What do you— Come up there? Onto the reliquary altar? No, no possible way."

"Shall I bring it down, then?"

"No! Don't touch it!" Kelly glanced wildly around. He spied a heavy, brocaded chair near the wall, used by the celebrant while hymns were sung during Mass. He dragged it over and stepped onto it. She extended a hand to help him but he placed his palms flat on the altar and swung himself up with surprising athletic grace.

Standing beside her on the narrow marble shelf, he gave her a resentful glance and then shifted his attention to the reliquary itself. After a moment he said, "See those scrolls inside?" She leaned nearer to look. "They're authentications, blessings, prayers. Maybe Damiani rolled up the Concordat and slipped it in with them. No one ever looks at those scrolls, once they're placed with a relic."

Livia peered skeptically at the beribboned, wax-sealed papers. "I don't think that's likely. They're very small.

The Concordat . . . But let's look at them. I imagine you'd prefer to handle them yourself?"

"I certainly would!" She stood aside, letting him be the one to test whether the reliquary was locked, which it wasn't; to ease open the front panel; and to slip out the five scrolls, fastidiously avoiding the saint's foot itself. He stared at the delicate cylinders; then, looking pale, he set his jaw and untied the ribbons and broke the sealing wax scroll by scroll. His face fell as he scanned each and put it aside, until they were all opened and read.

"I'm wrong," he finally said, deflated. "It's not here."

Livia glanced over the scrolls, all in Latin and none anything other than what it purported to be.

From below, Spencer spoke. "No," he said, "this is just too Mario to be wrong." Raising his eyebrows at Livia, he took a step forward. "May I join you up there?"

"No, you may not!" Kelly snapped.

Spencer sighed. "Then you do it. See if there's anything stuck up under the top. Not underfoot, you see. Overhead."

After a moment, with great care, the priest reached inside and felt around the peaked gold cover. He stopped still. Seconds later he drew his hand out again. In it was a single sheet of paper, folded small and yellowed with age.

◀◦▶

35

Raffaele Orsini sighed. He hated surveillance. Giulio Aventino didn't seem to mind when they had to sit for hours in a parked car or on a park bench, waiting for someone to appear or something to happen. Raffaele always found it painful, though he was grateful that right now he at least had a chair and a coffee.

To be fair, he had nothing against idling his time away in a café. Before their children were born, he and Elena had spent many pleasant hours over coffee and the morning *La Repubblica*. Even in the past few very busy years they'd made it a point to spend time together doing nothing in languid indolence. The trouble with surveillance was that to do it right you needed to look languid and indolent, while being anything but. Raffaele had found—Giulio had taught him, give the man his due—that often the vital information a surveillance yields comes from some event that takes place before the subject is spotted. It was important to note all comings and goings, to remember faces and clothes, cars and license plates, while lounging lazily and being bored to tears.

Automatically, partly to sharpen his skills of observation and partly to keep his mind from wandering, Raffaele, since he'd arrived, had been cataloging the people crossing the piazza, his fellow café guests, the infrequent cars, and the buzzing *motorini*. Since his subject, the dark-haired woman, had left the house and entered Santa Maria della Scala he'd been particularly focused on visitors coming and going from the church. There had been very few, just four laughing Americans with cameras and one skinny young man who'd been moping in that very café, a few tables over. The signs of lovesickness in him were unmistakable. He'd probably gone to pray to the Virgin to solve his romance problems. The Americans had come out already, consulting guidebooks and wandering away. Raffaele was confident he could describe them all if need be, equally sure he'd never be called upon to do so, and proud of the professionalism with which he committed them to memory just the same. He was wondering idly how many more people besides his surveillance subjects and the skinny young man were actually inside the church when a frantic old woman came out screaming.

36

With fingers he had to order to stop trembling, Thomas unfolded the paper he'd discovered wedged up into the reliquary's roof. It was a small single sheet, but until he'd flattened it completely, he held on to hope that he'd found the Concordat. Once he opened the last crease, though, that hope was gone.

Still, there could be no question that this paper was what they'd been sent here for.

It was another poem.

"Oh, my God," Spencer George breathed, staring up at the paper in Thomas's hand. Thomas didn't even bother to rebuke him for his blasphemy. "Mario, Mario," George whispered. "What were you up to?"

Livia Pietro leaned over the unfolded poem to examine it. She began to speak, but before she could, she and Spencer George both snapped their heads up.

"What?" said Thomas. "What's happening?"

Pietro shushed him. She stood still, listening, and then even Thomas heard it: a distant shrieking coming from outside the church. Pietro turned to him. "Replace those. We need to close these boxes."

"Those"? For a moment Thomas was lost. Then he realized she meant the prayers, the supplications of devout worshippers to the saint. Of course. What good would prayer do him now, in any case? Thomas slipped the scrolls back into the reliquary and shut the front. He swung the larger door closed, also, and, with the poem still in hand, jumped down. Pietro followed. He replaced the chair he'd climbed up on while Pietro stood still, frowning in concentration. Finally she spoke low. "He's here! The clerk. The incense, the candles—they're confusing me. But I think he's here."

"By 'clerk,'" asked Spencer George, "you mean the Noantri from the Vatican Library?"

Pietro nodded and Thomas demanded, "But what happened? Who's screaming?"

"I don't know. Be quiet." She tilted her head down, seeming to concentrate. "I don't know," she repeated. "But something bad's— Oh, no. Police."

"Gendarmes?"

"No. Carabinieri. Just came inside. Only one, but he's on his radio. He's called an ambulance."

"We have to see what's wrong." Thomas started for the gate.

"Excuse me, Father, but are you insane?" Spencer George stepped in front of him.

"I'm a priest. I might be able to help."

"You're not a doctor, I think. Believe me, if whatever happened needs a priest, they'll have no trouble finding one here."

"We can't just—"

"Father," Pietro said. "We have to. This poem. It must be sending us somewhere else. It's from the notebook. Did you see that?"

Thomas looked again at the unfolded sheet in his hand. Paper, ink, and handwriting, all the same. Something else, too, something added in graphite pencil beneath the inked poem: a row of letters. Thomas had no idea what they meant but it was clear Pietro was right. This leaf had been ripped from Damiani's notebook, too.

"It's sending us somewhere else," she repeated.

"Ah." Chuckling, Spencer George snapped his fingers. "Of course. For one thing, there's the matter of the missing leaves. There are seven of them, not just one." Thomas thought about the implications of this as the historian went on. "For another, Mario never did things by halves. Once he'd hidden something as important as the Concordat, he'd make sure it was difficult to find."

The two Noantri froze again and this time Thomas heard what they had: the two-note howl of an approaching siren. No: more than one siren. The ambulance and more police.

"Livia," said Spencer George, "you and the priest must leave." He handed over her shoulder bag. "Whatever happened, if it's important enough for a herd of Carabinieri, you don't want to get tangled up with them. I'll stay and if the subject comes up I'll explain that you two are long gone. And the clerk—he must have followed you. He'll need to be diverted, also."

"You said he'd been arrested." Thomas glared at Livia. "If he'd been arrested he couldn't have—"

"Yes, he could." Pietro dismissed Thomas, turned to George. "Spencer, we need you. Damiani's poems. You might know—"

George was shaking his head. "I told you, I hadn't seen any of them. They'd be as new to me as they will be to you. You know more about the churches of Trastevere than I do. Most importantly, you're the one charged by the Conclave with retrieving the lost Concordat. You, and your priest."

"I'm not her priest!" Thomas snapped. "And short of a little lockpicking and thievery, which they won't be looking for, what do we have to worry about? Why don't we just go out there, tell them we were back in here and don't know anything about whatever it is that went on, and—"

George waved Thomas silent. "If something dire has really happened, this church will be closed down. The authorities will interview everyone here and your search could be delayed for hours. Time, according to both of you for your different reasons, is critical. Your situation, Father, I'm sorry to say, doesn't move me, but I'm quite fond of Livia and I hate to think of the consequences to her if she does not succeed." He looked at them both. "Go now, before they—and that clerk—find you."

"And how are we supposed to get out?" Thomas demanded. "Tiptoe up a side aisle while you distract them with a juggling act in the nave?"

"That does sound like fun. But I'm sure there's a more sensible way." He looked up at the high, thin windows. Thomas followed his gaze. Neither John of the Cross nor Saint Teresa looked as if they'd moved on their hinges in five hundred years.

A bell began to toll in the monastery behind the church. It was a single note, repeated and clanging: not a call to prayer, but a declaration of calamity.

"Yes!" said Pietro suddenly. "Yes, there's another way. Father, come."

Thomas stood rooted to the stone floor. His eyes met Pietro's. A second of stillness, nothing but the tolling: then in a flash Pietro snatched the poem from his hand

and stuffed it in her shoulder bag. "Come with me. Or stay here with Spencer and at least buy me some time."

Stay with Spencer George, swear to whatever sneering lies he was going to tell? While Lorenzo's only chance at mortal life—and natural death, and the eternal blessed rest that followed upon that—vanished with this creature? As Livia Pietro slipped out of the Reliquary Chapel and behind the nave screen that separated cloistered monks from parishioners, Thomas sped after her.

37

Giulio Aventino couldn't decide whether to sigh in frustration, snarl in anger, or give in to a satisfied grin. He settled on the grin as he piloted his Fiat through the Trastevere traffic. His dominant emotion at the moment, he had to admit, was smugness. He'd come back to the station to find his sergeant, the well-heeled and pious Raffaele Orsini, out doing the bidding of his cardinal uncle. Not entirely Raffaele's fault, of course: he'd quite properly taken the Cardinal's request to the *maresciallo*. Everything Raffaele did was quite proper. The boss, obviously seeing visions of himself on the Vatican's IOU list, had dispatched Raffaele to sit in a café watching someone the Cardinal, for some secret Vatican reason, wanted watched. Giulio didn't care about the Vatican and its secrets and he wouldn't have given a damn, except that he did.

Two damns.

Damn the *maresciallo* for sending Raffaele out on, basically, an extended coffee break, and thereby sticking Giulio with the mountain of unfiled witness reports on a case he and Raffaele had closed last week.

And damn the Vatican for thinking it could call at any time and the Carabinieri would jump because it said to.

No, three damns.

Damn the Vatican again, for being right.

Still, neither the Vatican's secrets nor the *maresciallo*'s naked ambition nor even the shorts-clad, bottled-water-slugging tourists ambling through the streets as though any car they ignored couldn't hit them quite pierced Giulio's satisfaction. Raffaele's little café break had turned, right under the sergeant's patrician nose, into a homicide. News of which had made the apoplectic *maresciallo* explode from his office and order Giulio Aventino to Santa Maria della Scala immediately, post-haste, and soonest, to go see how much of the situation he could salvage.

The boss, Giulio had noted, and here's where the satisfaction had begun, had showered a few damns of his own on the absent person of Raffaele Orsini.

38

Thomas Kelly was right on her heels as Livia slipped behind the carved wooden screen to the far side of the apse, then through the blue folds of a velvet curtain and around a chapel to an unremarkable door against the far wall. Anyone might think, she reflected, that people made a habit of slinking around Santa Maria della Scala without being seen. Of course, since an order of cloistered friars had lived here for six hundred years, they probably did. The lock on the door was easy and Thomas Kelly, though he tsked in obvious unhappiness when she picked it, had the sense not to speak until it was closed again and they were on the other side.

"What now?" he demanded in a whisper, glancing at a staircase that led up into dimness. "This doesn't look like a way out."

"No. We need to work out what this poem means before we go anywhere. This is a place where we won't be disturbed."

"What happened to 'you and your priest must leave'?"

"I'm not the one who said that. Look, Spencer can be hard to take, I know. But he has a marvelous mind and he's a loyal friend. And his work has been very important to the Noantri." At that the priest scowled. Without knowing why—did she really think Thomas Kelly would ever feel kindly toward her and her people? And did it matter if he did?—Livia went on, "Spencer studies the history of the Noantri, of our people. It's an odd thing, to have lives as long as ours but no sense of continuity *as a people*, no shared history, until a few hundred years ago. I could introduce you to Noantri who rode with Genghis Khan or sailed with Christopher Columbus. Others who helped build the Pyramids, Machu Picchu, the Great Wall of China. Each of them, for centuries, knew only that he was different from those around him. Knew only guilt and fear as he tried to satisfy hungers over which he had no control. Each knew only his own story, do you understand? Since the Concordat it's been possible for us to try to bring our stories together. That's Spencer's work: to help us begin to understand who we are as a people."

She stopped abruptly, feeling her cheeks grow hot. She'd never spoken to any of the Unchanged about her people's history and yearnings, the power of their need for connection, the relief and joy of Community. The few Unchanged outside the inner ranks of the Church who knew about their existence, and the even fewer who were considered friends, were nevertheless rarely presented with any evidence of Noantri misgiving, unhappiness, or doubt.

Livia brushed past Thomas Kelly and started up the curving stone stairs, though she noted as she did that his aversion seemed to have been neutralized, however briefly, by interest, as the scholar in him considered what she'd said.

She led the way up to a landing with a window in the left-side wall and glass-doored cabinets to the right. On the shelves stood ranks of bottles of red, blue, and amber liquids. Most bore labels describing the contents—*Perle della Saggezza*, *Tonico del Missionario*—in precise and fading script, though on a few of the more recent ones the labels were the work of that at-the-time cutting-edge technology, the manual typewriter. Livia briefly left Thomas Kelly to his surprised inspection of the shelves and worked on the lock on the door between the cabinets. Kelly didn't cluck his tongue this time, though he did catch his breath when she got the door open and they walked into the room beyond.

What had taken him by surprise was not, Livia knew, the trompe l'oeil drapery or the aged wooden counter, not the Murano glass bottles or the ceramic jars with their bright painted lids. This was the eighth or ninth time Livia had been in this room, and the glorious aroma that greeted a visitor as the door creaked back was one of the reasons to keep returning.

Thomas Kelly stood in awe, as most first-time visitors did, though Livia knew he couldn't parse the wave of scent as finely as she could: sweet columbine and spicy goldenrod, the faint rankness of deer's antlers and the astringent bite of arsenic. And so many, many more: the air was a tapestry of olfactory threads, thick and thin, sharp and soft, bile-bitter and honey-sweet. Over two hundred herbs, flowers, leaves and barks, fruit essences and tree saps, ground minerals, cracked bones, and crumbled earths were stored in this room, in drawers, in jars, and in bottles, waiting.

"What is this place?" Kelly breathed.

"The old pharmacy, from the fifteenth century."

"Is it still in use?"

"Not since 1954."

"But it looks so complete. So . . . ready."

She shook her head. "When it closed, the last apothecary monks just locked the door and walked away. Their order had been pharmacists to the popes for six hundred years. I think they didn't really believe they'd never be called on again."

Now Kelly turned to her. "You think. You knew those monks, didn't you? In 1954. You were here."

Livia faced him, calmly but squarely. "I'd moved away for a time, before the Second World War. We have to, every now and then, no matter how committed we may be to our hometowns. We stay away for years and change our identities before we return. We call it 'Cloaking.' It's our own kind of internal exile, and it's hard on us. But yes, by then I was back."

Once again, she'd told him more than she'd meant to. She braced for his shudder, even a curled lip of disgust; but to her surprise, they didn't come. Nor did a kind smile, or sympathetic eyes, but those would have been too much to ask. Kelly just nodded, as though an academic hypothesis had been confirmed, and returned his gaze to the room.

Above the counter where the apothecary friars had traded herbs and elixirs for customers' coins, a painted angel peered over the trompe l'oeil curtains. He was there, a monk had once told her, to ensure honest dealing.

39

Jorge Ocampo was running like the wind. He shouldn't, he knew. Anna said he must never let the Unchanged see the extent of his Noantri abilities. Their minds were small and they would get frightened; they would shun him, perhaps even attack him, if they felt him to be vastly different from themselves. She assured him they couldn't harm him if they did attack: any pain would be transitory, and in the centuries since the Concordat the Unchanged had lost the understanding of the effects of fire. Still, she said, if Jorge were to arouse suspicion, he would become less valuable to her. That was an alarming thought, but still he sped around the corner at Vicolo del Piede until he reached his goal: the abandoned cinema. The startled gasps as he raced past (*"Madonna!* Did you see that guy?"*) would reduce his value to Anna less, he was sure, than being identified as the man responsible for what had happened in Santa Maria della Scala.

The old theater sagged and creaked in the shade of the vines that colonized its flanks. That Vicolo del Piede was never busy was one of the reasons Jorge had chosen this place for his private hideaway. Even Anna didn't know he came here. The street was empty now, as usual, no one to see him leap onto a sill and slip through a half-open window.

Immediately, as it always did, the still darkness of the derelict interior quieted Jorge's heart. His Noantri eyes adjusted immediately to the low light that seeped through the few filthy, cracked windows, but even if they hadn't that would have been all right; he knew every inch of this theater. No films had been shown at Il Pasquino for a decade, but as so often happened in Rome, though the building was now useless it had not been demolished. It had merely been abandoned, as those who'd loved it had moved on to something new.

Anna. He had to call Anna. What would he say? He had to tell her the truth, but he so dreaded her inevitable fury—Anna could detonate with an incendiary heat, just like an Argentinian girl—that though he forced himself to take out his cell phone, he couldn't, for a moment, go further. He gripped the phone tightly and sat where he always did: third row, right side, on the aisle, the seat he'd taken every chance he'd had at any of the movie houses on Avenida Corrientes, back home. Before he'd gotten involved with his brothers of La Guerra Sucia, before he'd met Anna and become part of an even bigger revolutionary movement, Jorge's happiest hours had been spent in the dark theaters of Buenos Aires. Even with the torn upholstery and the spiders and the musty smell, even with no film to watch on the ripped and mildewed screen, Jorge felt more at home in Il Pasquino than anywhere else in Rome.

Oh, how he wanted to go home. He yearned for the day when Anna's plans were accomplished and they could fly off to Argentina, finally together, with only each other to think about. Anna would always be concerned with the welfare of the Noantri, of course, and he would always support her in her efforts on behalf of her people. *Their* people! How many times had she reprimanded him, reminded him that he was Noantri, too, now and forever? But once the last obstacle to Noantri rule had been removed, he and Anna would be free to change their priorities, to trade this necessary work of freedom fighting for the joy of each other's arms.

And though he'd made a bad mistake today, Anna would know how to fix it. She'd give him new instructions, he'd carry them out faithfully, and her plans would not really be disrupted. They'd continue on their path to victory, and home.

Feeling much calmer now, he lifted his phone.

40

◇

Anna Jagiellon threw her phone into her shoulder bag as though to dash it to pieces against the rocks inside. Of course there were no rocks and the phone nestled comfortably next to her makeup kit. She really shouldn't be blaming the phone, anyway, just because that idiot simpering Argentinian was always on the other end. What a mistake he was. It had seemed like a good idea at the time, making Jorge Ocampo Noantri. He already followed her around like a puppy dog, the skinny premed student (premed, because Che had been a doctor: always one for hero worship, Jorge) enraptured by the fiery foreigner. Her Hungarian heritage, which she'd alternately hidden and revealed as she cycled through identities in the years she'd spent in Argentina, had been on full display at the university at the moment Juan Perón returned to power in 1973. They'd all been Communists, all the hottest boys and fiercest girls, out to change the world, and Anna was ever their most articulate organizer, their bravest leader. Oh, the slogans she'd written, the speeches she'd made! On the streets she'd marched and chanted and then, with the others—as though such things could harm her—fled from the tear gas and the bullets down backstreets and twisting alleys. In smoky rooms packed with eager, sweating young bodies, all leaning forward to hear her, to see her, she'd shown them the beauty of the world that could be, the world being kept from them by the rich and the powerful.

They were fools, of course, but that wasn't their fault. The Unchanged, Anna had found, only grew into anything resembling wisdom as they neared their own deaths. Not that it was the approaching obliteration that brought about understanding. Quite the contrary, it was, simply, the years. Wisdom took decades to bloom, and most of the Unchanged were not allotted anything like sufficient time. That might be sad, but it was true. Anna's fellow Party members, her comrade leaders and her wide-eyed followers, were fools because they were young.

Anna had also been young, many years ago, when John Zápolya ascended to the throne of Hungary and Anna was torn from the life that was rightfully hers. Silk and velvet, meat and wine and music, were replaced overnight by sackcloth and filth, coarse bread and foul water. Though she was her father's natural, not legitimate, child, Anna was nevertheless the only remaining heir to the house of Jagiellon, and as such had, of course, to be exterminated. The golden-haired daughter of the soon-to-be extinguished royal line was thrown into a stinking cell where her wishes meant nothing and her degradation was complete.

Until what she thought was to be her final night on earth, with her execution scheduled for dawn. The priest had come to hear her confession in her last hours. Anna had refused to speak to him. They had been a devout family, hearing Mass daily in the palace chapel, taking

Holy Communion. Her father was the patron of the monastery on the hill. That the God they'd worshipped with such certainty had allowed this carnage and desolation, and that one of his priests was now offering *Anna* forgiveness—no, no, the man should be on his knees, begging her for hers! She'd turned away stonily, and he'd crept out, and Anna waited in exhausted relief for the dawn and her release from this hell.

Near midnight—as on so many horrific nights before—the jangle of keys heralded a visit by a man intent on having his way with the once-virginal daughter of the dead king. By now long past numb, and intent on the longed-for dawn, Anna just stared at the wall as the man settled in the dirty straw beside her and said he was a friend, a former courtier of her father's, and was here to help. He was lying, she was sure: all her father's intimates had surely been put to death, or had fled. Why he said it, she didn't know. Some of them did, the men who came into her cell. Some of them spoke to her as though to persuade her there was, somewhere, a reason she should not hate them for what they were about to do. She despised those men even more than the ones who silently and roughly threw her on the straw and took her as they wanted.

So she didn't speak to this man, didn't look at him, and when he came close she didn't move. She'd learned to respond as little as she could; in the beginning she'd fought them, but they had always conquered her and her ineffectual struggles only inflamed their lust. Her sole power was in impassiveness and scorn.

The man took her chin gently in his hand, turned her head to face him. He looked into her eyes. She found herself strangely captivated, and was not sure if she could have moved in any case when finally he took her by her shoulders, laid her softly in the straw, and leaned over her. She felt his mouth on her throat, his soft lips, and then a searing, fiery pain engulfed her. It blazed through her as though she were plunging into boiling oil. She lost sight and hearing, could feel nothing but this agonizing Fire. She tried to scream but no sound came. Just when she thought she'd go mad from the pain, it started to fade, and when she could see again, she found the man's eyes still on hers. She found also that she could hear the newborn squeak of a baby mouse in its nest inside the walls, and she could smell the aroma of roast meat from the guard's quarters across the courtyard.

He sat her up, this courtier, took her hands, and told her what he was. What she now was. Stunned and unbelieving, she took him for mad. He told her not to fear the dawn. He stroked her hair and, leaning forward again, kissed her. His mouth on hers awoke in her such a clamor of yearning, such vast, unknown pleasure, that it was almost pain again. She still hadn't spoken when he stood and left, locking her cell behind him.

She sat immobile, staring where he'd gone, until they came for her at dawn. Her hands were bound behind her, her eyes blindfolded, and she was hanged, not with a sharp, merciful snap of the neck, but a slow, terrifying strangulation. She fought, kicking, writhing, but darkness flowed gradually in and she was gone. Her last thought was, **At least it's over.**

Until she awoke on silk sheets in a room filled with daylight glowing softly through lace curtains. The courtier sat beside her in a velvet chair. He smiled and she reached her hand to his.

*   *   *

Anna shook herself to bring her thoughts back to this world. Enough memories, enough time-wasting! Each phone call from Jorge brought worse news than the last. She could see no help for it now: she had to involve herself directly, or this golden chance might be lost. If the Church, or the Conclave, recovered the Concordat, another such opportunity could be centuries away. But Jorge was no longer a useful tool. He was a liability, calling attention to himself, and so potentially to her and their movement.

Jorge, the stupid fool, had killed a monk.

4I

◀◯▶

"Esposito? Come in here a minute."

The *soprintendente*'s command came without urgency, as though it were a request; but the man never raised his voice. Some of Luigi Esposito's fellow Gendarmes had the idea from his manner that their boss was fundamentally unconcerned, with his work, theirs, or anything else, that he was just marking time until he was pensioned off. As so many of them were. But Luigi had learned to read the *soprintendente*'s inflections and the look in his eyes. That's why, though he was just a Naples street kid, he'd become a *vice assistente* when his fellows were still—and would always be—uniformed Gendarmes.

Luigi rose from his desk, where three windows open on his computer linked him to the Web sites of various law enforcement agencies specializing in art and antiquities theft. Educating himself about the ins and outs of this crime specialty seemed an obvious next step. Especially since he had no suspects to process, no interviews to conduct, and no actual physical evidence to examine.

Well, not entirely no evidence. He'd made a search of the Library passage both the clerk and the black-haired woman had used—and a man claiming to be a priest, one Father Thomas Kelly, a researcher from Boston—

and come up with the clerk's Library smock. That he'd thrown it off, obviously the better to blend in, plus the fact that he and the other two had used the same escape route, made it even more glaringly obvious to Luigi that this was a ring of highly professional thieves. Though it was also clear, from the reported fight in the *Manoscritti* Reading Room, that something had gone wrong with this particular attempt at larceny. Maybe the priest really was a priest, and had been trying to prevent the theft? And had chased after the woman to get the stolen book back? But if so, where was he? Why hadn't he come forward? No, to Luigi it seemed more likely that the priest, real or bogus, was a member of the ring, involved up to his clerical collar.

Luigi followed his boss into his office, where the *soprintendente* dropped his round, rumpled body into his desk chair and said, "Close the door. Take a look at this."

Luigi pushed the door shut and took the sheet of paper the *soprintendente* handed him. It was a printout of an incident report, one from a steady stream that flowed through the *soprintendente*'s computer all day. The Rome *polizia*, the Italian Carabinieri, and the Vatican Gendarmerie kept one another informed of goings-on in their jurisdictions throughout the day. (And into the endlessly silent Vatican night, when, during Luigi's stints as watch officer, reading the reports of the other police agencies was sometimes the only thing that kept him awake.) It was a professional courtesy, though Luigi couldn't imagine a cop or a Carabiniere scanning the Holy See's crime news with any serious interest.

Glancing over the other agencies' reports was part of the *soprintendente*'s duties, though, and he performed this office faithfully. Luigi knew, from his boss's sharp blue eyes combined with the weary set of his shoulders, that the *soprintendente* had once seen himself sailing the wild seas of true law enforcement, before he'd gotten becalmed in the backwater of the Vatican. It made Luigi wonder how he, Luigi, would survive once he got promoted to a supervisory position and spent all day doing Vatican paperwork, his nose pressed to the glass of actual policing.

Then he read the printout, and his heart skipped a beat.

"That description," the *soprintendente* said. As usual, his manner was casual, but now his eyes were narrowed. "Of their person of interest. Reminiscent of the man you had in here earlier, wouldn't you say?"

Luigi swallowed. "Very much so, sir."

The *soprintendente* stared wordlessly at Luigi for long enough that Luigi found he had to force himself to meet the pale gaze and not squirm. Finally the man spoke. "You don't have the seniority, and unless I'm wrong, you haven't worked with the Carabinieri before." He wasn't wrong and he knew he wasn't, so Luigi said nothing. "But if it's the same man, you might be of use. I've spoken to the detective in charge, a man named Giulio Aventino. He's on his way to the church. Santa Maria della Scala." The *soprintendente* gestured to the printout. "His sergeant's already there. He was nearby on some kind of surveillance, I don't know what, when the incident occurred. They'll meet you at the scene."

Trying to appear cool and professional though he'd already nearly crushed the printout in his grip, Luigi said, "Yes, sir!" and headed for the door.

"Esposito?" The *soprintendente* waited for Luigi to

stop and turn. "It's their case. They're willing to have us send someone because it's a homicide of a churchman in a church. You're the obvious choice because of the suspect." **Whom, on the instructions of the Cardinal Librarian, I ordered you to release, and I'm now making it up to you.** Luigi wasn't sure he saw that in the *soprintendente*'s eyes, but he hoped so. "But Santa Maria della Scala's not the Vatican," his boss went on. "It's Italy. You're there to help. To help *them*, Esposito."

Luigi nodded. Anything for a fellow cop. Though, he thought as he loped through the station to the door, if *Vice Assistente* Luigi Esposito of the Gendarmerie were to be any help to a homicide detective of the Carabinieri, it was just possible he might find he was helping himself.

42

◄◦►

Thomas read Mario Damiani's cryptic words with, a tiny corner of his mind was pleased to note, less befuddlement than he'd felt in the Vatican Library when first faced with the poet's works. He was beginning to get inside Damiani's head, he thought. These lines, he was sure, would soon yield to serious and methodical consideration and offer up their meaning.

If he could bring serious and methodical consideration to bear.

The truth was, leaning here on the worn wooden counter beside Livia Pietro, under the scrutiny of a painted angel peeking over a painted curtain, Thomas was having trouble concentrating. Part of it was the distraction created by the aromas swirling through the room. How many weeks, months perhaps, had it been since anyone had opened that door, before he and Pietro had, well, broken in? In all that time the sunlight of summer, now fading to autumn, had continued to fall through the ancient windows. In the quiet warmth, spices, medicinal herbs, flowers, and oils had released their intoxicating scents into the air.

The aromas were part of it, but the other part was that Thomas was noticing them.

Father Thomas Kelly was famous for his scholarly

focus, which was another way of saying he was an ab-
sentminded professor. Though fond of flowers and sunshine, he generally took as little notice of them while
working as he did of howling winter storms and broken
water pipes—each of which had landed him in trouble in
the past, to the great amusement of his colleagues.
("Until your feet got wet? Seriously?") Faced with a task
as monumentally important as the one he was involved
in now, it seemed inexplicable to Thomas that he was
thinking about scent.

And even more ridiculous, he realized, that he was
thinking about thinking about scent. He was distracted
by his own distraction. While Lorenzo's life, and death,
and afterlife, hung in the balance.

Thomas shifted position, leaning closer to the unfolded paper. Pietro raised her eyebrows as he crowded
her, but said nothing. Together they read:

Sarve Reggina, madre de la sorgente
de nasscita e de morte, fragrante ojjo ner core
de le lanterne, tutto d'oro, potente
drento. Ave all'anima, ar piede, a la tera
ch'aregge sordati e ssuore, peregrini ner gnente.

Ave, Maria, mother of the source
of birth and death, and fragrant, flowing oil
that fuels the lanterns, golden, and the force
within. Ave, the soul, the foot, the soil
'neath nuns and soldiers, pilgrims on their course.

Just below the last line of the poem: the letters T I V
A C, in heavy lead pencil, all uppercase.

At first neither of them spoke. The soft air of the

apothecary enfolded them in scent and silence. Finally, Pietro tentatively offered, "Maria. Foot, again. Soil. Pilgrimage. Well, they're pilgrimage poems. And these." She pointed, not touching the paper. "What do you suppose this means?"

"T-I-V-A-C?" With equal uncertainty, Thomas said, "Nothing I can see. Maybe it's initials? Something Spencer George would understand?"

"I suppose. Though we can't very well ask him right now."

"And," Thomas realized, "we can't be sure Damiani wrote them. Uppercase letters, lead, not ink—someone else might have done it."

"In Damiani's notebook? I got the feeling from Spencer that Damiani never showed his notebooks to anyone. But all right, let's let that go for now and focus on the poem."

If only I could focus, Thomas thought. But he redoubled his efforts and stared at the words. And slowly found himself drawn in, absorbed in the old, familiar way, until he all but felt the connections being made in his brain between what he was learning now, and what he already knew. "Something else," he said slowly, as his synapses sizzled and clicked. "Soil, foot, you're right, pilgrimage, but something else . . . Maria, yes, so another church dedicated to Mary. But: Source. Oil. Soldiers, the soldiers are important . . . Lanterns . . . golden lanterns . . . No! Not the lanterns are golden! The oil is golden. The oil. Where the oil bubbled up." He saw the light go on in Pietro's eyes and wondered if it was mirrored in his own.

43

Livia refolded Damiani's poem, slipped it into the pages of her own notebook, and zipped the notebook and poem into her bag. The Conclave had been right: having the priest with her was paying off. She was a little surprised at herself for, well, being surprised. The Conclave carried a collective wisdom of thousands of years. Behind them were centuries of debate and study. It was their responsibility to be right. And—with the single, glaring exception of her defying of the Law to make Jonah Noantri—Livia had, since her own Change, always taken it as an article of personal faith that they were. Livia wanted nothing more than a quiet, assimilated life, lived undiscovered among the Unchanged and openly among her own kind; she'd never wanted anything else, except Jonah, and allowing herself to want him was her great error and still her greatest regret.

In silence she led the priest back out of the apothecary—though she caught him casting a look of disappointment on the shelves and bottles, the jars and the drawers he'd had no chance to explore—and across the vestibule to a hallway on the right. She made quick work of the lock on the first door, to, she noticed, no reaction at all from Thomas Kelly. The room held old equipment for crushing and distilling herbs, fascinating devices, and the priest appeared even more pained here, to have to pass them all by. But he made no comment as she crossed to the dusty window, unlatched it, and peered out. Ten feet below lay a courtyard that was even now planted in a formal pattern, though no longer with herbs the monks were cultivating for future use, just with ornamental flowers and shrubs. She pulled the window wide.

"Wait." Thomas Kelly finally spoke, the edginess back in his voice. She'd expected it would return, but still she sighed; his disapproval and objections were wearying. "You can't be planning to go out that way?"

"It's not a far drop. There's a fig tree here." She smiled. "Even a priest in a jacket and collar should be able to make it."

"That's not the point! We can't go through there. It's the monastery garden. They'll see us."

"The monks? They're all in the church. The bells called them. Look around: there's no one anywhere."

Kelly's face changed. "I should—I should go, too. To see if—"

"No." She turned to look at him full-on. "Father, whatever it was, there's nothing you can do. You and I have a task, as important to you as it is to me. Let's concentrate on it." With that she sat on the windowsill, swung her legs over it, and leapt to the ground. She hadn't needed the help of the fig tree but turned expecting to find Thomas Kelly clambering clumsily down its branches—if he decided to come along at all. She was surprised to see the priest, after hesitating, ignore the tree and grasp the sill, lowering himself on outstretched arms until he let go his handhold and dropped lightly beside her.

As he stood dusting his hands, Livia said, "Nicely done."

"We humans aren't completely without our physical abilities."

She sighed. "Can't we have a truce?" When he didn't answer, she turned away from him. "All right." She surveyed the walled garden. "Now we need to find a way out to the street."

Kelly gave her a pitying look and spun briskly, heading to his left. Livia caught up with him. "Where are you going?"

"Out."

"How do you know it's this way?"

"It's a monastery. I'm a priest."

She couldn't argue with that. She followed, and it turned out he was right. He marched confidently through a small door into a cool, dim corridor, then led her along a smooth-worn stone floor past walls hung with crucifixes and a dark, not very good but clearly deeply felt painting of Santa Teresa. After a brief moment of decision at the intersection with a wider corridor he turned right. A few yards later they reached another door and, through it, a small vestibule. Livia's heart pounded when she saw the sliding scrollwork screen and the desk in the tiny room beyond it, but the vestibule and room were as empty as the corridors. Thomas Kelly crossed to the outer door, eased it open, took a cautious look out, and gestured impatiently as though she were dragging her feet. They issued onto Via del Mattonato, behind the church. No one was about as they hurried away.

"That was impressive," Livia said.

"Tradesman's entrance," was Kelly's short answer.

But after a moment he relented, adding, "The Discalced Carmelites are a semicloistered order. Their contact with the outside world is carefully controlled."

"They have a big gate right smack through the rear wall into the monastery."

"That would have been added recently. For trucks. Originally a tradesman would have brought his wares on his back or by handcart as far as the vestibule we just came out of. He'd have been paid by the monk behind the screen and gone off. Then other friars would have been summoned to collect the delivery. Which, you can be sure, is a similar system to the one they use now for the trucks. It's only when the monks are performing their pastoral duties that they have contact with outsiders."

Kelly had assumed the pedantic tones of the university lecturer again, but Livia took care to keep her amusement to herself. To her surprise, though, the corners of the priest's mouth lifted into a small smile.

"What's funny?" she asked.

"You might be the only woman ever to have walked that hallway."

"Don't tell the monks—they'll be scandalized."

Still smiling, Kelly nodded. Then, as if he'd caught himself in an error, his face flushed and he said, "Much more than scandalized if they knew what you really were. What I'd brought to their consecrated halls."

Livia sighed once again. "Give it a rest, Father." She strode past him and then, without looking back, turned down a *vicolo* so narrow it was always in shadow. She kept a few paces ahead of Thomas Kelly as they covered the short distance to the Basilica of Santa Maria in Trastevere.

44

<hr>

Giulio Aventino had to admit that, notwithstanding the Armani jacket, the elegant two-day scruff, and the cardinal uncle, Raffaele Orsini had done an excellent job at the Santa Maria della Scala crime scene. Once you got past the fact that he'd sat drinking coffee in the café across the piazza while it became a crime scene, of course. Raffaele had called in the coroner and the forensics team, used some of the responding officers to secure the church and some to fan out and hunt for the alleged perpetrator; and he'd held on to all the witnesses. That last must not have been easy in the case of the sour historian who was sitting in cold impatience, his arms folded, in a rear pew. He, according to the sergeant, had to have it explained to him that the forces of law and good represented by the Carabinieri would be most grateful for his continuing cooperation. As would the substantial paperwork-generating bureaucratic machine of the civil state, which sadly the Carabinieri could not control once it was unleashed. Giulio nodded. Raffaele was very good at that sort of thing. Giulio himself would just have arrested the man if he'd tried to leave, and sorted it out later.

Not for the first time, Giulio considered the possibility that the *maresciallo* had created their partnership not only because of the things the junior detective could learn from the senior.

The other two witnesses, by contrast, were only too glad to stay. Black-clad *vecchie*, of a type Giulio's twenty-three years on the force had taught him to know well, they had not only been in the church when the homicide had occurred, they'd nearly seen it happen. They'd turned at the yell and the thud, seen the thin young man flee back up the aisle. It was their solemn duty, they assured him, to help the Carabinieri solve this horrible crime, this desecration, this tragedy that offered further proof, if any were needed, that today's young people were lost to God and running completely amok. No, they'd needed no persuasion to stay; in fact, Giulio suspected he'd need a pry bar to get these ladies out of the church in the end.

He'd listened patiently to each as she objected, disingenuously but huffily, to being made to go through her story again, having already told it to Raffaele. Then, being reassured of her value to the investigation, each launched into a blow-by-blow (". . . lighting candles for my late husband, such a good man, God rest his soul, he was Francesca's brother, we come every day . . .") that eventually wound round to the raised voices, the scuffle, the fall. By the time each of the ladies had told it twice, the story included bellowed blasphemous curses, an unprovoked vicious attack on a man of God by a wild-eyed degenerate, and a morbidly delighted grin lighting up the face of the killer ("I can never forget it, Madonna help me!"); but Giulio thought not. What he heard, between the self-importantly hysterical lines, played out like this: a young man rose from his knees at the rear of the church and sought access to an area in which he was not permitted; the old monk sought to prevent him; in an attempt to shove his way past, the young man had knocked the old monk down. The monk had hit his head on the ancient marble floor—on a gravestone marking a tomb below, but Giulio was long over the ironies that churches could offer—and died, either of the impact or of a heart attack caused by fright or agitation, the specific cause being for the coroner to determine.

Giulio, again from long experience of such matters, suspected the death had been an absurd accident. An overreaction, you might say, on the part of Fate. A satanic disciple, a specimen of today's amok youth with eyes like burning coals, would be unlikely to have been found on his knees at the back of the church to begin with. Had the young man stayed, and assuming he had no record of previous criminal violence, it was likely he'd have gotten a slap on the wrist: at worst, a six-month suspended sentence for assault. As it was, because he'd fled the scene, he was now a suspect in a homicide. The longer and harder the authorities looked for him and the more resources they expended, the angrier the judge they brought him before would be when he was finally caught.

It was that he had, in fact, fled that interested Giulio. That, and the fact that he'd been on his knees in prayer in the first place.

The coroner's men were ready to go, so Giulio dismissed the second *vecchia*, instructing one of the uniformed officers to escort the important lady out. As he'd expected, she balked at leaving, but her sanctimonious respect for authority overcame her desire to be at the center of any tragedy; and finally she went. As was his custom, Giulio went back to the body, lifting the linen

over the face for one final look. Raffaele Orsini, standing beside him, crossed himself. That made, since Giulio
had arrived, four times. Of course he'd counted; it was
one of the little delights of working with Raffaele, the
private side bets Giulio made daily about how the sergeant's piety would express itself. Since this case involved the death of a monk in a church, Giulio was
looking forward to some inspired devotion.

Giulio nodded to the coroner's team, who started the
process of packing the body up for transport. From Giulio's point of view there was nothing of note about the
body except the look of peace, even joy, on the old
monk's face. Giulio could tell the man had been bent
crooked with arthritis, which probably caused him constant pain; and at his age no doubt he had other health
problems as well. **As you will soon enough, Aventino,**
he told himself, **and at least this one died happy, expecting to meet his Maker.** As Giulio often did, he
considered the cheerless irony of how he and his fellow
realists (a word he vastly preferred to "nonbelievers,"
which implied something actually existed in which they
refused to believe) had outsmarted themselves. Men like
this monk—and Raffaele Orsini—might be deluded about
their own purpose, about God existing and having a
plan, and most of all, about the afterlife; but they generally died happy.

With a stifled sigh Giulio walked over to the pew
where the historian sat. The lemon face turned to look at
him.

"Well. The majesty of the law is finally prepared to
catechize me, is that it?"

Giulio enjoyed the deliberate misuse of the theological verb, partly because he heard, from the pew behind,

Raffaele sucking air disapprovingly between his teeth. "I'm sorry to have kept you waiting, sir," he said. "Professor Spencer George, is that correct?" Giulio pronounced the English badly but with obvious care, and then returned to Italian with equally obvious relief. "I'm Senior Investigator Giulio Aventino. It's an honor, sir. May I?" Without pausing for an answer Giulio dropped wearily into the pew. "It was those women. They were witnesses to the incident—which I take it you yourself were not, *Professore*?"

He waited, though they both knew he knew the answer. The historian forced out an exasperated "That's correct."

"As I thought. In any case, I needed personally to hear those women's accounts of the situation—as senior investigator on this case I can't rely on secondhand testimony, even from someone as reliable as my sergeant"—his nod to Raffaele, now leaning forward, caused the historian to swivel around to look—"but frankly, sir, it was also that until they were gone I knew I wouldn't be able to think straight. Very pious, of course, and no doubt women of great virtue, but exhausting, don't you find?"

None of this did the *professore* grace with an answer; and all of it was only barely true. Giulio had no special love for the doom-and-gloom sin-sniffing old ladies who came early to Mass and made a point of occupying the pews nearest the confessional, the better to eavesdrop on other people's transgressions. But they didn't make his head spin. Belying his carefully cultivated appearance, very little, in reality, made Giulio Aventino's head spin.

He peered at Spencer George and could tell the historian was seeing right through his rumpled-and-befuddled act. Excellent. George would conclude that Giulio, after having kept him cooling his heels for no good reason, was now making an inept attempt to cozy up to him for the purpose of manipulating him into lowering his guard. Being manipulated tended to irritate people. And, having so easily discovered Giulio's strategy, the *professore*—in any case no doubt accustomed to thinking of himself as smarter than everyone around him; Giulio could see that in the impatient thin lips and the arrogant set of the shoulders—would allow his own condescension free rein.

Irritated, impatient, and condescending. If any constellation of mind-sets was more likely to cause a suspect to make mistakes, Giulio hadn't yet come across it.

Not that Spencer George was a suspect, at least, not in the death of the monk, at least, not directly. But when Giulio had first arrived, after he'd seen the body and gotten the lay of the land, and before he'd questioned any of the witnesses, he'd taken his sergeant outside and had a hushed conversation with him on the church steps. Raffaele had filled him in, with exactly the mixture of apology and pride that Giulio had expected, on his surveillance mission for his cardinal uncle. Giulio, over the half-glasses perennially slipping down his nose as though they wanted to bury themselves in his mustache, had interrupted Raffaele's narrative to ask whether he was absolutely sure he hadn't noticed anything at all amiss about the visitors going in and out of the church. That was by way of reminding the sergeant that all of this had happened while he'd been lounging in the piazza outside on secondment to the Vatican, so perhaps a bit more apology and a touch less pride would have been appropriate.

Then, because they were, at the end of the day, partners, and because Raffaele, at bottom, had the makings of a good, solid cop—and because one of Raffaele's better points was that he never made excuses for his mistakes—Giulio had filled the sergeant in on what might turn out to be the intriguing next piece of what might turn out to be a larger puzzle: the anticipated arrival of a member of the Gendarmerie. ("Stop smirking, Raffaele, they're brothers in arms. If anyone should show respect to an officer from the Vatican I'd think it would be a cardinal's nephew.") The Gendarme, so Giulio had heard, had an interesting tale to tell about the homicide suspect who, after causing what Giulio was still sure was an accident, had so rapidly disappeared.

45

Raffaele Orsini was watching his partner work.

He himself had gotten Giulio Aventino's trademark soft-voiced, phrased-as-a-question, piercing-gaze-over-the-eyeglasses reprimand earlier, but he was the first to admit he'd deserved it. Not so much because of what had happened inside Santa Maria della Scala while he sat in the café outside—hadn't the *maresciallo* told him not to enter the church?—but because, though Giulio hadn't mentioned this, the thin young man they now thought of as their suspect must have exploded out of one of the church's main doors just as, through another, Raffaele had been charging in.

Raffaele had been forgiven, though, or at least considered properly chastised, and welcomed back into the fold. In fact, he'd proved his use already. Not only by his rapid, efficient, and book-proper handling of the crime scene. While the historian smoldered in the pew, Giulio Aventino patiently listened to the lamentations of the old ladies. Raffaele would have liked to stay and pick up some pointers on dealing with hysterical witnesses, but he'd been dispatched to run interference with the dyspeptic emissary launched in their direction by the Bishop. This vinegary *Monsignore* had arrived with a flurry and a frown, sent to ensure, in equal measure, that the search for the friar's killer was made a high Carabinieri priority, and that untoward behavior at the monastery of Santa Maria della Scala, should any come to light, not find its way into the official report. Raffaele had done a good job, he was pleased to say, of placating the priest while upholding the honor and independence of the Carabinieri. At the moment the *Monsignore*, in the company of the monastery's prior, was exploring the possibility that some valuable item might have gone missing (a suggestion that made the *Monsignore*'s eyes flash, as though Raffaele, by speaking the words, was in danger of bringing about the fact). After they'd gone off Raffaele had herded the rest of the monks— there were fourteen—into two pews not far from where the body lay. As a detective, he'd have been happier if they'd left the premises altogether, so as not to endanger the evidence; and his partner, as a nonbeliever, would probably be happier if they just vaporized. But Raffaele felt strongly that they had a right to sit in prayer and meditation near the corporeal remains of their brother, to keep vigil and ease his joyous trip into the presence of God.

Until the coroner's men took the body away, of course. Now the monks, on the orders of their prior, had returned to their cloister. The prior and the acidic *Monsignore* were inspecting the side chapels one by one. Uniformed officers, armed with a dialed-back version of the old ladies' descriptions, prowled the streets hunting down the thin young man. And Raffaele was in a rear pew taking lessons in interview technique.

He always enjoyed this process. In some ways observing Giulio with a witness was like watching a soccer game between unmatched teams. Each play unfolded uniquely, and so held individual interest; but the overall organization of the game was familiar and the outcome never in doubt.

"Now, *Professore*, please." Seeming both distracted and ready to be grateful, Giulio addressed the historian. "Tell me what you can about this incident. Where were you when it took place?" The answer, of course, Giulio already knew, as he could also, no doubt, predict the objection of Spencer George.

"What I told your sergeant—"

"Is what you told my sergeant. I'm sorry, sir, but it's my responsibility to hear all witness statements personally. As I did with those of the *vecchie*," he confided in a tone of shared misery.

"Yes, of course." Spencer George, his eye-roll making it clear he was yielding, unwillingly, to the inevitable, began his tale. It was essentially the same story he'd told Raffaele: he and two friends had entered the Reliquary Chapel at the end of the side aisle "to admire Santa Teresa's chopped-off foot," a phrase near enough to blasphemy that it caused Raffaele to suppress a shudder. George had remained after his friends had gone. He'd heard a scream, come into the main church, and seen the monk lying on the floor with an apparition in black hovering over him. Giulio lifted his eyebrows at this suggestion of the supernatural, until George went on to add, "I believe it was her sister-in-law who'd run howling outside."

"Ah." Giulio nodded and continued. "And the friends you were with, your fellow historians? Livia Pietro and Thomas Kelly? Where are they now?"

From the pause and the widening of the historian's eyes, Raffaele could tell the question had hit home. The *professore* had never been asked, or volunteered, the names or occupations of his companions.

And this was the point and had been all along: the point of keeping Spencer George waiting, of Giulio's pedantic civil servant act, to make him feel superior and therefore get careless.

In their brief conference when Giulio arrived, Raffaele had explained he'd been sent by the Cardinal to keep an eye on Livia Pietro; Giulio in turn told Raffaele about the theft at the Vatican Library and the red-haired American priest easily identified as one Thomas Kelly, who'd been with Pietro then. The third party involved in that fracas, it seemed, was a thin young man of suspiciously similar description to the suspect they were seeking now. The Gendarme detective on that case was on his way; but even without him, Raffaele and his senior partner could see something was going on here that required a more thorough explanation. And that this historian, now that he'd been thrown off-balance, might well be the one to give it.

46

Thomas Kelly realized he'd lost control of the situation once again. He'd boldly led their escape from the monastery, as he'd been the discoverer of the hiding place of the new poem. True, Pietro had chosen for them a serene and splendid retreat in which to decipher the verse, and also true, and more rankling, it had been Spencer George who'd prompted Thomas to check for the folded paper in the reliquary's roof. But as Thomas brought Livia Pietro through the hushed monastery corridors and out onto the street, and then along it, he'd felt less at sea than any time that day.

However, now she was ahead of him in a dark lane he wouldn't have thought to turn down. She knew the way to the Basilica of Santa Maria in Trastevere, and he didn't. He was sure she had no idea what to do when they got there, but neither had he, so they were even on that score.

And she was an unnatural creature with a nimble intellect, a great depth of learning, and an indelible physical presence. A creature who, to hear her tell it, felt a warm, benign joy in the company of others physiologically like herself. Whereas he was a man who'd given his merely human mind, body, and soul to a spiritual community he'd chosen: a Church he'd always understood, even in the days of his darkest doubts, to exist as a place of honest refuge from the evils of the world. About which characterization he was now, at best, unsure.

Where did that put the two of them on the relative-advantage scale?

He pondered that question as he followed Pietro, turning left and then right along narrow streets, then left again onto a busier one, until she suddenly stopped. She thrust out her arm so she could halt Thomas's progress, also. Shades of the Vatican Library. She peered from the mouth of the alley, and then, adjusting her hat and sunglasses, strode confidently into a wide piazza. Thomas followed—what else was he going to do?—as she strolled nonchalantly toward the fountain and then turned to survey the basilica's façade. Wide and imposing, it well suited the first church in Rome, in fact the first in the world, dedicated to Christ's mother. On the pediment the Madonna and Child were flanked by—if he remembered his art history (and he certainly wasn't going to ask Pietro)—a mosaic of ten female saints no one had ever been able to name. He craned up to see them as he trotted by the fountain and through the piazza. Pietro, he noticed, also looked up, with an air of familiarity and happiness, as though seeing old friends. Well, there you go. Maybe they weren't saints. Maybe they were all female Noantri. And maybe that wasn't the Infant Jesus and the Blessed Virgin at their center, it was Baby Damian and the Queen of the Night.

He considered issuing himself a reprimand for his cynical attitude but decided he had a right to it.

Inside the church Thomas's eyes had to adjust once again to the dimness while Pietro headed without pause down the center aisle. Unlike Santa Maria della Scala, he and Pietro didn't have this basilica practically to themselves. A few scattered worshippers were kneeling or sitting quietly in pews, and one or two stood in side chapels lighting candles, while dozens of visitors, some with guidebooks, some without, prowled the splendid aisles.

Now capable of seeing, Thomas hurried after Pietro, passing between rows of columns of which no two were alike. They'd come from Roman and even Egyptian buildings, he recalled his art history lecturer saying, and he remembered thinking at the time that this reuse of structural elements was a physical manifestation of the supplanting of pagan thoughts and fears by the sheltering truth his faith offered. Resolutely, he turned his gaze away from the columns and from the astounding ceiling with its gold coffers and devotional paintings, there to remind the flock what awaited them in heaven above if only their faith, while they remained below, stayed strong.

Refusing equally to think about the implications of that and to allow himself another cynical interior remark, Thomas stepped to Livia Pietro's side. She stood at a marble railing supported on open stone grillwork; the railing bore a stone plaque. *Fons Olei*, the bronze letters read, marking the spot where, two thousand years before, the miracle responsible for the basilica's existence had occurred. Oil had bubbled up out of the ground here. According to legend, the Jewish residents of Trastevere had recalled an ancient prophecy and hailed the flow as a sign, a herald of the appearance of the Messiah. A few decades later word came from Bethlehem that a Virgin had brought forth a Son; there followed tales of signs and miracles, and later of the Son's sacrifice for love of his Father's flock. The nascent Church declared the prophecy of the oil fulfilled. The building in which it had occurred—by then a social club for retired Roman soldiers—was recognized as sanctified ground, razed, and rebuilt to the glory of the Lord.

That the oil was now understood to have been petroleum, a substance unknown to the locals at the time but not uncommon in the area, and that the ancient Jewish prophecy appeared to be a back-formation of which no trace could be found before the bubbling of the oil, had never bothered Thomas before this.

Pietro turned to Thomas. "*Fons Olei,*" she said. "We're here. What now?"

"It's astounding how you people keep expecting me to know what to do next."

She pursed her lips. "You're right. I'm sorry. I was less expecting than hoping, actually."

In Latin it's the same word, he thought, but didn't speak, just squatted and fingered the bronze letters, feeling around their edges. Maybe something had been slipped behind one; but Pietro had apparently had the same thought and already discarded it. "Those letters are too new. They were put there after Damiani's time. You can tell by the typeface."

Thomas could tell no such thing, but she was the expert. Still on his haunches, he examined the marble railing. He ran his gaze along the floor's intricate mosaics, seeking a break in the pattern, a hidden instruction. Nothing presented itself as a hiding place, with one exception: the open stone grillwork on which the railing rested. Behind it, the steps to the altar rose. A piece of paper shoved through the grillwork would have fallen to the floor and could count on resting in that lightless cavern until the entire basilica crumbled to dust. Or until the paper rotted away from mold and damp. Or was devoured by dark-dwelling beetles. From the experience Thomas could claim of Mario Damiani—limited but intense—sliding the next poem, if that's what they were here for, through the grillwork to lie in the dirt was far too slapdash a choice.

Nevertheless, he pressed his face to one of the openings, for a closer look. He felt Pietro kneel beside him, heard her rummage in her bag, and suddenly the area under the steps was illuminated by a bright light. Pietro peered through an opening beside him as he searched the cavern with methodical care.

It was totally, completely empty.

Thomas stuck his hand through the railing anyway. He felt around: perhaps there was a way to fasten something, attach the paper to the back of the grillwork. If so, he'd have to search behind every opening, a tedious process at best. But the masons had been conscientious. The rear side of the stone, though never intended to be seen, was polished to as smooth a finish as the front.

Thomas stood slowly and Pietro straightened up beside him.

"I thought you could see in the dark," he said, unhappily belligerent.

"Better than you. But light always helps."

He saw her drop her cell phone back into her bag.

"That's not a flashlight," he said uselessly.

"On the iPhone. It's an app." She zipped the bag. "You can't really be as disgusted as you look. That a Noantri would have the newest technology?"

With a pang of guilt Thomas realized what he'd been

doing. Ruefully grateful she hadn't taken his bait, he said, almost by way of apology, "Some people think it all comes from the devil anyway. There's nothing here. What are we going to do?"

Pietro looked around, as though hoping for inspiration from the columns, the ceiling, the swirling patterned Cosmatesque floors. Doing that, she reminded Thomas of someone, and then he realized: himself.

"Is it possible Damiani didn't mean this church?" she asked.

"No." Thomas shook his head. "'Fragrant, flowing oil.' This is the place."

"But the oil . . . If he was leading us to the oil . . ."

Thomas stared at the bronze letters, and then spun to look at her. "There's no oil here. There was. There once was. But if he was leading us to the oil, he didn't mean here."

"But we just agreed, he had to mean here. This church."

"*Basilica*. This basilica. But not here." Rapidly, he turned and started up the aisle, pausing at each side chapel, glancing inside. Pietro didn't ask what he was looking for, just trotted beside him. He reached the narthex and gazed at the front wall, then turned to cross to the left-side aisle. He stopped before he'd taken a step. There it was. Across the narthex, in the side wall, maybe ten feet above the floor, a small golden door in a carved stone frame. Pietro followed his gaze.

"What is it?" she asked.

"An aumbry. A lot of older churches have them but they're not used anymore. This one might not have been opened for years." He barked a humorless laugh. "I'd have said, 'not within living memory,' but—"

"What's in it?"

Right. Serious. This was all serious. "Chalices and other requisites for administering the sacraments. Sacraments like the anointing of the sick." He turned to her. "Requisites like holy oil."

47

◦━◦━◦

Livia stared in wonder at Thomas Kelly. An aumbry. She'd never even heard of an aumbry.

Thomas Kelly turned away from her look to focus, with a frown, on the golden door set high above their heads. He clearly saw the location as an obstacle.

She didn't.

"Father," she said, "it'll take me two minutes if it's locked, one if it's not. Can you give me that?"

"What are you—" The priest's face darkened. He glanced at the offering box at shoulder height directly under the golden door. "You can't be serious."

"If it will hold me."

"No. No, that's—" He stopped himself. "What am I worried about? Such a minor desecration." His sarcastic tone made it clear the words weren't intended for her. After a moment's pause, Thomas Kelly, looking as though his stomach hurt, turned and walked across the narthex and back up the right-side aisle.

He fell. The priest tripped and plowed into a group of tourists, nearly knocking one man over, clumsily recovering, tripping again in his attempt to aid the man and his flummoxed friends. Voices were raised in apology and forgiveness, Thomas Kelly was straightening the man's coat, and then a small exclamation, more apology, and three people in the group fell to their knees. They weren't, Livia realized, praying. They were attempting to recover the contents of a purse knocked away in the confusion.

She looked around. The raised voices and flailing arms had claimed the attention of most people in the church. Good, but it wouldn't last. This leap was higher than the last one she'd made, and the landing area was a nine-inch box. A stretch even for a Noantri, but what choice did she have? She lightly vaulted up, prepared for the box to give, but it didn't. Balancing herself, she reached to test the golden door. She was ready with her pick and shim but the door wasn't locked. Well, really, ten feet above the floor in a basilica, why would it be? She eased it open.

Inside: a pearly marble niche, a shallow gold shelf, a graceful Murano glass flask of pale yellow oil.

And nothing else.

How could this be? Were they wrong? **No,** she heard Spencer's voice in her head. **This is just too Mario to be wrong.**

Then what?

The glass flask, the gold shelf, the marble niche. The glass was clear, the oil was pure, the shelf sat firmly on the pearl gray marble.

Except behind the flask the marble wasn't gray.

There, it was black. And it didn't look like marble.

She reached in and removed the stoppered flask with her left hand, taking care not to spill the holy oil. With her other hand she felt the niche's rear wall. No, not stone. Leather. Wedged into the niche, almost the exact dimensions of the rear wall. An unobservant priest replenishing the holy oil would never notice it. She ran a finger around the edge, found a raised corner, peeled it gently toward her. It came away easily.

It was a book cover. Matching exactly the front cover of Damiani's poetry notebook.

Fluttering out from behind it came a single sheet of now-familiar paper.

48

◄○►

Thomas heard a shout. He whipped around in time to see Livia Pietro, paper and something else in hand, leap down from the offering box, shove a ten-euro note in it, and dash out the basilica's door. The aumbry was open, the holy oil sitting untroubled within. Three men, clearly more troubled, gave chase, tearing after Pietro while voices echoed around the church in confusion and in umbrage. Thomas's little commotion was suddenly so sixty seconds ago.

Now, if someone steals something from a basilica, shouldn't a priest chase after her? The same as if she steals from, oh, say, the Vatican Library? With a final shamefaced smile to the people he'd been bouncing off of, Thomas ran out the door.

The three chasing men were nowhere to be seen. Neither was Pietro. There was no way they would catch her, Thomas was sure. She could probably fly, or something. No, of course she couldn't. She could run very fast, was all.

What, Thomas? You're starting to buy the nothing-supernatural-about-it line? Careful there.

Well, whether or not she was supernatural, he wasn't. He had complete confidence that her pursuers wouldn't find her. But could he? A cold fear struck him: What if they'd been wrong about how many missing poems they needed to lead them to the Concordat? What if the paper she'd just found was the final one? If she'd realized it would take her to the document and she didn't need him anymore? If so, she'd find it on her own and deliver it to her Conclave. To *her* people. And Lorenzo?

Lorenzo would be condemned.

Thomas stood in the piazza, staring around helplessly. Resolute tourists headed into the basilica while indolent locals strolled toward cafés. Pigeons swooped in to perch on the fountain. A little white dog barked at a big black one, which looked down with amused disdain. Nothing offered a clue to Pietro's course.

Thomas's heart sank.

Against it, in his breast pocket, his phone began to vibrate.

He almost dropped it fumbling it out. A local number that he didn't recognize. Lorenzo's abductors? He thumbed it on and practically shouted, "Thomas Kelly!"

"I know that, Father. Are you coming?"

For a moment Thomas couldn't speak. "I— *Professoressa*?"

"Try to call me 'Livia.' I'm on Via dei Fienaroli, just past where it intersects with Via della Cisterna. Can you find that?"

"I'm— I will. Stay there. Don't leave!"

"If I were going to leave," he heard her sigh, "why would I have called you?"

49

At the sound of the door latch Lorenzo Cardinal Cossa turned from the open window. Jonah Richter stood on the threshold, golden hair tousled, hands in his trouser pockets, wearing that confident grin Lorenzo despised. Truth be told, there was nothing about the man Lorenzo didn't despise. Starting with the fact that he wasn't a man.

Richter took a few steps into the room, but, as though he were humoring Lorenzo, did not closely approach. "Don't you find it chilly with all the windows open?"

"This room reeks of your kind."

"So strange—before you knew I was Noantri, you didn't complain that I smelled. My stench seems to have arisen simultaneously with your knowledge. What do you make of that?"

"What do you want?"

"I've come to report the hunt is going well."

Lorenzo didn't answer.

"It seems," Richter went on, "that Mario Damiani was a complicated fellow. The trail's longer than it appeared. My historian and your priest have been to two churches and they're on their way to a third."

"What are they finding?" Lorenzo asked in spite of himself.

"I'm not sure. My people can't get that close without being detected by Livia."

Lorenzo turned his back on Richter to gaze out the window again. The room was on the top floor of a building on the Janiculum Hill, and the view was grand. "There. As I said: you stink."

Richter actually laughed. "We can, in fact, detect one another by scent, but we don't feel about it the way you seem to. In any case—" He stopped as his cell phone rang. Lorenzo turned again to face him as Richter answered it and listened. His cheeriness faded into a thoughtful frown. "Thank you," he said, and clicked off. "I have to go," he told Lorenzo.

"Why, is this brilliant scheme malfunctioning?"

"Probably not. But a Noantri who isn't one of my people has been spotted twice in the vicinity of Livia and Kelly. I'd like to know what's going on."

"You can't even trust one another, is that it?"

Richter laughed again. "And you princes and priests of the Church—you can?"

He shut the door behind himself, the latch clicking loudly into place. Lorenzo stood looking where Richter had gone; then he turned once more to the open window and lit a cigar.

50

It took longer than it probably should have for Thomas to arrive at Via dei Fienaroli. That was the fault of the first man he'd asked, who helpfully gave detailed, incorrect directions. Via dei Fienaroli, in fact, was right around the corner from the Basilica of Santa Maria in Trastevere, and it intersected Via della Cisterna another fifty yards along. Via dei Fienaroli was a street so narrow it had no sidewalks. The doors of the shadowed, ancient houses opened directly to the road.

On which, when Thomas got there, no one could be seen.

Of course. She'd sent him on a wild-goose chase. She needed to make sure he couldn't follow her. It wasn't enough that she was an unnatural demon and he just a man, that this city was her home and he had trouble finding his way around it, that she had an entire Community surrounding and supporting her while he was alone with a secret he desperately wished he didn't know, that—

"Father Kelly?"

Not two feet beyond him a battered green door had opened. In the doorway stood a thin young woman with serious eyes and black curly hair. She wore loose white pants and a T-shirt, both of them streaked and

splattered with paint, plus a blue stripe on one bare arm
and, disarmingly, a smudge on the side of her nose.
Smiling, she said, "Father, please come in. Livia's upstairs. I'm Ellen Bird. I'd shake your hand, but I've been
told you'd probably rather I didn't."

Her English was American, with a New York tinge.
For a moment Thomas felt so relieved, so practically at
home, that he began to give her a big answering smile.
Then he realized what she must mean about not shaking
his hand.

He stepped back. "Are you—" **Seriously, Thomas?
What exactly are you going to ask her and how are
you going to explain the question if the answer's no?**

The answer, however, was not no. "Am I Noantri?
Yes. Please come in."

Thomas stared at Ellen Bird. Her curls, her clear skin,
her easy air: she might have been one of his undergraduates. This woman was Noantri? A—**go ahead and say
it, Thomas**—a vampire? There was nothing threatening
about her. She seemed to be nothing more—or less—
than a young American (judging from the paint
smudges, an artist) trying her luck in Rome. Not at all
like Spencer George, about whom Thomas had gotten
an ill feeling from the moment they met. Of course, he
reflected, that could have been because the man was arrogant, hostile, and snide. He'd known priests like that
whom he hadn't liked any better. Livia Pietro, on the
other hand, could be maddeningly manipulative, confusing, and pushy, but even once he knew what she was,
she emanated no air of menace. And this Ellen Bird
seemed refreshingly straightforward.

But evil was subtle.

"Father Kelly? We can't stand here all day."

No, they couldn't. Livia Pietro, and the new poem, and Lorenzo's fate, were waiting upstairs. Thomas squared his shoulders and, for the second time that day, entered a house whose inhabitants weren't human.

51

From the easy chair by the front window in Ellen's studio Livia heard the conversation on the street, heard the door shut, heard Ellen lead Thomas Kelly up the two flights in silence. He was a brave man, she decided. Brave, because he was obviously so frightened, so repulsed, but still he continued because he wanted to save his friend. That's what courage was about, she'd always believed: not the absence of terror, but the ability to go on in the face of it.

Ellen ushered Thomas Kelly into the room. She said, "I'll leave you two alone for a while," and went out. Kelly stopped and stared around, taking in the bright midday sun streaming through the skylight, the turmoil of pinned-up drawings and sketches, the two easels, each with a painting half-finished; then he turned his gaze to Livia. "Why are we here?"

"Lovely to see you, too, Father." He frowned. She felt a pang of guilt; she shouldn't tease him. "Please, sit down. Ellen's a friend of mine."

He didn't move from the doorway. "I didn't like what happened the last time we went to see one of your friends."

"I don't blame you. But don't worry. Ellen's not much like Spencer. There won't be any drama."

"Do you have friends everywhere? I suppose you do, a lot of friends. That must be what happens when you have centuries to get acquainted."

"I'm sorry. I know this is hard for you. Please," she said again. "Sit down."

He didn't, but his tone was a shade less belligerent when he said, "I saw you slip money into the collection box."

"Call it penance. That was a nice distraction in the aisle, by the way."

"Thank you," he said automatically, but he remained standing, clearly warring with himself. The scholar, she wondered, against the cleric? If so, the scholar won. Still without moving into the room, he said, "Tell me this. How many of you are there?"

"Of—?"

"Noantri." He made a face, as though tasting a lemon.

"We borrowed the word 'Noantri' centuries ago, from the native-born Trasteverians," she said calmly. "When we use it, we do mean our kind, but it's not a dirty word."

"Answer my question. How many *Noantri* are there?"

"Altogether, in the world? Probably ten thousand, give or take. A third of us here in Italy, half of that number in Rome, half of those in Trastevere."

"A third? Three thousand . . . three thousand . . ."

"Three thousand vampires, yes, Father. In Italy. We were once more scattered, and we can still be found everywhere, but we concentrate, for obvious reasons, in countries and cities with Catholic populations." Incomprehension clouded his face, so Livia added, "For the hospitals. For the blood."

Perplexity looked like it was about to give way to something worse, so she went on matter-of-factly, "And also, because once we started to gather, we found we very much liked living in Community. The comfort we feel in the presence of one another is something we never knew until the Concordat. In all the years Before, no Noantri was safe who wasn't furtive and hidden."

"Comfort?"

"We're kin, in a way. We feel it more physically than the Unchanged do, but everyone feels heartened in the presence of family."

This was too much for the scholar; the cleric reasserted himself. "Family? Blood relatives, you mean? That's a perverse angle on that concept." Thomas Kelly, his disgust reaffirmed, crossed the room and sat. "Let's get to work. You found another poem."

52

Livia Pietro had just unzipped her bag to draw out the new poem when the door opened. Thomas jumped but settled back again; it was Ellen Bird, bearing a tray. He marveled at himself: **It's okay, nothing to worry about, just a young vampire with some sandwiches.** He realized his coma-hallucination theory had long since faded away and he missed it.

"I know you're hungry, Father Kelly." Ellen Bird smiled, balanced the tray on an art-book pile, and left.

Thomas turned to Pietro. "She knows I'm hungry. How? She sensed my blood sugar falling? Smelled the stomach acid building up?"

"Maybe you have a lean and hungry look. But ask yourself this: If Ellen's Noantri senses did tell her something an Unchanged couldn't have known, is that a reason to reject her food?"

Part of Thomas felt it should have been. The other part reached for a napkin, a sandwich, and a bottle of beer.

"You can use that pile of books as a coffee table. Ellen doesn't care much for furniture," Pietro said, replacing the poem in her bag to keep it from damage. "Take a minute to eat. You'll do better when your blood sugar's up."

"You can tell, too?" She just smiled. Thomas examined the sandwich suspiciously. "What's in it?"

"I'm not going to dignify that with an answer."

She was offended. **Well, good. Oh, what, Thomas, now it's all right to offend people on purpose just because you don't like them?** He was startled to hear himself ask that, and reminded himself, **They're not people!** To which the response was even more surprising: **So?** No, really, now he was seriously confused, and Livia Pietro wasn't even doing it. It must be his blood sugar, which was, in fact, low, no matter who knew it. He looked again at the sandwich. It did look like standard Italian fare: salami, cheese, and tomato. But this was a Noantri household. The two parts of his mind were still quarreling when his mouth took a bite. Salty meat, smooth soft cheese, and sharp tomato perfectly set off the crumbly thick bread. A truly great sandwich, or he was starving, or both. He leaned down for a second bite, then stopped as Pietro reached for a sandwich, too.

"I thought you didn't eat. Eat food, I mean."

"We don't need it, no. But we can metabolize it, and the tastes and textures of food are like any other sensations—more powerful and nuanced since we became Noantri. Many of us enjoy eating. It's always been my habit to eat when my Unchanged friends do."

"To keep us company? Or to conceal yourself better?"

She replaced the sandwich on the tray. "I won't if it bothers you."

"No," he said. "No, go ahead. These are amazingly good. You don't want to miss them." He searched his own voice for sarcasm and unexpectedly found none. "Just leave me another two or three."

Pietro smiled. "Don't worry, Father."

"Thomas." That was even more unexpected. "I'd rather you called me Thomas."

"Only if you call me Livia."

"I don't know."

"Then I don't either. Father."

Thomas pulled away from her gaze, uncomfortable. He really needed to raise his blood sugar. He finished what he was holding in three more bites with no conversation in between, drank some beer, and reached for a second sandwich. Pietro was obviously letting him take the lead, set the rhythm, so, as much to break the silence as anything else, he spoke. "These paintings. And the ones in the entrance, and the hallways. I don't know much about art, but they seem quite good. Only, they're in so many different styles. For someone so young—" He stopped, realizing what he was saying.

"It takes some getting used to," Pietro said. Livia. He was going to try to start thinking of her as Livia. "For us, too. When we meet it's one of the first pieces of information we exchange. How long we've been Noantri. It situates us for one another. Ellen's from New York."

"I thought I heard that in her voice."

Pietro—Livia—shook her head. "Her original way of speaking would make her sound like a Brit. She was born in 1745. She's my Elder by about a hundred and fifty years."

"I . . ." Thomas paused, finished his beer. "I don't even know how to think about that."

"Don't try." Livia's voice was gentle. "As I said, it takes some getting used to. Now that your blood sugar's returning to normal, let's look at this poem."

53

◄◦►

Livia leaned forward and placed Mario Damiani's third poem on the art-book coffee table between herself and Thomas, holding it flat on its edges. Before she'd had a chance to work her way through the Romanesco lines, her cell phone rang. She rummaged it out of her bag.

"Livia, it's Spencer."

"Oh, good! Where are you? Are you all right? What happened in the church?"

"I'm home and I'm fine, thank you, apart from some minor psychological brutalization at the hands of the Carabinieri. And more to the point, the Gendarmerie."

"They were there, too?"

"I'm afraid so. The incident was unfortunately serious. That old monk was killed."

Livia drew a sharp breath. Thomas sent her a questioning look. "It's Spencer," she told him. "Spencer, Father Kelly's here with me. Tell me what happened."

"Am I on speaker?" Spencer asked carefully.

"No."

"Good. I'm sure it will be better if you tell him in your way, rather than if he hears it from me."

"That's considerate of you."

"You needn't sound so shocked. I'm not a total beast, Livia. In any case, what seems to have happened is that you were correct about the Vatican Library clerk. He was there, and he tried to follow us into the saint's foot chapel." That sounded more like the Spencer Livia knew.

"He must have come for the book," she said. "Who *is* he?"

"His name is Jorge Ocampo. Does that mean anything to you?"

"No. The police told you that?"

"No, they told each other that. Within my hearing. Careless of them." Except, of course, the Unchanged police officers had no way of knowing how far Spencer's Noantri auditory reach extended. "Ocampo is an Argentinian national." Which, since the clerk was Noantri, did not mean much. "The old monk sought to prevent him from following us. To give us, presumably, our meditative peace. There was an altercation, and the monk fell or was thrown to the ground. He hit his head and gained admission to heaven." Yes, definitely Spencer. "But listen closely, because this is the part that will prove important to you and your priest. Because a churchman died in a church, the Gendarmes sent a representative. A handsome young Neapolitan, who just happens to be the *vice assistente* who arrested this same clerk at the Colosseum Metro station this morning for theft of Vatican property. Though all they found on him of the stolen property was a tracking chip."

"Hmm."

"Don't hmm yet—there's more. The Neapolitan Gendarme has a theory which he's shared with the Carabinieri. It involves a large and well-organized ring of thieves specializing in antiquities, possibly international in scope and clearly effective enough to successfully steal from the Vatican. And to attempt, in the same day with the same personnel, a theft at Santa Maria della Scala."

"The same personnel?"

"The clerk, who was obviously the inside man on the earlier occasion, as he was employed at the Vatican Library. And an art historian, one Livia Pietro. And also— quite appallingly—a priest. An American named Thomas Kelly."

"Spencer. Are they serious?"

"The Gendarme is entirely serious and he seems to have sold this theory to the Carabinieri. They've become intent on catching the miscreants. It took all my powers of persuasion to convince them I barely know you, I was a touch surprised when you appeared at my door, I'd never met your priest before, and though I had no inkling of your intentions in visiting Santa Maria della Scala, I could assure them that your reputation and character were entirely spotless. You'd have been pleased, I think, to hear the fervor with which I defended your honor."

"Thank you."

"My pleasure. I told them their theory was flatly absurd, and that I was sure you would be able to clear up any misunderstanding as soon as you had the opportunity to speak with them. In order to help you restore your good name, I promised them that, though I had no earthly idea where you'd gone while I was praying over the withered extremity of the sainted Teresa, they could be sure that if I heard from you or of you, they'd be the first to know."

"Did they believe you?"

"I doubt it, but what does it matter? It's clear they also suspect me, which is why they were willing to share their innermost thoughts: so I'd know how much they know, shiver in my boots, and come clean. However, they had no grounds on which to take me into custody, though keeping me inside a church for over an hour was in my view punitive detention enough. I have no doubt they've set a watch on my home, so you're not to come here. However, if I can be of any assistance to your task by leading them around Robin Hood's barn, do let me know. And talking of your task, how are you progressing?"

"We found another poem, at Santa Maria in Trastevere. In an aumbry."

"In a what?"

"It's— Look it up. We're working on the poem now."

"I'm reaching for my dictionary. I'll leave you to it, but if the poem—or any other you find—doesn't yield to your combined powers, I'd be happy to help. And in any case, do be careful. Your names and faces are all the rage in law enforcement circles."

"Thanks, Spencer. You caught us just in time."

"I endeavor," Spencer drawled, "to give satisfaction."

54

◁○▷

Once again Thomas was having trouble concentrating.

This distraction, so new to him, had first fractured his scholarly focus in the ancient apothecary. There he'd found himself trying to unravel the air, to sort pine bark from rose petal, detach mint from mushroom. Now, leaning with Livia Pietro over Damiani's poem, his mind again popped with unmanageable thoughts and sensations. Partly, he knew, it was the unpleasant news conveyed by Spencer George: that he and Livia were wanted by the Carabinieri and that the old monk was dead. Thomas had said a brief prayer for the soul of Father Battista, though he suspected the friar didn't need the help of a priest as heavily compromised as Thomas Kelly to get into heaven. Guilt was an element of his distraction, too: though Livia had tried to assure him the monk's death wasn't their fault, of course it was. And of course, she knew it was. **What would it be like,** he suddenly wondered, **to live forever, to go through eternity accumulating loss and guilt, with no way to expiate, to make amends, to be forgiven? With no end in sight?** He glanced at Livia, her black hair falling about her face as she leaned forward, her arms wrapped around her in her own posture of concentration that, he realized, was already familiar to him.

Without looking up, she spoke. "The poem, Thomas. I know a lot has happened and it's not easy to deal with. But the poem is what's important now."

He was glad her gaze didn't stray from the torn notebook leaf, because he felt his face grow hot. He straightened his shoulders and stared down at the poem, too.

Dojje de morte? Er piaggnisteo de l'esse nati?
Frammezzo a le crature alate, l'api, l'uscelli,
le sonajjere d'angioli, eccosce volati
a spiarje l'estasi ne l'occhi bbelli,
da dove, simme và, posso scappà coll'ale 'mmacolate.

Death throes? The pure puling of being born?
Among the winged creatures, birds and bees
and hierarchies of angels, here we swarm,
look down upon her face in ecstasy,
whence, if I chose, could flee, both wings untorn.

Again, uppercase blunt lead-pencil letters along the bottom:

I F I D E.

Nothing. The words gave him nothing at all. Death or birth? Hierarchies of angels? Looking down in ecstasy, or looking down on a face in ecstasy? Who was looking? Whose face? Whose wings were untorn? Though that, of all the images here, was the only one that struck a bell in Thomas's mind; but it was a bell so faint that, try as he might, he was unable to call up any meaning.

The letters, though: they were a different matter.

With growing excitement he stared at them. The first set had made no sense; neither did these, but if you added them to the first ones, and then read them backward, they almost did.

"*Aedificavit,*" he said tentatively, trying it out. "'Built.'"

"Built?" Livia looked up. "Built what?"

"I don't know. But if you read these letters backward and then the first set backward, I mean if you read them *together*, they nearly spell *aedificavit*. 'Built.'"

"Nearly?"

"It's missing the initial *a*, but it's a compound letter, *ae,* so maybe he thought he could dispense with it. Or maybe it's in the next line! The *a*. On the next poem."

Livia was silent for a moment. "Are you saying this is a cumulative upside-down acrostic? In Latin?"

"From everything we know, that kind of thing would be right up Damiani's alley."

She nodded. "Yes, that's true. You could be right. It would answer the question of whether the penciled letters are his."

"But the poem itself," Thomas said. "Where to go now. What that means, I have no idea."

"That's all right." Livia smiled. "I do."

55

This time, Jorge Ocampo wasn't going to run. He would do nothing to call attention to himself. He'd covertly, stealthily make his way, an operative whose objective was to remain in deep cover while fulfilling his mission.

What was his mission?

He wasn't exactly sure.

Anna hadn't given him new instructions on the retrieval of the notebook or the surveillance of the *professoressa*. She hadn't told him what to do about the unalterable facts of what had happened in Santa Maria della Scala. She'd drawn in a sharp, angry breath when he'd told her about the accident, but she didn't yell, didn't berate him, didn't let loose that hot stream of vitriol she'd poured on his head on the few other occasions when he'd been unsuccessful at accomplishing a task. She really was unfair to him, Anna. He generally did quite well with the assignments she gave him, and he was—justly, he thought—proud of that. Like anyone, he had his moments of bad luck. Her impatience at those times, her lightning-fast willingness to reproach and blame him, really stung. It wasn't reasonable—it truly wasn't.

Although maybe she was changing. Maybe she was beginning to appreciate how hard he tried, and to understand that misfortune can happen to anyone. He'd expected a storm of anger, he'd braced for it, but instead he'd heard a silence, and then, "All right, Jorge. Are you out of sight?" When he'd assured her he'd taken cover, she asked where, and after he told her, she just said, "Stay there. I'm on my way."

So he'd settled into his velvet seat in the musty theater, waiting for Anna to come and tell him what to do. In the dark he drifted into a reverie, feeling her satin skin and silken hair, hearing the thrilling music of her voice as she whispered to him in his native Spanish. But a horn blared outside and startled him, and the dream vanished and would not come back. As he waited he found himself growing more and more uncomfortable. Il Pasquino was his private place. He didn't know what he should have said. "I'm not going to tell you where I am" hadn't occurred to him, and if it had, Anna wouldn't have put up with it. But he began to feel ill at ease about the idea of seeing Anna. Something in her voice . . . She was angry. She was hiding it, and he thought that sweet of her; clearly she knew the stress he was under and didn't want to upset him further. But she was angry.

And, he realized, disappointed.

That caused Jorge a new kind of pain, the thought that his Anna was disappointed in him. She'd sent him out to be her knight in shining armor, and he'd let her down. He came to a decision. He wasn't going to wait for her. Not right now. Not here, in his theater. He was going to leave Il Pasquino and steal along Vicolo del Piede, keeping to the shadows.

He had no instructions, that was true; but he was capable of formulating his own plans. He would find the *professoressa*. He would retrieve the notebook. He would complete his original assignment before he saw Anna again. Then his mistake in the church wouldn't loom so large. He'd never meant to hurt the old monk. He'd only been trying to move him out of the way. How could he have known he'd lose his balance and fall? After all, Anna was the one who'd drilled into him that he must never use any of his Noantri Blessings in a way that Mortals might notice. So it shouldn't be any surprise that he didn't know his own strength! And people fell all the time, even hit their heads, without dying. What had happened to the monk was definitely not Jorge's fault.

Anna had sounded worried about his safety, making sure he was out of sight, telling him to stay there. She wasn't acting as though what had happened in Santa Maria della Scala was very important.

But even if he couldn't be blamed for the monk's death, he knew it mattered. And he was going to make up for it.

Jorge peeked through the grimy window, waiting for a moment when the street was clear. His mind drifted again, this time not to Anna, but to the accident. It was a strange thing, what had happened to that old monk. The man had died, and Jorge wasn't so far from his own Change that he'd forgotten the terror of a Mortal anticipating that. But among the emotions passing across the old monk's face, Jorge, to his astonishment, hadn't found fear. What he'd seen—what he'd caused—was relief. Then, gratitude. Finally, to Jorge's astonishment, joy.

To his additional astonishment, Jorge found himself feeling a tiny, transitory twinge of envy.

Back to the window. One of a revolutionary's best weapons was an ability to focus on his mission despite distractions. Ah—now came Jorge's chance. The street was empty. Jorge slipped from the window and sauntered along, in his sunglasses and porkpie hat. He hadn't worn either in the church, and he'd had on a jacket he was leaving in the theater. Sauntering down the street, he blended in beautifully with all the other hipsters. His plan was to head back to the *professoressa*'s house. He'd watch, and surely she'd come home eventually. Then he'd get the notebook Anna wanted and everything would be as it had been before.

That was his plan. But when he hit the intersection with Via della Fonte D'Olio, an amazing thing happened.

The *professoressa*. She'd passed by there. He caught her scent.

She was wearing perfume, this lady, something complicated and tropical. He'd noticed it in the Library and felt a stab of longing; the girls back home wore perfume, but among the Noantri, his new Community, his home now, it was the fashion to shun such things. Anna never wore perfume, petulantly asking, when he'd wondered why, if the fragrance of her own skin was not enough for him. He hadn't mentioned it again.

This *professoressa*, though: the perfume he'd first detected in the Library—maybe gardenias, could that be right?—the scent he'd followed down the winding hidden corridor, and then faintly noted in Santa Maria della Scala (though there the flowers and incense overpowered it)—he could sense it now, trailing from the direction of the piazza.

She'd passed by, and recently.

His heart started to pound. He ordered himself to stay calm. Quickly, but no faster than a Mortal in a hurry would have jogged, he rushed up Via della Fonte D'Olio into the piazza. She was nowhere in sight, but her scent laced the air. The church—she must have gone into the church! Jorge trotted up the steps, and the moment he entered Santa Maria in Trastevere he knew two things: she'd been there, and she was gone.

Something had happened here, though it was over. He could feel the disturbance in the settling air, smell the ozone scent of sudden excitement, the fading but still strongly acrid aroma a jolt of adrenaline adds to sweat. On his left as he entered, a priest stood on a ladder locking a small golden door. The Catedral Metropolitana de Buenos Aires—a church he'd been in only once or twice, but oh, how beautiful it was—had a door like that. He'd wondered about it, but never asked anyone, because he liked his own answer. Symbolic sanctuary, he'd decided it meant, a reminder that the church would shelter all who came to it. He'd never seen the one back home open and regretted he hadn't arrived at Santa Maria in Trastevere just a few moments sooner, to see what was in them.

As the priest started down the ladder Jorge ordered himself to stop daydreaming. Revolutionary focus! This Church mumbo jumbo, it was oppressive, it was the enemy. He was only thinking about the Catedral Metropolitana because he missed home. The sooner he accomplished his mission, the sooner Anna and the others could establish Noantri rule, and the sooner he and Anna could return to Argentina. Jorge himself wasn't

interested in a position of power in the new order. He
didn't need it, because he'd have everything he wanted:
to be with Anna, for eternity.

With new resolve, Jorge turned and left the church.
He surveyed the streets issuing from the piazza, sniffed
the air, and hurried past the fountain to the other side.

56

◄◦►

Rome could be splendid in autumn, clear and bright. The air, even when cool, lacked the sharp edge of Jonah's native Berlin, but he had no argument with a day like today. Rome was a beautiful city. Livia had brought him to it. And Livia was here still.

Shadows and sunlight alternated as his taxi sped—or what passed for speed in Rome traffic—alongside the Tiber. From habit unwilling to risk exposing his Noantri nature—though why it should matter, this near his goal, he wasn't sure—he'd hailed a cab to take him down the Janiculum into Trastevere.

Livia and the priest were apparently inside San Francesco a Ripa, something he'd learned from the man he had watching them. Much as he loved the sight of Livia, Jonah had avoided tailing them himself to keep her from picking up his scent. Or the rhythm of his footsteps, or the sound of his breath. After all the time, and the depth of it, that they'd spent together, she'd know within seconds if he came near.

Now, though, he had to take the chance.

He'd been informed earlier that a Noantri, someone his agent didn't know, had raced by on Vicolo del Piede. It might have been just some newcomer unable to keep his light under the Conclave-required bushel and it was possible the incident had no bearing on Jonah or his plan, beyond underlining the satisfaction he'd feel when it succeeded. After the Concordat had been published and the Noantri all Unveiled, none of his people would ever again be forced into false modesty and painful mediocrity. That was what he'd been thinking; but another of his agents had called just now, as he'd stood with Cardinal Cossa, to say a man who sounded to Jonah very much like the same one who had passed by on Via di San Franceso a Ripa in the direction of the church—and to identify him as the clerk from the theft in the Vatican Library. Jonah had been told a third Noantri, besides Livia and the supercilious Spencer George, had been in Santa Maria della Scala, also; it was unclear whether that was again this same man, but Jonah was uneasy enough that he decided to come see for himself.

He understood that not only the Church, but the Conclave, would do everything in their power to thwart him, but he'd thought that at this point he had the upper hand with both.

This unknown Noantri, though, might be working for the Conclave. Jonah wouldn't put that past the Pontifex, to give Livia a task and then set a spy on her. The Noantri leader was a dark and secretive man who'd always made Jonah edgy, whose eyes seemed to see right into him, whom Jonah suspected uneasily of foreseeing Jonah's plan before he, Jonah, had ever had it fully formulated. Foreseeing it, but taking no preemptive action to stop it. As though he were giving Jonah every opportunity to do the right thing himself. This man, who'd emerged from the shadows to lead the Noantri as soon as the Concordat was signed, was an enigma even to his own. His steady voice had long led the opposition to

Unveiling. Jonah was well aware that the Pontifex had now ordered his death and also that the only reason that order was stayed was the Conclave's desire to find and reconceal the lost Concordat. If the Noantri stranger was in fact trailing Livia and the priest at the behest of the Conclave, that was a situation Jonah would have to handle.

Another worrisome possibility existed, also: that he was following Livia and Kelly for someone else. Within the Community, sentiment on the subject of Unveiling ran high on both sides of the line. At this sensitive point, it was imperative that no one, from either camp, interfere with Jonah's plan.

Now, Cardinal Cossa, he thought, as the taxi made the turn onto Viale di Trastevere: the Cardinal was a perfect example of everything that was wrong with the status quo. Because the Noantri were forced to remain hidden, Lorenzo Cossa was unfamiliar with them as people, as individuals; because he had only centuries of lies, tales, and legends by which to judge them, he feared and hated them. He couldn't tell reality from nonsense, claiming, for example, to be revolted by the smell of a Noantri, which Jonah knew no Mortal could detect. As opposed to Cossa's own omnipresent cigars, which could truly stink up a room.

What a sad man he was, too. Sad and bitter. As far as Jonah knew, it had been Cossa's life's goal to become Librarian and Archivist of the Vatican. Now he had. In the short time left to him—if he didn't become Noantri—you'd think he'd revel in the vast, varied collection under his control. The knowledge there, the connections to be made and understood, the possibilities! But he hadn't. He'd focused on the Concordat, set a team searching for it, brought in Thomas Kelly when they didn't find it. Cossa was angry, fearful, and disappointed, and from what Jonah could see, he loved nothing.

No. That was wrong. He did seem to love Thomas Kelly. Although of course Cardinal Cossa would never say anything of the sort to Jonah, still he could sense it in Cossa's voice, in the shift of his shoulders when Kelly was mentioned, in the fear in his eyes for Kelly in the current situation. Thomas Kelly was the son Lorenzo Cossa had never had. The prize pupil, the acolyte. Kelly had done well and Cossa was proud.

Soon, thought Jonah, Kelly would do even better. After which, Jonah would be rid of Lorenzo Cardinal Cossa once and for all.

And his revolting cigars.

57

◇

Jorge Ocampo walked slowly, casually up the shallow steps leading into San Francesco a Ripa. Livia Pietro's perfume trail had brought him straight here, and though Jorge knew following it would have been child's play for any Noantri, still he was pleased with himself. Not just for finding the *professoressa*, but for ensuring he'd be able to get close enough to relieve her of the notebook before *she* detected *him*. He'd stopped at a *farmacia* and bought cologne, not one of the powerful, manly scents he'd worn back home—though he'd been tempted—but a cheap, sharp, unpleasant toilet water no one but a stuffed-nosed Mortal could have enjoyed. He'd have to wash it off before he saw Anna again, of course, but the pungent junk should make an excellent mask as he approached Pietro. What she might be doing here, he didn't know, but it mattered not to Jorge. He was on a mission.

Briefly he considered remaining outside, waiting for his quarry to emerge. His last foray into a church had not gone well. No, he decided. Too many variables, too many chances for her to slip away. Or even just to do whatever she was here for, and keep him waiting. Jorge did not want to wait.

The church's doors stood open, welcoming tourists,

pilgrims, and the faithful. The fearful, Anna called them. Jorge's memories of the sweet incense and the echoing cool shadows in La Iglesia de Caacupé, the Buenos Aires church of his childhood, always brought him comfort. He supposed Anna must be right when she said the comfort sprang not from the presence of something ineffable and beyond his understanding, but from yielding to fear and surrendering rational thought, allowing scheming, power-hungry churchmen to deceive him, like millions of other sheep, into believing in that presence. She must be right, but he missed the comfort.

He sidled to the left as he entered, took off his shades, and looked around. At first glance it seemed that San Francesco a Ripa enclosed its visitors in a calm white interior, gilt-trimmed but sedate. Broad streams of sunlight poured from twelve round-topped windows, one over each arch, to crisscross the nave and reflect up off the patterned marble floor. People knelt or sat with bowed heads in some of the pews, and tourists with guidebooks ambled up and down the aisles.

Jorge had been in this church before, though, and he knew the serene nature of the nave and columns only served to emphasize the real pride of San Franceso a Ripa and the real reason to come here. The church was the final resting place of many wealthy and devout parishioners. Their memorials occupied the side chapels, where elaborate commissioned statuary commemorated their exemplary lives and their assured places in the world to come.

Seized with inspiration, Jorge slipped quietly over to, and up, the right-hand aisle, keeping his gaze on the side chapels opposite. Pietro was an art historian. The crowning glory of San Franceso a Ripa's funerary art was the chapel dedicated to Ludovica Albertoni. It depicted the deceased, surrounded by the heads of angels, at the moment of her departure from this life. To Jorge this work had always appeared more erotic than pious, more earthy than ethereal. He wasn't alone in thinking so, but no matter: the work was by Bernini, and in a church full of beautiful things, it stood head and shoulders above the rest.

And—obviously trying to elude him, because she'd changed into loose, cropped white pants, a white T-shirt, and a floppy canvas hat, and was carrying a different shoulder bag—Livia Pietro stood before it, looking up.

58

Five angels gazed out beyond their chapel and over the church, the joy on their faces inviting the congregation to share in the glory of Ludovica Albertoni's ascension to heaven. The sixth angel didn't join them; he was watching Ludovica as the ecstasy of what was happening filled and thrilled her.

"Here?" asked Thomas. "You're sure?"

"'Death throes? The pure puling of being born?'" Livia quoted. "This is Ludovica Albertoni at the moment of death. There's also always been a theory that it can be read as Saint Ann receiving the Immaculate Conception."

"Simultaneously?"

"He did that sort of thing, Bernini. And see there? 'Among the winged creatures . . . look down upon her face . . .' That one *putto*, he's the only one looking at her." As Thomas followed her pointing finger, she added, "Aren't they beautiful?"

They were, the light from Bernini's hidden window glowing on the angels' heads and on the tomb of the pious woman they were welcoming to paradise. Thomas didn't offer his critical assessment, though, asking instead, "If this is right, where could the poem be?"

Livia paused, then answered, "The only place I can think of is inside that head."

Thomas gazed skeptically at the sculpture. "But this was carved centuries before—"

"They're mounted on steel rods. The heads. They were made separately and installed once the sculpture was in place."

"They come off?"

"So I've read. I've never tried it." Still she didn't move, just stood gazing up at the flowing marble.

"Well?" Thomas said. "If that's where it is, shouldn't we go get it?" By "we" he meant she, and he was sure she knew it. She was clearly the better of the two of them at climbing on things.

Livia glanced around her. "I'm sorry. It's just . . . I'm always so taken with this work. You're right, of course. I'll need something to stand on. I wonder if there's a ladder in the sacristy—"

"What are you talking about? You can reach it from there."

"From where?" she said, so he pointed. Her eyes widened. "You can't be serious. Stand on a Bernini?"

Thomas stared at her. "You climbed onto Santa Teresa's altar. You stood on a collection box!"

Livia blinked. "But this is a Bernini."

They traded looks of mutual incomprehension. With a huffed breath, Thomas turned, approached the sculpture, and said to her, "Then this time you make the distraction." He took a quick look around. No one was near; this was the moment. Without waiting to see what Livia came up with, he slipped off his shoes, turned back to the beatified Ludovica and her angelic escort, grabbed a fold of her marble garment, and hoisted himself up.

59

Livia watched, appalled, as Thomas Kelly clambered across the supine marble body of Ludovica Albertoni to reach the angel head. On their way here, she and he had both made improvised efforts at disguise. She'd borrowed pants, a bag, and an *Io* ♥ *Nuova York* T-shirt from Ellen; she'd bought tiny round Yoko Ono sunglasses and braided and pinned up her hair under a floppy white canvas hat. Thomas had bought a *Roma* sweatshirt—black; he was still a priest—and a baseball cap. They'd both ditched their cells and bought new prepaid phones. Thomas had fought doing that, in case the Cardinal called him; when finally persuaded that their GPS chips were like neon signs ("Even when the phone is off?" "Yes, Father. Thomas. Yes, Thomas"), the first thing he did when he got the new phone was to call Lorenzo Cossa from it. And get no answer.

What all this meant was, Thomas Kelly wasn't wearing his clerical collar or tabbed shirt anymore. Crawling over the sculpture, he didn't even have that air of authority to separate him from a common vandal. Of course, climbing on a Bernini did just about make him a common vandal, so maybe any separation would've been beside the point. Livia wanted to shout at him to stop, to come down, to be careful, but she clamped her mouth shut: she certainly did not want to alert anyone else in the church to what was going on. A distraction. She needed to cause a distraction. She turned to leave the Albertoni chapel.

The distraction caused itself.

The Noantri clerk from the Library, Jorge Ocampo. The man who, according to Spencer, had killed the old monk. Jorge Ocampo stood right smack in front of her, grinning.

She'd barely registered his presence when he lunged for her. No, not for her. For her bag. He'd wrenched it off her shoulder before she realized what was happening. She reached for it, grabbing nothing but air. Holding the bag high, Ocampo spun away. Livia leapt and tackled him for the second time that day. They both went down, rolling, tangled in each other's clothes. Ocampo's sharp elbow slammed painfully into Livia's cheek. He stank of some disgusting cologne and was slimy with sweat; but though thin, he was strong and determined. She gave him a knee to the gut, tried to yank the bag back. His grip was like glue. He shoved her; her head smacked the chapel railing. She was stunned only for a second, less; but it was enough. Ocampo sprang to his feet and took off with her bag.

He collided, in the aisle, with a broad-shouldered, yellow-haired man.

Jonah.

Dumbfounded, Livia could only stare. Hallucination caused by concussion? Were hallucinations this detailed, carrying scent, glints of gold, the precise web of tiny wrinkles beside laughing eyes? For his part, Jonah, or his phantasm, had no time to acknowledge her presence or answer any of the thousand questions racing around in her head. Livia watched Ocampo try to shove Jonah aside, saw Jonah push back, then sweep his right fist into the clerk's chin and pump his left into his stomach. When Ocampo doubled over, Jonah grabbed the shoulder bag, but Ocampo held tight to the strap and punched Jonah's nose.

With a shout Thomas Kelly jumped from the sculpture to land beside her. He charged forward and grabbed the clerk's arm as Ocampo was pulling back for another blow. Ocampo spun around snarling and threw Thomas hard to the ground. He raised his leg to stomp Thomas's face. Thomas rolled; in that extra second Jonah slammed his fist into Ocampo's neck. The clerk staggered and loosened his grip on Livia's bag. Jonah yanked it away.

Livia suddenly realized that beyond all this chaos she could hear not only shouts and horrified screams, but sirens. They heralded the law; two officers burst into the church. She rose clumsily to her feet. Jonah, with a grin, tossed her her shoulder bag. He leaned down, helped Thomas up, and then yanked Ocampo to his feet, also. And socked him again. And then, instead of delivering a coup de grâce, he just stood, arms at his sides, and gave Ocampo an opening. The clerk couldn't resist. He threw a punch. Livia stood, openmouthed, until Thomas, shoes in one hand, grabbed her elbow with the other and dragged her down the aisle, saying, "Now that's what I call a distraction. Let's go."

60

The bread was nothing but crumbs, the *salumi* and *formaggio* gone. Giulio Aventino finished his coffee and signaled for another, and for a second for his sergeant, also. Raffaele Orsini drank *caffè macchiato*, into which he stirred sugar, producing a sweet, complicated drink. Giulio preferred the bitter simplicity of espresso. But that was Raffaele. Everything was multilayered and everything was for the best.

They sat at a café in the piazza opposite Santa Maria della Scala working the phones. Raffaele had been all for dashing out into the streets immediately, but Giulio had suggested mildly that they might do better if they knew which direction to dash in. Carabinieri and *polizia* all over Rome were on the lookout for the suspect, that Vatican Library clerk, and for his associates. Since Giulio and Raffaele both had street sources they cultivated for exactly this type of situation, why not explore whatever assistance the criminal underworld might be able to offer?

Before they'd settled in to run through their contact lists—Giulio wondered if Raffaele had a subfolder labeled "informant" on his cell phone, organized alphabetically or perhaps by specialty—Giulio had called the *maresciallo* to give him a report.

"The Curia's not happy, Aventino," the boss had said darkly.

Giulio stopped himself from asking why a holy friar gaining admission to heaven should displease the Vatican, saying instead, "We're doing what we can."

"Do it faster. Is the Gendarme any use? Or is he in the way? I could get him called off."

"No, don't. I think he's worth having around. But what you could do is tell Central to alert me to any odd goings-on in a church anywhere in the city."

If anyone else had spoken that way, the *maresciallo* would probably have reminded him who was boss. Giulio could hear the gritted teeth as he asked, "Why? Is something else about to happen?"

"I have no idea. Just a feeling."

The *maresciallo* allowed himself a snort, but Giulio didn't care and they both knew that.

"All right, but be judicious in what you respond to. I don't want you to waste your time on wild-goose chases."

"Oh? Well, in that case, we won't." Giulio clicked off.

The Gendarme, Luigi Esposito, had gone off on his own. He wasn't under Giulio's command, so Giulio couldn't stop him. Esposito had told them his own sources were better consulted in person. That could be true, but Giulio suspected the young man was just plain excited at the prospect of spending his time on the bustling workaday streets of Rome, instead of the sedate corridors and tourist-choked public rooms of the Holy See.

Giulio himself would have gone out of his mind there.

He'd admonished Raffaele when the sergeant had snickered at the news a Gendarme was coming to join them, but in the pecking order of Roman law enforcement there was no question the Gendarmerie was at the bottom. The Rome *polizia* crowded the middle step, as local lawmen did everywhere in Italy: clumsy, slow-moving bureaucracies at best, or in some places, corrupt and dangerous. The constabulary pinnacle, of course, was occupied by the Carabinieri. A branch of the Italian military, they were well trained and well armed, charged with fighting crime all over the country and occasionally overseas: on any given day you could find Carabinieri on secondment to other nations, and to international agencies; and Carabinieri had been called up for, and had died in, service in the Middle East. Giulio himself had served in Africa, many years ago, and he knew this about his partner: as devoted as Raffaele was to his job and his young family, if called up he'd go proudly. And acquit himself well, Giulio had no doubt. For all Raffaele's religious piety, Giulio had long suspected devotion to duty—to his family, to his job, to his country, and yes, to his Church—was Raffaele's real faith.

Giulio's own faith was simple: that he loved his wife and kids, and they were worth loving; that he was good at his job, and his job was worth doing. Anything else— the next life, or the one after that—would have to take care of itself.

What Luigi Esposito was devoted to, Giulio didn't know. But the young Gendarme had impressed Giulio with his energy, pleased him with his thoroughness, and more or less convinced him with his theory. More or less because hard evidence was the only thing that ever convinced Giulio Aventino of anything. But Esposito's stolen-art-ring idea intrigued him, and tentatively answered some otherwise confounding questions: What had gone on this morning at the Vatican Library? How was it connected to what had happened at Santa Maria della Scala? And why had Raffaele's cardinal uncle requested a surveillance of *Professoressa* Livia Pietro?

That last would have been easier to answer if the cardinal uncle would answer his cell phone, but even his secretary, Father Ateba, when reached at the Vatican, had no idea where Lorenzo Cossa might be.

Giulio nodded his thanks as the new coffees were delivered and dialed the next source on his list, the owner of a fine-art framing shop whom Giulio was sure, but had never tried hard to prove, had a sideline in forged Old Masters. The shop owner was grateful for Giulio's lack of diligence, and Giulio had long since calculated that the man's value as an informant vastly outweighed any potential gain from shutting down his operation, which, after all, only made fools of people drooling after bargains anyone without larceny in his heart would recognize as too good to be true. On this occasion the shop owner had nothing to add, though, beyond promising to contact Giulio immediately should the street start buzzing with tales of audacious, highly professional art thieves.

Giulio thumbed off the phone and grunted. "That makes seven," he said to Raffaele, whose phone was likewise temporarily idle. "And they all claim they haven't heard a thing. You finding anything?"

"*Niente di niente.* I'm beginning to wonder if Esposito's wrong. Or are these people just really good?"

"I've never known Roman crooks to be adept at hiding their traces."

"Well, only one of these three is even Italian."

"Supporting Esposito's international-gang theory.

Though you might expect Interpol would've had something on them, then." Which Esposito had said they didn't. The young Gendarme had searched the relevant databases—interesting to find someone so apparently techno-savvy in those hidebound holy halls—and found nothing. Giulio himself, a Luddite—nothing to be proud of but he was too old to change—had done some old-fashioned research: he'd called a friend, Paolo Lucca, who'd been promoted out of general larceny to the elite Nucleo Tutela Patrimonio Artistico, the Carabinieri's own stolen art bureau. Paolo was no help: none of the suspects were known to Il Nucleo. He was interested, but the only actual theft had occurred at the Vatican, outside Carabinieri jurisdiction. He'd promised to sniff around, and also, at Giulio's request, to look into unsolved cases involving Church-related art anywhere in the country.

"Around the world, come to that," Giulio told him. "These people may be new to Italy. You're buddy-buddy with the hotshots at Interpol, I assume."

"I thought you said you'd already checked with them."

"Checked their database. The Gendarme did. But—"

"But he doesn't know anyone over there and you're afraid if he calls them they won't give him the time of day."

"Am I wrong?"

"No. They're worse than we are. Though I have to admit, the last Gendarme I worked with was a bona fide idiot."

"This kid's sharp, Paolo. He's wasted over there."

Giulio sat back now and sipped his coffee. "I wonder what the point is."

Raffaele looked up. "Point of what?"

"These particular thefts. They've obviously got a specific agenda. And they're in a hurry."

"That could just be because they screwed up this morning and now they're exposed."

"Then why didn't they lay low for a while instead of heading over here? I wish I knew what they were looking for. A notebook from the Vatican Library, some target in the Reliquary Chapel . . ."

"Monsignor Conti said nothing was missing."

"That only means they failed. Possibly because they didn't want that irritating historian to know what they were up to and they couldn't get him to leave."

Raffaele grinned. "If that's it, I sympathize with them."

"What is it they're doing, Raffaele?" Giulio leaned back, staring at the sky. "What's the connection? Come on, you're the church guy. What do you see?"

"Nothing," Raffaele admitted. "But I wonder if they do."

"If they do what?"

"See the connection. Maybe all they have is a list."

Giulio was silent for a moment. "They're working for someone."

Raffaele noddded. "Not just theft, theft to order. For a client who doesn't want to wait."

"All right. I'll buy it. But that just makes the question: What's the client after?"

"I wonder," Raffaele said, "if the client's impatient enough—or important enough—that they're willing to risk going on now. Accident or not, they did kill someone."

From the table beside his coffee, Giulio's cell phone rang.

"*Ispettore*, this is Dispatch," a woman's voice said. "We've just sent two officers to a fight inside San Francesco a Ripa. There was a bulletin asking that you be alerted to—"

"Yes. Hold on." Giulio looked over at Raffaele. "San Francesco a Ripa. Close, right?" Raffaele nodded. "Thank you," Giulio told Dispatch.

He was about to click off when she said, "*Ispettore*? I have another report here, from an hour ago, before your bulletin came in. I didn't handle the call but when I saw what you wanted I looked back through our files just in case. There was a disturbance in Santa Maria in Trastevere. Nothing seems to be missing but our reports are that a woman stood on the collection box and opened the aumbry. Were you told about that?"

"No. Opened the what?"

"The aumbry, it says. I don't know either."

"But nothing's missing?"

"According to the priests, no."

"Thank you. Good work." By the time he said, "Keep me updated," he'd jumped up and dropped ten euros on the table. To Raffaele he shouted over his shoulder, "My car's closest. Call Esposito." They took off across the piazza, reached the Fiat, and yanked open the doors at the same moment. Raffaele was poking buttons on his cell phone as they climbed into the car. Giulio fired the engine and peeled out. To Raffaele, holding the phone between ear and shoulder and struggling to buckle his seat belt, Giulio added, "And what's an aumbry?"

61

◦

Livia Pietro tripped. Thomas, his heart pounding, had
to grab her to keep her from falling as they ran down San
Francesco a Ripa's center aisle. She kept turning to look
back; you'd think she'd never seen a fight before. He surveyed the narthex as they neared it. No one there but
horrified tourists. The two officers were charging down
the left aisle toward the Albertoni chapel, where the
clerk and the other man were still brawling. He and
Livia could make it out the door. Gripping her arm, he
tried to pull her along, but she dug in her heels and said,
"No!"

"No, what?"

"We can't leave."

"You made me leave Santa Maria della Scala, and you
were right! This is the same. We can't stay here. There's
nothing we can—"

"That's not what I mean. There are more police coming. I can hear them. They'll be pulling into the piazza
any second."

As if to prove her words, the wail of a siren and the
screech of brakes reached Thomas. Livia, with a look of
longing, had turned back toward the fight, which had
expanded: now both the clerk—Ocampo, was that his
name?—and the blond man were mixing it up with the

officers. Thomas tightened his grip on her arm. He stared around desperately, then said, "Come this way!"

The Catholic Church had, over the centuries, evolved many different practices for the administration of its sacraments, and reasons and explanations abounded for each choice. The sacrament of confession, for example: some theologians thought it best that the penitent's side of the confessional be open, with neither door nor drape. Thus the entire congregation could see a fellow believer offer contrition for his sins and seek absolution. They could be a support for him, he an example to them. There was an argument to be made in that direction, to be sure. Right now, however, Thomas was unutterably relieved that the designers of the ecclesiastical furnishings in San Francesco a Ripa had not shared this approach.

He hauled Livia down the center aisle toward the entrance and then over to the other side of the nave, about as far from the action as they could get. A confessional nestled between two chapels in the side aisle. The booth was of a weighty Baroque style, both priest and penitent hidden behind heavily carved wooden doors. Pulling open the penitent's side, he told Livia, "Get in!" and then, since she seemed frozen, casting yet another look at the scuffling men, he shoved her inside and shut the door on her. **Ah, Thomas, now we're forcing reluctant sinners into the confessional?** He yanked open the other door, jumped in, and pulled it to. Sitting on the narrow bench, he slid the panel, revealing the screen between them.

"What's going on?" he whispered as he pulled his shoes on. When she didn't answer he demanded, "The clerk—that was Ocampo, right?"

"Yes." Livia's own whisper was hoarse. "And Jonah."

"Jonah? Who, the blond man? I thought that was just a Good Samaritan helping you."

"No. Jonah."

"The man—the . . . Noantri—who started all this? The one you're looking for?"

He started to rise but she said, "Don't. Listen, you can hear it. They're both gone."

Now her voice only sounded sad. He paused, and listened, and found she was right. He heard shouts and clamoring voices, people vying to tell their versions of what they'd seen, what they'd heard. Other voices tried to calm things down, sort them out. Nothing sounded like thrown punches, kicks, flesh striking flesh.

"How do you know they're gone? Not just arrested?"

"Their footsteps when they ran."

"You heard them?"

Wearily, she said, "Of course."

Of course. Thomas sat back down. His skin felt oddly flushed and his heart still beat rapidly as he said, "What *happened*?"

"I don't know. I turned and he was there. Ocampo. He must still be after the notebook because he grabbed my bag."

"How did he find us?"

"I'm not sure. He might have caught my scent."

"Caught your—" Thomas realized that through the confessional screen he was catching her scent, too. Or perhaps not hers—he was human, after all—but the perfume she wore: a deep, gentle fragrance, as of a tropical garden where night flowers bloomed. "All right, fine!" He shook his head to clear it. "And this Jonah? How did *he* find us?"

"I don't know that, either. Or why. He must know what I've been told to do. And that the Conclave is prepared to . . . do it, if I fail. Why doesn't he just stay out of sight?"

"Are they working together?"

"Jonah and Ocampo? You mean, because they're both Noantri? If they are that's some show they just put on." She seemed to rouse herself, her voice beyond the screen taking on a sharper note.

Many questions elbowed one another in Thomas's head, about Jonah, about Livia, about the Noantri; and he felt he didn't want to ask them here, through the confessional screen. He wanted to see her face, look into her eyes. But another question had to be answered first. "Where are the police?"

"What?"

"Use your supersonic hearing! Are they still here?"

For a moment, silence from the other side of the screen. Then, "Yes. More of them. The two officers we saw, and also the man who called for the ambulance in Santa Maria della Scala. He's with someone else. And the Gendarme! From the Colosseum station, I think he's here, too." She drew a sharp breath. "Two of them are heading this way."

"All right," Thomas said. He tried to ignore the odd sensations he was feeling, tried to concentrate on the immediate problem. "Do you remember how this goes?"

"How what goes?"

"Confession. 'Bless me, Father, for I have sinned'? You said you were raised a Catholic. Or is even the memory of that something you've dispensed with?"

"Would you absolve a Noantri if one came to you?" she snapped. "Though in fact you probably have, more than once." Without giving him a chance to answer she intoned, *"Mi benedica, Padre, perché ho peccato."*

She didn't go on, so in soft, droning Italian, which he hoped was quiet enough to barely be heard by, and accentless enough to convince, any passing policeman, Thomas replied with the prompt. "How long has it been, my child, since your last confession?"

A pause; then, "Ninety-six years."

Thomas tried to swallow the choking sound he found himself making. He wasn't sure what to say, but this time, she didn't stop.

"I don't repent of the life I've lived or am living," she said, speaking low. "I'm aware that you think I should— the Unchanged have always thought so—but that belief is born from fear and ignorance."

Thomas started to protest, but was she that wrong? What did he know about her life—their life, these No-antri? And wasn't he, in fact, afraid? He said nothing, only listened as she went on. As, it occurred to him, a priest in a confessional is supposed to do.

"But I committed a great sin, and it's led to others," she said, drawing a slow breath. "I loved a man who wasn't mine to love. Without permission I brought him into my Community. We both could have been expelled, but instead the Community welcomed him. Now he's threatening to destroy it."

At a sound, Thomas glanced through the metal grill-work on the confessional door. The tiny holes that formed a cross showed him two men moving slowly up the aisle in their direction.

"This man you loved." Something inside him resented saying those words; what was wrong with him?

They had to keep talking, so he continued, "His actions aren't your fault."

"He's my responsibility. Because I brought him to us. It's one of our Laws. What's worse is, I've been ordered to stop him but I fear that I can't."

"Failure is never a sin."

"Failure to try, though? To do what's right? When it comes to it, I'm afraid I'll let him go. In fact I already did, just now. Instead of . . ." She trailed off.

Thomas paused, as understanding dawned. "Instead of killing him? Is that what you've been ordered to do?"

"It might be necessary."

"To take his life? How could failure to take a life ever be construed as a sin?" He frowned as another question came to him. "Wait. He's— How could that even be done? Throw him on a bonfire? Burn him at the stake?" Would she really do that? Just when he'd begun to think—

"No," she whispered. "There's another way."

"To destroy you? You people, I mean?"

With a faint trace of amusement in her voice she answered, "I'm glad you qualified that. Yes. I—"

She stopped for a moment. He glanced through the door panel. The men walking down the aisle were coming close.

"Don't speak," he said to Livia. "Just let me do this. We'll be fine."

62

————◦————

". . . in San Francesco a Ripa," Giulio Aventino was telling the *maresciallo*. Raffaele signaled him to keep his voice down—they were standing by an occupied confessional—but all Giulio did was walk a few steps farther down the aisle. They'd come over here for a little peace and quiet. Though the Carabinieri had finished their questioning, tourists and worshippers still milled around by the Albertoni chapel, each offering his own account and disputing the others. If past experience was anything to go on—and in police work, it always was—Raffaele knew the fight was growing in duration and danger with each retelling. By the time the story was told over this afternoon's coffee or tonight's red wine, there would have been knives, brass knuckles, and blood all over the Bernini. Meanwhile, the actual altercation had been over so fast that officers questioning tourists who'd been over here on the right side of the church had found that some hadn't even been aware of the fight and none had seen it.

"Over by the time we got here," Giulio was saying. "It seems to have been a purse-snatching. A tourist. No, some Good Samaritan stopped it. That was the fight. But the point is, the witness descriptions of the snatcher fit our suspect. There's a possibility here that he's just some kind of anticlerical nut job." **Which was funny,**

Raffaele thought, **coming from Giulio.** "Yes, you're absolutely right, sir. It would've been easier to know what he's up to if we'd laid our hands on him. You might ask the officers why they let him get away, once they're out of the hospital." Giulio rolled his eyes at Raffaele. "The Good Samaritan took off after him. Yes, of course we need to keep the search going, but I still think meanwhile— No, I'm not suggesting you provide protection to every church in Rome. Sir. Just to warn them. Yes. All right. Well, it might, but false alarms are better than another death, don't you think? Unless the Vatican doesn't care that we—" He held the phone away from his ear; Raffaele heard the *maresciallo* sputtering something about Giulio going too far. Giulio brought the phone back and sighed, "Yes. What? Yes, Esposito's his name, and yes, he's here, too. No, why? As long as they let him stay, I can use him. Yes. We will. No, we haven't, but we're trying. Thank you. Sir."

As Giulio sighed and pocketed the phone, Raffaele said, "He's not happy?"

"Have you ever known him happy? He wanted this wrapped up and it just gets worse. Come on, I need a smoke."

As the priest in the confessional continued to assign penance—judging from the length of the list, this was a prodigal with a wide gulf of time since his or her last confession and an impressive collection of sins—Raffaele and Giulio walked up the aisle and left the church, emerging into the bright autumn afternoon.

"Raffaele," Giulio said, cupping a Marlboro to light it, "you think we're wrong? Esposito's wrong? That this has nothing to do with stolen art, it really is just some lunatic with a grudge against the Church?"

"Lunatic? I've heard you use much more flattering words about people who feel that way."

"Be serious."

"You mean, is this just a wacko trying to create havoc, no worries about killing if someone gets in the way?"

Giulio nodded and blew a stream of smoke. "Il Nucleo, Interpol, all those bright bulbs, they never heard of this gang. It's the simplest explanation: there is no gang."

"I guess it's possible. But it doesn't explain what Cardinal Cossa wanted with Livia Pietro."

"The boss asked whether we'd reached him. Try him again." While Raffaele took out his phone, Giulio went on, "Maybe this guy's stalking Pietro because she's part of whatever fantasy he's working from. Maybe he has a particular thing about her and Cossa knew it, and wanted you to keep an eye on her to protect her? Or as a way to catch him? That tourist whose purse he went for has her general build, from what the witnesses say."

"Why didn't the Cardinal tell me that, then? I wish that tourist had hung around. She might be able to tell us something."

"Would you stay knowing you'd be wasting your next hour with us? If you weren't hurt and hadn't lost anything?"

"It would've been the right thing to do," Raffaele stoutly maintained. Giulio gave him the over-the-eyeglasses look, and Raffaele admitted, "But if I didn't do it, what I would probably do is head for the nearest café to calm my nerves."

"Hmm. Or wine bar."

While Raffaele dialed his uncle, Giulio dialed Dispatch, asking them to start a search for the intended victim in the cafés and wine bars near San Francesco a

Ripa. Raffaele waited until Giulio lowered his phone to say, "Voice mail. So you're thinking that Pietro—and the priest she was with—aren't involved in anything? That there's nothing to be involved in, just some nut?"

Giulio narrowed his eyes at Raffaele through the smoke from his cigarette. "No," he said after a pause. "No. It makes sense and it's simple, but no, I still think something bigger's going on here."

"Good." Raffaele grinned. "So do I. Look, here's Esposito."

63

"You can stop," Livia said, as Thomas droned on about Hail Marys and Our Fathers. "They're gone."

He did stop, and silence filled the confessional. In truth, Livia was grateful. She'd been growing oddly uncomfortable. The need for penance was something she felt acutely, and she was experiencing more than a touch of regret for the days—so long ago—when she believed some prayers and a few good deeds could wipe a slate clean.

"We'll have to wait before we go back," she said. "The Carabinieri are still outside. On the steps."

"Go back where?"

"To look for the poem, of course. Though this time we'll get a ladder. I'm not going to let you climb on the Bernini again."

"Don't worry about it."

"No, I'm serious. Shoes or no shoes, there's no—"

"I mean, don't worry, no one's going to climb on anything. I have it."

"You have— You found it? The poem?"

"That head was heavy, too." She could swear she heard him grinning. "I lifted it off and the sheet of paper was wrapped around the iron bar. It's a little rusty but I think it's readable. I put the head back, by the way."

"I should hope so! Read it to me."

"How about, 'Good work, Father Kelly'?"

"Good work, Father Kelly. Now read it to me!"

64

Through the confessional screen, Thomas read to Livia the poem he'd found inside the angel's head.

Ar penitente, quann'è arivato, ce vo' er zonno.
J'ammolla la dorce machina lì su la roccia
lisscia com'un guanciale, ppoi casca fonno
frammezzo a 'n zzoggno: du' lupi rampanti, 'na
    bboccia
granne ch'aribolle . . . E la nostra compaggnia ce stà
    'ntorno.

The penitent, at journey's end, needs sleep.
He lays the sweet machine upon the stone
that's smooth enough for pillow, falls to deep
dreaming: two gray wolves rampant, a cauldron . . .
And dreams lead to the company we keep.

"And there are more penciled letters. A M A E E. They're spread weirdly far apart, but they're here. And there's the *a*." Thomas had to force himself to keep his voice down. "The missing *a* from *aedificavit*. There it is."

"If you're right, maybe the next three letters—I mean, the three before, reading right to left—are *eam*. 'It.' 'Built it.'"

"All right, but who built what?"

"That other *e*—it must be part of another word. When we find the next poem, it will tell us."

It was oddly thrilling, he thought. Collaboration. Working with her to solve this puzzle. Building on each other's work, correcting, suggesting, adding. Up until now, all his scholarly work had been done alone. He taught, yes, and so was not lonely; but it was different with students. This joy of teamwork, of equals sparking off each other—he was feeling now an excitement he hadn't felt in years.

Which must be what explained his quickened heartbeat, the tingling in his skin.

"All right," he said. "I think the coast is clear. Let's go."

"Go where?"

"Upstairs, of course."

"Upstairs where?"

He was taken aback. "Really? You don't know? This one's so easy."

65

Luigi Esposito was delighted. He supposed he shouldn't have been, since the case had no breaks yet, but the Carabinieri were treating him like an equal—like a cop!—and he'd been right about that repellent Argentinian clerk. All a mistake, faulty alarm system, hogwash. It was like breathing fresh mountain air, to be working out here in the real world, where investigating crime was more important than maintaining decorum.

And Luigi had an idea.

He'd arrived at San Francesco a Ripa at almost the same moment as *Ispettore* Aventino and his sergeant, Orsini, which meant none of them had seen the purse-snatching, the fight, or the suspect blasting out of the church with the Good Samaritan after him. They found the two damaged officers groaning on the marble floor inside. Both the suspect and his pursuer, apparently, went flying across the piazza and disappeared up Via di San Francesco a Ripa. The suspect, from witness reports, was pulling ahead, which probably meant the Good Samaritan eventually gave up, patted himself on the back for the rescue, and went about his business. Carabinieri and *polizia* were out combing the area for the suspect; but they'd done that before, after he escaped from Santa Maria della Scala, and hadn't found a trace. Aventino had requested a bulletin go out to the churches of Rome, ostensibly a warning because the suspect was dangerous. Luigi had caught on, though, and was impressed: the *ispettore*, with that one move, had provided them with many thousands more eyes.

Luigi, though, was interested in a specific set of eyes.

He stood with Aventino and Orsini on the church steps near one of the potted palms, he and Aventino smoking, Orsini scanning the piazza. The sergeant was a man who was in his element in this job, Luigi thought. As he himself would be, if the job were his. They had finished interviewing everyone willing to stay and be interviewed—and everyone who thought they'd slink out the doors; because while the Carabinieri had worked the inside, Luigi, with the help of an officer he'd been lent (a uniformed officer with a brain! *Miracoloso!*) had ambushed the slinkers. Afterward, they'd compared notes. The Carabinieri had told Luigi about the ruckus with the aumbry in Santa Maria in Trastevere, and though it wasn't clear whether it was the same cast of characters involved in that one, they all agreed: the Vatican Library and three churches in the same day meant something big was going on.

"The historian," Luigi said. "I want to go back and talk to him."

Aventino squinted through the smoke from his cigarette. "The Englishman? Spencer George? We grilled him pretty thoroughly. You just caught the end."

"So you're satisfied he has nothing to do with this?"

"I'm never satisfied. We've got people watching him. I just don't have anything new to ask him yet."

"I'd like to try."

Orsini grinned. "A hunch?"

Luigi felt his face grow hot. "Not really, I—"

The *ispettore* shrugged. "Good cops play their hunches. Let us know what you find out."

"Yes, sir!" Luigi, thrilled to be just another cop on a case, playing a hunch, entrusted with the interrogation of a suspect under surveillance, loped to his car. Five minutes later he was back in Piazza della Scala, parking opposite Spencer George's door. He banged the bronze lion knocker and saw the curtain move aside in the upstairs window. For a moment he wondered what he'd do if the historian didn't let him in. He had no authority outside the Holy See, and even if he'd had, a citizen was under no obligation to speak to anyone in law enforcement unless he was under arrest. Or then, either, come to think of it: that's what lawyers were for.

But the door opened and Spencer George stood there, his expression as haughtily bored as it had been when he'd sat on the church pew a few hours ago. **Did his face ever change,** Luigi wondered, **or was this sneer permanent?** He was about to introduce himself when the historian spoke.

"Well. The gentleman from the Gendarmerie. Presumably you're here to ask yet more tiresome questions. I'd hope your position would create in you greater reserves of humility and courtesy than that of your secular peers, but I doubt it does. At least let's be comfortable. Please, come in."

66

Anna's blood started to boil.

Jorge had left the theater. She could tell by sniffing the air when she dropped in the open window: his scent was faded, dissipating in the musty room. She stared around her, picking out, in the dark, all the details Mortal eyes would have needed assistance to see. What was it about this place, Il Pasquino? Why had Jorge chosen to hide here? Dust, mold, and spiderwebs; torn curtains and bubbling plaster. Another object once valuable, now discarded, discounted, by myopic Mortals who found no worth in what they couldn't use right that instant. This had been a beautiful place once, she could tell, before it was chopped up, then closed and allowed to rot. Sleek art deco lines, comfortable wooden-armed seats, even a retractable roof. A place to relax and be transported to someone else's fantasy, where you'd be safe for an hour or two.

Maybe after she and her followers were successful and Noantri rule was established over a peaceful—a pacified—world, she'd reopen this theater. She'd name it after Jorge, she thought, smiling. L'Ocampo. He'd like that.

Too bad he wouldn't be around to see it.

◄○►

67

"Ignatius Loyola revered Saint Francis. Ignatius was the son of a noble family whose crest was two gray wolves, rampant, and a cauldron. And of course the wolf is associated with Francis, also." Thomas spoke rapidly, and had fallen back into university lecturer mode, Livia noted, as he led the way up the stone staircase to the left of the altar. To reach these stairs they'd had to cut through the sacristy. Livia had regretted Thomas's lack of ecclesiastical dress at that point, as she had when they left the confessional. She wasn't sure the priests and monks at San Francesco a Ripa would be pleased to see some guy in a sweatshirt climbing out of the box; but speaking through the screen, Thomas had brushed off her worry. "It's not an issue. There's no law about what I wear when. Anyway, my passport photo shows the full regalia. If anyone asks I'll tell them I'm on vacation, we were out sightseeing, and you were overcome with an urge to confess as soon as we walked in here. Believe me, they'll be thrilled." He paused. "I'll be lying, but they'll be thrilled."

"Lying? What about all the things I just told you?"

"We had to keep talking. You had to say something."

"I could have said lots of other things."

He was silent for a moment. "I'm sorry. I don't . . . I didn't . . . even if you were—"

"Oh, never mind. Father. We have work to do. Let's go."

As it happened, they weren't challenged leaving the confessional, or in the sacristy, or on their way up the stone stairway. A number of priests and monks could be seen in the aisles of the church itself, trying to restore tranquillity after the recent excitement. No one noticed Thomas and Livia making their calm way toward the altar. Of course, the two of them did—calmly—stick to as many shadows as they could find.

"Before he founded the Jesuit order—my order—Ignatius made a number of pilgrimages to sites associated with Francis. Including here." Thomas sounded odd to Livia. A peculiar note had found its way into his voice in the confessional, and she could still hear it now. And why was he going on about Ignatius Loyola and Francis? Was he offering what he had to offer—knowledge—as some sort of apology for accusing her of tendering meaningless words just so there would be something for the Carabinieri to hear? Although, to be honest, the raw truth of what she'd said had surprised her, too. Or was Thomas trying to convince her his deciphering of the poem had been correct? Why work so hard? She believed him, or at least, believed him enough to follow where that deciphering led and see if he was right. Still, he kept talking. "This was a Benedictine monastery church when Francis came here, on his visits to Rome to petition the Pope—Innocent the Third—to authorize his new order. He lodged in a tiny cell up these stairs. Nearly three centuries later Ignatius Loyola made a pilgrimage here, asking and receiving permission to sleep in the same room."

He stopped as they reached a small landing at the top.

Before them stood a wrought-iron gate, its lines and curlicues allowing a clear view, but no access, to the room beyond. Thomas stepped aside, motioning to the lock. He folded his hands and waited.

He'd certainly gotten used to this process fast, Livia thought, taking out her pick and shim. She didn't call him on it, though, saying instead, "How do you know this is where we're supposed to be? If Ignatius made all those pilgrimages to all those sites?"

"I made this particular one myself, my first time in Rome."

That wasn't actually enlightening, but Livia said nothing, concentrating on the lock. It was at least a century old, which meant her tools were almost too delicate for it, but after thirty seconds of careful work—the faint resistance of tumblers against her fingertips was her guide—she heard it click open. Swinging the gate aside, she stepped into the room. She almost brushed against Thomas on the narrow landing, but he drew back, pressing himself into the stone wall.

"I thought we were past that," she said.

"Past what?"

"You being afraid to touch me."

"I . . . I'm not . . ."

The oddness of his voice made her turn to face him. She saw his flushed cheeks, his wide pupils, and finally she understood.

"It's all right," she said quietly. "It's natural, in a way you don't know."

"What are you talking about? What is?" he croaked.

She stepped back, put more space between them. "Your desire."

"My *what*?"

"Father. You're a priest, but you're a man. I'm Noantri and I'm a woman. What you're feeling right now—" She stopped, looking for the right words. "Our bodies— Noantri bodies—exert a pull on the Unchanged. When I saw Jonah just now, everything I felt for him . . . You couldn't help but sense it, and it made you—" The dismay on his face was so total Livia understood three things: she was right; as funny as he looked, she mustn't laugh; and they'd better get back to work before he ran away again.

68

◄○►

In stunned disbelief, Thomas watched Livia step into Saint Francis's cell, into the room where that most pious and self-denying of saints had prayed and slept. The horror he felt was not because such an unnatural creature as she was defiling these hallowed stones. Exactly the opposite: it was partly because he realized he'd led her here with no hesitation, no disquiet whatsoever. Worse: with a sense of pride and pleasure. Showing off his cleverness, his erudition. To a Noantri? When had he become so cavalier about who she was, what she was?

And the other cause of his horror was the knowledge that she was right.

The rapid heartbeat, the tingling. The inability to stop talking, to be too near her, to look at her. How many ways, he wondered, could he deceive himself?

He'd felt desire before; of course he had. If ordination meant the end of human frailty, there would be no need for vows. He'd felt it, not acted upon it, confessed, and been absolved. Was what was happening now so different?

Yes.

It was stronger, richer, deeper. More immediate, more propulsive. Though he stood two yards from her, his fingertips could feel the silk of her skin, his palms the wildness her hair would offer if, as his hands longed to do, they reached to unfasten her braid. Her scent, that night-blooming jungle, permeated his senses, and every movement she made, every swing of hip or sweep of arm, arrested his gaze. He longed for her. He'd hidden this truth from himself behind a meandering excursus about Saint Ignatius Loyola; but now she'd said it, and he couldn't deny it. And to whom could he confess it? What would he even say? That he, who had vowed to yield to no such wordly hunger, now ached for the touch of a creature not even of this world, a being with no soul and no place in the afterlife?

And how could he confess it, until he really, truly, felt it was wrong?

Ignatius Loyola, who had stood in this very room, had founded an order based on intellectual rigor and natural law. Thomas had joined that order with joy. His life thus far had been spent fearlessly pursuing the truth, confident that the light of reason would chase away the shadows of superstition and ignorance. His Church had agreed, maintaining that belief in the supernatural was error and—even when, in former times of ignorance, indulged in by the Church itself—had ever been so. God's mystical nature and his miracles were one thing, not to be rationally understood; but demons, succubae, and other such creatures were mere metaphors, images useful to reveal the evil in all of us.

But here he was, Father Thomas Kelly, standing in Saint Francis's cell with one of those creatures, yearning for her touch.

Her claim, of course, was that her people were not supernatural, just humans with a virus in the blood. Maybe so, but that didn't change another fundamental point. The Church had always known about the Noan-tri. For centuries it had hunted them. That path, brutal as it was, made sense in the days of irrational belief. Then—still in those days—Martin the Fifth suddenly signed a document that began six hundred years of si-multaneously trafficking with the Noantri, and denying their existence. Six hundred years during which the Church had maintained a position it knew to be false.

What else, then, was false?

The efficacy of confession?

The sanctity of the Host?

The need for priestly celibacy?

An old familiar voice, one he'd thought he'd never hear again, came whispering back to him now.

Thomas—really?

69

Her back to Thomas, Livia stood facing the polished wood and painted saints of the tall altarpiece in Saint Francis's otherwise stark cell. She bit her lip to keep from speaking, planted her feet so she'd stay still, so she wouldn't spin around and demand that Thomas tell her why they were here and how to find the next poem. The priest was teetering on a narrow ledge, she sensed. And so was she.

She'd hidden it from herself behind the immediacy of effort: slipping from the confessional, working their way through the shadows to the sacristy, picking the lock. Listening to Thomas's discourse on saints and holy orders. Worrying about the oddness she sensed in him. Now, in the silence of the stone cell, she could no longer deny it.

Seeing Jonah, his grin and his broad shoulders, smelling his sweat, hearing his laugh, had thrown her into a cyclone of confusion.

She'd thought, for so long, that all that was behind her. Jonah had left her long ago. On a gray autumn afternoon, the entire world outside the windows dispirited, he'd gazed into her eyes across a gulf of disappointment, saying sadly that he could see she wouldn't change. That she'd always be content to follow the rules, to live in the past, to hide her Blessings and mimic the mediocrity of the Unchanged around her. The necessity of that, he said, had ended long ago, and he'd tried every way he could think of to show her he was right; but he realized now that she'd never understand. She was afraid, or she was comfortable, or she was uninterested in a longer, broader view of the world; whatever the chains that were holding her back, he couldn't let them bind him, too. The future was calling him forward, he said, and he kissed her and turned away.

She'd thought then that she'd understood who and what he was. She'd mourned their love, staggered under a weight of loss and guilt, but she'd come back to Italy, to Rome, and started life anew. Through the years since, she hadn't seen him. She hadn't heard from him, or even about him. She'd lived each day still believing she was right and he was wrong. Believing that over the years, as he deepened in understanding of the life he now had, the life of her people, he'd come to realize that.

It would be too late for them then, was too late for them from the moment he strode out the door without looking back, leaving her in the chill of a dusk that came too early. Her victory would be hollow, so personally meaningless that she never thought of it as a victory at all. But she did feel comfort imagining Jonah settling into a rich, fruitful Noantri life. Picturing him some-where back at his work, studying, exploring, endlessly immersed in beauty: it was their love of art that had brought them together, had given rise to their love of each other. She'd hoped he'd think of her now and then, and that the memory would be a warm one.

But now, suddenly, frighteningly, she wondered.

It was the confessional that had opened the floodgate of her questions, not what she'd said to Thomas as much as the small dark booth itself. Hiding behind a heavy door, concealing herself in fear—this was the Noantri life. This was the life the Concordat had brought about. Yes, and Community; yes, and assimilation, which brought with it the gift of normal days, of street corner cafés and neighbors who knew her, students to teach and a house to maintain. And friendship, people she loved among both Noantri and Unchanged.

But would all this not still be possible if the Noantri Unveiled?

Maybe Jonah was right. Maybe science was ready to lead the way to Unchanged acceptance of her people, once they were understood to be no threat; and maybe the fear she and every Noantri now felt, not of discovery by the Unchanged as in the days Before, but of the wrath of the Conclave, could be banished forever.

Facing the altarpiece, Livia could not shake off this new idea: that she could find Jonah and tell him she understood now and was ready to join him. That she could disobey the Conclave. Jonah—she knew this from the look she'd just seen in his eyes—would embrace her. He would publish the contents of the Concordat. The Noantri would Unveil, and a new day would begin.

The outlines of that new day, just starting to emerge from the swirl of sensations she was feeling, were shattered by a loud pop.

Before her, the saints on the tall painted panels began to move. She stepped back in instinctive alarm as, with piercing creaks, the panels slowly rotated, vanishing into the altarpiece. The low light in the cell bounced off a moving forest of gold, silver, and glass, which slowed and came to a stop facing her: reliquaries, dozens of them, hidden behind what she hadn't even known were doors.

70

"What . . . ," Livia sputtered. "How did you . . . ?"

"I told you," Thomas said. "I've made this pilgrimage before." He stepped back to the middle of the room, leaving open the small door on the altarpiece where the switch was hidden.

"'He lays the sweet machine upon the stone.' There." Thomas pointed to a recess in the wall, where an unimposing rock was locked away behind a grate, to be viewed and venerated like the precious object it was. "Francis's pillow. Ignatius used it, too. The sweet machine, *la dorce machina*, that would be his body. But there's another machine here, too. This one. That's what it's called, *La Macchina*. Thomas of Spoleto built it in 1704 to house relics Lorenzo di Medici donated to this church."

"But—it still works?"

"It's spring-loaded. As long as the friars replace the springs every few decades, it's fine. I think they need to oil the hinges, though. It shouldn't creak like that."

"And Lorenzo di Medici? He was a fan of Saint Francis? That's a stretch."

"Desperation to get into heaven makes strange bedfellows."

"Desperation of any kind does that, I suppose. Like you and me."

He looked at her. He had to be able, he'd decided, to look at her, if they were to continue. And they had to continue. Lorenzo may have lied to Thomas, the Church may have lied to everyone, but Lorenzo was still a man and even if it were remotely possible that the Noantri were actually people, just a different kind of people, still, becoming one was the sort of choice a man should be able to make for himself. Not have made for him by someone who considered him an enemy.

"Yes." Steadily, he returned her gaze. "Like you and me." He kept his eyes on hers, found he could, in fact, look at her, and was relieved (though he already regretted the choice of the word "bedfellows"). It might not be wise, though, to stand too near her. He took a step forward, toward the newly revealed shelves of caskets, boxes, stands, and tiny treasure chests in which rested particles of bone and hair that had once been living, breathing saints.

"Well," Livia said, "I'm very impressed." She moved forward to stand at the altar also, but to his relief she kept a space between them. "But there must be over a hundred reliquaries here." She stepped up on the small stone ledge where the altarpiece sat. Reaching out, she tentatively pushed and pulled at half a dozen of the gold and silver cases. "They're fastened down. Some of them seem to be built in. It would take us hours to remove them all and search them, or search behind them or under them. How—" She stopped. "I'm sorry. I was about to ask you what we should do next."

Thomas nodded and didn't take his eyes off the reliquaries. He'd been trying to get inside the head of Mario Damiani; this might be a good time for the famous Thomas Kelly laser-beam concentration, that blazing focus that allowed for no distractions. "If I were leaving a poem for you"—he felt a flush of heat in his cheeks—"I'd try to think what you'd be likely to look for. Something that meant a lot to the two of us—the two of them, I mean. If I were Mario. That meant a lot to them—to Damiani and Spencer George. What would that be? You knew them."

"Only Spencer." He could tell she was trying to keep amusement out of her voice.

"Yes, I know that. But he—they—" He swallowed. "Or maybe, not something they shared, but something Damiani would expect Spencer George to expect him to think of . . ."

"A place," she said, taking over. "A saint, a name. This was Damiani, so a pun, a joke, an elliptical reference. Maybe—"

Bees, Thomas thought, trying desperately to detour his brain away from the sound of her voice. **Swarm.** It meant something. Those were the words that had led them to Ludovica Albertoni, not to this cell, but still . . . **Wings untorn.** Nothing about the Ludovica tomb particularly called for bee imagery. It was odd, almost forced, in a way nothing of Damiani's had been before this. **Bees . . .**

"Virgil!" he burst out.

"What? Where?"

"Virgil. He thought bees were immortal. That a hive could come back to life after a plague wiped it out. That would've appealed to Damiani, wouldn't it? To one of your people?" The words tumbled out so fast Thomas nearly tripped over them. "He wrote about it. Virgil did. A whole beekeeping manual. Part of a larger work called *Farmers.* In English, it's called that. Virgil wrote it in

Latin but he titled it in Greek." He grinned. "'Farmers,' in Greek. He called it the *Georgics*."

Livia stared at him. "You're amazing. I've spent the last century among academics, but you're amazing. Can all Jesuits do this?"

Thomas turned away to hide the glow of pride suffusing his cheeks. **Honestly, Thomas. A female vampire is impressed by your intellect and that makes you blush?** Add that to the ever-growing list of things to take into the confessional next time he had the chance. He scanned the reliquaries. Each bore a small silver plate inscribed in tiny, flowing script. The low light made them hard for him to read. He knew she could do better, and it wasn't thirty seconds before she pointed and said, "There." Thomas leaned forward to examine one of the larger, more elaborate of the boxes, a gold castle flying a tiny gold flag. The silver script spelled out a name that should have been obvious to them from the start. With his erudition, his love of wordplay—and his love of Spencer—Damiani had chosen images for the poem to the erotic Ludovica sculpture that would have made his lover smile. They were Noantri, the lovers, and they were homosexuals; Thomas supposed he'd have to add to his list of items to take into the confessional the fact that he hoped, when this was over, the historian got a chance to see the poem, and that it did make him smile.

"It's a toe bone," Livia said, gently rocking the golden castle to see if it could be removed. "From the left foot of Saint George."

71

Over his coffee cup, Spencer George considered his visitor. The young Gendarme from Naples was unself-consciously handsome, with his sharp nose, dark eyes, and quick, catlike movements. He was clearly making an effort to appear cool and professional, but Luigi Esposito projected an excitement like a badly banked fire, ready to blaze up at any moment. Spencer found that refreshing. Why the stifling boredom that must attend a year-in, year-out daily presence in those musty Vatican rooms had not smothered in the young man all trace of enthusiasm for anything, Spencer couldn't answer. He didn't seem to be burning with the fervor of faith. It was unlikely he'd chosen the Gendarmerie out of a calling to serve the Holy See, and thereby the Church; but if his vocation was police work, could it really be fulfilling to spend his days chasing pickpockets and confidence men around Saint Peter's Square?

Probably not, which might be one explanation for the heat in Luigi Esposito's cheeks as he confronted Spencer: the business that had brought him here was real police business, a meaty investigation, a problem that would engage what Spencer gauged as the young man's considerable intelligence—and his even more considerable ambition. Whether a successful resolution to the situation would satisfy Esposito's hopes, Spencer didn't know; he'd still be a Gendarme, after all. Nevertheless, the opportunity this case had handed him couldn't be one he came across very often, and Esposito was pursuing it for all he was worth.

Even if he was headed in the wrong direction.

A smile tugged the corner of Spencer's mouth as he considered the other possible reason for the young man's bright-eyed animation. Spencer had had a number of lovers since he'd lost Mario, men both Noantri and Unchanged. Come to that, he'd had many before Mario, too. Mario was the anomaly, the miracle, the one great love Spencer had thought he'd never find, immortality notwithstanding. After Mario was gone Spencer had spent many years—decades—alone, a recluse among his papers and books, a Noantri hermit monk whose work was enough for him. But what good is eternal life, if one doesn't live it? Finally the voice of Mario in Spencer's head, berating him, demanding that he reenter the world and the Community, was too much to bear. Spencer had started to live in the world again. The voice of Mario had of course been right. Spencer had renewed old friendships, found new ones—Livia Pietro, for example—and taken lovers. None of these liaisons were serious and he hadn't pretended they were, to himself or his partners. Nevertheless, he'd enjoyed them.

As he'd enjoy a dalliance with this Neapolitan detective. And if Esposito's heartbeat, temperature, and adrenaline level—all of which Spencer could discern—were any guide, the detective, although Spencer suspected he himself might not know it, would likely enjoy it, too.

However, it was not to be. To hide a sigh, Spencer

sipped at his coffee. Too much was at stake—not least, the life Livia had made for herself in the wake of her unfortunate love affair, a life Spencer knew she treasured. Any entanglement between himself and this Vatican detective would create far too many complications in an already precarious situation. The effect of the Noantri body on the Unchanged—especially an Unchanged with his own hungers—was not something Spencer could control, but he could certainly refrain from flirtatious cues, and refuse to respond to any the Gendarme might deliberately or, more likely, involuntarily, offer.

He replaced his cup into the saucer with a small clink, recrossed his legs, and gave the detective an affronted stare. "Let me see if I understand," he said coldly. "The barely credible theory put forward this morning by you and your Carabinieri counterparts—the idea that, one, a ring of art-and-antiquities thieves has been responsible for the recent unpleasantness, and two, that the eminently respectable and highly regarded *Professoressa* Livia Pietro is a member of it—has become firmly entrenched and is the basis for your continuing investigation. Is this correct?"

Luigi Esposito replaced his coffee cup also, leaned back in his chair, and crossed his legs, too. "Please remind me, *Professore*. Where is it you teach?"

Mirroring, Spencer thought. **Put your subject at ease, make him feel you're on the same side underneath it all. A good approach. Better than the bogus befuddlement of that mustached Carabiniere, in any case.** "I'm retired," he responded stiffly.

"Yes, of course, I'm sorry." The Gendarme looked around with a lazy gaze. "You have so many unusual and interesting objects here." He swung his sharp eyes back to Spencer. "Antiquities."

Spencer raised an eyebrow. "Are you a connoisseur?"

"No, no." The young man smiled. "I'm just a cop. But I've done a little studying on my own. I try to better myself. Connoisseurship on a Gendarme's pay—it's just not possible. I'm impressed that you've managed to do so well on an academic's salary. This, for example." He tapped the glass top of the small display table where his coffee rested. Under it lay an open bronze hinge, highly polished to show off the delicate vines winding over its surface. "It's beautiful. It must be an important piece?"

Well played. A little self-deprecation, a touch of flattery, the tiniest hint of suspicion, and redirect my attention before I bristle. "You're correct. It's from the door to the Cathedral in Constance. It was in place when the Council of Constance was held." The Gendarme's face was an expectant blank. Spencer continued, "Where the Church's Great Schism was finally ended, and the papal line of succession that's been followed to this day was clarified and established."

Esposito raised his eyebrows. "I got the impression earlier, *Professore,* that you don't highly value the Church."

"How observant of you. However, a historian certainly can't ignore it." Not, at least, a Noantri historian. Particularly the moment in Church history from which sprang the papacy of Martin the Fifth and the beginning of a new era for all Noantri.

"Well. As I said, even a cop can see it's beautiful. How did you come by it?"

"Come by it?" Spencer leaned forward for the silver coffeepot. He refilled Esposito's cup, mostly so he could watch the grace with which the young man added and then stirred his cream and sugar. "*Vice Assistente* Esposito, I'm getting the uncomfortable feeling you're questioning the provenance of my collection."

"Oh, no, sir, not at all. Just, you're clearly a resourceful and dedicated collector."

"And you're clearly a police officer with more urgent issues on which to spend your time than a retired professor's pieces." He couldn't stop himself from adding, "No matter how impressive."

As the Gendarme gave him a rueful smile, Spencer could feel the young man's body temperature rise a fraction. "I'm afraid that's true. But it's occurred to me, *Professore,* that you might be able to tell me where to look."

I certainly could, Spencer thought, but said, "I don't follow." **Well, sometimes I do, and sometimes I lead.**

Esposito leaned confidentially forward. "There's no question in my mind that a reputable academic like yourself would only deal with the most respectable merchants."

"Of course."

"I also have no doubt that you're well-known in certain circles."

How true, though they might be different circles from the ones you're thinking about.

"I'm sure, sir," the Gendarme went on, "that, because of your tastes and interests, you've been approached more than once by people much shadier than the ones you usually deal with."

Yes, and if one is careful, they can be rather fun. "I see." Spencer nodded as though he'd just caught on.

"And you were wondering whether I might be able to supply you with the names of some of these . . . shadier people. I must say I'm relieved. I was beginning to worry that you thought I myself was caught up in this international theft ring you're postulating. Which, by the way, I still find hard to credit."

"The ring? Or *Professoressa* Pietro's involvement in it? Or maybe the American priest's?"

"The involvement of an American priest in any sort of criminal activity would not come as a shock, I assure you. Livia Pietro's would. I suppose it's possible you could be right, though, no matter how dubious I find the proposition." **There are other propositions I'd accept sooner, but never mind.** "Very well. I believe I can, after all, be of some service to the Gendarmerie. Let me make you a list."

———◇———

72

Climbing the stairs in the run-down building in the Pigneto district, Giulio heard his cell phone ring. He pulled it out. To Raffaele he said, "It's Esposito." To the Gendarme: "How did it go? Learn anything?"

"He gave me a list of shady dealers who might fence stolen art. I think they ought to be followed up but I don't expect anything to come of it."

"Okay, I can get someone on it. Unless you have people who can do it?" After all, it was Esposito's find.

"They'd be me," Esposito answered shortly.

"Fine. I'll give my boss your number. Someone'll call for the list. That's all?"

"Not exactly." Esposito's grin came through loud and clear. "I insisted that he himself wasn't under suspicion, oh no way. That we overworked cops only wanted the help of an upstanding citizen like himself. That we felt lucky to have him as a resource."

"Did he buy it?"

"Of course not. In fact he tried to distract me by coming on to me."

"Why, that old dog."

"As you say. I pretended to pretend not to notice."

"Esposito, you're confusing me," said Giulio, who wasn't in the least confused.

"I'm sure," Esposito said cheerfully. "Anyway, I'm hoping now he'll tip his hand."

"If he has one to tip."

"He does." The Gendarme sounded completely confident. "I'm not sure how deeply he's involved, but there's no question he's hiding something. I know you have a man here, but I'd like to stay on him myself. I have a feeling things could get interesting."

It didn't escape Giulio's notice that the idea was phrased as a request, as though Esposito were under Giulio's authority. They both knew that wasn't the case, and that Esposito could stay if he wanted, or go if he wanted. "You have any experience with surveillance?"

"Not here. On the force in Naples, though."

And I bet you're good at it, Giulio thought. "Okay, go ahead. I'll get my man reassigned." Freeing up a Carabiniere—that should make the *maresciallo* happy. "Let me know right away if anything breaks. Hey, Esposito," Giulio said as a thought struck him. "I don't suppose he gave you anything I could use to get a wiretap warrant?"

"I fished for it, but no such luck. But he's probably using a cell phone anyway."

"True. All right, give me a call when you have something." He was going to add, **Or when you want to be relieved,** but he had a feeling that wouldn't be for a long time.

"I will. If you don't mind my asking, what are you up to?"

Giulio wasn't used to that question from anyone except his partner and his boss. But it had been asked deferentially enough; and the kid had earned an answer. "I had search warrants for Livia Pietro's house and Jorge

Ocampo's flat. And through your boss, for the priest's room in the Vatican. Pietro's and Kelly's places haven't given us anything, but we got a call from the team going through Ocampo's place. Orsini and I just got here."

"Anything good?"

"We're about to walk in the door. Don't worry, Esposito, we'll let you know."

At the top of the stairs he handed his cell phone to an officer, telling him to get the last number that called it to the *maresciallo* and explaining why. The officer was clearly pleased to have a reason to bring himself to the attention of the big boss, and Giulio was equally pleased to avoid him.

Raffaele was waiting for Giulio in the hallway. "Esposito found something?"

"Not yet. He set the guy up. He's pretty good, Raffaele. He's wasted over there." They'd reached the top floor, where the ceilings and the rents were lower than for the other dumps in this exhausted building. The door at the end of the hall was open. An officer standing at it waved Giulio and Raffaele in.

Dingy, rank-smelling, its chipped tile floor sticky under their shoes, Ocampo's one room was more of a mess than even Carabinieri executing a search warrant could have made. Giulio grinned to himself as the dapper Raffaele wrinkled his nose.

"What do you have?" he asked the officer in charge.

"Over here, sir."

Over there, indeed. Giulio would have spotted it himself as soon as he turned around. A wall of photos, a vase of fresh flowers on the shelf below. A silk scarf under the vase. The scarf, the flowers, and the blond girl in the photos were all of them far too high-class for a man who lived in a room like this.

"Who is she?"

"Her name's Anna. That's all we know so far." The officer tapped one of the photos, where the margin was carefully labeled *Anna en la playa*.

"We'd better find her. She might be in danger. This guy just went from thief to serious nutcase."

"Or not," Raffaele said. "Look. The guy—Ocampo—he's in half these pictures with her."

Giulio looked again. It was true. Smiling, sometimes with their arms around each other, Ocampo and this Anna looked out at them from a café, from someone's living room, from a tree-lined street. The girl seemed perfectly happy, even smug, while Ocampo himself had a grateful puppy-dog air. Giulio's thinking started down an entirely different path. "You know what? Find her anyway."

73

---◈---

The notebook leaf from the toe-bone reliquary cracked along one of its folds as Livia smoothed it out on the altarpiece. The art historian in her winced and wanted to fold it up again and get it to a conservator as fast as possible. She pushed that thought aside and read along with Thomas.

> *Er pollarolo co' la frebre se scopre e prega. Lei fa*
> *   miracoli.*
> *S'appiccia 'na cannula, se fanno cappelle e cori*
> *de marmo barocco. Li giardinieri, i vinajjoli,*
> *li mercanti, ricopreno 'sto paradiso d'ori.*
> *Ma cqui, non tutti l'alati spiccano voli.*

The fevered farmer uncloaks, prays. She cures.
A lamp is lit and tended, chapels built,
Baroque and marble. Vintners, gardeners,
and merchants gild this Eden to the hilt.
But here, not all the winged creatures soar.

Below, the five block letters:

TNAMA

"Amante," Thomas said. "If you add that other *e*. If it were Italian it would be 'lover.' . . ."

"But the rest makes no sense if it's Italian." Livia concentrated on the page. "In Latin it's 'loving,' or depending on what comes next, 'being loved.' The *eam* would imply there's a feminine object in the sentence somewhere." She thought for a moment, then took her cell phone out.

"Livia," came Spencer's dry voice. "A joy to hear from you. How are you progressing?"

"Damiani's poems are leading us from church to church," Livia told him. "We're in San Francesco a Ripa now." That Jonah had also been here, and that she'd made no move to try to stop him from leaving, she didn't add.

"Ah, Mario."

"And there's another thing. Each poem we've found has five penciled letters on it. They seem to form some sort of puzzle, maybe an acrostic, reading back to front and bottom to top. In Latin."

Spencer laughed. "I don't mind admitting to you that he was, occasionally, a trial to live with."

"I can believe it. The words we have so far are *amante eam aedificavit*. Do you have any idea what that means?"

'Loving it, built' . . . Feminine form . . . Nothing comes to mind, no."

"Or, stretching, 'being loved, built.' Did you ever build anything together? Or did you build something for him?"

"Livia, I rarely built him a sandwich. And though I'd readily agree I'm no Neanderthal, I'm hardly a woman. I suppose it might refer to an earlier lover, but I don't know who that might have been. If he was ever inclined toward your fair sex, I'm unaware of it."

"All right, it was a long shot. There's at least one more church to go. Maybe we'll figure it out there."

"Call me if you need me. What's the next church?"

"We don't know yet. These poems aren't easy to translate."

"I imagine not. Livia, take care. I've just had a visit from an adorable Gendarme, the same gentleman whose acquaintance you made earlier today. Apparently the narrative of an international art-theft ring has developed a galloping momentum among the forces of the law, and you and your priest have been elevated to leadership positions in this criminal circle. There's some possibility this fascinating theory can be turned to your advantage, but for now I'd recommend looking over your shoulder at all times."

Livia thanked Spencer for his warning and pocketed the phone.

"He's no help?" Thomas asked.

"No. But while we were talking I had a thought." She pointed to the poem. "'Vintners, gardeners, and merchants.' If you were heading from here to the river, one way to go would take you by Santa Maria dell'Orto. It was a guild church—an *Arciconfraternita* that incorporated guilds of small-holding farmers, livestock breeders, and wine sellers. Could that—?"

"Yes!" Thomas interrupted with a shout. With a guilty look he dropped his voice. "'She cures'! That church—it was founded on the site of a miracle. The Blessed Virgin appeared and cured a dying farmer."

"All right." Livia folded the poem back into her bag.

"Come on, let's get out of here before someone wants to know what we're up to in Saint Francis's cell."

Pretending she hadn't seen him blush, Livia started down the stone steps. Thomas followed.

"The winged creatures," he whispered as they made their way to the back of the church. "The ones that don't soar. More bees?"

From the shadows just inside the door Livia peered out onto the piazza. No Carabinieri. She gestured to Thomas and trotted down the steps, quick-walking away down the street to the right. "Not more bees," she said as he hurried to catch up with her. "A turkey."

74

Thomas stood beside Livia in a recessed doorway on Via Anicia. Across the street the deepening afternoon had already cast the Baroque façade of Santa Maria dell'Orto into shadow, silhouetting the pyramidal obelisks on its roofline against an intense blue sky. The pace they'd maintained on the way here had been fast, Thomas too intent on breathing to speak; but now that they were staring across at this façade, he said to her, "The turkey's a New World bird. You don't have those in Italy."

"We do. In there. It's enormous. Condor-size. The guilds that made up the *Arciconfraternita* used to compete to make the most impressive donations. The poultry guild trumped everyone when it presented a robing cabinet for the sacristy with a giant turkey on it, to commemorate the arrival in Italy of the first pairs of turkeys for breeding purposes." She added, "They didn't catch on."

"You know," Thomas said, gazing across the street, "you sound just like me."

She grinned. "That's not a good thing, I take it?"

"No. You've seen this turkey?"

"My first area of specialization was representations of the New World in European art."

So, thought Thomas. **I was in Boston studying**

your world while you were here, studying mine. But no, not "while": Livia's studies had been decades earlier. And he might have been studying Italy, but in no way had he been studying her world.

He realized she was waiting for him to speak. "The turkey's on the robing cabinet?" he managed.

"'The fevered farmer uncloaks.' That's bound to be it."

"All right, I'm convinced. So, how will we get in? Can you pick a lock that big?"

"As a matter of fact, no. I'd need heftier tools. I'm impressed you know that."

"I had a cousin," Thomas said.

"I'd like to hear about him."

"Her."

"Even more. But as for getting in, it shouldn't be a problem. It's open until six."

"Open? Santa Maria dell'Orto? It's been closed to the public for years. I've never been inside, any of the times I've been in Rome."

"It's not only open now, it's in use. It was restored a few years ago. Saved by the Japanese."

"I'm sorry?"

"Japanese Catholic expats. They've made it their home church. They—" She stopped as the church doors swung wide. A portly priest with wavy white hair came to stand in the doorway, dressed in his vestments for Mass, ready to greet and chat with worshippers as they filed out. About two dozen did, all of them Asian.

"Well, thank you, Japan," Thomas said, then froze at the unexpected echo of Lorenzo's voice. **The future of the Church lies in Africa. In Latin America. In Asia! Do you know why? Because they believe.**

"Thomas? Are you all right?"

"I— What? Yes, I'm fine." Thomas shook off the picture in his mind! Lorenzo's sharp, determined face, his ornate office, his hand gesturing with the ever-present cigar.

"I'm fine. But look—we may have a problem."

He pointed across the street, where the priest stood on the pavement chatting with the last of the parishioners.

"What's that?"

"They've just finished Mass. As soon as everyone's gone the priest will be heading back to the sacristy. He'll disrobe. Maybe there's even a sacristan, in which case they'll probably chat. Unless he's in a hurry to get somewhere, it could take a while before the sacristy's empty."

Livia said nothing, but he felt her eyes on him. He looked over at her. "What?"

"Nothing. I was giving you space. You look like a man with a plan."

Slowly, he nodded. "Do you know where the sacristy is?"

"Left of the altar."

"All right," Thomas said. They watched as the priest took the hand of an old woman, the last of the worshippers to leave the church. "I'll distract him. You wander around as though you're looking at the church while you wait for me, then head back there. I'll buy you as much time as I can."

"What are you—" Livia began, but the old woman started down the street and the priest turned to head back into Santa Maria dell'Orto.

"Let's go," Thomas said, and stepped from the doorway into the street. "Father?" he called in soft Italian as he approached.

The priest turned, his round face open, waiting.

"*Buonasera*, Father. I'm Thomas—O'Brien. Father Thomas O'Brien, SJ. From Boston."

The two men shook hands as the white-haired priest said, "Well, all the way from Boston? A pleasure, Father O'Brien. Marcello Franconi. I was in Boston, oh, ten years ago now. For a conference. A beautiful city."

"It is, but nothing compares to Rome."

Father Franconi smiled almost ruefully, as a kind parent would who can't deny that his child is the most extraordinary in town but doesn't want to embarrass the parents of lesser children.

"This is my friend," Thomas went on. "Ellen Bird. She's a painter."

"*Signora* Bird."

"Father." Livia shook the priest's hand. In Italian more American-accented than Thomas's, she said, "I'm from New York, but I've been living in Rome for many years."

"I came over to see her," Thomas said. "To visit. Father, I—I'm glad I saw you here. I want you to hear my confession."

Father Franconi's face registered mild surprise. He looked from Thomas to Livia, and in his eyes a new light dawned. "Of course, my son."

"Thank you. A priest's work is never done, is it?"

"Until we've all attained the Kingdom of Heaven, I suppose it never will be. Please, come this way." They entered the church, Thomas and Father Franconi making use of the holy water font. Father Franconi closed the doors behind them. "*Signora* Bird, make yourself comfortable while you wait. You're a painter? You're welcome to view the church. You might find a few things of interest. We have some fine Zuccari frescoes. Father O'Brien, please come this way."

An old Asian man sat waiting near the altar. Father Franconi called across the church to him in Japanese. The old man answered, then, at Father Franconi's response, smiled and bowed. He headed for the door as Father Franconi said to Thomas, "We don't have the budget for a sacristan but Kaoru's retired and he enjoys helping. Actually he's invaluable. I just told him to go home, though. If I can't get out of these by myself by now, I never should have been wearing them in the first place."

He led Thomas to a confessional to the right of the church doors. That was good: as far from the sacristy as they could get. They entered, Thomas kneeling on the penitent's side this time, not sitting on the confessor's.

"Bless me, Father, for I have sinned."

"How long has it been since your last confession?"

Thomas thought. Yesterday; but that was a lifetime ago. That was a different man. This Thomas Kelly, the one who stole books and consorted with vampires, who unsealed reliquaries and climbed Berninis, who knew his friend had been hiding a world-shattering truth from him for decades and his Church had been double-dealing for six hundred years—this Thomas Kelly had never been to confession.

"Father O'Brien?" came Father Franconi's quiet voice through the screen.

Right. Father Kelly wasn't confessing this afternoon. Father O'Brien was, and he could say anything he wanted. He could make stuff up. "Three days."

Father Franconi said nothing, waiting for Thomas to explain what had driven him into the confessional at Santa Maria dell'Orto all the way from Boston.

Thomas had to speak. He opened his mouth, unsure what he was going to say, something to buy Livia time. What he heard, in his own voice, was, "Lust, Father. I've been—experiencing lust." **Wait. This was just a diversion. Father O'Brien was supposed to be making stuff up.**

"Your friend," Father Franconi said. "*Signora* Bird." Not phrased as a question, but not an accusation, either.

"Yes."

"Have you acted upon these feelings?"

"No. No. I haven't touched her. She says it's natural, it's not my fault, but—" **But she's a vampire, so what does she know?**

"She's aware of your feelings for her, then?"

"I didn't tell her, but she knows."

"Well, she's a wise woman. Of course it's natural. The Lord places temptation in our path so we can have the privilege of overcoming it. If you haven't acted on your feelings you're well on your way to defeating them."

"But I . . ." Thomas stopped, unclear on what he'd been about to say.

"But you still feel bad. Especially that you came all the way to Rome."

Bad that I came to Rome isn't the half of it. "Yes, Father."

"'I should have known better,' you're thinking. 'I should have stayed home. What was I expecting?' Is that it?"

I know what I was expecting. I was expecting to be of service to my friend and my Church. "Pretty much."

"But something called you here."

A friendship based on a shocking and enormous lie. "Yes."

"Has it occurred to you that what you're experiencing right now is part of God's purpose for you?"

"I don't see how, Father."

"You're doubting yourself. Your vocation. The need for priestly celibacy. You're thinking, in a different world—perhaps a better world—you might be able to serve your Church and yield to this temptation, also."

Actually, I'm thinking I might as well yield to it, since I don't see any possible way—or reason—to go on serving my Church. Thomas didn't speak. Father Franconi waited, then went on.

"The Lord knows what you're going through, Father O'Brien. Do you think he doesn't see you struggle? Yes, the vows you took were written by men. Poverty, chastity, obedience. They might as easily have been self-improvement, fecundity, and silliness." At the surprise of that, Thomas laughed. "Very good, Father O'Brien. You haven't lost your sense of perspective. Here's my point: they might as easily have been, but they weren't. And when you took your vows, it wasn't to the men who wrote them that you dedicated yourself. It was to God. You promised God you'd live your life in a certain way. He was pleased to receive your vows, and he stands ready to help you live up to them. This is not about what should be or could be. It's about what is."

Again, Thomas didn't answer, this time for a completely different reason. He couldn't. He was thinking: God knew. About the Noantri, about the Church's perfidy. Of course he did. Some would say, *and permitted it?* but Thomas was unconcerned on that score. As Father Franconi had said, we make our own choices; God gives us that privilege. The point was, whatever God's unknowable plan for the Universe, the Noantri were part of it. Part of it because the devil had sent them to test the faithful, or part of it for some other purpose: it didn't matter. What the Church said and did about their existence might be at odds with reality, even at odds with God's intentions, but if there was anything a Jesuit was prepared for it was living with, investigating, even celebrating, that very contradiction.

Another thing Father Franconi had said: Thomas's vows had been made to God. Not to the Church. How simple. How basic. As long as he was a priest he'd keep his vows. His relationship to the Church, and therefore to the priesthood, once all this was over, was a different question. He didn't have to negotiate that path now. That thought filled him with a relief so profound it was like the cessation of pain.

"Of course," he said. "The struggle's the whole point, isn't it, Father?"

"Well, I don't think God's especially pleased that you're struggling. But as long as you have something to struggle against, I'm sure he's proud that you're doing it. Are you ready for the Act of Contrition?"

"What's my penance, Father?"

"None, I think." Thomas could hear the other priest smile. "You paid this account in advance."

"Thank you, Father," Thomas said, and began, "My God, I am heartily sorry . . ."

75

◁○▷

Raffaele couldn't believe it. He'd finally gotten a hit.

Once there was nothing more to be learned at Jorge Ocampo's squalid flat—which was not that long after they'd gotten there—Raffaele and Giulio Aventino had hit the streets. They'd taken copies (Giulio, on paper; Raffaele, in his iPhone) of photos of Ocampo and his ladylove. She turned out to be a comparative literature student at La Sapienza by the name of Anna Jagiellon. She also turned out to be nowhere to be found, including in the Russian poetry seminar where her paper on Akhmatova was supposed to have been presented today. The two detectives went out to show the photos around, to see what they could see.

The Carabinieri had a number of uniformed officers doing the same, of course, and in the general way of things detectives were too valuable to waste on this kind of canvassing. As Giulio had pointed out, however, it was either do the photos or go back to the station and discuss with the *maresciallo* the current situation: that Ocampo had slipped through their fingers twice already; that Livia Pietro and Thomas Kelly had completely eluded them; and that furthermore they were basing their investigation on the idea that either they had a serial anti-clerical nutcase on their hands, who might or might not be after the aforementioned elusive Pietro (who was in no way, however, a cleric); or they were chasing an international art-theft ring of which the aforementioned Pietro might or might not be a part, in a conspiracy theory promulgated by, horror of horrors, a Gendarme. Raffaele had considered the possible outcomes of such a conversation and agreed the street was preferable. They'd split up, each taking a direction out from San Francesco a Ripa, the last church where Ocampo had been seen.

The calls from churches, monasteries, and convents had been coming thick and fast. Raffaele couldn't tell if the ordained and avowed who were burning up the tip line were worried for their own safety and that of their treasures, or were merely trying to be of service to the authorities. Whichever it was, Carabinieri officers had been crisscrossing Rome all afternoon responding to reports of collection boxes jacked open and tourists' wallets disappearing, which were the kind of thing usually the province of the Rome *polizia*; and also, stories of strange men lurking in church doorways and loud arguments on basilica steps, which on a normal Rome day wouldn't get reported at all.

However, the clerics, to whom Raffaele was used to turning for spiritual but never before for professional help, had provided nothing. The only thing these calls had yielded was a sense, disquieting to Raffaele, that church-related disturbances were much more of a quotidian occurrence than he'd thought.

What had borne Raffaele promising fruit was exactly what, in his experience, usually did: two pretty girls drinking wine at a café table, in this case on Via della Luce. Both nodded emphatically when he showed them Ocampo's picture.

"Half an hour, maybe?" The brunette cast a heavily made-up glance at her redheaded companion for confirmation. "He was in a hurry."

"Running?" Raffaele asked.

"No, walking fast, and he kept looking behind him like someone was following him."

The Good Samaritan, Raffaele thought, wishing he had a photo of that man, too. "Was anyone?"

"I don't think so."

"But you're sure it was him?"

"He was gross," the redhead sniffed. "All sweaty. And some kind of awful cologne."

"Sickening," her friend agreed.

"And the way he looked at us when he went by. Like if he weren't in a rush he'd sit right down and buy us a drink."

"I guess I shouldn't try that, huh?" Raffaele grinned.

"Don't flirt. You're on duty," the girl said, but she smiled.

"Did you see where he went?"

"Seriously? I didn't even look at him." A toss of the red hair.

The brunette pointed north. "That way. I think he turned left a couple of blocks up."

"You watched where he was going that far?"

She nodded, then shrugged as the redhead stared. "I don't know, something about him—he was just *interesting*, okay?"

The redhead rolled her eyes.

"How about this woman?" Raffaele intervened, swiping to the photo of Anna Jagiellon. "Was she with him?"

Both girls leaned forward to see. Their eyes met in surprise. "Not with him," the brunette said. "But a few minutes ago. Going the same direction. They know each other?"

"Was she who was following him?" asked the red-head. "That he was afraid of?"

Raffaele didn't answer that, but asked, "The same direction?"

The brunette nodded. The redhead, to prove she could be as helpful to the Carabinieri as her friend—or maybe, to draw Raffaele's attention back to herself—said, "She turned left up there, too. I don't know if it was the same street—"

"It was," the brunette confirmed. The redhead scowled.

"You're sure it was this girl?" Raffaele asked.

"Absolutely. She's, like, completely hot. I mean, not that we're— But she—" The brunette blushed prettily. Raffaele tried not to smile.

"A girl who looks like that," the redhead clarified, "other girls notice."

Raffaele thanked them, walked a few paces away, and called Giulio. "Looks like we're right. Whatever it is, she's involved. Not only wasn't he stalking her, right now it seems like she's looking for him." He boiled the conversation down.

"You're sure they have the right people?"

"They called him gross and brought up the cologne. Her, they were checking out the competition. Girls don't miss much when they're doing that."

"Good work. Keep going. I'll join you as soon as I can get there."

Raffaele pocketed the phone and continued up Via della Luce to the corner the girls had indicated. He stopped a few more times, showing the photos, closing in, once again, on Jorge Ocampo.

76

Livia was examining a side-chapel ceiling in Santa Maria dell'Orto when the two priests stepped from the confessional. She walked to the back of the church, where they stood talking.

"Thanks for waiting," Thomas said to her.

She smiled. "I'd never interfere with the confessional. I just hope your penance doesn't involve giving up coffee—I'm desperate. Father Franconi, your Zuccaris are truly beautiful. And wonderfully restored."

"Thank you. I'm glad you enjoyed them. Please come back to our church. We celebrate Mass every day at four." He added, "There's an excellent café around the corner."

Father Franconi's smile followed them out the church doors. They walked purposefully in the direction he'd pointed them, American tourists in search of caffeine. As soon as she heard the church doors creak shut Livia said to Thomas, "Your blood pressure's about to blow the top of your head off. Relax. I have it."

"The poem? You do?"

"You gave me just about enough time. I guess you found something to talk about."

"Yes. No problem. It was fine. Fine. The turkey's still there?"

"On top of the wardrobe, almost touching the ceiling. Beautifully carved, but huge. I had to tilt the whole thing over. Luckily it's so heavy it just sits up there. They don't fasten it down."

"It's that heavy, but you— Right. Never mind."

She smiled. "The poem was under the base, as far from any of the edges as it could be."

"Did you read it? What does it say?"

"No. I barely made it out of the sacristy when I heard the confessional doors open. It's in my bag. Let's go get coffee."

She saw Thomas pick up on her thought: they needed to get off the street, and two people bending over a page in a café would arouse no suspicions. Besides which, he looked like a man who could use a restorative drink.

At the café they ordered *macchiati*. Once the waiter had brought them and gone back behind the glass counter, Livia unfolded the sheet of paper on the marble table. Thomas leaned to read it.

Nun se po' vvedé la bbellezza de 'sto vorto bbello
come nun se vede pe' gnente l'effimerità
de la musica: e uno, e tre, li diti senz'anello
indicano la grazzia de l'incorrotta santità.
La su' anima lucente rischiara 'sto spazzio poverello.

We cannot see the beauty of the face
that turns, music's ephemerality,
and one, and three, the fingers gesture grace
and point toward incorrupt sanctity.
Her lucent soul illumes this tiny space.

Below, the expected penciled letters:

R B O R T

Brow furrowed in concentration, Thomas looked from the poem to the letters, back and forth. Livia was about to speak when he blurted, "Bramante! If you add the *b* and the *r*. Going backward. *Bramante eam aedificavit.* 'Bramante made it.' Not *amante*. Nothing to do with lovers. Bramante. Something Bramante made."

"Well, that doesn't narrow it down much." Donato Bramante, the architect who brought the High Renaissance style to Rome, had held, among other posts, that of papal architect to Julius the Second. Still, it was something; and there were more words to come. "And the *t r o*?"

"I don't know. The next word. I mean, the word before. Whichever of Bramante's buildings Damiani used."

"Good. Now finish up so we can go."

"But the poem—"

"Yes. Let's go."

"Wait. You know where this poem's sending us?"

"Of course. You don't?"

"I have no idea."

"Seriously?" She sat back, grinning. "And I had no idea about Saint Francis's cell. Believe me, this one's as easy as you said that one was."

77

This time, Jorge was doing it differently. Slowly, methodically. Scientifically.

For one thing, he had to. After he'd escaped the ambush at San Francesco a Ripa, he'd zigzagged through the neighborhood, partly to throw that interfering blond Noantri off his trail. He'd stopped and bought more cologne to aid the purpose, and that and his evasive maneuvers seemed to have worked, because that smirking man was nowhere to be seen.

The other reason for Jorge's serpentine, systematic progress was to pick up the trail of Livia Pietro. There were only so many streets leading away from San Francesco a Ripa. Unless she was still inside, she had to have left by one of them; and if she were still inside, sooner or later she'd come out. And leave by one of them.

He was on Via Anicia, in fact, heading back in the direction of San Francesco a Ripa to start again, when he got a strong whiff of Pietro's gardenia perfume and the perspiration and skin-scent under it. She'd been here, and fairly recently. He looked back to make sure the blond man wasn't behind him and then picked up his pace. It was an easy trail to follow, for a talented operative like himself. Sticking to the late afternoon shadows, he arrived at, not surprisingly, another church. It was Santa Maria dell'Orto; and it was closed. Why all these churches? Jorge wondered. Was Pietro like him, a Noantri who still missed the comfort of the stained glass and the wooden pews, the wise homily and the glimpse of heaven? Anna said heaven was an outdated and ridiculous concept, a crutch for fearful Mortals. Of course she was right, but Jorge, as he peered down the long, indistinct tunnel of his endless future, sometimes wished he could lean on that crutch just a little bit, even now.

But back to work! Risking leaving the shadows, Jorge worked his way through the intersection in front of the church. Pietro, he decided, had been here, but she wasn't here now. She'd arrived along Via Anicia, but she'd left along Via della Madonna dell'Orto. Her scent was stronger there. Fresher. Madonna dell'Orto, walled on both sides and running east to the river, at this time of day didn't provide much concealing shadow. So be it. Jorge strode into the middle of the street and boldly made his way.

78

———◦〇◦———

Thomas followed Livia through the open gate and into the shadowed garden in front of Santa Cecilia. The streets they'd traveled to get here had been quiet, but when they shut the gate the walled garden surrounded them with a different kind of silence. Thomas stopped for a moment, surprised to feel his heartbeat slow down, his breathing calm. He felt suddenly apart, serenely separated from the tumult his life had turned into on this day.

Almost, he realized with a start, he felt an echo of the old peace.

The basilica's open doors welcomed visitors, but when Thomas and Livia entered they found themselves nearly alone. The air was soft with fading incense; it whispered to Thomas of Asia, of desert caravans and distant cities. Three votive candles flickered in a side chapel. There, a woman knelt before the rail. No one else was about.

Livia didn't hesitate. She trotted up the center aisle. Thomas followed her to the stone rail that stood in front of what he privately considered one of the most beautiful works in Rome. He wasn't an art historian, so maybe he was wrong, but he'd come out of his way on previous trips to Rome just to spend time with this: Stefano Maderno's breathtaking, delicate statue of Saint Cecilia, head so oddly turned away from those who looked on her.

Livia knelt before the statue, and Thomas, though sure she was just inspecting the marble for possible poem locations, knelt with her.

"You're sure it's this one?" he asked.

"There's no question. '. . . the beauty of the face / that turns . . . and one, and three, the fingers gesture grace.'" Livia pointed to Cecilia's hands, their gentle fingers raised to signal the holy trinity. "And," Livia added, "she was one of us."

"What?" He couldn't have heard her correctly. "Cecilia— You're telling me—"

Livia nodded. "They tried three times to chop off her head. They didn't quite succeed, but in any Unchanged the damage and blood loss would surely have caused death. Not only didn't Cecilia die, she remained conscious. It was only after she was allowed to take Communion that she slipped into a coma. The next day they declared her dead and buried her. Stefano Maderno had her disinterred twelve hundred years later, to use her remains as a model for this work. They were intact, undecayed. As you see."

Thomas stared, first at Livia, then at the pure white marble sculpture of the saint. Could this possibly be true? "Is this . . . You said it could take a very long time . . ."

"Yes. In some cases, hundreds of years. Cecilia's Renewal was almost complete when she was disinterred."

"Maderno . . . How did he . . . Why . . . no. I know."

"Yes. Maderno also. They'd known each other two millennia before. In, I believe, Greece. He'd been to her grave. He could tell she was nearly ready. That's why he put himself forward for the commission."

Thomas nodded, a part of him astonished, not by this news, but by his lack of astonishment at it.

"Look." Livia brought him back to the moment, gesturing in the direction of the woman in the side chapel, who rose and turned. "She's leaving. This may be the best chance we'll get."

79

As soon as the woman who'd been praying in the side chapel stepped out the church door, Livia was up and over the railing. She'd done this a number of times over the years, waiting her chance to be alone in order to study Maderno's Cecilia. The basilican authorities made it almost impossible to get close to this sculpture. Even to the Unchanged, the evident tenderness, Maderno's skill and joy as he made this piece, was so captivating that the marble cried out to be touched, to be taken in with more senses than just sight. Even the way sound echoed off the stone folds of Cecilia's shroud . . . Livia stopped herself. This was not the time to get lost in the beauty of this work.

Thomas, as usual, was a beat behind her. He'd probably never lose his instinctive horror of trespassing, of breaking the rules. He did seem to have lost a good deal of his horror of her people, though. He'd taken her revelation that Cecilia was both saint and Noantri with a minimum of aversion and no disbelief she could detect.

As he stepped over the railing, she knelt and ran her fingertips along the line at Cecilia's throat. That would have been the obvious spot for a Noantri to hide something for a Noantri to find; but the line was as she remembered: a chiseled groove in the solid stone, filled with a thin layer of gold. She moved on, exploring the flowing marble garments, the cavity made by Cecilia's arms resting in front of her torso, the space under her lifted left foot. Livia's fingertips thrilled to every alteration in texture, rough to smooth; her muscles followed Maderno's hammering, his tapping, his polishing. Her delight in experiencing, skin to stone, the cool curves of Maderno's work was so great that it threatened to derail her urgent search.

Or maybe it already had. She was carefully searching the cavity at the statue's feet when Thomas said, "Um, Livia?" She turned to see him prying his key-ring penknife into a small gap at the statue's base. As she watched he dug the blade into a slip of paper and slid it out.

"Oh," she said.

Gingerly, Thomas unfolded the familiar page. He looked up at her. "It's the last." He turned it for her to see. It held no poem. The paper was blank but for five block letters printed in graphite.

EPORP

The last! No new poem, no next church to go to. They had it all, now—the entire puzzle. This final piece would lead them to the Concordat. Heart pounding, Livia knelt beside Thomas. *"Pro,"* she said, reading backward as they had learned to do. "If that's the first word, and the *p e* goes with what we already had, the word before it is *Petro*." She looked up to see the dismay she suddenly felt echoed on Thomas's face.

"'For Peter'?" he said. "'For Peter Bramante made it'?"

Livia sat back on her heels. "Saint Peter's? He hid the Concordat in Saint Peter's?"

For some moments they sat in silence. Saint Peter's, the Vatican church, was Donato Bramante's grandest work. A huge basilica where the Popes themselves worshipped, it held side chapels, underground rooms and tombs, hundreds of statues, plaques, paintings, gold and silver and precious woods, multiple levels, even tiers to its giant dome. How would you search Saint Peter's? Where would you begin?

"That would be so like Damiani, wouldn't it?" Livia asked rhetorically. "Once he got it out of the Vatican Library, he didn't take it anywhere. Just around the corner. To Saint Peter's. But where?"

Thomas made no answer, just shook his head.

"Maybe when we get there," she said. "Maybe something will jump out at us."

Thomas looked as unconvinced as she was, but what else could they do? She stood. He didn't, though. Still crouched beside the sculpture, he said, "He wrote it backward." Frowning at the floor, which she was sure he wasn't seeing, he asked, "Why did he write it backward?"

"As extra insurance? If you didn't have the whole thing—"

"You need the whole thing no matter what direction it goes in."

She said nothing, to give him space to follow his thought. He took a pencil from his back pocket, then searched in vain for a piece of paper. Wordlessly, she slipped Damiani's notebook from her shoulder bag and offered it to him.

He didn't reach for it. "Write in that? I can't."

"Damiani would've wanted us to."

"But it's from the Vatican Library."

"The Bernini," she said, "Santa Teresa's relic box. Saint George's."

He met her eyes, sighed, took the notebook, and opened it to a blank page. He tapped the pencil on it a few times, then wrote:

PROPETROBRAMANTEEAMAEDIFICAVIT

He stared at the line of letters, then separated them into the words they made:

PRO PETRO BRAMANTE EAM AEDIFICAVIT

"Was he telling us to rearrange the words? Once we have it all, to run it backward? But it's Latin. Word order doesn't matter." He did it anyway.

AEDIFICAVIT EAM BRAMANTE PETRO PRO

"Or, each word backward? No. That just gives us Latin gibberish."

Livia realized he was talking as much to himself as to her.

"But he did do it backward," Thomas went on. "There must be a reason."

Livia withdrew the poems themselves from the zippered pocket of the bag and spread them on the floor in front of the statue. Well, if anyone could help with understanding poems, it would be Santa Cecilia. She read the poems over, taking in the lettered additions. Then she stopped reading, and just looked. Slowly, she said, "If you see it purely as pattern, each line is just below the bottom line of its poem, and the same width."

Thomas turned to her, to the poems, back to her. "As pattern?"

"As graphics. Not meaning."

"All right," he said. "Go on."

"I don't know. But some are stretched out, some are squished up. To me that implies each line's supposed to be kept as a block." She gathered the poems and lapped them over one another, then covered the words of the first poem with her hand. Now only the letters were visible.

TIVAC

IFIDE

AMAEE

TNAMA

RBORT

EPORP

"Maybe," she said, "some other kind of acrostic? The first letter of each line, or the second, or from one corner to another . . ." She trailed off, seeing nothing at all.

Thomas also stared at the letters, absently tapping his pencil on the marble floor. Beyond its rhythmic sound, Livia's Noantri senses heard a rustle of wind in the courtyard trees, saw the tiny change in the shadows as the votive flames danced. The spices in the faint incense brought her an odd comfort, a connection to distant lands, other times. She realized that, as much time as she'd spent here with Maderno's sculpture, she had never focused on the other works in this church. Maybe, after all this was concluded, once they found the Concordat and her world, so recently upended, was set right again—Upended. Set right. *"Thomas!"* The pencil-tapping abruptly stopped. "It's not backward. It's upside down!"

He stared.

She said, "'For Peter Bramante it made.' Upside down. For Peter, upside down!"

He leapt to his feet and hugged her.

80

◄◦►

Jorge had been right.

He didn't take the time to pat himself on the back, though. As a disciplined guerilla fighter, he shrugged off his satisfaction, not letting it interfere with his strategy. He'd followed Pietro's scent along Via di San Michele to Santa Cecilia and arrived at the perfect moment. He was pondering how to make his incursion—he wasn't afraid of churches, of course not, no matter how many, and how dangerous, the obstacles the opposition had thrown into his course already today—when the *professoressa* and the priest came flying out. It was pitiable to watch the priest try to keep up with her, even more pathetic to watch such a graceful and talented Noantri holding herself back for the convenience of a Mortal. Not that any of that mattered. Jorge's path was clear. Now that they were on the street, he'd just trail them to someplace uncrowded, pounce, and wrest the notebook from her. He took off, staying a safe distance behind, ready to drop back if she seemed to be aware of him or speed up if they turned.

Which they did, left on Via dei Genovesi and left again on Viale di Trastevere. The route they chose, avoiding broad piazzas and skulking in shadows, underlined to Jorge that they were up to no good. That, plus the shamefaced, embarrassed air about them both—the priest more than Pietro, but both—as they exited the church, the way they barely looked at each other and took obvious care not to touch. Jorge didn't know the nature of their wrongdoing and he didn't care: Anna would know; Anna would explain to him what all this was about once, in glowing triumph, he handed her the notebook. He wondered where Anna was, whether she was mad he hadn't waited at the theater, but he decided she must not be because she hadn't called. She probably knew he'd seized the initiative, taken the opportunity to continue his mission. She had faith in him; she was waiting.

Pietro and the priest rushed through the piazza in front of Santa Maria in Trastevere, keeping to the far side of the fountain from the church, she with her hat pulled down, he pretending to shade his eyes but clearly just hiding his face with his hand. Jorge followed as they worked their way to Vicolo della Frusta and then started on the steps up the Janiculum. He gave them a head start and then trotted up the steps himself. They must be going this way to avoid the road, where they'd be more likely to be seen. Probably, since whatever they were doing involved churches, they were making for San Pietro in Montorio, but a good agent would never assume such a thing. Jorge would catch up with them closer to the top; for now, better to hang back. He let some people pass him. Mortals, they were, huffing and puffing on the steps: a French-speaking couple holding hands, three teenage boys in soccer uniforms (how long had it been since Jorge himself had kicked a ball around? he suddenly wondered), and a thin, hatchet-faced older man who'd find himself able to breathe better, Jorge decided, if he threw away his cigar. Focusing on his task, Jorge realized he must really be spooked, because even though they'd left San Francesco a Ripa far behind, he couldn't get over the sense that that blond Noantri was nearby. Well, continuing in the face of fear was the mark of heroism. Not that Jorge was afraid. Far from it. His hanging back on the steps was strategic. He could do that because there wasn't much chance that his quarry would escape him. Actually, there was no chance. Finally, on the Janiculum Hill, Jorge would get what he'd been hoping for.

81

---◄◊►---

Spencer George, having seen the young Gendarme to the door and pressed his hand in perhaps a more fond farewell than their short acquaintance called for, had been settled in his easy chair deep in thought when Livia's call came. After speaking with her, he'd spent some more time the same way, unmoving, eyes focused on nothing. Now he stood, walked slowly about his house, looking at this and that, contemplating an etching or a bit of silver. Finally he returned to his study. He rang for coffee, and when it had come and he had enjoyed it, he took out his cell phone and made a call.

"*Salve,*" came the voice at the other end of the line.

"*Salve. Sum Spencer George. Quid aegis?*"

"*Hic nobis omnibus bene est. Quomodo auxilium vobis dare possumus?*" **All is well here,** came the response. **How may we be of service?**

82

Trotting up the last of the steep steps to the courtyard above, Livia slowed. Not that she'd been running at any speed, not for her: she'd had to hold herself back to make sure Thomas stayed with her. For an Unchanged—especially a bookish priest—he had impressive stamina and speed; still, a part of her wanted to race ahead and let him catch up when he could. He knew where they were going, after all. But that would be unfair. It might even make him think she was planning to abscond with the Concordat and leave him empty-handed. She didn't want to worry him, and this discovery was as much his as hers.

What she was, in fact, planning to do with the Concordat when they found it, Livia wasn't sure. Thomas was desperate to hand it over to the Noantri who'd abducted his friend the Cardinal. She needed to take it to the Conclave to obey her instructions—and to save Jonah. Incompatible goals, and though her Noantri strength would give her an easy victory if it came to a wrestling match, the thought of that, after this past day, left her decidedly queasy.

Well, they didn't have it yet. That was a bridge they'd have to cross later. She wondered if Thomas was thinking about that moment, too.

She stopped to wait for him. He jogged up beside her, then leaned over for a moment, hands on knees, catching his breath. He straightened, but didn't speak. Together, wordlessly, they started toward their goal.

Saint Peter's, a mile away at the opposite end of the same long ridge where they were standing, was indisputably Donato Bramante's most magnificent and monumental building. But this one before them now, this tiny chapel, this Tempietto, was arguably his best.

For Peter Bramante made it, Damiani's acrostic had read. Upside down.

Simon Peter, the first Pope, the rock upon whom Jesus built his church, was martyred in Rome. Modern scholarship located the site of his death as, in fact, the ground on which Saint Peter's now stood; but in Bramante's day, and on through Mario Damiani's, Peter was believed to have died on the Janiculum Hill. Ferdinand and Isabella of Spain commissioned Bramante to create a chapel on what was thought to be the very site. The site where Peter, sentenced to crucifixion and considering himself unworthy to share the fate of his Lord, made a final request, which was granted: that he be crucified upside down.

Livia entered the open gate and stepped into the cloister between San Pietro in Montorio and what had been its monastery, now the Spanish Academy. Crossing the courtyard, she reached the Tempietto and started up the steps, Thomas beside her. They stood for a moment in the faultless colonnade, then entered the single, circular room. Spare, with statuary in wall niches, soft light from high windows glowing off the polished marble floor, the perfect chapel invited contemplation and prayer. It offered proof that though men and women might be incurably flawed, their works occasionally rose to flawlessness; it suggested, therefore, that while sadly not perfectable, people had the power to rise also, to be better than they, until a moment ago, had been.

Perfection, however, Livia thought, gazing around, did not allow for change. For addition or subtraction. It did not, for example, suggest within itself a hiding place.

"Below," Thomas said, as though in response. His voice was completely calm, completely sure. "The place itself."

As soon as he said it she knew he was right. They went back out and around to the Tempietto's far side, where two symmetrical staircases led down to a level below the upper chapel floor. At the bottom where the staircases joined again, light slipped through a locked iron gate to glance off a wide glass disk in the floor at the precise center of the chapel above. The glass covered a brick cistern dug, legendarily, on the very spot where Peter's cross had been driven into the earth.

This time when Livia picked the lock, Thomas watched her eagerly. She pulled open the creaking gate and started through it, but he placed a gentle hand on her arm. "May I go?"

She stopped at once. "Of course."

83

Hurrying up the steps, Jorge reached the hairpin above Via Garibaldi and started to make the turn. As he came around, his heart, already pounding, surged into another dimension. He whispered, "Anna." Because Anna was here.

She stood just above him, slender and steady, her head cocked, her arms folded. Sunlight blazed in her long pale hair, outlined her slim hips, limned her hat like the dark halos edged in gold on the paintings of saints. Anna! She'd come to be with him in his moment of triumph, to share in the victory his cunning was about to bring them. Desire leapt desperately in him, all the more wild because the sight of her was unexpected. His skin longed for hers. His body ached with the need to enfold her, to surround her and have her enclose him in her heat, her ferocity. More than anything he'd ever wanted, Jorge wanted to touch her at this moment.

He didn't. He forced his arms still, ordered his feet not to move. Discipline was critical for a revolutionary fighter. Their goal was near. The scents in the air told him the *professoressa* and the priest had just passed this way. They would follow, they would have them. He saw the scene, knew with certainty how it would be. He'd leap out in ambush, battle them both, and defeat them.

The priest was nothing, the Noantri woman a challenge, but Jorge had no doubt of his success. He'd deliver up the notebook to his Anna. He'd planned to rush to her, bearing it victoriously through the streets. But she was here, standing in the sunlight on the rough stone steps. She was here to watch proudly while her Jorge slew dragons for her.

"*Buonasera*, Jorge." She smiled.

Italian, he thought, puzzled. She'd addressed him in Italian. Usually they spoke Spanish, their private language. Italian was the language she used for the others, sometimes English if she had to, but alone together, she and Jorge shared the melodic, flowing tones of his home. He didn't know why she'd done it—maybe the excitement, she must feel it, too—but he answered in Spanish, as he'd always done.

"Anna. You're so beautiful. Anna, it's almost over."

"Yes," she said. "I know."

A flash of movement on the steps far above caught his eye. The *professoressa* and the priest, arriving at the top. He turned to Anna, to tell her.

She was right there: she'd moved much, much closer. She was still smiling. Her teeth were bared.

"*Buenas tardes*, Jorge," she whispered. "*Adiós.*"

"Anna? They're— Anna, what—"

He stopped as she embraced him. How could he speak? In the warmth of her arms he shivered in an all-consuming ecstasy. It drained away his will. Joyfully, he surrendered his ability to talk, to move, even to want to move. As always when Anna held him, rapture transported him, a bliss so overpowering it was almost pain.

Then it was pain. First, a tiny, tearing twinge, where a moment ago her velvet lips had been kissing his throat.

Slowly, from there, a burn began to spread; he felt it reach his side, his stomach, across his hips, replacing with fiery agony the unfathomable joy he'd just known.

"Anna." He wasn't even sure if he'd really said it, if she could hear him.

"*Adiós,*" she murmured again in his ear. "I'll find them myself, Jorge. I can keep looking. Alone. I don't need you."

Find them? They're very near. You don't need to look. They're just above . . . He tried to tell her, but the fire inside him was unbearable, and he couldn't speak.

She stepped back. Blood smeared her smile, his blood.

The Lord had retasted the Disciple's blood.

Through the excruciating anguish that engulfed him now, Jorge understood. He felt Anna lift him, knew the moment she threw his agonized body over the railing down to Via Garibaldi far below. The pain didn't stop; no, it amplified beyond bearing, but Jorge found himself feeling something else, something that drew his attention away from his agony. As he fell he was suffused with joy, a bliss to match, to far outshine, both the pain, and even the ecstasy, of moments before. Of any of his time with Anna, since their first, transcendent night. His Anna had given him a gift. She'd bestowed on him a final blessing, one that exceeded all the Noantri Blessings he'd ever had. Into his mind flashed the face of the old monk, the man he'd killed in the church, that man's joy and relief, and Jorge understood this gift was one he'd hoped for, yearned for, but never dared admit even to himself. But his Anna knew, and because she loved him, she'd sacrificed her own need for him, given up the dream of a life together on the broad boulevards of Buenos Aires. She'd put her own desires aside to grant Jorge's unspoken, barely imagined wish.

Anna had reinfected him, and soon, now, now, he was going to die.

84

"If this is wrong," Giulio huffed, "and I'm running up the Janiculum for no reason—"

"I'm running right with you," Raffaele Orsini threw back. "And I smoke more."

"You're fifteen years younger. And," Giulio added, "three steps behind."

Despite burning lungs and aching legs, Giulio had to smile as Raffaele shot past him. No one could say his partner wasn't competitive. They'd trailed Jorge Ocampo and Anna Jagiellon through Trastevere, getting enough confirmation on the photos they were showing to determine that, though not together, both were heading up the Janiculum Hill. Giulio had already sent a car to the top, but because there were places to turn off before you got there, Giulio had decided he and Raffaele would follow.

All right, no more talk. Giulio put his head down, got a rhythm, and kept it going, afraid if he slowed he'd stop and never get started again. Step pump step pump step—

"Wait!"

That shout sounded like it came from Raffaele's last breath. Giulio called on a reserve he hadn't known he had and pushed on up to come even with the sergeant.

Raffaele had stopped at a place where the curve of the roadway below became visible. Panting, he pointed over the railing. Jorge Ocampo, eyes open and staring, lay in a lake of blood.

"I guess we can stop running," Raffaele wheezed. "Or one of us can." He grinned, then said, "I'll go check. He may still be alive. He might be able to tell us something."

Giulio, peering down at the broken body, clutched Raffaele's arm as the sergeant turned to head back down the steps. "Raffaele. Don't go near him. Go up above and stop traffic. No one comes down this road."

"What—"

"Go!" Giulio himself turned and jogged down the steps, stopping where they crossed the road below the place where Ocampo lay. He pulled out his cell phone as he ran and called Dispatch. "I need Hazmat," he said. "On Via Garibaldi where it hits Via Mameli, near where the steps go up the Janiculum. Close the road up and down, the staircase, too. Anyone at the top, make them stay. Contact the American Academy, the Spanish Academy, everyone else. No one goes up or down until this is cleared."

"Understood, *Ispettore*," came the cool voice. "Details on the threat? Do you need the Bomb Squad?"

"No. Hemorrhagic fever."

"I'm sorry?"

"Hazmat will know."

He positioned himself in the roadway below the body, ready to wave off traffic. He hadn't been there thirty seconds when his phone rang.

"Raffaele," he said. "Where are you?"

"Where the hell do you think? Up the damn hill, stopping traffic. What the hell's going on?"

"Did you go near the body?"

"Did you tell me not to?"

"Do you always do what I tell you? He could be highly contagious, Raffaele."

"Contagious? With what?"

Giulio repeated himself. "Hemorrhagic fever. Can you see him from where you are?"

"Yes."

"Then look. He's bleeding. From every orifice. Eyes, ears, mouth. Asshole. He didn't get those injuries in a fall. Look at his skin."

A pause. "Looks like someone beat the crap out of him."

"No. Subcutaneous bleeding. Every cell in his body's ruptured. We saw this in Zaire. He probably threw himself over the wall. The pain must have driven him mad."

Another pause, longer. "And it's contagious?"

"There are half a dozen types, maybe more. They're all contagious. Some are virulent. You've heard of Ebola?"

"Shit! Are you serious? This guy has Ebola?"

"There are others." Giulio tried to sound reassuring. "Not nearly so bad. But until we know which one this is . . ." He trailed off when he heard sirens in the distance. They grew louder as they neared.

"Giulio," Raffaele said, "could he— You said the pain drove him mad. Could all this, what he's been doing all day . . ."

"I don't know. Whether it affects the brain like that—I don't know how these things progress."

"What about all the people he came into contact with?"

Giulio just shook his head. The potential public health crisis was enormous, but he didn't see any reason to say that. "Hazmat's on the way," he told Raffaele. "They'll wrap him up and get him out of here. You and I will have to go with them, to . . . get checked out." Listening to the sirens down below, there was another thing Giulio didn't see any reason to say: that while most of the hemorrhagic fevers weren't fatal, this one clearly was; and that though some of them would pass on their own after a time, none of them could be cured.

85

Thomas stepped over the threshold and onto the marble floor under the Tempietto, into one of Christendom's most sacred sites. Across the room, at a small altar, an eternal flame steadily burned, fed by a reservoir of oil. The only light beyond that came through the open door behind him where Livia now stood and faintly through the grate in the floor above. This late in the day, no one but he and Livia had been in the upper chapel, and they were alone here in the lower one, too. He paused, breathing the quiet air. Saint Peter had not died here, may never have even set foot here; but relics and churches, paintings and sculptures and holy places, were all just tools, all serving the same purpose: to bring a seeking soul into awareness of the divine. Despite his knowledge, despite the new truths lately learned and old lies newly revealed, Thomas, standing here, couldn't help but feel a deep, cool comfort, a calm and quiet joy.

He understood: faith had created this joy. Not his faith alone; the true belief of pilgrims over centuries that this place was sacred had sanctified it. Faith had brought holiness into being.

Thomas had rarely felt so strongly the desire to fall to his knees in grateful prayer. But this thought came to him also: belief of a different kind could work to equally powerful, and disastrous, ends. Lorenzo, and countless church-men before him, believed the Noantri to be evil, knew them as Satan's creatures. Had acted upon this belief, had hunted and annihilated them—and in the process, set itself as the enemy of men and women of every kind whom the Church, lost in an overgrowth of fear whose roots were its fear of the Noantri, had also considered *other*. Had done great evil in the name of eradicating evil.

Thomas himself had held to this belief just a few hours earlier. Yet Livia, and Ellen Bird, even Spencer George—and Mario Damiani, and Saint Cecilia herself!—all you had to do was look with open and clear eyes to see the truth.

And the Noantri who had abducted Lorenzo? Without whose demands Thomas would not be here on this holy ground? Yes, they were evil. Proving only that there were malevolent forces at work in the world, in the hearts of Noantri as well as the hearts of churchmen. In the hearts of all people—his, and Livia's. People.

These thoughts were well worth serious reflection, deep contemplation. Not here, though, and not now.

Thomas knelt, but not in prayer. He bent over the thick glass disk, scrabbling for a fingerhold around its edges. He was prepared to work it, to heft it loose. It surprised him by giving without much difficulty, though at two inches thick and three feet wide it made him work to lift it out. Livia could have done it easily, but if any-thing today had been Thomas's job, it was this. He rolled the glass cover aside, laid it carefully down. The cistern below appeared not as deep as he was tall. Its di-ameter was the same as the glass cover, perhaps three feet, and its dirt floor was rough in the dim light. With a glance back at Livia, Thomas dropped inside it.

86

Forcing himself to be calm, Jonah Richter watched from behind a column in the cloister as Livia and Father Kelly entered the Tempietto's lower chapel. Things were unfolding beautifully. When Livia and Kelly exploded out of Santa Cecilia and started doubling back, Jonah knew at once the hunt had entered a new phase. Though he'd been observing them all day, he'd never gotten close enough to learn what their search was based on; still, it was clear the geographical pattern they were following had radically changed. Closer and closer they'd crept to the river, and then suddenly they were running back through Trastevere and up the Janiculum Hill.

Whoever had stolen the Concordat had hidden it well. All of Rome would be demolished and rebuilt, urban-renewed and modernized, before a stone of the Tempietto was ever changed. Silently, Jonah thanked the brave Noantri who'd done it, who'd made possible the coming Unveiling. He had no idea who that had been. That the Concordat was missing at all he'd only learned when like-minded Noantri working in and around the Vatican had begun to whisper to him of odd, esoteric inquiries and recondite trail-following initiated by the new Librarian, Lorenzo Cardinal Cossa. Jonah was the first to grasp the meaning of the Cardinal's research, the only one to arrive at a plan for turning the situation to their use.

This had all taken time, but time was something Jonah had in abundance. He did acknowledge the irony of impatience such as his in someone for whom time unrolled endlessly, world without end, amen. Impetuosity was a trait from his Unchanged days. It had caused him to leave engineering studies for art history, led him to act on his attraction to his dark-haired thesis adviser, though she was clearly at least a decade older. (Such a breathtaking understatement!) It drove him, once he knew, to ask, beg, plead with her to make him Noantri: the world was so huge, so much to be seen, tasted, lived—far more than one meager human lifetime would allow. She'd been reluctant, but once his Change had been accomplished, she'd taken almost as much pleasure in it as he. In their lovemaking, their studies, their play, she was always the more measured, considered, he the more eager and rash. She'd known much better how to choose the routes and byways, metaphorical and real; but once started along them, he could always outrun her.

And he was impatient now: impatient to Unveil, impatient to live freely in the world as the man he was, to stop pretending, stop lying. Impatient to feel Livia's arms around him once again; because she would certainly recognize, once his plans had succeeded—as she always had in all the unorthodox paths he'd taken them down—that the only thing that had been holding her back was an old and burdensome fear.

Impatience, though, could sink him now. He could barely stay still, lurking ridiculously behind this column, but he had to. He'd known that once he made his threat, the Conclave would set Livia on his trail, his and the Concordat's, and that she'd start by searching for it, not him. He knew her that well. He hadn't counted on Father Kelly being of any real use, though he'd admittedly gone to some lengths to keep him around. What he had counted on, and he'd apparently been right, was that if anyone could find the Concordat—the Cardinal Librarian having failed—his Livia could.

———<o>———

87

Livia watched Thomas sit on the edge of the cistern for a moment, and then slip down. The pit appeared to be about five feet deep; the chapel floor was level with his shoulders. He crouched, disappearing. She waited until impatience got the better of her. She stepped forward and, looking down, said, "What can you see?"

"Nothing. You're in my light."

She rummaged in her bag, stooped, and handed him her new cell phone. It didn't have the flashlight app but the screen was bright. He took his out, too, and trained them together on the cistern floor. No spot stood out from another, but it had been a century and a half since Damiani had hidden the Concordat. Livia was already working out various schemes for digging into the packed earth when Thomas turned the beams to the brick walls. They were five feet high, making a circle three feet in diameter. Livia searched her geometry training, itself from a century back. If she was right, something over two hundred bricks would need to be painstakingly examined, pulled and prodded to see if any were loose.

But suddenly Thomas stopped the back-and-forth movement of the light, stood for a moment in thought, and then swung the light to a line of bricks in a chosen direction.

"What are you doing?" Livia asked.

"Southeast. Toward Jerusalem. Look!"

How like Damiani. The sacred dimension of Peter's journey might have eluded him, but not its geographical one. There, on a brick exactly halfway down the wall in the row facing Jerusalem, was scratched a small upside-down cross.

88

———◇———

Thomas handed Livia both phones. Without a word she sat and held the light steady on the marked brick. He crouched, felt around the mortar joint, found a tiny protruding angle. The brick put up no objection as he wriggled it back and forth. It slid forward until he could get a real grip on it, then eased out into his waiting hand. He slipped his other hand into the crevice its absence created.

A curved wall like this, Thomas knew, would be three or four bricks deep; his hand should have had no more than a three-inch cavity to search before bumping into the next brick. But the two bricks behind the marked one had been removed, leaving a miniature cavern. He felt around and found it immediately: a metal tube. He examined it as he drew it out. Lead, from the dullness of it, six inches long, two inches in diameter, sealed in red wax around its cap.

He looked wordlessly up at Livia. She nodded.

With his thumbnail he pried the wax from the seam. A little wriggling and the cap came loose. Inside the tube was a rolled and folded parchment. Thomas slid it out.

"It may be brittle," Livia warned.

Afraid she was right, he loosened its tight spiral but

didn't try to flatten it out. Instead he pulled the outside edge away just enough to see two florid, flowing signatures in ink.

"*Martinus V, Pontifex Maximus,*" he said. "And here—*Pontifex Aliorum*? The Pope of the Others? Who—"

"'The Pope of the Others,'" Livia repeated calmly. "Our Pontifex. He leads the Noantri, and always has. We—" Without warning, she leapt to her feet and spun around. "Stay down!" she shouted.

Of course Thomas didn't. He stood up just in time to see a man trotting down the steps from the Tempietto's upper level. He knew him: the blond Noantri from San Francesco a Ripa. Jonah Richter, the man who'd started all this.

Richter stepped over the threshold into the small room. The eternal flame flickered shadows across his features. He gazed at Livia with a smile brash but also surprisingly tender. "Hello, Livia."

"Jonah." In that one word Thomas heard anguish: love, fear, longing, loss.

"It'll be all right now," Richter said, with gentle reassurance. "Give it to me."

That voice. Thomas realized he knew it. Before he could stop himself he blurted, "You're the man on the phone! You kidnapped Lorenzo!"

Richter looked down at Thomas, standing in the cistern, and laughed. "Father Kelly, we meet at last. An odd situation, but it's a pleasure."

"It's certainly not! Where's the Cardinal? If you've— If he's—" He wasn't sure how to put it. Before he found the words, Livia spoke.

"Jonah. How did you know we were here? And in the church, before?"

Richter nodded, confirming. "I've been following you."

"The Concordat." Her voice held marvel, not accusation. "You never had it. You never knew where it was."

"No." Richter's smile softened. "But I knew you could find it."

Sparks flew from her words: "I was trying to save *you*!"

"Proving I was right. You've never stopped loving me. Or I you. Give it to me, Livia, and we'll be together again. Together, and free. To live as we please. That's all I ever wanted."

"That's why . . . all this? The threat to reveal it, everything? You suddenly thought, Oh, I know, I'll get the Conclave to scare Livia to death and she'll go out and find the lost Concordat, and I'll steal it from her and make us all Unveil?"

He shook his head. "I wish I could claim that sort of inspiration. No, I learned the new Librarian was hunting for it. Before that I didn't even know it was missing. But you can see, it presented a golden opportunity."

"I can't." Her shoulders fell. When she spoke all fire was gone. She sounded small and sad. "All *I* wanted was the life I had. My home, my work." She paused. "You. But you ended that."

"For a while. But now we can have it forever. Give me the Concordat, and we can start a new life. Together. In the sun. Livia, please."

Thomas calmly rerolled the Concordat and replaced it in the tube, making sure the cap was tight. Tube in hand, he muscled himself out of the cistern as though he were leaving a swimming pool. He straightened, stood next to Livia, and, facing Richter, said, "No."

89

————◇————

"Father," said Jonah. Livia saw him smile at Thomas, saw his smile change. "I understand. You want to negotiate. The Concordat for your friend the Cardinal. Fine. Give it to me and I'll tell you where he is. I promise you, he's"—Jonah's grin broadened—"as you last saw him. So, please."

Talking to Livia, Jonah had been caring, wry, the man she'd never—as he'd known—stopped loving. But as he spoke to Thomas, Livia heard a new note in his voice. His confidence spilled into smug superiority, his resolve into threat. Did he not hear himself?

Momentarily the Tempietto dissolved and Livia was back standing before the Conclave. Rosa Cartelli's shrill fears of terror and of fire if the Noantri Unveiled were balanced by the Pontifex's calm words: *The time will come, but it is not come yet.* The Pontifex, whose understanding of their lives was fathomless and clear: this was what he'd meant. This was the true peril of Unveiling. The greatest danger came not from the Unchanged, was not to the temporal existence of the Noantri. It arose from within, and what was at risk was their very souls. Her people would have much to offer an Unveiled world; but the change she was seeing in Jonah right now was the proof that they were not ready. The Concordat's demand for secrecy, she was suddenly sure, was the very thing that kept the swagger out of the Noantri step.

"No," she said. "What you want is wrong."

"His reasons are wrong," said a new voice. "Twisted as they can be. But his request will be fulfilled."

90

Thomas spun to face the doorway. At the sight of the thin form silhouetted there his heart leapt. "*Lorenzo!* Thank God! You're free!"

The Cardinal, dressed in street clothes and without clerical collar—but carrying a lit cigar—smiled as he stepped into the room. "Thomas. You've done well." He turned to the openmouthed Jonah Richter. "You didn't seriously think I'd stay shut up in that foul-smelling attic waiting for you to come back?"

Richter recovered himself, laughed, and made Lorenzo a mock bow. "Your Eminence. You have to admit I was right, though. It worked."

"It wouldn't have been necessary in the first place if you'd had the least modicum of self-control. How like your kind, though: the arrogance of Satan himself. Thomas, bravo. I'm humbled by your devotion and proud of your erudition. Now please give the Concordat to me."

"Lorenzo." Thomas felt the way he often did translating a fragment of text: he understood the words but couldn't get them to make sense. "How did you get free?"

"He obviously walked out my door." Richter's tone was merry. "The same way he walked in."

"I'm sorry, Thomas," said Lorenzo. "We had to improvise. You'd quit the search and were leaving Rome. Jonah had great faith in *Professoressa* Pietro and was perfectly happy to let you go, but I knew better. You were the key." Lorenzo turned a sour eye on Livia, as though she'd been holding Thomas back. Then: "Thomas. The document. Please." He put out his hand.

"Wait. I don't understand. The phone call . . . Your abduction . . ."

"Catch up, Father!" Richter said. His thumb waggled from Lorenzo to himself.

"Desperation makes strange bedfellows," Lorenzo said matter-of-factly. "Jonah came to me and, after I'd controlled my disgust at his very presence, convinced me the Concordat was more likely to be found if a Noantri was also on the trail. This one, to be precise." He pointed the cigar at Livia. "I was revolted, but it was efficient. Thomas, let's get out of here. It's unbearable to be this close to them for long."

Richter shrugged. "Livia, he thinks we smell funny. This from a man who can't go anywhere without a stinking cigar. To have a flame always nearby, that's it, isn't it, Your Eminence? God, you Mortals are so easy to read. Fine, take it and go. It amounts to the same thing."

Thomas looked from one man to the other. "It does? How can that be? *You* want to make it public. Lorenzo—" He stopped as he met Lorenzo's eyes.

In a voice of infinite patience, Lorenzo spoke. "I told you once: centuries ago, a great mistake was made. It can't be undone, but it can be corrected."

"But the Church—if the world knows about this agreement, that the Church and the Noantri—"

"Yes." Lorenzo stood relaxed and straight, like a man

relieved of a burden. "The Church we know, compromised and corrupt, will finally fall."

"And our people"—Jonah Richter smiled at Livia—"will be free."

"Not for long!" Lorenzo spun on Richter in sudden, savage rage. "The new Church that rises will be fearless and mighty! The Church the Savior intended! It will put an end to your filthy kind!" He turned to Thomas; his voice dropped to a plea. "You understand, don't you? All evil flows from them. In God's image, but not human. Among us, not of us, degrading us, destroying us. Mocking the promise of the Resurrection. *They must be stopped!"*

Thomas felt shaky, as though engulfed by a tide that might sweep him away. This was the Lorenzo he knew, the friend he loved, raging against coming disaster as so often before. But this time he was wrong.

Whatever the true colors of Livia's people, whatever the depth of their hearts and the desires inside them—however evil one or another of them might be, as one or another of Thomas's people might also be—the Noantri nature was not as Lorenzo believed.

"No," he said. "Lorenzo—"

"Give it to me!" Lorenzo grasped for the tube in Thomas's hand. Thomas pulled his arm back but no need: Richter seized Lorenzo, flinging him into the altar. The shadows from the eternal flame bounced and danced, though the lamp stayed aright. Richter lunged, clamped a vise grip on Thomas's wrist. He tried to pry the tube loose and would have succeeded but Livia wrapped him from behind in a bear hug. Thomas yanked his hand from Richter's fingers as Richter, with an earthquake roar, blasted free, throwing Livia to the floor.

Richter leapt on Thomas and the two stumbled back. Thomas felt a sickening thud as his head slammed into the wall. Dizzy, pinned by Richter's weight, he stretched his arm, lifting the tube as high as he could; he was taller than Richter and the man couldn't reach it. Richter laughed. He stopped trying for the tube, instead wrapping both hands around Thomas's throat. He squeezed and shook. Fiery knives sliced through Thomas's skull every time the back of his head hit the stone again. Tiny red lights burst behind his eyes and he knew he'd lost. He couldn't breathe; he couldn't think. The tube began to slip from his fingers. His straining lungs begged for air. **Our Father, who art in heaven . . .**

"NO!" A howl echoed off the stone walls. *"Leave him alone!"* Thomas could barely make out Lorenzo staggering toward them. The Cardinal's face purpled with effort as he tried to pull Richter away. He had no effect at all; then, with wonder, Thomas saw Lorenzo—rail-thin, seventy-three, and never a street fighter—make fists and hammer at Richter's head and face.

The blows were ineffectual but Lorenzo was relentless. *"Let go of him!"* he rasped, and finally Richter turned, snarling. Thomas slipped down the wall as Richter dropped his grip and faced the Cardinal. A second's pause; then one roundhouse punch to the jaw was all it took to lift Lorenzo into the air and hurl him across the room.

———◇———

91

Livia, winded when Jonah threw her to the floor, pulled in deep breaths. She shook off her daze and looked up just in time to see the Cardinal, flying off Jonah's fist, crash headfirst into a wall. Jonah spared himself a moment to grin in satisfaction. Then he turned back to where Thomas lay gasping on the floor. He reached down for the tube that had dropped from Thomas's grip; but that moment was all Livia needed.

Leaping up, she tackled Jonah as she had the clerk at the Metro station. The tube flew from Jonah's hand and bounced across the room. They rolled and wrestled; in the end he was stronger, though, and leveraged himself on top of her, pinning her down. Looking into her eyes, he grinned. "This was not how I imagined myself back in this position." He leaned down and quickly kissed her. She lost her breath again. Then he jumped up, scanning for the tube. Livia shook off another, much different kind of daze, and followed his eyes. She saw him redden in anger: Thomas had recovered enough to crawl across the floor and grasp the tube, pulling it protectively close.

"Father," Jonah said. "Don't be silly. You'll only get hurt more."

Thomas couldn't do more than shake his head as he

lay on the floor, hugging the tube to him. When Jonah leaned down to take it, Thomas held it tight, engaging with all his remaining strength in what Livia knew would be a losing tug-of-war.

She leapt up. "Jonah!" He turned to face her. "Leave it! It isn't time!"

He grinned again. A bead of sweat made a trail down his temple. "No. If I can't make you understand, my darling, I'll continue without you. Once we've Unveiled, you'll know. You'll thank me and come back to me. We have time. I can wait." He reached down again and, with a grunt, yanked the tube from Thomas's weakened grip. "Now move aside," he said, but she filled the doorway and stood. "Livia. If we fight, I'll win."

"Still. I can't let you take it."

"Come with me." His voice was soft. "I became Noantri to be with you. You took on this task to save me, you say. So come with me now."

"And to save our people."

"This will free our people."

"It will destroy them."

He took a step toward her. "There's only one way you could stop me."

She said nothing.

"But you won't do it."

"I will," she said, but she knew he was right.

Another step, and he put a hand on her arm, as if to gently tug her aside. She shook it off and stood firm. "I don't want to hurt you," he said.

Before she could answer Thomas lunged up from the floor, grasping for the tube in Jonah's hand. A second late, Jonah pulled his hand away but he'd lost his grip. The tube flew through the air again, this time landing on the altar shelf. Jonah sprang toward it, stretched for it, but Thomas grabbed at his leg and he tripped. Flailing clumsily, trying simultaneously to kick Thomas away and to reach the tube, Jonah knocked the lamp over. Oil spilled down his arm, and in horror Livia watched flame catch fabric. She rushed forward, threw her arms around him to smother the fire, but he had the Concordat in his hand now and he broke free. The back of his jacket blazed as he leapt for the door.

"No!" she shouted. "If you run the air will feed the flames! Drop! Roll!"

She raced out the door, through the courtyard, and down the steps, wild with fear as she saw the flames engulf him. If she could only catch up to him she could stop him, wrap him in her arms, choke off the fire; but he'd always been able to outrun her.

92

Livia had run after Jonah Richter. Thomas should have followed. She might need his help to wrest the Concordat from Richter's hands. But Thomas could barely stand, certainly couldn't run.

And there was something else.

Staggering to his feet, Thomas crossed the chapel to where Lorenzo lay, his head at an odd angle but otherwise sprawled like a man relaxing in the sun.

"Lorenzo. Father!"

Lorenzo opened his eyes.

"Thank God!" Thomas breathed, fumbling for his phone. "I'm calling for help."

"Thomas." Lorenzo's voice was faint. "Find the Magdalene."

"What? No, don't talk. Help will be here—"

"I can't move," Lorenzo whispered. "I can't feel my arms, my legs. Thomas, let me go. But find the Magdalene."

"What do you mean?"

"This isn't all. The Church you love . . . the Concordat wouldn't have . . . it would have been built anew. Stronger, purer. But it won't . . . you must find . . . find . . ." Slowly, his eyes closed. His lips continued to move, though no sound reached Thomas.

"No. No, Father, please. Lorenzo!" But there was nothing more.

Thomas knelt motionless on the cold marble, trying to will Lorenzo to open his eyes, to speak. Finally, rousing himself, he looked around. Oil from the now-extinguished eternal flame dripped from the altar onto the floor. He stumbled over, dipped his fingers in it, muttered the prayer consecrating it to God's holy purposes. Returning to Lorenzo's side, he traced the sign of the cross on Lorenzo's forehead, and began: "Through this holy unction and his own most tender mercy may God pardon thee . . ."

93

Livia stepped slowly into the chapel under the Tempietto to find Thomas praying over the body of Lorenzo Cossa. In her hand she held the lead tube; in her heart, the indelible sight of Jonah, at the bottom of the steep steps, on his knees as the fire consumed him. His arms were raised high, one hand a triumphal fist; the other, holding the tube, suddenly hurled it out of the flames with what must have been his last strength.

By the time she'd reached him, nothing could be done. He was charred, devoured, destroyed, turning to ash in the still-dancing flames. She'd stood, numb, watching the fire die down. She'd said his name once; then, carefully, methodically, as though it were someone else doing it, she'd turned away and searched until she found the lead tube. Clutching it to her, she'd started back up the hill.

In the chapel, she knelt beside Thomas. After a few moments he turned to look at her.

"I'm so sorry," she said.

His eyes held a question that she answered with a shake of her head.

"I'm sorry, too," he told her.

In the silence, she opened her arms for him. He moved into her embrace. In the dim chapel, they shared their sorrow.

94

Anna had watched Jorge twist and flail as he fell. His descent wasn't long and he'd hit the ground hard. It didn't matter. The fall was camouflage. Since he was a Noantri, the impact wouldn't have killed him; but what she'd done would, whether he'd fallen or not. She'd seen it begin. As he lay on the asphalt, tiny drops of blood started to leak from his eyes. There would be more, and then from his mouth, nose, and ears. His skin would turn purple, as though he'd been bruised all over. His internal organs, too, would bleed. Anna had given him a great gift some decades ago. He'd been unworthy of it, and now she had taken it back.

She'd wanted to stay and watch, because although this was a process much discussed among the Noantri, very few had actually seen it. Fascinated as she was, though, she knew she'd better move on. Jorge's body would be discovered soon, and it would be just as well if she weren't around.

Where was she going? She hadn't decided, but it would be far. What she'd said about finding Pietro and the priest was bold talk, and with time she knew she could, but right now she wasn't in a position to look. So far the Conclave didn't seem to know that she'd been trying to thwart their plans; been trying, in fact, to usurp their power. At this point, she judged them likely to win. That idiot Jorge had put her and her faction too far behind. She had no idea where to go to pick up the chase now. To stay in the game she'd have to regroup, and she had a feeling the clock was running out.

She could live with that. She could live with that, she thought with a smile, for a very long time. Her followers were determined that the Noantri should Unveil, and their numbers grew with each passing year. When Anna decided their strength was sufficient, she'd step forward and confront the Conclave directly. She wouldn't need the lost Concordat for that.

Anna had cast one last glance at the dying Jorge, whose blood was by then seeping along the street to flow in little rivulets down the hill. She headed in the same direction, down, saying good-bye to La Sapienza, to comparative lit, and, with a sigh, to the Serb professor she'd had her eye on. And to Anna Jagiellon, she supposed, for a while. That was all right. It was a big world.

Trotting down the steps, she found herself wondering two things: Why the foul cologne, which had made him so much easier to find? And why, when Jorge's bloody dying eyes met hers, had she read in them, not pain, not anger, but gratitude, and joy?

95

Thomas walked beside Livia in the silence under the trees. The winding way through the Orto Botanico led them down the hill far from the sirens and flashing lights. Leaving the Tempietto they found something had happened, something so big, one wide-eyed tourist told another, that the road down the Janiculum had been closed and they all had to stay up top. The six tourists on the overlook argued among themselves, agreeing the problem was clearly terrorism, debating only what kind: domestic, foreign, bombs, bio-agents. Livia had relayed all this to Thomas as she'd listened in, unnoticed, from the cloister.

"We can't stay here," he said. "How will we get down?"

"Don't worry. Come."

He followed as she turned and headed in the other direction, back around the cloister to the road along the top of the hill.

Thomas, dazed and bruised, moved slowly. Walking at all was an effort, but he found, for the first time today, it didn't take any extra work to keep up with Livia. Her steps were as fatigued as his; she appeared also weary, also dispirited. The Noantri body, he'd learned, could restore itself, come back rapidly from almost any injury. The Noantri heart, it seemed, not so.

She'd led him to the gates of the Orto Botanico, Rome's Botanical Garden. They'd been prepared to climb the fence in case the Orto had been shut down, but in typical Roman style, either the word that no one was to go up or down the Janiculum hadn't reached the Orto, or more likely, it had been received with a shrug and was being ignored. They paid their entrance fee, hoping the young man in the booth wasn't on the look-out for fugitives. As it turned out, he was not, being barely sentient enough to notice customers. They headed down the curving pathway where fallen leaves whispered underfoot. The tracery of branches revealed the fading autumn afternoon, as though the tree canopy had given up trying to hide the sky. The few blooms still to be seen had withered; even the bamboo grove was fading from green to yellow.

Whatever had happened on the road they'd have to learn later. They couldn't afford to be seen by the *polizia* or Carabinieri; and they couldn't afford to wait. Richter was gone beyond recognition, an unexplained blaze exhausted to a smoking mound of ashes on a flight of stone steps; but Lorenzo's body would not lie in the chapel long without someone, a sightseer or caretaker, stumbling upon it.

Lorenzo's body. Lorenzo had lied to Thomas and used him, had betrayed his trust and had intended to betray the Church. But anger, indignation, resentment, even relief that Lorenzo's plans had been thwarted— Thomas felt none of these. Instead, walking under empty branches, he searched himself, searched their fifteen years of friendship, for the failing. What in

Thomas had made Lorenzo unwilling to trust him with this secret, unable to share his knowledge and his fears? They could have debated, talked, studied over it. They could have found another path. Why had it come to this?

96

Seated at the café in Piazza della Scala, Luigi Esposito had to admit to himself that he might be wrong. Wrong about Spencer George's involvement in whatever was going on? No. The man was so clearly hiding something that Luigi suspected the uniformed *scemi* he'd been stuck with this morning could've seen it. But it was possible he was wrong about the value of a surveillance. It had been an hour since he'd left the interview with the historian and the man had not emerged. If nothing happened in the next hour or so, no one in or out, maybe the most useful thing Luigi could do would be to go back to the office and dig into George's life. People peddling stolen art didn't exist in vacuums. He'd find another path.

These were the thoughts running through his head when his cell phone rang. He didn't need to check the screen; he'd thought it prudent to give the *soprintendente* his own ring tone.

"Esposito, where are you?"

"Piazza della Scala, sir. Still on the surveillance."

"Leave. Your car's close?"

"Yes, sir, but—"

"Take it, not a cab. Go to the Ambulatorio di Medicina Tropicale. On Via Portuense. The emergency room. Tell them who you are."

"The emergency room? Who's there?"

"You. They're waiting for you."

"I— Sir, what are you talking about? I'm fine."

"Maybe not. That Argentinian, your suspect? He's dead. Of a hemorrhagic fever."

"A what?"

"Deadly and contagious. The officers you had with you this morning are already there. So are the Carabinieri you're working with, and from what you say they had no physical contact with him."

"No, they didn't. But, sir, he—"

"Esposito. It's an order. They'll keep you until they finish the autopsy and isolate the virus. It's not just for you. It's to keep you from infecting anyone else. I'm sure you're fine," he said, in tones that made it clear he wasn't. "But go."

This wasn't happening, Luigi thought. He had a case! A real crime to solve. A theory that was right, he knew it was. Two Carabinieri detectives who respected him. This was his chance—this was his blue uniform—

"Esposito! Do I have to send an ambulance to find you?"

"No." Luigi cast a last, longing glance at Spencer George's door. "Sir. Not necessary. I'm on my way."

97

◆—◇—◆

Neither Livia nor Thomas had spoken since they entered the Orto Botanico; their silence continued as they emerged at the bottom of the hill and made their way through Trastevere. Livia kept them to the less-traveled, more-shadowed streets, though they saw few Carabinieri or *polizia*; whatever had happened on the Janiculum seemed to have drawn all the law officers in Rome. Livia's thoughts, unbidden but uncontrollable, kept returning to that long-ago violet evening, to the cobalt cloth in the candlelit room, to the moment she'd given in to her own desires, and his, and made Jonah Noantri.

The fault was hers. He wasn't strong enough, and if she'd brought the request to the Conclave, as the Law required, they would have told her that. She had ignored the Law, because she already knew.

She'd done it, as she'd revealed herself to him at all, because she was afraid of losing him. Now he was lost: to her, to the world. To himself.

Thomas hadn't asked where they were going, but as they reached the middle of the Ponte Sisto, Livia stopped and faced him. "The place where the Conclave meets is just over the bridge."

Thomas leaned on the stone balustrade and watched the Tiber flow. "You intend to give the Concordat to them?"

"They'll keep it hidden. I wasn't sure that was still necessary, even as late as this morning. But now . . ." She leaned beside him, trying to marshal an argument. This was his Church's copy; by rights it should be returned. Still staring out over the water, he held up a hand to stop her.

"I agree. I don't know how many in the Church know it exists, but Lorenzo can't be the only one who feels— who felt as he did. About your people. I don't think we can return it to the Church."

"Jonah wasn't alone, either," she said quietly. "The Conclave will protect both copies. Until it's time."

He nodded and straightened, and they walked on.

98

Father Thierry Ateba unlocked the Librarian's office suite, entered, and closed the ornate door behind. He crossed himself as though in the presence of death, although the death of Cardinal Cossa, of which Father Ateba had just learned, had occurred within the hour on the Janiculum Hill, not here. The room, of course, did not know its occupant was gone forever, and the Cardinal's open books, his papers, and his humidor all sat as he had left them, awaiting his return.

It would fall to Father Ateba, as Lorenzo Cossa's personal secretary, to sort and organize these items, to separate Cardinal Cossa's possessions from those of the Church and ensure that each item was ultimately disposed of as it must be. It would take time, but meticulousness and patience were two of Father Ateba's virtues. He glanced about the room, unconsciously planning his strategy for where to begin, how to conscientiously, efficiently fulfill this final responsibility. After his work was complete, he himself would no longer be needed here. The new Librarian and Archivist would bring with him his own assistant.

Father Ateba moved to the window and threw it open to rid the air of the lingering smell of cigar smoke: not offensive, but an odor he had never liked. Turning back to the room, he regarded the books and papers on the late Cardinal's desk. Father Ateba had been made privy to the work the Cardinal was doing, and he wondered if the new Librarian would want to continue it.

He walked to the desk, the obvious place to begin. First, though, now that he was alone here where he wouldn't be disturbed, one other task demanded his attention. As he'd been requested to do when he'd received the sad news, he took his cell phone from his jacket pocket and pressed in a number. He was greeted by a voice familiar to him for many, many years.

"Salve."

"Salve. Sum Thierry Ateba. Quid aegis?"

"Hic nobis omnibus bene est. Quomodo auxilium vobis dare possumus?"

99

"You've done well, Livia," said a deep, slow voice. "And you, Father Kelly. The Noantri thank you."

Thomas nodded, unable to speak. As he'd walked with Livia through the twilight from the Ponte Sisto to Santa Maria dell'Orazione e Morte, she'd told him where they were going and what to expect. She'd tried to prepare him, but how could he have been prepared for this? This morning he'd have laughed at the idea that vampires existed. Twelve hours later he was standing beside one, in front of thirteen more, in the light of two great candelabra in the basement of a bone church.

Arrayed before him, robed in black, were what had been described as the most powerful figures in the Noantri world. Their College of Cardinals, in a way. He suddenly realized: their ruling body! Body, now *that* was funny. A laugh threatened to explode out of him; understanding himself to be on the edge of a cliff of exhaustion, shock, and grief-fueled wildness, he clamped his jaw shut and forced himself to be still.

"We will keep this copy of the Concordat safe," the voice went on. "As we have the other, all these years." The speaker was the Noantri leader, the Pontifex Aliorum. It was he himself who had signed the Concordat. He spoke in English; Livia had said that would be the case, out of courtesy to Thomas. His was the first voice heard in the room since Livia had presented the lead tube, along with Mario Damiani's notebook and its missing pages. The Pontifex had passed the notebook to the woman on his right and opened the tube in silence and with great care. Once he'd unfolded the document, Thomas could have sworn he saw the man's face lose some of its somber tension, though you couldn't say he relaxed. Probably—like Lorenzo—this man never relaxed. He'd passed the document, also, to the woman on his right; each Counsellor had taken it in turn and looked it over while Livia and Thomas stood before them.

"The time will come when our peoples—yours, Father, and ours—will be released from the requirements of this agreement. On that day, your names will be spoken in praise. Until then, what's happened must remain our secret." He regarded Thomas. "Father Kelly, you've lost a friend today. Please accept our deepest sympathy, and understand none among us sought this outcome."

Again, Thomas could only nod. The Pontifex turned his attention to Livia.

"Livia, you've also suffered a loss. That it was inevitable makes it no less tragic. We offer our sympathy to you, also."

"Thank you, Lord," Livia said, her voice quiet but steady.

A long moment of silence followed. All eyes rested on Livia as the Pontifex said, *"Mandatum exsecuta es et opus perfectum est."* **You have followed your instructions and your task is complete.** It was a formal acknowledgment, no doubt part of a ritual centuries old. What other rituals, Thomas wondered, were observed here?

"Officio perfungi mihi gratum est." Livia responded formally. **I am grateful to be of service.** She took a breath and, switching back to English, she said, "Lord, might I make a request?"

The Pontifex traded glances with the woman beside him. He nodded. "Speak."

"Thank you, Lord. The circumstances of the day have left many questions in the Unchanged world. The Carabinieri are searching for Father Kelly and myself. Jonah's—" Thomas saw her swallow and blink back tears. She recovered and continued, "His death will go unnoticed by the Unchanged, but two men, churchmen, are also dead."

"And a Noantri who certainly has not gone unnoticed," said the woman beside the Pontifex. "The clerk from the Library. On the Janiculum Hill. You didn't know?"

Livia gasped. "Not unnoticed? Was he—"

She stopped as the woman nodded. "Yes. His Lord destroyed him."

Thomas wasn't sure of the significance of that, but Livia clearly was. She paled. "Who is that?"

"A woman named Anna Jagiellon. She made him without our consent, and has done this without it, also. She will be dealt with."

"On the Janiculum." Thomas was surprised to hear his own voice. The Counsellors turned to him. "Is that why the emergency vehicles were there?"

A rotund man answered, someone who hadn't previously spoken. "Yes. The death of a Noantri, when brought about this way, resembles some of the more frightening human illnesses." Unlike the other two, this man spoke English—American English—without a trace of an accent. No, Thomas realized: with an accent like his own. A Boston Noantri, from Southie. Thomas set that aside, to think about later. "The body was removed and will be autopsied," the man said. "Nothing, of course, will be found."

"The microbe?" Thomas asked.

The man smiled. "Ever the scholar, eh, Father Kelly? The autoimmune reaction triggered by reexposure—the cause of death—destroys the microbe. Nothing," he repeated, "will be found."

Thomas felt questions arising in his mind in infinite number, but their sheer quantity prevented his articulating any single one.

"Father Kelly," the Pontifex said, "your curiosity regarding our natures is obvious. So is your weariness. Perhaps you'd prefer to renew our dialogue at some future time? Because of your services to the Noantri this day, I speak for each member of this Conclave, including myself, when I say we will be pleased to make ourselves available to you for further discussion, whenever you choose. We have held these dialogues from time to time, through the years, with friends of the Noantri. You are one."

As exhausted and grief-stricken as he was, Thomas still understood the value of the gift he'd just been given. "Yes," he said. "I'd welcome that. Thank you."

The Pontifex turned back to Livia.

"You, too, are weary. But you have a request to make of us?"

"Yes, Lord," Livia said. "I, of course, will leave Rome, but I'm concerned about Ellen Bird and Spencer George. Most of all, about Father Kelly. The authorities will continue their investigations, and I don't want

Spencer's or Ellen's lives interrupted. And Thomas—
Father Kelly—can't just change identities and vanish, as
we can. Nor, I think, would he want to." Her gaze
briefly met Thomas's, then returned to the Counsellors.
"If there's any way the Conclave can . . . affect the
course of the authorities' processes? I'm not sure what
I'm asking you to do, but . . ." She trailed off.

"There is no reason for you to leave Rome," the Pontifex said. "Or to Cloak."

"The Carabinieri have been looking for us since Father Battista died in Santa Maria della Scala. Spencer told
me that. And surely someone will have seen us near the
Tempietto. We're suspects and, at this point, fugitives."

"At the moment, yes. But you have a very good friend
in Spencer George. He contacted us a few hours ago,
with a clever proposal. Arrangements have already been
made."

"Arrangements, Lord?"

The Pontifex looked to the woman on his right.

"The Carabinieri and the Gendarmerie are in fact
looking for you," she said, "though their theories about
the basis of your involvement keep changing." In her dry
voice Thomas heard her disdain for the quotidian forces
of the law. "What they are sure of is the existence of an
international ring of art thieves. Spencer George has
elected himself head of this cabal. When his home is
searched, as it will soon be, many valuable items belonging to the Vatican will be found. They're being selected
as we speak, from the office of the Cardinal Librarian,
and will be scattered about. They will include this notebook. Certain other treasures will also be found, which
will be traced back to other collections. On those items

the provenance marks are recent and false, provided by Spencer George himself. Evidence planted in certain places will make it clear that you, Livia, were aiding Father Kelly in a search, instigated by Cardinal Cossa, to find the leader of this criminal organization, and to do it with utmost discretion, in order that the Vatican not be embarrassed by the ease with which its collections have apparently been raided. The Holy See, realizing you were both in service to the Cardinal, will intervene with the Carabinieri on your behalf."

"I . . ."

Livia seemed no more able to take all this in than Thomas was himself. The woman continued.

"Ellen Bird, if she's noticed at all, will be considered an ally of yours and therefore of the Vatican's. The unfortunate death of Father Battista will be ascribed—correctly, I think?—to Jorge Ocampo, now dead himself, and a member of this ring of thieves, though his murderous behavior will most likely be attributed not to the requirements of larceny but to a mental instability brought about by the infectious fever that killed him. Cardinal Cossa"—she gave Thomas a brief, piercing look—"will be thought to have been slain in a confrontation with these thieves. Whose leader, by the time this has all been worked out—the Carabinieri and Gendarmerie detectives involved in the case being temporarily indisposed—will be found to have fled the country."

"Leader?" Livia asked. "Spencer? Fled the country?"

"He'll be traceable for a time, to give the authorities something to do. His ultimate plan, once he's finally disappeared, is to spend some years in America."

"Spencer?" Livia repeated. "America?"

"He expressed a desire to see the New World."

"The New . . ." A pause. "Yes, I see. And his collection?"

"The most valuable pieces—valuable to the Noantri, I mean—will be found to have unassailable provenance. They, and his home, will turn out to be not strictly Dr. George's possessions, but actually those of a distant cousin in Wales. This cousin will continue to pay the taxes and costs of upkeep on the home and will visit occasionally. A number of years hence he will, I believe, retire to Italy."

She settled back in her chair with a satisfied huff. The Pontifex spoke. "You have, as I said, a very good friend in Spencer George." With a small smile, he added, "As does the Gendarme detective. Apparently the entire idea of an art-theft ring was his. Dr. George feels he's wasted on the Gendarmerie and has requested that, in return for Dr. George's participation in this scheme, we arrange for the young man to be reassigned—transferred to the Carabinieri. If, of course, he's willing to go."

"I see," said Livia again. "So, I may just . . . go home?"

"You may, but I wouldn't suggest that you do, just yet. You and Father Kelly will be cleared of all suspicion shortly, but not until the various detectives become available, sometime tomorrow. Until then your house is being watched by officers who have instructions to bring you in for questioning. I assume you'd rather avoid that eventuality?"

"Very much so, Lord."

"Well, then. As I'm sure you know, we maintain a number of residences throughout Rome for the convenience of visitors. May we offer you both our hospitality this evening?"

In fitful sleep that night, Livia was haunted by shadowy, oppressive dreams; between them, lying awake, by the image of Jonah engulfed in fire. Arising with the sun, she showered, then chose gray slacks and a soft blue sweater from among the items they'd been told would be waiting at the spacious apartment on Via Giulia for their use. "You both look rather the worse for wear," had been Rosa Cartelli's assessment.

Livia made her way into the kitchen. She and Thomas had been met the night before by a friendly young Noantri—though, from his manner of speech, Elder to her, Livia thought—who had shown them their rooms and served a light supper of *pasta al limone* before retiring discreetly to his own apartment across the hall. Now, at this early hour, she expected to be alone; but she found Thomas already at the table in the bright room. He was drinking a cappuccino, and grounds in the sink indicated it wasn't his first.

"Good morning," Livia said, smiling softly. "How are you doing?"

She could see he'd also had a shower; his wet hair was neatly combed and parted. The purple bruises from Jonah's hands were visible above the collar of a new sweatshirt, plain and black. He considered her question as though it were complex and arcane. At last he said, "I'm not the same man I was yesterday, that's for sure."

"I hope," she said, "that I like this man as well as I liked that one. Do you want more coffee?"

At his nod, she opened a ceramic canister and spooned coffee into the *moka* pot. She put it on the stove and unwrapped the blue and white paper around the *cornetti* that sat in a bowl in the center of the table. In a small pitcher she steamed milk and drizzled it into their coffee cups. Bringing the coffee to the table, she sat down across from him. "Were you able to sleep?"

"Not really."

"I'm not surprised. It will be a long time, for both of us, I think."

He nodded, reached for a *cornetto*. He ate; she leaned back in her chair and sipped her coffee, looking beyond him to the window and the glorious blue sky. In this quiet moment, in this bright, airy place her people maintained to shelter their own, she began to feel, not the end of her shock and sadness over what had happened yesterday, but the possibility of that end. The Noantri sense of time and thus of potential was different from that of the Unchanged. To Livia's people, even to the Eldest, the future was always longer than the past. Thomas's relationship to his own history was quite different, but she hoped he could feel some echo of optimism, too.

"There's something else," he said.

She turned from the window. "Something else?"

"That kept me awake. Not just what happened. What Lorenzo said."

Livia thought back, found nothing to fasten on. "What did he say?"

"As he was . . . The last thing he said to me was that the Church would have been built anew after the revelation of the Concordat. But he seemed to be trying to tell me there was another secret, something even more dangerous. He died . . . before he could tell me more. But he said, 'Find the Magdalene.'"

"The Magdalene? Do you have any idea what he meant?"

Thomas shook his head.

Tentatively, Livia said, "There are artworks all over Rome, paintings and sculptures, depicting Mary Magdalene. Hundreds, I'd guess. But there's only one church dedicated to her. Santa Maria Maddalena, near the Pantheon. Could he have wanted us to go there? You, wanted you to go. He wouldn't have wanted anything from me."

Thomas met her eyes. "I'm sorry," he said. "Hate like his . . . I always thought he was such a good man. Tough, and often angry, but at heart so good."

"The tragedy," she said softly, "is that he thought so, too. He meant to do good. He thought he was. So few people are wicked by their own lights. Thomas, you loved him. And he loved you. Remember that."

"He used me," Thomas said bitterly. "My studies—my focus on the period around the Risorgimento—it was his idea. Our friendship, keeping me close—it was all so I'd be ready for this. For when he had the chance to find the Concordat."

"Because he thought it was important. He thought the Church you both loved needed him, needed you, to do this." She put her hand over his. "And I doubt if your friendship was any less real, or less deep, for all that."

"How real? He didn't trust me enough to tell me about the Concordat. About your people."

She was quiet a moment. "I trusted Jonah enough to tell him. It was wrong."

Thomas entwined his fingers with hers. They sat in silence for a long time.

"I want to go there," Thomas said. "To Santa Maria Maddalena."

Livia met his eyes. "What I was instructed to do, I've done," she said. "Whatever the Cardinal's words meant, he intended them for you. If you want to go without me, I'll understand."

"No," Thomas said, without pause. "I'd like you to come."

101

They walked through the fresh Rome morning along streets just waking for the day. Their footsteps, in rhythm with one another, were purposeful but no longer racing, no longer furtive. Thomas tried to soothe the heaviness in his heart and the confusion in his mind by not thinking at all, not about where they were going or about what had happened yesterday. He watched shopkeepers put out their signs and sidewalk racks, café owners wipe off tables and bustle out with coffee for early customers; but the extraordinary choreography of everyday activity, usually a source of delight to him, today didn't provide enough distraction. He turned to something else, something that had always worked: the search for knowledge.

"May I ask you something? Some things?" he said to Livia.

"Of course."

"About your people?"

"I just hope I know the answers. It might really be Spencer you want."

"No, it's not your history. It's your . . . your nature, I suppose you'd say." They walked on, Thomas organizing his thoughts, welcoming the calm that came with focus. "Stop me if I get too personal. Can you . . . have children?"

"No." A few steps later, she added, "Some Noantri, who either didn't know that when they were made, or thought they didn't care, find it a source of great sadness later on." She paused again. "There are children among us. Or rather, Noantri who were made when they were children. Since the Concordat it's been an unforgivable infraction of the Law to do that, and even before, it's something most Noantri would have balked at. But these people—no more than a dozen or so—were made long ago. They occupy a special place in our Community—one or two of them are among the Eldest."

Thomas reflected upon that. Everything he'd learned this past day would take so much reflection. "Is anyone ever sorry?"

"About becoming Noantri?"

"Because it's irreversible. And . . . endless."

He thought he knew her answer: that she'd say absolutely not, that with senses enhanced and all the time in the world to study, to hone, to learn, to love, what could anyone regret?

"Yes," she said quietly. "This life becomes a burden for some. Many people find they never actually wanted to live forever. What they wanted was not to die."

They turned a corner, had to part for a large group of small children in two ragged, giggling lines. When the little ones had been herded past by their frazzled guardians, Thomas and Livia came together again.

"This time yesterday," he said, "I didn't know you existed. Tell me, are there—others?"

"Other Noantri?" Livia looked confused. "Besides those of us you've met? Of course."

"No, no. Other . . . I'd have said, 'supernatural beings,' but . . ."

Livia laughed. "I see. You want to know if I party with werewolves and zombies? Dance with skeletons, go hiking with Bigfoot?"

"I . . ." Thomas felt himself reddening. "When you put it that way, it does sound idiotic."

"It's not idiotic." Her voice softened. "I just don't know. There have always been legends—we hear them just as you do. But there've been legends about us, too: that we turn into bats, that we can't be seen in mirrors. On book covers we're shown with eyes like red-hot coals, in films with skin like dirty snow. Some of those ideas, we're guilty of fostering, once they start making the rounds. Bram Stoker, who was one of us, did us a great service. Stories about us had started to circulate, interest had been renewed. It was a daring move to write *Dracula*. Some Noantri were horrified, but it turned out to be brilliant. He made us seem at once completely outlandish, and identifiable. Anyone who could go out in daylight, who didn't have pointy teeth and didn't smell like rank earth, couldn't possibly be a vampire. Those kinds of myths allow us to live among the Unchanged more easily. I'd imagine if other"—she paused—"other varieties of people, people with different natures, do exist, they're not much like the stories about them, either."

Pondering that, the meaning and possibilities, how wide the world was and how narrow human knowledge, Thomas found himself beside Livia rounding the corner into Piazza della Rotonda without being quite sure how they'd gotten there. To their right, the Pantheon itself, one of the world's truest gems of architectural creation. To their left, a café, people relaxing with a morning coffee or using the coffee to rev up for the day: contradictory uses, the same pleasure. Livia led the way past tourists getting an early start and up a little street called Via della Rosetta. A few short, shadowy blocks, and then straight ahead rose the elaborate Baroque façade of Santa Maria Maddalena, golden limestone glowing.

Thomas and Livia entered the open church doors, stepped through the small entry on the right into the sanctuary. Thomas dipped his fingers in the font of holy water and crossed himself, Livia waiting for this brief ritual to be complete before, together, they walked forward. Reaching the last row of pews, they stopped. Soaring marble, polished wood, gilt and silver and a blood-red cross in the stained glass of the rose window; but nothing offered a direction, a hint of what Lorenzo might have meant.

"Damiani's notebook," Thomas said. "Maybe there was a poem . . . ?"

But Livia shook her head. "They were all in Trastevere, the places he wrote about."

Thomas hadn't really expected that to work. "Well," he said, scanning the ornate ceiling, the patterned floor, the side chapels with their marble tombs, none of which sparked any flashes of inspiration, "I guess it's time to ask someone."

"Ask what?" Livia said, but Thomas was already striding down the center aisle.

102

<hr />

Livia followed Thomas to the front of the church, where a black-robed monk whose habit bore a large crimson cross laid an altar cloth in one of the side chapels.

"*Buongiorno*, Father," Thomas said, and continued in Italian. "Thomas Kelly, SJ, and *Professoressa* Livia Pietro. Do you have a moment? We have some questions about this church."

The monk turned his lean, unsmiling face to them. "Emilio Creci. I'll be glad to help." Meeting his eyes, "glad" was not the first word that sprang to Livia's mind.

"Thank you." Thomas smiled, not reacting to the monk's frostiness. "We're both historians, Livia and I. We were advised to come here by . . . another historian, who has since died. We're hoping to honor his guidance, but we don't know what it was he particularly wanted us to study. I'm sure your church has many treasures, but does anything stand out to you, something a pair of bookish academics might have been sent to see?" He spoke with a self-deprecating diffidence, clearly calculated to make the other man feel both superior and impatient. This wasn't exactly flimflam, Livia thought, but it could without fear of contradiction be called misdirection. What he'd said over breakfast was true: Thomas Kelly wasn't the same man he'd been yesterday.

And, Livia was delighted to find, she liked this one even better.

Father Creci shrugged. "We're a poor order, dedicated to the sick. This church is grand, but in Rome"—he smiled thinly—"undistinguished. Like many of the smaller orders, we're . . . honored with the responsibility of maintaining a property whose demands threaten to outstrip our resources. Not a problem I believe Jesuits encounter often?"

Oho, thought Livia. **Sibling rivalry: so that's his problem.**

Thomas smiled beneficently. "If that's the case, you're due even more praise, Father." He spread his hands to indicate the gleaming marble and glowing stained glass, the elaborate side chapels and polished wood pews. The church's rococo interior was wild with gilt and Technicolor frescoes: in Livia's opinion, over the top, but admirable nonetheless. "The beauty of Santa Maria Maddalena—and of the obvious treasures here—is a testament to you and your brothers," Thomas said. "You must spend a great deal of time working here. Each of you must come to know this church intimately."

Thomas was obviously trying to steer the conversation back to the church building and its contents, but Father Creci still had a point to make.

"As much as needed. As I said, our mission is to the indigent sick. The resources I spoke of include our time. We resist as well as we can being caught up in the needs of the material world."

"And yet you serve your immediate material world— your obligation to this church—so well."

"Thank you," said the monk. He was forced to acknowledge the compliment, but rose to the defense of his fellows and how they spent their time. "The endowment helps a great deal, of course."

Thomas and Livia glanced at each other. "Endowment?" Thomas asked.

"Strictly for the upkeep of the church and its possessions. Not for our ministry, which is always in need."

"Really?" Thomas murmured. "How narrow. Who is your benefactor?"

"We've never known," the monk answered with a combination of resentment and pride. "The endowment dates to 1601. It enabled us to maintain our first church, and later build this one. We're charged with the particular responsibility of the Maddalena statue, but in return for constant vigilance with regard to that, the endowment enables us to provide for, as you say, this immediate material world, while allowing my brothers and myself to focus on our true calling."

Livia felt her pulse quickening, but she didn't speak, letting Thomas continue. Betraying no excitement, he said, "The Maddalena statue? An endowment—that must be an important piece."

"To us it is, for the freedom its upkeep allows us. It dates from the late fifteenth century. Personally—though of course I haven't a Jesuit's erudition, so I can only think what I think—I find it neither good nor particularly beautiful. It was of obvious value to someone in 1601, however."

Smiling, Thomas asked, "May we see it?"

103

The grudging Father Creci led them across the front of the church to a chapel on the right. Tucked in a corner on a two-foot marble plinth stood a large wooden statue of Mary Magdalene. Life-size, Livia thought, if you took into account people's smaller stature then. Of course, it wasn't made in Mary's time; it was made in the fifteenth century. Still, people were smaller during the Renaissance, also. It was an ongoing source of needling from the Elder Noantri to the Newer, if one of the relatively few made in the nineteenth and twentieth centuries should show himself to be no physical match for a smaller, slighter—but no less everlasting—senior.

Examining the statue with a practiced eye, Livia found herself agreeing with the belligerently untutored monk. As a work of art, it wasn't very good. Its proportions were off, its carving in some places clumsy. The iconography was here: the long loose hair, the left hand holding the unguent jar, that marvelous contradiction signaling Mary Magdalene's dual nature—her debased early life as a prostitute and her later devotion, because it was that same costly unguent with which she washed Christ's feet. This Magdalene wore no jewels or gold chains, and neither her clothing nor the body beneath it could be called voluptuous. Those facts and the half-closed eyes and pensive face told Livia the sculptor was depicting Mary after her repentance and conversion.

"Livia," Thomas said, in casual tones that belied the rise in his pulse rate and adrenaline level, which Livia could feel, and which echoed her own. "I think this might be it, don't you? What we were sent to see."

"It could be," Livia answered, putting doubt into her voice although she felt none. She turned and smiled at the monk. "Father Creci, you're obviously dedicated to your mission and we've already taken you from it for too long. Might we be allowed to spend some time with your sculpture? I understand you have a great deal to do. I think I speak for Father Kelly, also, when I say your devotion to your ministry is inspiring. If I may be allowed to make an offering?" She slipped three one-hundred-euro notes from her wallet. "Or shall I place this in the offering box on our way out?"

The monk all but snatched the bills from her hand. "No, no need to trouble yourself. I'll take care of it. Thank you. Yes, please, take as much time as you like. If you have any further questions, don't hesitate to ask."

They watched him walk quickly away, a bit more bounce in his step now than before.

"Do you think he thought I wasn't actually going to stuff the bills in the box?" Livia asked Thomas.

"I'm sure of it." Thomas grinned. He turned his attention to the statue and his face grew serious. "If this is it, what Lorenzo meant, what about it did he mean?"

"I don't know," Livia said slowly, considering the piece. "Either its iconography conceals something . . ."

"Or it conceals something."

"Another Damiani poem?"

"Possible," said Thomas. "Personally, I hope not. I'd like to think we're done with that."

Livia walked slowly around, leaned to peer behind the statue. She put out a tentative hand, felt it, pushed gently. Firmly positioned on its base, solid and tremendously heavy, it didn't move. Returning to the front, she stood and looked, letting her eyes move slowly over the piece, as the art historian in her would with any new work.

The statue's face wasn't beautiful: elongated and flat, with a high forehead, a crooked nose, a cleft chin. The folds of cloth, so often a breathtaking element of Renaissance art, were uninteresting, and the unguent jar was held at a strange angle. The face had an undeniable power, its emotions growing deeper and more complex the longer Livia regarded it. The force exerted by it, though, required time spent before it. In a church—and a city—so full of glories, this statue would almost assuredly have passed unnoticed through the centuries; Livia herself, whose vocation gave her reason to be familiar with many more pieces than most people could claim, couldn't recall having seen it before. A strange piece to carry its own endowment.

Unless that were the point.

"The face is beautiful," Thomas said. "No, I don't mean beautiful. But I can't stop looking at it."

"I think the sculptor felt the same way about his model." The tiny contractions in Livia's muscles were showing her the artist's path through the work. "Thomas, look at this. The jar is tipping—if you really carried oil like that, you'd spill it. And the right hand—it looks like it's pointing straight to it."

"Does that mean something?"

"Maybe not. Or maybe it's saying what the jar holds is important. And isn't liquid." She looked around. The few resolute early tourists they'd passed on their way up the aisle might make their eventual way to this chapel, but right now, none were near. Livia handed Thomas her shoulder bag and stepped up lightly onto the plinth. Balancing easily, she ran her hands over the unguent jar. She rapped with her knuckles, listening for a change of tone. "Thomas?" she said quietly. "It's hollow."

———◦———

104

Thomas watched Livia explore the unguent jar on the wooden statue of Mary Magdalene. He found himself oddly calm, his heart no longer pounding with the urgency and fright of the day before. Whatever they found—if there was anything to find—might reveal to him the meaning of Lorenzo's final words. Or those words might remain forever a mystery. Of more importance to Thomas was his own mystery: Would he be able to forgive Lorenzo for his betrayal? For his hate?

Livia's searching hands suddenly stopped still. After a moment she repositioned herself, gripped the jar with her left hand, and placed her right on its carved lid. Thomas could see the slow, steady force she was using in the set of her shoulders. The lid didn't move. Livia dropped her arms and stared at it. "Thomas? In my bag there's a vial. Can you hand it to me?"

Thomas, not used to rummaging through a woman's handbag, spent a minute finding it. "This?"

"Yes. It's the scent I use. Not really a perfume. An essential oil." She took the vial he handed her, unscrewed the top, and poured the oil carefully on the seam between the jar and its lid. The heady scent of gardenias wafted down to Thomas as the oil perched on the surface of the wood and then gradually began to seep in.

Livia restoppered the vial and handed it back down. Slowly, she started to work at the lid again. Nothing, nothing, nothing—then, finally, Thomas could see it begin to give. With calm patience Livia pressured it, pushing down, turning, until at last, millimeter by millimeter, she was able to unscrew it. Slowly and deliberately, she took the lid off, reached into the hollow jar, and removed a rolled, beribboned, wax-sealed scroll.

———◇———

Standing at the back of the church, he could see only that Livia Pietro and Thomas Kelly had been escorted by a monk to the Magdalene chapel. But he didn't need to be near to see—to know—what they were doing. When he'd gotten the call telling him they'd left the apartment, he'd gone out, too, into the fresh Rome morning. He didn't try to follow them. Anywhere they had it in mind to go was their own business and they had his blessing. Anywhere but here. He came straight to Santa Maria Maddalena, hoping that they wouldn't appear, but knowing they would.

He'd never been sure how much of the truth Lorenzo Cossa knew. It was possible, he'd thought, that though the contents of the document Livia Pietro and Thomas Kelly had just found were known to the Cardinal, its hiding place might not be. It had also seemed possible that, even if he knew, he hadn't had a chance to pass his knowledge on. When Livia and Kelly walked into the church, though, that possibility was lost. He took heart when it became clear that they didn't know what next step to take, but the resourcefulness they'd proved yesterday came into play here, too. He wasn't sure how they'd done it, and it didn't matter: once they'd found the statue, it was all but assured they'd find the treasure it held.

This day was a long time coming, but it was always bound to come. He'd been given, not instructions to follow, but the immeasurable honor and immense responsibility of deciding what to do when it came. He'd pondered the question long and hard, never coming to a conclusion. Now he'd reached one. Now he had to.

Stepping from the shadows, the Pontifex strode forward.

106

———◇———

Thomas sank slowly onto the marble plinth. Livia stood beside him, the unrolled vellum scroll from the unguent jar in her hand. Around him Santa Maria Maddalena faded, became a still photograph, a frozen stage set. Nothing lived, moved, breathed. He was ice-cold. The words he'd just read—he wanted to never have seen them; if that wasn't possible, to instantly forget them. But they swam before his eyes and, though he'd never heard them spoken, they sounded in his head.

Roma profecturi hoc testamentum relinquimus. Nobis praesentibus non erat opus talibus litteris; nos ipsi vitaque nostra pro testibus veritatis erant. Quamquam ex hac urbe discedimus, testimonium illud manet. Sumus etiamnunc inter vos. Estote certi: si necessarium fiet, nos revelabimus naturamque nostram duplicem manifestabimus, id quod non prius necessarium erit quam aut Ecclesia aut Noantri pacto inter duas nostras gentes valenti deficiant. Ad quod tempus— utinam ne veniat—fidem servabimus atque occultum tenebimus et pactum et nostram ipsorum naturam.

Preparing to depart from Rome, we leave behind this Testament. While we remained, no such document was required. The proof of its truth was ourselves and our lived lives. Though we leave this city, that proof remains. We are still among you. If necessary, be sure we will reveal ourselves, and make our dual natures known. That necessity will not arise until the day either the Church or the Noantri fail to conform to the Concordat between our peoples. Until such time—may it never come!—we will honor our vows, revealing neither the secret of the Concordat nor the secret of our own natures.

Below this brief, world-changing text, a date:

DIE DOMINICA XXII APRILIS ANNO DOMINI MDCI

Sunday, 22 April, the Year of Our Lord 1601.

and the signatures.

On the left, *Maria Magdalena*.

On the right, *Jesus Nazarenus*.

Mary Magdalene.

Jesus of Nazareth.

This was what it was, then: the secret Lorenzo had thought the Church could not survive. Thomas wasn't sure he'd survive it himself. *Dual natures*. Could this document be real? Could it be authenticated? But even as the scholar in him, desperate for a handhold, asked the question, the priest knew it was beside the point. The Concordat existed; the Noantri existed. Even if this Testament couldn't be proved real by any science known to man, its revelation, with its signatures and its date, would force the Concordat and the Noantri into the light. The ensuing whirlwind would bring down the Church, and who knew what would fall with it? If the . . . if the signatories . . . Thomas couldn't bring himself to say their names, even in his own head. **Come on, Father Kelly, you're a Jesuit,** he told himself. **You don't fear knowledge.** If he hadn't been frozen, he'd have laughed. Had he been just a tiny bit proud of how he'd accepted the Noantri, even come to respect and feel fondness for them, in so short a time? **Then accept this, Father Kelly: your Savior is also . . . is also . . .**

"So that's it." Someone spoke, a warm voice penetrating the ice in which Thomas was locked. Slowly, he looked up. Livia, appearing as shaken as he was, stared at the scroll in her hand. "That's the reason," she breathed. "Why Martin the Fifth signed the Concordat at all. What forced him into it. They did. It was this."

Yes, Thomas thought. **Fine.** That question now was answered. What of it? What did such a thing matter now, when . . .

"Yes." Another voice, dark and quiet. Thomas turned; Livia gasped. Before them stood the man—the Noantri—who'd sat at the center of the Conclave yesterday. The Pontifex Aliorum. The Pope of the Others. The Noantri ruler.

"Yes," he said again. The Pontifex stepped closer, pointing to the document Livia held. "You now know the final secret."

A long silence; then Thomas, to his surprise, heard a ghost of his own voice. "Who else . . ."

"Only the Conclave," the Pontifex replied. "No other Noantri, and no one in the Church, have this knowledge. The Church has swirled with dark rumors for centuries, stories of another document even more dangerous than the Concordat. But that the Concordat—and we—exist is perilous enough for the Church."

"But Lorenzo knew. How?"

The Pontifex turned his dark gaze on Thomas. He waited; then he spoke. "Ending the persecution of the Noantri, and accepting the help we could give him, brought Martin the Fifth to power over the rival line of Popes then at Avignon. If he had lost that struggle, the Antipope John would have reigned. John was his papal name. He was born Baldassare Cossa."

"Cossa," Thomas repeated. He felt simultaneously that vast knowledge was being revealed to him, and that he was unbearably stupid.

"Lorenzo Cardinal Cossa was descended from Baldassare's brother's line. The Cossas, believing the Church illegitimate from the moment the Concordat was signed, have been determined to regain the papacy since."

"Regain? Lorenzo? He'd have . . . made himself Pope?"

"A spy in the retinue of Martin the Fifth brought the knowledge of this"—again, a gesture at the document—"to Baldassare Cossa. Once the Avignon Popes lost the struggle for power, the Cossa family understood what they'd need to regain it: both the Concordat and this Testament. It's an odd irony that, though it is the Noantri to whom time is no enemy, the Cossas have been willing to wait as long as necessary, passing this knowledge from father to son."

"And Lorenzo also passed it on?"

"We think not—except to you."

Thomas felt the meaning of the Pontifex's words as a physical blow.

"It took more than one hundred and fifty years after the signing of the Concordat to bring the entire Church into line. The last man executed by fire died in 1600. The resulting outcry ended the practice and convinced Jesus and Mary that they could vanish again—could return the Church, and the choice to believe and follow, to men.

"They wrote this Testament. The Noantri were told of its existence, and that it had been placed in the care of the Order of Saint Camillus, chosen because of their humble devotion to the infirm and the dying. We were not told what form the Testament took nor where it was placed. The friars were given to understand their work would be supported as long as they took especial care of this statue, without a reason given."

"But surely," Thomas said, "you must have deduced its location. Why not take it into your care? Why leave it here for . . . for someone to find?" By which he meant, **For me to find, and read, and learn.** He meant, **Why force this unwanted knowledge upon me?**

The Pontifex nodded. "We had. But it wasn't ours to move. It was done thus to assure that its keeping would be in the hands of both parties. The Noantri have kept watch over this church since that time, and the friars, over the statue. All was well until the ascendancy of Lorenzo Cossa. He felt himself uniquely positioned for the search for the Concordat."

"He positioned himself. He positioned me."

"Thomas?" Livia said. "What I said before, I still think it's true. The Cardinal believed himself to be doing good."

Thomas didn't answer.

In the silence, Livia turned to the Pontifex. "Lord. This knowledge—you understand what a tremendous shock it is. To us both."

"Of course. It will take time to fully understand it."

"May I ask—"

"When the Savior," Thomas interrupted, needing to know the answer to the question Livia was having trouble framing—or maybe her question was different, but he didn't care; it was this he needed to know—"when he promised eternal life, was it this he meant? Endless human existence? Not transcendent heavenly life, eternally with the Father?" Did he also, then, lie?

"No," the Pontifex said calmly. "The opposite. He was ready to die for his flock, Father Kelly, to prove his faith and sustain yours. He nearly did. When he was cut down from the cross he was thought to be dead. But Mary Magdalene was Noantri. She knew he still lived—barely, but lived." He gazed at the wooden statue. "Art and legend have always depicted Mary as miserable and debased until she met Jesus of Nazareth. That was indeed her condition, but not because she was a prostitute—she was not. At that time, the Noantri, with no understanding of what we were, no knowledge of others like ourselves, lived constrained, degraded, furtive lives. The preaching of Jesus, the promise that the least among us could be redeemed, was a revelation to Mary. When he was on the edge of death, she struggled with her newfound faith, and realized she could in her way give him what he'd given her: the promise of eternal life."

"And if he chose not to accept her gift . . ."

The Pontifex nodded again. "She could restore him to his mortality."

"But he chose to remain," Thomas whispered.

"As always, he assented to what he saw as the will of his Father."

The grand church dedicated to the lowliest of Jesus's followers fell completely silent. Not a footfall or a whisper interposed itself, waiting for Thomas to say, "So he is still here."

"Yes."

"Where?" Thomas had never wanted the answer to a question as much as he wanted this one.

The Pontifex smiled and spoke softly. "I don't know."

Thomas, stricken, could not reply.

"Understand," the Pontifex said, "that he could have revealed himself at any moment before the writing of this Testament—or any moment since. But from the start of time, good has rarely come from religion. When it comes, it comes from faith. The Concordat was an attempt to set the Church founded in his name—a Church founded on faith—back onto a righteous path. Ultimately, though, each of us, Unchanged and Noantri, must choose our own way. If any good is to come of religion, faith must guide that choice, and faith does not merely allow—it absolutely *requires*—a lack of proof."

In his head, Thomas heard his own earlier thoughts: **If God's existence could be "proved," what was man offering God? Faith was what God asked of man. The only thing man has, and the only thing God wants.**

Faith was our single gift to him.

107

———⟨◦⟩———

What Livia felt now, she'd felt only once before, at the moment of her own Change: that the world had been revealed to her as overflowing, churning, mad with color and sound and scent, with promises she'd never thought to ask for and answers to questions she'd never thought to ask. This kaleidoscopic symphony, this vast, endless tapestry was before her now, again, in this silent church. What a gift! What a marvel, to live in such a world!

But a question grew in her, and with it a fear. One question that did have to be asked.

"Lord," she addressed the Pontifex, "what do you intend to do?"

"I?"

"Now that Father Kelly and I have come upon this knowledge."

He regarded them without words for quite some time. "From the moment I was asked to lead our people," he said quietly, "it was clear this day would sometime come. I have given much thought to this question and never found an answer. Even as I stepped forward to speak with you here, I was not sure what my duty required. Now, I am." He paused. "Father Kelly. Livia. The choice is yours."

Livia had to swallow before she could speak. "Ours, Lord?"

"As faith was put in me, I put mine in you to make the correct choice. If you choose a path that I would not have, my faith will continue to guide me as we travel that path. Reveal what you know, or hide this secret again. I await your decision."

Livia was struck dumb, unable even to think. She stood motionless, staring at the Pontifex, the dark eyes that seemed to see into her. For a few long moments, that was all. Then Thomas spoke.

"We will replace it."

Slowly, he rose from the plinth and faced them. "I can't claim to understand the meaning of what we've learned today. That will take a long time, perhaps a lifetime, of contemplation and prayer." Unexpectedly, he smiled. "My lifetime. Not yours."

"I think," Livia said, "mine, also."

Thomas met her eyes and went on. "That this document was written at all tells me there will come a time when these facts will be revealed. That it was hidden tells me that that time will come at the choosing of someone much greater than myself. Sir, your faith in us is an honor that will forever humble me. But the choice is not, in fact, ours. Jesus of Nazareth chose to keep this secret. Until he chooses otherwise, it will remain a secret."

The Pontifex nodded slowly, but said, "Others— Unchanged, or Noantri—might one day discover what you have."

"Then they will make their choices. I've made mine."

Wordlessly, Livia handed the scroll to the Pontifex. He took it and glanced over it, a ghost of a smile playing on his lips. Then he rerolled it and, as lightly as she had, he stepped onto the marble plinth, removed the jar's cap, and slipped the scroll inside. No one said anything until he was standing beside them again. Then it was the Pontifex who spoke.

"Thank you."

Nothing else needed to be said. He turned to leave them. Before he could take a step, though, Thomas said, "Sir?"

The Pontifex turned back.

"May I ask something?"

"You may."

"Thank you. You speak as one who . . . knew them. Knew him."

"I did. And loved them both. My own Change dates from not long before his. Father Kelly, you know my story, though it's not as you've long thought."

To Thomas's puzzled look, the Pontifex continued.

"I also was thought to be in the arms of death. I also was brought back to this world. Jesus of Nazareth, however, did not accomplish that 'miracle.' It has been attributed to him, but in truth it was brought about by the same Noantri who later performed his. Mary Magdalene. She who was also"—he smiled again—"despite what biblical scholars say, Mary of Bethany. My sister."

The Pontifex's smile broadened as understanding dawned in Thomas's eyes, though Livia herself didn't quite believe it until she heard him say it.

"I am Lazarus."

Then he turned in the aisle, and was gone.

POSTSCRIPT

◄◦►

NOTABLE NOANTRI—A BRIEF LIST

Most Noantri, of course, take some pains not to become famous. The spotlight makes disappearing, and reappearing in another place as another person—a necessity of eternal life—more difficult. Some, however, especially those in the arts, are unable to avoid public notice; and some frankly enjoy both the acclaim, and the thrill of danger that comes with it. Listed on the following pages are some men and women claimed by the Noantri as their own. It must be said that the siren song of fame is heard, perhaps, more clearly in some nations than in others; thus it will be noted that this list is heavy with Americans. The birth dates given for some here are the actual date of birth of the person before his or her Change; for others, they are the birth date associated with the identity we have come to know—a false date, in other words. Which are which are facts deeper in the Noantri Archive than your scribe was permitted to go.

Sam Cabot
January 1, 2013

Khachatur Abovian, b. 1809, Armenian writer.

Al-Hakim bi-Amr Allah, b. 996, sixth Fatimid caliph.

Theodosia Burr Alston, b. June 21, 1783, daughter of U.S. vice president Aaron Burr.

Dorothy Arnold, b. 1884, American socialite.

Benjamin Bathurst, b. March 18, 1784, British diplomat.

Ambrose Bierce, b. June 24, 1842, American writer.

Captain James William Boyd, b. 1822, Confederate States of America military officer.

Matthew Brady, b. 1822, American photographer.

Giordano Bruno, b. 1548, Dominican friar, mathematician, astronomer, philosopher.

John Cabot, b. 1450, Italian explorer.

Saint Cecilia, b. second century AD, Roman, Catholic martyr and saint, patroness of poets and musicians.

Thomas P. "Boston" Corbett, b. 1832, Union Army soldier.

Hart Crane, b. July 21, 1899, American poet.

Joseph Force Crater, b. January 5, 1889, New York judge.

Arthur Cravan (Favian Avenarius Lloyd), b. May 22, 1887, Swiss boxer, poet, surrealist figure.

Emilio de' Cavalieri, b. 1550, Italian composer.

Amelia Earhart, b. July 24, 1897, American aviatrix.

The Eight Taoist Immortals, b. during Tang or Song Dynasty, Chinese "mythological" characters.

Carlo Gesualdo, b. March 8, 1566, Italian composer.

Franz Greiter, b. 1918, Austrian scientist, inventor of sunscreen.

Jesus of Nazareth, b. 1 AD, central figure of Christianity.

Louis Aimé Augustin Le Prince, b. August 28, 1841, French inventor.

Romualdo Locatelli, b. 1905, Italian painter.

Thomas Lynch, Jr., b. August 5, 1749, American patriot, signer of the U.S. Declaration of Independence.

Stefano Maderno, b. 1576, Italian sculptor.

Mary Magdalene, b. first century AD, early disciple of Jesus of Nazareth.

Philip Mazzei, b. December 25, 1730, Italian physician, confidant of Thomas Jefferson, originator of the phrase "All men are created equal."

Methuselah, b. 1,656 years after creation, figure mentioned in Hebrew Bible.

Nefertiti, b. 1370 BC, "Great Royal Wife" of Pharaoh Akhenaten.

Ivan Nikitin, b. 1690, Russian painter.

Qin Shi Huang, b. 259 BC, Chinese emperor.

The Seven Sleepers of Ephesus, b. 250, Christian martyrs.

Spartacus, b. 109 BC, Thracian rebel slave.

Bram Stoker, b. November 8, 1847, Irish novelist.

Horace Sumner, b. 1826, American passenger on ill-fated ship on which Margaret Fuller (American writer) was lost.

Jan van Eyck, b. 1390, Flemish painter.

Yellow Emperor or Huangdi, b. 2724 BC, Chinese emperor, reigned 2696–2598 BC.

ACKNOWLEDGMENTS

Without the hard work of many people, this book would not exist. For that, Sam Cabot would like to thank Damiano Abeni, Dana Cameron, Moira Egan, Conor Fitzgerald, Massimo Gatto, Tom Govero, Betsy Harding, the late Royal Huber, Tyler Lansford, Dermot O'Connell, Franco Onorati, Ingrid Rowland, Tom Savage, Barbara Shoup, the secret map-maker, and all the believers and nonbelievers at Rancho Obsesso. Sam would also like to offer a particular tip of the biretta to Steve Axelrod of the Axelrod Agency, and to David Rosenthal, Vanessa Kehren, and the fine folks at Blue Rider. *Grazie.*

Without the electricity of Art Workshop International in Assisi, Sam Cabot would not exist. For that, Carlos Dews and S. J. Rozan would like to thank Edith Isaac-Rose, Bea Kreloff, Charles Kreloff, Chris Spencer, and the Hotel Giotto. *Pax et bonum.*

Read on for a preview of
the next thrilling book in
the Secrets Series,
SKIN OF THE WOLF
by Sam Cabot
Coming in hardcover from
Blue Rider Press in August 2014.

Brittany Williams slid the box with the Ohtahyohnee mask into its place on the shelf. The holding room was almost empty; most of the items for the upcoming auctions were already on display. Not quite all: as usual, Native Art had only been given three galleries. Not like Old Masters, which always got a full floor when their big show came up. Or Asian Art, actually three separate departments with three specialists, eight assistants, and two entire floors for two whole weeks in the spring. No, Native Art didn't even have enough space to exhibit all their pieces, and Brittany and Estelle were expected to do everything themselves.

Estelle was a genius, though. The pieces not on display were the ones buyers would be least likely to be familiar with, pieces they might have to be talked through to understand. Making people have to ask to see them was a way to ensure that either Estelle or Brittany would be right there to explain and extol. Brittany had gotten a French doctor interested in a Spokane doll yesterday and she'd made sure Estelle knew it. If he bought it, Brittany wouldn't get a commission—God forbid Sotheby's should work like that, as though any of this were about anything besides money—but Estelle would remember. Even in the backwater that Native Art had turned out to be, it was all about people knowing how good you were. And this Ohtahyohnee: according to Estelle the owner insisted it not be shown until the last-possible minute, which by Sotheby's policy was the day before the auction. This was the star item for Friday, slated to go on display tomorrow morning. Brittany didn't believe for a minute an owner would hold a piece back that way, especially one causing a big stir. The first Eastern tribe wolf mask to be auctioned in, like, ever? As much as they liked making money, owners liked to show off. There was a lot of *nyaah, nyaah* in the collecting world, and this was an absolutely primo opportunity for it. But holding it back was pure Estelle. The only way to create more demand than its existence did was to tell people you had it and then not let anyone near it.

Okay, Estelle might be a genius, but she abused her assistant just like every other specialist. She was out to dinner kissing some German museum director's ass, and Brittany would be here late into the night yet again, getting ready for tomorrow.

She went into the inner office and sat at the computer to key in Estelle's scrawled notes of the people who'd come to see pieces today. After that, she'd be last-minuting all the oh so fascinating preauction details: making sure there were enough black velvet cloths of all the right sizes for the sale pedestals, dusting and polishing each piece one final time. Things no one with an art history degree—and God knew, no one with a trust fund—should have to do.

B-o-o-o-oring. She yawned. She'd perk right up with a little coke and a night of clubbing, but no way that would happen. Unless she quit. Which she'd thought about. She didn't want to wake up one morning and find she was like Estelle and her friends from this afternoon. Dried-up old prunes, not even cougars, just three single, sexless, middle-aged women. Well, that Italian one, there was something about her. She could have been hot, but she didn't do anything to help herself, and God, what was she, like, fifty?

Brittany didn't want to give Daddy the satisfaction of quitting, though. He hadn't minded that she'd majored in art history, but he'd been incredulous when she'd actually taken a job. It wouldn't last, he'd sneered to Mom. Some Switzerland ski trip or Caribbean beach would beckon, and she'd follow like the airhead she'd always been. She wasn't cut out for working.

So she stayed, because screw him. But maybe she really should reconsider the native thing. The art was okay, but with Old Masters or Contemporary or even American Outsider, you had a whole gallery scene in addition to the museums and auction houses. You didn't have to be a Slave of Sotheby's, the assistants' name for themselves, which all the specialists knew, and didn't care about. Sure, there were Native Art galleries, but not in New York. They were in the Southwest or in places like Seattle, and no way she was going there. It wasn't like she particularly loved this art, not like Estelle did. And Katherine Cochran—she was even weirder. Brittany suspected they actually bought into it, thought some of the pieces were alive and had powers. Brittany always took care to look thoughtful when they talked like that, but seriously? No, she had to get out of here. No one ever said a Koons had superpowers. Not all that many people even said they were any good. Brittany had only gotten into Native Art in the first place because of that Chippewa guy Stan from junior year. God, he was hot, and she'd really gotten to Daddy with that one. He'd have been happier if she'd hooked up with a Jew or an Irish potato farmer.

She looked up when she heard the outer door click

open. The Jamaican guard Harold, this was his night. She'd taken a run at him but he didn't want to lose his job. Maybe she should try harder. He was big, with broad shoulders—and talk about pissing off Daddy! And he was early tonight, so maybe he wasn't as immune to her as he pretended. She swept her golden hair off her forehead—at $300 every few weeks, it had better be golden—so it would fall back into place when she looked up. Harold would pass through the storeroom and then, seeing her light on, stick his head in here. She recrossed her legs to reveal a little more thigh.

He didn't show up, though. She didn't hear the outer door shut again, so he must still have been in the storeroom. What was taking him so long? He couldn't be, like, afraid that she'd make another pass? She smiled. Or maybe he was trying to figure out a line to use, because he'd decided to do her, but he wanted her to understand it was his idea. As if. She stood, tugged the neckline of her sweater a little lower, and went into the storeroom.

Nothing to be seen. "Harold?" A sense, then, that someone had just frozen, that movement had stopped. God, what a coward he was. She stepped up the aisle in her red-soled Louboutins, shoes that turned men to jelly even on women not as beautiful as she. She made a right and halted. Wait. What? She didn't get what she was seeing, couldn't grasp this. The Ohtahyohnee's box was open; the mask grimaced up at her. Standing over it, staring down, quivering in taut-muscled rage, was a huge gray dog. *How the hell did that get in here?* Brittany started to tiptoe backward. Her stiletto heel caught the rug, and she stumbled against a shelf. Just a tiny clunk, but the dog whipped its giant head in her direction. Its eyes glowed, and its lips peeled back in a hungry, insane smile. Brittany took two more slow steps back while the dog just stood. Then it crouched to spring.

Brittany spun and dashed for the office, but the Louboutins weren't made for running and she tripped. She tried to scramble up from her knees, but the dog crashed into her, knocked her down. Its breath stank. It weighed a ton. She struggled, but the mouth slavered and the teeth gleamed, and for the first—and last—time in her life, Brittany was prey.

"In a general sort of way," Spencer George announced, burrowing more deeply into his coat, "I do not enjoy this weather. In case you wondered." His eyes watered as yet another blast of cold air hit them.

Bare-headed and gloveless, the larger, younger man beside him laughed. "Why not? It's beautiful! Look at that moon—full tomorrow! Look how bright the stars are! When do you see that in the city? And listen to that wind! Come on, it's a gorgeous night."

"Michael, I am fully prepared to accept that for your people, priding yourselves as you do on your oneness with the natural world, it's conceivable shrieking wind and glowing stars are sufficient to neutralize the discomfort of numb toes and frostbitten ears. I would further stipulate that I myself am a decadent white man who long ago lost touch with Mother Earth." *Longer ago than you can imagine,* he added sourly to himself, *and I can't say I've missed her caress.* "I acceded to this absurd notion of a walk through Central Park purely out of my high regard for you and respect for your wishes. Also my fear that you'd change your mind about joining my friends and myself for a drink if I didn't."

"You weren't afraid of that." Michael grinned.

"That's true. It sounds good, though, doesn't it? It makes me appear unselfish and noble. Willing to suffer for those I cherish."

"Only if I believed it."

Spencer sighed. "Then what am I doing out here? Really, Michael, if this is your idea of a good time, we might be less compatible than I hoped. Talking of 'hoped,' did you see your mask, by the way? Was it as exceptional as you'd anticipated?"

Michael didn't speak immediately. With a small smile, he said, "It's beautiful."

"Hmm. Beautiful. I detect a note of disappointment, however. Are you—" He stopped as Michael grabbed hold of his arm. "What?"

"Shh." Michael stood still. His eyes narrowed and his nostrils flared. He turned his head slowly left, then right, and loosened his grip. "Go," he said.

"What are you—"

"Leave. Go home. I'll come soon."

Spencer didn't move and didn't answer. His own Noantri hearing, acute as it was, detected no sound beyond the howling wind and the hiss of the city's unceasing traffic. Nor did he scent anything unusual riding the rushing air. But he felt something: a current on his skin, a dark voltage new to him, but charged, unmistakably, with danger.

A roar blasted the night. A blur of movement: Spencer spun, but not in time. Something smashed into him, knocked him painfully to the ground. Something alive, he knew, because, while he lay on his back, breath knocked out, he saw it bound up and after Michael, who was racing away into the darkness under the trees.

*   *   *

Michael Bonnard took off along the darkest route he could find. He sprinted up and over a small hill, then loped down the far slope in great long strides. Icy wind whistled around him. He had to lead Edward away from Spencer.

This was Edward, no doubt. It astounded Michael to find him in the city—Edward hated the concrete streets, the crowds, the cars, the steel—but he was here and he was raging. On the bitter air Michael could smell Edward's scent, sense his heat, feel his fury. A fury so great, an anger so overpowering, that Edward had Shifted.

Disaster. For Edward it was always, always anger that triggered the Shift. Michael could use anger, but other states also: panic once, as a child; another time, the exhilaration of first love. It was harder for him, though, no matter what. His flashpoint was higher. For Michael the Shift had to be intentioned, a matter of determined will.

Plunging into a tangle of shrubs, he tore at his clothes, trying to free himself, trying at the same time to summon that overwhelming, cresting sensation that would be his own trigger. Anger. Fear. Shock. Whatever he could use. Michael didn't know why Edward had come here, what powerful need had driven him so far from home to a place he detested: but right now, Michael knew with certainty, Edward was burning for a kill and he was hunting.

Spencer gathered himself, drew a deep breath, used it to mutter an oath, and raced after Michael.

At the time of his Change, Spencer George had been a landed aristocrat with an estate in Sussex. He could ride a horse, wield a sword, shoot accurately with a flint-lock pistol, and creditably execute every dance in Ebreo da Pesaro's *De Practica*. Once he'd become Noantri, his grace, strength, and stamina had all increased. He was grateful for, and delighted in, that fact in the bedroom; but outside that sanctum, with the exceptions of shooting, swordplay, riding, and dancing, physical exertion had for five hundred years remained on Spencer's list of ways he would rather not spend his time.

Comparable to going to church.

But Michael was in trouble. Spencer ground his teeth as his pounding footfalls up a stone outcropping rattled his bones. He had no idea what had knocked him down—a rabid dog, perhaps?—but two things were unmistakable: Michael was heroically attempting to lead the danger away from Spencer, and Michael had no chance of out-running whatever this creature was.

Pausing at the top of the huge boulder, Spencer surveyed the undergrowth below. A wild rustle down to the right: Michael, hiding in a tangle of bushes at the center of a copse, his scent exaggerated by effort and fear. Why didn't he stay still? On the other hand, what good would it have done? Spencer could clearly see, even in the shadows, a large shape slinking slowly, patiently, toward the thicket.

Spencer inched down the rock toward the animal, which looked for all the world like a wolf. The trees and the brush cast wind-tossed shadows, though, confusing his sight. More to the point, this was New York City. A more likely explanation made the animal a husky or some other crossbred dog, possibly rabid, and certainly feral or it wouldn't be hunting in the park.

Spencer moved carefully and silently. His intent, once he'd put himself within the dog's striking distance, was to call attention to his presence. He would be an easier target than Michael in the thicket, and the beast would leap. Spencer, whose strength certainly equaled that of a large dog and whose Noantri body could withstand whatever physical insult the dog might inflict, would defeat it. Unfortunately, that would likely mean killing it. It wouldn't do merely to drive it away, back into the streets of the city, now that, rabid or not, it had reached the point of stalking human prey.

Explaining to Michael his victory over the thing might get tricky, but Spencer had had more than five hundred years' practice in such matters. If he was lucky, Michael would remain hidden in the undergrowth and see nothing, in which case no explanation beyond a lucky bash with a large branch might be required. Spencer's gaze scoured the ground for some such branch, and he found one and hefted it. Excellent: a weapon he could wield as he once had his saber. As he crept forward, his mind began to fill with the possible intimate consequences of this episode. Michael had acted courageously, leading the danger away from him, and he was about to play the hero himself, rescuing Michael. Adrenaline-fueled mutual gratitude and relief, in a warm bedroom on a cold night, offered a promising prospect. This ridiculous exertion might be worthwhile, after all.

Near the base of the rock he spied a flat shelf, perhaps three feet above the ground and ten feet from the dog. He leapt lightly down onto it, held his weapon at the ready, and called, *"Ahoy!"* The animal snapped its head up, snarling. Spencer braced for its spring.

But before it could move, Michael burst from the thicket, shouting. Not at him, at the dog. Spencer didn't know what he was saying, wasn't sure it was in a language he spoke, and didn't spend any time on the question: Michael was charging the dog, and Michael was naked.

Spencer found himself momentarily paralyzed, both by the sight—not entirely unfamiliar, but the relationship was new enough that he still found it breathtaking—and by the inability of his own mind to account for it. The animal similarly froze, torn between the two men, but Michael threw himself forward and tackled it, and its decision was made.

So was Spencer's. Michael might have suddenly lost his mind but that didn't mean he had to lose his life. Spencer hurled himself off the rock and onto the swirling mass of fur and flesh. The rich scent of earth, Michael's acrid sweat, and the aroma of blood—had the dog already made a kill?—assaulted him. He used the branch as a club, pounding its end on the dog's head, but the dog just snarled and shifted its weight, and the three of them rolled, tangled together, into the thicket. Brambles scratched Spencer's face. The combined bulk of the other two thudded onto his chest, and he realized three things.

One: the dog was huge. And coarse-furred, and gray. And muscular beyond expectation. This was no dog. This was a wolf.

Two: Michael was holding his own, clamping the wolf's jaws shut with powerful hands, but he had no weapon. What had he expected to do, talk to the beast?

Three: Michael was, in fact, talking to the beast. Half speaking, half chanting, and accomplishing nothing that Spencer could see beyond tiring himself out while the wolf thrashed, kicked, and clawed at him with razor paws.

With Spencer still on the bottom of the pile, the wolf stopped moving. For the briefest second it seemed to stare into Michael's eyes. Then it arched its back and dug its rear legs into the dirt. Snarling, it shook its head left, right, left, until with a roar it broke free. It stood, eyes glowing, jaws slavering. Then it lunged. Michael rolled desperately and lifted his arm in protection. The wolf rolled with him, and Spencer was freed. The wolf's pointed teeth, aiming for Michael's throat, instead clamped onto his naked shoulder. Blood began to flow; Spencer could smell it. Without rising, he kicked hard into the wolf's flank. The startled beast yelped, lost its grip on Michael and its footing. It stumbled, scrabbling to right itself.

Man and beast turned shocked eyes to Spencer.

He used the moment to jump to his feet and launch himself at the wolf. He aimed for the ears, vulnerable points on any animal. He'd yank the creature's head up, get its jaws away from Michael. Then he'd break its skull. If he was lucky he'd find a rock to use; but he could do it with his hands. That was his plan. But the wolf was astoundingly fast. By the time he reached it—a second? two?—it had spun to face him. Its huge head angled, and Spencer's own momentum drove him into the gaping jaws. They caught his throat. The pain almost blinded him but, choking, he seized the snout and lower jaw, one hand on each, and pulled them apart. Knife-sharp teeth pierced his fingers. He managed to loosen the wolf's grip and kicked at its belly, but his kick was weaker than before. He was dizzy; he was losing blood.

His hand on his own throat confirmed that the wolf had cut his jugular. In the long term—and for Spencer, what was not long-term?—nothing more than a nuisance, but here, now, with Michael in danger, Spencer felt the blood flowing between his fingers as a true loss, a failure, a tragedy. He tried to stand, but couldn't. A strange sound began behind him. He expected the wolf to lunge at him again, but its head lifted. It snarled, stood quivering. Spencer, lying on cold rock, turned his head painfully. The hallucinatory vision that met his eyes was Michael, naked, bleeding, bare feet planted on the soil, arms raised to the skies, howling at the moon.

THE HOUSE OF EARTH

Now available for the first time in paperback, the *House of Earth* trilogy brings together three engrossing, best-selling novels—*The Good Earth*, *Sons*, and *A House Divided*—in the epic saga of the House of Wang that follows three generations of farmers, warlords, merchants and students through the sweeping events of half a century.

"The mightiest monument of American letters."

—*Philadelphia Forum*

"An impressive achievement, revealing and rich in humanity."

—*The New York Times*

THE GOOD EARTH

"A comment upon the meaning and tragedy of life as it is lived in any age in any quarter of the globe."

—*The New York Times*

"One of the most important and revealing novels of our time."

—*Pittsburgh Post-Gazette*

THE GOOD EARTH
was originally published by The John Day Company, Inc.

Books by Pearl S. Buck

The Angry Wife
A Bridge for Passing
Come, My Beloved
Command the Morning
Death in the Castle
Dragon Seed
The Exile
Fighting Angel
The Goddess Abides
God's Men
The Good Earth
Hearts Come Home and Other Stories
The Hidden Flower
A House Divided
Imperial Woman
Kinfolk
Letter from Peking
The Living Reed
The Long Love
Mandala
The Mother
My Several Worlds
The New Year
Pavilion of Women
Peony
Portrait of a Marriage
Sons
The Three Daughters of Madame Liang
The Time Is Noon
The Townsman
Voices In the House

Published by POCKET BOOKS

PEARL S. BUCK

The
Good
Earth

PUBLISHED BY POCKET BOOKS NEW YORK

THE GOOD EARTH

John Day edition published 1931

POCKET BOOK edition published January, 1939

78th printing.....................January, 1975

L

This POCKET BOOK edition includes every word contained in the original, higher-priced edition. It is printed from brand-new plates made from completely reset, clear, easy-to-read type. POCKET BOOK editions are published by POCKET BOOKS, a division of Simon & Schuster, Inc., 630 Fifth Avenue, New York, N.Y. 10020. Trademarks registered in the United States and other countries.

Standard Book Number: 671-78798-5.

Printed in the U.S.A.

I am always glad when any of my books can be put into an inexpensive edition, because I like to think that any people who might wish to read them can do so. Surely books ought to be within the reach of everybody.

". . . This was what Vinteuil had done for the little phrase. Swann felt that the composer had been content (with the instruments at his disposal) to draw aside its veil, to make it visible, following and respecting its outlines with a hand so loving, so prudent, so delicate and so sure, that the sound altered at every moment, blunting itself to indicate a shadow, springing back into life when it must follow the curve of some more bold projection. And one proof that Swann was not mistaken when he believed in the real existence of this phrase was that anyone with an ear at all delicate for music would have at once detected the imposture had Vinteuil, endowed with less power to see and to render its forms, sought to dissemble (by adding a line, here and there, of his own invention) the dimness of his vision or the feebleness of his hand."—*Swann's Way*, by MARCEL PROUST.

The
Good
Earth

1

IT WAS Wang Lung's marriage day. At first, opening his eyes in the blackness of the curtains about his bed, he could not think why the dawn seemed different from any other. The house was still except for the faint, gasping cough of his old father, whose room was opposite to his own across the middle room. Every morning the old man's cough was the first sound to be heard. Wang Lung usually lay listening to it and moved only when he heard it approaching nearer and when he heard the door of his father's room squeak upon its wooden hinges.

But this morning he did not wait. He sprang up and pushed aside the curtains of his bed. It was a dark, ruddy dawn, and through a small square hole of a window, where the tattered paper fluttered, a glimpse of bronze sky gleamed. He went to the hole and tore the paper away.

"It is spring and I do not need this," he muttered.

He was ashamed to say aloud that he wished the house to look neat on this day. The hole was barely large enough to admit his hand and he thrust it out to feel of the air. A small soft wind blew gently from the east, a wind mild and murmurous and full of rain. It was a good omen. The fields needed rain for fruition. There would be no rain this day, but within a few days, if this wind continued, there would be water. It was good. Yesterday he had said to his father that if this brazen, glittering sunshine continued, the wheat could not fill in the ear. Now it was as if Heaven had chosen this day to wish him well. Earth would bear fruit.

He hurried out into the middle room, drawing on his blue outer trousers as he went, and knotting about the fullness at his waist his girdle of blue cotton cloth. He left his upper body bare until he had heated water to bathe himself. He went into the shed which was the kitchen, leaning against the house, and out of its dusk an ox twisted its head from behind the corner next the door and lowed at him deeply. The kitchen was made of earthen bricks as the house was, great squares of earth dug from their own fields, and thatched with straw from their own wheat. Out of their own earth had his grandfather in his youth fashioned also the oven, baked and black with many years of meal preparing. On top of this earthen structure stood a deep, round, iron cauldron.

This cauldron he filled partly full of water, dipping it with a half gourd from an earthen jar that stood near, but he dipped cautiously, for water was precious. Then, after a hesitation, he suddenly lifted the jar and emptied all the water into the cauldron. This day he would bathe his whole body. Not since he was a child upon his mother's knee had anyone looked upon his body. Today one would, and he would have it clean.

He went around the oven to the rear, and selecting a handful of the dry grass and stalks standing in the corner of the kitchen, he arranged it delicately in the mouth of the oven, making the most of every leaf. Then from an old flint and iron he caught a flame and thrust it into the straw and there was a blaze.

This was the last morning he would have to light the fire. He had lit it every morning since his mother died six years before. He had lit the fire, boiled water, and poured the water into a bowl and taken it into the room where his father sat upon his bed, coughing and fumbling for his shoes upon the floor. Every morning for these six years the old man had waited for his son to bring in hot water to ease him of his morning coughing. Now father and son could rest. There was a woman coming to the house. Never again would Wang Lung have to rise summer and winter at dawn to light the fire. He could lie in his bed and wait, and he also would have a bowl of water brought to him, and if the earth were fruitful there would be tea leaves in the water. Once in some years it was so.

And if the woman wearied, there would be her children to light the fire, the many children she would bear to Wang Lung. Wang Lung stopped, struck by the thought of children running in and out of their three rooms. Three rooms had always seemed much to them, a house half empty since his mother died. They were always having to resist relatives who were more crowded—his uncle, with his endless brood of children, coaxing, "Now, how can two lone men need so much room? Cannot father and son sleep together? The warmth of the young one's body will comfort the old one's cough."

But the father always replied, "I am saving my bed for my grandson. He will warm my bones in my age."

Now the grandsons were coming, grandsons upon grandsons! They would have to put beds along the walls and in the middle room. The house would be full of beds. The blaze in the oven died down while Wang Lung thought of all the beds there would be in the half empty house, and the water began to chill in the cauldron. The shadowy figure of the old man appeared in the doorway, holding his unbuttoned garments about him. He was coughing and spitting and he gasped,

"How is it that there is not water yet to heat my lungs?"

Wang Lung stared and recalled himself and was ashamed.

"This fuel is damp," he muttered from behind the stove. "The damp wind—"

The old man continued to cough perseveringly and would not cease until the water boiled. Wang Lung dipped some into a bowl, and then, after a moment, he opened a glazed jar that stood upon a ledge of the stove and took from it a dozen or so of the curled dried leaves and sprinkled them upon the surface of the water. The old man's eyes opened greedily and immediately he began to complain.

"Why are you wasteful? Tea is like eating silver."

"It is the day," replied Wang Lung with a short laugh. "Eat and be comforted."

The old man grasped the bowl in his shriveled, knotty fingers, muttering, uttering little grunts. He watched the leaves uncurl and spread upon the surface of the water, unable to bear drinking the precious stuff.

"It will be cold," said Wang Lung.

"True—true——" said the old man in alarm, and he began to take great gulps of the hot tea. He passed into an animal satisfaction, like a child fixed upon its feeding. But he was not too forgetful to see Wang Lung dipping the water recklessly from the cauldron into a deep wooden tub. He lifted his head and stared at his son.

"Now there is water enough to bring a crop to fruit," he said suddenly.

Wang Lung continued to dip the water to the last drop. He did not answer.

"Now then!" cried his father loudly.

3

"I have not washed my body all at once since the New Year," said Wang Lung in a low voice.

He was ashamed to say to his father that he wished his body to be clean for a woman to see. He hurried out, carrying the tub to his own room. The door was hung loosely upon a warped wooden frame and it did not shut closely, and the old man tottered into the middle room and put his mouth to the opening and bawled,

"It will be ill if we start the woman like this—tea in the morning water and all this washing!"

"It is only one day," shouted Wang Lung. And then he added, "I will throw the water on the earth when I am finished and it is not all waste."

The old man was silent at this, and Wang Lung unfastened his girdle and stepped out of his clothing. In the light that streamed in a square block from the hole he wrung a small towel from the steaming water and he scrubbed his dark slender body vigorously. Warm though he had thought the air, when his flesh was wet he was cold, and he moved quickly, passing the towel in and out of the water until from his whole body there went up a delicate cloud of steam. Then he went to a box that had been his mother's and drew from it a fresh suit of blue cotton cloth. He might be a little cold this day without the wadding of the winter garments, but he suddenly could not bear to put them on against his clean flesh. The covering of them was torn and filthy and the wadding stuck out of the holes, grey and sodden. He did not want this woman to see him for the first time with the wadding sticking out of his clothes. Later she would have to wash and mend, but not the first day. He drew over the blue cotton coat and trousers a long robe made of the same material—his one long robe, which he wore on feast days only, ten days or so in the year, all told. Then with swift fingers he unplaited the long braid of hair that hung down his back, and taking a wooden comb from the drawer of the small, unsteady table, he began to comb out his hair.

His father drew near again and put his mouth to the crack of the door.

"Am I to have nothing to eat this day?" he complained. "At my age the bones are water in the morning until food is given them."

"I am coming," said Wang Lung, braiding his hair quickly and smoothly and weaving into the strands a tasseled, black silk cord.

4

Then after a moment he removed his long gown and wound his braid about his head and went out, carrying the tub of water. He had quite forgotten the breakfast. He would stir a little water into corn meal and give it to his father. For himself he could not eat. He staggered with the tub to the threshold and poured the water upon the earth nearest the door, and as he did so he remembered he had used all the water in the cauldron for his bathing and he would have to start the fire again. A wave of anger passed over him at his father.

"That old head thinks of nothing except his eating and his drinking," he muttered into the mouth of the oven; but aloud he said nothing. It was the last morning he would have to prepare food for the old man. He put a very little water into the cauldron, drawing it in a bucket from the well near the door, and it boiled quickly and he stirred meal together and took it to the old man.

"We will have rice this night, my father," he said. "Meanwhile, here is corn."

"There is only a little rice left in the basket," said the old man, seating himself at the table in the middle room and stirring with his chopsticks the thick yellow gruel.

"We will eat a little less then at the spring festival," said Wang Lung. But the old man did not hear. He was supping loudly at his bowl.

Wang Lung went into his own room then, and drew about him again the long blue robe and let down the braid of his hair. He passed his hand over his shaven brow and over his cheeks. Perhaps he had better be newly shaven? It was scarcely sunrise yet. He could pass through the Street of the Barbers and be shaved before he went to the house where the woman waited for him. If he had the money he would do it.

He took from his girdle a small greasy pouch of grey cloth and counted the money in it. There were six silver dollars and a double handful of copper coins. He had not yet told his father he had asked friends to sup that night. He had asked his male cousin, the young son of his uncle, and his uncle for his father's sake, and three neighboring farmers who lived in the village with him. He had planned to bring back from the town that morning pork, a small pond fish, and a handful of chestnuts. He might even buy a few of the bamboo sprouts from the south and a little beef to stew with the cabbage he had raised in his own garden. But this only if there were any money left after the bean oil and the soybean sauce had been bought. If he shaved

5

his head he could not, perhaps, buy the beef. Well, he would shave his head, he decided suddenly.

He left the old man without speech and went out into the early morning. In spite of the dark red dawn the sun was mounting the horizon clouds and sparkled upon the dew on the rising wheat and barley. The farmer in Wang Lung was diverted for an instant and he stooped to examine the budding heads. They were empty as yet and waiting for the rain. He smelled the air and looked anxiously at the sky. Rain was there, dark in the clouds, heavy upon the wind. He would buy a stick of incense and place it in the little temple to the Earth God. On a day like this he would do it.

He wound his way in among the fields upon the narrow path. In the near distance the grey city wall arose. Within that gate in the wall through which he would pass stood the great house where the woman had been a slave girl since her childhood, the House of Hwang. There were those who said, "It is better to live alone than to marry a woman who has been slave in a great house." But when he had said to his father, "Am I never to have a woman?" his father replied, "With weddings costing as they do in these evil days and every woman wanting gold rings and silk clothes before she will take a man, there remain only slaves to be had for the poor."

His father had stirred himself, then, and gone to the House of Hwang and asked if there were a slave to spare.

"Not a slave too young, and above all, not a pretty one," he had said.

Wang Lung had suffered that she must not be pretty. It would be something to have a pretty wife that other men would congratulate him upon having. His father, seeing his mutinous face, had cried out at him,

"And what will we do with a pretty woman? We must have a woman who will tend the house and bear children as she works in the fields, and will a pretty woman do these things? She will be forever thinking about clothes to go with her face! No, not a pretty woman in our house. We are farmers. Moreover, who has heard of a pretty slave who was virgin in a wealthy house? All the young lords have had their fill of her. It is better to be first with an ugly woman than the hundredth with a beauty. Do you imagine a pretty woman will think your farmer's hands as pleasing as the soft hands of a rich man's son, and your sun-black face as beautiful as the golden skin of the others who have had her for their pleasure?"

Wang Lung knew his father spoke well. Nevertheless, he had to struggle with his flesh before he could answer. And then he said violently,

"At least, I will not have a woman who is pock-marked, or who has a split upper lip."

"We will have to see what is to be had," his father replied.

Well, the woman was not pock-marked nor had she a split upper lip. This much he knew, but nothing more. He and his father had bought two silver rings, washed with gold, and silver earrings, and these his father had taken to the woman's owner in acknowledgment of betrothal. Beyond this, he knew nothing of the woman who was to be his, except that on this day he could go and get her.

He walked into the cool darkness of the city gate. Water carriers, just outside, their barrows laden with great tubs of water, passed to and fro all day, the water splashing out of the tubs upon the stones. It was always wet and cool in the tunnel of the gate under the thick wall of earth and brick; cool even upon a summer's day, so that the melon vendors spread their fruits upon the stones, melons split open to drink in the moist coolness. There were none yet, for the season was too early, but baskets of small hard green peaches stood along the walls, and the vendor cried out,

"The first peaches of spring—the first peaches! Buy, eat, purge your bowels of the poisons of winter!"

Wang Lung said to himself,

"If she likes them, I will buy her a handful when we return." He could not realize that when he walked back through the gate there would be a woman walking behind him.

He turned to the right within the gate and after a moment was in the Street of Barbers. There were few before him so early, only some farmers who had carried their produce into the town the night before in order that they might sell their vegetables at the dawn markets and return for the day's work in the fields. They had slept shivering and crouching over their baskets, the baskets now empty at their feet. Wang Lung avoided them lest some recognize him, for he wanted none of their joking on this day. All down the street in a long line the barbers stood behind their small stalls, and Wang Lung went to the furthest one and sat down upon the stool and motioned to the barber who stood chattering to his neighbor. The barber came at once and began quickly to pour hot water, from a kettle on his pot of charcoal, into his brass basin.

7

"Shave everything?" he said in a professional tone.

"My head and my face," replied Wang Lung.

"Ears and nostrils cleaned?" asked the barber.

"How much will that cost extra?" asked Wang Lung cautiously.

"Four pence," said the barber, beginning to pass a black cloth in and out of the hot water.

"I will give you two," said Wang Lung.

"Then I will clean one ear and one nostril," rejoined the barber promptly. "On which side of the face do you wish it done?" He grimaced at the next barber as he spoke and the other burst into a guffaw. Wang Lung perceived that he had fallen into the hands of a joker, and feeling inferior in some unaccountable way, as he always did, to these town dwellers, even though they were only barbers and the lowest of persons, he said quickly,

"As you will—as you will——"

Then he submitted himself to the barber's soaping and rubbing and shaving, and being after all a generous fellow enough, the barber gave him without extra charge a series of skilful poundings upon his shoulders and back to loosen his muscles. He commented upon Wang Lung as he shaved his upper forehead,

"This would not be a bad-looking farmer if he would cut off his hair. The new fashion is to take off the braid."

His razor hovered so near the circle of hair upon Wang Lung's crown that Wang Lung cried out,

"I cannot cut it off without asking my father!" And the barber laughed and skirted the round spot of hair.

When it was finished and the money counted into the barber's wrinkled, water-soaked hand, Wang Lung had a moment of horror. So much money! But walking down the street again with the wind fresh upon his shaven skin, he said to himself,

"It is only once."

He went to the market, then, and bought two pounds of pork and watched the butcher as he wrapped it in a dried lotus leaf, and then, hesitating, he bought also six ounces of beef. When all had been bought, even to fresh squares of beancurd, shivering in a jelly upon its leaf, he went to a candlemaker's shop and there he bought a pair of incense sticks. Then he turned his steps with great shyness toward the House of Hwang.

8

Once at the gate of the house he was seized with terror. How had he come alone? He should have asked his father—his uncle—even his nearest neighbor, Ching—anyone to come with him. He had never been in a great house before. How could he go in with his wedding feast on his arm, and say, "I have come for a woman?"

He stood at the gate for a long time, looking at it. It was closed fast, two great wooden gates, painted black and bound and studded with iron, closed upon each other. Two lions made of stone stood on guard, one at either side. There was no one else. He turned away. It was impossible.

He felt suddenly faint. He would go first and buy a little food. He had eaten nothing—had forgotten food. He went into a small street restaurant, and putting two pence upon the table, he sat down. A dirty waiting boy with a shiny black apron came near and he called out to him, "Two bowls of noodles!" And when they were come, he ate them down greedily, pushing them into his mouth with his bamboo chopsticks, while the boy stood and spun the coppers between his black thumb and forefinger.

"Will you have more?" asked the boy indifferently.

Wang Lung shook his head. He sat up and looked about. There was no one he knew in the small, dark, crowded room full of tables. Only a few men sat eating or drinking tea. It was a place for poor men, and among them he looked neat and clean and almost well-to-do, so that a beggar, passing, whined at him,

"Have a good heart, teacher, and give me a small cash—I starve!"

Wang Lung had never had a beggar ask of him before, nor had any ever called him teacher. He was pleased and he threw into the beggar's bowl two small cash, which are one fifth of a penny, and the beggar pulled back with swiftness his black claw of a hand, and grasping the cash, fumbled them within his rags.

Wang Lung sat and the sun climbed upwards. The waiting boy lounged about impatiently. "If you are buying nothing more," he said at last with much impudence, "you will have to pay rent for the stool."

Wang Lung was incensed at such impudence and he would have risen except that when he thought of going into the great House of Hwang and of asking there for a woman, sweat broke out over his whole body as though he were working in a field.

9

"Bring me tea," he said weakly to the boy. Before he could turn it was there and the small boy demanded sharply,

"Where is the penny?"

And Wang Lung, to his horror, found there was nothing to do but to produce from his girdle yet another penny.

"It is robbery," he muttered, unwilling. Then he saw entering the shop his neighbor whom he had invited to the feast, and he put the penny hastily upon the table and drank the tea at a gulp and went out quickly by the side door and was once more upon the street.

"It is to be done," he said to himself desperately, and slowly he turned his way to the great gates.

This time, since it was after high noon, the gates were ajar and the keeper of the gate idled upon the threshold, picking his teeth with a bamboo sliver after his meal. He was a tall fellow with a large mole upon his left cheek, and from the mole hung three long black hairs which had never been cut. When Wang Lung appeared he shouted roughly, thinking from the basket that he had come to sell something.

"Now then, what?"

With great difficulty Wang Lung replied,

"I am Wang Lung, the farmer."

"Well, and Wang Lung, the farmer, what?" retorted the gateman, who was polite to none except the rich friends of his master and mistress.

"I am come—I am come——" faltered Wang Lung.

"That I see," said the gateman with elaborate patience, twisting the long hairs of his mole.

"There is a woman," said Wang Lung, his voice sinking helplessly to a whisper. In the sunshine his face was wet.

The gateman gave a great laugh.

"So you are he!" he roared. "I was told to expect a bridegroom today. But I did not recognize you with a basket on your arm."

"It is only a few meats," said Wang Lung apologetically, waiting for the gateman to lead him within. But the gateman did not move. At last Wang Lung said with anxiety,

"Shall I go alone?"

The gateman affected a start of horror. "The Old Lord would kill you!"

Then seeing that Wang Lung was too innocent he said, "A little silver is a good key."

Wang Lung saw at last that the man wanted money of him.

10

"I am a poor man," he said pleadingly.

"Let me see what you have in your girdle," said the gateman.

And he grinned when Wang Lung in his simplicity actually put his basket upon the stones and lifting his robe took out the small bag from his girdle and shook into his left hand what money was left after his purchases. There was one silver piece and fourteen copper pence.

"I will take the silver," said the gateman coolly, and before Wang Lung could protest the man had the silver in his sleeve and was striding through the gate, bawling loudly,

"The bridegroom, the bridegroom!"

Wang Lung, in spite of anger at what had just happened and horror at this loud announcing of his coming, could do nothing but follow, and this he did, picking up his basket and looking neither to the right nor left.

Afterwards, although it was the first time he had ever been in a great family's house, he could remember nothing. With his face burning and his head bowed, he walked through court after court, hearing that voice roaring ahead of him, hearing tinkles of laughter on every side. Then suddenly when it seemed to him he had gone through a hundred courts, the gateman fell silent and pushed him into a small waiting room. There he stood alone while the gateman went into some inner place, returning in a moment to say,

"The Old Mistress says you are to appear before her."

Wang Lung started forward, but the gateman stopped him, crying in disgust,

"You cannot appear before a great lady with a basket on your arm—a basket of pork and beancurd! How will you bow?"

"True—true——" said Wang Lung in agitation. But he did not dare to put the basket down because he was afraid something might be stolen from it. It did not occur to him that all the world might not desire such delicacies as two pounds of pork and six ounces of beef and a small pond fish. The gateman saw his fear and cried out in great contempt,

"In a house like this we feed these meats to the dogs!" and seizing the basket he thrust it behind the door and pushed Wang Lung ahead of him.

Down a long narrow veranda they went, the roofs supported by delicate carven posts, and into a hall the like of which Wang Lung had never seen. A score of houses such as his whole house could have been put into it and have disappeared, so wide were the spaces, so high the roofs. Lifting his head in wonder to see

11

the great carven and painted beams above him he stumbled upon the high threshold of the door and would have fallen except that the gateman caught his arm and cried out,

"Now will you be so polite as to fall on your face like this before the Old Mistress?"

And collecting himself in great shame Wang Lung looked ahead of him, and upon a dais in the center of the room he saw a very old lady, her small fine body clothed in lustrous, pearly grey satin, and upon the low bench beside her a pipe of opium stood, burning over its little lamp. She looked at him out of small, sharp, black eyes, as sunken and sharp as a monkey's eyes in her thin and wrinkled face. The skin of her hand that held the pipe's end was stretched over her little bones as smooth and as yellow as the gilt upon an idol. Wang Lung fell to his knees and knocked his head on the tiled floor.

"Raise him," said the old lady gravely to the gateman, "these obeisances are not necessary. Has he come for the woman?"

"Yes, Ancient One," replied the gateman.

"Why does he not speak for himself?" asked the old lady.

"Because he is a fool, Ancient One," said the gateman, twirling the hairs of his mole.

This roused Wang Lung and he looked with indignation at the gateman.

"I am only a coarse person, Great and Ancient Lady," he said. "I do not know what words to use in such a presence."

The old lady looked at him carefully and with perfect gravity and made as though she would have spoken, except that her hand closed upon the pipe which a slave had been tending for her and at once she seemed to forget him. She bent and sucked greedily at the pipe for a moment and the sharpness passed from her eyes and a film of forgetfulness came over them. Wang Lung remained standing before her until in passing her eyes caught his figure.

"What is this man doing here?" she asked with sudden anger. It was as though she had forgotten everything. The gateman's face was immovable. He said nothing.

"I am waiting for the woman, Great Lady," said Wang Lung in much astonishment.

"The woman? What woman? . . ." the old lady began, but the slave girl at her side stooped and whispered and the lady recovered herself. "Ah, yes, I forgot for the moment—a small affair—you have come for the slave called O-lan. I remember we

12

promised her to some farmer in marriage. You are that farmer?"

"I am he," replied Wang Lung.

"Call O-lan quickly," said the old lady to her slave. It was as though she was suddenly impatient to be done with all this and to be left alone in the stillness of the great room with her opium pipe.

And in an instant the slave appeared leading by the hand a square, rather tall figure, clothed in clean blue cotton coat and trousers. Wang Lung glanced once and then away, his heart beating. This was his woman.

"Come here, slave," said the old lady carelessly. "This man has come for you."

The woman went before the lady and stood with bowed head and hands clasped.

"Are you ready?" asked the lady.

The woman answered slowly as an echo, "Ready."

Wang Lung, hearing her voice for the first time, looked at her back as she stood before him. It was a good enough voice, not loud, not soft, plain, and not ill-tempered. The woman's hair was neat and smooth and her coat clean. He saw with an instant's disappointment that her feet were not bound. But this he could not dwell upon, for the old lady was saying to the gateman,

"Carry her box out to the gate and let them begone." And then she called Wang Lung and said, "Stand beside her while I speak." And when Wang had come forward she said to him, "This woman came into our house when she was a child of ten and here she has lived until now, when she is twenty years old. I bought her in a year of famine when her parents came south because they had nothing to eat. They were from the north in Shantung and there they returned, and I know nothing further of them. You see she has the strong body and the square cheeks of her kind. She will work well for you in the field and drawing water and all else that you wish. She is not beautiful but that you do not need. Only men of leisure have the need for beautiful women to divert them. Neither is she clever. But she does well what she is told to do and she has a good temper. So far as I know she is virgin. She has not beauty enough to tempt my sons and grandsons even if she had not been in the kitchen. If there has been anything it has been only a serving man. But with the innumerable and pretty slaves running freely about the courts, I doubt if there has been anyone. Take her and use her well. She is a good slave, although somewhat slow and

13

stupid, and had I not wished to acquire merit at the temple for my future existence by bringing more life into the world I should have kept her, for she is good enough for the kitchen. But I marry my slaves off if any will have them and the lords do not want them."

And to the woman she said,

"Obey him and bear him sons and yet more sons. Bring the first child to me to see."

"Yes, Ancient Mistress," said the woman submissively.

They stood hesitating, and Wang Lung was greatly embarrassed, not knowing whether he should speak or what.

"Well, go, will you!" said the old lady in irritation, and Wang Lung, bowing hastily, turned and went out, the woman after him, and after her the gateman, carrying on his shoulder the box. This box he dropped down in the room where Wang Lung returned to find his basket and would carry it no further, and indeed he disappeared without another word.

Then Wang Lung turned to the woman and looked at her for the first time. She had a square, honest face, a short, broad nose with large black nostrils, and her mouth was wide as a gash in her face. Her eyes were small and of a dull black in color, and were filled with some sadness that was not clearly expressed. It was a face that seemed habitually silent and unspeaking, as though it could not speak if it would. She bore patiently Wang Lung's look, without embarrassment or response, simply waiting until he had seen her. He saw that it was true there was not beauty of any kind in her face—a brown, common, patient face. But there were no pock-marks on her dark skin, nor was her lip split. In her ears he saw his rings hanging, the gold-washed rings he had bought, and on her hands were the rings he had given her. He turned away with secret exultation. Well, he had his woman!

"Here is this box and this basket," he said gruffly.

Without a word she bent over and picking up one end of the box she placed it upon her shoulder and, staggering under its weight, tried to rise. He watched her at this and suddenly he said,

"I will take the box. Here is the basket."

And he shifted the box to his own back, regardless of the best robe he wore, and she, still speechless, took the handle of the basket. He thought of the hundred courts he had come through and of his figure, absurd under its burden.

"If there were a side gate——" he muttered, and she nodded

14

after a little thought, as though she did not understand too quickly what he said. Then she led the way through a small unused court that was grown up with weed, its pool choked, and there under a bent pine tree was an old round gate that she pulled loose from its bar, and they went through and into the street.

Once or twice he looked back at her. She plodded along steadily on her big feet as though she had walked there all her life, her wide face expressionless. In the gate of the wall he stopped uncertainly and fumbled in his girdle with one hand for the pennies he had left, holding the box steady on his shoulder with the other hand. He took out two pence and with these he bought six small green peaches.

"Take these and eat them for yourself," he said gruffly.

She clutched them greedily as a child might and held them in her hand without speech. When next he looked at her as they walked along the margin of the wheat fields she was nibbling one cautiously, but when she saw him looking at her she covered it again with her hand and kept her jaws motionless.

And thus they went until they reached the western field where stood the temple to the earth. This temple was a small structure, not higher in all than a man's shoulder and made of grey bricks and roofed with tile. Wang Lung's grandfather, who had farmed the very fields upon which Wang Lung now spent his life, had built it, hauling the bricks from the town upon his wheelbarrow. The walls were covered with plaster on the outside and a village artist had been hired in a good year once to paint upon the white plaster a scene of hills and bamboo. But the rain of generations had poured upon this painting until now there was only a faint feathery shadow of bamboos left, and the hills were almost wholly gone.

Within the temple snugly under the roof sat two small, solemn figures, earthen, for they were formed from the earth of the fields about the temple. These were the god himself and his lady. They wore robes of red and gilt paper, and the god had a scant, drooping moustache of real hair. Each year at the New Year Wang Lung's father bought sheets of red paper and carefully cut and pasted new robes for the pair. And each year rain and snow beat in and the sun of summer shone in and spoiled their robes.

At this moment, however, the robes were still new, since the year was but well begun, and Wang Lung was proud of their spruce appearance. He took the basket from the woman's arm and carefully he looked about under the pork for the sticks of incense he had bought. He was anxious lest they were broken and thus make an evil omen, but they were whole, and when he had found them he stuck them side by side in the ashes of other sticks of incense that were heaped before the gods, for the whole neighborhood worshipped these two small figures. Then fumbling for his flint and iron he caught, with a dried leaf for tinder, a flame to light the incense.

Together this man and this woman stood before the gods of their fields. The woman watched the ends of the incense redden and turn grey. When the ash grew heavy she leaned over and with her forefinger she pushed the head of ash away. Then as though fearful for what she had done, she looked quickly at Wang Lung, her eyes dumb. But there was something he liked in her movement. It was as though she felt that the incense belonged to them both; it was a moment of marriage. They stood there in complete silence, side by side, while the incense smouldered into ashes; and then because the sun was sinking, Wang Lung shouldered the box and they went home.

At the door of the house the old man stood to catch the last rays of the sun upon him. He made no movement as Wang Lung approached with the woman. It would have been beneath him to notice her. Instead he feigned great interest in the clouds and he cried,

"That cloud which hangs upon the left horn of the new moon speaks of rain. It will come not later than tomorrow night." And then as he saw Wang Lung take the basket from the woman he cried again, "And have you spent money?"

Wang Lung set the basket on the table. "There will be guests tonight," he said briefly, and he carried the box into the room where he slept and set it down beside the box where his own clothes were. He looked at it strangely. But the old man came to the door and said volubly,

"There is no end to the money spent in this house!"

Secretly he was pleased that his son had invited guests, but he felt it would not do to give out anything but complaints before his new daughter-in-law lest she be set from the first in ways of extravagance. Wang Lung said nothing, but he went out and took the basket into the kitchen and the woman followed him there. He took the food piece by piece from the basket and laid it upon the ledge of the cold stove and he said to her,

16

"Here is pork and here beef and fish. There are seven to eat. Can you prepare food?"

He did not look at the woman as he spoke. It would not have been seemly. The woman answered in her plain voice,

"I have been kitchen slave since I went into the House of Hwang. There were meats at every meal."

Wang Lung nodded and left her and did not see her again until the guests came crowding in, his uncle jovial and sly and hungry, his uncle's son an impudent lad of fifteen, and the farmers clumsy and grinning with shyness. Two were men from the village with whom Wang Lung exchanged seed and labor at harvest time, and one was his next door neighbor, Ching, a small, quiet man, ever unwilling to speak unless he were compelled to it. After they had been seated about the middle room with demurring and unwillingness to take seats, for politeness, Wang Lung went into the kitchen to bid the woman serve. Then he was pleased when she said to him,

"I will hand you the bowls if you will place them upon the table. I do not like to come out before men."

Wang Lung felt in him a great pride that this woman was his and did not fear to appear before him, but would not before other men. He took the bowls from her hands at the kitchen door and he set them upon the table in the middle room and called loudly,

"Eat, my uncle and my brothers." And when the uncle, who was fond of jokes, said, "Are we not to see the moth-browed bride?" Wang Lung replied firmly, "We are not yet one. It is not meet that other men see her until the marriage is consummated."

And he urged them to eat and they ate heartily of the good fare, heartily and in silence, and this one praised the brown sauce on the fish and that one the well-done pork, and Wang Lung said over and over in reply,

"It is poor stuff—it is badly prepared."

But in his heart he was proud of the dishes, for with what meats she had the woman had combined sugar and vinegar and a little wine and soy sauce and she had skilfully brought forth all the force of the meat itself, so that Wang Lung himself had never tasted such dishes upon the tables of his friends.

That night after the guests had tarried long over their tea and had done with their jokes, the woman still lingered behind the stove, and when Wang Lung had seen the last guest away he went in and she cowered there in the straw piles asleep beside the ox. There was straw in her hair when he roused her, and when he called her she put up her arm suddenly in her sleep as though to defend herself from a blow. When she opened her eyes at last, she looked at him with her strange speechless gaze, and he felt as though he faced a child. He took her by the hand and led her into the room where that morning he had bathed himself for her, and he lit a red candle upon the table. In this light he was suddenly shy when he found himself alone with the woman and he was compelled to remind himself,

"There is this woman of mine. The thing is to be done."

And he began to undress himself doggedly. As for the woman, she crept around the corner of the curtain and began without a sound to prepare for the bed. Wang Lung said gruffly,

"When you lie down, put the light out first."

Then he lay down and drew the thick quilt about his shoulders and pretended to sleep. But he was not sleeping. He lay quivering, every nerve of his flesh awake. And when, after a long time, the room went dark, and there was the slow, silent, creeping movement of the woman beside him, an exultation filled him fit to break his body. He gave a hoarse laugh into the darkness and seized her.

2

THERE WAS this luxury of living. The next morning he lay upon his bed and watched the woman who was now wholly his own. She rose and drew about her her loosened garments and fastened them closely about her throat and waist, fitting them to her body with a slow writhe and twist. Then she put her feet into her cloth shoes and drew them on by the straps hanging at the back. The light from the small hole shone on her in a bar and he saw her face dimly. It looked unchanged. This was an astonishment to Wang Lung. He felt as though the night must have changed him; yet here was this woman rising from his bed as though she had risen every day of her life. The old man's cough rose querulously out of the dusky dawn and he said to her,

"Take to my father first a bowl of hot water for his lungs."

She asked, her voice exactly as it had been yesterday when she spoke, "Are there to be tea leaves in it?"

This simple question troubled Wang Lung. He would have liked to say, "Certainly there must be tea leaves. Do you think we are beggars?" He would have liked the woman to think that they made nothing of tea leaves in this house. In the House of Hwang, of course, every bowl of water was green with leaves. Even a slave, there, perhaps, would not drink only water. But he knew his father would be angry if on the first day the woman served tea to him instead of water. Besides, they really were not rich. He replied negligently, therefore,

"Tea? No—no—it makes his cough worse."

And then he lay in his bed warm and satisfied while in the kitchen the woman fed the fire and boiled the water. He would like to have slept, now that he could, but his foolish body, which he had made to arise every morning so early for all these years, would not sleep although it could, and so he lay there, tasting and savoring in his mind and in his flesh his luxury of idleness.

He was still half ashamed to think of this woman of his. Part of the time he thought of his fields and of the grains of the wheat and of what his harvest would be if the rains came and of the white turnip seed he wished to buy from his neighbor Ching if they could agree upon a price. But between all these thoughts which were in his mind every day there ran weaving and interweaving the new thought of what his life now was, and it occurred to him, suddenly, thinking of the night, to wonder if she liked him. This was a new wonder. He had questioned only of whether he would like her and whether or not she would be satisfactory in his bed and in his house. Plain though her face was and rough the skin upon her hands the flesh of her big body was soft and untouched and he laughed when he thought of it—the short hard laugh he had thrown out into the darkness the night before. The young lords had not seen, then, beyond that plain face of the kitchen slave. Her body was beautiful, spare and big boned yet rounded and soft. He desired suddenly that she should like him as her husband and then he was ashamed.

The door opened and in her silent way she came in bearing in both hands a steaming bowl to him. He sat up in bed and took it. There were tea leaves floating upon the surface of the water.

19

He looked up at her quickly. She was at once afraid and she said,

"I took no tea to the Old One—I did as you said—but to you I . . ."

Wang Lung saw that she was afraid of him and he was pleased and he answered before she finished, "I like it—I like it," and he drew his tea into his mouth with loud sups of pleasure.

In himself there was this new exultation which he was ashamed to make articulate even to his own heart, "This woman of mine likes me well enough!"

It seemed to him that during these next months he did nothing except watch this woman of his. In reality he worked as he always had. He put his hoe upon his shoulder and he walked to his plots of land and he cultivated the rows of grain, and he yoked the ox to the plow and he ploughed the western field for garlic and onions. But the work was luxury, for when the sun struck the zenith he could go to his house and food would be there ready for him to eat, and the dust wiped from the table, and the bowls and the chopsticks placed neatly upon it. Hitherto he had had to prepare the meals when he came in, tired though he was, unless the old man grew hungry out of time and stirred up a little meal or baked a piece of flat, unleavened bread to roll about a stem of garlic.

Now whatever there was, was ready for him, and he could seat himself upon the bench by the table and eat at once. The earthen floor was swept and the fuel pile replenished. The woman, when he had gone in the morning, took the bamboo rake and a length of rope and with these she roamed the countryside, reaping here a bit of grass and there a twig or a handful of leaves, returning at noon with enough to cook the dinner. It pleased the man that they need buy no more fuel.

In the afternoon she took a hoe and a basket and with these upon her shoulder she went to the main road leading into the city where mules and donkeys and horses carried burdens to and fro, and there she picked the droppings from the animals and carried it home and piled the manure in the dooryard for fertilizer for the fields. These things she did without a word and without being commanded to do them. And when the end of the day came she did not rest herself until the ox had been fed in the kitchen and until she had dipped water to hold to its muzzle to let it drink what it would.

And she took their ragged clothes and with thread she herself spun on a bamboo spindle from a wad of cotton she mended and contrived to cover the rents in their winter clothes. Their bedding she took into the sun on the threshold and ripped the coverings from the quilts and washed them and hung them upon a bamboo to dry, and the cotton in the quilts that had grown hard and grey from years she picked over, killing the vermin that had flourished in the hidden folds, and sunning it all. Day after day she did one thing after another, until the three rooms seemed clean and almost prosperous. The old man's cough grew better and he sat in the sun by the southern wall of the house, always half-asleep and warm and content.

But she never talked, this woman, except for the brief necessities of life. Wang Lung, watching her move steadily and slowly about the rooms on her big feet, watching secretly the stolid, square face, the unexpressed, half-fearful look of her eyes, made nothing of her. At night he knew the soft firmness of her body. But in the day her clothes, her plain blue cotton coat and trousers, covered all that he knew, and she was like a faithful, speechless serving maid, who is only a serving maid and nothing more. And it was not meet that he should say to her, "Why do you not speak?" It should be enough that she fulfilled her duty.

Sometimes, working over the clods in the fields, he would fall to pondering about her. What had she seen in those hundred courts? What had been her life, that life she never shared with him? He could make nothing of it. And then he was ashamed of his own curiosity and of his interest in her. She was, after all, only a woman.

But there is not that about three rooms and two meals a day to keep busy a woman who has been a slave in a great house and who has worked from dawn until midnight. One day when Wang Lung was hard pressed with the swelling wheat and was cultivating it with his hoe, day after day, until his back throbbed with weariness, her shadow fell across the furrow over which he bent himself, and there she stood, with a hoe across her shoulder.

"There is nothing in the house until nightfall," she said briefly, and without speech she took the furrow to the left of him and fell into steady hoeing.

The sun beat down upon them, for it was early summer, and her face was soon dripping with her sweat. Wang Lung had his coat off and his back bare, but she worked with her thin

21

garment covering her shoulders and it grew wet and clung to her like skin. Moving together in a perfect rhythm, without a word, hour after hour, he fell into a union with her which took the pain from his labor. He had no articulate thought of anything; there was only this perfect sympathy of movement, of turning this earth of theirs over and over to the sun, this earth which formed their home and fed their bodies and made their gods. The earth lay rich and dark, and fell apart lightly under the points of their hoes. Sometimes they turned up a bit of brick, a splinter of wood. It was nothing. Some time, in some age, bodies of men and women had been buried there, houses had stood there, had fallen, and gone back into the earth. So would also their house, some time, return into the earth, their bodies also. Each had his turn at this earth. They worked on, moving together—together—producing the fruit of this earth—speechless in their movement together.

When the sun had set he straightened his back slowly and looked at the woman. Her face was wet and streaked with the earth. She was as brown as the very soil itself. Her wet, dark garments clung to her square body. She smoothed a last furrow slowly. Then in her usual plain way she said, straight out, her voice flat and more than usually plain in the silent evening air,

"I am with child."

Wang Lung stood still. What was there to say to this thing, then! She stooped to pick up a bit of broken brick and threw it out of the furrow. It was as though she had said, "I have brought you tea," or as though she had said, "We can eat." It seemed as ordinary as that to her! But to him—he could not say what it was to him. His heart swelled and stopped as though it met sudden confines. Well, it was their turn at this earth!

He took the hoe suddenly from her hand and he said, his voice thick in his throat, "Let be for now. It is a day's end. We will tell the old man."

They walked home, then, she half a dozen paces behind him as befitted a woman. The old man stood at the door, hungry for his evening's food, which, now that the woman was in the house, he would never prepare for himself. He was impatient and he called out,

"I am too old to wait for my food like this!"

But Wang Lung, passing him into the room, said,

"She is with child already."

He tried to say it easily as one might say, "I have planted the seeds in the western field today," but he could not. Although he spoke in a low voice it was to him as though he had shouted the words out louder than he would.

The old man blinked for a moment and then comprehended, and cackled with laughter.

"Heh-heh-heh——" he called out to his daughter-in-law as she came, "so the harvest is in sight!"

Her face he could not see in the dusk, but she answered evenly,

"I shall prepare food now."

"Yes—yes—food——" said the old man eagerly, following her into the kitchen like a child. Just as the thought of a grandson had made him forget his meal, so now the thought of food freshly before him made him forget the child.

But Wang Lung sat upon a bench by the table in the darkness and put his head upon his folded arms. Out of this body of his, out of his own loins, life!

3

WHEN THE HOUR for birth drew near he said to the woman,

"We must have someone to help at the time—some woman."

But she shook her head. She was clearing away the bowls after the evening food. The old man had gone to his bed and the two of them were alone in the night, with only the light that fell upon them from the flickering flame of a small tin lamp filled with bean oil, in which a twist of cotton floated for a wick.

"No woman?" he asked in consternation. He was beginning now to be accustomed to these conversations with her in which her part was little more than a movement of head or hand, or at most an occasional word dropped unwillingly from her wide mouth. He had even come to feel no lack in such conversing. "But it will be odd with only two men in the house!" he continued. "My mother had a woman from the village. I know nothing of these affairs. Is there none in the great house, no old slave with whom you were friends, who could come?"

It was the first time he had mentioned the house from which she came. She turned on him as he had never seen her, her narrow eyes widened, her face stirred with dull anger.

"None in that house!" she cried out at him.

He dropped his pipe which he was filling and stared at her. But her face was suddenly as usual and she was collecting the chopsticks as though she had not spoken.

"Well, here is a thing!" he said in astonishment. But she said nothing. Then he continued in argument, "We two men, we have no ability in childbirth. For my father it is not fitting to enter your room—for myself, I have never even seen a cow give birth. My clumsy hands might mar the child. Someone from the great house, now, where the slaves are always giving birth . . ."

She had placed the chopsticks carefully down in an orderly heap upon the table and she looked at him, and after a moment's looking she said,

"When I return to that house it will be with my son in my arms. I shall have a red coat on him and red-flowered trousers and on his head a hat with a small gilded Buddha sewn on the front and on his feet tiger-faced shoes. And I will wear new shoes and a new coat of black sateen and I will go into the kitchen where I spent my days and I will go into the great hall where the Old One sits with her opium, and I will show myself and my son to all of them."

He had never heard so many words from her before. They came forth steadily and without break, albeit slowly, and he realized that she had planned this whole thing out for herself. When she had been working in the fields beside him she had been planning all this out! How astonishing she was! He would have said that she had scarcely thought of the child, so stilly had she gone about her work, day in and day out. And instead she saw this child, born and fully clothed, and herself as his mother, in a new coat! He was for once without words himself, and he pressed the tobacco diligently into a ball between his thumb and forefinger, and picking up his pipe he fitted the tobacco into the bowl.

"I suppose you will need some money," he said at last with apparent gruffness.

"If you will give me three silver pieces . . ." she said fearfully. "It is a great deal, but I have counted carefully and I will waste no penny of it. I shall make the cloth dealer give me the last inch to the foot."

Wang Lung fumbled in his girdle. The day before he had

sold a load and a half of reeds from the pond in the western field to the town market and he had in his girdle a little more than she wished. He put the three silver dollars upon the table. Then, after a little hesitation, he added a fourth piece which he had long kept by him on the chance of his wanting to gamble a little some morning at the tea house. But he never did more than linger about the tables and look at the dice as they clattered upon the table, fearful lest he lose if he played. He usually ended by spending his spare hours in the town at the storyteller's booth, where one may listen to an old tale and pay no more than a penny into his bowl when it was passed about.

"You had better take the other piece," he said, lighting his pipe between the words, blowing quickly at the paper spill to set it aflame. "You may as well make his coat of a small remnant of silk. After all, he is the first."

She did not at once take the money, but she stood looking at it, her face motionless. Then she said in a half-whisper,

"It is the first time I have had silver money in my hand."

Suddenly she took it and clenched it in her hand and hurried into the bedroom.

Wang Lung sat smoking, thinking of the silver as it had lain upon the table. It had come out of the earth, this silver, out of his earth that he ploughed and turned and spent himself upon. He took his life from this earth; drop by drop by his sweat he wrung food from it and from the food, silver. Each time before this that he had taken the silver out to give to anyone, it had been like taking a piece of his life and giving it to someone carelessly. But now for the first time such giving was not pain. He saw, not the silver in the alien hand of a merchant in the town; he saw the silver transmuted into something worth even more than itself—clothes upon the body of his son. And this strange woman of his, who worked about, saying nothing, seeming to see nothing, she had first seen the child thus clothed!

She would have no one with her when the hour came. It came one night, early, when the sun was scarcely set. She was working beside him in the harvest field. The wheat had borne and been cut and the field flooded and the young rice set, and now the rice bore harvest, and the ears were ripe and full after the summer rains and the warm ripening sun of early autumn. Together they cut the sheaves all day, bending and cutting with short-handled scythes. She had stooped stiffly, because of the burden she bore, and she moved more slowly than he, so that they cut unevenly, his row ahead, and hers behind. She began to cut more and more slowly as noon wore on to afternoon and evening, and he turned to look at her with impatience. She stopped and stood up then, her scythe dropped. On her face was a new sweat, the sweat of a new agony.

"It is come," she said. "I will go into the house. Do not come into the room until I call. Only bring me a newly peeled reed, and slit it, that I may cut the child's life from mine."

She went across the fields toward the house as though there were nothing to come, and after he had watched her he went to the edge of the pond in the outer field and chose a slim green reed and peeled it carefully and slit it on the edge of his scythe. The quick autumn darkness was falling then and he shouldered his scythe and went home.

When he reached the house he found his supper hot on the table and the old man eating. She had stopped in her labor to prepare them food! He said to himself that she was a woman such as is not commonly found. Then he went to the door of their room and he called out,

"Here is the reed!"

He waited, expecting that she would call out to him to bring it in to her. But she did not. She came to the door and through the crack her hand reached out and took the reed. She said no word, but he heard her panting as an animal pants which has run for a long way.

The old man looked up from his bowl to say,

"Eat, or all will be cold." And then he said, "Do not trouble yourself yet—it will be a long time. I remember well when the first was born to me it was dawn before it was over. Ah me, to think that out of all the children I begot and your mother bore, one after the other—a score or so—I forget—only you have lived! You see why a woman must bear and bear." And then he said again, as though he had just thought of it newly, "By this time tomorrow I may be grandfather to a man child!" He began to laugh suddenly and he stopped his eating and sat chuckling for a long time in the dusk of the room.

But Wang Lung stood listening at the door to those heavy animal pants. A smell of hot blood came through the crack, a sickening smell that frightened him. The panting of the woman within became quick and loud, like whispered screams, but she made no sound aloud. When he could bear no more and was about to break into the room, a thin, fierce cry came out and he forgot everything.

"Is it a man?" he cried importunately, forgetting the woman. The thin cry burst out again, wiry, insistent. "Is it a man?" he cried again, "tell me at least this—is it a man?"

And the voice of the woman answered as faintly as an echo, "A man!"

He went and sat down at the table then. How quick it had all been! The food was long cold and the old man was asleep on his bench, but how quick it had all been! He shook the old man's shoulder.

"It is a man child!" he called triumphantly. "You are grandfather and I am father!"

The old man woke suddenly and began to laugh as he had been laughing when he fell asleep.

"Yes—yes—of course," he cackled, "a grandfather—a grandfather—" and he rose and went to his bed, still laughing.

Wang Lung took up the bowl of cold rice and began to eat. He was very hungry all at once and he could not get the food into his mouth quickly enough. In the room he could hear the woman dragging herself about and the cry of the child was incessant and piercing.

"I suppose we shall have no more peace in this house now," he said to himself proudly.

When he had eaten all that he wished he went to the door again and she called to him to come in and he went in. The odor of spilt blood still hung hot upon the air, but there was no trace of it except in the wooden tub. But into this she had poured water and had pushed it under the bed so that he could hardly see it. The red candle was lit and she was lying neatly covered upon the bed. Beside her, wrapped in a pair of his old trousers, as the custom was in this part, lay his son.

He went up and for the moment there were no words in his mouth. His heart crowded up into his breast and he leaned over the child to look at it. It had a round wrinkled face that looked very dark and upon its head the hair was long and damp and black. It had ceased crying and lay with its eyes tightly shut.

He looked at his wife and she looked back at him. Her hair was still wet with her agony and her narrow eyes were sunken. Beyond this, she was as she always was. But to him she was touching, lying there. His heart rushed out to these two and he said, not knowing what else there was that could be said,

27

"Tomorrow I will go into the city and buy a pound of red sugar and stir it into boiling water for you to drink."

And then looking at the child again, this burst forth from him suddenly as though he had just thought of it, "We shall have to buy a good basketful of eggs and dye them all red for the village. Thus will everyone know I have a son!"

4

THE NEXT DAY after the child was born the woman rose as usual and prepared food for them but she did not go into the harvest fields with Wang Lung, and so he worked alone until after the noon hour. Then he dressed himself in his blue gown and went into the town. He went to the market and bought fifty eggs, not new laid, but still well enough and costing a penny for one, and he bought red paper to boil in the water with them to make them red. Then with the eggs in his basket he went to the sweet shop, and there he bought a pound and a little more of red sugar and saw it wrapped carefully into its brown paper, and under the straw string which held it the sugar dealer slipped a strip of red paper, smiling as he did so.

"It is for the mother of a new-born child, perhaps,"

"A first-born son," said Wang Lung proudly.

"Ah, good fortune," answered the man carelessly, his eye on a well-dressed customer who had just come in.

This he had said many times to others, even every day to someone, but to Wang Lung it seemed special and he was pleased with the man's courtesy and he bowed and bowed again as he went from the shop. It seemed to him as he walked into the sharp sunshine of the dusty street that there was never a man so filled with good fortune as he.

He thought of this at first with joy and then with a pang of fear. It did not do in this life to be too fortunate. The air and the earth were filled with malignant spirits who could not endure the happiness of mortals, especially of such as are poor. He turned abruptly into the candlemaker's shop, who sold incense also, and there he bought four sticks of incense, one for each person in his house, and with these four sticks he went into the small temple of the gods of the earth, and he thrust them into the cold ashes of the incense he had placed there before, he and his wife together. He watched the four sticks well lit and then went homeward, comforted. These two small, protective figures, sitting staidly under their small roof—what a power they had!

And then, almost before one could realize anything, the woman was back in the fields beside him. The harvests were past, and the grain they beat out upon the threshing floor which was also the dooryard to the house. They beat it out with flails, he and the woman together. And when the grain was flailed they winnowed it, casting it up from great flat bamboo baskets into the wind and catching the good grain as it fell, and the chaff blew away in a cloud with the wind. Then there were the fields to plant for winter wheat again, and when he had yoked the ox and ploughed the land the woman followed behind with her hoe and broke the clods in the furrows.

She worked all day now and the child lay on an old torn quilt on the ground, asleep. When it cried the woman stopped and uncovered her bosom to the child's mouth, sitting flat upon the ground, and the sun beat down upon them both, the reluctant sun of late autumn that will not let go the warmth of summer until the cold of the coming winter forces it. The woman and the child were as brown as the soil and they sat there like figures made of earth. There was the dust of the fields upon the woman's hair and upon the child's soft black head.

But out of the woman's great brown breast the milk gushed forth for the child, milk as white as snow, and when the child suckled at one breast it flowed like a fountain from the other, and she let it flow. There was more than enough for the child, greedy though he was, life enough for many children, and she let it flow out carelessly, conscious of her abundance. There was always more and more. Sometimes she lifted her breast and let it flow out upon the ground to save her clothing, and it sank into the earth and made a soft, dark, rich spot in the field. The child was fat and good-natured and ate of the inexhaustible life his mother gave him.

Winter came on and they were prepared against it. There had been such harvests as never were before, and the small,

29

three-roomed house was bursting. From the rafters of the thatched roof hung strings and strings of dried onions and garlic, and about the middle room and in the old man's room and in their own room were mats made of reeds and twisted into the shapes of great jars and these were filled full of wheat and rice. Much of this would be sold, but Wang Lung was frugal and he did not, like many of the villagers, spend his money freely at gambling or on foods too delicate for them, and so, like them, have to sell the grain at harvest when the price was low. Instead he saved it and sold it when the snow came on the ground or at the New Year when people in the towns will pay well for food at any price.

His uncle was always having to sell his grain before it was even well ripened. Sometimes he even sold it standing in the field to save himself the trouble of harvesting and threshing to get a little ready cash. But then his uncle's wife was a foolish woman, fat and lazy, and forever clamoring for sweet food and for this sort of thing and that and for new shoes bought in the town. Wang Lung's woman made all the shoes for himself and for the old man and for her own feet and the child's. He would not know what to make of it if she wished to buy shoes!

There was never anything hanging from the rafters in his uncle's crumbling old house. But in his own there was even a leg of pork which he had bought from his neighbor Ching when he killed his pig that looked as though it were sickening for a disease. The pig had been caught early before it lost flesh and the leg was a large one and O-lan had salted it thoroughly and hung it to dry. There were as well two of their own chickens killed and drawn and dried with the feathers on and stuffed with salt inside.

In the midst of all this plenty they sat in the house, therefore, when the winds of winter came out of the desert to the northeast of them, winds bitter and biting. Soon the child could almost sit alone. They had had a feast of noodles, which mean long life, on his month birthday, when he was a full moon of age, and Wang Lung had invited those who came to his wedding feast and to each he had given a round ten of the red eggs he had boiled and dyed, and to all those who came from the village to congratulate him he gave two eggs. And every one envied him his son, a great, fat, moony-faced child with high cheekbones like his mother. Now as winter came on he sat on the quilt placed on the earthen floor of the house instead of upon the fields, and they opened the door to the south for light, and the sun came in, and the wind on the north beat in vain against the thick earthen wall of the house.

The leaves were soon torn from the date tree on the threshold and from the willow trees and the peach trees near the fields. Only the bamboo leaves clung to the bamboos in the sparse clump to the east of the house, and even though the wind wrenched the stems double, the leaves clung.

With this dry wind the wheat seed that lay in the ground could not sprout and Wang Lung waited anxiously for the rains. And then the rains came suddenly out of a still grey day when the wind fell and the air was quiet and warm, and they all sat in the house filled with well-being, watching the rain fall full and straight and sink into the fields about the dooryard and drip from the thatched ends of the roof above the door. The child was amazed and stretched out his hands to catch the silver lines of the rain as it fell, and he laughed and they laughed with him and the old man squatted on the floor beside the child and said,

"There is not another child like this in a dozen villages. Those brats of my brother notice nothing before they walk." And in the fields the wheat seed sprouted and pushed spears of delicate green above the wet brown earth.

At a time like this there was visiting, because each farmer felt that for once Heaven was doing the work in the fields and their crops were being watered without their backs being broken for it, carrying buckets to and fro, slung upon a pole across their shoulders; and in the morning they gathered at this house and that, drinking tea here and there, going from house to house barefoot across the narrow path between the fields under great oiled paper umbrellas. The women stayed at home and made shoes and mended clothes, if they were thrifty, and thought of preparations for the feast of the New Year.

But Wang Lung and his wife were not frequent at visiting. There was no house in the village of small scattered houses, of which theirs was one of a half dozen, which was so filled with warmth and plenty as their own, and Wang Lung felt that if he became too intimate with the others there would be borrowing. New Year was coming and who had all the money he wanted for the new clothes and the feasting? He stayed in his house and while the woman mended and sewed he took his rakes of split bamboo and examined them, and where the string was broken he wove in new string made of hemp he grew himself, and where a prong was broken out he drove in cleverly a new bit of bamboo.

And what he did for the farm implements, his wife, O-lan, did for the house implements. If an earthen jar leaked she did not, as other women did, cast it aside and talk of a new one. Instead she mixed earth and clay and welded the crack and heated it slowly and it was as good as new.

They sat in their house, therefore, and they rejoiced in each other's approval, although their speech was never anything more than scattered words such as these:

"Did you save the seed from the large squash for the new planting?" Or, "We will sell the wheat straw and burn the bean stalks in the kitchen." Or perhaps rarely Wang Lung would say, "This is a good dish of noodles," and O-lan would answer in deprecation, "It is good flour we have this year from the fields."

From the produce, Wang Lung in this good year had a handful of silver dollars over and above what they needed and these he was fearful of keeping in his belt or of telling any except the woman what he had. They plotted where to keep the silver and at last the woman cleverly dug a small hole in the inner wall of their room behind the bed and into this Wang Lung thrust the silver and with a clod of earth she covered the hole, and it was as though there was nothing there. But to both Wang and O-lan it gave a sense of secret richness and reserve. Wang Lung was conscious that he had money more than he need spend, and when he walked among his fellows he walked at ease with himself and with all.

5

THE NEW YEAR approached and in every house in the village there were preparations. Wang Lung went into the town to the candlemaker's shop and he bought squares of red paper on which were brushed in gilt ink the letter for happiness and some with the letter for riches, and these squares he pasted upon his farm utensils to bring him luck in the New Year. Upon his plow and upon the ox's yoke and upon the two buckets in which he carried his fertilizer and his water, upon each of these he pasted a square. And then upon the doors of his house he pasted long strips of red paper brushed with mottoes of good luck, and over his doorway he pasted a fringe of red paper cunningly cut into a flower pattern and very finely cut. And he bought red paper to make new dresses for the gods, and this the old man did cleverly enough for his old shaking hands, and Wang Lung took them and put them upon the two small gods in the temple to the earth and he burned a little incense before them for the sake of the New Year. And for his house he bought also two red candles to burn on the eve of the year upon the table under the picture of a god, which was pasted on the wall of the middle room above where the table stood.

And Wang Lung went again into the town and he bought pork fat and white sugar and the woman rendered the fat smooth and white and she took rice flour, which they had ground from their own rice between their millstones to which they could yoke the ox when they needed to do so, and she took the fat and the sugar and she mixed and kneaded rich New Year's cakes, called moon cakes, such as were eaten in the House of Hwang.

When the cakes were laid out upon the table in strips, ready for heating, Wang Lung felt his heart fit to burst with pride. There was no other woman in the village able to do what his had done, to make cakes such as only the rich ate at the feast. In some of the cakes she had put strips of little red haws and spots of dried green plums, making flowers and patterns.

"It is a pity to eat these," said Wang Lung.

The old man was hovering about the table, pleased as a child might be pleased with the bright colors. He said,

"Call my brother, your uncle, and his children—let them see!"

But prosperity had made Wang Lung cautious. One could not ask hungry people only to see cakes.

"It is ill luck to look at cakes before the New Year," he replied hastily. And the woman, her hands all dusty with the fine rice flour and sticky with the fat, said,

"Those are not for us to eat, beyond one or two of the plain ones for guests to taste. We are not rich enough to eat white sugar and lard. I am preparing them for the Old Mistress at the

33

great house. I shall take the child on the second day of the New Year and carry the cakes for a gift."

Then the cakes were more important than ever, and Wang Lung was pleased that to the great hall where he had stood with so much timidity and in such poverty his wife should now go as visitor, carrying his son, dressed in red, and cakes made as these were, with the best flour and sugar and lard.

All else at that New Year sank into insignificance beside this visit. His new coat of black cotton cloth which O-lan had made, when he had put it on, only made him say to himself,

"I shall wear it when I take them to the gate of the great house."

He even bore carelessly the first day of the New Year when his uncle and his neighbors came crowding into the house to wish his father and himself well, all boisterous with food and drink. He had himself seen to it that the colored cakes were put away into the basket lest he might have to offer them to common men, although he found it very hard when the plain white ones were praised for their flavor of fat and sugar not to cry out,

"You should see the colored ones!"

But he did not, for more than anything he wished to enter the great house with pride.

Then on the second day of the New Year, when it is the day for women to visit each other, the men having eaten and drunk well the day before, they rose at dawn and the woman dressed the child in his red coat and in the tiger-faced shoes she had made, and she put on his head, freshly shaven by Wang Lung himself on the last day of the old year, the crownless red hat with the small gilt Buddha sewed on front, and she set him upon the bed. Then Wang Lung dressed himself quickly while his wife combed out afresh her long black hair and knotted it with the brass pin washed with silver which he had bought for her, and she put on her new coat of black that was made from the same piece as his own new robe, twenty-four feet of good cloth for the two, and two feet of cloth thrown in for good measure, as the custom is at cloth shops. Then he carrying the child and she the cakes in the basket, they set out on the path across the fields, now barren with winter.

Then Wang Lung had his reward at the great gate of the House of Hwang, for when the gateman came to the woman's call he opened his eyes at all he saw and he twirled the three long hairs on his mole and cried out,

"Ah, Wang the farmer, three this time instead of one!" And then seeing the new clothes they all wore and the child who was a son, he said further, "One has no need to wish you more fortune this year than you have had in the last."

Wang Lung answered negligently as one speaks to a man who is scarcely an equal, "Good harvests—good harvests—" and he stepped with assurance inside the gate.

The gateman was impressed with all he saw and he said to Wang Lung,

"Do you sit within my wretched room while I announce your woman and son within."

And Wang Lung stood watching them go across the court, his wife and his son, bearing gifts to the head of a great house. It was all to his honor, and when he could no longer see them when they had dwindled down the long vista of the courts one inside the other, and had turned at last wholly out of sight, he went into the gateman's house and there he accepted as a matter of course from the gateman's pock-marked wife the honorable seat to the left of the table in the middle room, and he accepted with only a slight nod the bowl of tea which she presented to him and he set it before him and did not drink of it, as though it were not good enough in quality of tea leaves for him.

It seemed a long time before the gateman returned, bringing back again the woman and child. Wang Lung looked closely at the woman's face for an instant trying to see if all were well, for he had learned now from that impassive square countenance to detect small changes at first invisible to him. She wore a look of heavy content, however, and at once he became impatient to hear her tell of what had happened in those courts of the ladies into which she could not go, now that he had no business there.

With short bows, therefore, to the gateman and to his pock-marked wife he hurried O-lan away and he took into his own arms the child who was asleep and lying all crumpled in his new coat.

"Well?" he called back to her over his shoulder as she followed him. For once he was impatient with her slowness. She drew a little nearer to him and said in a whisper,

"I believe, if one should ask me, that they are feeling a pinch this year in that house."

She spoke in a shocked tone as one might speak of gods being hungry.

35

"What do you mean?" said Wang Lung, urging her.

But she would not be hastened. Words were to her things to be caught one by one and released with difficulty.

"The Ancient Mistress wore the same coat this year as last. I have never seen this happen before. And the slaves had no new coats." And then after a pause she said, "I saw not one slave with a new coat like mine." And then after a while she said again, "As for our son, there was not even a child among the concubines of the Old Master himself to compare to him in beauty and in dress."

A slow smile spread over her face and Wang Lung laughed aloud and he held the child tenderly against him. How well he had done—how well he had done! And then as he exulted he was smitten with fear. What foolish thing was he doing, walking like this under an open sky, with a beautiful man child for any evil spirit passing by chance through the air to see! He opened his coat hastily and thrust the child's head into his bosom and he said in a loud voice,

"What a pity our child is a female whom no one could want and covered with smallpox as well! Let us pray it may die."

"Yes—yes——" said his wife as quickly as she could, understanding dimly what a thing they had done.

And being comforted with these precautions they had now taken, Wang Lung once more urged his wife.

"Did you find out why they are poorer?"

"I had but a moment for private talk with the cook under whom I worked before," she replied, "but she said, 'This house cannot stand forever with all the young lords, five of them, spending money like waste water in foreign parts and sending home woman after woman as they weary of them, and the Old Lord living at home adding a concubine or two each year, and the Old Mistress eating enough opium every day to fill two shoes with gold.'"

"Do they indeed!" murmured Wang Lung, spellbound.

"Then the third daughter is to be married in the spring," continued O-lan, "and her dowry is a prince's ransom and enough to buy an official seat in a big city. Her clothes she will have of nothing but the finest satins with special patterns woven in Soochow and Hangchow and she will have a tailor sent from Shanghai with his retinue of under tailors lest she find her clothes less fashionable than those of the women in foreign parts."

"Whom will she marry, then, with all this expense?" said Wang Lung, struck with admiration and horror at such pouring out of wealth.

"She is to marry the second son of a Shanghai magistrate," said the woman, and then after a long pause she added, "They must be getting poorer for the Old Mistress herself told me they wished to sell land—some of the land to the south of the house, just outside the city wall, where they have always planted rice each year because it is good land and easily flooded from the moat around the wall."

"Sell their land!" repeated Wang Lung, convinced. "Then indeed are they growing poor. Land is one's flesh and blood."

He pondered for a while and suddenly a thought came to him and he smote the side of his head with his palm.

"What have I not thought of!" he cried, turning to the woman. "We will buy the land!"

They stared at each other, he in delight, she in stupefaction.

"But the land—the land——" she stammered.

"I will buy it!" he cried in a lordly voice. "I will buy it from the great House of Hwang!"

"It is too far away," she said in consternation. "We would have to walk half the morning to reach it."

"I will buy it," he repeated peevishly as he might repeat a demand to his mother who crossed him.

"It is a good thing to buy land," she said pacifically. "It is better certainly than putting money into a mud wall. But why not a piece of your uncle's land? He is clamoring to sell that strip near to the western field we now have."

"That land of my uncle's," said Wang Lung loudly, "I would not have it. He has been dragging a crop out of it in this way and that for twenty years and not a bit has he put back of manure or bean cake. The soil is like lime. No, I will buy Hwang's land."

He said "Hwang's land" as casually as he might have said "Ching's land,"—Ching, who was his farmer neighbor. He would be more than equal to these people in the foolish, great, wasteful house. He would go with the silver in his hand and he would say plainly,

"I have money. What is the price of the earth you wish to sell?" Before the Old Lord he heard himself saying and to the Old Lord's agent, "Count me as anyone else. What is the fair price? I have it in my hand."

And his wife, who had been a slave in the kitchens of that

37

proud family, she would be wife to a man who owned a piece of the land that for generations had made the House of Hwang great. It was as though she felt his thought for she suddenly ceased her resistance and she said,

"Let it be bought. After all, rice land is good, and it is near the moat and we can get water every year. It is sure."

And again the slow smile spread over her face, the smile that never lightened the dullness of her narrow black eyes, and after a long time she said,

"Last year this time I was slave in that house."

And they walked on, silent with the fullness of this thought.

6

THIS PIECE of land which Wang Lung now owned was a thing which greatly changed his life. At first, after he had dug the silver from the wall and taken it to the great house, after the honor of speaking as an equal to the Old Lord's equal was past, he was visited with a depression of spirit which was almost regret. When he thought of the hole in the wall now empty that had been filled with silver he need not use, he wished that he had his silver back. After all, this land, it would take hours of labor again, and as O-lan said, it was far away, more than a *li* which is a third of a mile. And again, the buying of it had not been quite so filled with glory as he had anticipated. He had gone too early to the great house and the Old Lord was still sleeping. True, it was noon, but when he said in a loud voice,

"Tell his Old Honor I have important business—tell him money is concerned!" the gateman had answered positively,

"All the money in the world would not tempt me to wake the old tiger. He sleeps with his new concubine, Peach Blossom, whom he has had but three days. It is not worth my life to waken him." And then he added somewhat maliciously, pulling at the hairs on his mole, "And do not think that silver will waken him——he has had silver under his hand since he was born."

In the end, then, it had had to be managed with the Old Lord's agent, an oily scoundrel whose hands were heavy with the money that stuck to them in passing. So it seemed sometimes to Wang Lung that after all the silver was more valuable than the land. One could see silver shining.

Well, but the land was his! He set out one grey day in the second month of the new year to look at it. None knew yet that it belonged to him and he walked out to see it alone, a long square of heavy black clay that lay stretched beside the moat encircling the wall of the town. He paced the land off carefully, three hundred paces lengthwise and a hundred and twenty across. Four stones still marked the corners of the boundaries, stones set with the great seal character of the House of Hwang. Well, he would have that changed. He would pull up the stones later and he would put his own name there——not yet, for he was not ready for people to know that he was rich enough to buy land from the great house, but later, when he was more rich, so that it did not matter what he did. And looking at that long square of land he thought to himself,

"To those at the great house it means nothing, this handful of earth, but to me it means how much!"

Then he had a turn of his mind and he was filled with a contempt for himself that a small piece of land should seem so important. Why, when he had poured out his silver proudly before the agent the man had scraped it up carelessly in his hands and said,

"Here is enough for a few days of opium for the old lady, at any rate."

And the wide difference that still lay between him and the great house seemed suddenly impassable as the moat full of water in front of him, and as high as the wall beyond, stretching up straight and hoary before him. He was filled with an angry determination, then, and he said to his heart that he would fill that hole with silver again and again until he had bought from the House of Hwang enough land so that this land would be less than an inch in his sight.

And so this parcel of land became to Wang Lung a sign and a symbol.

Spring came with blustering winds and torn clouds of rain and for Wang Lung the half-idle days of winter were plunged into long days of desperate labor over his land. The old man looked after the child now and the woman worked with the man from dawn until sunset flowed over the fields, and when Wang Lung perceived one day that again she was with child, his first thought was of irritation that during the harvest she would be unable to work. He shouted at her, irritable with fatigue,

"So you have chosen this time to breed again, have you!"

She answered stoutly.

"This time it is nothing. It is only the first that is hard."

Beyond this nothing was said of the second child from the time he noticed its growth swelling her body until the day came in autumn when she laid down her hoe one morning and crept into the house. He did not go back that day even for his noon meal, for the sky was heavy with thunder clouds and his rice lay dead ripe for gathering into sheaves. Later before the sun set she was back beside him, her body flattened, spent, but her face silent and undaunted. His impulse was to say,

"For this day you have had enough. Go and lie upon your bed." But the aching of his own exhausted body made him cruel, and he said to himself that he had suffered as much with his labor that day as she with her childbirth, and so he only asked between the strokes of his scythe,

"Is it male or female?"

She answered calmly,

"It is another male."

They said nothing more to each other, but he was pleased, and the incessant bending and stooping seemed less arduous, and working on until the moon rose above a bank of purple clouds, they finished the field and went home.

After his meal and after he had washed his sunburnt body in cool water and had rinsed his mouth with tea, Wang Lung went in to look at his second son. O-lan had lain herself upon the bed after the cooking of the meal and the child lay beside her—a fat, placid child, well enough, but not so large as the first one. Wang Lung looked at him and then went back to the middle room well content. Another son, and another and another each year—one could not trouble with red eggs every year; it was enough to do it for the first. Sons every year; the house was full of good fortune—this woman brought him nothing but good fortune. He shouted to his father,

"Now, Old One, with another grandson we shall have to put the big one in your bed!"

The old man was delighted. He had for a long time been desiring this child to sleep in his bed and warm his chilly old flesh with the renewal of young bones and blood, but the child would not leave his mother. Now, however, staggering in with feet still unsteady with babyhood, he stared at this new child beside his mother, and seeming to comprehend with his grave eyes that another had his place, he allowed himself without protest to be placed in his grandfather's bed.

And again the harvests were good and Wang Lung gathered silver from the selling of his produce and again he hid it in the wall. But the rice he reaped from the land of the Hwangs brought him twice as much as that from his own rice land. The earth of that piece was wet and rich and the rice grew on it as weeds grow where they are not wanted. And everyone knew now that Wang Lung owned this land and in his village there was talk of making him the head.

7

WANG LUNG's uncle began at this time to become the trouble which Wang Lung had surmised from the beginning that he might be. This uncle was the younger brother of Wang Lung's father, and by all the claims of relationship he might depend upon Wang Lung if he had not enough for himself and his family. So long as Wang Lung and his father were poor and scantily fed the uncle made muster to scratch about on his land and gather enough to feed his seven children and his wife and himself. But once fed none of them worked. The wife would not stir herself to sweep the floor of their hut, nor did the children trouble to wash the food from their faces. It was a disgrace that as the girls grew older and even to marriageable age they still ran about the village street and left uncombed their rough sun-browned hair, and sometimes even talked to men. Wang Lung,

41

meeting his oldest girl cousin thus one day, was so angered for the disgrace done to his family that he dared to go to his uncle's wife and say,

"Now, who will marry a girl like my cousin, whom any man may look on? She has been marriageable these three years and she runs about and today I saw an idle lout on the village street lay his hand on her arm and she answered him only with brazen laughter!"

His uncle's wife had nothing active in her body except her tongue and this she now loosed upon Wang Lung.

"Well, and who will pay for the dowry and for the wedding and for the middleman's fees? It is all very well for those to talk who have more land than they know what to do with and who can yet go and buy more land from the great families with their spare silver, but your uncle is an unfortunate man and he has been so from the first. His destiny is evil and through no fault of his own. Heaven wills it. Where others can produce good grain, for him the seed dies in the ground and nothing but weeds spring up, and this though he break his back!"

She fell into loud, easy tears, and began to work herself up into a fury. She snatched at her knot of hair on the back of her head and tore down the loose hairs about her face and she began to scream freely,

"Ah, it is something you do not know—to have an evil destiny! Where the fields of others bear good rice and wheat, ours bear weeds; where the houses of others stand for a hundred years, the earth itself shakes under ours so that the walls crack; where others bear men, I, although I conceive a son, will yet give birth to a girl—ah, evil destiny!"

She shrieked aloud and the neighbor women rushed out of their houses to see and to hear. Wang Lung stood stoutly, however, and would finish what he came to say.

"Nevertheless," he said, "although it is not for me to presume to advise the brother of my father, I will say this: it is better that a girl be married away while she is yet virgin, and whoever heard of a bitch dog who was allowed on the streets who did not give birth to a litter?"

Having spoken thus plainly, he went away to his own house and left his uncle's wife screaming. He had it in his mind to buy more land this year from the House of Hwang and more land year after year as he was able, and he dreamed of adding a new room to his house and it angered him that as he saw himself and his sons rising into a landed family, this shiftless brood of his cousins should be running loose, bearing the same name as his own.

The next day his uncle came to the field where he was working. O-lan was not there, for ten moons had passed since the second child was born and a third birth was close upon her, and this time she was not so well and for a handful of days she had not come to the fields and so Wang Lung worked alone. His uncle came slouching along a furrow, his clothes never properly buttoned about him, but caught together and held insecurely with his girdle, so that it always seemed that if a gust of wind blew at him he might suddenly stand naked. He came to where Wang Lung was and he stood in silence while Wang Lung hoed a narrow line beside the broad beans he was cultivating. At last Wang Lung said maliciously and without looking up,

"I ask your pardon, my uncle, for not stopping in my work. These beans, must, if they are to bear, as you know, be cultivated twice and thrice. Yours, doubtless, are finished. I am very slow—a poor farmer—never finishing my work in time to rest."

His uncle understood perfectly Wang Lung's malice, but he answered smoothly,

"I am a man of evil destiny. This year out of twenty seed beans, one came up, and in such a poor growth as that there is no use in putting the hoe down. We shall have to buy beans this year if we eat them," and he sighed heavily.

Wang Lung hardened his heart. He knew that his uncle had come to ask something of him. He put his hoe down into the ground with a long even movement and with great care, breaking up the tiniest clod in the soft earth already well cultivated. The bean plants stood erect in thrifty order, casting as they stood little fringes of clear shadow in the sunshine. At last his uncle began to speak.

"The person in my house has told me," he said, "of your interest in my worthless oldest slave creature. It is wholly true what you say. You are wise for your years. She should be married. She is fifteen years old and for these three or four years could have given birth. I am terrified constantly lest she conceive by some wild dog and bring shame to me and to our name. Think of this happening in our respectable family, to me, the brother of your own father!"

Wang Lung put his hoe down hard into the soil. He would

43

have liked to have spoken plainly. He would have liked to have said,

"Why do you not control her, then? Why do you not keep her decently in the house and make her sweep and clean and cook and make clothes for the family?"

But one cannot say these things to an older generation. He remained silent, therefore, and hoed closely about a small plant and he waited.

"If it had been my good destiny," continued his uncle mournfully, "to have married a wife as your father did, one who could work and at the same time produce sons, as your own does also, instead of a woman like mine, who grows nothing but flesh and gives birth to nothing but females and that one idle son of mine who is less than a male for his idleness, I, too, might have been rich now as you are. Then might I have, willingly would I have, shared my riches with you. Your daughters I would have wed to good men, your son would I have placed in a merchant's shop as apprentice and willingly paid the fee of guaranty—your house would I have delighted to repair, and you I would have fed with the best I had, you and your father and your children, for we are of one blood."

Wang Lung answered shortly,

"You know I am not rich. I have the five mouths to feed now and my father is old and does not work and still he eats, and another mouth is being born in my house at this very moment, for aught I know."

His uncle replied shrilly,

"You are rich—you are rich! You have bought the land from the great house at the gods know what heavy price—is there another in the village who could do this thing?"

At this Wang Lung was goaded to anger. He flung down his hoe and he shouted suddenly, glaring at his uncle,

"If I have a handful of silver it is because I work and my wife works, and we do not, as some do, sit idling over a gambling table or gossiping on doorsteps never swept, letting the fields grow to weeds and our children go half-fed!"

The blood flew into his uncle's yellow face and he rushed at his nephew and slapped him vigorously on both cheeks.

"Now that," he cried, "for speaking so to your father's generation! Have you no religion, no morals, that you are so lacking in filial conduct? Have you not heard it said that in the Sacred Edicts it is commanded that a man is never to correct an elder?"

Wang Lung stood sullen and immoveable, conscious of his fault but angry to the bottom of his heart against this man who was his uncle.

"I will tell your words to the whole village!" screamed his uncle in a high cracked voice of fury. "Yesterday you attack my house and call aloud in the streets that my daughter is not a virgin; today you reproach me, who if your father passes on, must be as your own father to you! Now may my daughters all not be virgins, but not from one of them would I hear such talk!" And he repeated over and over, "I will tell it to the village—I will tell it to the village . . ." until at last Wang Lung said unwillingly, "What do you want me to do?"

It touched his pride that this matter might indeed be called out before the village. After all, it was his own flesh and blood.

His uncle changed immediately. Anger melted out of him. He smiled and he put his hand on Wang Lung's arm.

"Ah, I know you—good lad—good lad——" he said softly. "Your old uncle knows you—you are my son. Son, a little silver in this poor old palm—say, ten pieces, or even nine, and I could begin to have arrangements with a matchmaker for that slave of mine. Ah, you are right! It is time—it is time!" He sighed and shook his head and he looked piously to the sky.

Wang Lung picked up his hoe and threw it down again.

"Come to the house," he said shortly. "I do not carry silver on me like a prince," and he strode ahead, bitter beyond speech because some of the good silver with which he had planned to buy more land was to go into this palm of his uncle's, from whence it would slip on to the gambling table before night fell.

He strode into the house, brushing out of his way his two small sons who played, naked in the warm sunshine, about the threshold. His uncle, with easy good nature, called to the children and took from some recess in his crumpled clothing a copper coin for each child. He pressed the small fat shining bodies to him, and putting his nose into their soft necks he smelled of the sun-browned flesh with easy affection.

"Ah, you are two little men," he said, clasping one in either arm.

But Wang Lung did not pause. He went into the room where he slept with his wife and the last child. It was very dark, coming in as he did from the outer sunshine, and except for the bar of light from the hole, he could see nothing. But the smell of warm blood which he remembered so well filled his nostrils and he called out sharply,

45

"What now—has your time come?"

The voice of his wife answered from the bed more feebly than he had ever heard her speak,

"It is over once more. It is only a slave this time—not worth mentioning."

Wang Lung stood still. A sense of evil struck him. A girl! A girl was causing all this trouble in his uncle's house. Now a girl had been born into his house as well.

He went without reply then to the wall and felt for the roughness which was the mark of the hiding place and he removed the clod of earth. Behind it he fumbled among the little heap of silver and he counted out nine pieces.

"Why are you taking the silver out?" said his wife suddenly in the darkness.

"I am compelled to lend it to my uncle," he replied shortly.

His wife answered nothing at first and then she said in her plain, heavy way,

"It is better not to say lend. There is no lending in that house. There is only giving."

"Well I know that," replied Wang Lung with bitterness. "It is cutting my flesh out to give to him and for nothing except that we are of a blood."

Then going out into the threshold he thrust the money at his uncle and he walked quickly back to the field and there he fell to working as though he would tear the earth from its foundations. He thought for the time only of the silver; he saw it poured out carelessly upon a gambling table, saw it swept up by some idle hand—his silver, the silver he had so painfully collected from the fruits of his fields, to turn it back again for more earth for his own.

It was evening before his anger was spent and he straightened himself and remembered his home and his food. And then he thought of that new mouth come that day into his house and it struck him, with heaviness, that the birth of daughters had begun for him, daughters who do not belong to their parents, but are born and reared for other families. He had not even thought, in his anger at his uncle, to stop and see the face of this small, new creature.

He stood leaning upon his hoe and he was seized with sadness. It would be another harvest before he could buy that land now, a piece adjoining the one he had, and there was this new mouth in the house. Across the pale, oyster-colored sky of twilight a flock of crows flew, sharply black, and whirred over him, cawing loudly. He watched them disappear like a cloud into the trees about his house, and he ran at them, shouting and shaking his hoe. They rose again slowly, circling and re-circling over his head, mocking him with their cries, and they flew at last into the darkening sky.

He groaned aloud. It was an evil omen.

8

IT SEEMED as though once the gods turn against a man they will not consider him again. The rains, which should have come in early summer, withheld themselves, and day after day the skies shone with fresh and careless brilliance. The parched and starving earth was nothing to them. From dawn to dawn there was not a cloud, and at night the stars hung out of the sky, golden and cruel in their beauty.

The fields, although Wang Lung cultivated them desperately, dried and cracked, and the young wheat stalks, which had sprung up courageously with the coming of spring and had prepared their heads for the grain, when they found nothing coming from the soil or the sky for them, ceased their growing and stood motionless at first under the sun and at last dwindled and yellowed into a barren harvest. The young rice beds which Wang Lung sowed at first were squares of jade upon the brown earth. He carried water to them day after day after he had given up the wheat, the heavy wooden buckets slung upon a bamboo pole across his shoulders. But though a furrow grew upon his flesh and a callus formed there as large as a bowl, no rain came.

At last the water in the pond dried into a cake of clay and the water even in the well sunk so low that O-lan said to him,

"If the children must drink and the old man have his hot water the plants must go dry."

Wang Lung answered with anger that broke into a sob,

47

"Well, and they must all starve if the plants starve." It was true that all their lives depended upon the earth.

Only the piece of land by the moat bore harvest, and this because at last when summer wore away without rain, Wang Lung abandoned all his other fields and stayed the day out at this one, dipping water from the moat to pour upon the greedy soil. This year for the first time he sold his grain as soon as it was harvested, and when he felt the silver upon his palm he gripped it hard in defiance. He would, he told himself, in spite of gods and drought, do that which he had determined. His body he had broken and his sweat he had spilled for this handful of silver and he would do what he would with it. And he hurried to the House of Hwang and he met the land agent there and he said without ceremony,

"I have that with which to buy the land adjoining mine by the moat."

Now Wang Lung had heard here and there that for the House of Hwang it had been a year verging upon poverty. The old lady had not had her dole of opium to the full for many days and she was like an old tigress in her hunger so that each day she sent for the agent and she cursed him and struck his face with her fan, screaming at him,

"And are there not acres of land left, yet?" until he was beside himself.

He had even given up the moneys which ordinarily he held back from the family transactions for his own use, so beside himself had he been. And as if this were not enough, the Old Lord took yet another concubine, a slave who was the child of a slave who had been his creature in her youth, but who was now wed to a man servant in the house, because the Old Lord's desire for her failed before he took her into his room as concubine. This child of the slave, who was not more than sixteen, he now saw with fresh lust, for as he grew old and infirm and heavy with flesh he seemed to desire more and more women who were slight and young, even to childhood, so that there was no slaking his lust. As the Old Mistress with her opium, so he with his lusts, and there was no making him understand there was not money for jade earrings for his favorites and not gold for their pretty hands. He could not comprehend the words "no money," who all his life had but to reach out his hand and fill it as often as he would.

And seeing their parents thus, the young lords shrugged their shoulders and said there must still be enough for their

48

lifetime. They united in only one thing and this was to berate the agent for his ill management of the estates, so that he who had once been oily and unctuous, a man of plenty and of ease, was now become anxious and harried and his flesh gone so that his skin hung upon him like an old garment.

Neither had Heaven sent rain upon the fields of the House of Hwang, and there, too, there were no harvests, and so when Wang Lung came to the agent crying, "I have silver," it was as though one came saying to the hungry, "I have food."

The agent grasped at it, and where there had been dickering and tea-drinking, now the two men spoke in eager whispers, and more quickly than they could speak whole words, the money passed from one hand to the other and papers were signed and sealed and the land was Wang Lung's.

And once again Wang Lung did not count the passing of silver, which was his flesh and his blood, a hard thing. He bought with it the desire of his heart. He had now a vast field of good land, for the new field was twice as large as the first. But more to him than its dark fertility was the fact that it had belonged once to the family of a prince. And this time he told no one, not even O-lan, what he had done.

Month passed into month and still no rain fell. As autumn approached the clouds gathered unwillingly in the sky, small, light clouds, and in the village street one could see men standing about, idle and anxious, their faces upturned to the sky, judging closely of this cloud and that, discussing together as to whether any held rain in it. But before sufficient clouds could gather for promise, a bitter wind rose out of the northwest, the acrid wind of the distant desert, and blew the clouds from the sky as one gathers dust from a floor with a broom. And the sky was empty and barren, and the stately sun rose each morning and made its march and set solitary each night. And the moon in its time shone like a lesser sun for clearness.

From his fields Wang Lung reaped scanty harvest of hardy beans, and from his corn field, which he had planted in despair when the rice beds had yellowed and died before ever the plants had been set into the watered field, he plucked short stubby ears with the grains scattered here and there. There was not a bean lost in the threshing. He set the two little boys to sifting the dust of the threshing floor between their fingers after he and the woman had flailed the bean vines, and he shelled the corn upon the floor in the middle room, watching sharply every grain that flew wide. When he would have put the cobs away for fuel, his wife spoke out,

"No—do not waste them in burning. I remember when I was a child in Shantung when years like this came, even the cobs we ground and ate. It is better than grass."

When she had spoken they all fell silent, even the children. There was foreboding in these strange brilliant days when the land was failing them. Only the girl child knew no fear. For her there were the mother's two great breasts as yet filled for her needs. But O-lan, giving her suck, muttered,

"Eat, poor fool—eat, while there is yet that which can be eaten."

And then, as though there were not enough evil, O-lan was again with child, and her milk dried up, and the frightened house was filled with the sound of a child continually crying for food.

If one had asked Wang Lung,

"And how are you fed through the autumn?" he would have answered, "I do not know—a little food here and there."

But there was none to ask him that. None asked of any other in the whole countryside, "How are you fed?" None asked anything except of himself, "How shall I be fed this day?" And parents said, "How shall we be fed, we and our children?"

Now Wang Lung's ox he had cared for as long as he could. He had given the beast a bit of straw and a handful of vines as long as these lasted and then he had gone out and torn leaves from the trees for it until winter came and these were gone. Then since there was no land to plough, since seed, if it were planted only dried in the earth, and since they had eaten all their seed, he turned the ox out to hunt for itself, sending the eldest boy to sit upon its back all day and hold the rope passed through its nostrils so that it would not be stolen. But latterly he had not dared even to do this, lest men from the village, even his neighbors, might overcome the lad and seize the ox for food, and kill it. So he kept the ox on the threshold until it grew lean as its skeleton.

But there came a day when there was no rice left and no wheat left and there were only a few beans and a meager store of corn, and the ox lowed with its hunger and the old man said,

"We will eat the ox, next."

Then Wang Lung cried out, for it was to him as though one

50

said, "We will eat a man next." The ox was his companion in the fields and he had walked behind and praised it and cursed it as his mood was, and from his youth he had known the beast, when they had bought it a small calf. And he said,

"How can we eat the ox? How shall we plough again?"

But the old man answered, tranquil enough,

"Well, and it is your life or the beast's, and your son's life or the beast's and a man can buy an ox again more easily than his own life."

But Wang Lung would not that day kill it. And the next day passed and the next and the children cried out for food and they would not be comforted and O-lan looked at Wang Lung, beseeching him for the children, and he saw at last that the thing was to be done. So he said roughly,

"Let it be killed then, but I cannot do it."

He went into the room where he slept and he laid himself upon the bed and he wrapped the quilt about his head that he might not hear the beast's bellowing when it died.

Then O-lan crept out and she took a great iron knife she had in the kitchen and she cut a great gash in the beast's neck, and thus she severed its life. And she took a bowl and caught its blood to cook for them to eat in a pudding, and she skinned and hacked to pieces the great carcass, and Wang Lung would not come out until the thing was wholly done and the flesh was cooked and upon the table. But when he tried to eat the flesh of his ox his gorge rose and he could not swallow it and he drank only a little of the soup. And O-lan said to him,

"An ox is but an ox and this one grew old. Eat, for there will be another one day and far better than this one."

Wang Lung was a little comforted then and he ate a morsel and then more, and they all ate. But the ox was eaten at last and the bones cracked for the marrow, and it was all too quickly gone, and there was nothing left of it except the skin, dried and hard and stretched upon the rack of bamboo O-lan had made to hold it spread.

At first there had been hostility in the village against Wang Lung because it was supposed that he had silver which he was hiding and food stored away. His uncle, who was among the first to be hungry, came importuning to his door, and indeed the man and his wife and his seven children had nothing to eat. Wang Lung measured unwillingly into the skin of his uncle's robe a small heap of beans and a precious handful of corn. Then he said with firmness,

"It is all I can spare and I have first my old father to consider, even if I had no children."

When his uncle came again Wang Lung cried out,

"Even filial piety will not feed my house!" and he sent his uncle empty away.

From that day his uncle turned against him like a dog that has been kicked, and he whispered about the village in this house and in that,

"My nephew there, he has silver and he has food, but he will give none of it to us, not even to me, and to my children, who are his own bones and flesh. We can do nothing but starve."

And as family after family finished its store in the small village and spent its last coin in the scanty markets of the town, and the winds of winter came down from the desert, cold as a knife of steel and dry and barren, the hearts of the villagers grew distraught with their own hunger and with the hunger of their pinched wives and crying children, and when Wang Lung's uncle shivered about the streets like a lean dog and whispered from his famished lips, "There is one who has food—there is one whose children are fat, still," the men took up poles and went one night to the house of Wang Lung and beat upon the door. And when he had opened to the voices of his neighbors, they fell upon him and pushed him out of the doorway and threw out of the house his frightened children, and they fell upon every corner, and they scrabbled every surface with their hands to find where he had hidden his food. Then when they found his wretched store of a few dried beans and a bowlful of dried corn they gave a great howl of disappointment and despair, and they seized his bits of furniture, the table and the benches and the bed where the old man lay, frightened and weeping.

Then O-lan came forward and spoke, and her plain, slow voice rose above the men,

"Not that—not that yet," she called out. "It is not yet time to take our table and the benches and the bed from our house. You have all our food. But out of your own houses you have not sold yet your table and your benches. Leave us ours. We are even. We have not a bean or a grain of corn more than you—no, you have more than we, now, for you have all of ours. Heaven will strike you if you take more. Now, we will go out together and hunt for grass to eat and bark from the trees, you for your children, and we for our three children, and for this fourth who is to be born in such times." She pressed her hand to her belly as she spoke, and the men were ashamed before her and went out one by one, for they were not evil men except when they starved.

One lingered, that one called Ching, a small, silent yellow man with a face like an ape's in the best of times, and now hollowed and anxious. He would have spoken some good word of shame, for he was an honest man and only his crying child had forced him to evil. But in his bosom was a handful of beans he had snatched when the store was found and he was fearful lest he must return them if he spoke at all, and so he only looked at Wang Lung with haggard, speechless eyes and he went out.

Wang Lung stood there in his dooryard where year after year he had threshed his good harvests, and which had lain now for many months idle and useless. There was nothing left in the house to feed his father and his children—nothing to feed this woman of his who besides the nourishment of her own body had this other one to feed into growth, this other one who would, with the cruelty of new and ardent life, steal from the very flesh and blood of its mother. He had an instant of extreme fear. Then into his blood like soothing wine flowed this comfort. He said in his heart,

"They cannot take the land from me. The labor of my body and the fruit of the fields I have put into that which cannot be taken away. If I had the silver, they would have taken it. If I had bought with the silver to store it, they would have taken it all. I have the land still, and it is mine."

9

WANG LUNG, sitting at the threshold of his door, said to himself that now surely something must be done. They could not remain here in this empty house and die. In his lean body, about which he daily wrapped more tightly his loose girdle, there was a determination to live. He would not thus, just when he was coming into the fullness of a man's life, suddenly be robbed of it by a stupid fate. There was such anger in him now

53

as he often could not express. At times it seized him like a frenzy so that he rushed out upon his barren threshing floor and shook his arms at the foolish sky that shone above him, eternally blue and clear and cold and cloudless.

"Oh, you are too wicked, you Old Man in Heaven!" he would cry recklessly. And if for an instant he were afraid, he would the next instant cry sullenly, "And what can happen to me worse than that which has happened!"

Once he walked, dragging one foot after another in his famished weakness, to the temple of the earth, and deliberately he spat upon the face of the small, imperturbable god who sat there with his goddess. There were no sticks of incense now before this pair, nor had there been for many moons, and their paper clothes were tattered and showed their clay bodies through the rents. But they sat there unmoved by anything and Wang Lung gnashed his teeth at them and walked back to his house groaning and fell upon his bed.

They scarcely rose at all now, any of them. There was no need, and fitful sleep took the place, for a while, at least, of the food they had not. The cobs of the corn they had dried and eaten and they stripped the bark from trees and all over the countryside people were eating what grass they could find upon the wintry hills. There was not an animal anywhere. A man might walk for a handful of days and see not an ox nor an ass nor any kind of beast or fowl.

The children's bellies were swollen out with empty wind, and one never saw in these days a child playing upon the village street. At most the two boys in Wang Lung's house crept to the door and sat in the sun, the cruel sun that never ceased its endless shining. Their once rounded bodies were angular and bony now, sharp small bones like the bones of birds, except for their ponderous bellies. The girl child never even sat alone, although the time was past for this, but lay uncomplaining hour after hour wrapped in an old quilt. At first the angry insistence of her crying had filled the house, but she had come to be quiet, sucking feebly at whatever was put into her mouth and never lifting up her voice. Her little hollowed face peered out at them all, little sunken blue lips like a toothless old woman's lips, and hollow black eyes peering.

This persistence of the small life in some way won her father's affection, although if she had been round and merry as the others had been at her age he would have been careless of her for a girl. Sometimes, looking at her he whispered softly,

"Poor fool—poor little fool———" And once when she essayed a weak smile with her toothless gums showing, he broke into tears and took into his lean hard hand her small claw and held the tiny grasp of her fingers over his forefinger. Thereafter he would sometimes lift her, all naked as she lay, and thrust her inside the scant warmth of his coat against his flesh and sit with her so by the threshold of the house, looking out over the dry, flat fields.

As for the old man, he fared better than any, for if there was anything to eat he was given it, even though the children were without. Wang Lung said to himself proudly that none should say in the hour of death he had forgotten his father. Even if his own flesh went to feed him the old man should eat. The old man slept day and night, and ate what was given him and there was still strength in him to creep about the dooryard at noon when the sun was warm. He was more cheerful than any of them and he quavered forth one day in his old voice that was like a little wind trembling among cracked bamboos,

"There have been worse days—there have been worse days. Once I saw men and women eating children."

"There will never be such a thing in my house," said Wang Lung, in extremest horror.

There was a day when his neighbor Ching, worn now to less than the shadow of a human creature, came to the door of Wang Lung's house and he whispered from his lips that were dried and black as earth,

"In the town the dogs are eaten and everywhere the horses and the fowls of every sort. Here we have eaten the beasts that ploughed our fields and the grass and the bark of trees. What now remains for food?"

Wang Lung shook his head hopelessly. In his bosom lay the slight, skeleton-like body of his girl child, and he looked down into the delicate bony face, and into the sharp, sad eyes that watched him unceasingly from his breast. When he caught those eyes in his glance, invariably there wavered upon the child's face a flickering smile that broke his heart.

Ching thrust his face nearer.

"In the village they are eating human flesh," he whispered. "It is said your uncle and his wife are eating. How else are they living and with strength enough to walk about—they, who, it is known, have never had anything?"

Wang Lung drew back from the death-like head which Ching

55

had thrust forward as he spoke. With the man's eyes close like this, he was horrible. Wang Lung was suddenly afraid with a fear he did not understand. He rose quickly as though to cast off some entangling danger.

"We will leave this place," he said loudly. "We will go south! There are everywhere in this great land people who starve. Heaven, however wicked, will not at once wipe out the sons of Han."

His neighbor looked at him patiently. "Ah, you are young," he said sadly. "I am older than you and my wife is old and we have nothing except one daughter. We can die well enough."

"You are more fortunate than I," said Wang Lung. "I have my old father and these three small mouths and another about to be born. We must go lest we forget our nature and eat each other as the wild dogs do."

And then it seemed to him suddenly that what he said was very right, and he called aloud to O-lan, who lay upon the bed day after day without speech, now that there was no food for the stove and no fuel for the oven.

"Come, woman, we will go south!"

There was cheer in his voice such as none had heard in many moons, and the children looked up and the old man hobbled out from his room and O-lan rose feebly from her bed and came to the door of their room and clinging to the door frame she said,

"It is a good thing to do. One can at least die walking."

The child in her body hung from her lean loins like a knotty fruit and from her face every particle of flesh was gone, so that the jagged bones stood forth rock-like under her skin. "Only wait until tomorrow," she said. "I shall have given birth by then. I can tell by this thing's movements in me."

"Tomorrow, then," answered Wang Lung, and then he saw his wife's face and he was moved with a pity greater than any he had had for himself. This poor creature was dragging forth yet another!

"How shall you walk, you poor creature!" he muttered, and he said unwillingly to his neighbor Ching, who still leaned against the house by the door, "If you have any food left, for a good heart's sake give me a handful to save the life of the mother of my sons, and I will forget that I saw you in my house as a robber."

Ching looked at him ashamed and he answered humbly,

"I have never thought of you with peace since that hour. It

was that dog, your uncle, who enticed me, saying that you had good harvests stored up. Before this cruel heaven I promise you that I have only a little handful of dried red beans buried beneath the stone of my doorway. This I and my wife placed there for our last hour, for our child and ourselves, that we might die with a little food in our stomachs. But some of it I will give to you, and tomorrow go south, if you can. I stay, I and my house. I am older than you and I have no son, and it does not matter whether I live or die."

And he went away and in a little while he came back, bringing tied in a cotton kerchief a double handful of small red beans, mouldy with the soil. The children clambered about at the sight of the food, and even the old man's eyes glistened, but Wang Lung pushed them away for once and he took the food in to his wife as she lay and she ate a little of it, bean by bean, unwilling except that her hour was upon her and she knew that if she had not any food she would die in the clutches of her pain.

Only a few of the beans did Wang Lung hide in his own hand and these he put into his own mouth and he chewed them into a soft pulp and then putting his lips to the lips of his daughter he pushed into her mouth the food, and watching her small lips move, he felt himself fed.

That night he stayed in the middle room. The two boys were in the old man's room and in the third room O-lan gave birth alone. He sat there as he had sat during the birth of his first-born son and listened. She would not even yet have him near her at her hour. She would give birth alone, squatting over the old tub she kept for the purpose, creeping about the room afterwards to remove the traces of what had been, hiding as an animal does the birth stains of its young.

He listened intently for the small sharp cry he knew so well, and he listened with despair. Male or female, it mattered nothing to him now—there was only another mouth coming which must be fed.

"It would be merciful if there were no breath," he muttered, and then he heard the feeble cry—how feeble a cry!—hang for an instant upon the stillness. "But there is no mercy of any kind in these days," he finished bitterly, and he sat listening.

There was no second cry, and over the house the stillness became impenetrable. But for many days there had been stillness everywhere, the stillness of inactivity and of people,

57

each in his own house, waiting to die. This house was filled with such stillness. Suddenly Wang Lung could not bear it. He was afraid. He rose and went to the door of the room where O-lan was and he called into the crack and the sound of his own voice heartened him a little.

"You are safe?" he called to the woman. He listened. Suppose she had died as he sat there! But he could hear a slight rustling. She was moving about and at last she answered, her voice a sigh,

"Come!"

He went in, then, and she lay there upon the bed, her body scarcely raising the cover. She lay alone.

"Where is the child?" he asked.

She made a slight movement of her hand upon the bed and he saw upon the floor the child's body.

"Dead!" he exclaimed.

"Dead," she whispered.

He stooped and examined the handful of its body—a wisp of bone and skin—a girl. He was about to say, "But I heard it crying—alive——" and then he looked at the woman's face. Her eyes were closed and the color of her flesh was the color of ashes and her bones stuck up under the skin—a poor silent face that lay there, having endured to the utmost, and there was nothing he could say. After all, during these months he had had only his own body to drag about. What agony of starvation this woman had endured, with the starved creature gnawing at her from within, desperate for its own life!

He said nothing, but he took the dead child into the other room and laid it upon the earthen floor and searched until he found a bit of broken mat and this he wrapped about it. The round head dropped this way and that and upon the neck he saw two dark, bruised spots, but he finished what he had to do. Then he took the roll of matting, and going as far from the house as he had strength, he laid the burden against the hollowed side of an old grave. This grave stood among many others, worn down and no longer known or cared for, on a hillside just at the border of Wang Lung's western field. He had scarcely put the burden down before a famished, wolfish dog hovered almost at once behind him, so famished that although he took up a small stone and threw it and hit its lean flank with a thud, the animal would not stir away more than a few feet. At last Wang Lung felt his legs sinking beneath him and covering his face with his hands he went away.

"It is better as it is," he muttered to himself, and for the first time was wholly filled with despair.

The next morning when the sun rose unchanging in its sky of varnished blue it seemed to him a dream that he could ever have thought of leaving his house with these helpless children and this weakened woman and this old man. How could they drag their bodies over a hundred miles, even to plenty? And who knew whether or not even in the south there was food? One would say there was no end to this brazen sky. Perhaps they would wear out all their last strength only to find more starving people and these strangers to them as well. Far better to stay where they could die in their beds. He sat desponding on the threshold of the door and gazed bleakly over the dried and hardened fields from which every particle of anything which could be called food or fuel had been plucked.

He had no money. Long ago the last coin was gone. But even money would do little good now, for there was no food to buy. He had heard earlier that there were rich men in the town who were hoarding food for themselves and for sale to the very rich, but even this ceased to anger him. He did not feel this day that he could walk to the town, even to be fed without money. He was, indeed, not hungry.

The extreme gnawing in his stomach which he had had at first was now past and he could stir up a little of the earth from a certain spot in one of his fields and give it to the children without desiring any of it for himself. This earth they had been eating in water for some days—goddess of mercy earth, it was called, because it had some slight nutritious quality in it, although in the end it could not sustain life. But made into a gruel it allayed the children's craving for a time and put something into their distended, empty bellies. He steadfastly would not touch the few beans that O-lan still held in her hand, and it comforted him vaguely to hear her crunching them, one at a time, a long time apart.

And then, as he sat there in the doorway, giving up his hope and thinking with a dreamy pleasure of lying upon his bed and sleeping easily into death, someone came across the fields—men walking toward him. He continued to sit as they drew near and he saw that one was his uncle and with him were three men whom he did not know.

"I have not seen you these many days," called his uncle with loud and affected good humor. And as he drew nearer he said in the same loud voice, "And how well you have fared! And your father, my elder brother, he is well?"

Wang Lung looked at his uncle. The man was thin, it is true, but not starved, as he should be. Wang Lung felt in his own shriveled body the last remaining strength of life gathering into a devastating anger against this man, his uncle.

"How you have eaten—how you have eaten!" he muttered thickly. He thought nothing of these strangers or of any courtesy. He saw only his uncle with flesh on his bones, still. His uncle opened wide his eyes and threw up his hands to the sky.

"Eaten!" he cried. "If you could see my house! Not a sparrow even could pick up a crumb there. My wife—do you remember how fat she was? How fair and fat and oily her skin? And now she is like a garment hung on a pole—nothing but the poor bones rattling together in her skin. And of our children only four are left—the three little ones gone—gone—and as for me, you see me!" He took the edge of his sleeve and wiped the corner of each eye carefully.

"You have eaten," repeated Wang Lung dully.

"I have thought of nothing but of you and of your father, who is my brother," retorted his uncle briskly, "and now I prove it to you. As soon as I could, I borrowed from these good men in the town a little food on the promise that with the strength it gave me I would help them to buy some of the land about our village. And then I thought of your good land first of all, you, the son of my brother. They have come to buy your land and to give you money—food—life!" His uncle, having said these words, stepped back and folded his arms with a flourish of his dirty and ragged robes.

Wang Lung did not move. He did not rise nor in any way recognize the men who had come. But he lifted his head to look at them and he saw that they were indeed men from the town, dressed in long robes of soiled silk. Their hands were soft and their nails long. They looked as though they had eaten and blood still ran rapidly in their veins. He suddenly hated them with an immense hatred. Here were these men from the town, having eaten and drunk, standing beside him whose children were starving and eating the very earth of the fields; here they were, come to squeeze his land from him in his extremity. He looked up at them sullenly, his eyes deep and enormous in his bony, skull-like face.

"I will not sell my land," he said.

His uncle stepped forward. At this instant the younger of Wang Lung's two sons came creeping to the doorway upon his hands and knees. Since he had so little strength in these latter days the child at times had gone back to crawling as he used in his babyhood.

"Is that your lad?" cried the uncle, "the little fat lad I gave a copper to in the summer?"

And they all looked at the child and suddenly Wang Lung, who through all this time had not wept at all, began to weep silently, the tears gathering in great knots of pain in his throat and rolling down his cheeks.

"What is your price?" he whispered at last. Well, there were these three children to be fed—the children and the old man. He and his wife could dig themselves graves in the land and lie down in them and sleep. Well, but here were these.

And then one of the men from the city spoke, a man with one eye blind and sunken in his face, and unctuously he said,

"My poor man, we will give you a better price than could be got in these times anywhere for the sake of the boy who is starving. We will give you . . ." he paused and then he said harshly, "we will give you a string of a hundred pence for an acre!"

Wang Lung laughed bitterly. "Why, that," he cried, "that is taking my land for a gift. Why, I pay twenty times that when I buy land!"

"Ah, but not when you buy it from men who are starving," said the other man from the city. He was a small, slight fellow with a high thin nose, but his voice came out of him unexpectedly large and coarse and hard.

Wang Lung looked at the three of them. They were sure of him, these men! What will not a man give for his starving children and his old father! The weakness of surrender in him melted into an anger such as he had never known in his life before. He sprang up and at the men as a dog springs at an enemy.

"I shall never sell the land!" he shrieked at them. "Bit by bit I will dig up the fields and feed the earth itself to the children and when they die I will bury them in the land, and I and my wife and my old father, even he, we will die on the land that has given us birth!"

He was weeping violently and his anger went out of him as suddenly as a wind and he stood shaking and weeping. The men stood there smiling slightly, his uncle among them, unmoved.

This talk was madness and they waited until Wang's anger was spent.

And then suddenly O-lan came to the door and spoke to them, her voice flat and commonplace as though every day such things were.

"The land we will not sell, surely," she said, "else when we return from the south we shall have nothing to feed us. But we will sell the table and the two beds and the bedding and the four benches and even the cauldron from the stove. But the rakes and the hoe and the plow we will not sell, nor the land."

There was some calmness in her voice which carried more strength than all Wang Lung's anger, and Wang Lung's uncle said uncertainly,

"Will you really go south?"

At last the one-eyed man spoke to the others and they muttered among themselves and the one-eyed man turned and said,

"They are poor things and fit only for fuel. Two silver bits for the lot and take it or leave it."

He turned away with contempt as he spoke, but O-lan answered tranquilly,

"It is less than the cost of one bed, but if you have the silver give it to me quickly and take the things."

The one-eyed man fumbled in his girdle and dropped into her outstretched hand the silver and the three men came into the house and between them they took out the table and the benches and the bed in Wang Lung's room first with its bedding, and they wrenched the cauldron from the earthern oven in which it stood. But when they went into the old man's room Wang Lung's uncle stood outside. He did not wish his older brother to see him, nor did he wish to be there when the old man was laid on the floor and the bed taken from under him. When all was finished and the house was wholly empty except for the two rakes and the two hoes and the plow in one corner of the middle room, O-lan said to her husband,

"Let us go while we have the two bits of silver and before we must sell the rafters of the house and have no hole into which we can crawl when we return."

And Wang Lung answered heavily, "Let us go."

But he looked across the fields at the small figures of the men receding and he muttered over and over, "At least I have the land—I have the land."

10

THERE WAS nothing to do but to pull the door tight upon its wooden hinges and fasten the iron hasp. All their clothes they had upon them. Into each child's hands O-lan thrust a rice bowl and a pair of chopsticks and the two little boys grasped at them eagerly and held them tight as a promise of food to come. Thus they started across the fields, a dreary small procession moving so slowly that it seemed they would never be to the wall of the town.

The girl Wang Lung carried in his bosom until he saw that the old man would fall and then he gave the child to O-lan and stooping under his father he lifted him on his back and carried him, staggering under the old man's dry, wind-light frame. They went on in complete silence past the little temple with the two small stately gods within, who never noticed anything that passed. Wang Lung was sweating with his weakness in spite of the cold and bitter wind. This wind never ceased to blow on them and against them, so that the two boys cried of its cold. But Wang Lung coaxed them saying,

"You are two big men and you are travellers to the south. There is warmth there and food every day, white rice every day for all of us and you shall eat and you shall eat."

In time they reached the gate of the wall, resting continually every little way, and where Wang Lung had once delighted in its coolness now he clenched his teeth against the gust of wintry wind that swept furiously through its channel, as icy water will rush between cliffs. Beneath their feet the mud was thick and speared through with needles of ice and the little boys could make no headway and O-lan was laden with the girl and desperate under the weight of her own body. Wang Lung staggered through with the old man and set him down and then went back and lifted each child and carried him through, and then when it was over at last his sweat poured out of him like rain, spending all his strength with it, so that he had to lean for a long time against the damp wall, his eyes shut and his breath coming and going quickly, and his family stood shivering and waiting about him.

They were close to the gate of the great house now, but it was locked fast, the iron doors reared full to their height and the stone lions grey and windbitten on either side. Upon the doorsteps lay cowering a few dingy shapes of men and women who gazed, famished, upon the closed and barred gate, and when Wang Lung passed with his miserable little procession one cried out in a cracked voice,

"The hearts of these rich are hard like the hearts of the gods. They have still rice to eat and from the rice they do not eat they are still making wine, while we starve."

And another moaned forth,

"Oh, if I had an instant's strength in this hand of mine I would set fire to the gates and to those houses and courts within, even though I burned in the fire. A thousand curses to the parents that bore the children of Hwang!"

But Wang Lung answered nothing to all this and in silence they went on towards the south.

When they had passed through the town and had come out on the southern side, and this they did so slowly that it was evening and near to darkness, they found a multitude of people going toward the south. Wang Lung was beginning to think of what corner of the wall they had better choose for sleeping as well as they could huddled together, when he suddenly found himself and his family caught in a multitude, and he asked of one who pressed against him,

"Where is all this multitude going?"

And the man said,

"We are starving people and we are going to catch the firewagon and ride to the south. It leaves from yonder house and there are wagons for such as we for the price of less than a small silver piece."

Firewagons! One had heard of them. Wang Lung in days past in the tea shop had heard men tell of these wagons, chained one to the other and drawn neither by man nor beast, but by a machine breathing forth fire and water like a dragon.

64

He had said to himself many times then that on a holiday he would go and see it, but with one thing and another in the fields there was never time, he being well to the north of the city. Then there was always distrust of that which one did not know and understand. It is not well for a man to know more than is necessary for his daily living.

Now, however, he turned doubtfully to the woman and said, "Shall we also then go on this firewagon?"

They drew the old man and the children a little away from the passing crowd and looked at each other anxiously and afraid. At the instant's respite the old man sank upon the ground and the little boys lay down in the dust, heedless of the feet trampling everywhere about them. O-lan carried the girl child still, but the child's head hung over her arm with such a look of death on its closed eyes that Wang Lung, forgetting all else, cried out,

"Is the little slave already dead?"

O-lan shook her head.

"Not yet. The breath flutters back and forth in her. But she will die this night and all of us unless——"

And then as if she could say no other word she looked at him, her square face exhausted and gaunt. Wang Lung answered nothing but to himself he thought that another day of walking like this one and they would all be dead by night, and he said with what cheer there was to be found in his voice,

"Up, my sons, and help the grandfather up. We will go on the firewagon and sit while we walk south."

But whether or not they could have moved none knows, had there not come thundering out of the darkness a noise like a dragon's voice and two great eyes puffing fire out, so that everyone screamed and ran. And pressing forward in the confusion they were pushed hither and thither, but always clinging desperately together, until they were pushed somehow in the darkness and in the yelling and crying of many voices into a small open door and into a box-like room, and then with an incessant roaring the thing in which they rode tore forth into the darkness, bearing them in its vitals.

11

WITH HIS two pieces of silver Wang Lung paid for a hundred miles of road and the officer who took his silver from him gave him back a handful of copper pence, and with a few of these Wang Lung bought from a vendor, who thrust his tray of wares in at a hole in the wagon as soon as it stopped, four small loaves of bread and a bowl of soft rice for the girl. It was more than they had to eat at one time for many days, and although they were starved for food, when it was in their mouths desire left them and it was only by coaxing that the boys could be made to swallow. But the old man sucked perseveringly at the bread between his toothless gums.

"One must eat," he cackled forth, very friendly to all who pressed about him as the firewagon rolled and rocked on its way. "I do not care that my foolish belly is growing lazy after all these days of little to do. It must be fed. I will not die because it does not wish to work." And men laughed suddenly at the smiling, wizened little old man, whose sparse white beard was scattered all over his chin.

But not all the copper pence did Wang Lung spend on food. He kept back all he was able to buy mats to build a shed for them when they reached the south. There were men and women in the firewagon who had been south in other years; some who went each year to the rich cities of the south to work and to beg and thus save the price of food. And Wang Lung, when he had grown used to the wonder of where he was and to the astonishment of seeing the land whirl by the holes in the wagon, listened to what these men said. They spoke with the loudness of wisdom where others are ignorant.

"First you must buy six mats," said one, a man with coarse,

hanging lips like a camel's mouth. "These are two pence for one mat, if you are wise and do not act like a country bumpkin, in which case you will be charged three pence, which is more than is necessary, as I very well know. I cannot be fooled by the men in the southern cities, even if they are rich." He wagged his head and looked about for admiration. Wang Lung listened anxiously.

"And then?" he urged. He sat squatting upon his haunches on the bottom of the wagon, which was, after all, only an empty room made of wood and with nothing to sit upon, and the wind and the dust flying up through the cracks in the floor.

"Then," said the man more loudly still, raising his voice above the din of the iron wheels beneath them, "then you bind these together into a hut and then you go out to beg, first smearing yourself with mud and filth to make yourselves as piteous as you can."

Now Wang Lung had never in his life begged of any man and he disliked this notion of begging of strange people in the south.

"One must beg?" he repeated.

"Ah, indeed," said the coarse-mouthed man, "but not until you have eaten. These people in the south have so much rice that each morning you may go to a public kitchen and for a penny hold as much as you can in your belly of the white rice gruel. Then you can beg comfortably and buy beancurd and cabbage and garlic."

Wang Lung withdrew a little from the others and turned himself about to the wall and secretly with his hand in his girdle he counted out the pence he had left. There was enough for the six mats and enough each for a penny for rice and beyond that he had three pence left. It came over him with comfort that thus they could begin the new life. But the notion of holding up a bowl and begging of anyone who passed continued to distress him. It was very well for the old man and for the children and even for the women, but he had his two hands.

"Is there no work for a man's hands?" he asked of the man suddenly, turning about.

"Aye, work!" said the man with contempt, and he spat upon the floor. "You can pull a rich man in a yellow ricksha if you like, and sweat your blood out with heat as you run and have your sweat freeze into a coat of ice on you when you stand waiting to be called. Give me begging!" And he cursed a round curse, so that Wang Lung would not ask anything of him further.

But still it was a good thing that he had heard what the man said, for when the firewagon had carried them as far as it would and had turned them out upon the ground, Wang Lung had ready a plan and he set the old man and the children against a long grey wall of a house, which stood there, and he told the woman to watch them, and he went off to buy the mats, asking of this one and that where the market streets lay. At first he could scarcely understand what was said to him, so brittle and sharp was the sound which these southerners made when they spoke, and several times when he asked and they did not understand, they were impatient, and he learned to observe what sort of man he asked of and to choose one with a kindlier face, for these southerners had tempers which were quick and easily ruffled.

But he found the mat shop at last on the edge of the city and he put his pennies down upon the counter as one who knew the price of the goods and he carried away his roll of mats. When he returned to the spot where he had left the others, they stood there waiting, although when he came the boys cried out at him in relief, and he saw that they had been filled with terror in this strange place. Only the old man watched everything with pleasure and astonishment and he murmured at Wang Lung,

"You see how fat they all are, these southerners, and how pale and oily are their skins. They eat pork every day, doubtless."

But none who passed looked at Wang Lung and his family. Men came and went along the cobbled highway to the city, busy and intent and never glancing aside at beggars, and every little while a caravan of donkeys came pattering by, their small feet fitting neatly to the stones, and they were laden with baskets of brick for the building of houses and with great bags of grain crossed upon their swaying backs. At the end of each caravan the driver rode on the hindermost beast, and he carried a great whip, and this whip he cracked with a terrific noise over the backs of the beasts, shouting as he did so. And as he passed Wang Lung each driver gave him a scornful and haughty look, and no prince could have looked more haughty than these drivers in their rough work coats as they passed by the small group of persons, standing wondering at the edge of the roadway. It was the especial pleasure of each driver, seeing how strange Wang Lung and his family were, to crack his whip just as he passed them, and the sharp explosive cut of the air made them leap up, and seeing them leap the drivers guffawed, and Wang Lung was angry when this happened two and three times and he turned away to see where he could put his hut.

There were already other huts clinging to the wall behind them, but what was inside the wall none knew and there was no way of knowing. It stretched out long and grey and very high, and against the base the small mat sheds clung like fleas to a dog's back. Wang Lung observed the huts and he began to shape his own mats this way and that, but they were stiff and clumsy things at best, being made of split reeds, and he despaired, when suddenly O-lan said,

"That I can do. I remember it in my childhood."

And she placed the girl upon the ground and pulled the mats thus and thus, and shaped a rounded roof reaching to the ground and high enough for a man to sit under and not strike the top, and upon the edges of the mats that were upon the ground she placed bricks that were lying about and she sent the boys to picking up more bricks. When it was finished they went within and with one mat she had contrived not to use they made a floor and sat down and were sheltered.

Sitting thus and looking at each other, it seemed less than possible that the day before they had left their own house and their land and that these were now a hundred miles away. It was a distance vast enough to have taken them weeks of walking and at which they must have died, some of them, before it was done.

Then the general feeling of plenty in this rich land, where no one seemed even hungered, filled them and when Wang Lung said, "Let us go and seek the public kitchens," they rose up almost cheerfully and went out once more, and this time the small boys clattered their chopsticks against their bowls as they walked, for there would soon be something to put into them. And they found soon why the huts were built to that long wall, for a short distance beyond the northern end of it was a street and along the street many people walked carrying bowls and buckets and vessels of tin, all empty, and these persons were going to the kitchens for the poor, which were at the end of the street and not far away. And so Wang Lung and his family mingled with these others and with them they came at last to two great buildings made of mats, and everyone crowded into the open end of these buildings.

Now in the rear of each building were earthen stoves, but

larger than Wang Lung had ever seen, and on them iron cauldrons as big as small ponds; and when the great wooden lids were pried up, there was the good white rice bubbling and boiling, and clouds of fragrant steam rose up. Now when the people smelled this fragrance of rice it was the sweetest in the world to their nostrils, and they all pressed forward in a great mass and people called out and mothers shouted in anger and fear lest their children be trodden upon and little babies cried, and the men who opened the cauldrons roared forth,

"Now there is enough for every man and each in his turn!"

But nothing could stop the mass of hungry men and women and they fought like beasts until all were fed. Wang Lung caught in their midst could do nothing but cling to his father and his two sons and when he was swept to the great cauldron he held out his bowl and when it was filled threw down his pence, and it was all he could do to stand sturdily and not be swept on before the thing was done.

Then when they had come to the street again and stood eating their rice, he ate and was filled and there was a little left in his bowl and he said,

"I will take this home to eat in the evening."

But a man stood near who was some sort of a guard of the place for he wore a special garment of blue and red, and he said sharply,

"No, and you can take nothing away except what is in your belly." And Wang Lung marvelled at this and said,

"Well, if I have paid my penny what business is it of yours if I carry it within or without me?"

The man said then,

"We must have this rule, for there are those whose hearts are so hard that they will come and buy this rice that is given for the poor—for a penny will not feed any man like this—and they will carry the rice home to feed to their pigs for slop. And the rice is for men and not for pigs."

Wang Lung listened to this in astonishment and he cried,

"Are there men as hard as this!" And then he said, "But why should any give like this to the poor and who is it that gives?"

The man answered then,

"It is the rich and the gentry of the town who do it, and some do it for a good deed for the future, that by saving lives they may get merit in heaven, and some do it for righteousness that men may speak well of them."

"Nevertheless it is a good deed for whatever reason," said

Wang Lung, "and some must do it out of a good heart." And then seeing that the man did not answer him, he added in his own defense, "At least there are a few of these?"

But the man was weary of speaking with him and he turned his back, and he hummed an idle tune. The children tugged at Wang Lung then, and Wang Lung led them all back to the hut they had made, and there they laid themselves down and they slept until the next morning, for it was the first time since summer they had been filled with food, and sleep overcame them with fullness.

The next morning it was necessary that there be more money for they spent the last copper coin upon the morning's rice. Wang Lung looked at O-lan, doubtful as to what should be done. But it was not with the despair with which he had looked at her over their blank and empty fields. Here with the coming and going of well-fed people upon the streets, with meat and vegetables in the markets, with fish swimming in the tubs in the fish market, surely it was not possible for a man and his children to starve. It was not as it was in their own land, where even silver could not buy food because there was none. And O-lan answered him steadily, as though this were the life she had known always,

"I and the children can beg and the old man also. His grey hairs will move some who will not give to me."

And she called the two boys to her, for, like children, they had forgotten everything except that they had food again and were in a strange place, and they ran to the street and stood staring at all that passed, and she said to them,

"Each of you take your bowls and hold them thus and cry out thus——"

And she took her empty bowl in her hand and held it out and called piteously,

"A heart, good sir—a heart, good lady! Have a kind heart—a good deed for your life in heaven! The small cash—the copper coin you throw away—feed a starving child!"

The little boys stared at her, and Wang Lung also. Where had she learned to cry thus? How much there was of this woman he did not know! She answered his look saying,

"So I called when I was a child and so I was fed. In such a year as this I was sold a slave."

Then the old man, who had been sleeping, awoke, and they gave him a bowl and the four of them went out on the road to beg. The woman began to call out and to shake her bowl at every passerby. She had thrust the girl child into her naked bosom, and the child slept and its head bobbed this way and that as she moved, running hither and thither with her bowl outstretched before her. She pointed to the child as she begged and she cried loudly,

"Unless you give, good sir, good lady—this child dies—we starve—we starve——" And indeed the child looked dead, its head shaking this way and that, and there were some, a few, who tossed her unwillingly a small cash.

But the boys after a while began to take the begging as play and the elder one was ashamed and grinned sheepishly as he begged, and then their mother perceiving it dragged them into the hut and she slapped them soundly upon their jaws and she scolded them with anger.

"And do you talk of starving and then laugh at the same time! You fools, starve then!" And she slapped them again and again until her own hands were sore and until the tears were running freely down their faces and they were sobbing and she sent them out again saying,

"Now you are fit to beg! That and more if you laugh again!"

As for Wang Lung, he went into the streets and asked hither and thither until he found a place where jinrickshas were for hire and he went in and hired one for the day for the price of half a round of silver to be paid at night and then dragged the thing after him out to the street again.

Pulling this rickety, wooden wagon on its two wheels behind him, it seemed to him that everyone looked at him for a fool. He was as awkward between its shafts as an ox yoked for the first time to the plow, and he could scarcely walk; yet must he run if he were to earn his living, for here and there and everywhere through the streets of this city men ran as they pulled other men in these. He went into a narrow side street where there were no shops but only doors of homes closed and private, and he went up and down for a while pulling to accustom himself, and just as he said to himself in despair that he had better beg, a door opened, and an old man, spectacled and garbed as teacher, stepped forth and hailed him.

Wang Lung at first began to tell him that he was too new at it to run, but the old man was deaf, for he heard nothing of what Wang Lung said, only motioning to him tranquilly to lower the shafts and let him step in, and Wang Lung obeyed, not knowing what else to do, and feeling compelled to it by the deafness of the old man and by his well-dressed and learned looks. Then the old man, sitting erect, said,

"Take me to the Confucian temple," and there he sat, erect and calm, and there was that in his calmness which allowed no question, so that Wang started forward as he saw others do, although he had no faintest knowledge of where the Confucian temple stood.

But as he went he asked, and since the road lay along crowded streets, with the vendors passing back and forth with their baskets and women going out to market, and carriages drawn by horses, and many other vehicles like the one he pulled, and everything pressing against another so that there was no possibility of running, he walked as swiftly as he was able, conscious always of the awkward bumping of his load behind him. To loads upon his back he was used, but not to pulling, and before the walls of the temple were in sight his arms were aching and his hands blistered, for the shafts pressed spots where the hoe did not touch.

The old teacher stepped forth out of the riksha when Wang Lung lowered it as he reached the temple gates, and feeling in the depths of his bosom he drew out a small silver coin and gave it to Wang Lung saying,

"Now I never pay more than this, and there is no use in complaint." And with this he turned away and went into the temple.

Wang Lung had not thought to complain for he had not seen this coin before, and he did not know for how many pence it could be changed. He went to a rice shop near by where money is changed, and the changer gave him for the coin twenty-six pence, and Wang Lung marvelled at the ease with which money comes in the south. But another ricksha puller stood near and leaned over as he counted and he said to Wang Lung,

"Only twenty-six. How far did you pull that old head?" And when Wang told him, the man cried out, "Now there is a small-hearted old man! He gave you only half the proper fare. How much did you argue for before you started?"

"I did not argue," said Wang Lung. "He said 'Come' and I came."

The other man looked at Wang Lung pityingly.

"Now there is a country lout for you, pigtail and all!" he called out to the bystanders. "Someone says come and he comes, and he never asks, this idiot born of idiots, 'How much will you give me if I come!' Know this, idiot, only white foreigners can be taken without argument! Their tempers are like quick lime, but when they say 'Come' you may come and trust them, for they are such fools they do not know the proper price of anything, but let the silver run out of their pockets like water." And everyone listening, laughed.

Wang Lung said nothing. It was true that he felt very humble and ignorant in all this crowd of city people, and he pulled his vehicle away without a word in answer.

"Nevertheless, this will feed my children tomorrow," he said to himself stubbornly, and then he remembered that he had the rent of the vehicle to pay at night and that indeed there was not yet half enough to do that.

He had one more passenger during the morning and with this one he argued and agreed upon a price and in the afternoon two more called to him. But at night, when he counted out all his money in his hand he had only a penny above the rent of the ricksha, and he went back to his hut in great bitterness, saying to himself that for labor greater than the labor of a day in a harvest field he had earned only one copper penny. Then there came flooding over him the memory of his land. He had not remembered it once during this strange day, but now the thought of it lying back there, far away, it is true, but waiting and his own, filled him with peace, and so he came to his hut.

When he entered there he found that O-lan had for her day's begging received forty small cash, which is less than five pence, and of the boys, the elder had eight cash and the younger thirteen, and with these put together there was enough to pay for the rice in the morning. Only when they put the younger boy's in with all, he howled for his own, and he loved the money he had begged, and slept with it that night in his hand and they could not take it from him until he gave it himself for his own rice.

But the old man had received nothing at all. All day long he had sat by the roadside obediently enough, but he did not beg. He slept and woke and stared at what passed him, and when he grew weary he slept again. And being of the older generation, he could not be reproved. When he saw that his hands were empty he said merely.

"I have plowed and I have sown seed and I have reaped harvest and thus have I filled my rice bowl. And I have beyond this begotten a son and son's sons."

74

And with this he trusted like a child that now he would be fed, seeing that he had a son and grandsons.

12

Now AFTER the first sharpness of Wang Lung's hunger was over and he saw that his children daily had something to eat, and he knew there was every morning rice to be had, and of his day's labor and of O-lan's begging there was enough to pay for it, the strangeness of his life passed, and he began to feel what this city was, to whose fringes he clung. Running about the streets every day and all day long he learned to know the city after a fashion, and he saw this and that of its secret parts. He learned that in the morning the people he drew in his vehicle, if they were women, went to the market, and if they were men, they went to the schools and to the houses of business. But what sort of schools these were he had no way of knowing, beyond the fact that they were called such names as "The Great School of Western Learning" or as "The Great School of China," for he never went beyond the gates, and if he had gone in well he knew someone would have come to ask him what he did out of his place. And what houses of business they were to which he drew men he did not know, since when he was paid it was all he knew.

And at night he knew that he drew men to big tea houses and to places of pleasure, the pleasure that is open and streams out upon the streets in the sound of music and of gaming with pieces of ivory and bamboo upon a wooden table, and the pleasure that is secret and silent and hidden behind walls. But none of these pleasures did Wang Lung know for himself, since his feet crossed no threshold except that of his own hut, and his road was always ended at a gate. He lived in the rich city as alien as a rat in a rich man's house that is fed on scraps thrown away, and hides here and there and is never a part of the real life of the house.

So it was that, although a hundred miles are not so far as a thousand, and land road never so far as water road, yet Wang Lung and his wife and children were like foreigners in this southern city. It is true that the people who went about the streets had black hair and eyes as Wang Lung and all his family had, and as all did in the country where Wang Lung was born, and it is true that if one listened to the language of these southerners it could be understood, if with difficulty.

But Anhwei is not Kiangsu. In Anhwei, where Wang Lung was born, the language is slow and deep and it wells from the throat. But in the Kiangsu city where they now lived the people spoke in syllables which splintered from their lips and from the ends of their tongues. And where Wang Lung's fields spread out in slow and leisurely harvest twice a year of wheat and rice and a bit of corn and beans and garlic, here in the farms about the city men urged their land with perpetual stinking fertilizing of human wastes to force the land to a hurried bearing of this vegetable and that besides their rice.

In Wang Lung's country a man, if he had a roll of good wheat bread and a sprig of garlic in it, had a good meal and needed no more. But here the people dabbled with pork balls and bamboo sprouts and chestnuts stewed with chicken and goose giblets and this and that of vegetables, and when an honest man came by smelling of yesterday's garlic, they lifted their noses and cried out, "Now here is a reeking, pig-tailed northerner!" The smell of the garlic would make the very shopkeepers in the cloth shops raise the price of blue cotton cloth as they might raise the price for a foreigner.

But then the little village of sheds clinging to the wall never became a part of the city or of the countryside which stretched beyond, and once when Wang Lung heard a young man haranguing a crowd at the corner of the Confucian temple, where any man may stand, if he has the courage to speak out, and the young man said that China must have a revolution and must rise against the hated foreigners, Wang Lung was alarmed and slunk away, feeling that he was the foreigner against whom the young man spoke with such passion. And when on another day he heard another young man speaking—for this city was full of young men speaking—and he said at his street corner that the people of China must unite and must educate themselves in these times, it did not occur to Wang Lung that anyone was speaking to him.

It was only one day when he was on the street of the silk

markets looking for a passenger that he learned better than he had known, and that there were those who were more foriegn than he in this city. He happened on this day to pass by the door of a shop from whence ladies sometimes came after purchasing silks within, and sometimes thus he secured one who paid him better than most. And on this day someone did come out on him suddenly, a creature the like of whom he had never seen before. He had no idea of whether it was male or female, but it was tall and dressed in a straight black robe of some rough harsh material and there was the skin of a dead animal wrapped about its neck As he passed, the person, whether male or female, motioned to him sharply to lower the shafts and he did so, and when he stood erect again, dazed at what had befallen him, the person in broken accents directed that he was to go to the Street of Bridges. He began to run hurriedly, scarcely knowing what he did, and once he called to another puller whom he knew casually in the day's work,

"Look at this—what is this I pull?"

And the man shouted back at him,

"A foreigner—a female from America—you are rich——"

But Wang Lung ran as fast as he could for fear of the strange creature behind him, and when he reached the Street of Bridges he was exhausted and dripping with his sweat.

This female stepped out then and said in the same broken accents, "You need not have run yourself to death," and left him with two silver pieces in his palm, which was double the usual fare.

Then Wang Lung knew that this was indeed a foreigner and more foreign yet than he in this city, and that after all people of black hair and black eyes are one sort and people of light hair and light eyes of another sort, and he was no longer after that wholly foreign in the city.

When he went back to the hut that night with the silver he had received still untouched, he told O-lan and she said,

"I have seen them. I always beg of them, for they alone will drop silver rather than copper into my bowl."

But neither Wang Lung nor his wife felt that the foreigner dropped silver because of any goodness of heart but rather because of ignorance and not knowing that copper is more correct to give to beggars than silver.

Nevertheless, through this experience Wang Lung learned what the young men had not taught him, that he belonged to his own kind, who have black hair and black eyes.

Clinging thus to the outskirts of the great, sprawling, opulent city it seemed that at least there could not be any lack of food. Wang Lung and his family had come from a country where if men starve it is because there is no food, since the land cannot bear under a relentless heaven. Silver in the hand was worth little because it could buy nothing where nothing was.

Here in the city there was food everywhere. The cobbled streets of the fish market were lined with great baskets of big silver fish, caught in the night out of the teeming river; with tubs of small shining fish, dipped out of a net cast over a pool; with heaps of yellow crabs, squirming and nipping in peevish astonishment; with writhing eels for gourmands at the feasts. At the grain markets there were such baskets of grain that a man might step into them and sink and smother and none know it who did not see it; white rice and brown and dark yellow wheat and pale gold wheat, and yellow soybeans and red beans and green broad beans and canary-colored millet and grey sesame. And at the meat markets whole hogs hung by their necks, split open the length of their great bodies to show the red meat and the layers of goodly fat, the skin soft and thick and white. And duck shops hung row upon row, over their ceilings and in their doors, the brown baked ducks that had been turnd slowly on a spit before coals and the white salted ducks and the strings of duck giblets, and so with the shops that sold geese and pheasant and every kind of fowl.

As for the vegetables, there was everything which the hand of man could coax from the soil; glittering red radishes and white, hollow lotus root and taro, green cabbages and celery, curling bean sprouts and brown chestnuts and garnishes of fragrant cress. There was nothing which the appetite of man might desire that was not to be found upon the streets of the markets of that city. And going hither and thither were the vendors of sweets and fruits and nuts and of hot delicacies of sweet potatoes browned in sweet oils and little delicately spiced balls of pork wrapped in dough and steamed, and sugar cakes made from glutinous rice, and the children of the city ran out to the vendors of these things with their hands full of pennies and they bought and they ate until their skins glistened with sugar and oil.

Yes, one would say that in this city there could be none who starved.

Still, every morning a little after dawn Wang Lung and his family came out of their hut and with their bowls and chopsticks they made a small group in a long procession of people, each issuing from his hut, shivering in clothes too thin for the damp river fog, walking curved against the chill morning wind to the public kitchens, where for a penny a man may buy a bowl of thin rice gruel. And with all Wang Lung's pulling and running before his ricksha and with all O-lan's begging, they never could gain enough to cook rice daily in their own hut. If there was a penny over and above the price of the rice at the kitchens for the poor, they bought a bit of cabbage. But the cabbage was dear at any price, for the two boys must go to hunt for fuel to cook it between the two bricks O-lan had set up for a stove, and this fuel they had to snatch by handsful as they could from the farmers who carried the loads of reed and grass into the city fuel markets. Sometimes the children were caught and cuffed soundly and one night the elder lad, who was more timid than the younger and more ashamed of what he did, came back with an eye swollen shut from the blow of a farmer's hand. But the younger lad grew adept and indeed more adept at petty thieving than at begging.

To O-lan this was nothing. If the boy could not be without laughing and play, let them steal to fill their bellies. But Wang Lung, although he had no answer for her, felt his gorge rise at this thievery of his sons, and he did not blame the elder when he was slow at the business. This life in the shadow of the great wall was not the life Wang Lung loved. There was his land waiting for him.

One night he came late and there was in the stew of cabbage a good round piece of pork. It was the first time they had had flesh to eat since they killed their own ox, and Wang Lung's eyes widened.

"You must have begged of a foreigner this day," he said to O-lan. But she, according to her habit, said nothing. Then the younger boy, too young for wisdom and filled with his own pride of cleverness, said,

"I took it—it is mine, this meat. When the butcher looked the other way after he had sliced it from the big piece upon the counter, I ran under an old woman's arm who had come to buy it and seized it and ran into an alley and hid in a dry water jar at a back gate until Elder Brother came."

"Now will I not eat this meat!" cried Wang Lung angrily. "We will eat meat that we can buy or beg, but not that which we steal. Beggars we may be but thieves we are not." And he took the meat out of the pot with his two fingers and threw it

79

upon the ground and was heedless of the younger lad's howling.

Then O-lan came forward in her stolid fashion and she picked up the meat and washed it off with a little water and thrust it back into the boiling pot.

"Meat is meat," she said quietly.

Wang Lung said nothing then, but he was angry and afraid in his heart because his sons were growing into thieves here in this city. And although he said nothing when O-lan pulled the tender cooked flesh apart with her chopsticks, and although he said nothing when she gave great pieces of it to the old man and to the boys and even filled the mouth of the girl with it and ate of it herself, he himself would have none of it, contenting himself with the cabbage he had bought. But after the meal was over he took his younger son into the street out of hearing of the woman and there behind a house he took the boy's head under his arm and cuffed it soundly on this side and that, and would not stop for the lad's bellowing.

"There and there and there!" he shouted. "That for a thief!"

But to himself he said when he had let the lad go snivelling home,

"We must get back to the land."

13

DAY BY DAY beneath the opulence of this city Wang Lung lived in the foundations of poverty upon which it was laid. With the food spilling out of the markets, with the streets of the silk shops flying brilliant banners of black and red and orange silk to announce their wares, with rich men clothed in satin and in velvet, soft-fleshed rich men with their skin covered with garments of silk and their hands like flowers for softness and perfume and the beauty of idleness, with all of these for the regal beauty of the city, in that part where Wang Lung lived there was not food enough to feed savage hunger and not clothes enough to cover bones.

Men labored all day at the baking of breads and cakes for feasts for the rich and children labored from dawn to midnight and slept all greasy and grimed as they were upon rough pallets on the floor and staggered to the ovens next day, and there was not money enough given them to buy a piece of the rich breads they made for others. And men and women labored at the cutting and contriving of heavy furs for the winter and of soft light furs for the spring and at the thick brocaded silks, to cut and shape them into sumptuous robes for the ones who ate of the profusion at the markets, and they themselves snatched a bit of coarse blue cotton cloth and sewed it hastily together to cover their bareness.

Wang Lung living among these who labored at feasting others, heard strange things of which he took little heed. The older men and women, it is true, said nothing to anyone. Greybeards pulled rickshas, pushed wheelbarrows of coal and wood to bakeries and palaces, strained their backs until the muscles stood forth like ropes and they pushed and pulled the heavy carts of merchandise over the cobbled roads, ate frugally of their scanty food, slept their brief nights out, and were silent. Their faces were like the face of O-lan, inarticulate, dumb. None knew what was in their minds. If they spoke at all it was of food or of pence. Rarely was the word silver upon their lips because rarely was silver in their hands.

Their faces in repose were twisted as though in anger, only it was not anger. It was the years of straining at loads too heavy for them which had lifted their upper lips to bare their teeth in a seeming snarl, and this labor had set deep wrinkles in the flesh about their eyes and their mouths. They themselves had no idea of what manner of men they were. One of them once, seeing himself in a mirror that passed on a van of household goods, had cried out, "There is an ugly fellow!" And when others laughed at him loudly he smiled painfully, never knowing at what they laughed, and looking about hastily to see if he had offended someone.

At home in the small hovels where they lived, around Wang Lung's hovel, heaped one upon another, the women sewed rags together to make a covering for the children they were forever

81

breeding, and they snatched at bits of cabbage from farmers' fields and stole handfuls of rice from the grain markets, and gleaned the year round the grass on the hillsides; and at harvest they followed the reapers like fowls, their eyes piercing and sharp for every dropped grain or stalk. And through these huts passed children; they were born and dead and born again until neither mother or father knew how many had been born or had died, and scarcely knew even how many were living, thinking of them only as mouths to be fed.

These men and these women and these children passed in and out of the markets and the cloth shops and wandered about the countryside that bordered on the city, the men working at this and that for a few pence and the women and children stealing and begging and snatching, and Wang Lung and his woman and his children were among them.

The old men and the old women accepted the life they had. But there came a time when the male children grew to a certain age, before they were old and when they ceased to be children, and then they were filled with discontent. There was talk among the young men, angry, growling talk. And later when they were fully men and married and the dismay of increasing numbers filled their hearts, the scattered anger of their youth became settled into a fierce despair and into a revolt too deep for mere words because all their lives they labored more severely than beasts, and for nothing except a handful of refuse to fill their bellies. Listening to such talk one evening Wang Lung heard for the first time what was on the other side of the great wall to which their rows of huts clung.

It was at the end of one of those days in late winter when for the first time it seems possible that spring may come again. The ground about the huts was still muddy with the melting snow and the water ran into the huts so that each family had hunted here and there for a few bricks upon which to sleep. But with the discomfort of the damp earth there was this night a soft mildness in the air and this mildness made Wang Lung exceedingly restless so that he could not sleep at once as was his wont after he had eaten, so that he went out to the street's edge and stood there idle.

Here his old father habitually sat squatting on his thighs and leaning against the wall and here he sat now, having taken his bowl of food there to sup it, now that the children filled the hut to bursting when they were clamoring. The old man held in one hand the end of a loop of cloth which O-lan had torn from her girdle, and within this loop the girl child staggered to and fro without falling. Thus he spent his days looking after this child who had now grown rebellious at having to be in her mother's bosom as she begged. Besides this, O-lan was again with child and the pressure of the larger child upon her from without was too painful to bear.

Wang Lung watched the child falling and scrambling and falling again and the old man pulling at the loop ends, and standing thus he felt upon his face the mildness of the evening wind and there arose within him a mighty longing for his fields.

"On such a day as this," he said aloud to his father, "the fields should be turned and the wheat cultivated."

"Ah," said the old man tranquilly, "I know what is in your thought. Twice and twice again in my years I have had to do as we did this year and leave the fields and know that there was no seed in them for fresh harvests."

"But you always went back, my father."

"There was the land, my son," said the old man simply.

Well, they also would go back, if not this year, then next, said Wang to his own heart. As long as there was the land! And the thought of it lying there waiting for him, rich with the spring rains, filled him with desire. He went back to the hut and he said roughly to his wife.

"If I had anything to sell I would sell it and go back to the land. Or if it were not for the old head, we would walk though we starved. But how can he and the small child walk a hundred miles? And you, with your burden!"

O-lan had been rinsing the rice bowls with a little water and now she piled them in a corner of the hut and looked up at him from the spot where she squatted.

"There is nothing to sell except the girl," she answered slowly.

Wang Lung's breath caught.

"Now, I would not sell a child!" he said loudly.

"I was sold," she answered very slowly. "I was sold to a great house so that my parents could return to their home."

"And would you sell the child, therefore?"

"If it were only I, she would be killed before she was sold . . . the slave of slaves was I! But a dead girl brings nothing. I would sell this girl for you—to take you back to the land."

"Never would I," said Wang Lung stoutly, "not though I spent my life in this wilderness."

But when he had gone out again the thought, which never

alone would have come to him, tempted him against his will. He looked at the small girl, staggering persistently at the end of the loop her grandfather held. She had grown greatly on the food given her each day, and although she had as yet said no word at all, still she was plump as a child will be on slight care enough. Her lips that had been like an old woman's were smiling and red, and as of old she grew merry when he looked at her and she smiled.

"I might have done it," he mused, "if she had not lain in my bosom and smiled like that."

And then he thought again of his land and he cried out passionately.

"Shall I never see it again! With all this labor and begging there is never enough to do more than feed us today."

Then out of the dusk there answered him a voice, a deep burly voice,

"You are not the only one. There are a hundred hundred like you in this city."

The man came up, smoking a short bamboo pipe, and it was the father of the family in the hut next but two to Wang Lung's hut. He was a man seldom seen in the daylight, for he slept all day and worked at night pulling heavy wagons of merchandise which were too large for the streets by day when other vehicles must continually pass each other. But sometimes Wang Lung saw him come creeping home at dawn, panting and spent, and his great knotty shoulders drooping. Wang Lung passed him thus at dawn as he went out to his own ricksha pulling, and sometimes at dusk before the night's work the man came out and stood with the other men who were about to go into their hovels to sleep.

"Well, and is it forever?" asked Wang Lung bitterly.

The man puffed at his pipe thrice and then spat upon the ground. Then he said,

"No, and not forever. When the rich are too rich there are ways, and when the poor are too poor there are ways. Last winter we sold two girls and endured, and this winter, if this one my woman bears is a girl, we will sell again. One slave I have kept—the first. The others it is better to sell than to kill, although there are those who prefer to kill them before they draw breath. This is one of the ways when the poor are too poor. When the rich are too rich there is a way, and if I am not mistaken, that way will come soon." He nodded and pointed

84

with the stem of his pipe to the wall behind them. "Have you seen inside that wall?"

Wang Lung shook his head, staring. The man continued,

"I took one of my slaves in there to sell and I saw it. You would not believe it if I told you how money comes and goes in that house. I will tell you this—even the servants eat with chopsticks of ivory bound with silver, and even the slave women hang jade and pearls in their ears and sew pearls upon their shoes, and when the shoes have a bit of mud upon them or a small rent comes such as you and I would not call a rent, they throw them away, pearls and all!"

The man drew hard on his pipe and Wang Lung listened, his mouth ajar. Over this wall, then, there were indeed such things!

"There is a way when men are too rich," said the man, and he was silent for a time and then as though he had said nothing he added indifferently,

"Well, work again," and was gone into the night.

But Wang Lung that night could not sleep for thinking of silver and gold and pearls on the other side of this wall against which his body rested, his body clad in what he wore day after day, because there was no quilt to cover him and only a mat upon bricks beneath him. And temptation fell on him again to sell the child, so that he said to himself,

"It would be better perhaps that she be sold into a rich house so that she can eat daintily and wear jewels, if it be that she grow up pretty and please a lord." But against his own wish he answered himself and he thought again, "Well, and if I did, she is not worth her weight in gold and rubies. If she bring enough to take us back to the land, where will come enough to buy an ox and a table and a bed and the benches once more? Shall I sell a child that we may starve there instead of here? We have not even seed to put into the land."

And he saw nothing of the way of which the man spoke when he said, "There is a way, when the rich are too rich."

14

Spring seethed in the village of huts. Out to the hills and the grave lands those who had begged now could go to dig the small green weeds, dandelions and shepherd's purse that thrust up feeble new leaves, and it was not necessary as it had been to snatch at vegetables here and there. A swarm of ragged women and children issued forth each day from the huts, and with bits of tin and sharp stones or worn knives, and with baskets made of twisted bamboo twigs or split reeds they searched the countrysides and the roadways for the food they could get without begging and without money. And every day O-lan went out with this swarm, O-Lan and the two boys.

But men must work on, and Wang Lung worked as he had before, although the lengthening warm days and the sunshine and sudden rains filled everyone with longings and discontents. In the winter they had worked and been silent, enduring stolidly the snow and ice under their bare, straw-sandalled feet, going back at dark to their huts and eating without words such food as the day's labor and begging had brought, falling heavily to sleep, men, women and children, together, to gain that for their bodies which the food was too poor and too scanty to give. Thus it was in Wang Lung's hut and well he knew it must be so in every other.

But with the coming of spring talk began to surge up out of their hearts and to make itself heard on their lips. In the evening when the twilight lingered they gathered out of their huts and talked together, and Wang Lung saw this one and that of the men who had lived near him and whom through the winter he had not known. Had O-lan been one to tell him things he might have heard, for instance, of this one who beat his wife, of that one who had a leprous disease that ate his cheeks out, of that one who was king of a gang of thieves. But she was silent beyond the spare questions and answers she asked and gave, and so Wang Lung stood diffidently on the edge of the circle and listened to the talk.

Most of these ragged men had nothing beyond what they took in the day's labor and begging, and he was always conscious that he was not truly one of them. He owned land and his land was waiting for him. These others thought of how they might tomorrow eat a bit of fish, or of how they might idle a bit, and even how they might gamble a little, a penny or two, since their days were alike all evil and filled with want and a man must play sometimes, though desperate.

But Wang Lung thought of his land and pondered this way and that, with the sickened heart of deferred hope, how he could get back to it. He belonged, not to this scum which clung to the walls of a rich man's house; nor did he belong to the rich man's house. He belonged to the land and he could not live with any fullness until he felt the land under his feet and followed a plow in the springtime and bore a scythe in his hand at harvest. He listened, therefore, apart from the others, because hidden in his heart was the knowledge of the possession of his land, the good wheat land of his fathers, and the strip of rich rice land which he had bought from the great house.

They talked, these men, always and forever of money; of what pence they had paid for a foot of cloth, and of what they had paid for a small fish as long as a man's finger, or of what they could earn in a day, and always at last of what they would do if they had the money which the man over the wall had in his coffers. Every day the talk ended with this:

"And if I had the gold that he has and the silver in my hand that he wears every day in his girdle and if I had the pearls his concubines wear and the rubies his wife wears . . ."

And listening to all the things they would do if they had these things, Wang Lung heard only of how much they would eat and sleep, and of what dainties they would eat that they had never yet tasted, and of how they would gamble in this great tea shop and in that, and of what pretty women they would buy for their lust, and above all, how none would ever work again, even as the rich man behind the wall never worked.

Then Wang Lung cried out suddenly,

"If I had the gold and the silver and the jewels, I would buy land with it, good land, and I would bring forth harvests from the land!"

At this they united in turning on him and in rebuking him,

"Now here is a pig-tailed country bumpkin who understands nothing of city life and of what may be done with money. He would go on working like a slave behind an ox or an ass!" And each one of them felt he was more worthy to have the riches than was Wang Lung, because they knew better how to spend it.

But this scorn did not change the mind of Wang Lung. It only made him say to himself instead of aloud for others to hear,

"Nevertheless, I would put the gold and the silver and the jewels into good rich lands."

And thinking this, he grew more impatient every day for the land that was already his.

Being possessed continually by this thought of his land, Wang Lung saw as in a dream the things that happened about him in the city every day. He accepted this strangeness and that without questioning why anything was, except that in this day this thing came. There was, for an example, the paper that men gave out here and there, and sometimes even to him.

Now Wang Lung had never in his youth or at any time learned the meaning of letters upon paper, and he could not, therefore, make anything out of such paper covered with black marks and pasted upon city gates or upon walls or sold by the handful or even given away. Twice had he had such paper given him.

The first time it was given by a foreigner such as the one he had pulled unwittingly in his ricksha one day, only this one who gave him the paper was a man, very tall, and lean as a tree that has been blown by bitter winds. This man had eyes as blue as ice and a hairy face, and when he gave the paper to Wang Lung it was seen that his hands were also hairy and red-skinned. He had, moreover, a great nose projecting beyond his cheeks like a prow beyond the sides of a ship and Wang Lung although frightened to take anything from his hand, was more frightened to refuse, seeing the man's strange eyes and fearful nose. He took what was thrust at him, then, and when he had courage to look at it after the foreigner had passed on, he saw on the paper a picture of a man, white-skinned, who hung upon a crosspiece of wood. The man was without clothes except for a bit about his loins, and to all appearances he was dead, since his head drooped upon his shoulder and his eyes were closed above his bearded lips. Wang Lung looked at the pictured man in horror and with increasing interest. There were characters beneath, but of these he could make nothing.

He carried the picture home at night and showed it to the old man. But he also could not read and they discussed its possible meaning, Wang Lung and the old man and the two boys. The two boys cried out in delight and horror,

"And see the blood streaming out of his side!"

And the old man said,

"Surely this was a very evil man to be thus hung."

But Wang Lung was fearful of the picture and pondered as to why a foreigner had given it to him, whether or not some brother of this foreigner's had not been so treated and the other brethren seeking revenge. He avoided, therefore, the street on which he had met the man and after a few days, when the paper was forgotten, O-lan took it and sewed it into a shoe sole together with other bits of paper she picked up here and there to make the soles firm.

But the next time one handed a paper freely to Wang Lung it was a man of the city, a young man well clothed, who talked loudly as he distributed sheets hither and thither among the crowds who swarm about anything new and strange in a street. This paper bore also a picture of blood and death, but the man who died this time was not white-skinned and hairy but a man like Wang Lung himself, a common fellow, yellow and slight and black of hair and eye and clothed in ragged blue garments. Upon the dead figure a great fat one stood and stabbed the dead figure again and again with a long knife he held. It was a piteous sight and Wang Lung stared at it and longed to make something of the letters underneath. He turned to the man beside him and he said,

"Do you know a character or two so that you may tell me the meaning of this dreadful thing?"

And the man said,

"Be still and listen to the young teacher; he tells us all."

And so Wang Lung listened, and what he heard was what he had never heard before.

"The dead man is yourselves," proclaimed the young teacher, "and the murderous one who stabs you when you are dead and do not know it are the rich and the capitalists, who would stab you even after you are dead. You are poor and downtrodden and it is because the rich seize everything."

Now that he was poor Wang Lung knew full well but he had

heretofore blamed it on a heaven that would not rain in its season, or having rained, would continue to rain as though rain were an evil habit. When there was rain and sun in proportion so that the seed would sprout in the land and the stalk bear grain, he did not consider himself poor. Therefore he listened in interest to hear further what the rich men had to do with this thing, that heaven would not rain in its season. And at last when the young man had talked on and on but had said nothing of this matter where Wang Lung's interest lay, Wang Lung grew bold and asked,

"Sir, is there any way whereby the rich who oppress us can make it rain so that I can work on the land?"

At this the young man turned on him with scorn and replied,

"Now how ignorant you are, you who still wear your hair in a long tail! No one can make it rain when it will not, but what has this to do with us? If the rich would share with us what they have, rain or not would matter none, because we would all have money and food."

A great shout went up from those who listened, but Wang Lung turned away unsatisfied. Yes, but there was the land. Money and food are eaten and gone, and if there is not sun and rain in proportion, there is again hunger. Nevertheless, he took willingly the papers the young man gave him, because he remembered that O-lan had never enough paper for the shoe soles, and so he gave them to her when he went home, saying,

"Now there is some stuff for the shoe soles," and he worked as before.

But of the men in the huts with whom he talked at evening there were many who heard eagerly what the young man said, the more eagerly because they knew that over the wall there dwelt a rich man and it seemed a small thing that between them and his riches there was only this layer of bricks, which might be torn down with a few knocks of a stout pole, such as they had, to carry their heavy burdens every day upon their shoulders.

And to the discontent of the spring there was now added the new discontent which the young man and others like him spread abroad in the spirits of the dwellers in the huts, the sense of unjust possession by others of those things which they had not. And as they thought day after day on all these matters and talked of them in the twilight, and above all as day after day their labor brought in no added wage, there arose in the hearts of the young and the strong a tide as irresistible as the tide of the river, swollen with winter snows—the tide of the fullness of savage desire.

But Wang Lung, although he saw this and he heard the talk and felt their anger with a strange unease, desired nothing but his land under his feet again.

Then in this city out of which something new was always springing at him, Wang Lung saw another new thing he did not understand. He saw one day, when he pulled his ricksha empty down a street looking for a customer, a man, seized as he stood by a small band of armed soldiers, and when the man protested, the soldiers brandished knives in his face, and while Wang Lung watched in amazement, another was seized and another, and it came to Wang Lung that those who were seized were all common fellows who worked with their hands, and while he stared, yet another man was seized, and this one a man who lived in the hut nearest his own against the wall.

Then Wang Lung perceived suddenly out of his astonishment that all these men seized were as ignorant as he as to why they were thus being taken, willy nilly, whether they would or not. And Wang Lung thrust his ricksha into a side alley and he dropped it and darted into the door of a hot water shop lest he be next and there he hid, crouched low behind the great cauldrons, until the soldiers passed. And then he asked the keeper of the hot water shop the meaning of the thing he had seen, and the man, who was old and shriveled with the steam rising continually about him out of the copper cauldrons of his trade, answered with indifference.

"It is but another war somewhere. Who knows what all this fighting to and fro is about? But so it has been since I was a lad and so will it be after I am dead and well I know it."

"Well, and but why do they seize my neighbor, who is as innocent as I who have never heard of this new war?" asked Wang Lung in great consternation. And the old man clattered the lids of his cauldrons and answered,

"These soldiers are going to battle somewhere and they need carriers for their bedding and their guns and their ammunition and so they force laborers like you to do it. But what part are you from? It is no new sight in this city."

"But what then?" urged Wang Lung breathless. "What wage—what return——"

Now the old man was very old and he had no great hope in

91

anything and no interest in anything beyond his cauldrons and he answered carelessly,

"Wage there is none and but two bits of dry bread a day and a sup from a pond, and you may go home when the destination is reached if your two legs can carry you."

"Well, but a man's family——" said Wang Lung, aghast.

"Well, and what do they know or care of that?" said the old man scornfully, peering under the wooden lid of the nearest cauldron to see if the water bubbled yet. A cloud of steam enveloped him and his wrinkled face could scarcely be seen peering into the cauldron. Nevertheless he was kindly, for when he came forth again out of the steam he saw what Wang Lung could not see from where he crouched, that once more the soldiers approached, searching the streets from which now every able-bodied working man had fled.

"Stoop yet more," he said to Wang Lung. "They are come again."

And Wang Lung crouched low behind the cauldrons and the soldiers clattered down the cobbles to the west, and when the sound of their leathern boots was gone Wang Lung darted out and seizing his ricksha he ran with it empty to the hut.

Then to O-lan, who had but just returned from the roadside to cook a little of the green stuff she had gathered, he told in broken, panting words what was happening and how nearly he had not escaped, and as he spoke this new horror sprang up in him, the horror that he be dragged to battlefields and not only his old father and his family left alone to starve, but he dying upon a battlefield and his blood spilled out, and nevermore able to see his own land. He looked at O-lan haggardly and he said,

"Now am I truly tempted to sell the little slave and go north to the land."

But she, after listening, mused and said in her plain and unmoved way,

"Wait a few days. There is strange talk about."

Nevertheless, he went out no more in the daylight but he sent the eldest lad to return the ricksha to the place from where he hired it and he waited until the night came and he went to the houses of merchandise and for half what he had earned before he pulled all night the great wagonloads of boxes, to each wagon a dozen men pulling and straining and groaning. And the boxes were filled with silks and with cottons and with fragrant tobacco, so fragrant that the smell of it leaked through the wood. And there were great jars of oils and of wines.

All night through the dark streets he strained against the ropes, his body naked and streaming with sweating, and his bare feet slipping on the cobbles, slimy and wet as they were with the dampness of the night. Before them to show the way ran a little lad carrying a flaming torch and in the light of this torch the faces and the bodies of the men and the wet stones glistened alike. And Wang Lung came home before dawn, gasping and too broken for food until he had slept. But during the bright day when the soldiers searched the street he slept safely in the furthermost corner of the hut behind a pile of straw O-lan gathered to make a shield for him.

What battles there were or who fought which other one Wang Lung did not know. But with the further coming of spring the city became filled with the unrest of fear. All during the days carriages drawn by horses pulled rich men and their possessions of clothing and satin-covered bedding and their beautiful women and their jewels to the river's edge where ships carried them away to other places, and some went to that other house where firewagons came and went. Wang Lung never went upon the streets in the day, but his sons came back with their eyes wide and bright, crying,

"We saw such an one and such an one, a man as fat and monstrous as a god in a temple, and his body covered with many feet of yellow silk and on his thumb a great gold ring set with green stone like a piece of glass, and his flesh was all bright with oil and eating!"

Or the elder cried,

"And we have seen such boxes and boxes and when I asked what was in them one said, 'There is gold and silver in them, but the rich cannot take all they have away, and some day it will all be ours.' Now, what did he mean by this, my father?" And the lad opened his eyes inquisitively to his father.

But when Wang Lung answered shortly, "How should I know what an idle city fellow means?" the lad cried wistfully,

"Oh, I wish we might go even now and get it if it is ours. I should like to taste a cake. I have never tasted a sweet cake with sesame seed sprinkled on the top."

The old man looked up from his dreaming at this and he said as one croons to himself,

"When we had a good harvest we had such cakes at the autumn feast, when the sesame had been threshed and before it was sold we kept a little back to make such cakes."

And Wang Lung remembered the cakes that O-lan had once

made at the New Year's feast, cakes of rice flour and lard and sugar, and his mouth watered and his heart pained him with longing for that which was passed.

"If we were only back on our land," he muttered.

Then suddenly it seemed to him that not one more day could he lie in this wretched hut, which was not wide enough for him even to stretch his length in behind the pile of straw, nor could he another night strain the hours through, his body bent against a rope cutting into his flesh, and dragging the load over the cobble stones. Each stone he had come to know now as a separate enemy, and he knew each rut by which he might evade a stone and so use an ounce less of his life. There were times in the black nights, especially when it rained and the streets were wet and more wet than usual, that the whole hatred of his heart went out against these stones under his feet, these stones that seemed to cling and to hang to the wheels of his inhuman load.

"Ah, the fair land!" he cried out suddenly and fell to weeping so that the children were frightened and the old man, looking at his son in consternation, twisted his face this way and that under his sparse beard, as a child's face twists when he sees his mother weep.

And again it was O-lan who said in her flat plain voice,

"Yet a little while and we shall see a thing. There is talk everywhere now."

From his hut where Wang Lung lay hid he heard hour after hour the passing of feet, the feet of soldiers marching to battle. Lifting sometimes a very little the mat which stood between them and him, he put one eye to the crack and he saw these feet passing, passing, leather shoes and cloth-covered legs, marching one after the other, pair by pair, score upon score, thousands upon thousands. In the night when he was at his load he saw their faces flickering past him, caught for an instant out of the darkness by the flaming torch ahead. He dared ask nothing concerning them, but he dragged his load doggedly, and he ate hastily his bowl of rice, and slept the day fitfully through in the hut behind the straw. None spoke in those days to any other. The city was shaken with fear and each man did quickly what he had to do and went into his house and shut the door.

There was no more idle talk at twilight about the huts. In the market places the stalls where food had been were now empty. The silk shops drew in their bright banners and closed the fronts of their great shops with thick boards fitting one into the other solidly, so that passing through the city at noon it was as though the people slept.

It was whispered everywhere that the enemy approached and all those who owned anything were afraid. But Wang Lung was not afraid, nor the dwellers in the huts, neither were they afraid. They did not know for one thing who this enemy was, nor had they anything to lose since even their lives were no great loss. If this enemy approached let him approach, seeing that nothing could be worse than it now was with them. But every man went on his own way and none spoke openly to any other.

Then the managers of the houses of merchandise told the laborers who pulled the boxes to and fro from the river's edge that they need come no more, since there were none to buy and sell in these days at the counters, and so Wang Lung stayed in his hut day and night and was idle. At first he was glad, for it seemed his body could never get enough rest and he slept as heavily as a man dead. But if he did not work neither did he earn, and in a few short days what they had of extra pence was gone and again he cast about desperately as to what he could do. And as if it were not enough of evil to befall them, the public kitchens closed their doors also and those who had in this way provided for the poor went into their own houses and shut the doors and there was no food and no work, and no one passing upon the streets of whom anyone could beg.

Then Wang Lung took his girl child into his arms and he sat with her in the hut and he looked at her and said softly,

"Little fool, would you like to go to a great house where there is food and drink and where you may have a whole coat to your body?"

Then she smiled, not understanding anything of what he said, and put up her small hand to touch with wonder his staring eyes and he could not bear it and he cried out to the woman,

"Tell me, and were you beaten in that great house?"

And she answered him flatly and somberly,

"Every day was I beaten."

And he cried again,

"But was it just with a girdle of cloth or was it with bamboo or rope?"

And she answered in the same dead way,

"I was beaten with a leather thong which had been halter for one of the mules, and it hung upon the kitchen wall."

Well he knew that she understood what he was thinking, but he put forth his last hope and he said,

"This child of ours is a pretty little maid, even now. Tell me, were the pretty slaves beaten also?"

And she answered indifferently, as though it were nothing to her this way or that,

"Aye, beaten or carried to a man's bed, as the whim was, and not to one man's only but to any that might desire her that night, and the young lords bickered and bartered with each other for this slave or that and said, 'Then if you tonight, I tomorrow,' and when they were all alike wearied of a slave the men servants bickered and bartered for what the young lords left, and this before a slave was out of childhood—if she were pretty."

Then Wang Lung groaned and held the child to him and said over and over to her softly, "Oh, little fool—oh, poor little fool." But within himself he was crying as a man cries out when he is caught in a rushing flood and cannot stop to think, "There is no other way—there is no other way——"

Then suddenly as he sat there came a noise like the cracking of heaven and every one of them fell unthinking on the ground and hid their faces, for it seemed as though the hideous roar would catch them all up and crush them. And Wang Lung covered the girl child's face with his hand, not knowing what horror might appear to them out of this dreadful din, and the old man called out into Wang Lung's ear, "Now this I have never heard before in all my years," and the two boys yelled with fear.

But O-lan, when silence had fallen as suddenly as it had gone, lifted her head and said, "Now that which I have heard of has come to pass. The enemy has broken in the gates of the city." And before any could answer her there was a shout over the city, a rising shout of human voices, at first faint, as one may hear the wind of a storm approaching, and gathering in a deep howl, louder and more loud as it filled the streets.

Wang Lung sat erect then, on the floor of his hut, and a strange fear crept over his flesh, so that he felt it stirring among the roots of his hair, and everyone sat erect and they all stared at each other waiting for something they knew not. But there was only the noise of the gathering of human beings and each man howling.

Then over the wall and not far from them they heard the sound of a great door creaking upon its hinges and groaning as it opened unwillingly, and suddenly the man who had talked to Wang Lung once at dusk and smoked a short bamboo pipe, thrust his head in at the hut's opening and cried out,

"Now do you still sit here? The hour has come—the gates of the rich man are open to us!" And as if by magic of some kind O-lan was gone, creeping out under the man's arm as he spoke.

Then Wang Lung rose up, slowly and half dazed, and he set the girl child down and he went out and there before the great iron gates of the rich man's house a multitude of clamoring common people pressed forward, howling together the deep, tigerish howl that he had heard, rising and swelling out of the streets, and he knew that at the gates of all rich men there pressed this howling multitude of men and women who had been starved and imprisoned and now were for the moment free to do as they would. And the great gates were ajar and the people pressed forward so tightly packed together that foot was on foot and body wedged tightly against body so that the whole mass moved together as one. Others hurrying from the back caught Wang Lung and forced him into the crowd so that whether he would or not he was taken forward with them, although he did not himself know what his will was, because he was so amazed at what had come about.

Thus was he swept along over the threshold of the great gates, his feet scarcely touching the ground in the pressure of people, and like the continuous roar of angry beasts there went on all around the howling of the people.

Through court after court he was swept, into the very inner courts, and of those men and women who had lived in the house he saw not one. It was as though here were a palace long dead except that early lilies bloomed among the rocks of the gardens and the golden flowers of the early trees of spring blossomed upon bare branches. But in the rooms food stood upon a table and in the kitchens fire burned. Well this crowd knew the courts of the rich, for they swept past the front courts, where servants and slaves lived and where the kitchens are, into the inner courts, where the lords and ladies have their dainty beds and where stand their lacquered boxes of black and red and gold, their boxes of silken clothing, where carved tables and chairs are, and upon the walls painted scrolls. And upon these treasures the crowd fell, seizing at and tearing from each other what was revealed in every newly opened box or closet, so that clothing and bedding and curtains and dishes passed from hand to hand, each hand snatching that which another held, and none stopping to see what he had.

Only Wang Lung in the confusion took nothing. He had never in all his life taken what belonged to another, and not at once could he do it. So he stood in the middle of the crowd at first, dragged this way and that, and then coming somewhat to his senses, he pushed with perseverance toward the edge and found himself at last on the fringe of the multitude, and here he stood, swept along slightly as little whirlpools are at the edge of a pool of current; but still he was able to see where he was.

He was at the back of the innermost court where the ladies of the rich dwell, and the back gate was ajar, that gate which the rich have for centuries kept for their escape in such times, and therefore called the gate of peace. Through this gate doubtless they had all escaped this day and were hidden here and there through the streets, listening to the howling in their courts. But one man, whether because of his size or whether because of his drunken heaviness of sleep, had failed to escape, and this one Wang Lung came upon suddenly in an empty inner room from whence the mob had swept in and out again, so that the man, who had been hidden in a secret place and not been found, now crept out, thinking he was alone, to escape. And thus Wang Lung, always drifting away from the others until he too was alone, came upon him.

He was a great fat fellow, neither old nor young, and he had been lying naked in his bed, doubtless with a pretty woman, for his naked body gaped through a purple satin robe he held about him. The great yellow rolls of his flesh doubled over his breasts and over his belly and in the mountains of his cheeks his eyes were small and sunken as a pig's eyes. When he saw Wang Lung he shook all over and yelled out as though his flesh had been stuck with a knife, so that Wang Lung, weaponless as he was, wondered and could have laughed at the sight. But the fat fellow fell upon his knees and knocked his head on the tiles of the floor and he cried forth,

"Save a life—save a life—do not kill me. I have money for you—much money——"

It was this word "money" which suddenly brought to Wang Lung's mind a piercing clarity. Money! Aye, and he needed that! And again it came to him clearly, as a voice speaking, "Money—the child saved—*the land!*"

He cried out suddenly in a harsh voice such as he did not himself know was in his breast,

"Give me the money then!"

And the fat man rose to his knees, sobbing and gibbering, and feeling for the pocket of the robe, and he brought forth his yellow hands dripping with gold and Wang Lung held out the end of his coat and received it. And again he cried out in that strange voice that was like another man's,

"Give me more!"

And again the man's hands came forth dripping with gold and he whimpered,

"Now there is none left and I have nothing but my wretched life," and he fell to weeping, his tears running like oil down his hanging cheeks.

Wang Lung, looking at him as he shivered and wept, suddenly loathed him as he had loathed nothing in his life and he cried out with the loathing surging up in him,

"Out of my sight, lest I kill you for a fat worm!"

This Wang Lung cried, although he was a man so softhearted that he could not kill an ox. And the man ran past him like a cur and was gone.

Then Wang Lung was left alone with the gold. He did not stop to count it, but thrust it into his bosom and went out of the open gate of peace and across the small back streets to his hut. He hugged to his bosom the gold that was yet warm from the other man's body and to himself he said over and over,

"We go back to the land—tomorrow we go back to the land!"

15

BEFORE A HANDFUL of days had passed it seemed to Wang Lung that he had never been away from his land, as indeed, in his heart he never had. With three pieces of the gold he bought good seed from the south, full grains of wheat and of rice and of corn, and for very recklessness of riches he bought seeds the like of which he had never planted before, celery and lotus for his pond and great red radishes that are stewed with pork for a feast dish and small red fragrant beans.

With five gold pieces he bought an ox from a farmer ploughing in the field, and this before ever he reached his own land. He saw the man ploughing and he stopped and they all stopped, the old man and the children and the woman, eager as they were to reach the house and the land, and they looked at the ox. Wang Lung had been struck with its strong neck and noticed at once the sturdy pulling of its shoulder against the wooden yoke and he called out,

"That is a worthless ox! What will you sell it for in silver or gold, seeing that I have no animal and am hard put to it and willing to take anything?"

And the farmer called back,

"I would sooner sell my wife than this ox which is but three years old and in its prime," and he ploughed on and would not stop for Wang Lung.

Then it seemed to Wang Lung as if out of all the oxen the world held he must have this one, and he said to O-lan and to his father,

"How is it for an ox?"

And the old man peered and said, "It seems a beast well castrated."

And O-lan said, "It is a year older than he says."

But Wang Lung answered nothing because upon this ox he had set his heart because of its sturdy pulling of the soil and because of its smooth yellow coat and its full dark eye. With this ox he could plough his fields and cultivate them and with this ox tied to his mill he could grind the grain. And he went to the farmer and said,

"I will give you enough to buy another ox and more, but this ox I will have."

At last after bickering and quarrelling and false starts away the farmer yielded for half again the worth of an ox in those parts. But gold was suddenly nothing to Wang Lung when he looked at this ox, and he passed it over to the farmer's hand and he watched while the farmer unyoked the beast, and Wang Lung led it away with a rope through its nostrils, his heart burning with his possession.

When they reached the house they found the door torn away and the thatch from the roof gone and within their hoes and rakes that they had left were gone, so only the bare rafters and the earthen walls remained, and even the earthen walls were worn down with the belated snows and the rains of winter and early spring. But after the first astonishment all this was as nothing to Wang Lung. He went away to the town and he bought a good new plow of hard wood and two rakes and two hoes and mats to cover the roof until they could grow thatch again from the harvest.

Then in the evening he stood in the doorway of his house and looked across the land, his own land, lying loose and fresh from the winter's freezing, and ready for planting. It was full spring and in the shallow pool the frogs croaked drowsily. The bamboos at the corner of the house swayed slowly under a gentle night wind and through the twilight he could see dimly the fringe of trees at the border of the near field. They were peach trees, budded most delicately pink, and willow trees thrusting forth tender green leaves. And up from the quiescent, waiting land a faint mist rose, silver as moonlight, and clung about the tree trunks.

At first and for a long time it seemed to Wang Lung that he wished to see no human being but only to be alone on his land. He went to no houses of the village and when they came to him, those who were left of the winter's starving, he was surly with them.

"Which of you tore away my door and which of you have my rake and my hoe and which of you burned my roof in his oven?" Thus he bawled at them.

And they shook their heads, full of virtue; and this one said, "It was your uncle," and that one said, "Nay, with bandits and robbers roving over the land in these evil times of famine and war, how can it be said that this one or that stole anything? Hunger makes thief of any man."

Then Ching, his neighbor, came creeping forth from his house to see Wang Lung and he said,

"Through the winter a band of robbers lived in your house and preyed upon the village and the town as they were able. Your uncle, it is said, knows more of them than an honest man should. But who knows what is true in these days? I would not dare to accuse any man."

This man was nothing but a shadow indeed, so close did his skin stick to his bones and so thin and grey had his hair grown, although he had not yet reached forty-five years of his age. Wang Lung stared at him awhile and then in compassion he said suddenly,

"Now you have fared worse than we and what have you eaten?"

And the man sighed forth in a whisper,

"What have I not eaten? Offal from the streets like dogs when we begged in the town and dead dogs we ate and once before she died my woman brewed some soup from flesh I dared not ask what it was, except that I knew she had not the courage to kill, and if we ate it was something she found. Then she died, having less strength than I to endure, and after she died I gave the girl to a soldier because I could not see her starve and die also." He paused and fell silent and after a time he said, "If I had a little seed I would plant once more, but no seed have I."

"Come here!" cried Wang Lung roughly and dragged him into the house by the hand and he bade the man hold up the ragged tail of his coat and into it Wang Lung poured from the store of seed he had brought from the south. Wheat he gave him and rice and cabbage seed and he said,

"Tomorrow I will come and plough your land with my good ox."

Then Ching began to weep suddenly and Wang Lung rubbed his own eyes and cried out as if he were angry, "Do you think I have forgotten that you gave me that handful of beans?" But Ching could answer nothing, only he walked away weeping and weeping without stop.

It was joy to Wang Lung to find that his uncle was no longer in the village and where he was none knew certainly. Some said he had gone to a city and some said he was in far distant parts with his wife and his son. But there was not one left in his house in the village. The girls, and this Wang Lung heard with stout anger, were sold, the prettiest first, for the price they could bring, but even the last one, who was pock-marked, was sold for a handful of pence to a soldier who was passing through to battle.

Then Wang Lung set himself robustly to the soil and he begrudged even the hours he must spend in the house for food and sleep. He loved rather to take his roll of bread and garlic to the field and stand there eating, planning and thinking, "Here shall I put the black-eyed peas and here the young rice beds." And if he grew too weary in the day he laid himself into a furrow and there with the good warmth of his own land against his flesh, he slept.

And O-lan in the house was not idle. With her own hands she lashed the mats firmly to the rafters and took earth from the fields and mixed it with water and mended the walls of the house, and she built again the oven and filled the holes in the floor that the rain had washed.

Then she went into the town one day with Wang Lung and together they bought beds and a table and six benches and a great iron cauldron and then they bought for pleasure a red clay teapot with a black flower marked on it in ink and six bowls to match. Last of all they went into an incense shop and bought a paper god of wealth to hang on the wall over the table in the middle room, and they bought two pewter candlesticks and a pewter incense urn and two red candles to burn before the god, thick red candles of cow's fat and having a slender reed through the middle for wick.

And with this, Wang Lung thought of the two small gods in the temple to the earth and on his way home he went and peered in at them, and they were piteous to behold, their features washed from their faces with rain and the clay of their bodies naked and sticking through the tatters of their paper clothes. None had paid any heed to them in this dreadful year and Wang Lung looked at them grimly and with content and he said aloud, as one might speak to a punished child,

"Thus it is with gods who do evil to men!"

Nevertheless, when the house was itself again, and the pewter candlesticks gleaming and the candles burning in them shining red, and the teapot and the bowls upon the table and the beds in their places with a little bedding once more, and fresh paper pasted over the hole in the room where he slept and a new door hung upon its wooden hinges, Wang Lung was afraid of his happiness. O-lan grew great with the next child; his children tumbled like brown puppies about his threshold and against the southern wall his old father sat and dozed and smiled as he slept; in his fields the young rice sprouted as green as jade and more beautiful, and the young beans lifted their hooded heads from the soil. And out of the gold there was still enough left to feed them until the harvest, if they ate sparingly. Looking at the blue heaven above him and the white clouds driving across it, feeling upon his ploughed fields as upon his own flesh the sun and rain in proportion, Wang Lung muttered unwillingly,

"I must stick a little incense before those two in the small temple. After all, they have power over earth."

16

ONE NIGHT as Wang lay with his wife he felt a hard lump the size of a man's closed hand between her breasts and he said to her,

"Now what is this thing you have on your body?"

He put his hand to it and he found a cloth-wrapped bundle that was hard yet moved to his touch. She drew back violently at first and then when he laid hold of it to pluck it away from her she yielded and said,

"Well, look at it then, if you must," and she took the string which held it to her neck and broke it and gave him the thing.

It was wrapped in a bit of rag and he tore this away. Then suddenly into his hand fell a mass of jewels and Wang Lung gazed at them stupefied. There were such a mass of jewels as one had never dreamed could be together, jewels red as the inner flesh of watermelons, golden as wheat, green as young leaves in spring, clear as water trickling out of the earth. What the names of them were Wang did not know, having never heard names and seen jewels together in his life. But holding them there in his hand, in the hollow of his brown hard hand, he knew from the gleaming and the glittering in the half-dark room that he held wealth. He held it motionless, drunk with color and shape, speechless, and together he and the woman stared at what he held. At last he whispered to her, breathless,

"Where—where—"

And she whispered back as softly,

"In the rich man's house. It must have been a favorite's treasure. I saw a brick loosened in the wall and I slipped there carelessly so no other soul could see and demand a share. I pulled the brick away, caught the shining, and put them into my sleeve."

"Now how did you know?" he whispered again, filled with admiration, and she answered with the smile on her lips that was never in her eyes,

"Do you think I have not lived in a rich man's house? The rich are always afraid. I saw robbers in a bad year once rush into the gate of the great house and the slaves and the concubines and even the Old Mistress herself ran hither and thither and each had a treasure that she thrust into some secret place already planned. Therefore I knew the meaning of a loosened brick."

And again they fell silent, staring at the wonder of the stones. Then after a long time Wang Lung drew in his breath and said resolutely,

"Now treasure like this one cannot keep. It must be sold and put into safety—into land, for nothing else is safe. If any knew of this we should be dead by the next day and a robber would carry the jewels. They must be put into land this very day or I shall not sleep tonight."

He wrapped the stones in the rag again as he spoke and tied them hard together with the string, and opening his coat to thrust them into his bosom, by chance he saw the woman's face. She was sitting cross-legged upon the bed at its foot and her heavy face that never spoke of anything was moved with a dim yearning of open lips and face thrust forward.

"Well, and now what?" he asked, wondering at her.

"Will you sell them all?" she asked in a hoarse whisper.

"And why not then?" he answered, astonished. "Why should we have jewels like this in an earthen house?"

"I wish I could keep two for myself," she said with such helpless wistfulness, as of one expecting nothing, that he was moved as he might be by one of his children longing for a toy or for a sweet.

"Well, now!" he cried in amazement.

"If I could have two," she went on humbly, "only two small ones—two small white pearls even . . ."

"Pearls!" he repeated, agape.

"I would keep them —I would not wear them," she said, "only keep them." And she dropped her eyes and fell to twisting a bit of the bedding where a thread was loosened, and she waited patiently as one who scarcely expects an answer.

Then Wang Lung, without comprehending it, looked for an instant into the heart of this dull and faithful creature, who had labored all her life at some task at which she won no reward

105

and who in the great house had seen others wearing jewels which she never even felt in her hand once.

"I could hold them in my hand sometimes," she added, as if she thought to herself.

And he was moved by something he did not understand and he pulled the jewels from his bosom and unwrapped them and handed them to her in silence, and she searched among the glittering colors, her hard brown hand turning over the stones delicately and lingeringly until she found the two smooth white pearls, and these she took, and tying up the others again, she gave them back to him. Then she took the pearls and she tore a bit of the corner of her coat away and wrapped them and hid them between her breasts and was comforted.

But Wang Lung watched her astonished and only half understanding, so that afterwards during the day and on other days he would stop and stare at her and say to himself,

"Well now, that woman of mine, she has those two pearls between her breasts still, I suppose." But he never saw her take them out or look at them and they never spoke of them at all.

As for the other jewels, he pondered this way and that, and at last he decided he would go to the great house and see if there were more land to buy.

To the great house he now went and there was in these days no gateman standing at the gate, twisting the long hairs of his mole, scornful of those who could not enter past him into the House of Hwang. Instead the great gates were locked and Wang Lung pounded against them with both fists and no one came. Men who passed in the streets looked up and cried out at him,

"Aye, you may pound now and pound again. If the Old Lord is awake he may come and if there is a stray dog of a slave about she may open, if she is inclined to it."

But at last he heard slow footsteps coming across the threshold, slow wandering footsteps that halted and came on by fits, and then he heard the slow drawing of the iron bar that held the gate and the gate creaked and a cracked voice whispered,

"Who is it?"

Then Wang Lung answered, loudly, although he was amazed,

"It is I, Wang Lung!"

Then the voice said peevishly,

"Now who is an accursed Wang Lung?"

And Wang Lung perceived by the quality of the curse that it was the Old Lord himself, because he cursed as one accustomed to servants and slaves. Wang Lung answered, therefore, more humbly than before.

"Sir and lord, I am come on a little business, not to disturb your lordship, but to talk a little business with the agent who serves your honor."

Then the Old Lord answered without opening any wider the crack through which he pursed his lips,

"Now curse him, that dog left me many months ago and he is not here."

Wang Lung did not know what to do after this reply. It was impossible to talk of buying land directly to the Old Lord, without a middleman, and yet the jewels hung in his bosom hot as fire, and he wanted to be rid of them and more than that he wanted the land. With the seed he had he could plant as much land again as he had, and he wanted the good land of the House of Hwang.

"I came about a little money," he said hesitatingly.

At once the Old Lord pushed the gates together.

"There is no money in this house," he said more loudly than he had yet spoken. "The thief and robber of an agent—and may his mother and his mother's mother be cursed for him—took all that I had. No debts can be paid."

"No—no——" called Wang Lung hastily, "I came to pay out, not to collect debt."

At this there was a shrill scream from a voice Wang Lung had not yet heard and a woman thrust her face suddenly out of the gates.

"Now that is a thing I have not heard for a long time," she said sharply, and Wang Lung saw a handsome, shrewish, high-colored face looking out at him. "Come in," she said briskly and she opened the gates wide enough to admit him and then behind his back, while he stood astonished in the court, she barred them securely again.

The Old Lord stood there coughing and staring, a dirty grey satin robe wrapped about him, from which hung an edge of bedraggled fur. Once it had been a fine garment, as anyone could see, for the satin was still heavy and smooth, although stains and spots covered it, and it was wrinkled as though it had been used as a bedgown. Wang Lung stared back at the Old Lord, curious, yet half-afraid, for all his life he half-feared the people in the great house, and it seemed impossible that the

Old Lord, of whom he had heard so much, was this old figure, no more dreadful than his old father, and indeed less so for his father was a cleanly and smiling old man, and the Old Lord, who had been fat, was now lean, and his skin hung in folds about him and he was unwashed and unshaven and his hand was yellow and trembled as he passed it over his chin and pulled at his loose old lips.

The woman was clean enough. She had a hard, sharp face, handsome with a sort of hawk's beauty of high bridged nose and keen bright black eyes and pale skin stretched too tightly over her bones, and her cheeks and lips were red and hard. Her black hair was like a mirror for smooth shining blackness, but from her speech one could perceive she was not of the lord's family, but a slave, sharp voiced and bitter tongued. And besides these two, the woman and the Old Lord, there was not another person in the court where before men and women and children had run to and fro on their business of caring for the great house.

"Now about money," said the woman sharply. But Wang Lung hesitated. He could not well speak before the Old Lord and this the woman instantly perceived as she perceived everything more quickly than speech could be made about it, and she said to the old man shrilly, "Now off with you!"

And the aged lord, without a word, shambled silently away, his old velvet shoes flapping and off at his heels, coughing as he went. As for Wang Lung, left alone with this woman, he did not know what to say or do. He was stupefied with the silence everywhere. He glanced into the next court and still there was no other person, and about the court he saw heaps of refuse and filth and scattered straw and branches of bamboo trees and dried pine needles and the dead stalks of flowers, as though not for a long time had anyone taken a broom to sweep it.

"Now then, wooden head!" said the woman with exceeding sharpness, and Wang Lung jumped at the sound of her voice, so unexpected was its shrillness. "What is your business? If you have money, let me see it."

"No," said Wang Lung with caution, "I did not say that I had money. I have business."

"Business means money," returned the woman, "either money coming in or money going out, and there is no money to go out of his house."

"Well, but I cannot speak with a woman," objected Wang

Lung mildly. He could make nothing of the situation in which he found himself, and he was still staring about him.

"Well, and why not?" retorted the woman with anger. Then she shouted at him suddenly, "Have you not heard, fool, that there is no one here?"

Wang Lung stared at her feebly, unbelieving, and the woman shouted at him again, "I and the Old Lord—there is no one else!"

"Where then?" asked Wang Lung, too much aghast to make sense in his words.

"Well, and the Old Mistress is dead," retorted the woman. "Have you not heard in the town how bandits swept into the house and how they carried away what they would of the slaves and of the goods? And they hung the Old Lord up by his thumbs and beat him and the Old Mistress they tied in a chair and gagged her and everyone ran. But I stayed. I hid in a gong half full of water under a wooden lid. And when I came out they were gone and the Old Mistress sat dead in her chair, not from any touch they had given her but from fright. Her body was a rotten reed with the opium she smoked and she could not endure the fright."

"And the servants and the slaves?" gasped Wang Lung. "And the gateman?"

"Oh, those," she answered carelessly, "they were gone long ago—all those who had feet to carry them away, for there was no food and no money by the middle of the winter. Indeed," her voice fell to a whisper, "there are many of the men servants among the bandits. I saw that dog of a gateman myself—he was leading the way, although he turned his face aside in the Old Lord's presence, still I knew those three long hairs of his mole. And there were others, for how could any but those familiar with the great house know where jewels were hid and the secret treasure stores of things not to be sold? I would not put it beneath the old agent himself, although he would consider it beneath his dignity to appear publicly in the affair, since he is a sort of distant relative of the family."

The woman fell silent and the silence of the courts was heavy as silence can be after life has gone. Then she said,

"But all this was not a sudden thing. All during the lifetime of the Old Lord and of his father the fall of this house has been coming. In the last generation the lords ceased to see the land and took the moneys the agents gave them and spent it carelessly as water. And in these generations the strength of the land has gone from them and bit by bit the land has begun to go also."

"Where are the young lords?" asked Wang Lung, still staring about him, so impossible was it for him to believe these things.

"Hither and thither," said the woman indifferently. "It is good fortune that the two girls were married away before the thing happened. The elder young lord when he heard what had befallen his father and his mother sent a messenger to take the Old Lord, his father, but I persuaded the old head not to go. I said, 'Who will be in the courts, and it is not seemly for me, who am only a woman.'"

She pursed her narrow red lips virtuously as she spoke these words, and cast down her bold eyes, and again she said, when she had paused a little, "Besides, I have been my lord's faithful slave for these several years and I have no other house."

Wang Lung looked at her closely then and turned quickly away. He began to perceive what this was, a woman who clung to an old and dying man because of what last thing she might get from him. He said with contempt,

"Seeing that you are only a slave, how can I do business with you?"

At that she cried out at him, "He will do anything I tell him."

Wang Lung pondered over this reply. Well, and there was the land. Others would buy it through this woman if he did not.

"How much land is there left?" he asked her unwillingly, and she saw instantly what his purpose was.

"If you have come to buy land," she said quickly, "there is land to buy. He has a hundred acres to the west and to the south two hundred that he will sell. It is not all in one piece but the plots are large. It can be sold to the last acre."

This she said so readily that Wang Lung perceived she knew everything the old man had left, even to the last foot of land. But still he was unbelieving and not willing to do business with her.

"It is not likely the Old Lord can sell all the land of his family without the agreement of his sons," he demurred.

But the woman met his words eagerly.

"As for that, the sons have told him to sell when he can. The land is where no one of the sons wishes to live and the country is run over with bandits in these days of famine, and they have all said, 'We cannot live in such a place. Let us sell and divide the money.'"

"But into whose hand would I put the money?" asked Wang Lung, still unbelieving.

"Into the Old Lord's hand, and whose else?" replied the woman smoothly. But Wang Lung knew that the Old Lord's hand opened into hers.

He would not, therefore, talk further with her, but turned away saying, "Another day—another day—" and he went to the gate and she followed him, shrieking after him into the street,

"This time tomorrow—this time or this afternoon—all times are alike!"

He went down the street without answer, greatly puzzled and needing to think over what he had heard. He went into the small tea shop and ordered tea of the slavey and when the boy had put it smartly before him and with an impudent gesture had caught and tossed the penny he paid for it, Wang Lung fell to musing. And the more he mused the more monstrous it seemed that the great and rich family, who all his own life and all his father's and grandfather's lives long had been a power and a glory in the town, were now fallen and scattered.

"It comes of their leaving the land," he thought regretfully, and he thought of his own two sons, who were growing like young bamboo shoots in the spring, and he resolved that on this very day he would make them cease playing in the sunshine and he would set them to tasks in the field, where they would early take into their bones and their blood the feel of the soil under their feet, and the feel of the hoe hard in their hands.

Well, but all this time here were these jewels hot and heavy against his body and he was continually afraid. It seemed as though their brilliance must shine through his rags and someone cry out,

"Now here is a poor man carrying an emperor's treasure!"

And he could not rest until they were changed into land. He watched, therefore, until the shopkeeper had a moment of idleness and he called to the man and said,

"Come and drink a bowl at my cost, and tell me the news of the town, since I have been a winter away."

The shopkeeper was always ready for such talk, especially if he drank his own tea at another's cost, and he sat down readily at Wang Lung's table, a small weasel-faced man with a twisted and crossed left eye. His clothes were solid and black with grease down the front of his coat and trousers, for besides tea he sold food also, which he cooked himself, and he was fond of saying, "There is a proverb, 'A good cook has never a clean

111

coat,' " and so he considered himself justly and necessarily filthy. He sat down and began at once,

"Well, and beyond the starving of people, which is no news, the greatest news was the robbery at the House of Hwang."

It was just what Wang Lung hoped to hear and the man went on to tell him of it with relish, describing how the few slaves left had screamed and how they had been carried off and how the concubines that remained had been raped and driven out and some even taken away, so that now none cared to live in that house at all. "None," the man finished, "except the Old Lord, who is now wholly the creature of a slave called Cuckoo, who has for many years been in the Old Lord's chamber, while others came and went, because of her cleverness."

"And has this woman command, then?" asked Wang Lung, listening closely.

"For the time she can do anything," replied the man. "And so for the time she closes her hand on everything that can be held and swallows all that can be swallowed. Some day, of course, when the young lords have their affairs settled in other parts they will come back and then she cannot fool them with her talk of a faithful servant to be rewarded, and out she will go. But she has her living made now, although she live to a hundred years."

"And the land?" asked Wang Lung at last, quivering with his eagerness.

"The land?" said the man blankly. To this shopkeeper land meant nothing at all.

"Is it for sale?" said Wang Lung impatiently.

"Oh, the land!" answered the man with indifference, and then as a customer came in he rose and called as he went, "I have heard it is for sale, except the piece where the family are buried for these six generations," and he went his way.

Then Wang Lung rose also, having heard what he came to hear, and he went out and approached again the great gates and the woman came to open to him and he stood without entering and he said to her,

"Tell me first this, will the Old Lord set his own seal to the deeds of sale?"

And the woman answered eagerly, and her eyes were fastened on his,

"He will—he will—on my life!"

Then Wang Lung said to her plainly,

"Will you sell the land for gold or for silver or for jewels?"

112

And her eyes glittered as she spoke and she said,
"I will sell it for jewels!"

17

Now WANG LUNG had more land than a man with an ox can plough and harvest, and more harvest than one man can garner and so he built another small room to his house and he bought an ass and he said to his neighbor Ching,

"Sell me the little parcel of land that you have and leave your lonely house and come into my house and help me with my land." And Ching did this and was glad to do it.

The heavens rained in season then; and the young rice grew and when the wheat was cut and harvested in heavy sheaves, the two men planted the young rice in the flooded fields, more rice than Wang Lung had ever planted he planted this year, for the rains came in abundance of water, so that lands that were before dry were this year fit for rice. Then when this harvest came he and Ching alone could not harvest it, so great it was, and Wang Lung hired two other men as laborers who lived in the village and they harvested it.

He remembered also the idle young lords of the fallen great house as he worked on the land he had bought from the House of Hwang, and he bade his two sons sharply each morning to come into the fields with him and he set them at what labor their small hands could do, guiding the ox and the ass, and making them, if they could accomplish no great labor, at least to know the heat of the sun on their bodies and the weariness of walking back and forth along the furrows.

But O-lan he would not allow to work in the fields for he was no longer a poor man, but a man who could hire his labor done if he would, seeing that never had the land given forth such harvests as it had this year. He was compelled to build yet another room to the house to store his harvests in, or they would not have had space to walk in the house. And he bought three pigs and a flock of fowls to feed on the grains spilled from the harvests.

Then O-lan worked in the house and made new clothes for each one and new shoes, and she made coverings of flowered cloth stuffed with warm new cotton for every bed, and when all was finished they were rich in clothing and in bedding as they had never been. Then she laid herself down upon her bed and gave birth again, although still she would have no one with her; even though she could hire whom she chose, she chose to be alone.

This time she was long at labor and when Wang Lung came home at evening he found his father standing at the door and laughing and saying,

"An egg with a double yolk this time!"

And when Wang Lung went into the inner room there was O-lan upon the bed with two new-born children, a boy and a girl as alike as two grains of rice. He laughed boisterously at what she had done and then he thought of a merry thing to say,

"So this is why you bore two jewels in your bosom!"

And he laughed again at what he had thought of to say, and O-lan, seeing how merry he was, smiled her slow, painful smile.

Wang Lung had, therefore, at this time no sorrow of any kind, unless it was this sorrow, that his eldest girl child neither spoke nor did those things which were right for her age, but only smiled her baby smile still when she caught her father's glance. Whether it was the desperate first year of her life or the starving or what it was, month after month went past and Wang Lung waited for the first words to come from her lips, even for his name which the children called him, "da-da." But no sound came, only the sweet, empty smile, and when he looked at her he groaned forth,

"Little fool—my poor little fool—"

And in his heart he cried to himself,

"If I had sold this poor mouse and they found her thus they would have killed her!"

And as if to make amends to the child he made much of her and took her into the field with him sometimes and she followed him silently about, smiling when he spoke and noticed her there.

In these parts, where Wang Lung had lived all his life and his father and his father's father had lived upon the land, there were famines once in five years or so, or if the gods were lenient, once in seven or eight or even ten years. This was because the heavens rained too much or not at all, or because the river to the north, because of rains and winter snows in distant mountains, came swelling into the fields over the dykes which had been built by men for centuries to confine it.

Time after time men fled from the land and came back to it, but Wang Lung set himself now to build his fortunes so securely that through the bad years to come he need never leave his land again but live on the fruits of the good years, and so subsist until another year came forth. He set himself and the gods helped him and for seven years there were harvests, and every year Wang Lung and his men threshed far more than could be eaten. He hired more laborers each year for his fields until he had six men and he built a new house behind his old one, a large room behind a court and two small rooms on each side of the court beside the large room. The house he covered with tiles, but the walls were still made of the hard tamped earth from the fields, only he had them brushed with lime and they were white and clean. Into these rooms he and his family moved, and the laborers, with Ching at their head, lived in the old house in front.

By this time Wang Lung had thoroughly tried Ching, and he found the man honest and faithful, and he set Ching to be his steward over the men and over the land and he paid him well, two silver pieces a month besides his food. But with all Wang Lung's urging Ching to eat and eat well, the man still put no flesh on his bones, remaining always a small, spare, lean man of great gravity. Nevertheless he labored gladly, pottering silently from dawn until dark, speaking in his feeble voice if there was anything to be said, but happiest and liking it best if there were nothing and he could be silent; and hour after hour he lifted his hoe and let it fall, and at dawn and sunset he would carry to the fields the buckets of water or of manure to put upon the vegetable rows.

But still Wang Lung knew that if any one of the laborers slept too long each day under the date trees or ate more than his share of the beancurd in the common dish or if any bade his wife or child come secretly at harvest time and snatch handfuls of the grain that was being beaten out under the flails, Ching would, at the end of the year when master and man feast together after the harvest, whisper to Wang Lung,

"Such an one and such an one do not ask back for the next year."

And it seemed that the handful of peas and of seed which had passed between these two men made them brothers, except that Wang Lung, who was the younger, took the place of the elder, and Ching never wholly forgot that he was hired and lived in a house which belonged to another.

By the end of the fifth year Wang Lung worked little in his fields himself, having indeed to spend his whole time, so increased were his lands, upon the business and the marketing of his produce, and in directing his workmen. He was greatly hampered by his lack of book knowledge and of the knowledge of the meaning of characters written upon a paper with a camel's hair brush and ink. Moreover, it was a shame to him when he was in a grain shop where grain was bought and sold again, that when a contract was written for so much and for so much of wheat or rice, he must say humbly to the haughty dealers in the town,

"Sir, and will you read it for me, for I am too stupid."

And it was a shame to him that when he must set his name to the contract another, even a paltry clerk, lifted his eyebrows in scorn and, with his brush pointed on the wet ink block, brushed hastily the characters of Wang Lung's name; and greatest shame that when the man called out for a joke,

"Is it the dragon character Lung or the deaf character Lung, or what?" Wang Lung must answer humbly,

"Let it be what you will, for I am too ignorant to know my own name."

It was on such a day one harvest time after he had heard the shout of laughter which went up from the clerks in the grain shop, idle at the noon hour and all listening to anything that went on, and all lads scarcely older than his sons, that he went home angrily over his own land saying to himself,

"Now, not one of those town fools has a foot of land and yet each feels he can laugh a goose cackle at me because I cannot tell the meanings of brush strokes over paper." And then as his indignation wore away, he said in his heart, "It is true that this is a shame to me that I cannot read and write. I will take my elder son from the fields and he shall go to a school in the town and he shall learn, and when I go into the grain markets he will read and write for me so that there may be an end of this hissing laughter against me, who am a landed man."

This seemed to him well and that very day he called to him his elder son, a straight tall lad of twelve years now, looking like his mother for his wide face bones and his big hands and feet but with his father's quickness of eye, and when the boy stood before him Wang Lung said,

"Come out of the fields from this day on, for I need a scholar in the family to read the contracts and to write my name so that I shall not be ashamed in the town."

The lad flushed a high dark red and his eyes shone.

"My father," he said, "so have I wished for these last two years that I might do, but I did not dare to ask it."

Then the younger boy when he heard of it came in crying and complaining, a thing he was wont to do, for he was a wordy, noisy lad from the moment he spoke at all, always ready to cry out that his share was less than that of others, and now he whined forth to his father,

"Well, and I shall not work in the fields, either, and it is not fair that my brother can sit at leisure in a seat and learn something and I must work like a hind, who am your son as well as he!"

Then Wang Lung could not bear his noise and he would give him anything if he cried loudly enough for it, and he said hastily,

"Well and well, go the both of you, and if Heaven in its evil take one of you, there will be the other one with knowledge to do the business for me."

Then he sent the mother of his sons into the town to buy cloth to make a long robe for each lad and he went himself to a paper and ink shop and he bought paper and brushes and two ink blocks, although he knew nothing of such things, and being ashamed to say he did not, was dubious at everything the man brought forward to show him. But at last all was prepared and arrangements made to send the boys to a small school near the city gate kept by an old man who had in past years gone up for government examinations and failed. In the central room of his house therefore he had set benches and tables and for a small sum at each feast day in the year he taught boys in the classics, beating them with his large fan, folded, if they were idle or if they could not repeat to him the pages over which they pored from dawn until sunset.

Only in the warm days of spring and summer did the pupils have a respite for then the old man nodded and slept after he had eaten at noon, and the dark small room was filled with the sound of his slumber. Then the lads whispered and played and drew pictures to show each other of this naughty thing and that, and snickered to see a fly buzzing about the old man's hanging, open jaw, and laid wagers with each other as to whether the fly would enter the cavern of his mouth or not. But when the old teacher opened his eyes suddenly—and there was no telling when he would open them as quickly and secretly as though he had not slept—he saw them before they were aware, and then laid about him with his fan, cracking this skull and that. And hearing the cracks of his stout fan and the cries of the pupils, the neighbors said,

"It is a worthy old teacher, after all." And this is why Wang Lung chose the school for the one where his sons should go to learn.

On the first day when he took them there he walked ahead of them, for it is not meet that father and son walk side by side, and he carried a blue kerchief filled with fresh eggs and these eggs he gave to the old teacher when he arrived. And Wang Lung was awed by the old teacher's great brass spectacles and by his long loose robe of black and by his immense fan, which he held even in winter, and Wang Lung bowed before him and said,

"Sir, here are my two worthless sons. If anything can be driven into their thick brass skulls it is only by beating them, and therefore if you wish to please me, beat them to make them learn." And the two boys stood and stared at the other boys on benches, and these others stared back at the two.

But going home again alone, having left the two lads, Wang Lung's heart was fit to burst with pride and it seemed to him that among all the lads in the room there were none equal to his two lads for tallness and robustness and bright brown faces. Meeting a neighbor coming from the village as he passed through the town gate, he answered the man's inquiry,

"This day I am back from my sons' school." And to the man's surprise he answered with seeming carelessness, "Now I do not need them in the fields and they may as well learn a stomachful of characters."

But to himself he said, passing by,

"It would not surprise me at all if the elder one should become a prefect with all this learning!"

And from that time on the boys were no longer called Elder and Younger, but they were given school names by the old teacher, and this old man, after inquiring into the occupation of their father, erected two names for the sons; for the elder, Nung En, and for the second Nung Wen, and the first word of each name signified one whose wealth is from the earth.

18

THUS WANG LUNG built the fortunes of his house and when the seventh year came and the great river to the north was too heavy with swollen waters, because of excessive rains and snows in the northwest where its source was, it burst it's bounds and came sweeping and flooding all over the lands of that region. But Wang Lung was not afraid. He was not afraid although two-fifths of his land was a lake as deep as a man's shoulders and more.

All through the late spring and early summer the water rose and at last it lay like a great sea, lovely and idle, mirroring cloud and moon and willows and bamboo whose trunks stood submerged. Here and there an earthen house, abandoned by the dwellers, stood up until after days of the water it fell slowly back into the water and the earth. And so it was with all houses that were not, like Wang Lung's built upon a hill, and these hills stood up like islands. And men went to and from town by boat and by raft, and there were those who starved as they ever had.

But Wang Lung was not afraid. The grain markets owed him money and his store-rooms were yet filled full with harvests of the last two years and his houses stood high so that the water was a long way off and he had nothing to fear.

But since much of the land could not be planted he was more idle than he had ever been in his life and being idle and full of good food he grew impatient when he had slept all he could sleep and done all there was to be done. There were, besides, the laborers, whom he hired for a year at a time, and it was foolish for him to work when there were those who ate his rice while they were half idle waiting day after day for the waters to recede. So after he had bade them mend the thatching of the old house and see to the setting of the tiles where the new roof leaked and had commanded them to mend the hoes and the rakes and the plows and to feed the cattle and to buy ducks to herd upon the water and to twist hemp into ropes—all those things which in the old days he did himself when he tilled his land alone—his own hands were empty and he did not know what to do with himself.

Now a man cannot sit all day and stare at a lake of water covering his fields, nor can he eat more than he is able to hold at one time, and when Wang Lung had slept, there was an end to sleeping. The house, as he wandered about it impatiently, was silent, too silent for his vigorous blood. The old man grew very feeble now, half blind and almost wholly deaf, and there was no need of speech with him except to ask if he were warm and fed or if he would drink tea. And it made Wang Lung impatient that the old man could not see how rich his son was and would always mutter if there were tea leaves in his bowl, "A little water is well enough and tea like silver." But there was no telling the old man anything for he forgot it at once and lived drawn into his own world and much of the time he dreamed he was a youth again and in his own fullness and he saw little of what passed him now.

The old man and the elder girl, who never spoke at all but sat beside her grandfather hour after hour, twisting a bit of cloth, folding and re-folding it and smiling at it, these two had nothing to say to a man prosperous and vigorous. When Wang Lung had poured the old man a bowl of tea and had passed his hand over the girl's cheek and received her sweet, empty smile, which passed with such sad swiftness from her face, leaving empty the dim and unshining eyes, there was nothing left. He always turned away from her with a moment's stillness, which was his daughter's mark of sadness on him, and he looked to his two younger children, the boy and the girl which O-lan had borne together, and who now ran about the threshold merrily.

But a man cannot be satisfied with the foolishness of little children and after a brief time of laughter and teasing they went off to their own games and Wang Lung was alone and filled with restlessness. Then it was that he looked at O-lan, his wife, as a man looks at the woman whose body he knows thoroughly and to satiation and who has lived beside him so closely that there is nothing he does not know of her and nothing new which he may expect or hope from her.

And it seemed to Wang Lung that he looked at O-lan for the first time in his life and he saw for the first time that she was a woman whom no man could call other than she was, a dull and common creature, who plodded in silence without thought of how she appeared to others. He saw for the first time that her hair was rough and brown and unoiled and that her face was large and flat and coarse-skinned, and her features too large altogether and without any sort of beauty or light. Her eyebrows were scattered and the hairs too few, and her lips were too wide, and her hands and feet were large and spreading. Looking at her thus with strange eyes, he cried out at her,

"Now anyone looking at you would say you were the wife of a common fellow and never of one who has land which he hires men to plow!"

It was the first time he had ever spoken of how she seemed to him and she answered with a slow painful gaze. She sat upon a bench threading a long needle in and out of a shoe sole and she stopped and held the needle poised and her mouth gaped open and showed her blackened teeth. Then as if she understood at last that he had looked at her as a man at a woman, a thick red flush crept up over her high cheek bones and she muttered,

"Since those two last ones were born together I have not been well. There is a fire in my vitals."

And he saw that in her simplicity she thought he accused her because for more than seven years she had not conceived. And he answered more roughly than he meant to do,

"I mean, cannot you buy a little oil for your hair as other women do and make yourself a new coat of black cloth? And those shoes you wear are not fit for a land proprietor's wife, such as you now are."

But she answered nothing, only looked at him humbly and without knowing what she did, and she hid her feet one over the other under the bench on which she sat. Then, although in his heart he was ashamed that he reproached this creature who through all these years had followed him faithfully as a dog, and although he remembered that when he was poor and labored in the fields himself she left her bed even after a child was born and came to help him in the harvest fields, yet he could not stem the irritation in his breast and he went on ruthlessly, although against his inner will,

"I have labored and have grown rich and I would have my wife look less like a hind. And those feet of yours—"

He stopped. It seemed to him that she was altogether hideous, but the most hideous of all were her big feet in their loose cotton cloth shoes, and he looked at them with anger so that she thrust them yet farther under the bench. And at last she said in a whisper,

"My mother did not bind them, since I was sold so young. But the girl's feet I will bind—the younger girl's feet I will bind."

But he flung himself off because he was ashamed that he was angry at her and angry because she would not be angry in return but only was frightened. And he drew his new black robe on him, saying fretfully,

"Well, and I will go to the tea shop and see if I can hear anything new. There is nothing in my house except fools and a dotard and two children."

His ill-temper grew as he walked to the town because he remembered suddenly that all these new lands of his he could not have bought in a lifetime if O-lan had not seized the handful of jewels from the rich man's house and if she had not given them to him when he commanded her. But when he remembered this he was the more angry and he said as if to answer his own heart rebelliously,

"Well, and but she did not know what she did. She seized them for pleasure as a child may seize a handful of red and green sweets, and she would have hidden them forever in her bosom if I had not found it out."

Then he wondered if she still hid the pearls between her breasts. But where before it had been strange and somehow a thing for him to think about sometimes and to picture in his mind, now he thought of it with contempt, for her breasts had grown flabby and pendulous with many children and had no beauty, and pearls between them were foolish and a waste.

But all this might have been nothing if Wang Lung were still a poor man or if the water was not spread over his fields. But he had money. There was silver hidden in the walls of his house and there was a sack of silver buried under a tile in the floor of his new house and there was silver wrapped in a cloth in the box in his room where he slept with his wife and silver sewed into the mat under their bed and his girdle was full of silver and he had no lack of it. So that now, instead of it passing from him like life blood draining from a wound, it lay in his girdle burning his fingers when he felt of it, and eager to be spent on this or that, and he began to be careless of it and to think what he could do to enjoy the days of his manhood.

Everything seemed not so good to him as it was before. The tea shop which he used to enter timidly, feeling himself but a common country fellow, now seemed dingy and mean to him. In the old days none knew him there and the tea boys were impudent to him, but now people nudged each other when he came in and he could hear a man whisper to another,

"There is that man Wang from the Wang village, he who bought the land from the House of Hwang that winter the Old Lord died when there was the great famine. He is rich, now."

And Wang Lung, hearing this sat down with seeming carelessness, but his heart swelled with pride at what he was. But on this day when he had reproached his wife even the deference he received did not please him and he sat gloomily drinking his tea and feeling that nothing was as good in his life as he had believed. And then he thought suddenly to himself,

"Now why should I drink my tea at this shop, whose owner is a cross-eyed weasel and whose earnings are less than the laborers upon my land, I who have land and whose sons are scholars?"

And he rose up quickly and threw his money on the table and went out before any could speak to him. He wandered forth upon the streets of the town without knowing what it was he wished. Once he passed by a story-teller's booth and for a little while he sat down upon the end of a crowded bench and listened to the man's tale of old days in the Three Kingdoms, when warriors were brave and cunning. But he was still restless and he could not come under the man's spell as the others did and the sound of the little brass gong the man beat wearied him and he stood up again and went on.

Now there was in the town a great tea shop but newly opened and by a man from the south, who understood such business, and Wang Lung had before this passed the place by, filled with horror at the thought of how money was spent there in gambling and in play and in evil women. But now, driven by his unrest from idleness and wishing to escape from the reproach of his own heart when he remembered that he had been unjust to his wife, he went toward this place. He was compelled by his restlessness to see or to hear something new. Thus he stepped across the threshold of the new tea shop into the great, glittering room, full of tables and open to the street as it was, and he went in, bold enough in his bearing and trying to be the more bold because his heart was timid and he remembered that only in the last few years was he more than a poor man who had not at any time more than a silver piece or two, ahead, and a man who had even labored at pulling a ricksha on the streets of a southern city.

At first he did not speak at all in the great tea house but he bought his tea quietly and drank it and looked about him with wonder. This shop was a great hall and the ceiling was set about with gilt and upon the walls there were scrolls hung made of white silk and painted with the figures of women. Now these women Wang Lung looked at secretly and closely and it seemed to him they were women in dreams for none on earth had he seen like them. And the first day he looked at them and drank his tea quickly and went away.

But day after day while the waters held on his land he went to this tea shop and bought tea and sat alone and drank it and stared at the pictures of the beautiful women, and each day he sat longer, since there was nothing for him to do on his land or in his house. So he might have continued for many days on end, for in spite of his silver hidden in a score of places he was still a country-looking fellow and the only one in all that rich tea shop who wore cotton instead of silk and had a braid of hair down his back such as no man in a town will wear. But one evening when he sat drinking and staring from a table near the back of the hall, someone came down from a narrow stair which clung to the furthermost wall and led to the upper floor.

Now this tea shop was the only building in all that town which had an upper floor, except the Western Pagoda, which stood five stories high outside the West Gate. But the pagoda was narrow and more narrow toward the top, while the second floor of the tea shop was as square as that part of the building which stood upon the ground. At night the high singing of women's voices and light laughter floated out of the upper windows and the sweet strumming of lutes struck delicately by the hands of girls. One could hear the music streaming into the streets, especially after midnight, although where Wang Lung sat the clatter and noise of many men drinking tea and the sharp bony click of dice and sparrow dominoes muffled all else.

Thus it was that Wang Lung did not hear behind him on this night the footsteps of a woman creaking upon the narrow stair, and so he started violently when one touched him on the shoulder, not expecting that any would know him here. When he looked up it was into a narrow, handsome, woman's face, the face of Cuckoo, the woman into whose hands he had poured the jewels that day he bought land, and whose hand had held steady the Old Lord's shaking one and helped him to set aright his seal upon the deed of the sale. She laughed when she saw him, and her laughter was a sort of sharp whispering.

"Well, and Wang the farmer!" she said, lingering with malice on the word farmer, "and who would think to see you here!"

It seemed to Wang Lung then that he must prove at any cost to this woman that he was more than a mere country fellow, and he laughed and said too loudly,

"Is not my money as good to spend as another man's? And money I do not lack in these days. I have had good fortune."

Cuckoo stopped at this, her eyes narrow and bright as a snake's eyes, and her voice smooth as oil flowing from a vessel.

"And who has not heard it? And how shall a man better spend the money he has over and above his living than in a place like this, where rich men take their joy and elegant lords gather to take their joy in feasting and pleasure? There is no such wine as ours—have you tasted it, Wang Lung?"

"I have only drunk tea as yet," replied Wang Lung and he was half ashamed. "I have not touched wine or dice."

"Tea!" she exclaimed after him, laughing shrilly. "But we have tiger bone wine and dawn wine and wine of fragrant rice—why need you drink tea?" And as Wang Lung hung his head she said softly and insidiously,

"And I suppose you have not looked at anything else, have you, eh?—No pretty little hands, no sweet-smelling cheeks?"

Wang Lung hung his head yet lower and the red blood rushed into his face and he felt as though everyone near looked at him with mockery and listened to the voice of the woman. But when he took heart to glance about from under his lids, he saw no one paying any heed and the rattling of dice burst out anew and so he said in confusion,

"No—no—I have not—only tea—"

Then the woman laughed again and pointed to the painted silken scrolls and said,

"There they are, their pictures. Choose which one you wish to see and put the silver in my hand and I will place her before you."

"Those!" said Wang Lung, wondering. "I thought they were pictures of dream women, of goddesses in the mountain of Kwen Lwen, such as the story tellers speak of!"

"So they are dream women," rejoined Cuckoo, with mocking good humor, "but dreams such as a little silver will turn into flesh." And she went on her way, nodding and winking at the servants standing about and motioning to Wang Lung as at one of whom she said, "There is a country bumpkin!"

But Wang Lung sat staring at the pictures with a new interest. Up this narrow stairway then, in the rooms above him, there were these women in flesh and blood, and men went up to them—other men than he, of course, but men! Well, and if he were not the man he was, a good and working man, a man with a wife and sons, which picture would he, pretending as a child pretends that he might do a certain thing, pretending then, which would he pretend to take? And he looked at every painted face closely and with intensity as though each were real. Before this they had all seemed equally beautiful, before this when there had been no question of choosing. But now there were clearly some more beautiful than others, and out of the score and more he chose three most beautiful, and out of the three he chose again and he chose one most beautiful, a small, slender thing, a body light as a bamboo and a little face as pointed as a kitten's face, and one hand clasping the stem of a lotus flower in bud, and the hand as delicate as the tendril of a fern uncurled.

He stared at her and as he stared a heat like wine poured through his veins.

"She is like a flower on a quince tree," he said suddenly aloud, and hearing his own voice he was alarmed and ashamed and he rose hastily and put down his money and went out and into the darkness that had now fallen and so to his home.

But over the fields and the water the moonlight hung, a net of silver mist, and in his body his blood ran secret and hot and fast.

19

Now if the waters had at this time receded from Wang Lung's land, leaving it wet and smoking under the sun, so that in a few days of summer heat it would need to have been ploughed and harrowed and seed put in, Wang Lung might never have gone again to the great tea shop. Or if a child had fallen ill or the old man had reached suddenly to the end of his days, Wang Lung might have been caught up in the new thing and so forgotten the pointed face upon the scroll and the body of the woman slender as a bamboo.

But the waters lay placid and unmoved except for the slight summer wind that rose at sunset, and the old man dozed and the two boys trudged to school at dawn and were away until evening and in his house Wang Lung was restless and he avoided the eyes of O-lan who looked at him miserably as he went here and there and flung himself down in a chair and rose from it without drinking the tea she poured and without smoking the pipe he had lit. At the end of one long day, more long than any other, in the seventh month, when the twilight lingered murmurous and sweet with the breath of the lake, he stood at the door of his house, and suddenly without a word he turned abruptly and went into his room and put on his new coat, even the coat of black shining cloth, as shining almost as silk, that O-lan made for feast days, and with no word to anyone he went over the narrow paths along the water's edge and through the fields until he came to the darkness of the city gate and through this he went and through the streets until he came to the new tea shop.

There every light was lit, bright oil lamps which are to be bought in the foreign cities of the coast, and men sat under the lights drinking and talking, their robes open to the evening coolness, and everywhere fans moved to and fro and good laughter flowed out like music into the street. All the gayety which Wang Lung had never had from his labor on the land was held here in the walls of this house, where men met to play and never to work.

Wang Lung hesitated upon the threshold and he stood in the bright light which streamed from the open doors. And he might have stood there and gone away, for he was fearful and timid in his heart still, although his blood was rushing through his body fit to burst his veins, but there came out of the shadows on the edge of the light a woman who had been leaning idly against the doorway and it was Cuckoo. She came forward when she saw a man's figure, for it was her business to get customers for the women of the house, but when she saw who it was, she shrugged her shoulders and said,

"Ah, it is only the farmer!"

Wang was stung with the sharp carelessness in her voice, and his sudden anger gave him a courage he had not otherwise, so that he said,

"Well, and may I not come into the house and may I not do as other men?"

And she shrugged herself again and laughed and said,

"If you have the silver that other men have, you may do as they do."

And he wished to show her that he was lordly and rich enough to do as he liked, and he thrust his hand into his girdle and brought it out full of silver and he said to her,

"Is it enough and is it not enough?"

She stared at the handful of silver and said then without further delay,

"Come and say which one you wish."

And Wang Lung, without knowing what he said, muttered forth,

"Well, and I do not know that I want anything." And then his desire overcame him and he whispered, "That little one— that one with the pointed chin and the little small face, a face like a quince blossom for white and pink, and she holds a lotus bud in her hand."

The woman nodded easily and beckoning him she threaded her way between the crowded tables, and Wang Lung followed her at a distance. At first it seemed to him that every man looked up and watched him but when he took courage to see he saw that none paid him any heed, except for one or two who called out, "Is it late enough, then, to go to the women?" and another called, "Here is a lusty fellow who needs must begin early!"

But by this time they were walking up the narrow straight stairway, and this Wang Lung did with difficulty, for it was the first time he had ever climbed steps in a house. Nevertheless, when they reached the top, it was the same as a house on the earth, except that is seemed a mighty way up when he passed a window and looked into the sky. The woman led the way down a close dark hall, then, and she cried as she went,

"Now here is the first man of the night!"

All along the hall doors opened suddenly and here and there girls' heads showed themselves in patches of light, as flowers burst out of their sheaths in the sun, but, Cuckoo called cruelly,

"No, not you—and not you—no one has asked for any of you! This one is for the little pink-faced dwarf from Soochow —for Lotus!"

A ripple of sound ran down the hall, indistinct, derisive, and one girl, ruddy as a pomegranate, called out in a big voice,

"And Lotus may have this fellow—he smells of the fields and of garlic!"

This Wang Lung heard, although he disdained to answer, although her words smote him like a dagger thrust because he feared that he looked indeed what he was, a farmer. But he went on stoutly when he remembered the good silver in his girdle, and at last the woman struck a closed door harshly with the flat palm of her hand and went in without waiting and there upon a bed covered with a flowered red quilt, sat a slender girl.

If one had told him there were small hands like these he would not have believed it, hands so small and bones so fine and fingers so pointed with long nails stained the color of lotus buds, deep and rosy. And if one had told him that there could be feet like these, little feet thrust into pink satin shoes no longer than a man's middle finger, and swinging childishly over the bed's edge—if anyone had told him he would not have believed it.

He sat stiffly on the bed beside her, staring at her, and he saw that she was like the picture and having seen the picture he would have known her if he had met her. But most of all her hand was like the painted hand, curling and fine and white as milk. Her two hands lay curling into each other upon the pink

129

and silken lap of her robe, and he would not have dreamed that they were to be touched.

He looked at her as he had looked at the picture and he saw the figure slender as bamboo in its tight short upper coat; he saw the small pointed face set in its painted prettiness above the high collar lined with white fur; he saw the round eyes, the shape of apricots, so that now at last he understood what the story-tellers meant when they sang of the apricot eyes of the beauties of old. And for him she was not flesh and blood but the painted picture of a woman.

Then she lifted that small curling hand and put it upon his shoulder and she passed it slowly down the length of his arm, very slowly. And although he had never felt anything so light, so soft as that touch, although if he had not seen it, he would not have known that it passed, he looked and saw the small hand moving down his arm, and it was as though fire followed it and burned under through his sleeve and into the flesh of his arm, and he watched the hand until it reached the end of his sleeve and then it fell with an instant's practiced hesitation upon his bare wrist and then into the loose hollow of his hard dark hand. And he began to tremble, not knowing how to receive it.

Then he heard laughter, light, quick, tinkling as the silver bell upon a pagoda shaking in the wind, and a little voice like laughter said,

"Oh, and how ignorant you are, you great fellow? Shall we sit here the night through while you stare?"

And at that he seized her hand between both of his, but carefully, because it was like a fragile dry leaf, hot and dry, and he said to her imploringly and not knowing what he said,

"I do not know anything—teach me!"

And she taught him.

Now Wang Lung became sick with the sickness which is greater than any a man can have. He had suffered under labor in the sun and he had suffered under the dry icy winds of the bitter desert and he had suffered from starvation when the fields would not bear and he had suffered from the despair of laboring without hope upon the streets of a southern city. But under none of these did he suffer as he now did under this slight girl's hand.

Every day he went to the tea shop; every evening he waited until she would receive him, and every night he went in to her.

Each night he went in and each night again he was the country fellow who knew nothing, trembling at the door, sitting stiffly beside her, waiting for her signal of laughter, and then fevered, filled with a sickened hunger, he followed slavishly, bit by bit, her unfolding, until the moment of crisis, when, like a flower that is ripe for plucking, she was willing that he should grasp her wholly.

Yet never could he grasp her wholly, and this it was which kept him fevered and thirsty, even if she gave him his will of her. When O-lan had come to his house it was health to his flesh and he lusted for her robustly as a beast for its mate and he took her and was satisfied and he forgot her and did his work content. But there was no such content now in his love for this girl, and there was no health in her for him. At night when she would have no more of him, pushing him out of the door petulantly, with her small hands suddenly strong on his shoulders, his silver thrust into her bosom, he went away hungry as he came. It was as though a man, dying of thirst, drank the salt water of the sea which, though it is water, yet dries his blood into thirst and yet greater thirst so that in the end he dies, maddened by his very drinking. He went in to her and he had his will of her again and again and he came away unsatisfied.

All during that hot summer Wang Lung loved thus this girl. He knew nothing of her, whence she came or what she was; when they were together he said not a score of words and he scarcely listened to the constant running of her speech, light and interspersed with laughter like a child's. He only watched her face, her hands, the postures of her body, the meaning of her wide sweet eyes, waiting for her. He had never enough of her, and he went back to his house in the dawn, dazed and unsatisfied.

The days were endless. He would not sleep any more upon his bed, making a pretense of heat in the room, and he spread a mat under the bamboos and slept there fitfully, lying awake to stare into the pointed shadows of the bamboo leaves, his breast filled with a sweet sick pain he could not understand.

And if any spoke to him, his wife or his children, or if Ching came to him and said, "The waters will soon recede and what is there we should prepare of seed?" he shouted and said,

"Why do you trouble me?"

And all the time his heart was like to burst because he could not be satisfied of this girl.

Thus as the days went on and he lived only to pass the day until the evening came, he would not look at the grave faces of O-lan and of the children, suddenly sober in their play when he approached, nor even at his old father who peered at him and asked,

"What is this sickness that turns you full of evil temper and your skin as yellow as clay?"

And as these days went past to the night, the girl Lotus did what she would with him. When she laughed at the braid of his hair, although part of every day he spent in braiding and in brushing it, and said, "Now the men of the south do not have these monkey tails!" he went without a word and had it cut off, although neither by laughter or scorn had anyone been able to persuade him to it before.

When O-lan saw what he had done she burst out in terror,

"You have cut off your life!"

But he shouted at her,

"And shall I look an old-fashioned fool forever? All the young men of the city have their hair cut short."

Yet he was afraid in his heart of what he had done, and yet so he would have cut off his life if the girl Lotus had commanded it or desired it, because she had every beauty which had ever come into his mind to desire in a woman.

His good brown body that he washed but rarely, deeming the clean sweat of his labor washing enough for ordinary times, his body he now began to examine as if it were another man's, and he washed himself every day so that his wife said, troubled,

"You will die with all this washing!"

He bought sweet-smelling soap in the shop, a piece of red scented stuff from foreign parts, and he rubbed it on his flesh, and not for any price would he have eaten a stalk of garlic, although it was a thing he had loved before, lest he stink before her.

And none in his house knew what to make of all these things.

He bought also new stuffs for clothes, and although O-lan had always cut his robes, making them wide and long for good measure and sewing them stoutly this way and that for strength, now he was scornful of her cutting and sewing and he took the stuffs to a tailor in the town and he had his clothes made as the men in the town had theirs, light grey silk for a robe, cut neatly to his body and with little to spare, and over this a black satin sleeveless coat. And he bought the first shoes he had

had in his life not made by a woman, and they were black velvet shoes such as the Old Lord had worn flapping at his heels.

But these fine clothes he was ashamed to wear suddenly before O-lan and his children. He kept them folded in sheets of brown oiled paper and he left them at the tea shop with a clerk he had come to know, and for a price the clerk let him go into an inner room secretly and put them on before he went up the stairs. And beyond this he bought a silver ring washed with gold for his finger, and as hair grew where it had been shaved above his forehead, he smoothed it with a fragrant foreign oil from a small bottle for which he had paid a whole piece of silver.

But O-lan looked at him in astonishment and did not know what to make from all this, except that one day after staring at him for a long time as they ate rice at noon, she said heavily,

"There is that about you which makes me think of one of the lords in the great house."

Wang Lung laughed loudly then and he said,

"And am I always to look like a hind when we have enough and to spare?"

But in his heart he was greatly pleased and for that day he was more kindly with her than he had been for many days.

Now the money, the good silver, went streaming out of his hands. There was not only the price he must pay for his hours with the girl, but there was the pretty demanding of her desires. She would sigh and murmur, as though her heart were half broken with her desire,

"Ah me—ah me!"

And when he whispered, having learned at last to speak in her presence, "What now, my little heart?" she answered, "I have no joy today in you because Black Jade, that one across the hall from me, has a lover who gave her a gold pin for her hair, and I have only this old silver thing, which I have had forever and a day."

And then for his life's sake he could not but whisper to her, pushing aside the smooth black curve of her hair that he might have the delight of seeing her small long-lobed ears,

"And so will I buy a gold pin for the hair of my jewel."

For all these names of love she had taught him, as one teaches new words to a child. She had taught him to say them to her and he could not say them enough for his own heart, even while he stammered them, he whose speech had all his life been only of planting and of harvests and of sun and rain.

Thus the silver came out of the wall and out of the sack, and O-lan, who in the old days might have said to him easily enough, "And why do you take the money from the wall," now said nothing, only watching him in great misery, knowing well that he was living some life apart from her and apart even from the land, but not knowing what life it was. But she had been afraid of him from that day on which he had seen clearly that she had no beauty of hair or of person, and when he had seen her feet were large, and she was afraid to ask him anything because of his anger that was always ready for her now.

There came a day when Wang Lung returned to his house over the fields and he drew near to her as she washed his clothes at the pool. He stood there silent for a while and then he said to her roughly, and he was rough because he was ashamed and would not acknowledge his shame in his heart,

"Where are those pearls you had?"

And she answered timidly, looking up from the edge of the pool and from the clothes she was beating upon a smooth flat stone,

"The pearls? I have them."

And he muttered, not looking at her but at her wrinkled, wet hands,

"There is no use in keeping pearls for nothing."

Then she said slowly,

"I thought one day I might have them set in earrings," and fearing his laughter she said again, "I could have them for the younger girl when she is wed."

And he answered her loudly, hardening his heart,

"Why should that one wear pearls with her skin as black as earth? Pearls are for fair women!" And then after an instant's silence he cried out suddenly, "Give them to me—I have need of them!"

Then slowly she thrust her wet wrinkled hand into her bosom and she drew forth the small package and she gave it to him and watched him as he unwrapped it; and the pearls lay in his hand and they caught softly and fully the light of the sun, and he laughed.

But O-lan returned to the beating of his clothes and when tears dropped slowly and heavily from her eyes she did not put up her hand to wipe them away; only she beat the more steadily with her wooden stick upon the clothes spread over the stone.

20

AND THUS it might have gone forever until all the silver was spent had not that one, Wang Lung's uncle, returned suddenly without explanation of where he had been or what he had done. He stood in the door as though he had dropped from a cloud, his ragged clothes unbuttoned and girdled loosely as ever about him, and his face as it always was but wrinkled and hardened with the sun and the wind. He grinned widely at them all as they sat about the table at their early morning meal, and Wang Lung sat agape, for he had forgotten that his uncle lived and it was like a dead man returning to see him. The old man his father blinked and stared and did not recognize the one who had come until he called out,

"Well, and Elder Brother and his son and his sons and my sister-in-law."

Then Wang Lung rose, dismayed in his heart but upon the surface of his face and voice courteous.

"Well, and my uncle and have you eaten?"

"No," replied his uncle easily, "but I will eat with you."

He sat himself down, then, and he drew a bowl and chopsticks to him and he helped himself freely to rice and dried salt fish and to salted carrots and to the dried beans that were upon the table. He ate as though he were very hungry and none spoke until he supped down loudly three bowls of the thin rice gruel, cracking quickly between his teeth the bones of the fish and the kernels of the beans. And when he had eaten he said simply and as though it was his right,

"Now I will sleep, for I am without sleep these three nights."

Then when Wang Lung, dazed and not knowing what else to do, led him to his father's bed, his uncle lifted the quilts and felt of the good cloth and of the clean new cotton and he looked at the wooden bedstead and at the good table and at the great wooden chair which Wang Lung had bought for his father's room, and he said,

"Well, and I heard you were rich but I did not know you were as rich as this," and he threw himself upon the bed and drew the quilt about his shoulders, all warm with summer though it was, and everything he used as though it was his own, and he was asleep without further speech.

Wang Lung went back to the middle room in great consternation for he knew very well that now his uncle would never be driven forth again, now that he knew Wang Lung had wherewith to feed him. And Wang Lung thought of this and thought of his uncle's wife with great fear because he saw that they would come to his house and none could stop them.

As he feared so it happened. His uncle stretched himself upon the bed at last after noon had passed and he yawned loudly three times and came out of the room, shrugging the clothes together upon his body and he said to Wang Lung,

"Now I will fetch my wife and my son. There are the three of us mouths, and in this great house of yours it will never be missed what we eat and the poor clothes we wear."

Wang Lung could do nothing but answer with sullen looks, for it is a shame to a man when he has enough and to spare to drive his own father's brother and son from the house. And Wang Lung knew that if he did this it would be a shame to him in the village where he was now respected because of his prosperity and so he did not dare to say anything. But he commanded the laborers to move altogether into the old house so that the rooms by the gate might be left empty and into these that very day in the evening his uncle came, bringing his wife and his son. And Wang Lung was exceedingly angry and the more angry because he must bury it all in his heart and answer with smiles and welcome his relatives. This, although when he saw the fat smooth face of his uncle's wife he felt fit to burst with his anger and when he saw the scampish, impudent face of his uncle's son, he could scarcely keep his hand down from slapping it. And for three days he did not go into the town because of his anger.

Then when they were all accustomed to what had taken place and when O-lan had said to him, "Cease to be angry. It is a thing to be borne," and Wang Lung saw that his uncle and his uncle's wife and son would be courteous enough for the sake of their food and their shelter, then his thoughts turned more violently than ever to the girl Lotus and he muttered to himself,

"When a man's house if full of wild dogs he must seek peace elsewhere."

And all the old fever and pain burned in him and he was still never satisfied of his love.

Now what O-lan had not seen in her simplicity nor the old man because of the dimness of his age nor Ching because of his friendship, the wife of Wang Lung's uncle saw at once and she cried out, the laughter slanting from her eyes,

"Now Wang Lung is seeking to pluck a flower somewhere." And when O-lan looked at her humbly, not understanding, she laughed and said again, "The melon must always be split wide open before you can see the seeds, eh? Well, then, plainly, your man is mad over another woman!"

This Wang Lung heard his uncle's wife say in the court outside his window as he lay dozing and weary in his room one early morning, exhausted with his love. He was quickly awake, and he listened further, aghast at the sharpness of this woman's eyes. The thick voice rumbled on, pouring like oil from her fat throat.

"Well, and I have seen many a man, and when one smooths his hair and buys new clothes and will have his shoes velvet all of a sudden, then there is a new woman and that is sure."

There came a broken sound from O-lan, what it was she said he could not hear, but his uncle's wife said again,

"And it is not to be thought, poor fool, that one woman is enough for any man, and if it is a weary hard-working woman who has worn away her flesh working for him, it is less than enough for him. His fancy runs elsewhere the more quickly, and you, poor fool, have never been fit for a man's fancy and little better than an ox for his labor. And it is not for you to repine when he has money and buys himself another to bring her to his house, for all men are so, and would my old do-nothing also, except the poor wretch has never had enough silver in his life to feed himself even."

This she said and more, but no more than this did Wang Lung hear upon his bed, for his thought stopped at what she had said. Now suddenly did he see how to satisfy his hunger and his thirst after this girl he loved. He would buy her and bring her to his house and make her his own so that no other man could come in to her and so could he eat and be fed and drink and be satisfied. And he rose up at once from his bed and he went out and motioned secretly to the wife of his uncle and he said, when she had followed him outside the gate and under the date tree where none could hear what he had to say,

"I listened and heard what you said in the courts and you are right. I have need of more than that one and why should I not, seeing that I have land to feed us all?"

She answered volubly and eagerly,

"And why not, indeed? So have all men who have prospered. It is only the poor man who must needs drink from one cup." Thus she spoke, knowing what he would say next, and he went on as she had planned,

"But who will negotiate for me and be the middleman? A man cannot go to a woman and say, 'Come to my house.' "

To this she answered instantly,

"Now do you leave this affair in my hands. Only tell me which woman it is and I will manage the affair."

Then Wang Lung answered unwillingly and timidly, for he had never spoken her name aloud before to anyone,

"It is the woman called Lotus."

It seemed to him that everyone must know and have heard of Lotus, forgetting how only a short two summers' moons before he had not known she lived. He was impatient, therefore, when his uncle's wife asked further,

"And where her home?"

"Now where," he answered with asperity, "where except in the great tea shop on the main street of the town?"

"The one called the House of Flowers?"

"And what other?" Wang Lung retorted.

She mused awhile, fingering her pursed lower lip, and she said at last,

"I do not know anyone there. I shall have to find a way. Who is the keeper of this woman?"

And when he told her it was Cuckoo, who had been slave in the great house, she laughed and said,

"Oh, that one? Is that what she did after the Old Lord died in her bed one night! Well, and it is what she would do."

Then she laughed again, a cackling "Heh—heh—heh—" and she said easily,

"That one! But it is a simple matter, indeed. Everything is plain. That one! From the beginning that one would do anything, even to making a mountain, if she could feel silver enough in her palm for it."

And Wang Lung, hearing this, felt his mouth suddenly dry and parched and his voice came from him in a whisper,

"Silver, then! Silver and gold! Anything to the very price of my land!"

Then from a strange and contrary fever of love Wang Lung would not go again to the great tea house until the affair was arranged. To himself he said,

"And if she will not come to my house and be for me only, cut my throat and I will not go near her again."

But when he thought the words, "if she will not come," his heart stood still with fear, so that he continually ran to his uncle's wife saying,

"Now, lack of money shall not close the gate." And he said again, "Have you told Cuckoo that I have silver and gold for my will?" and he said, "Tell her she shall do no work of any kind in my house but she shall wear only silken garments and eat shark's fins if she will every day," until at last the fat woman grew impatient and cried out at him, rolling her eyes back and forth,

"Enough and enough! Am I a fool, or is this the first time I have managed a man and a maid? Leave me alone and I will do it. I have said everything many times."

Then there was nothing to do except to gnaw his fingers and to see the house suddenly as Lotus might see it and he hurried O-lan into this and that, sweeping and washing and moving tables and chairs, so that she, poor woman, grew more and more terror stricken for well she knew by now, although he said nothing, what was to come to her.

Now Wang Lung could not bear to sleep any more with O-lan and he said to himself that with two women in the house there must be more rooms and another court and there must be a place where he could go with his love and be separate. So while he waited for his uncle's wife to complete the matter, he called his laborers and commanded them to build another court to the house behind the middle room, and around the court three rooms, one large and two small on either side. And the laborers stared at him, but dared not reply and he would not tell them anything, but he superintended them himself, so that he need not talk with Ching even of what he did. And the men dug the earth from the fields and made the walls and beat them down, and Wang Lung sent to the town and bought tiles for the roof.

Then when the rooms were finished and the earth smoothed and beaten down for a floor, he had bricks bought and the men set them closely together and welded them with lime and there was a good brick floor to the three rooms for Lotus. And Wang Lung bought red cloth to hang at the doors for curtains and he bought a new table and two carved chairs to put on either side and two painted scrolls of pictured hills and water to hang upon the wall behind the table. And he bought a round red lacquered comfit dish with a cover, and in this he put sesame cakes and larded sweets and he put the box on the table. Then he bought a wide and deep carven bed, big enough for a small room in itself, and he bought flowered curtains to hang about it. But in all this he was ashamed to ask O-lan anything, and so in the evenings his uncle's wife came in and she hung the bed curtains and did the things a man is too clumsy for doing.

Then all was finished and there was nothing to do, and a moon of days had passed and the thing was not yet complete. So Wang Lung dallied alone in the little new court he had built for Lotus and he thought of a little pool to make in the center of the court, and he called a laborer and the man dug a pool three feet square and set it about with tiles, and Wang Lung went into the city and bought five goldfish for it. Then he could think of nothing more to be done, and again he waited impatient and fevered.

During all this time he said nothing to anyone except to scold the children if they were filthy at their noses or to roar out at O-lan that she had not brushed her hair for three days and more, so that at last one morning O-lan burst into tears and wept aloud, as he had never seen her weep before, even when they starved, or at any other time. He said harshly, therefore,

"Now what, woman? Cannot I say comb out your horse's tail of hair without this trouble over it?"

But she answered nothing except to say over and over, moaning,

"I have borne you sons—I have borne you sons—"

And he was silenced and uneasy and he muttered to himself for he was ashamed before her and so he let her alone. It was true that before the law he had no complaint against his wife, for she had borne him three good sons and they were alive, and there was no excuse for him except his desire.

Thus it went until one day his uncle's wife came and said,

"The thing is complete. The woman who is keeper for the

master of the tea house will do it for a hundred pieces of silver on her palm at one time, and the girl will come for jade earrings and a ring of jade and a ring of gold and two suits of satin clothes and two suits of silk clothes and a dozen pairs of shoes and two silken quilts for her bed."

Of all this Wang Lung heard only this part, "The thing is complete—" and he cried out,

"Let it be done—let it be done—" and he ran into the inner room and he got out silver and poured it into her hands, but secretly still, for he was unwilling that anyone should see the good harvests of so many years go thus, and to his uncle's wife he said, "And for yourself take a good ten pieces of silver."

Then she made a feint of refusal, drawing up her fat body and rolling her head this way and that and crying in a loud whisper,

"No, and I will not. We are one family and you are my son and I am your mother and this I do for you and not for silver." But Wang Lung saw her hand outstretched as she denied, and into it he poured the good silver and he counted it well spent.

Then he bought pork and beef and mandarin fish and bamboo sprouts and chestnuts, and he bought a snarl of dried birds' nests from the south to brew for soup, and he bought dried shark's fins and every delicacy he knew he bought and then he waited, if that burning, restless impatience within him could be called a waiting.

On a shining glittering fiery day in the eighth moon, which is the last end of summer, she came to his house. From afar Wang Lung saw her coming. She rode in a closed sedan chair of bamboo borne upon men's shoulders and he watched the sedan moving this way and that upon the narrow paths skirting the fields, and behind it followed the figure of Cuckoo. Then for an instant he knew fear and he said to himself,

"What am I taking into my house?"

And scarcely knowing what he did he went quickly into the room where he had slept for these many years with his wife and he shut the door and there in the darkness of the room he waited in confusion until he heard his uncle's wife calling loudly for him to come out, for one was at the gate.

Then abashed and as though he had never seen the girl before he went slowly out, hanging his head over his fine clothes, and his eyes looking here and there, but never ahead. But Cuckoo hailed him merrily,

"Well, and I did not know we would be doing business like this!"

Then she went to the chair which the men had set down and she lifted the curtain and clucked her tongue and she said,

"Come out, my Lotus Flower, here is your house and here your lord."

And Wang Lung was in an agony because he saw upon the faces of the chair men wide grins of laughter and he thought to himself,

"Now these are loafers from the town streets and they are worthless fellows," and he was angry that he felt his face hot and red and so he would not speak aloud at all.

Then the curtain was lifted and before he knew what he did he looked and he saw sitting in the shadowy recess of the chair, painted and cool as a lily, the girl Lotus. He forgot everything, even his anger against the grinning fellows from the town, everything but that he had bought this woman for his own and she had come to his house forever, and he stood stiff and trembling, watching as she rose, graceful as though a wind had passed over a flower. Then as he watched and could not take his eyes away, she took Cuckoo's hand and stepped out, keeping her head bowed and her eyelids drooped as she walked, tottering and swaying upon her little feet, and leaning upon Cuckoo. And as she passed him she did not speak to him, but she whispered only to Cuckoo, faintly,

"Where is my apartment?"

Then his uncle's wife came forward to her other side and between them they led the girl into the court and into the new rooms that Wang Lung had built for her. And of all Wang Lung's house there was none to see her pass, for he had sent the laborers and Ching away for the day to work on a distant field, and O-lan had gone somewhere he knew not and had taken the two little ones with her and the boys were in school and the old man slept against the wall and heard and saw nothing, and as for the poor fool, she saw no one who came and went and knew no face except her father's and her mother's. But when Lotus had gone in Cuckoo drew the curtains after her.

Then after a time Wang Lung's uncle's wife came out, laughing a little maliciously, and she dusted her hands together as though to free them of something that clung to them.

"She reeks of perfume and paint, that one," she said still laughing. "Like a regular bad one she smells." And then she
142

said with a deeper malice, "She is not so young as she looks, my nephew! I will dare to say this, that if she had not been on the edge of an age when men will cease soon to look at her, it is doubtful whether jade in her ears and gold on her fingers and even silk and satin would have tempted her to the house of a farmer, and even a well-to-do farmer." And then seeing the anger on Wang Lung's face at this too plain speaking she added hastily, "But beautiful she is and I have never seen another more beautiful and it will be as sweet as the eight-jeweled rice at a feast after your years with the thick-boned slave from the House of Hwang."

But Wang Lung answered nothing, only he moved here and there through the house and he listened and he could not be still. At last he dared to lift the red curtain and to go into the court he had built for Lotus and then into the darkened room where she was and there he was beside her for the whole day until night.

All this time O-lan had not come near the house. At dawn she had taken a hoe from the wall and she called the children and she took a little cold food wrapped up in a cabbage leaf and she had not returned. But when night came on she entered, silent and earth-stained and dark with weariness, and the children silent behind her, and she said nothing to anyone, but she went into the kitchen and prepared food and set it upon the table as she always did, and she called the old man and put the chopsticks in his hand and she fed the poor fool and then she ate a little with the children. Then when they slept and Wang Lung still sat at the table dreaming she washed herself for sleeping and at last she went into her accustomed room and slept alone upon her bed.

Then did Wang Lung eat and drink of his love night and day. Day after day he went into the room where Lotus lay indolent upon her bed and he sat beside her and watched her at all she did. She never came forth in the heat of the early autumn days, but she lay while the woman Cuckoo bathed her slender body with lukewarm water and rubbed oil into her flesh and perfume and oil into her hair. For Lotus had said wilfully that Cuckoo must stay with her as her servant and she paid her prodigally so that the woman was willing enough to serve one instead of a score, and she and Lotus, her mistress, dwelt apart from the others in the new court that Wang Lung had made.

All day the girl lay in the cool darkness of her room, nibbling sweetmeats and fruits, and wearing nothing but single garments of green summer silk, a little tight coat cut to her waist and wide trousers beneath, and thus Wang Lung found her when he came to her and he ate and drank of his love.

Then at sunset she sent him away with her pretty petulance, and Cuckoo bathed and perfumed her again and put on her fresh clothes, soft white silk against her flesh and peach-colored silk outside, the silken garments that Wang Lung had given, and upon her feet Cuckoo put small embroidered shoes, and then the girl walked into the court and examined the little pool with its five gold fish, and Wang Lung stood and stared at the wonder of what he had. She swayed upon her little feet and to Wang Lung there was nothing so wonderful for beauty in the world as her pointed little feet and her curling helpless hands.

And he ate and drank of his love and he feasted alone and he was satisfied.

21

IT WAS not to be supposed that the coming of this one called Lotus and of her serving woman Cuckoo into Wang Lung's house could be accomplished altogether without stir and discord of some sort, since more than one woman under one roof is not for peace. But Wang Lung had not foreseen it. And even though he saw by O-lan's sullen looks and Cuckoo's sharpness that something was amiss, he would not pay heed to it and he was careless of anyone so long as he was still fierce with his desire.

Nevertheless, when day passed into night, and night changed into dawn, Wang Lung saw that it was true the sun rose in the morning, and this woman Lotus was there, and the moon rose in its season and she was there for his hand to grasp when it would, and his thirst of love was somewhat slaked and he saw things he had not seen before.

For one thing, he saw that there was trouble at once between O-lan and Cuckoo. This was an astonishment to him, for he was prepared for O-lan to hate Lotus, having heard many times of such things, and some women will even hang themselves upon a beam with a rope when a man takes a second woman into the house, and others will scold and contrive to make his life worthless for what he has done, and he was glad that O-lan was a silent woman for at least she could not think of words against him. But he had not foreseen that whereas she would be silent of Lotus, her anger would find its vent against Cuckoo.

Now Wang Lung had thought only of Lotus and when she begged him,

"Let me have this woman for my servant, seeing that I am altogether alone in the world, for my father and my mother died when I could not yet talk and my uncle sold me as soon as I was pretty to a life such as I have had, and I have no one."

This she said with her tears, always abundant and ready and glittering in the corners of her pretty eyes, and Wang Lung could have denied her nothing she asked when she looked up at him so. Besides, it was true enough that the girl had no one to serve her, and it was true she would be alone in his house, for it was plain enough and to be expected that O-lan would not serve the second one, and she would not speak to her or notice that she was in the house at all. There was only the uncle of Lotus then, and it was against Wang Lung's stomach to have that one peeping and prying and near to Lotus for her to talk to of him, and so Cuckoo was as good as any and he knew no other woman who would come.

But it seemed that O-lan, when she saw Cuckoo, grew angry with a deep and sullen anger that Wang Lung had never seen and did not know was in her. Cuckoo was willing enough to be friends, since she had her pay from Wang Lung, albeit she did not forget that in the great house she had been in the lord's chamber and O-lan a kitchen slave and one of many. Nevertheless, she called out to O-lan well enough when first she saw her,

"Well, and my old friend, here we are in a house together again, and you mistress and first wife—my mother—and how things are changed!"

But O-lan stared at her and when it came into her understanding who it was and what she was, she answered nothing but she put down the jar of water she carried and she went into the middle room where Wang Lung sat between his times of love, and she said to him plainly,

"What is this slave woman doing in our house?"

Wang Lung looked east and west. He would have liked to speak out to say in a surly voice of master, "Well, and it is my house and whoever I say may come in, she shall come in, and who are you to ask?" But he could not because of some shame in him when O-lan was there before him, and his shame made him angry, because when he reasoned it, there was no need for shame and he had done no more than any man may do who has silver to spare.

Still, he could not speak out, and he only looked east and west and feigned to have mislaid his pipe in his garments, and he fumbled in his girdle. But O-lan stood there solidly on her big feet and waited and when he said nothing she asked again plainly in the same words,

"What is this slave woman doing in our house?"

Then Wang Lung seeing she would have an answer, said feebly,

"And what is it to you?"

And O-lan said,

"I bore her haughty looks all during my youth in the great house and her running into the kitchen a score of times a day and crying out 'now tea for the lord'—'now food for the lord'—and it was always this is too hot and that is too cold, and that is badly cooked, and I was too ugly and too slow and too this and too that. . ."

But still Wang Lung did not answer, for he did not know what to say.

Then O-lan waited and when he did not speak, the hot, scanty tears welled slowly into her eyes, and she winked them to hold back the tears, and at last she took the corner of her blue apron and wiped her eyes and she said at last,

"It is a bitter thing in my house, and I have no mother's house to go back to anywhere."

And when Wang Lung was still silent and answered nothing at all, but he sat down to his pipe and lit it, and he said nothing still, she looked at him piteously and sadly out of her strange dumb eyes that were like a beast's eyes that cannot speak, and then she went away, creeping and feeling for the door because of her tears that blinded her.

Wang Lung watched her as she went and he was glad to be alone, but still he was ashamed and he was still angry that he was ashamed and he said to himself and he muttered the words aloud and restlessly, as though he quarreled with someone,

"Well, and other men are so and I have been good enough to

146

her, and there are men worse than I." And he said at last that O-lan must bear it.

But O-lan was not finished with it, and she went her way silently. In the morning she heated water and presented it to the old man, and to Wang Lung if he were not in the inner court she presented tea, but when Cuckoo went to find hot water for her mistress the cauldron was empty and not all her loud questionings would stir any response from O-lan. Then there was nothing but that Cuckoo must herself boil water for her mistress if she would have it. But then it was time to stir the morning gruel and there was not space in the cauldron for more water and O-lan would go steadily to her cooking, answering nothing to Cuckoo's loud crying,

"And is my delicate lady to lie thirsting and gasping in her bed for a swallow of water in the morning?"

But O-lan would not hear her; only she pushed more grass and straw into the bowels of the oven, spreading it as carefully and as thriftily as ever she had in the old days when one leaf was precious enough because of the fire it would make under food. Then Cuckoo went complaining loudly to Wang Lung and he was angry that his love must be marred by such things and he went to O-lan to reproach her and he shouted at her,

"And cannot you add a dipperful of water to the cauldron in the mornings?"

But she answered with a sullenness deeper than ever upon her face,

"I am not slave of slaves in this house at least."

Then he was angry beyond bearing and he seized O-lan's shoulder and he shook her soundly and he said,

"Do not be yet more of a fool. It is not for the servant but for the mistress."

And she bore his violence and she looked at him and she said simply,

"And to that one you gave my two pearls!"

Then his hand dropped and he was speechless and his anger was gone and he went away ashamed and he said to Cuckoo,

"We will build another stove and I will make another kitchen. The first wife knows nothing of the delicacies which the other one needs for her flower-like body and which you also enjoy. You shall cook what you please in it."

And so he bade the laborers build a little room and an earthen stove in it and he bought a good cauldron. And Cuckoo

147

was pleased because he said, "You shall cook what you please in it."

As for Wang Lung, he said to himself that at last his affairs were settled and his women at peace and he could enjoy his love. And it seemed to him freshly that he could never tire of Lotus and of the way she pouted at him with the lids drooped like lily petals over her great eyes, and at the way laughter gleamed out of her eyes when she glanced up at him.

But after all this matter of the new kitchen became a thorn in his body, for Cuckoo went to the town every day and she bought this and that of expensive foods that are imported from the southern cities. There were foods he had never even heard of: lichee nuts and dried honey dates and curious cakes of rice flour and nuts and red sugar, and horned fish from the sea and many other things. And these all cost money more than he liked to give out, but still not so much, he was sure, as Cuckoo told him, and yet he was afraid to say, "You are eating my flesh," for fear she would be offended and angry at him, and it would displease Lotus, and so there was nothing he could do except to put his hand unwillingly to his girdle. And this was a thorn to him day after day, and because there was none to whom he could complain of it, the thorn pierced more deeply continually, and it cooled a little of the fire of love in him for Lotus.

And there was yet another small thorn that sprang from the first, and it was that his uncle's wife, who loved good food, went often into the inner court at meal times, and she grew free there, and Wang Lung was not pleased that out of his house Lotus chose this woman for friend. The three women ate well in the inner courts, and they talked unceasingly, whispering and laughing, and there was something that Lotus liked in the wife of his uncle and the three were happy together, and this Wang Lung did not like.

But still there was nothing to be done, for when he said gently and to coax her,

"Now, Lotus, my flower, and do not waste your sweetness on an old fat hag like that one. I need it for my own heart, and she is a deceitful and untrustworthy creature, and I do not like it that she is near you from dawn to sunset."

Lotus was fretful and she answered peevishly, pouting her lips and hanging her head away from him,

"Now and I have no one except you and I have no friends and I am used to a merry house and in yours there is no one except the first wife who hates me and these children of yours who are a plague to me, and I have no one."

Then she used her weapons against him and she would not let him into her room that night and she complained and said,

"You do not love me for if you did you would wish me to be happy."

Then Wang Lung was humbled and anxious and he was submissive and he was sorry and he said,

"Let it be only as you wish and forever."

Then she forgave him royally and he was afraid to rebuke her in any way for what she wished to do, and after that when he came to her Lotus, if she were talking or drinking tea or eating some sweetmeat with his uncle's wife, would bid him wait and was careless with him, and he strode away, angry that she was unwilling for him to come in when this other woman sat there, and his love cooled a little, although he did not know it himself.

He was angry, moreover, that his uncle's wife ate of the rich foods that he had to buy for Lotus and that she grew fat and more oily than she had been, but he could say nothing for his uncle's wife was clever and she was courteous to him and flattered him with good words, and rose when he came into the room.

And so his love for Lotus was not whole and perfect as it had been before, absorbing utterly his mind and his body. It was pierced through and through with small angers which were the more sharp because they must be endured and because he could no longer go even to O-lan freely for speech, seeing that now their life was sundered.

Then like a field of thorns springing up from one root and spreading here and there, there was yet more to trouble Wang Lung. One day his father, whom one would say saw nothing at any time so drowsy with age he was, woke suddenly out of his sleeping in the sun and he tottered, leaning on his dragon-headed staff which Wang Lung had bought for him on his seventieth birthday, to the doorway where a curtain hung between the main room and the court where Lotus walked. Now the old man had never noticed the door before nor when the court was built and seemingly he did not know whether anyone had been added to the house or not, and Wang Lung never told him, "I have another woman," for the old man was too deaf to make anything out of a voice if it told him something new and of which he had not thought.

But on this day he saw without reason this doorway and he

went to it and drew the curtain, and it happened that it was at an hour of evening when Wang Lung walked with Lotus in the court, and they stood beside the pool and looked at the fish, but Wang Lung looked at Lotus. Then when the old man saw his son standing beside a slender painted girl he cried out in his shrill cracked voice,

"There is a harlot in the house!" and he would not be silent although Wang Lung, fearing lest Lotus grow angry—for this small creature could shriek and scream and beat her hands together if she were angered at all—went forward and led the old man away into the outer court and soothed him, saying,

"Now calm your heart, my father. It is not a harlot but a second woman in the house."

But the old man would not be silent and whether he heard what was said or not no one knew only he shouted over and over, "There is a harlot here!" And he said suddenly, seeing Wang Lung near him, "And I had one woman and my father had one woman and we farmed the land." And again he cried out after a time, "I say it is a harlot!"

And so the old man woke from his aged and fitful sleeping with a sort of cunning hatred against Lotus. He would go to the doorway of her court and shout suddenly into the air,

"Harlot!"

Or he would draw aside the curtain into her court and then spit furiously upon the tiles. And he would hunt small stones and throw them with his feeble arm into the little pool to scare the fish, and in the mean ways of a mischievous child he expressed his anger.

And this too made a disturbance in Wang Lung's house, for he was ashamed to rebuke his father, and yet he feared the anger of Lotus, since he had found she had a pretty petulant temper that she loosed easily. And this anxiety to keep his father from angering her was wearisome to him and it was another thing to make of his love a burden to him.

One day he heard a shriek from the inner courts and he ran in for he heard it was the voice of Lotus, and there he found that the two younger children, the boy and the girl born alike, had between them led into the inner court his elder daughter, his poor fool. Now the four other children were constantly curious about this lady who lived in the inner court, but the two elder boys were conscious and shy and knew well enough why she was there and what their father had to do with her, although they never spoke of her unless to each other secretly. But the two younger ones could never be satisfied with their peepings and their exclamations, and sniffing of the perfume she wore and dipping their fingers in the bowls of food that Cuckoo carried away from her rooms after she had eaten.

Lotus complained many times to Wang Lung that his children were a plague to her and she wished there were a way to lock them out so that she need not be plagued with them. But this he was not willing to do, and he answered her in jest,

"Well, and they like to look at a lovely face as much as their father does."

And he did nothing except to forbid them to enter her courts and when he saw them they did not, but when he did not see them they ran in and out secretly. But the elder daughter knew nothing of anything, but only sat in the sun against the wall of the outer court, smiling and playing with her bit of twisted cloth.

On this day, however, the two elder sons being away at school, the two younger children had conceived the notion that the fool must also see the lady in the inner courts, and they had taken her hands and dragged her into the court and she stood before Lotus, who had never seen her and sat and stared at her. Now when the fool saw the bright silk of the coat Lotus wore and the shining jade in her ears, she was moved by some strange joy at the sight and she put out her hands to grasp the bright colors and she laughed aloud, a laugh that was only sound and meaningless. And Lotus was frightened and screamed out, so that Wang Lung came running in, and Lotus shook with her anger and leaped up and down on her little feet and shook her finger at the poor laughing girl and cried out,

"I will not stay in this house if that one comes near me, and I was not told that I should have accursed idiots to endure and if I had known it I would not have come—filthy children of yours!" and she pushed the little gaping boy who stood nearest her, clasping his twin sister's hand.

Then the good anger awoke in Wang Lung, for he loved his children, and he said roughly,

"Now I will not hear my children cursed, no and not by any one and not even my poor fool, and not by you who have no son in your womb for any man." And he gathered the children together and said to them, "Now go out, my son and my daughter, and come no more to this woman's court, for she does not love you and if she does not love you she does not love your father, either." And to the elder girl he said with great gentleness, "And you, my poor fool, come back to your place in the sun." And she smiled and he took her by the hand and led her away.

For he was most angry of all that Lotus dared to curse this child of his and call her idiot, and a load of fresh pain for the girl fell upon his heart, so that for a day and two days he would not go near Lotus, but he played with the children and he went into the town and he bought a circle of barley candy for his poor fool and he comforted himself with her baby pleasure in the sweet sticky stuff.

And when he went in to Lotus again neither of them said anything that he had not come for two days, but she took special trouble to please him, for when he came his uncle's wife was there drinking tea, and Lotus excused herself and said,

"Now here is my lord come for me and I must be obedient to him for this is my pleasure," and she stood until the woman went away.

Then she went up to Wang Lung and took his hand and drew it to her face and she wooed him. But he, although he loved her again, loved her not so wholly as before, and never again so wholly as he had loved her.

There came a day when summer was ended and the sky in the early morning was clear and cold and blue as sea water and a clean autumn wind blew hard over the land, and Wang Lung woke as from a sleep. He went to the door of his house and he looked over his fields. And he saw that the waters had receded and the land lay shining under the dry cold wind and under the ardent sun.

Then a voice cried out in him, a voice deeper than love cried out in him for his land. And he heard it above every other voice in his life and he tore off the long robe he wore and he stripped off his velvet shoes and his white stockings and he rolled his trousers to his knees and he stood forth robust and eager and he shouted,

"Where is the hoe and where the plow? And where is the seed for the wheat planting? Come, Ching, my friend—come—call the men—I go out to the land!"

22

As HE had been healed of his sickness of heart when he came from the southern city and comforted by the bitterness he had endured there, so now again Wang Lung was healed of his sickness of love by the good dark earth of his fields and he felt the moist soil on his feet and he smelled the earthy fragrance rising up out of the furrows he turned for the wheat. He ordered his laborers hither and thither and they did a mighty day of labor, plowing here and plowing there, and Wang Lung stood first behind the oxen and cracked the whip over their backs and saw the deep curl of earth turning as the plow went into the soil, and then he called to Ching and gave him the ropes, and he himself took a hoe and broke up the soil into fine loamy stuff, soft as black sugar, and still dark with the wetness of the land upon it. This he did for the sheer joy he had in it and not for any necessity, and when he was weary he lay down upon his land and he slept and the health of the earth spread into his flesh and he was healed of his sickness.

When night came and the sun had gone blazing down without a cloud to dim it, he strode into his house, his body aching and weary and triumphant, and he tore aside the curtain that went into the inner court and there Lotus walked in her silken robes. When she saw him she cried out at the earth upon his clothes and shuddered when he came near her.

But he laughed and he seized her small, curling hands in his soiled ones and he laughed again and said,

"Now you see that your lord is but a farmer and you a farmer's wife!"

Then she cried out with spirit,

"A farmer's wife am I not, be you what you like!"

153

And he laughed again and went out from her easily.

He ate his evening rice all stained as he was with the earth and unwillingly he washed himself even before he slept. And washing his body he laughed again, for he washed it now for no woman, and he laughed because he was free.

Then it seemed to Wang Lung as though he had been for a long time away and there were suddenly a multitude of things he had to do. The land clamored for ploughing and planting and day after day he labored at it, and the paleness which the summer of his love had set on his flesh darkened to a deep brown under the sun and his hands, which had peeled off their calloused parts under the idleness of love, hardened again where the hoe pressed and where the plow handles set their mark.

When he came in at noon and at night he ate well of the food which O-lan prepared for him, good rice and cabbage and beancurd, and good garlic rolled into wheat bread. When Lotus held her small nose under her hand at his coming and cried out at his reek, he laughed and cared nothing and he breathed out his stout breath at her and she must bear it as she could for he would eat of what he liked. And now that he was full of health again and free of the sickness of his love he could go to her and be finished with her and turn himself to other things.

So these two women took their place in his house: Lotus for his toy and his pleasure and to satisfy his delight in beauty and in smallness and in the joy of her pure sex, and O-lan for his woman of work and the mother who had borne his sons and who kept his house and fed him and his father and his children. And it was a pride to Wang Lung in the village that men mentioned with envy the woman in his inner court; it was as though men spoke of a rare jewel or an expensive toy that was useless except that it was sign and symbol of a man who had passed beyond the necessity of caring only to be fed and clothed and could spend his money on joy if he wished.

And foremost among the men in the village who exclaimed over his prosperity was his uncle, for his uncle in these days was like a dog who fawns and desires to win favor. He said,

"There is my nephew, who keeps such an one for his pleasure as none of we common men have even seen." And again he said, "And he goes in to his woman, who wears robes of silk and satin like a lady in a great house. I have not seen it, but my woman tells me." And again he said, "My nephew, the son of my brother, is founding a great house and his sons will be the sons of a rich man and they need not work all their lives long."

Then men of the village, therefore, looked upon Wang Lung with increasing respect and they talked to him no more as to one of themselves but as to one who lived in a great house, and they came to borrow money of him at interest and to ask his advice concerning the marriage of their sons and daughters, and if any two had a dispute over the boundary of a field, Wang Lung was asked to settle the dispute and his decison was accepted, whatever it was.

Where Wang Lung had been busy with his love, then, he was now satisfied of it and was busied with many things. The rains came in season and the wheat sprouted and grew and the year turned to winter and Wang Lung took his harvests to the markets, for he saved his grain until prices were high, and this time he took with him his eldest son.

Now there is a pride a man has when he sees his eldest son reading aloud the letters upon a paper and putting the brush and ink to paper and writing that which may be read by others, and this pride Wang Lung now had. He stood proudly and saw this happen and he would not laugh when the clerks, who had scorned him before, now cried out,

"Pretty characters the lad makes and he is a clever one!"

No, Wang Lung would not pretend it was anything out of the common that he had a son like this, although when the lad said sharply as he read, "Here is a letter that has the wood radical when it should have the water radical," Wang Lung's heart was fit to burst with pride, so that he was compelled to turn aside and cough and spit upon the floor to save himself. And when a murmur of surprise ran among the clerks at his son's wisdom he called out merely,

"Change it, then! We will not put our name to anything wrongly written."

And he stood proudly and watched while his son took up the brush and changed the mistaken sign.

When it was finished and his son had written his father's name on the deed of sale of the grain and upon the receipt of the moneys, the two walked home together, father and son, and the father said within his heart that now his son was a man and his eldest son, and he must do what was right for his son, and he must see to it that there was a wife chosen and betrothed for his son so that the lad need not go begging into a great house as he had and pick up what was left there and what no one wanted, for his son was the son of a man who was rich and who owned land in his right.

Wang Lung set himself, therefore, to the seeking of a maid who might be his son's wife, and it was no slight task, for he would have no one who was a common and ordinary female. He talked of it one night to Ching, after the two of them had been alone in the middle room, taking account of what must be bought for spring planting and of what they had of their own seed. He talked not as one who expects great help, for he knew Ching was too simple, but still he knew the man was faithful as a good dog is faithful to its master, and it was relief to speak what he thought to such an one.

Ching stood humbly as Wang Lung sat at the table and spoke, for in spite of Wang Lung's urging, he would not, now that Wang Lung had become rich, sit in his presence as though they were equal, and he listened with fixed attention as Wang Lung spoke of his son and of the one he sought, and when Wang Lung was finished, Ching sighed and he said in his hesitant voice that was scarcely more than a whisper,

"And if my poor girl were here and sound you might have her for nothing at all and my gratitude, too, but where she is I do not know, and it may be she is dead and I do not know."

Then Wang Lung thanked him, but he forebore to say what was in his heart, that for his son there must be one far higher than the daughter of such an one as Ching, who although a good man was, besides that, only a common farmer on another's land.

Wang Lung kept his own counsel, therefore, only listening here and there in the tea shop when maids were spoken of, or men prosperous in the town who had daughters for marriage. But to his uncle's wife he said nothing, guarding his purpose from her. For she was well enough when he had need of a woman from a tea house for himself. She was such an one to arrange a matter like that. But for his son he would have no one like his uncle's wife, who could not know anyone he considered fit for his eldest son.

The year deepened into snow and the bitterness of winter and the New Year's festival came and they ate and drank, and men came to see Wang Lung, not only from the countryside but now from the town also, to wish him fortune, and they said,

"Well, and there is no fortune we can wish you greater than you have, sons in your house and women and money and land."

And Wang Lung, dressed in his silken robe with his sons in

good robes beside him on either hand, and sweet cakes and watermelon seeds and nuts upon the table, and red paper signs pasted upon his doors everywhere for the New Year and coming prosperity, knew that his fortune was good.

But the year turned to spring and the willows grew faintly green and the peach trees budded pink, and Wang Lung had not yet found the one he sought for his son.

Spring came in long, warm days scented with blossoming plum and cherry, and the willow trees sprouted their leaves fully and unfolded them, and the trees were green and the earth was moist and steaming and pregnant with harvest, and the eldest son of Wang Lung changed suddenly and ceased to be a child. He grew moody and petulant and would not eat this and that and he wearied of his books, and Wang Lung was frightened and did not know what to make of it and talked of a doctor.

There was no correction that could be made of the lad at all, for if his father said to him with anything beyond coaxing, "Now eat of the good meat and rice," the lad turned stubborn and melancholy, and if Wang Lung was angry at all, he burst into tears and fled from the room.

Wang Lung was overcome with surprise and he could make nothing of it, so that he went after the lad and he said gently as he was able,

"I am your father and now tell me what is in your heart." But the lad did nothing except sob and shake his head violently.

Moreover, he took a dislike to his old teacher and would not in the mornings rise out of his bed to go to school unless Wang Lung bawled at him or even beat him, and then he went sullenly and sometimes he spent whole days idling about the streets of the town, and Wang Lung only knew it at night, when the younger boy said spitefully,

"Elder Brother was not in school today."

Wang Lung was angry at his eldest son then and he shouted at him,

"And am I to spend good silver for nothing?"

And in his anger he fell upon the boy with a bamboo and beat him until O-lan, the boy's mother, heard it and rushed in from the kitchen and stood between her son and his father so that the blows rained upon her in spite of Wang Lung's turning this way and that to get at the boy. Now the strange thing was that whereas the boy might burst into weeping at a chance rebuke, he stood these beatings under the bamboo without a sound, his face carven and pale as an image. And Wang Lung could make nothing of it, although he thought of it night and day.

He thought of it one evening thus after he had eaten his night's food, because on that day he had beaten his eldest son for not going to the school, and while he thought, O-lan came into the room. She came in silently and she stood before Wang Lung and he saw she had that which she wished to say. So he said,

"Say on. What is it, mother of my son?"

And she said, "It is useless for you to beat the lad as you do. I have seen this thing come upon the young lords in the courts of the great house, and it came on them melancholy, and when it came the Old Lord found slaves for them if they had not found any for themselves and the thing passed easily."

"Now and it need not be so," answered Wang Lung in argument. "When I was a lad I had no such melancholy and no such weepings and tempers, and no slaves, either."

O-lan waited and then she answered slowly, "I have not indeed seen it thus except with young lords. You worked on the land. But he is like a young lord and he is idle in the house."

Wang Lung was surprised, after he had pondered a while, for he saw truth in what she said. It was true that when he himself was a lad there was no time for melancholy, for he had to be up at dawn for the ox and out with the plow and the hoe and at harvest he must needs work until his back broke, and if he wept he could weep for no one heard him, and he could not run away as his son ran away from school, for if he did there was nothing for him to eat on return, and so he was compelled to labor. He remembered all this and he said to himself,

"But my son is not thus. He is more delicate than I was, and his father is rich and mine was poor, and there is no need for his labor, for I have labor in my fields, and besides, one cannot take a scholar such as my son is and set him to the plow."

And he was secretly proud that he had a son like this and so he said to O-lan,

"Well, and if he is like a young lord it is another matter. But I cannot buy a slave for him. I will betroth him and we will marry him early, and there is that to be done."

Then he rose and went in to the inner court.

Now Lotus, seeing Wang Lung distraught in her presence, and thinking of things other than her beauty, pouted and said,

"If I had known that in a short year you could look at me and not see me, I would have stayed in the tea house." And she turned her head away as she spoke and looked at him out of the corner of her eyes so that he laughed and seized her hand and he put it against his face and smelled of its fragrance and he answered,

"Well, and a man cannot always think of the jewel he has sewn on his coat, but if it were lost he could not bear it. These days I think of my eldest son and of how his blood is restless with desire and he must be wed and I do not know how to find the one he should wed. I am not willing that he marry any of the daughters of the village farmers, nor is it meet, seeing that we bear the common name of Wang. Yet I do not know one in the town well enough to say to him, 'Here is my son and there is your daughter,' and I am loath to go to a professional match-maker, lest there be some bargain she has made with a man who has a daughter deformed or idiot."

Now Lotus, since the eldest son had grown tall and graceful with young manhood, looked on the lad with favor and she was diverted with what Wang Lung said to her and she replied, musing,

"There was a man who used to come in to me at the great tea house, and he often spoke of his daughter, because he said she was such an one as I, small and fine, but still only a child, and he said, 'And I love you with a strange unease as though you were my daughter; you are too like her, and it troubles me for it is not lawful,' and for this reason, although he loved me best, he went to a great red girl called Pomegranate Flower."

"What sort of man was this?" asked Wang Lung.

"He was a good man and his silver was ready and he did not promise without paying. We all wished him well, for he was not begrudging, and if a girl was weary sometimes he did not bawl out as some did that he had been cheated, but he always said courteously as a prince might, or some might from a learned and noble house, 'Well, and here is the silver, and rest, my child, until love blooms again.' He spoke very prettily to us." And Lotus mused until Wang Lung said hastily to waken her, for he did not like her to think on her old life,

"What was his business, then, with all this silver?"

And she answered,

"Now and I do not know but I think he was master of a grain market, but I will ask Cuckoo who knows everything about men and their money."

Then she clapped her hands and Cuckoo ran in from the kitchen, her high cheeks and nose flushed with the fire, and Lotus asked her,

"Who was that great, large, goodly man who came to me and then to Pomegranate Flower, because I was like his little daughter, so that it troubled him, although he ever loved me best?"

And Cuckoo answered at once, "Ah, and that was Liu, the grain dealer. Ah, he was a good man! He left silver in my palm whenever he saw me."

"Where is his market?" asked Wang Lung, although idly, because it was woman's talk and likely to come to nothing.

"In the street of the Stone Bridge," said Cuckoo.

Then before she finished the words Wang Lung struck his hands together in delight and he said,

"Now then, that is where I sell my grain, and it is a propitious thing and surely it can be done," and for the first time his interest was awake, because it seemed to him a lucky thing to wed his son to the daughter of the man who bought his grain.

When there was a thing to be done, Cuckoo smelled the money in it as a rat smells tallow, and she wiped her hands upon her apron and she said quickly,

"I am ready to serve the master."

Wang Lung was doubtful, and doubting, he looked at her crafty face, but Lotus said gaily,

"And that is true, and Cuckoo shall go and ask the man Liu, and he knows her well and the thing can be done, for Cuckoo is clever enough, and she shall have the match-maker's fee, if it is well done."

"That will I do!" said Cuckoo heartily and she laughed as she thought of the fee of good silver on her palm, and she untied her apron from her waist and she said busily, "Now and at once will I go, for the meat is ready except for the moment of cooking and the vegetables are washed."

But Wang Lung had not pondered the matter sufficiently and it was not to be decided so quickly as this and he called out,

"No, and I have decided nothing. I must think of the matter for some days and I will tell you what I think."

The women were impatient, Cuckoo for the silver and Lotus because it was a new thing and she would hear something new to amuse her, but Wang Lung went out, saying,

"No, it is my son and I will wait."

And so he might have waited for many days, thinking of this and that, had not one early morning, the lad, his eldest son, come home in the dawn with his face hot and red with wine drinking, and his breath was fetid and his feet unsteady. Wang Lung heard him stumbling in the court and he ran out to see who it was, and the lad was sick and vomited before him, for he was unaccustomed to more than the pale mild wine they made from their own rice fermented, and he fell and lay on the ground in his vomit like a dog.

Wang Lung was frightened and he called for O-lan, and together they lifted the lad up and O-lan washed him and laid him upon the bed in her own room, and before she was finished with him the lad was asleep and heavy as one dead and could answer nothing to what his father asked.

Then Wang Lung went into the room where the two boys slept together, and the younger was yawning and stretching and tying his books into a square cloth to carry to school, and Wang Lung said to him,

"Was your elder brother not in the bed with you last night?"

And the boy answered unwillingly,

"No."

There was some fear in his look and Wang Lung, seeing it, cried out at him roughly,

"Where was he gone?" and when the boy would not answer, he took him by the neck and shook him and cried, "Now tell me all, you small dog!"

The boy was frightened at this, and he broke out sobbing and crying and said between his sobs,

"And Elder Brother said I was not to tell you and he said he would pinch me and burn me with a hot needle if I told and if I do not tell he gives me pence."

And Wang Lung, beside himself at this, shouted out,

"Tell what, you who ought to die?"

And the boy looked about him and said desperately, seeing that his father would choke him if he did not answer,

"He has been away three nights altogether, but what he does I do not know, except that he goes with the son of your uncle, our cousin."

Wang Lung loosed his hand then from the boy's neck and he flung him aside and he strode forth into his uncle's rooms, and there he found his uncle's son, hot and red of face with wine, even as his own son, but steadier of foot, for the young man was older and accustomed to the ways of men. Wang Lung shouted at him,

"Where have you led my son?"

And the young man sneered at Wang Lung and he said,

"Ah, that son of my cousin's needs no leading. He can go alone."

But Wang Lung repeated it and this time he thought to himself that he would kill this son of his uncle's now, this impudent scampish face, and he cried in a terrible voice,

"Where has my son been this night?"

Then the young man was frightened at the sound of his voice and he answered sullenly and unwillingly, dropping his impudent eyes,

"He was at the house of the whore who lives in the court that once belonged to the great house."

When Wang Lung heard this he gave a great groan, for the whore was one well known of many men and none went to her except poor and common men, for she was no longer young and she was willing to give much for little. Without stopping for food he went out of his gate and across his fields, and for once he saw nothing of what grew on his land, and noted nothing of how the crop promised, because of the trouble his son had brought to him. He went with his eyes fixed inward, and he went through the gate of the wall about the town, and he went to the house that had been great.

The heavy gates were swung back widely now, and none ever closed them upon their thick iron hinges, for any who would might come and go in these days, and he went in, and the courts and the rooms were filled with common people, who rented the rooms, a family of common people to a room. The place was filthy and the old pines hewed down and those left standing were dying, and the pools in the courts were choked with refuse.

But he saw none of this. He stood in the court of the first house and he called out,

"Where is the woman called Yang, who is a whore?"

There was a woman there who sat on a three-legged stool, sewing at a shoe sole, and she lifted her head and nodded toward a side door opening on the court and she took up her sewing again, as though many times she had been asked this question by men.

Wang Lung went to the door and he beat on it, and a fretful voice answered,

"Now go away, for I am done my business for this night and must sleep, since I work all night."

But he beat again, and the voice cried out, "Who is it?"

He would not answer, but he beat yet again, for he would go in whether or not, and at last he heard a shuffling and a woman opened the foor, a woman none too young and with a weary face and hanging, thick lips, and coarse white paint on her forehead and red paint she had not washed from her mouth and cheeks, and she looked at him and said sharply,

"Now I cannot before tonight and if you like you may come as early as you will then in the night, but now I must sleep."

But Wang Lung broke roughly into her talking, for the sight of her sickened him and the thought of his son here he could not bear, and he said,

"It is not for myself—I do not need such as you. It is for my son."

And he felt suddenly in his throat a thickening of weeping for his son. Then the woman asked,

"Well, and what of your son?"

And Wang Lung answered and his voice trembled,

"He was here last night."

"There were many sons of men here last night," replied the woman, "and I do not know which was yours."

Then Wang Lung said, beseeching her,

"Think and remember a little slight young lad, tall for his years, but not yet a man, and I did not dream he dared to try a woman."

163

And she, remembering, answered,

"Were there two, and was one a young fellow with his nose turned to the sky at the end and a look in his eye of knowing everything, and his hat over one ear? And the other, as you say, a tall big lad, but eager to be a man!"

And Wang Lung said, "Yes—yes—that is he—that is my son!"

"And what of your son?" said the woman.

Then Wang Lung said earnestly,

"This: if he ever comes again, put him off—say you desire men only—say what you will—but every time you put him off I will give you twice the fee of silver on your palm!"

The woman laughed then and carelessly and she said in sudden good humor,

"And who would not say aye to this, to be paid for not working? And so I say aye also. It is true enough that I desire men and little boys are small pleasure." And she nodded at Wang Lung as she spoke and leered at him and he was sickened at her coarse face and he said hastily,

"So be it, then."

He turned quickly and he walked home, and as he walked he spat and spat again to rid him of his sickness at the memory of the woman.

On this day, therefore, he said to Cuckoo,

"Let it be as you said. Go to the grain merchant and arrange the matter. Let the dowry be good but not too great if the girl is suitable and if it can be arranged."

When he had said this to Cuckoo he went back to the room and he sat beside his sleeping son and he brooded, for he saw how fair and young the boy lay there, and he saw the quiet face, asleep and smooth with its youth. Then when he thought of the weary painted woman and her thick lips, his heart swelled with sickness and anger and he sat there muttering to himself.

And as he sat O-lan came in and stood looking at the boy, and she saw the clear sweat standing on his skin and she brought vinegar in warm water and washed the sweat away gently, as they used to wash the young lords in the great house when they drank too heavily. Then seeing the delicate childish face and the drunken sleep that even the washing would not awaken, Wang Lung rose and went in his anger to his uncle's room, and he forgot the brother of his father and he remembered only that this man was father to the idle, impudent young

164

man who had spoiled his own fair son, and he went in and he shouted,

"Now I have harbored an ungrateful nest of snakes and they have bitten me!"

His uncle was sitting leaning over a table eating his breakfast, for he never rose until midday, seeing there was no work he had to do, and he looked up at these words and he said lazily,

"How now?"

Then Wang Lung told him, half-choking, what had happened, but his uncle only laughed and he said,

"Well, and can you keep a boy from becoming a man? And can you keep a young dog from a stray bitch?"

When Wang Lung heard this laughter he remembered in one crowded space of time all that he had endured because of his uncle; how of old his uncle had tried to force him to the selling of his land, and how they lived here, these three, eating and drinking and idle, and how his uncle's wife ate of the expensive foods Cuckoo bought for Lotus, and now how his uncle's son had spoiled his own fair lad, and he bit his tongue between his teeth and he said,

"Now out of my house, you and yours, and no more rice will there be for any of you from this hour, and I will burn the house down rather than have it shelter you, who have no gratitude even in your idleness!"

But his uncle sat where he was and ate on, now from this bowl and now from that, and Wang Lung stood there bursting with his blood, and when he saw his uncle paid no heed to him, he stepped forward with his arm upraised. Then the uncle turned and said,

"Drive me out if you dare."

And when Wang Lung stammered and blustered, not understanding, "Well—and what —well and what—" his uncle opened his coat and showed him what was against its lining.

Then Wang Lung stood still and rigid, for he saw there a false beard of red hair and a length of red cloth, and Wang Lung stared at these things, and the anger went out of him like water and he shook because there was no strength left in him.

Now these things, the red beard and the red length of cloth were sign and symbol of a band of robbers who lived and marauded toward the northwest, and many houses had they burned and women they had carried away, and good farmers they had bound with ropes to the threshold of their own houses and men found them there next day, raving mad if they lived and burnt and crisp as roasted meat if they were dead. And Wang Lung stared and his eyes hung out of his head, and he turned and went away without a word. And as he went he heard his uncle's whispered laughter as he stooped again over his rice bowl.

Now Wang Lung found himself in such a coil as he had never dreamed of. His uncle came and went as before, grinning a little under the sparse and scattered hairs of his grey beard, his robes wrapped and girdled about his body as carelessly as ever, and Wang Lung sweated chilly when he saw him but he dared not speak anything except courteous words for fear of what his uncle might do to him. It was true that during all these years of his prosperity and especially during the years when there were no harvests or only very little and other men had starved with their children, never had bandits come to his house and his lands, although he had many times been afraid and had barred the doors stoutly at night. Until the summer of his love he had dressed himself coarsely and had avoided the appearance of wealth, and when among the villagers he heard stories of marauding he came home and slept fitfully and listened for sounds out of the night.

But the robbers never came to his house and he grew careless and bold and he believed he was protected by heaven and that he was a man of good fortune by destiny, and he grew heedless of everything, even of incense of the gods, since they were good enough to him without, and he thought of nothing except of his own affairs and of his land. And now suddenly he saw why he had been safe and why he would be safe so long as he fed the three of his uncle's house. When he thought of this he sweated heavy cold sweat, and he dared to tell no one what his uncle hid in his bosom.

But to his uncle he said no more of leaving the house, and to his uncle's wife he said with what urging he could muster,

"Eat what you like in the inner courts and here is a bit of silver to spend."

And to his uncle's son he said, although the gorge rose in his throat, yet he said,

"Here is a bit of silver, for young men will play."

But his own son Wang Lung watched and he would not allow him to leave the courts after sundown, although the lad grew angry and flung himself about and slapped the younger

166

children for nothing except his own ill-humor. So was Wang Lung encompassed about with his troubles.

At first Wang Lung could not work for thinking of all the trouble that had befallen him, and he thought of this trouble and that, and he thought, "I could turn my uncle out and I could move inside the city wall where they lock the great gates every night against robbers," but then he remembered that every day he must come to work on his fields, and who could tell what might happen to him as he worked defenseless, even on his own land? Moreover, how could a man live locked in a town and in a house in the town, and he would die if he were cut off from his land. There would surely come a bad year, moreover, and even the town could not withstand robbers, as it had not in the past when the great house fell.

And he could go into the town and go to the court where the magistrate lived and say to him,

"My uncle is one of the Redbeards."

But if he did this, who would believe him, who would believe a man when he told such a thing of his own father's brother? It was more likely that he would be beaten for his unfilial conduct rather than his uncle suffer, and in the end he would go in fear of his life, for if the robbers heard of it, they would kill him for revenge.

Then as if this were not enough Cuckoo came back from the grain merchant and although the affair of the betrothal had gone well, the merchant Liu was not willing that anything should take place now except the exchange of the betrothal papers, for the maid was too young for marriage, being but fourteen years old, and it must wait for another three years. Wang Lung was dismayed at three more years of this lad's anger and idleness and mooning eyes, for he would not go to school now two days out of ten, and Wang Lung shouted at O-lan that night when he ate,

"Well, and let us betroth these other children as soon as we are able, and the sooner the better, and let us marry them as soon as they begin to yearn, for I cannot have this over again three more times!"

And the next morning he had not slept but a little through the night, and he tore off his long robes and kicked off his shoes, and as was his wont when the affairs of his house became too deep for him, he took a hoe and he went to his fields, and he went through the outer court where the eldest girl sat smiling

167

and twisting her bit of cloth through her fingers and smoothing it, and he muttered,

"Well, and that poor fool of mine brings me more comfort than all the others put together."

And he went out to his land day after day for many days.

Then the good land did again its healing work and the sun shone on him and healed him and the warm winds of summer wrapped him about with peace. And as if to cure him of the root of his ceaseless thought of his own troubles, there came out of the south one day a small slight cloud. At first it hung on the horizon small and smooth as a mist, except it did not come hither and thither as clouds blown by the wind do, but it stood steady until it spread fanwise up into the air.

The men of the village watched it and talked of it and fear hung over them, for what they feared was this, that locusts had come out of the south to devour what was planted in the fields. Wang Lung stood there also, and he watched, and they gazed and at last a wind blew something to their feet, and one stooped hastily and picked it up and it was a dead locust, dead and lighter than the living hosts behind.

Then Wang Lung forgot everything that troubled him. Women and sons and uncle, he forgot them all, and he rushed among the frightened villagers, and he shouted at them,

"Now for our good land we will fight these enemies from the skies!"

But there were some who shook their heads, hopeless from the start, and these said,

"No, and there is no use in anything. Heaven has ordained that this year we shall starve, and why should we waste ourselves in struggle against it, seeing that in the end we must starve?"

And women went weeping to the town to buy incense to thrust before the earth gods in the little temple, and some went to the big temple in the town, where the gods of heaven were, and thus earth and heaven were worshipped.

But still the locusts spread up into the air and on over the land.

Then Wang Lung called his own laborers and Ching stood silent and ready beside him and there were others of the younger farmers, and with their own hands these set fire to certain fields and they burned the good wheat that stood almost ripe for cutting and they dug wide moats and ran water into them from the wells, and they worked without sleeping. O-lan brought them food and the women brought their men food, and the men ate standing in the field, gulping it down as beasts do, as they worked night and day.

Then the sky grew black and the air was filled with the deep still roar of many wings beating against each other, and upon the land the locusts fell, flying over this field and leaving it whole, and falling upon that field, and eating it as bare as winter. And men sighed and said "So Heaven wills," but Wang Lung was furious and he beat the locusts and trampled on them and his men flailed them with flails and the locusts fell into the fires that were kindled and they floated dead upon the waters of the moats that were dug. And many millions of them died, but to those that were left it was nothing.

Nevertheless, for all his fighting Wang Lung had this as his reward: the best of his fields were spared and when the cloud moved on and they could rest themselves, there was still wheat that he could reap and his young rice beds were spared and he was content. Then many of the people ate the roasted bodies of the locusts, but Wang Lung himself would not eat them, for to him they were a filthy thing because of what they had done to his land. But he said nothing when O-lan fried them in oil and when the laborers crunched them between their teeth and the children pulled them apart delicately and tasted them, afraid of their great eyes. But as for himself he would not eat.

Nevertheless, the locusts did this for him. For seven days he thought of nothing but his land, and he was healed of his troubles and his fears, and he said to himself calmly,

"Well, and every man has his troubles and I must make shift to live with mine as I can, and my uncle is older than I and he will die, and three years must pass as they can with my son and I shall not kill myself."

And he reaped his wheat and the rains came and the young green rice was set into the flooded fields and again it was summer.

24

ONE DAY after Wang Lung had said to himself that peace was in his house, his eldest son came to him as he returned at noon from the land, and the lad said,

"Father, if I am to be a scholar, there is no more that this old head in the town can teach me."

Wang Lung had dipped from the cauldron in the kitchen a basin of boiling water and into this he dipped a towel and wrung it and holding it steaming against his face he said,

"Well, and how now?"

The lad hesitated and then he went on,

"Well, and if I am to be a scholar, I would like to go to the south to the city and enter a great school where I can learn what is to be learned."

Wang Lung rubbed the towel about his eyes and his ears and with his face all steaming he answered his son sharply, for his body ached with his labor in the fields,

"Well, and what nonsense is this? I say you cannot go and I will not be teased about it, for I say you cannot go. You have learning enough for these parts."

And he dipped the cloth in again and wrung it.

But the young man stood there and stared at his father with hatred and he muttered something and Wang Lung was angry for he could not hear what it was, and he bawled at his son,

"Speak out what you have to say!"

Then the young man flared at the noise of his father's voice and he said,

"Well, and I will, then, for go south I will, and I will not stay in this stupid house and be watched like a child, and in this little town which is no better than a village! I will go out and learn something and see other parts."

Wang Lung looked at his son and he looked at himself, and his son stood there in a pale long robe of silver grey linen, thin and cool for the summer's heat, and on his lip were the first black hairs of his manhood, and his skin was smooth and golden and his hands under his long sleeves were soft and fine as a woman's. Then Wang Lung looked at himself and he was thick and stained with earth and he wore only trousers of blue cotton cloth girt about his knees and his waist and his upper body was naked, and one would have said he was his son's servant rather than his father. And this thought made him scornful of the young man's tall fine looks, and he was brutal and angry and he shouted out,

"Now then, get into the fields and rub a little good earth on yourself lest men take you for a woman, and work a little for the rice you eat!"

And Wang Lung forgot that he had ever had pride in his son's writing and in his cleverness at books, and he flung himself out, stamping his bare feet as he walked and spitting upon the floor coarsely, because the fineness of his son angered him for the moment. And the lad stood and looked at him with hatred, but Wang Lung would not turn back to see what the lad did.

Nevertheless, that night when Wang Lung went into the inner courts and sat beside Lotus as she lay upon the mat on her bed where Cuckoo fanned her as she lay, Lotus said to him idly as of a thing of no account, but only something to say,

"That big lad of yours is pining and desires to go away."

Then Wang Lung, remembering his anger against his son, said sharply,

"Well, and what is it to you? I will not have him in these rooms at his age."

But Lotus made haste to reply, "No—no—it is Cuckoo who says it." And Cuckoo made haste to say, "Anyone can see the thing and a lovely lad he is and too big for idleness and longing."

Wang Lung was led aside by this and he thought only of his anger against his son and he said,

"No, and he shall not go. I will not spend my money foolishly." And he would not speak of it any more and Lotus saw he was peevish from some anger, and she sent Cuckoo away and suffered him there alone.

Then for many days there was nothing said and the lad seemed suddenly content again, but he would not go to school any more and this Wang Lung allowed him, for the boy was nearly eighteen and large like his mother in frame of bones, and he read in his own room when his father came into the house and Wang Lung was content and he thought to himself,

"It was a whim of his youth and he does not know what he wants and there are only three years—it may be a little extra silver will make it two, or even one, if the silver is enough. One of these days when the harvests are well over and the winter wheat planted and beans hoed, I will see to it."

Then Wang Lung forgot his son, for the harvests, except what the locusts had consumed, were fair enough and by now he had gained once more what he had spent on the woman Lotus. His gold and his silver were precious to him once more, and at times he marvelled secretly at himself that he had ever spent so freely upon a woman.

Still, there were times when she stirred him sweetly, if not so strongly as at first, and he was proud to own her, although he saw well enough that what his uncle's wife had said was true, that she was none too young for all her smallness of stature, and she never conceived to bear a child for him. But for this he cared nothing, since he had sons and daughters, and he was willing enough to keep her for the pleasure she gave him.

As for Lotus, she grew lovelier as her fullness of years came on, for if before she had had a fault, it was her birdlike thinness that made too sharp the lines of her little pointed face and hollowed too much her temples. But now under the food which Cuckoo cooked for her, and under the idleness of her life with one man only, she became soft and rounded in body, and her face grew full and smooth at the temples, and with her wide eyes and small mouth she looked more than ever like a plump little cat. And she slept and ate and took on her body this soft smooth flesh. If she was no longer the lotus bud, neither was she more than the full-blown flower, and if she was not young, neither did she look old, and youth and age were equally far fom her.

With his life placid again and the lad content, Wang Lung might have been satisfied except that one night when he sat late and alone, reckoning on his fingers what he could sell of his corn and what he could sell of his rice, O-lan came softly into the room. This one, with the passing of the years had grown lean and gaunt and the rock-like bones of her face stood forth

172

and her eyes were sunken. If one asked her how she did she said no more than this,

"There is a fire in my vitals."

Her belly was as great as though with child these three years, only there was no birth. But she rose at dawn and she did her work and Wang Lung saw her only as he saw the table or his chair or a tree in the court, never even so keenly as he might see one of the oxen drooping its head or a pig that would not eat. And she did her work alone and spoke no more than she could escape speaking with the wife of Wang Lung's uncle, and she never spoke at all to Cuckoo. Never once had O-lan gone into the inner courts, and rarely, if Lotus came out to walk a little in a place other than her own court, O-lan went into her room and sat until one said, "She is gone." And she said nothing but she worked at her cooking and at the washing at the pool even in the winter when the water was stiff with ice to be broken. But Wang Lung never thought to say,

"Well, and why do you not with the silver I have to spare, hire a servant or buy a slave?"

It did not occur to him that there was any need of this, although he hired laborers for his fields and to help with the oxen and asses and with the pigs he had, and in the summers when the river flooded, he hired men for the time to herd the ducks and geese he fed upon the waters.

On this evening, then, when he sat alone with only the red candles in the pewter stands alight, she stood before him and looked this way and that, and at last she said,

"I have something to say."

Then he stared at her in surprise and he answered,

"Well, and say on."

And he stared at her and at the shadowed hollows of her face and he thought again how there was no beauty in her and how for many years had he not desired her.

Then she said in a harsh whisper,

"The eldest son goes too often into the inner courts. When you are away he goes."

Now Wang Lung could not at first grasp what she said thus whispering and he leaned forward with his mouth agape and he said,

"What, woman?"

She pointed mutely to her son's room and pursed her thick dry lips at the door of the inner court. But Wang Lung stared at her, robust and unbelieving.

"You dream!" he said finally.

She shook her head at this, and, the difficult speech halting on her lips, she said further,

"Well, and my lord, come home unexpectedly." And again, after a silence, "It is better to send him away, even to the south." And then she went to the table and took his bowl of tea and felt of it and spilled the cool tea on the brick floor and filled the bowl again from the hot pot, and as she came she went, silent, and left him sitting there agape.

Well, and this woman, she was jealous he said to himself. Well, and he would not trouble about this, with his lad content and reading every day in his own room, and he rose and laughed and put it away from him, laughing at the small thoughts of women.

But when he went in that night to lie beside Lotus and when he turned upon the bed she complained and was petulant and she pushed him away saying,

"It is hot and you stink and I wish you would wash yourself before you come to lie beside me."

She sat up, then, and pushed her hair fretfully back from her face and she shrugged her shoulders when he would have drawn her to him, and she would not yield to his coaxing. Then he lay still and he remembered that she had yielded unwillingly these many nights, and he had thought it her whim and the heavy hot air of departing summer that depressed her, but now the words of O-lan stood out sharply and he rose up roughly and said,

"Well, and sleep alone then, and cut my throat if I care!"

He flung himself out of the room and strode into the middle room of his own house and he put two chairs together and stretched himself on them. But he could not sleep and he rose and went out of his gate and he walked among the bamboos beside the house wall, and there he felt the cool night wind upon his hot flesh, and there was the coolness of coming autumn in it.

Then he remembered this, that Lotus had known of his son's desire to go away, and how had she known? And he remembered that of late his son had said nothing of going away but had been content, and why was he content? And Wang Lung said to his heart, fiercely,

"I will see the thing for myself!"

And he watched the dawn come ruddy out of a mist over his land.

When the dawn was come and the sun showed a gold rim over the edge of the fields, he went in and he ate, and then he went out to oversee his men as his custom was in times of harvest and planting, and he went here and there over his land, and at last he shouted loudly, so that anyone in his house might hear,

"Now I am going to the piece by the moat of the town and I shall not be back early," and he set his face to the town.

But when he had gone half-way and reached as far as the small temple he sat down beside the road on a hillock of grass that was an old grave, now forgotten, and he plucked a grass and twisted it in his fingers and he meditated. Facing him were the small gods and on the surface of his mind he noted how they stared at him and how of old he had been afraid of them, but now he was careless, having become prosperous and in no need of gods, so that he scarcely saw them. Underneath he thought to himself, over and over,

"Shall I go back?"

Then suddenly he remembered the night before when Lotus had pushed him away, and he was angry because of all he had done for her and he said to himself,

"Well I know that she would not have lasted many years more at the tea house, and in my house she is fed and clothed richly."

And in the strength of his anger he rose and he strode back to his house by another way and he went secretly into his house and stood at the curtain that hung in the door to the inner court. And listening, he heard the murmuring of a man's voice, and it was the voice of his own son.

Now the anger that arose in Wang Lung's heart was an anger he had not known in all his life before, although as things had prospered with him and as men came to call him rich, he had lost his early timidity of a country fellow, and had grown full of small sudden angers, and he was proud even in the town. But this anger now was the anger of one man against another man who steals away the loved woman, and when Wang Lung remembered that the other man was his own son, he was filled with a vomiting sickness.

He set his teeth then, and he went out and chose a slim, supple bamboo from the grove and he stripped off the branches, except for a cluster of small branches at the top, thin and hard as cord, and he ripped off the leaves. Then he went in softly and suddenly he tore aside the curtain and there was his son,

175

standing in the court, and looking down at Lotus, who sat on a small stool at the edge of the pool. And Lotus was dressed in her peach-colored silk coat, such as he had never seen her dressed in by the light of the morning.

These two talked together, and the woman laughed lightly and looked at the young man from the corner of her eyes, her head turned aside, and they did not hear Wang Lung. He stood and stared at them, his face whitening and his lips lifted back and snarling from his teeth, and his hands tightened about the bamboo. And still the two did not hear him and would not, except that the woman Cuckoo came out and saw him and shrieked and they saw.

Then Wang Lung leaped forward and he fell on his son, lashing him, and although the lad was taller than he, he was stronger from his labor in the fields and from the robustness of his mature body, and he beat the lad until the blood streamed down. When Lotus screamed and dragged at his arm he shook her off, and when she persisted, screaming, he beat her also and he beat her until she fled and he beat the young man until he stooped cowering to the ground, and covered his torn face in his hands.

Then Wang Lung paused and his breath whistled through his parted lips and the sweat poured down his body until he was drenched and he was weak as though with an illness. He threw down his bamboo and he whispered to the boy, panting,

"Now get you to your room and do not dare to come out of it until I am rid of you, lest I kill you!"

And the boy rose without a word and went out.

Wang Lung sat on the stool where Lotus had sat and he put his head in his hands and closed his eyes and his breath came and went in great gasps. No one drew near him and he sat thus alone until he was quieted and his anger gone.

Then he rose wearily and he went into the room and Lotus lay there on her bed, weeping aloud, and he went up to her and he turned her over, and she lay looking at him and weeping and there on her face lay the swollen purple mark of his whip.

And he said to her with great sadness,

"So must you ever be a whore and go a-whoring after my own sons!"

And she cried more loudly at this and protested,

"No, but I did not, and the lad was lonely and came in and you may ask Cuckoo if he ever came nearer to my bed than you saw him in the court!"

Then she looked at him frightened and piteous and she reached for his hand and drew it across the welt on her face and she whimpered.

"See what you have done to your Lotus—and there is no man in the world except you, and if it is your son, it is only your son, and what is he to me!"

She looked up at him, her pretty eyes swimming in her clear tears, and he groaned because this woman's beauty was more than he could wish and he loved her when he would not. And it seemed to him suddenly that he could not bear to know what had passed between these two and he wished never to know and it was better for him if he did not. So he groaned again and he went out. He passed his son's room and he called without entering.

"Well, and now put your things in the box and tomorrow go south to what you will and do not come home until I send for you."

Then he went on and there was O-lan sitting sewing on some garment of his, and when he passed she said nothing, and if she had heard the beating and the screaming, she made no sign of it. And he went on and out to his fields and into the high sun of noon, and he was spent as with the labor of a whole day.

25

WHEN THE eldest son was gone Wang Lung felt the house was purged of some surcharge of unrest and it was a relief to him. He said to himself that it was a good thing for the young man to be gone, and now he could look to his other children and see what they were, for what with his own troubles and the land which must be planted and harvested in season whatever might happen elsewhere, he hardly knew what he had for children after his eldest son. He decided, moreover, that he would early take the second lad out of school and he would apprentice him to a trade and not wait for the wildness of young manhood to catch him and make him a plague in the house as the older one had been.

Now the second son of Wang Lung was as unlike the elder as two sons in a house may be. Where the elder was tall and big-boned and ruddy faced as men of the north are and like his mother, this second one was short and slight and yellow-skinned, and there was that in him which reminded Wang Lung of his own father, a crafty, sharp, humorous eye, and a turn for malice if the moment came for it. And Wang Lung said,

"Well, and this boy will make a good merchant and I will take him out of school and see if he can be apprenticed in the grain market. It will be a convenient thing to have a son there where I sell my harvests and he can watch the scales and tip the weight a little in my favor."

Therefore he said to Cuckoo one day,

"Now go and tell the father of my eldest son's betrothed that I have something to say to him. And we should at any rate drink a cup of wine together, seeing that we are to be poured into one bowl, his blood and mine."

Cuckoo went, then, and came back saying,

"He will see you when you wish and if you can come to drink wine this noon it is well, and if you wish it he will come here instead."

But Wang Lung did not wish the town merchant to come to his house because he feared he would have to prepare this and that, and so he washed himself and put on his silk coat and he set out across the fields. He went first to the Street of Bridges, as Cuckoo had told him, and there before a gate which bore the name of Liu he stopped. Not that he knew the word himself, but he guessed the gate, two doors to the right of the bridge, and he asked one who passed and the letter was the letter of Liu. It was a respectable gate built plainly of wood, and Wang Lung struck it with the palm of his hand.

Immediately it opened and a woman servant stood there, wiping her wet hands on her apron as she spoke to ask who he was, and when he answered his name, she stared at him, and led him into the first court where the men lived and she took him into a room and bade him seat himself, and she stared at him again, knowing he was the father of the betrothed of the daughter of the house. Then she went out to call her master.

Wang Lung looked about him carefully, and he rose and felt of the stuffs of the curtains in the doorway, and examined the wood of the plain table, and he was pleased, for there was evidence of good living but not of extreme wealth. He did not want a rich daughter-in-law lest she be haughty and disobedient and cry for this and that of food and clothes and turn aside his son's heart from his parents. Then Wang sat down again and waited.

Suddenly there was a heavy step and a stout elderly man entered and Wang Lung rose and bowed and they both bowed, looking secretly at each other, and they liked each other, each respecting the other for what he was, a man of worth and prosperity. Then they seated themselves and they drank of the hot wine which the servant woman poured out for them, and they talked slowly of this and that, of crops and prices and what the price would be for rice this year if the harvest were good. And at last Wang Lung said,

"Well, and I have come for a thing and if it is not your wish, let us talk of other things. But if you have need for a servant in your great market, there is my second son, and a sharp one he is, but if you have no need of him, let us talk of other things."

Then the merchant said with great good humor,

"And so I have such need of a sharp young man, if he reads and writes."

And Wang Lung answered proudly,

"My sons are both good scholars and they can each tell when a letter is wrongly written, and whether the wood or the water radical is right."

"That is well," said Liu. "And let him come when he will and his wages at first are only his food until he learns the business, and then after a year if he do well, he may have a piece of silver at the end of every moon, and at the end of three years three pieces, and after that he is no longer apprentice, but he may rise as he is able in the business. And besides this wage, there is whatever fee he may extract from this buyer and that seller, and this I say nothing about if he is able to get it. And because our two families are united, there is no fee of guaranty I will ask of you for his coming."

Wang Lung rose then, well-pleased, and he laughed and said,

"Now we are friends, and have you no son for my second daughter?"

Then the merchant laughed richly, for he was fat and well-fed, and he said,

"I have a second son of ten whom I have not betrothed yet. How old is the girl?"

Wang Lung laughed again and answered,

"She is ten on her next birthday and she is a pretty flower."

Then the two men laughed together and the merchant said,

"Shall we tie ourselves together with a double rope?"

Then Wang Lung said no more, for it was not a thing that could be discussed face to face beyond this. But after he had bowed and gone away well-pleased, he said to himself, "The thing may be done," and he looked at his young daughter when he came home and she was a pretty child and her mother had bound her feet well, so that she moved about with small graceful steps.

But when Wang Lung looked at her thus closely he saw the marks of tears on her cheeks, and her face was a shade too pale and grave for her years, and he drew her to him by her little hand and he said,

"Now why have you wept?"

Then she hung her head and toyed with a button on her coat and said, shy and half-murmuring,

"Because my mother binds a cloth about my feet more tightly every day and I cannot sleep at night."

"Now I have not heard you weep," he said wondering.

"No," she said simply, "and my mother said I was not to weep aloud because you are too kind and weak for pain and you might say to leave me as I am, and then my husband would not love me even as you do not love her."

This she said as simply as a child recites a tale, and Wang Lung was stabbed at hearing this, that O-lan had told the child he did not love her who was the child's mother, and he said quickly,

"Well, and today I have heard of a pretty husband for you, and we will see if Cuckoo can arrange the matter."

Then the child smiled and dropped her head, suddenly a maid and no more a child. And Wang Lung said to Cuckoo on that same evening when he was in the inner court,

"Go and see if it can be done."

But he slept uneasily beside Lotus that night and he woke and fell to thinking of his life and of how O-lan had been the first woman he had known and how she had been a faithful servant beside him. And he thought of what the child said, and he was sad, because with all her dimness O-lan had seen the truth in him.

In the near days after this he sent his second son away into the town and he signed the papers for the second girl's betrothal and the dowry was decided upon and the gifts of clothing and jewelry for her marriage day were fixed. Then Wang Lung rested and he said to his heart,

"Well, and now all my children are provided for, and my poor fool can do nothing but sit in the sun with her bit of cloth and the youngest boy I will keep for the land and he shall not go to school, since two can read and it is enough."

He was proud because he had three sons and one was a scholar and one a merchant and one a farmer. He was content, then, and he gave over thinking any more about his children. But whether he would or not there came into his mind the thought of the woman who had borne them for him.

For the first time in his years with her Wang Lung began to think about O-lan. Even in the days of her new-coming he had not thought of her for herself and not further than because she was a woman and the first he had known. And it seemed to him that with this thing and that he had been busy and without time to spare, and only now, when his children were settled and his fields cared for and quiet under the coming of winter, and now, when his life with Lotus was regulated and she was submissive to him since he had beat her, now it seemed to him he had time to think of what he would and he thought of O-lan.

He looked at her, not because she was woman this time, and not that she was ugly and gaunt and yellow-skinned. But he looked at her with some strange remorse, and he saw that she had grown thin and her skin was sere and yellow. She had always been a dark woman, her skin ruddy and brown when she worked in the fields. Yet now for many years she had not gone into the fields except perhaps at harvest time, and not then for two years and more, for he disliked her to go, lest men say,

"And does your wife still work on the land and you rich?"

Nevertheless, he had not thought why she had been willing at last to stay in the house and why she moved slowly and more slowly about, and he remembered, now that he thought of it, that in the mornings sometimes he heard her groaning when she rose from her bed and when she stooped to feed the oven, and only when he asked, "Well, and what is it?" did she cease suddenly. Now, looking at her and at the strange swelling she had on her body, he was stricken with remorse, although he did not know why, and he argued with himself.

"Well, and it is not my fault if I have not loved her as one loves a concubine, since men do not." And to himself he said for comfort, "I have not beat her and I have given her silver when she asked for it."

But still he could not forget what the child had said and it pricked him, although he did not know why, seeing that, when he came to argue the matter out, he had always been a good husband to her and better than most.

Because he could not be rid of this unease toward her, then, he kept looking at her as she brought in his food or as she moved about, and when she stooped to sweep the brick floor one day after they had eaten, he saw her face turn grey with some inner pain, and she opened her lips and panted softly, and she put her hand to her belly, although still stooping as though to sweep. He asked her sharply,

"What is it?"

But she averted her face and answered meekly,

"It is only the old pain in my vitals."

Then he stared at her and he said to the younger girl,

"Take the broom and sweep, for your mother is ill." And to O-lan he said more kindly than he had spoken to her in many years, "Go in and lie on your bed, and I will bid the girl bring you hot water. Do not get up."

She obeyed him slowly and without answer, and she went in to her room and he heard her dragging about it, and at last she lay down and moaned softly. Then he sat listening to this moaning until he could not bear it, and he rose and went in to the town to ask where a doctor's shop was.

He found a shop recommended to him by a clerk in the grain market where his second son now was, and he went to it. There the doctor sat idle over a pot of tea. He was an old man with a long grey beard and brass spectacles large as an owl's eyes over his nose, and he wore a dirty grey robe whose long sleeves covered his hands altogether. When Wang Lung told him what his wife's symptoms were, he pursed his lips and opened a drawer of the table at which he sat, and he took out a bundle wrapped in a black cloth and he said,

"I will come now."

When they came to O-lan's bed she had fallen into a light sleep and the sweat stood like dew on her upper lip and on her forehead, and the old doctor shook his head to see it. He put forth a hand as dried and yellowed as an ape's hand and he felt for her pulse, and then after he had held it for a long time, he shook his head again gravely, saying,

182

"The spleen is enlarged and the liver diseased. There is a rock as large as a man's head in the womb; the stomach is disintegrated. The heart barely moves and doubtless there are worms in it."

At these words Wang Lung's own heart stopped and he was afraid and he shouted out angrily,

"Well, and give her medicine, can you not?"

O-lan opened her eyes as he spoke and looked at them, not understanding and drowsy with pain. Then the old doctor spoke again,

"It is a difficult case. If you do not wish guarantee of recovery, I will ask for fee ten pieces of silver and I will give you a prescription of herbs and a tiger's heart dried in it and the tooth of a dog, and these boil together and let her drink the broth. But if you wish complete recovery guaranteed, then five hundred pieces of silver."

Now when O-lan heard the words, "five hundred pieces of silver" she came suddenly out of her languor and she said weakly,

"No, and my life is not worth so much. A good piece of land can be bought for so much."

Then when Wang Lung heard her say this all his old remorse smote him and he answered her fiercely,

"I will have no death in my house and I can pay the silver."

Now when the old doctor heard him say, "I can pay the silver," his eyes shone greedily enough, but he knew the penalty of the law if he did not keep his word and the woman died, and so he said, although with regret,

"Nay, and as I look at the color of the whites of her eyes, I see I was mistaken. Five thousand pieces of silver must I have if I guarantee full recovery."

Then Wang Lung looked at the doctor in silence and in sad understanding. He had not so many pieces of silver in the world unless he sold his land, but he knew that even though he sold his land it was no avail, for it was simply that the doctor said, "The woman will die."

He went out with the doctor, therefore, and he paid him the ten pieces of silver, and when he was gone Wang Lung went into the dark kitchen where O-lan had lived her life for the most part, and where, now that she was not there, none would see him, and he turned his face to the blackened wall, and he wept.

26

But there was no sudden dying of life in O-lan's body. She was scarcely past the middle of her span of years, and her life would not easily pass from her body, so that she lay dying on her bed for many months. All through the long months of winter she lay dying and upon her bed, and for the first time Wang Lung and his children knew what she had been in the house, and how she made comfort for them all and they had not known it.

It seemed now that none knew how to light the grass and keep it burning in the oven, and none knew how to turn a fish in the cauldron without breaking it or burning one side black before the other side was cooked, and none knew whether sesame oil or bean were right for frying this vegetable or that. The filth of the crumbs and dropped food lay under the table and none swept it unless Wang Lung grew impatient with the smell of it and called in a dog from the court to lick it up or shouted at the younger girl to scrape it up and throw it out.

And the youngest lad did this and that to fill his mother's place with the old man his grandfather, who was helpless as a little child now, and Wang Lung could not make the old man understand what had happened that O-lan no longer came to bring him tea and hot water and to help him lie down and stand up, and he was peevish because he called her and she did not come, and he threw his bowl of tea on the ground like a wilful child. At last Wang Lung led him in to O-lan's room and showed him the bed where she lay, and the old man stared out of his filmed and half blind eyes, and he mumbled and wept because he saw dimly that something was wrong.

Only the poor fool knew nothing, and only she smiled and twisted her bit of cloth as she smiled. Yet one had to think of her to bring her in to sleep at night and to feed her and to set her in the sun in the day and to lead her in if it rained. All this one of them had to remember. But even Wang Lung himself forgot, and once they left her outside through a whole night, and the next morning the poor wretch was shivering and crying in the early dawn, and Wang Lung was angry and cursed his son and daughter that they had forgotten the poor fool who was their sister. Then he saw that they were but children trying to take their mother's place and not able to do it, and he forebore and after that he saw to the poor fool himself night and morning. If it rained or snowed or a bitter wind blew he led her in and he let her sit among the warm ashes that dropped from the kitchen stove.

All during the dark winter months when O-lan lay dying Wang Lung paid no heed to the land. He turned over the winter's work and the men to the government of Ching, and Ching labored faithfully, and night and morning he came to the door of the room where O-lan lay and he asked twice each day thus in his piping whisper how she did. At last Wang Lung could not bear it because every day and every night he could only say,

"Today she drank a little soup from a fowl," or "today she ate a little thin gruel of rice."

So he commanded Ching to ask no more but to do the work well, and it would be enough.

All during the cold dark winter Wang Lung sat often beside O-lan's bed, and if she were cold he lit an earthen pot of charcoal and set it beside her bed for warmth, and she murmured each time faintly,

"Well, and it is too expensive."

At last one day when she said this he could not bear it and he burst forth,

"This I cannot bear! I would sell all my land if it could heal you."

She smiled at this and said in gasps, whispering,

"No, and I would not—let you. For I must die—sometime anyway. But the land is there after me."

But he would not talk of her death and he rose and went out when she spoke of it.

Nevertheless because he knew she must die and it was his duty, he went one day into the town to a coffin-maker's shop and he looked at every coffin that stood there ready to be bought, and he chose a good black one made from heavy and hard wood. Then the carpenter, who waited for him to choose, said cunningly,

"If you take two, the price is a third off for the two, and why do you not buy one for yourself and know you are provided?"

"No, and my sons can do it for me," answered Wang Lung, and then he thought of his own father and he had not yet a coffin for the old man and he was struck with the thought and he said again, "But there is my old father and he will die one day soon, weak as he is on his two legs and deaf and half blind, and so I will take the two."

And the man promised to paint the coffins again a good black and send them to Wang Lung's house. So Wang Lung told O-lan what he had done, and she was pleased that he had done it for her, and had provided well for her death.

Thus he sat by her many hours of the day, and they did not talk much for she was faint, and besides there had never been talk between them. Often she forgot where she was as he sat there in stillness and silence, and sometimes she murmured of her childhood, and for the first time Wang Lung saw into her heart, although even now only through such brief words as these,

"I will bring the meats to the door only—and well I know I am ugly and cannot appear before the great lord—" And again she said, panting, "Do not beat me—I will never eat of the dish again—" And she said over and over, "My father—my mother —my father—my mother——" and again and again, "Well I know I am ugly and cannot be loved—"

When she said this Wang Lung could not bear it and he took her hand and he soothed it, a big hard hand, stiff as though it were dead already. And he wondered and grieved at himself most of all because what she said was true, and even when he took her hand, desiring truly that she feel his tenderness towards her, he was ashamed because he could feel no tenderness, no melting of the heart such as Lotus could win from him with a pout of her lips. When he took this stiff dying hand he did not love it, and even his pity was spoiled with repulsion towards it.

And because of this, he was more kind to her and he bought her special food and delicate soups made of white fish and the hearts of young cabbages. Moreover, he could not take his pleasure of Lotus, for when he went in to her to distract his mind from its despair over this long agony of dying, he could

186

not forget O-lan, and even as he held Lotus, he loosed her, because of O-lan.

There were times when O-lan woke to herself and to what was about her and once she called for Cuckoo, and when in great astonishment Wang Lung summoned the woman, O-lan raised herself trembling upon her arm, and she said plainly enough,

"Well, and you may have lived in the courts of the Old Lord, and you were accounted beautiful, but I have been a man's wife and I have borne him sons, and you are still a slave."

When Cuckoo would have answered angrily to this, Wang Lung besought her and led her out, saying,

"That one does not know what words mean, now."

When he went back into the room, O-lan still leaned her head upon her arms and she said to him,

"After I am dead that one nor her mistress neither is to come into my room or touch my things, and if they do, I will send my spirit back for a curse." Then she fell into her fitful sleep, and her head dropped upon the pillow.

But one day before the New Year broke, she was suddenly better, as a candle flickers brightly at its end, and she was herself as she had not been and she sat up in bed and twisted her hair for herself, and she asked for tea to drink, and when Wang Lung came she said,

"Now the New Year is coming and there are no cakes and no meats ready, and I have thought of a thing. I will not have that slave in my kitchen, but I would have you send for my daughter-in-law, who is betrothed to our eldest son. I have not seen her yet, but when she comes I will tell her what to do."

Wang Lung was pleased at her strength, although he cared nothing for festivities on this year, and he sent Cuckoo in to beseech Liu, the grain merchant, seeing how sad the case was. And after a while Liu was willing when he heard that O-lan would not live the winter out, perhaps, and after all the girl was sixteen and older than some who go to their husband's houses.

But because of O-lan there were no feasting. The maiden came quietly in a sedan chair, except that her mother and an old servant came with her, and her mother went back when she had delivered the maiden to O-lan, but the servant remained for the maiden's use.

Now the children were moved from the room where they had slept and the room was given to the new daughter-in-law, and all was arranged as it should be. Wang Lung did not speak with the maiden, since it was not fitting, but he inclined his head gravely when she bowed, and he was pleased with her, for she knew her duty and she moved about the house quietly with her eyes downcast. Moreover, she was a goodly maid, fair enough, but not too fair so as to be vain over it. She was careful and correct in all her behavior, and she went into O-lan's room and tended her, and this eased Wang Lung of his pain for his wife, because now there was a woman about her bed, and O-lan was very content.

O-lan was content for three days and more and then she thought of another thing and she said to Wang Lung when he came in the morning to see how she did through the night,

"There is another thing before I can die."

To this he replied angrily,

"You cannot speak of dying and please me!"

She smiled slowly then, the same slow smile that ended before it reached her eyes, and she answered,

"Die I must, for I feel it in my vitals waiting, but I will not die before my eldest son comes home and before he weds this good maid who is my daughter-in-law, and well she serves me, holding the hot water basin steadily and knowing when to bathe my face when I sweat in pain. Now I want my son to come home, because I must die, and I want him to wed this maid first, so that I may die easily, knowing your grandson is stirred into life and a great grandson for the old one."

Now these were many words for her at any time, even in health, and she said them more sturdily than she had said anything for many moons, and Wang Lung was cheered at the strength in her voice and with what vigor she desired this, and he would not cross her, although he would have liked more time for a great wedding for his eldest son. He only said heartily to her therefore,

"Well, and we will do this thing, and today I will send a man south and he shall search for my son and bring him home to be wed. And then you must promise me that you will gather your strength again and give over dying and grow well, for the house is like a cave for beasts without you."

This he said to please her and it pleased her, although she did not speak again, but lay back and closed her eyes, smiling a little.

Wang Lung despatched the man, therefore, and told him,

"Tell your young lord that his mother is dying and her spirit cannot rest in ease until she sees him and sees him wed, and if he values me and his mother and his home, he must come back before he draws another breath, for on the third day from now I will have feasts prepared and guests invited and he will be wed."

And as Wang Lung said, so he did. He bade Cuckoo provide a feast as best she could, and she was to call in cooks from the shop in town to help her, and he poured silver into her hands and he said,

"Do as it would have been done in the great house at such an hour, and there is more silver than this."

Then he went into the village and invited guests, men and women, everyone whom he knew, and he went into the town and invited whom he knew at the tea shops and at the grain markets and everyone whom he knew. And he said to his uncle,

"Ask whom you will for my son's marriage, any of your friends or any of your son's friends."

This he said because he remembered always who his uncle was and Wang Lung was courteous to his uncle and treated him as an honored guest, and so he had done from the hour when he knew who his uncle was.

On the night of the day before his marriage, Wang Lung's eldest son came home, and he came striding into the room and Wang Lung forgot all that the young man had troubled him when he was at home. For two years and more had passed since he saw this son of his, and here he was and no longer a lad, but a tall man and a goodly one, with a great square body and high ruddy cheeks and short black hair, shining and oiled. And he wore a long dark red gown of satin such as one finds in the shops of the south, and a short black velvet jacket without sleeves, and Wang Lung's heart burst with pride to see his son, and he forgot everything except this, his goodly son, and he led him to his mother.

Then the young man sat beside his mother's bed and the tears stood in his eyes to see her thus, but he would not say anything except cheerful things such as these, "You look twice as well as they said and years away from death." But O-lan said simply,

"I will see you wed and then I must die."

Now the maid who was to be wed must not of course be seen by the young man and Lotus took her into the inner court to prepare her for marriage, and none could do this better than Lotus and Cuckoo and the wife of Wang Lung's uncle. These three took the maid and on the morning of her wedding day they washed her clean from head to foot, and bound her feet freshly with new white cloths under her new stockings, and Lotus rubbed into her flesh some fragrant almond oil of her own. Then they dressed her in garments she had brought from her home; white flowered silk next her sweet virgin flesh and then a light coat of sheep's wool of the finest and most curling kind, and then the red satin garments of marriage. And they rubbed lime upon her forehead and with a string tied skilfully they pulled out the hairs of her virginity, the fringe over her brow, and they made her forehead high and smooth and square for her new estate. Then they painted her with powder and with red paint, and with a brush they drew out in two long slender lines her eyebrows, and they set upon her head the bride's crown and the beaded veil, and upon her small feet they put shoes, embroidered, and they painted her fingertips and scented the palms of her hands, and thus they prepared her for marriage. To everything the maid was acquiescent, but reluctant and shy as was proper and correct for her.

Then Wang Lung and his uncle and his father and the guests waited in the middle room and the maid came in supported by her own slave and by the wife of Wang Lung's uncle, and she came in modestly and correctly with her head bowed, and she walked as though she were unwilling to wed a man and must be supported to it. This showed her great modesty and Wang Lung was pleased and said to himself that she was a proper maid.

After this Wang Lung's eldest son came in dressed as he had been in his red robe and his black jacket and his hair was smooth and his face fresh shaven. Behind him came his two brothers, and Wang Lung, seeing them, was fit to burst with pride at this procession of his goodly sons, who were to continue after him the life of his body. Now the old man, who had not understood what was happening at all and could hear only the fragments of what was shouted to him, now suddenly he understood, and he cackled out with cracked laughter and he said over and over in his piping old voice,

"There is a marriage and a marriage is children again and grandchildren!"

And he laughed so heartily that the guests all laughed to see his mirth and Wang Lung thought to himself that if only O-lan had been up from her bed it would have been a merry day.

All this time Wang Lung looked secretly and sharply at his

son to see if he glanced at the maid, and the young man did glance secretly and from the corner of his eyes, but it was enough, for he grew pleased and merry in his ways and Wang said proudly to himself,

"Well, and I have chosen one he likes for him."

Then the young man and the maid together bowed to the old man and to Wang Lung, and then they went into the room where O-lan lay, and she had caused herself to be dressed in her good black coat and she sat up when they came in and on her face there burned two fiery spots of red, which Wang Lung mistook for health, so that he said loudly, "Now she will be well, yet!"

And the two young persons went up and bowed to her and she patted the bed and said,

"Sit here and drink the wine and eat the rice of your marriage, for I would see it all and this will be your bed of marriage since I am soon to be finished with it and carried away."

Now none would answer her when she spoke thus but the two sat down side by side, shy and in silence of each other, and the wife of Wang Lung's uncle came in fat and important with the occasion, bearing two bowls of hot wine, and the two drank separately, and then mingled the wine of the two bowls and drank again, thus signifying that the two were now one, and they ate rice and mingled the rice and this signified that their life was now one, and thus they were wed. Then they bowed again to O-lan and to Wang Lung and then they went out and together they bowed to the assembled guests.

Then the feasting began and and the rooms and the courts were filled with tables and with the smell of cooking and with the sound of laughter, for the guests came from far and wide, those whom Wang Lung had invited and with them many whom Wang Lung had never seen, since it was known he was a rich man and food would never be missed or counted in his house at such a time. And Cuckoo had brought cooks from the town to prepare the feast, for there were to be many delicacies such as cannot be prepared in a farmer's kitchen and the town cooks came bearing great baskets of food ready cooked and only to be heated, and they made much of themselves and flourished their grimy aprons and bustled here and there in their zeal. And everyone ate more and yet more and drank all they were able to hold, and they were all very merry.

O-lan would have all the doors open and the curtains drawn so that she could hear the noise and the laughter and could smell the food, and she said again and again to Wang Lung, who came often to see how she did,

"And has everyone wine? And is the sweet rice dish in the middle of the feast very hot and have they put full measure of lard and sugar into it and the eight fruits?"

When he assured her that everything was as she wished it, she was content and lay listening.

Then it was over and the guests were gone and night came. And with the silence over the house and with the ebbing of merriment strength passed from O-lan and she grew weary and faint and she called to her the two who had been wed that day and she said,

"Now I am content and this thing in me may do as it will. My son, look to your father and your grandfather, and my daughter, look to your husband and your husband's father and his grandfather and the poor fool in the court, there is she. And you have no duty to any other."

This last she said, meaning Lotus, to whom she had never spoken. Then she seemed to fall into a fitful sleep, although they waited for her to speak further, and once more she roused herself to speak. Yet when she spoke it was as though she did not know they were there or indeed where she was, for she said, muttering and turning her head this way and that and her eyes closed,

"Well, and if I am ugly, still I have borne a son; although I am but a slave there is a son in my house." And again she said, suddenly, "How can that one feed him and care for him as I do? Beauty will not bear a man sons!"

And she forgot them all and lay muttering. Then Wang Lung motioned to them to go away, and he sat beside her while she slept and woke, and he looked at her. And he hated himself because even as she lay dying he saw how wide and ghastly her purpled lips drew back from her teeth. Then as he looked she opened her eyes wide and it seemed there was some strange mist over them, for she stared at him full and stared again, wondering and fixing her eyes on him, as though she wondered who he was. Suddenly her head dropped off the round pillow where it lay, and she shuddered and was dead.

Once she lay dead it seemed to Wang Lung that he could not bear to be near O-lan, and he called his uncle's wife to wash the body for burial, and when it was finished he would not go in again, but he allowed his uncle's wife and his eldest son and his daughter-in-law to lift the body from the bed and set it into the great coffin he had bought. But to comfort himself he busied himself in going to the town and calling men to seal the coffin according to custom and he went and found a geomancer and asked him for a lucky day for burials. He found a good day three months hence and it was the first good day the geomancer could find, so Wang Lung paid the man and went to the temple in the town and he bargained with the abbot there and rented a space for a coffin for three months, and there was O-lan's coffin brought to rest until the day of burial, for it seemed to Wang Lung he could not bear to have it under his eyes in the house.

Then Wang Lung was scrupulous to do all that should be done for the one dead, so he caused mourning to be made for himself and for his children, and their shoes were made of coarse white cloth, which is the color of mourning, and about their ankles they bound bands of white cloth, and the women in the house bound their hair with white cord.

After this Wang Lung could not bear to sleep in the room where O-lan had died and he took his possessions and moved altogether into the inner court where Lotus lived and he said to his eldest son,

"Go with your wife into that room where your mother lived and died, who conceived and bore you, and beget there your own sons."

So the two moved into it and were content.

Then as though death could not easily leave the house where it had come once, the old man, Wang Lung's father, who had been distraught ever since he saw them putting the stiff dead body of O-lan into the coffin, lay down on his bed one night for sleeping, and when the second daughter came in to him in the morning to bring him his tea, there he lay on his bed, his scattered old beard thrust up into the air, and his head thrown back in death.

She cried out at the sight and ran crying to her father and Wang Lung came in and found the old man so; his light, stiff old body was dry and cold and thin as a gnarled pine tree and he had died hours before, perhaps as soon as he had laid himself upon the bed. Then Wang Lung washed the old man himself and he laid him gently in the coffin he had bought for him and he had it sealed and he said,

"On the same day we will bury these two dead from our house and I will take a good piece of my hill land and we will bury them there together and when I die I will be laid there also."

So he did what he said he would do. When he had sealed the old man's coffin he set it upon two benches in the middle room and there it stood until the appointed day came. And it seemed to Wang Lung that it was a comfort to the old man to be there, even dead, and he felt near to his father in the coffin, for Wang Lung grieved for his father, but not unto death, because his father was very old and full of years, and for many years had been but half alive.

Then on the day appointed by the geomancer in the full of the spring of the year Wang Lung called priests from the Taoist temple and they came dressed in their yellow robes and their long hair knotted on their crowns, and he called priests from the Buddhist temples and they came in their long grey robes, their heads shaven and set with the nine sacred scars, and these priests beat drums and chanted the whole night through for the two who were dead. And whenever they stopped their chanting Wang Lung poured silver into their hands and they took breath again and chanted and did not cease until dawn rose.

Now Wang Lung had chosen a good place in his fields under a date tree upon a hill to set the graves, and Ching had the graves dug and ready and a wall of earth made about the graves, and there was space within the walls for the body of Wang Lung and for each of his sons and their wives, and there was space for sons' sons, also. This land Wang Lung did not begrudge, even though it was high land and good for wheat, because it was a sign of the establishment of his family upon their own land. Dead and alive they would rest upon their own land.

Then on the appointed day after the priests had finished the night of chanting, Wang Lung dressed himself in a robe of white sackcloth and he gave a robe like it to his uncle and his uncle's son, and to his own sons each a robe, and to his son's wife and to his own two daughters. He called chairs from the town to carry them, for it was not meet that they walk to the place of burial as though he were a poor man and a common fellow. So for the first time he rode on men's shoulders and behind the coffin where O-lan was. But behind his father's coffin his uncle rode first. Even Lotus, who in O-lan's lifetime could not appear before her, now that O-lan was dead, she came riding in a chair in order that before others she might

194

appear dutiful to the first wife of her husband. So for his uncle's wife and for his uncle's son Wang Lung hired chairs also and for all of them he had robes of sackcloth, and even for the poor fool he made a robe and hired a chair and put her in it, although she was sorely bewildered and laughed shrilly when there should have been only weeping.

Then mourning and weeping loudly they went to the graves, the laborers and Ching following and walking and wearing white shoes. And Wang Lung stood beside the two graves. He had caused the coffin of O-lan to be brought from the temple and it was put on the ground to await the old man's burial first. And Wang Lung stood and watched and his grief was hard and dry, and he would not cry out loud as others did for there were no tears in his eyes, because it seemed to him that what had come about was come about, and there was nothing to be done more than he had done.

But when the earth was covered over and the graves smoothed, he turned away silently and he sent away the chair and he walked home alone with himself. And out of his heaviness there stood out strangely but one clear thought and it was a pain to him, and it was this, that he wished he had not taken the two pearls from O-lan that day when she was washing his clothes at the pool, and he would never bear to see Lotus put them in her ears again.

Thus thinking heavily, he went on alone and he said to himself,

"There in that land of mine is buried the first good half of my life and more. It is as though half of me were buried there, and now it is a different life in my house."

And suddenly he wept a little, and he dried his eyes with the back of his hand, as a child does.

27

DURING ALL this time Wang Lung had scarcely thought of what the harvests were, so busy had he been with the wedding feasts and funerals in his house, but one day Ching came to him and he said,

"Now that the joy and sorrow are over, I have that to tell you about the land."

"Say on, then," Wang Lung answered. "I have scarcely thought whether I had land or not these days except to bury my dead in."

Ching waited in silence for a few minutes in respect to Wang Lung when he spoke thus, and then he said softly,

"Now may Heaven avert it, but it looks as though there would be such a flood this year as never was, for the water is swelling up over the land, although it is not summer yet, and too early for it to come like this."

But Wang Lung said stoutly,

"I have never had any good from that old man in heaven, yet. Incense or no incense, he is the same in evil. Let us go and see the land." And as he spoke he rose.

Now Ching was a fearful and timid man and however bad the times were he did not dare as Wang Lung did to exclaim against Heaven. He only said "Heaven wills it," and he accepted flood and drought with meekness. Not so Wang Lung. He went out on his land, on this piece and that, and he saw it was as Ching said. All those pieces along the moat, along the waterways, which he had bought from the Old Lord of the House of Hwang, were wet and mucky from the full water oozing up from the bottom, so that the good wheat on this land had turned sickly and yellow.

The moat itself was like a lake and the canals were rivers, swift and curling in small eddies and whirlpools, and even a fool could see that with summer rains not yet come, there would be that year a mighty flood and men and women and children starving again. Then Wang Lung ran hastily here and there over his land and Ching came silently as a shadow behind him, and they estimated together which land could be planted to rice and which land before the young rice could be put on it would already be under water. And looking at the canals brimming already to the edge of their banks, Wang Lung cursed and said,

"Now that old man in heaven will enjoy himself, for he will look down and see people drowned and starving and that is what the accursed one likes."

This he said loudly and angrily so that Ching shivered and said,

"Even so, he is greater than anyone of us and do not talk so, my master."

But since he was rich Wang Lung was careless, and he was as angry as he liked and he muttered as he walked homeward to think of the water swelling up over his land and over his good crops.

Then it all came to pass as Wang Lung had foreseen. The river to the north burst its dykes, its furthermost dykes first, and when men saw what had happened, they hurried from this place to that to collect money to mend it, and every man gave as he was able, for it was to the interest of each to keep the river within its bounds. The money they entrusted, then, to the magistrate in the district, a man new and just come. Now this magistrate was a poor man and had not seen so much money in his lifetime before, being only newly risen to his position through the bounty of his father, who had put all the money he had and could borrow to buy this place for his son, so that from it the family might acquire some wealth. When the river burst again the people went howling and clamoring to this magistrate's house, because he had not done what he promised and mended the dykes, and he ran and hid himself because the money he had spent in his own house, even three thousand pieces of silver. And the common people burst into his house howling and demanding his life for what he had done, and when he saw he would be killed he ran and jumped into the water and drowned himself, and thus the people were appeased.

But still the money was gone, and the river burst yet another dyke and another before it was content with the space it had for itself, and then it wore away these walls of earth until none could tell where a dyke had been in that whole country and the river swelled and rolled like a sea over all the good farming land, and the wheat and the young rice were at the bottom of the sea.

One by one the villages were made into islands and men watched the water rising and when it came within two feet of their doorways they bound their tables and beds together and put the doors of their houses upon them for rafts, and they piled what they could of their bedding and their clothes and their women and children on these rafts. And the water rose into the earthern houses and softened the walls and burst them apart and they melted down into the water and were as if they had never been. And then as if water on earth drew water from heaven it rained as though the earth were in drought. Day after day it rained.

Wang Lung sat in his doorway and looked out over the waters that were yet far enough from his house that was built on a high wide hill. But he saw the waters covering his land and he watched lest it cover the new made graves, but it did not, although the waves of the yellow clay-laden water lapped about the dead hungrily.

There were no harvests of any kind that year and everywhere people starved and were hungry and were angry at what had befallen them yet again. Some went south, and some who were bold and angry and cared nothing for what they did joined the robber bands that flourished everywhere in the countryside. These even tried to beleaguer the town so that the townspeople locked the gates of the wall continually except for one small gate called the western water gate, and this was watched by soldiers and locked at night also. And besides those who robbed and those who went south to work and to beg, even as Wang Lung had once gone with his old father and his wife and children, there were others who were old and tired and timid, and who had no sons, like Ching, and these stayed and starved and ate grass and what leaves they could find on high places and many died upon the land and water.

Then Wang Lung saw that a famine such as he had never seen was upon the land, for the water did not recede in time to plant the wheat for winter and there could be no harvest then the next year. And he looked well to his own house and to the spending of money and food, and he quarreled heartily with Cuckoo because for a long time she would still buy meat every day in the town, and he was glad at last, since there must be flood, that the water crept between his house and the town so that she could no longer go to market when she would, for he would not allow the boats to be put forth except when he said, and Ching listened to him and not to Cuckoo, for all her sharpness of tongue.

Wang Lung allowed nothing to be bought and sold after the winter came except what he said, and he husbanded carefully all that they had. Every day he gave out to his daughter-in-law what food was needed in the house for that day, and to Ching he gave out what the laborers should have, although it hurt him to feed idle men, and it hurt him so greatly that at last when winter cold came and the water froze over, he bade the men begone to the south to beg and to labor until the spring came, when they might return to him. Only to Lotus he gave secretly sugar and oil, because she was not accustomed to hardship. Even on the New Year they did eat but a fish they caught themselves in the lake and a pig they killed from the farm.

Now Wang Lung was not so poor as he wished to seem, for he had good silver hidden away in the walls where his son slept with his wife, though his son and daughter-in-law did not know it, and he had good silver and even some gold hidden in a jar at the bottom of the lake under his nearest field, and he had some hidden among the roots of the bamboos, and he had grains from the year before which he had not sold at market, and there was no danger of starvation in his house.

But all around him there were people starving, and he remembered the cries of the starving at the gate of the great house once when he passed, and he knew that there were many who hated him well because he had still that which he could eat and feed to his children, and so he kept his gates barred and he let none in whom he did not know. But still he knew very well that even this could not have saved him in these times of robbers and lawlessness if it had not been for his uncle. Well did Wang Lung know that if it had not been for his uncle's power he would have been robbed and sacked for his food and for his money and for the women in his house. So he was courteous to his uncle and to his uncle's son and to his uncle's wife and the three were like guests in his house and they drank tea before others and dipped first with their chopsticks into the bowls at mealtime.

Now these three saw well enough that Wang Lung was afraid of them and they grew haughty and demanded this and that and complained of what they ate and drank. And especially did the woman complain, for she missed the delicacies she had eaten in the inner courts and she complained to her husband and the three of them complained to Wang Lung.

Now Wang Lung saw that although his uncle himself grew old and lazy and careless and would not have troubled to complain if he had been let alone, yet the young man, his son, and his wife goaded him, and one day when Wang Lung stood at the gate he heard these two urging the old man,

"Well, and he has money and food, and let us demand silver of him." And the woman said, "We will never have such a hold as this again, for well he knows that if you were not his uncle and the brother of his father he would be robbed and sacked and his house left empty and a ruin, since you stand next to the head of the Redbeards."

Wang Lung standing there secretly and hearing this grew so angry that his skin was like to burst on him, but he was silent with great effort and he tried to plan what he could do with these three, but he could think of nothing to do. When, therefore, his uncle came to him next day saying, "Well, and my good nephew, give me a handful of silver to buy me a pipe and a bit of smoke and my woman is ragged and needs a new coat," he could say nothing but he handed the old man the five pieces of silver from his girdle, although he gnashed his teeth secretly, and it seemed to him that never in the old days when silver was rare with him had it gone from him so unwillingly.

Then before two days were passed his uncle was at him again and again for silver and Wang Lung shouted at last,

"Well, and shall we all starve soon?"

And his uncle laughed and said carelessly,

"You are under a good heaven. There are men less rich than you who hang from the burnt rafters of their houses."

When Wang Lung heard this, cold sweat broke out on him and he gave the silver without a word. And so, although they went without meat in the house, these three must eat meat, and although Wang Lung himself scarcely tasted tobacco, his uncle puffed unceasingly at his pipe.

Now Wang Lung's eldest son had been engrossed in his marriage and he scarcely saw what happened except that he guarded his wife jealously from the gaze of his cousin so that now these two were no longer friends but enemies. Wang Lung's son scarcely let his wife stir from their room except in the evenings when the other man was gone with his father and during the day he made her stay shut in the room. But when he saw these three doing as they would with his father he grew angry, for he was of a quick temper, and he said,

"Well, and if you care more for these three tigers than you do for your son and his wife, the mother of your grandsons, it is a strange thing and we had better set up our house elsewhere."

Wang Lung told him plainly then what he had told no one,

"I hate these three worse than my life and if I could think of a way I would do it. But your uncle is lord of a horde of wild robbers, and if I feed him and coddle him we are safe, and no one can show anger toward them."

Now when the eldest son heard this he stared until his eyes hung out of his head, but when he had thought of it for a while he was more angry than ever and he said,

"How is this for a way? Let us push them all into the water one night. Ching can push the woman for she is fat and soft and helpless, and I will push the young one my cousin, whom I hate enough for he is always peeping at my wife, and you can push the man."

But Wang Lung could not kill; although he would rather have killed his uncle than his ox, he could not kill even when he hated and he said,

"No, and even if I could do this thing, to push my father's brother into the water I would not, for if the other robbers heard of it what should we do, and if he lives we are safe, and if he is gone we are become as other people who have a little and so are in danger in such times as these."

Then the two of them fell silent, each thinking heavily what to do, and the young man saw that his father was right and death was too easy for the trouble and that there must be another way. And Wang Lung spoke aloud at last, musing,

"If there were a way that we could keep them here but make them harmless and undesiring what a thing it would be, but there is no such magic as this!"

Then the young man smote his two hands together and cried out,

"Well, and you have told me what to do! Let us buy them opium to enjoy, and more opium, and let them have their will of it as rich people do. I will seem to be friends with my cousin again and I will entice him away to the tea house in the town where one can smoke and we can buy it for my uncle and his wife."

But Wang Lung, since he had not thought of the thing first himself, was doubtful.

"It will cost a great deal," he said slowly, "for opium is as dear as jade."

"Well, and it is dearer than jade to have them at us like this," the young man argued, "and to endure besides their haughtiness and the young man peeping at my wife."

But Wang Lung would not at once consent, for it was not so easy a thing to do, and it would cost a good bag of silver to do it.

It is doubtful whether the thing would ever have been done and they would have gone as they were until the waters chose to recede had not a thing happened.

This thing was that the son of Wang Lung's uncle cast his eyes upon the second daughter of Wang Lung, who was his cousin and by blood the same as his sister. Now the second daughter of Wang Lung was an exceedingly pretty girl, and she looked like the second son who was a merchant, but with her smallness and lightness, and she had not his yellow skin. Her skin was fair and pale as almond flowers and she had a little low nose and thin red lips and her feet were small.

Her cousin laid hold of her one night when she passed alone through the court from the kitchen. He laid hold of her roughly and he pressed his hand into her bosom and she screamed out, and Wang Lung ran out and beat the man about the head, but he was like a dog with a piece of stolen meat that he would not drop, so that Wang Lung had to tear his daughter away. Then the man laughed thickly and he said,

"It is only play and is she not my sister? Can a man do any evil with his sister?" But his eyes glittered with lust as he spoke and Wang Lung muttered and pulled the girl away and sent her into her own room.

And Wang Lung told his son that night what had come about, and the young man was grave and he said,

"We must send the maid into the town to the home of her betrothed; even if the merchant Liu says it is a year too evil for wedding we must send her, lest we cannot keep her virgin with this hot tiger in the house."

So Wang Lung did. He went the next day into the town and to the house of the merchant and he said,

"My daughter is thirteen years old and no longer a child and she is fit for marriage."

But Liu was hesitant and he said,

"I have not enough profit this year to begin a family in my house."

Now Wang Lung was ashamed to say, "There is the son of my uncle in the house and he is a tiger," so he said only,

"I would not have the care of this maid upon me, because her mother is dead and she is pretty and is of an age to conceive, and my house is large and full of this and that, and I cannot watch her every hour. Since she is to be your family, let her virginity be guarded here, and let her be wed soon or late as you like."

Then the merchant, being a lenient and kindly man, replied,

"Well, and if this is how it is, let the maid come and I will speak to my son's mother, and she can come and be safe here in the courts with her mother-in-law, and after the next harvest or so, she can be wed."

Thus the matter was settled and Wang Lung was well content, and he went away.

But on his way back to the gate in the wall, where Ching held a boat waiting for him, Wang Lung passed a shop where tobacco and opium are sold, and he went in to buy himself a little shredded tobacco to put in his water pipe in the evenings, and as the clerk had it on the scales, he said half unwillingly to the man,

"And how much is your opium if you have it?"

And the clerk said,

"It is not lawful in these days to sell it over the counter, and we do not sell it so, but if you wish to buy it and have the silver, it is weighed out in the room behind this, an ounce for a silver piece."

Then Wang Lung would not think further what he did, but he said quickly,

"I will take six ounces of it."

28

THEN AFTER the second daughter was sent away and Wang Lung was free of his anxiety about her, he said to his uncle one day,

"Since you are my father's brother, here is a little better tobacco for you."

And he opened the jar of opium and the stuff was sticky and sweet smelling and Wang Lung's uncle took it and smelled of it, and he laughed and was pleased and he said,

"Well now, I have smoked it a little but not often before this, for it is too dear, but I like it well enough."

And Wang Lung answered him, pretending to be careless,

"It is only a little I bought once for my father when he grew old and could not sleep at night and I found it today unused and I thought, 'There is my father's brother, and why should he not have it before me, who am younger and do not need it yet?' Take it then, and smoke it when you wish or when you have a little pain."

Then Wang Lung's uncle took it greedily, for it was sweet to smell and a thing that only rich men used, and he took it and bought a pipe and he smoked the opium, lying all day upon his bed to do it. Then Wang Lung saw to it that there were pipes bought and left here and there and he pretended to smoke himself, but he only took a pipe to his room and left it there cold. And his two sons in the house and Lotus he would not allow to touch the opium, saying as his excuse that it was too dear, but he urged it upon his uncle and upon his uncle's wife and son, and the courts were filled with the sweetish smell of the smoke, and the silver for this Wang Lung did not begrudge because it bought him peace.

Now as the winter wore away and the waters began to recede so that Wang Lung could walk abroad over his land it happened one day that his eldest son followed him and said to him proudly,

"Well, and there will soon be another mouth in the house and it will be the mouth of your grandson."

Then Wang Lung, when he heard this, turned himself about and he laughed and he rubbed his hands together and said,

"Here is a good day, indeed!"

And he laughed again, and went to find Ching and tell him to go to the town to buy fish and good food and he sent it in to his son's wife and said,

"Eat, make strong the body of my grandson."

Then all during the spring Wang Lung had the knowledge of this birth to come for his comfort. And when he was busy about other things he thought of it, and when he was troubled he thought of it and it was a comfort to him.

And as the spring grew into summer, the people who had gone away from the floods came back again, one by one and group by group, spent and weary with the winter and glad to be back, although where their houses had been there was nothing now but the yellow mud of the water-soaked land. But out of this mud houses could be fashioned again, and mats bought to roof them, and many came to Wang Lung to borrow money, and he loaned it at high interest, seeing how greatly it was in demand, and the security he always said must be land. And with the money they borrowed they planted seed upon the earth that was fat with the richness of the dried water, and when they needed oxen and seed and plows and when they could borrow no more money, some sold land and part of their fields that they might plant what was left. And of these Wang Lung bought land and much land, and he bought it cheaply, since money men must have.

But there were some who would not sell their land, and when they had nothing wherewith to buy seed and plow and oxen, they sold their daughters, and there were those who came to Wang Lung to sell, because it was known he was rich and powerful and a man of good heart.

And he, thinking constantly of the child to come and of others to come from his sons when they were all wed, bought five slaves, two about twelve years of age with big feet and strong bodies, and two younger to wait upon them all and fetch and carry, and one to wait on the person of Lotus, for Cuckoo grew old and since the second girl was gone there had been none other to work in the house. And the five he bought in one day, for he was a man rich enough to do quickly what he decided upon.

Then one day many days later a man came bearing a small delicate maid of seven years or so, wanting to sell her, and Wang Lung said he would not have her at first, for she was so small and weak. But Lotus saw her and fancied her and she said pettishly,

"Now this one I will have because she is so pretty and the other one is coarse and smells like goat's meat and I do not like her."

And Wang Lung looked at the child and saw her pretty frightened eyes and her piteous thinness and he said partly to humor Lotus and partly that he might see the child fed and fattened,

"Well, and let it be so if you wish it."

So he bought the child for twenty pieces of silver and she lived in the inner courts and slept on the foot of the bed where Lotus slept.

Now it seened to Wang Lung that he could have peace in his house. When the waters receded and summer came and the land was to be planted to good seed, he walked hither and thither and looked at every piece and he discussed with Ching the quality of each piece of soil and what change there should be of crops for the fertility of the land. And whenever he went he took with him his youngest son, who was to be on the land after him, that the lad might learn. And Wang Lung never looked to see how the lad listened and whether he listened or not, for the lad walked with his head downcast and he had a sullen look on his face, and no one knew what he thought.

But Wang Lung did not see what the lad did, only that he walked there in silence behind his father. And when everything was planned Wang Lung went back to his house well content and he said to his own heart,

"I am no longer young and it is not necessary for me to work any more with my hands since I have men on my land and my sons and peace in my house."

Yet when he went into his house there was no peace. Although he had given his son a wife and although he had bought slaves enough to serve them all, and although his uncle and his uncle's wife were given enough of opium for their pleasure all day, still there was no peace. And again it was because of his uncle's son and his own eldest son.

It seemed as though Wang Lung's eldest son could never give over his hatred of his cousin or his deep suspicion of his cousin's evil. He had seen well enough with his own eyes in his youth that the man, his cousin, was full of all sorts of evil, and things had come to pass where Wang Lung's son would not even leave the house to go to the tea shop unless the cousin went also, and he watched the cousin and left only when he left. And he suspected the man of evil with the slaves and even of evil in the inner court with Lotus, although this was idle, for Lotus grew fatter and older every day and had long since given over caring for anything except her foods and her wines and would not have troubled to look at the man had he come near, and she was even glad when Wang Lung came to her less and less with his age.

Now when Wang Lung entered with his youngest son from the fields, his eldest son drew his father aside and he said,

"I will not endure that fellow my cousin in the house any more with his peepings and his lounging about with his robes unbuttoned and his eyes on the slaves." He did not dare to say further what he thought, "And even he dares to peep into the inner courts at your own woman," because he remembered with a sickness in his vitals that he himself had once hung about this woman of his father's, and now seeing her fat and older as she was, he could not dream that he had ever done this thing and he was bitterly ashamed of it and would not for anything have recalled it to his father's memory. So he was silent of that, and mentioned only the slaves.

Wang Lung had come in robustly from the fields and in high humor because the water was off the land and the air dry and warm and because he was pleased with his youngest son that he had gone with him, and he answered, angry at this fresh trouble in his house,

"Well, and you are a foolish child to be forever thinking of this. You have grown fond and too fond of your wife and it is not seemly, for a man ought not to care for his wife that his parents gave him above all else in the world. It is not meet for a man to love his wife with a foolish and overweening love, as though she were a harlot."

Then the young man was stung with this rebuke of his father against him, for more than anything he feared any who accused him of behavior that was not correct, as though he were common and ignorant, and he answered quickly,

"It is not for my wife. It is because it is unseemly in my father's house."

But Wang Lung did not hear him. He was musing in anger and he said again,

"And am I never to be done with all this trouble in my house between male and female? Here am I passing into my age and my blood cools and I am freed at last from lusts and I would have a little peace, and must I endure the lusts and jealousies of my sons?" And then after a little silence, he shouted again, "Well, and what would you have me do?"

Now the young man had waited patiently enough for his father's anger to pass, for he had something to say, and this

Wang Lung saw clearly when he shouted, "What would you have me do?" The young man then answered steadily,

"I wish we could leave this house and that we could go into the town and live. It is not meet that we go on living in the country like hinds and we could go and we could leave my uncle and his wife and my cousin here and we could live safely in the town behind the gates."

Wang Lung laughed bitterly and shortly when his son said this, and he threw the desire of the young man aside for something worthless and not to be considered.

"This is my house," he said stoutly, seating himself at the table and drawing his pipe toward him from where it stood "and you may live in it or not. My house and my land it is, and if it were not for the land we should all starve as the others did, and you could not walk about in your dainty robes idle as a scholar. It is the good land that has made you something better than a farmer's lad."

And Wang Lung rose and tramped about loudly in the middle room and he behaved roughly and he spat upon the floor and acted as a farmer may, because although one side of his heart triumphed in his son's fineness, the other side was robust and scornful of him and this although he knew he was secretly proud of his son, and proud because none who looked at this son could dream that he was but one generation removed from the land itself.

But the eldest son was not ready to give over. He followed his father saying,

"Well, and there is the old great house of the Hwangs. The front part of it is filled with this and that of common people but the inner courts are locked and silent and we could rent them and live there peacefully and you and my youngest brother could come to and fro to the land and I would not be angered by this dog, my cousin." And then he persuaded his father and he allowed the tears to come into his eyes and he forced them upon his cheeks and did not wipe them away and he said again "Well, and I try to be a good son and I do not gamble and smoke opium and I am content with the woman you have given me and I ask a little of you and it is all."

Now whether the tears would have alone moved Wang Lung he did not know, but he was moved by the words of his son when he said "the great house of the Hwangs."

Never had Wang Lung forgotten that once he had gone crawling into that great house and stood ashamed in the

208

presence of those who lived there so that he was frightened of even the gateman, and this had remained a memory of shame to him all his life and he hated it. Through all his life he had the sense that he was held in the eyes of men a little lower than those who lived in the town, and when he stood before the Old Mistress of the great house, this sense became crisis. So when his son said, "We could live in the great house," the thought leaped into his mind as though he saw it actually before his eyes, "I could sit on that seat where that old one sat and from whence she bade me stand like a serf, and now I could sit there and so call another into my presence." And he mused and he said to himself again, "This I could do if I wished."

And he toyed with the thought and he sat silent and he did not answer his son, but he put tobacco in his pipe and lit it with a spill that stood ready and he smoked and he dreamed of what he could do if he wished. So not because of his son and not because of his uncle's son he dreamed that he could live in the House of Hwang, which was to him forever the great house.

Therefore although he was not willing at first to say that he would go or that he would change anything, yet thereafter he was more than ever displeased with the idleness of his uncle's son, and he watched the man sharply and he saw that it was true he did cast eyes at the maids and Wang Lung muttered and said,

"Now I cannot live with this lustful dog in my house."

And he looked at his uncle and he saw that he grew thin as he smoked his opium and his skin was yellow with opium and he was bent and old and he spat blood when he coughed; and he looked at his uncle's wife and she was a cabbage of a woman who took eagerly to her opium pipe and was satisfied with it and drowsy; and these were little trouble enough now, and the opium had done what Wang Lung wished it would do.

But here was the uncle's son, this man, still unwed, and a wild beast for his desires, and he would not yield to opium easily as the two old ones had done and take out his lusts in dreams. And Wang Lung would not willingly let him wed in the house, because of the spawn he would breed and one like him was enough. Neither would the man work, since there was no need and none to drive him to it, unless the hours he spent away at night could be called work. But even these grew less frequent, for as men returned to the land order came back to the villages and to the town and the robbers withdrew to the hills in the northwest, and the man would not go with them, preferring to live on Wang Lung's bounty. Thus he was a thorn in the household and he hung about everywhere, talking and idling and yawning, and half dressed even at noon.

One day, therefore, when Wang Lung went into the town to see his second son at the grain market he asked him,

'Well, my second son, what say you of the thing your elder brother desires, that we move into the town to the great house if we can rent part of it?"

The second son was grown a young man by now and he had grown smooth and neat and like the other clerks in the shop, although still small of stature and yellow-skinned and with crafty eyes, and he answered smoothly,

"It is an excellent thing and it would suit me well, for then I could wed and have my wife there also and we would all be under one roof as a great family is."

Now Wang Lung had done nothing toward the wedding of this son, for he was a cool youth and cool-blooded and there had never been any sign of lust in him and Wang Lung had much else to trouble him. Now, however, he said in some shame, for he knew he had not done well by his second son, "Well, now I have said to myself this long time that you should be wed, but what with this thing and that I have not had time, and with this last famine and having to avoid all feasting—but now that men may eat again, the thing shall be done."

And he cast about secretly in his mind where he should find a maid. The second son said then,

"Well, and wed I will then, for it is a good thing and better than spending money on a jade when the need comes, and it is right for a man to have sons. But do not get me a wife from a house in town, such as my brother has, for she will talk forever of what was in her father's house and make me spend money and it will be an anger to me."

Wang Lung heard this with astonishment, for he had not known that his daughter-in-law was thus, seeing only that she was a woman careful to be correct in her behavior and fair enough in her looks. But it seemed to him wise talk and he was rejoiced that his son was sharp and clever for the saving of money. This lad he had, indeed, scarcely known at all, for he grew up weak beside the vigor of the elder brother, and except for his piping tales he was not a child or a youth to whom one would pay great heed, so that when he went into the shop, Wang Lung forgot him day after day, except to answer when anyone asked him how many children he had, "Well, and I have three sons."

Now he looked at the youth, his second son, and he saw his smooth-cut hair, oiled and flat, and his clean gown of small-patterned grey silk, and he saw the youth's neat movements and steady, secret eyes and he said to himself in his surprise,

"Well, and this also is my son!" And aloud he said, "What sort of a maid would you have, then?"

Then the young man answered as smoothly and steadily as if he had the thing planned before,

"I desire a maid from a village, of good landed family and without poor relatives, and one who will bring a good dowry with her, neither plain nor fair to look upon, and a good cook, so that even though there are servants in the kitchen she may watch them. And she must be such a one that if she buys rice it will be enough and not a handful over and if she buys cloth the garment will be well cut so that the scraps of cloth left over should lie in the palm of her hand. Such an one I want."

Now Wang Lung was the more astonished when he heard this talk, for here was a young man whose life he had not seen, even though it was his own son. It was not such blood as this that ran in his own lusty body when he was young, nor in the body of his eldest son; yet he admired the wisdom of the young man and he said laughing,

"Well, and I shall seek such a maid and Ching shall look for her among the villages."

Still laughing, he went away and he went down the street of the great house and he hesitated between the stone lions and then, since there was none to stop him, he went in and the front courts were as he remembered them when he came in to seek the whore whom he feared for his son. The trees were hung with drying clothes and women sat everywhere gossiping as they drove their long needles back and forth through shoe soles they made, and children rolled naked and dusty upon the tiles of the courts and the place reeked with the smell of common people who swarm into the courts of the great when the great are gone. And he looked towards the door where the whore had lived, but the door stood ajar and another lived there now, an old man, and for this Wang Lung was glad and he went on.

Now Wang Lung in the old days when the great family were there would have felt himself one of these common people and against the great and half hating, half fearful of them. But now that he had land and that he had silver and gold hidden safely away, he despised these people who swarmed everywhere, and he said to himself that they were filthy and he picked his way among them with his nose up and breathing lightly because of the stink they made. And he despised them and was against them as though he himself belonged to the great house.

He went back through the courts, although it was for idle curiosity and not because he had decided anything, but still he went on and at the back he found a gate locked into a court and beside it an old woman drowsing, and he looked and he saw that this was the pock-marked wife of the man who had been gateman. This astonished him, and he looked at her, whom he had remembered as buxom and middleaged, now haggard and wrinkled and white haired, and her teeth were yellow snags loose in her jaws, and looking at her thus he saw in a full moment how many and how swift were the years that had passed since he was a young man coming with his first-born son in his arms, and for the first time in his life Wang Lung felt his age creeping upon him.

Then he said somewhat sadly to the old woman,

"Wake and let me into the gate."

And the old woman started up blinking and licking her dry lips, and she said,

"I am not to open except to such as may rent the whole inner courts."

And Wang Lung said suddenly,

"Well, and so I may, if the place please me."

But he did not tell her who he was, only he went in after her and he remembered the way well and he followed her. There the courts stood in silence; there the little room where he had left his basket; here the long verandas supported by the delicate, red-varnished pillars. He followed her into the great hall itself, and his mind went back how quickly over the years past when he had stood there waiting to wed a slave of the house. There before him was the great carven dais where the old lady had sat, her fragile, tended body wrapped in silvery satin.

And moved by some strange impulse he went forward and he sat down where she had sat and he put his hand on the table and from the eminence it gave him he looked down on the bleary face of the old hag who blinked at him and waited in silence for what he would do. Then some satisfaction he had longed for all his days without knowing it swelled up in his heart and he smote the table with his hand and he said suddenly,

"This house I will have!"

29

IN THESE DAYS when Wang Lung had decided a thing he could not do it quickly enough. As he grew older he grew impatient to have done with things and to sit in the latter part of the day at peace and idle and to watch the late sun and sleep a little after he had strolled about his land. So he told his elder son what he had decided and he commanded the young man to arrange the matter, and he sent for his second son to come and help with the moving and on a day when they were ready they moved, first Lotus and Cuckoo and their slaves and goods, and then Wang Lung's eldest son and his wife and their servants and the slaves.

But Wang Lung himself would not go at once, and he kept with him his youngest son. When the moment came for leaving the land whereon he was born he could not do it easily nor so quickly as he had thought and he said to his sons when they urged him,

"Well then, prepare a court for me to use alone and on a day that I wish I will come, and it will be a day before my grandson is born, and when I wish I can come back to my land."

And when they urged him yet again, he said,

"Well, and there is my poor fool and whether to take her with me or not I do not know, but take her I must, for there is no one who will see if she is fed or not unless I do it."

This Wang Lung said in some reproach to the wife of his eldest son, for she would not suffer the poor fool near her, but was finicking and squeamish and she said, "Such an one should not be alive at all, and it is enough to mar the child in me to look at her." And Wang Lung's eldest son remembered the dislike of

213

his wife and so now he was silent and said no more. Then Wang Lung repented his reproach and he said mildly,

"I will come when the maid is found who is to wed the second son, for it is easier to stay here where Ching is until the matter is completed."

The second son, therefore, gave over his urging.

There was left in the house, then, none but the uncle and his wife and son and Ching and the laboring men, besides Wang Lung and his youngest son and the fool. And the uncle and his wife and son moved into the inner courts where Lotus had been and they took it for their own, but this did not grieve Wang Lung unduly, for he saw clearly there were not many days of life left for his uncle and when the idle old man was dead Wang Lung's duty to that generation was over and if the younger man did not do as he was told none would blame Wang Lung if he cast him out. Then Ching moved into the outer rooms and the laborers with him, and Wang Lung and his son and the fool lived in the middle rooms, and Wang Lung hired a stout woman to be servant to them.

And Wang Lung slept and rested himself and took no heed of anything, for he was suddenly very weary and the house was peaceful. There was none to trouble him, for his youngest son was a silent lad who kept out of his father's way and Wang Lung scarcely knew what he was, so silent a lad was he.

But at last Wang Lung stirred himself to bid Ching find a maid for his second son to wed.

Now Ching grew old and withered and lean as a reed, but there was the strength of an old and faithful dog in him yet, although Wang Lung would no longer let him lift a hoe in his hand or follow the oxen behind the plow. But still he was useful for he watched the labor of others and he stood by when the grain was weighed and measured. So when he heard what Wang Lung wished him to do he washed himself and put on his good blue cotton coat and he went hither and thither to this village and that and he looked at many maidens and at last he came back and he said,

"Now would I lief have to choose a wife for myself than for your son. But if it were I and I young, there is a maid three villages away, a good, buxom, careful maid with no fault except a ready laugh, and her father is willing and glad to be tied to your family by his daughter. And the dowry is good for these times, and he has land. But I said I could give no promise until you gave it."

It seemed to Wang Lung then that this was good enough and he was anxious to be done with it and so he gave his promise and when the papers were come he set his mark to them, and he was relieved and he said,

"Now there is but one more son and I am finished with all this wedding and marrying and I am glad I am so near my peace."

And when it was done and the wedding day set, he rested and sat in the sun and slept even as his father had done before him.

Then it seemed to Wang Lung that as Ching grew feeble with age and since he himself grew heavy and drowsy with his food and his age and his third son was yet too young for responsibility, that it would be well to rent some of his farthest fields to others in the village. This Wang Lung did, then, and many of the men in the villages near by came to Wang Lung to rent his land and to become his tenants, and the rent was decided upon, half of the harvest to go to Wang Lung because he owned the land, and half to the one who hired because of his labor, and there were other things which each must furnish besides: Wang Lung certain stores of manure and beancake and of sesame refuse from his oil mill after the sesame was ground, and the tenant to reserve certain crops for the use of Wang Lung's house.

And then, since there was not the need for his management that there had been, Wang Lung went sometimes into the town and slept in the court which he caused to be prepared for him, but when day came he was back upon his land, walking through the gate in the wall about the town as soon as it was open after dawn came. And he smelled the fresh smell of the fields and when he came to his own land he rejoiced in it.

Then as if the gods were kind for the once and had prepared peace for his old age his uncle's son, who grew restless in the house now quiet and without women save for the stout serving woman who was wife to one of the laborers, this uncle's son heard of a war to the north and he said to Wang Lung,

"It is said there is a war to the north of us and I will go and join it for something to do and to see. This I will if you will give me silver to buy more clothes and my bedding and a foreign firestick to put over my shoulder."

Then Wang Lung's heart leaped with pleasure but he hid his pleasure artfully and he demurred in pretense and he said,

"Now you are the only son of my uncle and after you there are none to carry on his body and if you go to war what will happen?"

But the man answered, laughing,

"Well, and I am no fool and I will not stand anywhere that my life is in danger. If there is to be a battle I will go away until it is over. I wish for a change and a little travel and to see foreign parts before I am too old to do it."

So Wang Lung gave him the silver readily and this time again the giving was not hard so that he poured the money out into the man's hand and he said to himself,

"Well, and if he likes it there is an end to this curse in my house, for there is always a war somewhere in the nation." And again he said to himself, "Well, and he may even be killed, if my good fortune holds, for sometimes in wars there are those who die."

He was in high good humor, then, although he concealed it, and he comforted his uncle's wife when she wept a little to hear of her son's going, and he gave her more opium and lit her pipe for her and he said,

"Doubtless he will rise to be a military official and honor will come to us all through him."

Then at last there was peace, for there were only the two old sleeping ones in the house in the country besides his own, and in the house in the town the hour grew near for the birth of Wang Lung's grandson.

Now Wang Lung, as this hour drew near, stayed more and more in the house in town and he walked about the courts and he could never have done with musing on what had happened, and he could never have his fill of wonder at this, that here in these courts where the great family of Hwang had once lived now he lived with his wife and his sons and their wives and now a child was to be born of a third generation.

And his heart swelled within him so that nothing was too good for his money to buy and he bought lengths of satin and of silk for them all for it looked ill to see common cotton robe upon the carved chairs and about the carved tables of southern blackwood, and he bought lengths of good blue and black cotton for the slaves so not one of them needed to wear a garment ragged. This he did, and he was pleased when the friends that his eldest son had found in the town came into the courts and proud that they should see all that was.

And Wang Lung took it into his heart to eat dainty foods, and he himself, who once had been well satisfied with good wheaten bread wrapped about a stick of garlic, now that he slept late in the day and did not work with his own hands on the land, now he was not easily pleased with this dish and that, and he tasted winter bamboo and shrimps' roe and southern fish and shellfish from the northern seas and pigeons' eggs and all those things which rich men use to force their lagging appetites. And his sons ate and Lotus also, and Cuckoo, seeing all that had come about, laughed and said,

"Well, and it is like the old days when I was in these courts, only this body of mine is withered and dried now and not fit even for an old lord."

Saying this, she glanced slyly at Wang Lung and laughed again, and he pretended not to hear her lewdness, but he was pleased, nevertheless, that she had compared him to the Old Lord.

So with this idle and luxurious living and rising when they would and sleeping when they would, he waited for his grandson. Then one morning he heard the groans of a woman and he went into the courts of his eldest son and his son met him and said,

"The hour is come, but Cuckoo says it will be long, for the woman is narrowly made and it is a hard birth."

So Wang Lung went back to his own court and he sat down and listened to the cries, and for the first time in many years he was frightened and felt the need of some spirit's aid. He rose and went to the incense shop and he bought incense and he went to the temple in the town where the goddess of mercy dwells in her gilded alcove and he summoned an idling priest and gave him money and bade him thrust the incense before the goddess saying,

"It is ill for me, a man, to do it, but my first grandson is about to be born and it is a heavy labor for the mother, who is a town woman and too narrowly made, and the mother of my son is dead, and there is no woman to thrust in the incense."

Then as he watched the priest thrust it in the ashes of the urn before the goddess he thought with sudden horror, "And what if it be not a grandson but a girl!" and he called out hastily,

"Well, and if it is a grandson I will pay for a new red robe for the goddess, but nothing will I do if it is a girl!"

He went out in agitation because he had not thought of this thing, that it might be not a grandson but a girl, and he went and bought more incense, although the day was hot and in the streets the dust was a span's depth, and he went out in spite of this to the small country temple where the two sat who watched over fields and land and he thrust the incense in and lit it and he muttered to the pair,

"Well now, and we have cared for you, my father and I and my son, and now here comes the fruit of my son's body, and if it is not a son there is nothing more for the two of you."

Then having done all he could, he went back to the courts very spent, and he sat down at his table and he wished for a slave to bring him tea and for another to bring him a towel dipped and wrung from steaming water to wipe his face, but though he clapped his hands none came. No one heeded him and there was running to and fro, but he dared to stop no one to ask what sort of a child had been born or even if any had been born. He sat there dusty and spent and no one spoke to him.

Then at last when it seemed to him it must soon be night, so long he had waited, Lotus came in waddling upon her small feet because of her great weight and leaning upon Cuckoo, and she laughed and said loudly

"Well, and there is a son in the house of your son, and both mother and son are alive. I have seen the child and it is fair and sound."

Then Wang Lung laughed also and he rose and he slapped his hands together and laughed again and he said,

"Well, and I have been sitting here like a man with his own first son coming and not knowing what to do of this and that and afraid of everything."

And then when Lotus had gone on to her room and he sat again he fell to musing and he thought to himself,

"Well, and I did not fear like this when that other one bore her first, my son." And he sat silent and musing and he remembered within himself that day and how she had gone alone into the small dark room and how alone she had borne him sons and again sons and daughters and she bore them silently, and how she had come to the fields and worked beside him again. And here was this one, now the wife of his son, who cried like a child with her pains, and who had all the slaves running in the house, and her husband there by her door.

And he remembered as one remembers a dream long past how O-lan rested from her work a little while and fed the child richly and the white rich milk ran out of her breast and spilled upon the ground. And this seemed too long past ever to have been.

Then his son came in smiling and important and he said loudly,

"The man child is born, my father, and now we must find a woman to nurse him with her breasts, for I will not have my wife's beauty spoiled with the nursing and her strength sapped with it. None of the women of position in the town do so."

And Wang Lung said sadly, although why he was sad he did not know,

"Well, and if it must be so, let it be so, if she cannot nurse her own child."

When the child was a month old Wang Lung's son, its father, gave the birth feasts, and to it he invited guests from the town and his wife's father and mother, and all the great of the town. And he had dyed scarlet many hundreds of hens' eggs, and these he gave to every guest and to any who sent guests, and there was feasting and joy through the house, for the child was a goodly fat boy and he had passed his tenth day and lived and this was a fear gone, and they all rejoiced.

And when the birth feast was over Wang Lung's son came to his father and he said,

"Now that there are the three generations in this house, we should have the tablets of ancestors that great families have, and we should set the tablets up to be worshipped at the feast days for we are an established family now."

This pleased Wang Lung greatly, and so he ordered it and so it was carried out, and there in the great hall the row of tablets was set up, his grandfather's name on one and then his father's, and the spaces left empty for Wang Lung's name and his son's when they should die. And Wang Lung's son bought an incense urn and set it before the tablets.

When this was finished Wang Lung remembered the red robe he had promised the goddess of mercy and so he went to the temple to give the money for it.

And then, on his way back, as if the gods cannot bear to give freely and not hide sting somewhere in the gift one came running from the harvest fields to tell him that Ching lay dying suddenly and had asked if Wang Lung would come to see him die. Wang Lung hearing the panting runner, cried angrily,

"Now I suppose that accursed pair in the temple are jealous

219

because I gave a red robe to a town goddess and I suppose they do not know they have no power over childbirth and only over land."

And although his noon meal stood ready for him to eat he would not take up his chopsticks, although Lotus called loudly to him to wait until after the evening sun came; he would not stay for her, and he went out. Then when Lotus saw he did not heed her she sent a slave after him with an umbrella of oiled paper, but so fast did Wang Lung run that the stout maid had difficulty in holding the umbrella over his head.

Wang Lung went at once to the room where Ching had been laid and he called out loudly to anyone,

"Now how did all this come about?"

The room was full of laborers crowding about and they answered in confusion and haste,

"He would work himself at the threshing . . ." "We told him not at his age . . ." "There was a laborer who is newly hired . . ." "He could not hold the flail rightly and Ching would show him . . ." "It is labor too hard for an old man . . ."

Then Wang Lung called out in a terrible voice,

"Bring me this laborer!"

And they pushed the man in front before Wang Lung, and he stood there trembling and his bare knees knocking together, a great, ruddy, coarse, country lad, with his teeth sticking out in a shelf over his lower lip and round dull eyes like an ox's eyes. But Wang Lung had no pity on him. He slapped the lad on both his cheeks and he took the umbrella from the slave's hand and he beat the lad about the head, and none dared stop him lest his anger go into his blood and at his age poison him. And the bumpkin stood it humbly, blubbering a little and sucking his teeth.

Then Ching moaned from the bed where he lay and Wang Lung threw down the umbrella and he cried out,

"Now this one will die while I am beating a fool!"

And he sat down beside Ching and took his hand and held it, and it was as light and dry and small as a withered oak leaf and it was not possible to believe that any blood ran through it, so dry and light and hot it was. But Ching's face, which was pale and yellow every day, was now dark and spotted with his scanty blood, and his half-opened eyes were filmed and blind and his breath came in gusts. Wang Lung leaned down to him and said loudly in his ear,

"Here am I and I will buy you a coffin second to my father's only!"

But Ching's ear were filled with his blood, and if he heard Wang Lung he made no sign, but he only lay there panting and dying and so he died.

When he was dead Wang Lung leaned over him and he wept as he had not wept when his own father died, and he ordered a coffin of the best kind, and he hired priests for the funeral and he walked behind wearing white mourning. He made his eldest son, even, wear white bands on his ankles as though a relative had died, although his son complained and said,

"He was only an upper servant, and it is not suitable so to mourn for a servant."

But Wang Lung compelled him for three days. And if Wang Lung had had his way wholly, he would have buried Ching inside the earthen wall where his father and O-lan were buried. But his sons would not have it and they complained and said,

"Shall our mother and grandfather lie with a servant? And must we also in our time?"

Then Wang Lung, because he could not contend with them and because at his age he would have peace in his house, buried Ching at the entrance to the wall and he was comforted with what he had done, and he said,

"Well, and it is meet, for he has ever stood guardian to me against evil." And he directed his sons that when he himself died he should lie nearest to Ching.

Then less than ever did Wang Lung go to see his lands, because now Ching was gone it stabbed him to go alone and he was weary of labor and his bones ached when he walked over the rough fields alone. So he rented out all his land that he could and men took it eagerly, for it was known to be good land. But Wang Lung would never talk of selling a foot of any piece, and he would only rent it for an agreed price for a year at a time. Thus he felt it all his own and still in his hand.

And he appointed one of the laborers and his wife and children to live in the country house and to care for the two old opium dreamers. Then seeing his youngest son's wistful eyes, he said,

"Well, and you may come with me into the town, and I will take my fool with me too, and she can live in my court where I am. It is too lonely for you now that Ching is gone, and with him gone, I am not sure that they will be kind to the poor fool seeing there will be none to tell if she is beaten or ill fed. And

221

there is no one now to teach you concerning the land, now that Ching is gone."

So Wang Lung took his youngest son and his fool with him and thereafter he came scarcely at all for a long time to the house on his land.

30

Now to Wang Lung it seemed there was nothing left to be desired in his condition, and now he could sit in his chair in the sun beside his fool and he could smoke his water pipe and be at peace since his land was tended and the money from it coming into his hand without care from him.

And so it might have been if it had not been for that eldest son of his who was never content with what was going on well enough but must be looking aside for more. So he came to his father saying,

"There is this and that which we need in this house and we must not think we can be a great family just because we live in these inner courts. Now there is my younger brother's wedding due in a bare six months and we have not chairs enough to seat the guests and we have not bowls enough nor tables enough nor anything enough in these rooms. It is a shame, moreover, to ask guests to come through the great gates and through all that common swarm with their stinks and their noise, and with my brother wed and his children and mine to come we need those courts also."

Then Wang Lung looked at his son standing there in his handsome raiment and he shut his eyes and drew hard on his pipe and he growled forth,

"Well, and what now and what again?"

The young man saw his father was weary of him but he said stubbornly, and he made his voice a little louder,

"I say we should have the outer courts also and we should

have what befits a family with so much money as we have and good land as we have."

Then Wang Lung muttered into his pipe,

"Well, and the land is mine and you have never put your hand to it."

"Well, and my father," the young man cried out at this, "it was you who would have me a scholar and when I try to be a fitting son to a man of land you scorn me and would make a hind of me and my wife." And the young man turned himself away stormily and made as though he would knock his brains out against a twisted pine tree that stood there in the court.

Wang Lung was frightened at this, lest the young man do himself an injury, since he had been fiery always, and so he called out,

"Do as you like—do as you like—only do not trouble me with it!"

Hearing this, the son went away quickly lest his father change and he went well pleased. As quickly as he was able, then, he bought tables and chairs from Soochow, carved and wrought, and he bought curtains of red silk to hang in the doorways and he bought vases large and small and he bought scrolls to hang on the wall and as many as he could of beautiful women, and he bought curious rocks to make rockeries in the courts such as he had seen in southern parts, and thus he busied himself for many days.

With all this coming and going he had to pass many times through the outer courts, even every day, and he could not pass among the common people without sticking his nose up and he could not bear them, so that the people who lived there laughed at him after he had passed and they said,

"He has forgotten the smell of the manure in the dooryard on his father's farm!"

But still none dared to speak thus as he passed, for he was a rich man's son. When the feast came when rents are decided upon these common people found that the rent for the rooms and the courts where they lived had been greatly raised, because another would pay that much for them, and they had to move away. Then they knew it was Wang Lung's eldest son who had done this, although he was clever and said nothing and did it all by letters to the son of the old Lord Hwang in foreign parts, and this son of the Old Lord cared for nothing except where and how he could get the most money for the old house.

The common people had to move, then, and they move complaining and cursing because a rich man could do as h would and they packed their tattered possessions and wer away swelling with anger and muttering that one day the would come back even as the poor do come back when the ric are too rich.

But all this Wang Lung did not hear, since he was in the in ner courts and seldom came forth, since he slept and ate an took his ease as his age came on, and he left the thing in th hands of his eldest son. And his son called carpenters an clever masons and they repaired the rooms and the moon gate between the courts that the common people had ruined wit their coarse ways of living, and he built again the pools and h bought flecked and golden fish to put in them. And after it wa all finished and made beautiful as far as he knew beauty, h planted lotus and lilies in the pools, and the scarlet-berried bam boo of India and everything he could remember he had see in southern parts. And his wife came out to see what he ha done and the two of them walked about through every cour and room and she saw this and that still lacking, and he listene with great heed to all she said that he might do it.

Then people on the streets of the town heard of all tha Wang Lung's eldest son did, and they talked of what was bein done in the great house, now that a rich man lived there agai And people who had said Wang The Farmer now said Wan The Big Man or Wang The Rich Man.

The money for all these doings had gone out of Wang Lung hand bit by bit, so that he scarcely knew when it went, for th eldest son came and said,

"I need a hundred pieces of silver here"; or he said, "Ther is a good gate which needs only an odd bit of silver to men it as good as new"; or he said, "There is a place where a lon table should stand."

And Wang Lung gave him the silver bit by bit, as he sa smoking and resting in his court, for the silver came in easil from the land at every harvest and whenever he needed it, an so he gave it easily. He would not have known how much h gave had not his second son come into his court one mornin when the sun was scarcely over the wall and he said,

"My father, is there to be no end to all this pouring out c money and need we live in a palace? So much money lent out : twenty per cent would have brought in many pounds of silve and what is the use of all these pools and flowering trees that bear no fruit even, and all these idle, blooming lilies?"

Wang Lung saw that these two brothers would quarrel over this yet, and he said hastily, lest he never have any peace,

"Well, and it is all in honor of your wedding."

Then the young man answered, smiling crookedly and without any meaning of mirth,

"It is an odd thing for the wedding to cost ten times as much as the bride. Here is our inheritance, that should be divided between us when you are dead, being spent now for nothing but the pride of my elder brother."

And Wang Lung knew the determination of this second son of his and he knew he would never have done with him if talk began, so he said hastily,

"Well—well—I will have an end to it—I will speak to your brother and I will shut my hand. It is enough. You are right!"

The young man had brought out a paper on which was written a list of all the moneys his brother had spent, and Wang Lung saw the length of the list and he said quickly,

"I have not eaten yet and at my age I am faint in the morning until I eat. Another time for this." And he turned and went into his own room and so dismissed his second son.

But he spoke that same evening to his eldest son, saying,

"Have done with all this painting and polishing. It is enough. We are, after all, country folk."

But the young man answered proudly,

"That we are not. Men in the town are beginning to call us the great family Wang. It is fitting that we live somewhat suitably to that name, and if my brother cannot see beyond the meaning of silver for its own sake, I and my wife, we will uphold the honor of the name."

Now Wang Lung had not known that men so called his house, for as he grew older he went seldom even to the tea shops and no more to the grain markets since there was his second son to do his business there for him, but it pleased him secretly and so he said,

"Well, even great families are from the land and rooted in the land."

But the young man answered smartly,

"Yes, but they do not stay there. They branch forth and bear flowers and fruits."

Wang Lung would not have his son answering him too easily and quickly like this, so he said,

225

"I have said what I have said. Have done with pouring ou[t] silver. And roots, if they are to bear fruits, must be kept well i[n] the soil of the land."

Then since evening came on, he wished his son would g[o] away out of this court and into his own. He wished the youn[g] man to go away and leave him in peace in the twilight an[d] alone. But there was no peace for him with this son of his. Thi[s] son was willing to obey his father now for he was satisfied in th[e] rooms and the courts, at least for the time, and he had don[e] what he would do, but he began again,

"Well, let it be enough, but there is another thing."

Then Wang Lung flung his pipe down upon the ground an[d] he shouted,

"Am I never to be in peace?"

And the young man went on stubbornly,

"It is not for myself or for my son. It is for my younges[t] brother who is your own son. It is not fit that he grow up s[o] ignorant. He should be taught something."

Wang Lung stared at this for it was a new thing. He had lon[g] ago settled the life of his youngest son, what it was to be, an[d] he said now,

"There is no need for any more stomachsful of characters i[n] this house. Two is enough, and he is to be on the land when [I] am dead."

"Yes, and for this he weeps in the night, and this is why he i[s] so pale and so reedy a lad," answered the eldest son.

Now Wang Lung had never thought to ask his youngest so[n] what he wished to do with his life, since he had decided one so[n] must be on the land, and this that his eldest son had said struc[k] him between the brows and he was silent. He picked up hi[s] pipe from the ground slowly and pondered about his third son[.] He was a lad not like either of his brothers, a lad as silent as hi[s] mother, and because he was silent none paid any attention t[o] him.

"Have you heard him say this?" asked Wang Lung of hi[s] eldest son, uncertainly.

"Ask him for yourself, my father," replied the young man.

"Well, but one lad must be on the land," said Wang Lun[g] suddenly in argument and his voice was very loud.

"But why, my father?" urged the young man. "You are a ma[n] who need not have any sons like serfs. It is not fitting. Peopl[e] will say you have a mean heart. 'There is a man who makes hi[s] son into a hind while he lives like a prince.' So people will say."

226

Now the young man spoke cleverly for he knew that his father cared mightily what people said of him, and he went on,

"We could call a tutor and teach him and we could send him to a southern school and he could learn and since there is I in your house to help you and my second brother in his good trade, let the lad choose what he will."

Then Wang Lung said at last,

"Send him here to me."

After a while the third son came and stood before his father and Wang Lung looked at him to see what he was. And he saw a tall and slender lad, who was neither his father nor his mother, except that he had his mother's gravity and silence. But there was more beauty in him than there had been in his mother, and for beauty alone he had more of it than any of Wang Lung's children except the second girl who had gone to her husband's family and belonged no more to the house of Wang. But across the lad's forehead and almost a mar to his beauty were his two black brows, too heavy and black for his young, pale face, and when he frowned, and he frowned easily, these black brows met, heavy and straight, across his brow.

And Wang Lung stared at his son and after he had seen him well, he said,

"Your eldest brother says you wish to learn to read."

And the boy said, scarcely stirring his lips,

"Aye."

Wang Lung shook the ash from his pipe and pushed the fresh tobacco in slowly with his thumb.

"Well, and I suppose that means you do not want to work on the land and I shall not have a son on my own land, and I with sons and to spare."

This he said with bitterness, but the boy said nothing. He stood there straight and still in his long white robe of summer linen, and at last Wang Lung was angry at his silence and he shouted at him,

"Why do you not speak? Is it true you do not want to be on the land?"

And again the boy answered only the one word,

"Aye."

And Wang Lung looking at him said to himself at last that these sons of his were too much for him in his old age and they were a care and burden to him and he did not know what to

227

do with them, and he shouted again, feeling himself ill-used by these sons of his,

"What is it to me what you do? Get away from me!"

Then the boy went away swiftly and Wang Lung sat alone and he said to himself that his two girls were better after all than his sons, one, poor fool that she was, never wanted anything more than a bit of any food and her length of cloth to play with, and the other one married and away from his house. And the twilight came down over the court and shut him into it alone.

Nevertheless, as Wang Lung always did when his anger passed, he let his sons have their way, and he called his elder son and he said,

"Engage a tutor for the third one if he wills it, and let him do as he likes, only I am not to be troubled about it."

And he called his second son and said,

"Since I am not to have a son on the land it is your duty to see to the rents and to the silver that comes in from the land at each harvest. You can weigh and measure and you shall be my steward."

The second son was pleased enough for this meant the money would pass through his hands at least, and he would know what came in and he could complain to his father if more than enough was spent in the house.

Now this second son of his seemed more strange to Wang than any of his sons, for even at the wedding day, which came on, he was careful of the money spent on meats and on wine and he divided the tables carefully, keeping the best meats for his friends in the town who knew the cost of the dishes, and for the tenants and the country people who must be invited he spread tables in the courts, and to these he gave only the second best in meat and wine, since they daily ate coarse fare, and a little better was very good to them.

And the second son watched the money and the gifts that came in, and he gave to the slaves and servants the least that could be given them, so that Cuckoo sneered when into her hand he put a paltry two pieces of silver and she said in the hearing of many,

"Now a truly great family is not so careful of its silver and one can see that this family does not rightly belong in these courts."

The eldest son heard this, and he was ashamed and he was afraid of her tongue and he gave her more silver secretly and he

228

was angry with his second brother. Thus there was trouble between them even on the very wedding day when the guests sat about the tables and when the bride's chair was entering the courts.

And of his own friends the eldest son asked but a few of the least considered to the feast, because he was ashamed of his brother's parsimony and because the bride was but a village maid. He stood aside scornfully, and he said,

"Well, and my brother has chosen an earthen pot when he might, from my father's position, have had a cup of jade."

And he was scornful and nodded stiffly when the pair came and bowed before him and his wife as their elder brother and sister. And the wife of the eldest son was correct and haughty and bowed only the least that could be considered proper for her position.

Now of all of them who lived in these courts it seemed there was none wholly at peace and comfortable there except the small grandson who had been born to Wang Lung. Even Wang Lung himself, waking within the shadows of the great carved bed where he slept in his own room that was next to the court where Lotus lived, even he woke to dream sometimes that he was back in the simple, dark, earth-walled house where a man could throw his cold tea down where he would not splatter a piece of carven wood, and where a step took him into his own fields.

As for Wang Lung's sons, there was continual unrest, the eldest son lest not enough be spent and they be belittled in the eyes of men and lest the villagers come walking through the great gate when a man from the town was there to call, and so make them ashamed before him; and the second son lest there was waste and money gone; and the youngest son striving to make repair the years he had lost as a farmer's son.

But there was one who ran staggering hither and yon and content with his life and it was the son of the eldest son. This small one never thought of any other place than this great house and to him it was neither great nor small but only his house, and here was his mother and here his father and grandfather and all those who lived but to serve him. And from this one did Wang Lung secure peace, and he could never have enough of watching him and laughing at him and picking him up when he fell. He remembered also what his own father had done, and he delighted to take a girdle and put it about the child and walk, holding him thus from falling, and they went from court to court, and the child pointed at the darting fish in the pools and jabbered this and that and snatched the head of a flower and was at ease in the midst of everything, and only thus did Wang Lung find peace.

Nor was there only this one. The wife of the eldest son was faithful and she conceived and bore and conceived and bore regularly and faithfully, and each child as it was born had its slave. Thus Wang Lung each year saw more children in the courts and more slaves, so that when one said to him, "There is to be another mouth again in the eldest son's court," he only laughed and said,

"Eh—eh—well, there is rice and enough for all since we have the good land."

And he was pleased when his second son's wife bore also in her season, and she gave birth to a girl first as was fitting and it was seemly out of respect to her sister-in-law. Wang Lung, then, in the space of five years had four grandsons and three grand-daughters and the courts were filled with their laughter and their weeping.

Now five years is nothing in a man's life except when he is very young and very old, and if it gave to Wang Lung these others, it took away also that old dreamer, his uncle, whom he had almost forgotten except to see that he and his old wife were fed and clothed and had what they wished of opium.

On the winter of the fifth year it was very cold, more cold than any thirty years before, so that for the first time in Wang Lung's memory the moat froze about the wall of the town and men could walk back and forth on it. A continual icy wind blew also from the northeast and there was nothing, no garment of goatskin or fur, that could keep a man warm. In every room in the great house they burned braziers of charcoal and still it was cold enough to see a man's breath when he blew it out.

Now Wang Lung's uncle and his wife had long since smoked all the flesh off their bones and they lay day in and day out on their beds like two old dry sticks, and there was no warmth in them. And Wang Lung heard his uncle could not sit up even any more in his bed and he spat blood whenever he moved at all, and he went out to see and he saw there were not many hours left for the old man.

Then Wang Lung bought two coffins of wood good enough

but not too good, and he had the coffins taken into the room where his uncle lay that the old man might see them and die in comfort, knowing there was a place for his bones. And his uncle said, his voice a quavering whisper,

"Well, and you are a son to me and more than that wandering one of my own."

And the old woman said, but she was still stouter than the man,

"If I die before that son comes home, promise me you will find a good maid for him, so that he may have sons for us yet." And Wang Lung promised it.

What hour his uncle died Wang Lung did not know, except that he lay dead one evening when the serving woman went in to take a bowl of soup, and Wang Lung buried him on a bitter cold day when the wind blew the snow over the land in clouds, and he put the coffin in the family enclosure beside his father, only a little lower than his father's grave, but above the place where his own was to be.

Then Wang Lung caused mourning to be made for the whole family and they wore the sign of mourning for a year, not because any truly mourned the passing of this old man who had never been anything but a care to them, but because it is fitting so to do in a great family when a relative dies.

Then Wang Lung moved his uncle's wife into the town where she would not be alone, and he gave her a room at the end of a far court for her own, and he told Cuckoo to supervise a slave in the care of her, and the old woman sucked her opium pipe and lay on her bed in great content, sleeping day after day, and her coffin was beside her where she could see it for her comfort.

And Wang Lung marvelled to think that once he had feared her for a great fat blowsy country woman, idle and loud, she who lay there now shrivelled and yellow and silent, and as shrivelled and yellow as the Old Mistress had been in the fallen House of Hwang.

31

Now ALL HIS life long Wang Lung had heard of war here and there but he had never seen the thing come near except the once that he wintered in the southern city when he was young. It had never come nearer to him than that, although he had often heard men say from the time he was a child, "There is a war to the west this year," or they said, "War is to the east or the northeast."

And to him war was a thing like earth and sky and water and why it was no one knew but only that it was. Now and again he heard men say, "We will go to the wars." This they said when they were about to starve and would rather be soldiers than beggars; and sometimes men said it when they were restless at home as the son of his uncle had said it, but however this was, the war was always away and in a distant place. Then suddenly like a reasonless wind out of heaven the thing came near.

Wang Lung heard of it first from his second son who came home from the market one day for his noon rice and he said to his father,

"The price of grain has risen suddenly, for the war is to the south of us now and nearer every day, and we must hold our stores of grain until later for the price will go higher and higher as the armies come nearer to us and we can sell for a good price."

Wang Lung listened to this as he ate and he said,

"Well, and it is a curious thing and I shall be glad to see a war for what it is, for I have heard of it all my life and never seen it."

To himself then he remembered that once he had been afraid because he would have been seized against his will, but now he was too old for use and besides he was rich and the rich need not fear anything. So he paid no great heed to the matter beyond this and he was not moved by more than a little curiosity and he said to his second son,

"Do as you think well with the grain. It is in your hands."

And in the days to come he played with his grandchildren when he was in the mood, and he slept and ate and smoked and sometimes he went to see his poor fool who sat in a far corner of his court.

Then sweeping out of the northwest like a swarm of locusts there came one day in early summer a horde of men. Wang Lung's small grandson stood at the gate with a man servant to see what passed one fine sunny morning in early spring and when he saw the long ranks of grey-coated men, he ran back to his grandfather and he cried out,

"See what comes, Old One!"

Then Wang Lung went back to the gate with him to humor him, and there the men were filling the street, filling the town, and Wang Lung felt as though air and sunlight had been suddenly cut off because of the numbers of grey men tramping heavily and in unison through the town. Then Wang Lung looked at them closely and he saw that every man held an implement of some sort with a knife sticking out of the end, and the face of every man was wild and fierce and coarse; even though some were only lads, they were so. And Wang Lung drew the child to him hastily when he saw their faces and he murmured,

"Let us go and lock the gate. They are not good men to see, my little heart."

But suddenly, before he could turn, one saw him from among the men and shouted out at him,

"Ho there, my old father's nephew!"

Wang Lung looked up at this call, and he saw the son of his uncle, and he was clad like the others and dusty and grey, but his face was wilder and more fierce than any. And he laughed harshly and called out to his fellows,

"Here we may stop, my comrades, for this is a rich man and my relative!"

Before Wang Lung could move in his horror, the horde was pouring past him into his own gates and he was powerless in their midst. Into his courts they poured like evil filthy water, filling every corner and crack, and they laid themselves down on the floors and they dipped with their hands in the pools and drank, and they clattered their knives down upon carven tables and they spat where they would and shouted at each other.

Then Wang Lung, in despair over what had happened, ran back with the child to find his eldest son. He went into his son's courts and there his son sat reading a book and he rose when his father entered, and when he heard what Wang Lung gasped forth, he began to groan and he went out.

But when he saw his cousin he did not know whether to curse him or to be courteous to him. But he looked and he groaned forth to his father who was behind him,

"Every man with a knife!"

So he was courteous then and he said,

"Well, and my cousin, welcome to your home again."

And the cousin grinned widely and said,

"I have brought a few guests."

"They are welcome, being yours," said Wang Lung's eldest son, "and we will prepare a meal so that they may eat before they go on their way."

Then the cousin said, still grinning,

"Do, but make no haste afterwards, for we will rest a handful of days or a moon or a year or two, for we are to be quartered on the town until the war calls."

Now when Wang Lung and his son heard this they could scarcely conceal their dismay, but still it must be concealed because of the knives flashing everywhere through the courts, so they smiled what poor smiles they could muster and they said,

"We are fortunate—we are fortunate—"

And the eldest son pretended he must go to prepare and he took his father's hand and the two of them rushed into the inner court and the eldest son barred the door, and then the two, father and son, stared at each other in consternation, and neither knew what to do.

Then the second son came running and he beat upon the door and when they let him in he fell in and scarcely could save himself in his haste and he panted forth,

"There are soldiers everywhere in every house—even in the houses of the poor—and I came running to say you must not protest, for today a clerk in my shop, and I knew him well—he stood beside me every day at the counter—and he heard and went to his house and there were soldiers in the very room where his wife lay ill, and he protested and they ran a knife through him as though he were made of lard—as smoothly as that—and it came through him clean to the other side!

234

Whatever they wish we must give, but let us only pray that the war move on to other parts before long!"

Then the three of them looked at each other heavily, and thought of their women and of these lusty, hungry men. And the eldest son thought of his goodly, proper wife, and he said,

"We must put the women together in the innermost court and we must watch there day and night and keep the gates barred and the back gate of peace ready to be loosed and opened."

Thus they did. They took the women and the children and they put them all into the inner court where Lotus had lived alone with Cuckoo and her maids, and there in discomfort and crowding they lived. The eldest son and Wang Lung watched the gate day and night and the second son came when he could, and they watched as carefully by night as by day.

But there was that one, the cousin, and because he was a relative none could lawfully keep him out and he beat on the gate and he would come in and he walked about at will, carrying his knife shining and glittering and open in his hand. The eldest son followed him about, his face full of bitterness, but still not daring to say anything, for there was the knife open and glittering, and the cousin looked at this and that and appraised each woman.

He looked at the wife of the eldest son and he laughed his hoarse laugh and he said,

"Well, and it is a proper dainty bit you have, my cousin, a town lady and her feet as small as lotus buds!" And to the wife of the second son he said, "Well, here is a good stout red radish from the country—a piece of sturdy red meat!"

This he said because the woman was fat and ruddy and thick in the bone, but still not uncomely. And whereas the wife of the eldest son shrank away when he looked at her and hid her face behind her sleeve, this one laughed out, good humored and robust as she was, and she answered pertly,

"Well, and some men like a taste of hot radish, or a bite of red meat."

And the cousin answered back, promptly,

"That do I!" and he made as if to seize her hand.

All this time the eldest son was in agony of shame at this byplay between man and woman who ought not even to speak to each other, and he glanced at his wife because he was ashamed of his cousin and of his sister-in-law before her who had been more gently bred than he, and his cousin saw his timidity before his wife and said with malice,

"Well, and I had rather eat red meat any day than a slice of cold and tasteless fish like this other one!"

At this the wife of the eldest son rose in dignity and withdrew herself into an inner room. Then the cousin laughed coarsely and he said to Lotus, who sat there smoking her water pipe,

"These town women are too finicking, are they not, Old Mistress?" Then he looked at Lotus attentively and he said, "Well, and Old Mistress indeed, and if I did not know my cousin Wang Lung were rich I should know by looking at you, such a mountain of flesh you have become, and well you have eaten and how richly! It is only rich men's wives who can look like you!"

Now Lotus was mightily pleased that he called her Old Mistress, because it is a title that only the ladies of great families may have, and she laughed, deep and gurgling, out of her fat throat and she blew the ash out of her pipe and handed the pipe to a slave to fill again, and she said, turning to Cuckoo,

"Well, this coarse fellow has a turn for a joke!"

And as she said this she looked at the cousin out of her eyes coquettishly, although such glances, now that her eyes were no longer large and apricot-shaped in her great cheeks, were less coy than they once were, and seeing the look she gave him, the cousin laughed in uproar and cried out,

"Well, and it is an old bitch still!" and he laughed again loudly.

And all this time the eldest son stood there in anger and in silence.

Then when the cousin had seen everything he went to see his mother and Wang Lung went with him to show where she was. There she lay on her bed, asleep so her son could hardly wake her, but wake her he did, clapping the thick end of his gun upon the tiles of the floor at her bed's head. Then she woke and stared at him out of a dream, and he said impatiently,

"Well, and here is your son and yet you sleep on!"

She raised herself then in her bed and stared at him again and she said wondering,

"My son—it is my son——" and she looked at him for a long time and at last as though she did not know what else to do she proffered him her opium pipe, as if she could think of no greater good than this, and she said to the slave that tended her, "Prepare some for him."

And he stared back at her and he said,

"No, I will not have it."

Wang Lung stood there beside the bed and he was suddenly afraid lest this man should turn on him and say,

"What have you done to my mother that she is sere and yellow like this and all her good flesh gone?"

So Wang said hastily himself,

"I wish she were content with less, for it runs into a handful of silver a day for her opium, but at her age we do not dare to cross her and she wants it all." And he sighed as he spoke, and he glanced secretly at his uncle's son, but the man said nothing, only stared to see what his mother had become, and when she fell back and into her sleep again, he rose and clattered forth, using his gun as a stick in his hand.

None of the horde of idle men in the outer courts did Wang Lung and his family hate and fear as they did this cousin of theirs; this, although the men tore at the trees and the flowering shrubs of plum and almond and broke them as they would, and though they crushed the delicate carvings of chairs with their great leathern boots, and though they sullied with their private filth the pools where the flecked and golden fish swam, so that the fish died and floated on the water and rotted there, with their white bellies upturned.

For the cousin ran in and out as he would and he cast eyes at the slaves and Wang Lung and his sons looked at each other out of their eyes haggard and sunken because they dared not sleep. Then Cuckoo saw it and she said,

"Now there is only one thing to do, he must be given a slave for his pleasure while he is here, or else he will be taking where he should not."

And Wang Lung seized eagerly on what she said because it seemed to him he could not endure his life any more with all the trouble there was in his house, and so he said,

"It is a good thought."

And he bade Cuckoo go and ask the cousin what slave he would have since he had seen them all.

So Cuckoo did, then, and she came back and she said,

"He says he will have the little pale one who sleeps on the bed of the mistress."

Now this pale slave was called Pear Blossom and the one Wang Lung had bought in a famine year when she was small and piteous and half-starved, and because she was delicate always they had petted her and allowed her only to help Cuckoo

237

and to do the lesser things about Lotus, filling her pipe and pouring her tea, and it was thus the cousin had seen her.

Now when Pear Blossom heard this she cried out as she poured the tea for Lotus, for Cuckoo said it all out before them in the inner court where they sat, and she dropped the pot and it broke into pieces on the tiles and the tea all streamed out, but the maid did not see what she had done. She only threw herself down before Lotus and she knocked her head on the tiles and she moaned forth,

"Oh, my mistress, not I—not I— I am afraid of him for my life——"

And Lotus was displeased with her and she answered pettishly,

"Now he is only a man and a man is no more than a man with a maid and they are all alike, and what is this ado?" And she turned to Cuckoo and said, "Take this slave and give her to him."

Then the young maid put her hands together piteously and cried as though she would die of weeping and fear and her little body was all trembling with her fear, and she looked from this face to that, beseeching with her weeping.

Now the sons of Wang Lung could not speak against their father's wife, nor could their wives speak if they did not, nor could the youngest son, but he stood there staring at her, his hands clenched on his bosom and his brows drawn down over his eyes, straight and black. But he did not speak. The children and the slaves looked and were silent, and there was only the sound of this dreadful, frightened weeping of the young girl.

But Wang Lung was made uncomfortable by it, and he looked at the young girl doubtfully, not caring to anger Lotus, but still moved, because he had always a soft heart. Then the maid saw his heart in his face and she ran and held his feet with her hands and she bent her head down to his feet and wept on in great sobs. And he looked down at her and saw how small her shoulders were and how they shook and he remembered the great, coarse, wild body of his cousin, now long past his youth, and a distaste for the thing seized him and he said to Cuckoo, his voice mild,

"Well now, it is ill to force the young maid like this."

These words he said mildly enough, but Lotus cried out sharply,

"She is to do as she is told, and I say it is foolish, all this weeping over a small thing that must happen soon or late with all women."

But Wang Lung was indulgent and he said to Lotus,

"Let us see first what else can be done, and let me buy for you another slave if you will, or what you will, but let me see what can be done."

Then Lotus, who had long been minded for a foreign clock and a new ruby ring, was suddenly silent and Wang Lung said to Cuckoo,

"Go and tell my cousin the girl has a vile and incurable disease, but if he will have her with that, then well enough and she shall come to him, but if he fears it as we all do, then tell him we have another and a sound one."

And he cast his eyes over the slaves who stood about and they turned away their faces and giggled and made as if they were ashamed, all except one stout wench, who was already twenty or so, and she said with her face red and laughing,

"Well, and I have heard enough of this thing and I have a mind to try it, if he will have me, and he is not so hideous a man as some."

Then Wang Lung answered in relief,

"Well, go then!"

And Cuckoo said,

"Follow close behind me, for it will happen, I know, that he will seize the fruit nearest to him." And they went out.

But the little maid still clung to Wang Lung's feet, only now she ceased her weeping and lay listening to what took place. And Lotus was still angry with her, and she rose and went into her room without a word. Then Wang Lung raised the maid gently and she stood before him, drooping and pale, and he saw that she had a little, soft, oval face, egg-shaped, exceedingly delicate and pale, and a little pale red mouth. And he said kindly,

"Now keep away from your mistress for a day or two, my child, until she is past her anger, and when that other one comes in, hide, lest he desire you again."

And she lifted her eyes and looked at him full and passionately, and she passed him, silent as a shadow, and was gone.

The cousin lived there for a moon and a half and he had the wench when he would and she conceived by him and boasted in the courts of it. Then suddenly the war called and the horde went away quickly as chaff caught and driven by the wind, and there was nothing left except the filth and destruction they had wrought. And Wang Lung's cousin girded his knife to his waist and he stood before them with his gun over his shoulder and he said mockingly,

"Well, and if I come not back to you I have left you my second self and a grandson for my mother, and it is not every man who can leave a son where he stops for a moon or two, and it is one of the benefits of the soldier's life—his seed springs up behind him and others must tend it!"

And laughing at them all, he went his way with the others.

32

WHEN THE SOLDIERS were gone Wang Lung and his two elder sons for once agreed and it was that all trace of what had just passed must be wiped away, and they called in carpenters and masons again, and the men servants cleaned the courts, and the carpenters mended cunningly the broken carvings and tables, and the pools were emptied of their filth and clean fresh water put in, and again the elder son bought flecked and golden fish and he planted once more the flowering trees and he trimmed the broken branches of the trees that were left. And within a year the place was fresh and flowering again and each son had moved again into his own court and there was order once more everywhere.

The slave who had conceived by the son of Wang Lung's uncle he commanded to wait upon his uncle's wife as long as she lived, which could not be long now, and to put her into the coffin when she died. And it was a matter for joy to Wang Lung that this slave gave birth only to a girl, for if it had been a boy she would have been proud and have claimed a place in the family, but being a girl it was only slave bearing slave, and she was no more than before.

Nevertheless, Wang Lung was just to her as to all, and he said to her that she might have the old woman's room for her own if she liked when the old one was dead, and she could have the bed also, and one room and one bed would not be missed from the sixty rooms in the house. And he gave the slave a little silver, and the woman was content enough except for one thing, and this she told to Wang Lung when he gave her the silver.

"Hold the silver as dowry for me, my master," she said, "and if it is not a trouble to you, wed me to a farmer or to a good poor man. It will be merit to you, and having lived with a man, it is hardship to me to go back to my bed alone."

Then Wang Lung promised easily, and when he promised he was struck with a thought and it was this. Here was he promising a woman to a poor man, and once he had been a poor man come into these very courts for his woman. And he had not for half a lifetime thought of O-lan, and now he thought of her with sadness that was not sorrow but only heaviness of memory and things long gone, so far distant was he from her now. And he said heavily,

"When the old opium dreamer dies, I will find a man for you, then, and it cannot be long."

And Wang Lung did as he said. The woman came to him one morning and said,

"Now redeem your promise, my master, for the old one died in the early morning without waking at all, and I have put her in her coffin."

And Wang Lung thought what man he knew now on his land and he remembered the blubbering lad who had caused Ching's death, and the one whose teeth were a shelf over his lower lip, and he said,

"Well, and he did not mean the thing he did, and he is as good as any and the only one I can think of now."

So he sent for the lad and he came, and he was a man grown now, but still he was rude and still his teeth were as they were. And it was Wang Lung's whim to sit on the raised dais in the great hall and to call the two before him and he said slowly, that he might taste the whole flavor of the strange moment,

"Here, fellow, is this woman, and she is yours if you will have her, and none has known her except the son of my own uncle."

And the man took her gratefully, for she was a stout wench and good-natured, and he was a man too poor to wed except to such an one.

And Wang Lung came down off the dais and it seemed to him that now his life was rounded off and he had done all that he said he would in his life and more than he could ever have dreamed he could, and he did not know himself how it had all come about. Only now it seemed to him that peace could truly come to him and he could sleep in the sun. It was time for it, also, for he was close to sixty-five years of his age and his grandsons were like young bamboos about him, three the sons of his eldest son, and the eldest of these nearly ten years old, and two the sons of his second son. Well, and there was the third son to wed one day soon, and with that over there was nothing left to trouble him in his life, and he could be at peace.

But there was no peace. It seemed as though the coming of the soldiers had been like the coming of a swarm of wild bees that leave behind them stings wherever they can. The wife of the eldest son and the wife of the second son who had been courteous enough to each other until they lived in one court together, now had learned to hate each other with a great hatred. It was born in a hundred small quarrels, the quarrels of women whose children must live and play together and fight each other like cats and dogs. Each mother flew to the defense of her child, and cuffed the other's children heartily but spared her own, and her own had always the right in any quarrel, and so the two women were hostile.

And then on that day when the cousin had commended the country wife and laughed at the city wife, that had passed which could not be forgiven. The wife of the elder son lifted her head haughtily when she passed her sister-in-law and she said aloud one day to her husband as she passed,

"It is a heavy thing to have a woman bold and ill-bred in the family, so that a man may call her red meat and she laughs in his face."

And the second son's wife did not wait but she answered back loudly,

"Now my sister-in-law is jealous because a man called her only a piece of cold fish!"

And so the two fell to angry looks and hatred, although the elder, being proud of her correctness, would deal only in silent scorn, careful to ignore the other's very presence. But when her children would go out of their own court she called out,

"I would have you stay away from ill-bred children!"

This she called out in the presence of her sister-in-law who stood within sight in the next court, and that one would call out to her own children,

"Do not play with snakes or you will be bitten!"

So the two women hated each other increasingly, and the

thing was the more bitter because the two brothers did not love each other well, the elder always being fearful lest his birth and his family seem lowly in the eyes of his wife who was town bred and better born than he, and the younger fearful lest his brother's desire for expenditure and place lead them into wasting their heritage before it was divided. Moreover, it was a shame to the elder brother that the second brother knew all the money their father had and what was spent and the money passed through his hands, so that although Wang Lung received and dispensed all the moneys from his lands, still the second brother knew what it was and the elder did not, but must go and ask his father for this and that like a child. So when the two wives hated each other, their hatred spread to the men also and the courts of the two were full of anger and Wang Lung groaned because there was no peace in his house.

Wang Lung had also his own secret trouble with Lotus since the day when he had protected her slave from the son of his uncle. Ever since that day the young maid had been in disfavor with Lotus, and although the girl waited on her silently and slavishly, and stood by her side all day filling her pipe and fetching this and that, and rising in the night at her complaint that she was sleepless and rubbing her legs and her body to soothe her, still Lotus was not satisfied.

And she was jealous of the maid and she sent her from the room when Wang Lung came in and she accused Wang Lung that he looked at the maid. Now Wang Lung had not thought of the girl except as a poor small child who was frightened and he cared as he might care for his poor fool and no more. But when Lotus accused him he took thought to look and he saw it was true that the girl was very pretty and pale as a pear blossom, and seeing this, something stirred in his old blood that had been quiet these ten years and more.

So while he laughed at Lotus saying, "What—are you thinking I am still a-lust, when I do not come into your room thrice a year?" yet he looked sidelong at the girl and he was stirred.

Now Lotus, for all she was ignorant in all ways except the one, in the way of men with women she was learned and she knew that men when they are old will wake once again to a brief youth, and so she was angry with the maid and she talked of selling her to the tea house. But still Lotus loved her comfort and Cuckoo grew old and lazy and the maid was quick and

243

used about the person of Lotus and saw what her mistress needed before she knew it herself, and so Lotus was loath to part with her and yet she would part with her, and in this unaccustomed conflict Lotus was the more angry because of her discomfort and she was more hard than usual to live with. Wang Lung stayed away from her court for many days at a time because her temper was too ill to enjoy. He said to himself that he would wait, thinking it would pass, but meanwhile he thought of the pretty pale young maid more than he himself would believe he did.

Then as though there was not enough trouble with the women of his house all awry, there was Wang Lung's youngest son. Now his youngest son had been so quiet a lad, so bent on his belated books, that none thought of him except as a reedy slender youth with books always under his arm and an old tutor following him about like a dog.

But the lad had lived among the soldiers when they were there and he had listened to their tales of war and plunder and battle, and he listened rapt to it all, saying nothing. Then he begged novels of his old tutor, stories of the wars of the three kingdoms and of the bandits who lived in ancient times about the Swei Lake, and his head was full of dreams.

So now he went to his father and he said,

"I know what I will do. I will be a soldier and I will go forth to wars."

When Wang Lung heard this, he thought in great dismay that it was the worst thing that could yet happen to him and he cried out with a great voice,

"Now what madness is this, and am I never to have any peace with my sons!" And he argued with the lad and he tried to be gentle and kindly when he saw the lad's black brows gather into a line and he said, "My son, it is said from ancient times that men do not take good iron to make a nail nor a good man to make a soldier, and you are my little son, my best little youngest son, and how shall I sleep at night and you wandering over the earth here and there in a war?"

But the boy was determined and he looked at his father and drew down his black brows and he said only,

"I will go."

Then Wang Lung coaxed him and said,

"Now you may go to any school you like and I will send you to the great schools of the south or even to a foreign school to learn curious things, and you shall go anywhere you like for study if you will not be a soldier. It is a disgrace to a man like me, a man of silver and of land, to have a son who is a soldier." And when the lad was still silent, he coaxed again, and he said, "Tell your old father why you want to be a soldier?"

And the lad said suddenly, and his eyes were alight under his brows,

"There is to be a war such as we have not heard of—there is to be a revolution and fighting and war such as never was, and our land is to be free!"

Wang Lung listened to this in the greatest astonishment he had yet had from his three sons.

"Now what all this stuff is, I do not know," he said wondering. "Our land is free already—all our good land is free. I rent it to whom I will and it brings me silver and good grains and you eat and are clothed and are fed with it, and I do not know what freedom you desire more than you have."

But the boy only muttered bitterly,

"You do not understand—you are too old—you understand nothing."

And Wang Lung pondered and he looked at this son of his and he saw the suffering young face, and he thought to himself,

"Now I have given this son everything, even his life. He has everything from me. I have let him leave the land, even, so that I have not a son after me to see to the land, and I have let him read and write although there is no need for it in my family with two already." And he thought and he said to himself further, still staring at the lad. "Everything this son has from me."

Then he looked closely at his son and he saw that he was tall as a man already, though still reedy with youth, and he said, doubtfully, muttering and half-aloud, for he saw no sign of lust in the boy,

"Well, it may be he needs one thing more." And he said aloud then and slowly, "Well, and we will wed you soon, my son."

But the boy flashed a look of fire at his father from under his heavy gathered brows and he said scornfully,

"Then I will run away indeed, for to me a woman is not answer to everything as it is to my elder brother!"

Wang Lung saw at once that he was wrong and so he said hastily to excuse himself,

"No—no—we will not wed you—but I mean, if there is a slave you desire——"

And the boy answered with lofty looks and with dignity, folding his arms on his breast,

"I am not the ordinary young man. I have my dreams. I wish for glory. There are women everywhere." And then as though he remembered something he had forgotten, he suddenly broke from his dignity and his arms dropped and he said in his usual voice, "Besides, there never were an uglier set of slaves than we have. If I cared—but I do not—well, there is not a beauty in the courts except perhaps the little pale maid who waits on the one in the inner courts."

Then Wang knew he spoke of Pear Blossom and he was smitten with a strange jealousy. He suddenly felt himself older than he was—a man old and too thick of girth and with whitening hair, and he saw his son a man slim and young, and it was not for this moment father and son, but two men, one old and one young, and Wang Lung said angrily,

"Now keep off the slaves—I will not have the rotten ways of young lords in my house. We are good stout country folk and people with decent ways, and none of this in my house!"

Then the boy opened his eyes and lifted his black brows and shrugged his shoulders and he said to his father,

"You spoke of it first!" and then he turned away and went out.

Then Wang Lung sat there alone in his room by his table and he felt dreary and alone, and he muttered to himself,

"Well, and I have no peace anywhere in my house."

He was confused with many angers, but, although he could not understand why, this anger stood forth most clearly; his son had looked on a little pale young maid in the house and had found her fair.

33

WANG LUNG could not cease from his thought of what his youngest son had said of Pear Blossom and he watched the maid incessantly as she came and went and without his knowing it the thought of her filled his mind and he doted on her. But he said nothing to anyone.

One night in the early summer of that year, at the time when the night air is thick and soft with the mists of warmth and fragrance, he sat at rest in his own court alone under a flowering cassia tree and the sweet heavy scent of the cassia flowers filled his nostrils and he sat there and his blood ran full and hot like the blood of a young man. Through the day he had felt his blood so and he had been half of a mind to walk out on his land and feel the good earth under his feet and take off his shoes and his stockings and feel it on his skin.

This he would have done but he was ashamed lest men see him, who was no longer held a farmer within the gates of the town, but a landowner and a rich man. So he wandered restlessly about the courts and he stayed away altogether from the court where Lotus sat in the shade and smoked her water pipe, because well she knew when a man was restless and she had sharp eyes to see what was amiss. He went alone, then, and he had no mind to see either of his two quarreling daughters-in-law, nor even his grandchildren, in whom was his frequent delight.

So the day had passed very long and lonely and his blood was full and coursing under his skin. He could not forget his youngest son, how he had looked standing tall and straight and his black brows drawn together in the gravity of his youth, and he could not forget the maid. And to himself he said,

"I suppose they are of an age—the boy must be well on eighteen and she not over eighteen."

Then he remembered that he himself would before many years be seventy and he was ashamed of his coursing blood, and he thought,

"It would be a good thing to give the maid to the lad," and this he said to himself again and again, and everytime he said it the thing stabbed like a thrust on flesh already sore, and he could not but stab and yet he could not but feel the pain.

And so the day passed very long and lonely for him.

When night came he was still alone and he sat in his court alone and there was not one in all his house to whom he could go as friend. And the night air was thick and soft and hot with the smell of the flowers of the cassia tree.

And as he sat there in the darkness under the tree one passed

247

beside where he was sitting near the gate of his court where the tree stood, and he looked quickly and it was Pear Blossom.

"Pear Blossom!" he called, and his voice came in a whisper.

She stopped suddenly, her head bent in listening.

Then he called again and his voice would scarcely come from his throat,

"Come here to me!"

Then hearing him she crept fearfully through the gate and stood before him and he could scarcely see her standing there in the blackness, but he could feel her there and he put out his hand and laid hold of her little coat and he said, half choking,

"Child——!"

There he stopped with the word. He said to himself that he was an old man and it was a disgraceful thing for a man with grandsons and grand-daughters nearer to this child's age than he was, and he fingered her little coat.

Then she, waiting, caught from him the heat of his blood and she bent over and slipped, like a flower crumpling upon its stalk, to the ground, and she clasped his feet and lay there. And he said slowly,

"Child—I am an old man—a very old man——"

And she said, and her voice came out of the darkness like the very breath of the cassia tree,

"I like old men—I like old men—they are so kind—"

He said again, tenderly, stooping to her a little,

"A little maid like you should have a tall straight youth—a little maid like you!" And in his heart he added, "Like my son ——" but aloud he could not say it, because he might put the thought into her mind, and he could not bear it.

But she said,

"Young men are not kind—they are only fierce."

And hearing her small childish voice quavering up from about his feet his heart welled up in a great wave of love for this maid, and he took her and raised her gently, and then led her into his own courts.

When it was done, this love of his age astonished him more than any of his lusts before, for with all his love for Pear Blossom he did not seize upon her as he had seized upon the others whom he had known.

No, he held her gently and he was satisfied to feel her light youth against his heavy old flesh, and he was satisfied merely with the sight of her in the day and with the touch of her fluttering coat against his hand and with the quiet resting of her

248

body near him in the night. And he wondered at the love of old age, which is so fond and so easily satisfied.

As for her, she was a passionless maid and she clung to him as to a father, and to him she was indeed more than half child and scarcely woman.

Now the thing that Wang Lung had done did not quickly come out, for he said nothing at all, and why should he, being master in his own house?

But the eye of Cuckoo marked it first and she saw the maid slipping at dawn out of his court and she laid hold on the girl and laughed, and her old hawk's eyes glittered.

"Well!" she said. "And so it is the Old Lord over again!"

And Wang Lung in his room, hearing her, girded his robe about him quickly and he came out and smiled sheepishly and half proudly and he said muttering,

"Well, and I said she had better take a young lad and she would have the old one!"

"It will be a pretty thing to tell the mistress," Cuckoo said, then, and her eyes sparkled with malice.

"I do not know myself how the thing happened," answered Wang Lung slowly. "I had not meant to add another woman to my courts, and the thing came about of itself." Then when Cuckoo said, "Well, and the mistress must be told," Wang Lung, fearing the anger of Lotus more than anything begged Cuckoo and he said again, "Do you tell her, if you will, and if you can manage it without anger to my face I will give you a handful of money for it."

So Cuckoo, still laughing and shaking her head, promised, and Wang Lung went back to his court and he would not come forth for a while until Cuckoo came back and said,

"Well, and the thing is told, and she was angry enough until I reminded her she wanted and has wanted this long time the foreign clock you promised her, and she will have a ruby ring for her hand and a pair so that there will be one on each hand, and she will have other things as she thinks of them and a slave to take Pear Blossom's place, and Pear Blossom is not to come to her any more, and you are not to come soon either, because the sight of you sickens her."

And Wang Lung promised eagerly and he said,

"Get her what she wills and I do not begrudge anything."

And he was pleased that he need not see Lotus soon and until anger was cooled with the fulfillment of her wishes.

There were left yet his three sons, and he was strangely

ashamed before them of what he had done. And he said to himself again and again,

"Am I not master in my own house and may I not take my own slave I bought with my silver?"

But he was ashamed, and yet half proud too, as one feels himself who is still lusty and a man when others hold him to be only grandfather. And he waited for his sons to come into his court.

They came one by one, separately, and the second one came first. Now this one when he came talked of the land and of the harvest and of the summer drought which would this year divide the harvest by three. But Wang Lung considered nothing in these days of rain or drought, for if the harvest of the year brought him in little there was silver left from the year before and he kept his courts stuffed with silver and there was money owing to him at the grain markets and he had much money let out at high interest that his second son collected for him, and he looked no more to see how the skies were over his land.

But the second son talked on thus, and as he talked he looked here and there about the rooms with his eyes veiled and secret and Wang Lung knew that he looked for the maid to see if what he had heard was true, and so he called Pear Blossom from where she hid in the bed-room, and he called out,

"Bring me tea, my child, and tea for my son!"

And she came out, and her delicate pale face was rosy as a peach and she hung her head and crept about on her little silent feet, and the second son stared at her as if he had heard but could not believe until now.

But he said nothing at all except that the land was thus and so and this tenant and that must be changed at the end of the year, and the other one, because he smoked opium and would not gather from the land what it could bear. And Wang Lung asked his son how his children did, and he answered they had the hundred days' cough, but it was a slight thing now that the weather was warm.

This they talked back and forth drinking tea, and the second son took his fill of what he saw and he went away, and Wang Lung was eased of his second son.

Then the eldest son came in before the same day was half over and he came in tall and handsome and proud with the years of his maturity, and Wang Lung was afraid of his pride, and he did not call out Pear Blossom at first, but he waited and smoked his pipe. The eldest son sat there then stiff with his pride and his dignity and he asked after the proper manner for his father's health and for his welfare. Then Wang Lung answered quickly and quietly that he was well, and as he looked at his son his fear went out of him.

For he saw his eldest for what he was: a man big in body but afraid of his own town wife and more afraid of not appearing nobly born than of anything. And the robustness of the land that was strong in Wang Lung even when he did not know it swelled up in him, and he was careless again of this eldest son as he had been before, and careless of his proper looks, and he called easily of a sudden to Pear Blossom,

"Come, my child, and pour out tea again for another son of mine!"

This time she came out very cold and still and her small oval face was white as the flower of her name. Her eyes dropped as she came in and she moved stilly and did only what she was told to do and she went quickly out again.

Now the two men had sat silent while she poured the tea, but when she was gone and they lifted their bowls, Wang Lung looked fully into his son's eyes, and he caught there a naked look of admiration, and it was the look of one man who envies another man secretly. Then they drank their tea and the son said at last in a thick, uneven voice,

"I did not believe it was so."

"Why not?" replied Wang Lung tranquilly. "It is my own house."

The son sighed then and after a time he answered,

"You are rich and you may do as you like." And he sighed again and he said, "Well, I suppose one is not always enough for any man and there comes a day——"

He broke off, but there was in his look the tinge of a man who envies another man against his will, and Wang Lung looked and laughed in himself, for well he knew his eldest son's lusty nature and that not forever would the proper town wife he had hold the leash and some day the man would come forth again.

Then the eldest son said no more but he went his way as a man does who has had a new thought put into his head. And Wang sat and smoked his pipe and he was proud of himself that when he was an old man he had done what he wished.

But it was night before the youngest son came in and he

came alone also. Now Wang Lung sat in his middle room on the court and the red candles were lit on the table and he sat there smoking, and Pear Blossom sat silently on the other side of the table from him, and her hands were folded and quiet in her lap. Sometimes she looked at Wang Lung, fully and without coquetry as a child does, and he watched her and was proud of what he had done.

Then suddenly there was his youngest son standing before him, sprung out of the darkness of the court, and no one had seen him enter. But he stood there in some strange crouching way, and without taking thought of it, Wang Lung was reminded in a flash of memory of a panther he had once seen the men of the village bring in from the hills where they had caught it, and the beast was tied but he crouched for a spring, and his eyes gleamed, and the lad's eyes gleamed and he fixed them upon his father's face. And those brows of his that were too heavy and too black for his youth, he gathered fierce and black above his eyes. Thus he stood and at last he said in a low and surcharged voice,

"Now I will go for a soldier—I will go for a soldier——"

But he did not look at the girl, only at his father, and Wang Lung, who had not been afraid at all of his eldest son and his second son, was suddenly afraid of this one, whom he had scarcely considered from his birth up.

And Wang Lung stammered and muttered, and would have spoken, but when he took his pipe from his mouth, no sound came, and he stared at his son. And his son repeated again and again,

"Now I will go—now I will go——"

Suddenly he turned and looked at the girl once, and she looked back at him, shrinking, and she took her two hands and put them over her face so that she could not see him. Then the young man tore his eyes from her and he went in a leap from the room and Wang Lung looked out into the square of the darkness of the door, open into the black summer night, and he was gone and there was silence everywhere.

At last he turned to the girl and he said humbly and gently and with a great sadness and all his pride gone.

"I am too old for you, my heart, and well I know it. I am an old, old man."

But the girl dropped her hands from her face and she cried more passionately than he had ever heard her cry,

"Young men are so cruel—I like old men best!"

When the morning came of the next day Wang Lung's youngest son was gone and where he was gone no one knew.

34

THEN AS AUTUMN flares with the false heat of summer before it dies into the winter, so with the quick love Wang Lung had for Pear Blossom. The brief heat of it passed and passion died out of him; he was fond of her, but passionless.

With the passing of the flame out of him he was suddenly cold with an age and he was an old man. Nevertheless, he was fond of her, and it was a comfort to him that she was in his court and she served him faithfully and with a patience beyond her years, and he was always kind to her with a perfect kindness, and more and more his love for her was the love of father for daughter.

And for his sake she was even kind to his poor fool and this was comfort to him, so that one day he told her what had long been in his mind. Now Wang Lung had thought many times of what would come to his poor fool when he was dead and there was not another one except himself who cared whether she lived or starved, and so he had bought a little bundle of white poisonous stuff at the medicine shop, and he had said to himself that he would give it to his fool to eat when he saw his own death was near. But still he dreaded this more than the hour of his own death, and it was a comfort to him now when he saw Pear Blossom was faithful.

So he called her to him one day and he said,

"There is none other but you to whom I can leave this poor fool of mine when I am gone, and she will live on and on after me, seeing that her mind has no troubles of its own, and she has nothing to kill her and no trouble to worry her. And well I know that no one will trouble when I am gone to feed her or to bring

her out of the rain and the cold of winter or to set her in th
summer sun, and she will be sent out to wander on the stree
perhaps—this poor thing who has had care all her life from h
mother and from me. Now here is a gate of safety for her in th
packet, and when I die, after I am dead, you are to mix it in h
rice and let her eat it, that she may follow me where I am. An
so shall I be at ease."

But Pear Blossom shrank from the thing he held in his han
and she said in her soft way,

"I can scarcely kill an insect and how could I take this life
No, my lord, but I will take this poor fool for mine because yo
have been kind to me—kinder than any in all my life, and th
only kind one."

And Wang Lung could have wept for what she said becaus
not one had ever requited him like this, and his heart clung t
her and he said,

"Nevertheless, take it, my child, for there is none I trust as
do you, but even you must die one day—although I cannot sa
the words—and after you there is none—no, not one—and we
I know my sons' wives are too busy with their children and thei
quarrels and my sons are men and cannot think of such things.

So when she saw his meaning, Pear Blossom took the packe
from him and said no more and Wang Lung trusted her and wa
comforted for the fate of his poor fool.

Then Wang Lung withdrew more and more into his age an
he lived much alone except for these two in his courts, his poo
fool and Pear Blossom. Sometimes he roused himself a little an
he looked at Pear Blossom and he was troubled and said,

"It is too quiet a life for you, my child."

But she always answered gently and in great gratitude,

"It is quiet and safe."

And sometimes he said again,

"I am too old for you, and my fires are ashes."

But she always answered with a great thankfulness,

"You are kind to me and more I do not desire of any man."

Once when she said this Wang Lung was curious and h
asked her,

"What was it in your tender years that made you thus fearfu
of men?"

And looking at her for answer he saw a great terror in he
eyes and she covered them with her hands and she whispered,

"Every man I hate except you—I have hated every man, eve
254

my father who sold me. I have heard only evil of them and I hate them all."

And he said wondering,

"Now I should have said you had lived quietly and easily in my courts."

"I am filled with loathing," she said, looking away, "I am filled with loathing and I hate them all. I hate all young men."

And she would say nothing more, and he mused on it, and he did not know whether Lotus had filled her with tales of her life and had threatened her, or whether Cuckoo had frightened her with lewdness, or whether something had befallen her secretly that she would not tell him, or what it was.

But he sighed and gave over his questions, because above everything now he would have peace, and he wished only to sit in his court near these two.

So Wang Lung sat, and so his age came on him day by day and year by year, and he slept fitfully in the sun as his father had done, and he said to himself that his life was done and he was satisfied with it.

Sometimes, but seldom, he went into the other courts and sometimes, but more seldom, he saw Lotus, and she never mentioned the maid he had taken, but she greeted him well enough and she was old too and satisfied with the food and the wine she loved and with the silver she had for the asking. She and Cuckoo sat together now after these many years as friends and no longer as mistress and servant, and they talked of this and that, and most of all the old days with men and they whispered together of things they would not speak aloud, and they ate and drank and slept, and woke to gossip again before eating and drinking.

And when Wang Lung went, and it was very seldom, into his sons' courts, they treated him courteously and they ran to get tea for him and he asked to see the last child and he asked many times, for he forgot easily,

"How many grandchildren have I now?"

And one answered him readily,

"Eleven sons and eight daughters have your sons together."

And he, chuckling and laughing, said back,

"Add two each year, and I know the number, is it so?"

Then he would sit a little while and look at the children gathering around him to stare. His grandsons were tall lads now, and he looked at them, peering at them to see what they were, and he muttered to himself,

"Now that one has the look of his great-grandfather and there is a small merchant Liu, and here is myself when young."

And he asked them,

"Do you go to school?"

"Yes, grandfather," they answered in a scattered chorus, and he said again,

"Do you study the Four Books?"

Then they laughed with clear young scorn at a man so old as this and they said,

"No, grandfather, and no one studies the Four Books since the Revolution."

And he answered, musing,

"Ah, I have heard of a Revolution, but I have been too busy in my life to attend to it. There was always the land."

But the lads snickered at this, and at last Wang Lung rose, feeling himself after all but a guest in his sons' courts.

Then after a time he went no more to see his sons, but sometimes he would ask Cuckoo,

"And are my two daughters-in-law at peace after all these years?"

And Cuckoo spat upon the ground and she said,

"Those? They are at peace like two cats eyeing each other. But the eldest son wearies of his wife's complaints of this and that—too proper a woman for a man, she is, and always talking of what they did in the house of her father, and she wearies a man. There is talk of his taking another. He goes often to the tea shops."

"Ah?" said Wang Lung.

But when he would have thought of it his interest in the matter waned and before he knew it he was thinking of his tea and that the young spring wind smote cold upon his shoulders.

And another time he said to Cuckoo,

"Does any ever hear from that youngest son of mine where he is gone this long time?"

And Cuckoo answered, for there was nothing she did not know in these courts,

"Well, and he does not write a letter, but now and then one comes from the south and it is said he is a military official and great enough in a thing they call a Revolution there, but what it is I do not know—perhaps some sort of business."

And again Wang Lung said, "Ah?"

And he would have thought of it, but the evening was falling and his bones ached in the air left raw and chill when the sun withdrew. For his mind now went where it would and he could not hold it long to any one thing. And the needs of his old body for food and for hot tea were more keen than for anything. But at night when he was cold, Pear Blossom lay warm and young against him and he was comforted in his age with her warmth in his bed.

Thus spring wore on again and again and vaguely and more vaguely as these years passed he felt it coming. But still one thing remained to him and it was his love for his land. He had gone away from it and he had set up his house in a town and he was rich. But his roots were in his land and although he forgot it for many months together, when spring came each year he must go out on to the land; and now although he could no longer hold a plow or do anything but see another drive the plow through the earth, still he must needs go and he went. Sometimes he took a servant and his bed and he slept again in the old earthen house and in the old bed where he had begotten children and where O-lan had died. When he woke in the dawn he went out and with his trembling hands he reached and plucked a bit of budding willow and a spray of peach bloom and held them all day in his hand.

Thus he wandered one day in a late spring, near summer, and he went over his fields a little way and he came to the enclosed place upon a low hill where he had buried his dead. He stood trembling on his staff and he looked at the graves and he remembered them every one. They were more clear to him now than the sons who lived in his own house, more clear to him than anyone except his poor fool and except Pear Blossom. And his mind went back many years and he saw it all clearly, even his little second daughter of whom he had heard nothing for longer than he could remember, and he saw her a pretty maid as she had been in his house, her lips as thin and red as a shred of silk—and she was to him like these who lay here in the land. Then he mused and he thought suddenly,

"Well, and I shall be the next."

Then he went into the enclosure and he looked carefully and he saw the place where he would lie below his father and his uncle and above Ching and not far from O-lan. And he stared at the bit of earth where he was to lie and he saw himself in it and back in his own land forever. And he muttered,

"I must see to the coffin."

This thought he held fast and painfully in his mind and he went back to the town and he sent for his eldest son, and he said,

"There is something I have to say."

"Then say on," answered the son, "I am here."

But when Wang Lung would have said he suddenly could not remember what it was, and the tears stood in his eyes because he had held the matter so painfully in his mind and now it had slipped wilfully away from him. So he called Pear Blossom and he said to her,

"Child, what was it I wanted to say?"

And Pear Blossom answered gently,

"Where were you this day?"

"I was upon the land," Wang Lung replied, waiting, his eyes fixed on her face.

And she asked gently again,

"On what piece of land?"

Then suddenly the thing flew into his mind again and he cried, laughing out of his wet eyes,

"Well, and I do remember. My son, I have chosen my place in the earth, and it is below my father and his brother and above your mother and next to Ching, and I would see my coffin before I die."

Then Wang Lung's eldest son cried out dutifully and properly,

"Do not say that word, my father, but I will do as you say."

Then his son bought a carved coffin hewn from a great log of fragrant wood which is used to bury the dead in and for nothing else because that wood is as lasting as iron, and more lasting than human bones, and Wang Lung was comforted.

And he had the coffin brought into his room and he looked at it every day.

Then all of a sudden he thought of something and he said,

"Well, and I would have it moved out to the earthen house and there I will live out my few days and there I will die."

And when they saw how he had set his heart they did what he wished and he went back to the house on his land, he and Pear Blossom and the fool, and what servants they needed; and Wang Lung took up his abode again on his land, and he left the house in the town to the family he had founded.

Spring passed and summer passed into harvest and in the hot

autumn sun before winter comes Wang Lung sat where his father had sat against the wall. And he thought no more about anything now except his food and his drink and his land. But of his land he thought no more what harvest it would bring or what seed would be planted or of anything except of the land itself, and he stooped sometimes and gathered some of the earth up in his hand and he sat thus and held it in his hand, and it seemed full of life between his fingers. And he was content, holding it thus, and he thought of it fitfully and of his good coffin that was there; and the kind earth waited without haste until he came to it.

His sons were proper enough to him and they came to him every day or at most once in two days, and they sent him delicate food fit for his age, but he liked best to have one stir up meal in hot water and sup it as his father had done.

Sometimes he complained a little of his sons if they came not every day and he said to Pear Blossom, who was always near him,

"Well, and what are they so busy about?"

But if Pear Blossom said, "They are in the prime of life and now they have many affairs. Your eldest son has been made an officer in the town among the rich men, and he has a new wife, and your second son is setting up a great grain market for himself," Wang Lung listened to her, but he could not comprehend all this and he forgot it as soon as he looked out over his land.

But one day he saw clearly for a little while. It was a day on which his two sons had come and after they had greeted him courteously they went out and they walked about the house on to the land. Now Wang Lung followed them silently, and they stood, and he came up to them slowly, and they did not hear the sound of his footsteps nor the sound of his staff on the soft earth, and Wang Lung heard his second son say in his mincing voice,

"This field we will sell and this one, and we will divide the money between us evenly. Your share I will borrow at good interest, for now with the railroad straight through I can ship rice to the sea and I . . ."

But the old man heard only these words, "sell the land," and he cried out and he could not keep his voice from breaking and trembling with his anger,

"Now, evil, idle sons—sell the land! He choked and woul have fallen, and they caught him and held him up, and h began to weep.

Then they soothed him and they said, soothing him,

"No—no—we will never sell the land——"

"It is the end of a family—when they begin to sell the land, he said brokenly. "Out of the land we came and into it we mus go—and if you will hold your land you can live—no one can ro you of land——"

And the old man let his scanty tears dry upon his cheeks an they made salty stains there. And he stooped and took up handful of the soil and he held it and he muttered,

"If you sell the land, it is the end."

And his two sons held him, one on either side, each holdin his arm, and he held tight in his hand the warm loose earth And they soothed him and they said over and over, the elde son and the second son,

"Rest assured, our father, rest assured. The land is not to b sold."

But over the old man's head they looked at each other an smiled.

About the Author

PEARL S. BUCK devoted her life to the creation of better understanding between the peoples of Asia and the West. She was born in Hillsboro, West Virginia on June 26, 1892, but spent her childhood in China, where her parents were Presbyterian missionaries. Living in the historic city of Chianking, she learned Chinese before English. When she was fifteen she went to boarding school in Shanghai, her first formal schooling before she returned to America to enter Randolph-Macon College. After graduation in 1914, she married John Lossing Buck, a teacher of agriculture, and went to live in a town in North China. Here she lived for five years, gathering the memories that became the basis of *The Good Earth*.

The publication of her first article in the *Atlantic,* in 1923, confirmed a childhood interest in writing and led ultimately to her first novel, *East Wind, West Wind*. Less than a year later, the appearance of *The Good Earth* established her reputation. The novel was an extraordinary best seller and was awarded the Pulitzer Prize, translated into more than thirty languages, and made into a play and a motion picture. After that she wrote over eighty books, including such famous novels as *A House Divided, Dragon Seed, Pavilion of Women,* and *The Time is Noon*.

In addition to the Pulitzer Prize, Mrs. Buck was awarded the Nobel Prize for Literature in 1938, the Brotherhood Award of the National Conference of Christians and Jews, the Wesley Award for Distinguished Service to Humanity and more than a dozen honorary degrees from American colleges and universities. She died in Danby, Vermont on March 6, 1973.